MAY WE BE FORGIVEN

A.M. HOMES

MAY WE BE FORGIVEN

GRANTA

Granta Publications, 12 Addison Avenue, London W11 4QR

First published in Great Britain by Granta Books 2012
First published in the United States in 2012 by Viking Penguin, a member of Penguin Group
(USA) Inc. New York

A CIP catalogue record for this book is available from the British Library.

1 3 5 7 9 10 8 6 4 2

ISBN 978 1 84708 324 1 (hardback)
ISBN 978 1 84708 322 7 (trade paperback)

Set in Adobe Garamond Pro

Designed by Alissa Amell

Offset by Avon DataSet, Bidord on Avon, Warwickshire

Printed and bound by CPI Group (UK) Ltd, Croydon, CR0 4YY

For Claudia to whom I owe a debt of gratitude

MAY WE BE FORGIVEN

"May we be forgiven," an incantation, a prayer, the hope that somehow I come out of this alive. Was there ever a time you thought—I am doing this on purpose, I am fucking up and I don't know why.

Do you want my recipe for disaster?

The warning sign: last year, Thanksgiving at their house. Twenty or thirty people were at tables spreading from the dining room into the living room and stopping abruptly at the piano bench. He was at the head of the big table, picking turkey out of his teeth, talking about himself. I kept watching him as I went back and forth carrying plates into the kitchen—the edges of my fingers dipping into unnameable goo—cranberry sauce, sweet potatoes, a cold pearl onion, gristle. With every trip back and forth from the dining room to the kitchen, I hated him more. Every sin of our childhood, beginning with his birth, came back. He entered the world eleven months after me, sickly at first, not enough oxygen along the way, and was given far too much attention. And then, despite what I repeatedly tried to tell him about how horrible he was, he acted as though he believed he was a gift of the gods. They named him George. Geo, he liked to be called, like that was something cool, something scientific, mathematical, analytical. Geode, I called him—like a sedimentary rock. His preternatural confidence, his divinely arrogant head dappled with blond threads of hair lifted high drew the attention of others, gave the impression that he knew something. People solicited his opinions, his participation, while I never saw the charm. By the time we were ten and eleven, he was taller than me, broader, stronger. "You sure he's not the butcher's boy?" my father would ask jokingly. And no one laughed.

I was bringing in heavy plates and platters, casseroles caked with the debris of dinner, and no one noticed that help was needed—not George, not his two children, not his ridiculous friends, who were in fact in his employ, among them a weather girl and assorted spare anchormen and -women who sat stiff-backed and hair-sprayed like Ken and Barbie, not my Chinese-American wife, Claire, who hated turkey and never failed to remind us that her family used to celebrate with roast duck and sticky rice. George's wife, Jane, had been at it all day, cooking and cleaning, serving, and now scraping bones and slop into a giant trash bin.

Jane scoured the plates, piling dirty dishes one atop another and dropping the slimy silver into a sink of steamy soapy water. Glancing at me, she brushed her hair away with the back of her hand and smiled. I went back for more.

I looked at their children and imagined them dressed as Pilgrims, in black buckle-shoes, doing Pilgrim children chores, carrying buckets of milk like human oxen. Nathaniel, twelve, and Ashley, eleven, sat like lumps at the table, hunched, or more like curled, as if poured into their chairs, truly spineless, eyes focused on their small screens, the only thing in motion their thumbs—one texting friends no one has ever seen and the other killing digitized terrorists. They were absent children, absent of personality, absent of presence, and, except for holidays, largely absent from the house. They had been sent away to boarding schools at an age others might have deemed too young but which Jane had once confessed was out of a certain kind of necessity—there were allusions to nonspecific learning issues, failure to bloom, and the subtle implication that the unpredictable shifts in George's mood made living at home less than ideal.

In the background, two televisions loudly competed among themselves for no one's attention—one featuring football and the other the film *Mighty Joe Young*.

"I'm a company man, heart and soul," George says. "The network's President of Entertainment. I am ever aware, 24/7."

There is a television in every room; fact is, George can't bear to be alone, not even in the bathroom.

He also apparently can't bear to be without constant confirmation of his success. His dozen-plus Emmys have seeped out of his office and are now scattered around the house, along with various other awards and citations rendered in cut crystal, each one celebrating George's ability to parse popular culture, to deliver us back to ourselves—ever so slightly mockingly, in the format best known as the half-hour sitcom or the news hour.

The turkey platter was in the center of the table. I reached over my wife's shoulder and lifted—the tray was heavy and wobbled. I willed myself to stay strong and was able to carry out the mission while balancing a casserole of Brussels sprouts and bacon in the crook of my other arm.

The turkey, an "heirloom bird," whatever that means, had been rubbed, relaxed, herbed into submission, into thinking it wasn't so bad to be decapitated, to be stuffed up the ass with breadcrumbs and cranberries in some annual rite. The bird had been raised with a goal in mind, an actual date when his number would come up.

I stood in their kitchen picking at the carcass while Jane did the dishes, bright-blue gloves on, up to her elbows in suds. My fingers were deep in the bird, the hollow body still warm, the best bits of stuffing packed in. I dug with my fingers and brought stuffing to my lips. She looked at me—my mouth moist, greasy, my fingers curled into what would have been the turkey's g-spot if they had such things—lifted her hands out of the water and came towards me, to plant one on me. Not friendly. The kiss was serious, wet, and full of desire. It was terrifying and unexpected. She did it, then snapped off her gloves and walked out of the room. I was holding the counter, gripping it with greasy fingers. Hard.

Dessert was served. Jane asked if anyone wanted coffee and went back into the kitchen. I followed her like a dog, wanting more.

She ignored me.

"Are you ignoring me?" I asked.

She said nothing and then handed me the coffee. "Could you let me have a little pleasure, a little something that's just for myself?" She paused. "Cream and sugar?"

From Thanksgiving through Christmas and on into the new year, all I thought of was George fucking Jane. George on top of her, or, for a special occasion, George on the bottom, and once, fantastically, George having her from the back—his eyes fixed on the wall-mounted television—the ticker tape of news headlines trickling across the bottom of the screen. I couldn't stop thinking about it. I was convinced that, despite his charms, his excess of professional achievement, George wasn't very good in bed and that all he knew about sex he learned from the pages of a magazine read furtively while shitting. I thought of my brother fucking his wife—constantly. Whenever I saw Jane I was hard. I wore baggy pleated pants and double pairs of jockey shorts to contain my treasonous enthusiasm. The effort created bulk and, I worried, gave me the appearance of having gained weight.

It is almost eight o'clock on an evening towards the end of February when Jane calls. Claire is still at the office; she is always at the office. Another man would think his wife was having an affair; I just think Claire is smart.

"I need your help," Jane says.

"Don't worry," I say, before I even know what the worry is. I imagine her calling me from the kitchen phone, the long curly cord wrapping around her body.

"He's at the police station."

I glance at the New York skyline; our building is ugly, postwar white brick, dull, but we're up high, the windows are broad, and there's a small terrace where we used to sit and have our morning toast. "Did he do something wrong?"

"Apparently," she says. "They want me to come get him. Can you? Can you pick your brother up?"

"Don't worry," I say, repeating myself.

Within minutes I'm en route from Manhattan to the Westchester hamlet George and Jane call home. I phone Claire from the car; her voice mail picks up. "There's some kind of problem with George and I've got to pick him up and take him home to Jane. I had my dinner—I left some for you in the fridge. Call later."

A fight. On the way to the police station, that's what I'm thinking. George has it in him: a kind of atomic reactivity that stays under the surface until something triggers him and he erupts, throwing over a table, smashing his fist through a wall, or . . . More than once I've been the recipient of his frustrations, a baseball hurled at my back, striking me at kidney level and dropping me to my knees, a shove in my grandmother's kitchen hurling me backwards, through a full-length pane of glass as George blocks me from getting the last of the brownies. I imagine that he went out for a drink after work and got on the wrong side of someone.

Thirty-three minutes later, I park outside the small suburban police station, a white cake box circa 1970. There's a busty girlie calendar that probably shouldn't be in a police station, a jar of hard candy, two metal desks that sound like a car crash if you accidentally kick them, which I do, tipping over an empty bottle of diet Dr. Pepper. "I'm the brother of the man you called his wife about," I announce. "I'm here on behalf of George Silver."

"You're the brother?"

"Yes."

"We called his wife, she's coming to get him."

"She called me, I'm here to pick him up."

"We wanted to take him to the hospital but he wouldn't go; he kept repeating that he was a dangerous man and we should take him 'downtown,' lock him up, and be done with it. Personally, I think the man needs a doctor—you don't walk away from something like that unscathed."

"So he got into a fight?"

"Car accident, bad one. Doesn't appear he was under the influence, passed a breath test and consented to urine, but really he should see a doctor."

"Was it his fault?"

"He ran a red light, plowed into a minivan, husband was killed on impact, the wife was alive at the scene—in the back seat, next to the surviving boy. Rescue crew used the Jaws of Life to free the wife, upon release she expired."

"Her legs fell out of the car," someone calls out from a back office. "The boy is in fair condition. He'll survive," the younger cop says. "Your brother's in the rear, I'll get him."

"Is my brother being charged with a crime?"

"Not at the moment. There'll be a full investigation. Officers noted that he appeared disoriented at the scene. Take him home, get him a doctor and a lawyer—these things can get ugly."

"He won't come out," the younger cop says.

"Tell him we don't have room for him," the older one says. "Tell him the real criminals are coming soon and if he doesn't come out now they'll plug him up the bung hole in the night."

George comes out, disheveled. "Why are you here?" he asks me.

"Jane called, and besides, you had the car."

"She could have taken a taxi."

"It's late."

I lead George through the small parking lot and into the night, feeling compelled to take his arm, to guide him by his elbow—not sure if I'm preventing him from escaping or just steadying him. Either way, George doesn't pull away, he lets himself be led.

"Where's Jane?"

"At the house."

"Does she know?"

I shake my head no.

"It was awful. There was a light."

"Did you see the light?"

"I think I may have seen it but it was like it didn't make sense."

"Like it didn't apply to you?"

"Like I didn't know." He gets into the car. "Where's Jane?" he asks again.

"At the house," I repeat. "Buckle your belt."

Pulling into the driveway, the headlights cut through the house and catch Jane in the kitchen, holding a pot of coffee.

"Are you all right?" she asks when we are inside.

"How could I be," George says. He empties his pockets onto the kitchen counter. He takes off his shoes, socks, pants, boxers, jacket, shirt, undershirt, and stuffs all of it into the kitchen trash can.

"Would you like some coffee?" Jane asks.

Naked, George stands with his head tilted as if he's hearing something.

"Coffee?" she asks again, gesturing with the pot.

He doesn't answer. He walks from the kitchen through the dining room and into the living room, and sits in the dark—naked in a chair.

"Did he get into a fight?" Jane asks.

"Car accident. You'd better call your insurance company and your lawyer. Do you have a lawyer?"

"George, do we have a lawyer?"

"Do I need one?" he asks. "If I do, call Rutkowsky."

"Something is wrong with him," Jane says.

"He killed people."

There is a pause.

She pours George a cup of coffee and brings it into the living room along with a dish towel that she drapes over his genitals like putting a napkin in his lap.

The phone rings.

"Don't answer it," George says.

"Hello," she says.

"I'm sorry, he's not home right now, may I take a message?" Jane listens.

"Yes, I hear you, perfectly clear," she says and then hangs up. "Do you want a drink?" she asks no one in particular, and then pours one for herself.

"Who was it?" I ask.

"Friend of the family," she says, and clearly she means the family that was killed.

For a long time he sits in the chair, the dish towel shielding his privates, the cup of coffee daintily on his lap. Beneath him a puddle forms.

"George," Jane implores when she hears what sounds like water dripping, "you're having an accident."

Tessie, the old dog, gets up from her bed, comes over, and sniffs it.

Jane hurries into the kitchen and comes back with a wad of paper towels. "It will eat the finish right off the floor," she says.

Through it all George looks blank, like the empty husk left by a reptile who has shed his skin. Jane takes the coffee cup from George and hands it to me. She takes the wet kitchen towel from his lap, helps him to stand, and then wipes the back of his legs and his ass with paper towels. "Let me help you upstairs."

I watch as they climb the steps. I see my brother's body, slack, his stomach sagging slightly, the bones of his hips, his pelvis, his flat ass—all so white they appear to glow in the dark. As they climb I see below his ass and tucked between his legs his low, pinkish-purple nut sack swaying like an old lion.

I sit on their couch. Where is my wife? Isn't Claire curious to know what happened? Doesn't she wonder why I am not home?

The room smells like urine. The wet paper towels are on the floor. Jane doesn't come back to clean up the pee. I do it and then sit back down on the sofa.

I am staring through the dark at an old wooden tribal mask made with hemp hair and a feather and laced with tribal beads. I'm staring at this unfamiliar face that Nate brought back from a school trip to South Africa, and the mask seems to be staring back as though inhabited, wanting to say something—taunting me with its silence.

I hate this living room. I hate this house. I want to go home.

I text Claire and explain what's happened. She writes back, "I took advantage of your being gone and am still at the office; it sounds like you should stay the night in case things deteriorate further."

I dutifully sleep on the sofa with a small, smelly nap blanket covering my shoulders. Tessie, the dog, joins me, warming my feet.

In the morning there are hurried phone calls and hushed conversations; a copy of the accident report crawls out of the fax machine. We will take George to the hospital and they will look for something, some invisible explanation that will relieve him of responsibility.

"Am I going deaf or what the fuck is going on around here?" George wants to know.

"George," Jane says clearly. "We have to go to the hospital. Pack your bag." And he does.

I drive them. He sits next to me, wearing well-worn corduroy pants, a flannel shirt he's had for fifteen years. He's unevenly shaved.

I drive self-consciously, worried that his complacent mood might shift, that he might flash back, erupt, and try to grab the wheel. The seat belts are good, they discourage sudden movements.

"Simple Simon met a pieman, going to the fair. Said Simple Simon to the pieman, 'Let me taste your ware,'" George intones. "Simple Simon went a-fishing for to catch a whale; all the water he had got was in his mother's pail. Watch out," he says to me, "or you'll get what you asked for."

In the Emergency Room, Jane goes to the counter with their insurance information and the police report and explains that her husband was involved in a fatal car accident the evening before and appeared disoriented at the scene.

"That's not what happened," George bellows. "The fucking SUV was like a big white cloud in front of me, I couldn't see over it, couldn't see around it, I couldn't help but punch through it like a cheap piece of aluminum, like a fat fucking pillow. The airbag punched me back, slammed me, knocked the wind right outta me, and when I finally got out I saw people in the other car, pushed together like lasagna. The boy in the back didn't stop crying. I wanted to punch him, but his mother was looking at me, her eyes popping out of her head."

As George is talking, two large men make their way towards him from the rear. He doesn't see it coming. They grab him. He's strong. He fights back.

The next time we see George he's in a cubicle in the back of the Emergency Room, arms and legs tied to a gurney.

"Do you know why you're here?" a doctor asks him.

"I've got bad aim," George says.

"Can you remember what happened?"

"It's more like I'll never forget. I left work at about six-thirty, drove towards home, decided to stop for a bite, which is not something I normally do, but I was tired, I can admit that. I didn't see her. As soon as I realized I'd hit something, I stopped. I stayed with her. I held on to her. She was slipping out from under herself, fluid was leaking out, like a broken engine. I felt sick. And I hated her. I hated her for how stunned she looked, how gray, the pool forming beneath her—I didn't even know where exactly it was coming from. It started to rain. There were people with blankets—where did the blankets come from? I heard sirens. People in cars drove around us, I saw them staring."

"What is he talking about?" I ask, wondering whether I'm confused or George is entirely disoriented. "That's not what happened, that's not this accident, perhaps it's another one, but it's not his."

"George," Jane says. "I read the police report—that's not what happened. Are you thinking of something else? Something you dreamed or something you saw on television?"

George offers no clarification.

"Any history of mental or neurological symptoms?" the doctor asks. We all shake our heads. "What line of work are you in?"

"Law," George says. "I studied law."

"Why don't you leave him with us for now. We'll order some tests," the doctor says, "and then we'll talk further."

Again, I stay the night at George and Jane's house.

The next morning, on our way to see him, I wonder aloud, "Is this the right place for him, a psych ward?"

"It's the suburbs," she says. "How dangerous could a suburban psych ward be?"

He is alone in his room.

"Good morning," Jane says.

"Is it? I wouldn't know."

"Did you have your breakfast?" she asks, seeing the tray in front of him.

"It's dog food," he says, "Take it home to Tessie."

"Your breath stinks—did you brush your teeth?" I ask.

"Don't they do it for you?" George replies. "I've never been in a mental hospital before."

"It's not a mental hospital," Jane says. "You just happen to be in the mental unit."

"I can't go into the bathroom," he says. "I can't look at myself in the mirror—I can't." He begins to sound hysterical.

"Do you need me to help you? I can help you clean up," Jane says, opening the toilet kit they have left for him.

"Don't make her do this," I say. "You're not an infant—snap out of it—stop acting like a zombie."

He begins to cry. I am surprised at myself for the tone I'm taking with him. I walk out of the room. As I leave, Jane is running water on a washcloth.

In the evening, after work, Claire comes to the hospital, bringing Chinese food from the city for the four of us. For someone of Chinese descent, Claire is surprisingly indiscriminate about Chinese food—as far as she's concerned, it's all the same, variations on a theme. We reheat it in the microwave marked "For Patient Use—No Medical Products." We clean our hands with the bottles of foaming cleanser that are on every wall of every room. I worry about putting anything down, touching any surfaces—suddenly I fear I could be eating deadly germs. I look into the Chinese food and see a worm, which I discreetly show Claire.

"It's not a worm, it's a grain of rice."

"It's larva," I whisper.

"You're nuts." She uses her fork to extract the grain of rice.

"Does rice have eyes?" I ask.

"It's pepper," she says, wiping the eyes off.

"Where did the food come from?" I ask.

"The place on Third Avenue that you used to like," she says.

"The one the health department closed?" I ask with a measure of alarm.

"You have a big trip coming up," Jane says, distracting us.

"I'm going to China for a few days," Claire says.

"No one goes to China for 'a couple of days,'" George growls.

Claire does.

Refusing to eat, George will only allow himself to suck the hot mustard directly from the plastic packets—self-punishment. No one stops him. "More for me," I am tempted to say, but don't.

"When are you leaving?" Jane asks.

"Tomorrow."

I pass another packet of mustard to George.

Later, in private, Claire asks me if George and Jane have a gun. "If not, they should get one," she says.

"What are you saying? They should get a gun? That's how you end up dead, you get a gun and then someone shoots you."

"I'm just saying that I wouldn't be surprised if Jane comes home one night and the family of the people George hurt are waiting for her. He destroyed their lives, and they're going to want something back. Stay with her, don't leave her alone; Jane is vulnerable," Claire says. "Imagine if it were you; if you went nuts, wouldn't you want someone to stay with me and keep an eye on the house?"

"We live in an apartment with a doorman. If I went crazy, you'd be fine."

"That's true. If anything happened to you, I'd be perfectly okay, but Jane is not me. She needs someone. Also, you should visit the surviving boy. The lawyer is going to tell you not to, but do it anyway—George and Jane need to know what they're dealing with. There is a reason I run Asia," Claire says. "I'm always thinking." She taps the side of her head. Think. Think. Think.

And so the next day I visit the boy, more out of a kind of familial guilt and less out of the need to calculate the impossible cost of making the boy "whole." I stop at the gift shop, where the selection is limited to brightly colored carnations, religious necklaces, and candy. I pick a box of chocolates and powder-blue carnations. The boy is in the same hospital as George, in the pediatric unit—two floors higher. He is sitting up in bed, eating ice cream, his eyes fixed on the television—*SpongeBob SquarePants*. He is about nine years old, chunky, a single eyebrow arches across his face in the shape of the letter "M." His right eye is blackened, and a large patch on the side of his head has been shaved, and there's a meaty purple line of stitches exposed to the air. I give the gifts to the woman sitting with the boy, who tells me that he is doing as well as can be expected, there is always someone with him, a relative or one of the nurses.

"How much does he remember?" I ask.

"All of it," the woman says. "Are you from the insurance company?"

I nod—is a nod the same as a lie?

"Do you have everything you need?" I ask the boy.

He doesn't answer.

"I'll come back again in a few days," I say, anxious to leave. "If you think of anything, you'll let me know."

It's funny how quickly something becomes a routine, a way of doing business. I stay with Jane, and it is as though we are playing house. That night I take out the trash and lock the door; she makes a snack and asks if I'll come upstairs. We watch a little television and read. I read whatever it was that George had been reading, his newspapers and magazines, *Media Age, Variety, The Economist,* and a big history of Thomas Jefferson that sits beside the bed.

The accident happens and then it happens. It doesn't happen the night of the accident or the night we all visit. It happens the night after that, the night after Claire tells me not to leave Jane alone, the night after Claire leaves for China. Claire goes on her trip, George goes downhill, and then it happens. It's the thing that was never supposed to happen.

The evening visit to the hospital goes badly. For reasons that are not clear, George is locked in a padded room, his arms bound to his body. Jane and I take turns peering through the small window. He looks miserable. Jane asks to go in and see him, the nurse cautions her against it, but she insists. Jane goes to him, calls his name. George looks up at her; she sweeps his hair out of his face, wipes his furrowed brow; and he turns on her, pins her with his body and bites her again and again, her face, her neck, her hands, breaking the skin in several places. The aides rush in and pull him off of her. Jane is taken downstairs and treated in the Emergency Room, her wounds are cleaned and dressed and she's given some kind of a shot, like a rabies vaccination.

We go back to the house. Jane heats hundred-calorie brownies in the microwave, I scoop no-fat ice cream onto them, she sprays them with zero-calorie whipped cream, and I cheer them further with chocolate sprinkles. We snack in silence. I take out the trash and change out of my clothes, the same clothes I've been wearing for days, and put on a pair of his pajamas.

I hug her. I want to be comforting. I am in his pajamas, she is still dressed. I don't think anything will happen. "I apologize," I say, without knowing what I am saying. And then she is against me, she puts her hands on the sides of her skirt and slides it down. She pulls me towards her.

There was a time when I almost told Claire about Thanksgiving—in fact I tried to tell her, one night after sex, when I was feeling close to her. As I started to tell the story, Claire sat up straight and pulled the sheet tight against her body, and I backed away from what I was about to say. I changed it. I left out the kiss and just mentioned something about Jane brushing against me.

"You were in her way and she was trying to get past you and not get to you," Claire said.

I didn't mention that I felt the head of my cock pressing against my sister-in-law's hips, her thighs pressed together.

"Only you would think she was making a pass," Claire said, disgusted.

"Only me," I repeated. "Only me."

Jane pulls me to her; her hips are narrow. My hand slides down into her panties. It is a new jungle. She sighs. The feel of her, this private softness, is incredible. And I'm thinking, this is not really happening—is it?

Her mouth is on me; she reaches for something, some kind of cream, it starts cold and then goes warm. She strokes me, looking me in the eye. And then again her mouth is on me and there is no way to say no. She pulls my pajamas out from under, is quickly upon me, riding me. I explode.

Drenched in her scent, but too shaken to shower or to fall asleep in their bed, I wait until she is asleep and then go downstairs, to the kitchen, and wash myself with dish soap. I am in my brother's kitchen at three in the morning, soaping my cock at his sink, drying myself with a towel that says "Home Sweet Home." It happens again in the morning, when she finds me on the sofa, and then again in the afternoon, after we visit George. "What's the story with your hand?" George asks Jane the next day, noticing her bandages. He's back in his room, with no memory of the night before.

Jane starts to cry.

"You look like hell," he says. "Get some rest."

"It's been a difficult time," I say.

That evening we open a bottle of wine and do it again, more slowly, deliberately, intentionally.

The hospital lets him out, or more likely he simply decides to leave. Inexplicably, he is able to walk out unnoticed in the middle of the night. He comes home in a taxi, using money that he's found at the bottom of his pocket. He can't find his keys so he rings the bell and the dog barks.

Maybe I heard that part—the dog barking.

Or maybe he didn't ring the bell and maybe the dog didn't bark. Maybe

George took the spare key from inside the fake rock in the garden by the door, and, like an intruder, he came silently into his own house.

Maybe he came upstairs thinking he'd crawl into his bed, but his spot was taken. I don't know how long he stood there. I don't know how long he waited before he lifted the lamp from her side of the bed and smashed it onto her head.

That's when I woke up.

She is screaming. The one blow isn't enough. She tries to get up; the lamp isn't even broken. George looks at me and then picks the lamp up again and swings it at her. The porcelain vase that is the base explodes against her head. By then I am out of bed. He tosses aside what remained of the lamp—blood streaming down his fingers—picks up the telephone, and throws it to me.

"Call it in," he says.

I stand facing him, wearing his pajamas. We are the same, like mimes, we have the same gestures, the same faces, the family chin, my father's brow, the same mismatched selves. I am staring at him, not knowing how this is going to work out. A disturbing gurgling sound prompts me to dial the phone.

Accidentally, I drop the phone. I bend to pick it up, and my brother's foot catches me under the chin, kicking me hard; my head snaps back. I am down as he leaves the room. I see his hospital gown under his clothes, hanging out like some kind of tail. I hear George's heavy footfall as he goes down the stairs. Jane is making an alarming noise. I reach across the floor, pull the phone towards me, and dial "0." I dial "0" like it is a hotel, like I expect someone to answer. There is a long recording, a kind of spoken word essay about what the "0" button can do for you, and I realize it will be forever before a real person comes on. I hang up and after several shaky attempts am able to dial "911."

"A woman has been beaten. Hurry," I say, and give them the address.

I pull myself to standing, go into the bathroom, and get a washcloth, as though that will help, as though I can wipe the blood away. I can't even find the spot; her head is a mash, blood and hair and bone and lamp, and I just hold the washcloth and wait.

It takes forever. The fire truck comes first. The house shakes as it pulls up. I leave Jane and go to the window. They come across the grass in full fire gear, hats and coats, immune to the predawn spray of the irrigation system.

I don't know if he opens the door or they come in of their own accord.

"Upstairs," I shout.

Quickly they are upon her. One stands apart, talking as if narrating into his radio. "We've got a middle-aged woman, open head injury with exposed matter; bring long board, full air, medic bag; request paramedic and police support. Who is this woman?" the narrator asks.

"Jane. My brother's wife."

"Do you have a driver's license or other identification for her?"

"Her purse is downstairs."

"Relevant medical information, allergies, underlying conditions?"

"Does Jane have any medical problems?" I shout down.

"A lamp hit her on the head," my brother says.

"Anything else?"

"She takes a fuck of a lot of vitamins," George says.

"Is she pregnant?" the narrator asks.

Just the question makes me weak.

"She shouldn't be," George says, and I can't help but think that's got an edge to it.

"Stabilize the neck," one of the firemen says.

"It's not her neck, it's her head," I say.

"Stand back," the narrator says.

The paramedics arrive, slip an orange board under Jane, tape her to it with what looks like duct tape, and wrap her head in gauze—she looks like a mummy, a battle casualty, or maybe a Shriner en route to a convention.

Jane makes a noise, a low guttural growl, as five of them lift her and carry her out, leaving a trail of sterile debris and heavy footprints. Turning the corner, they knock into the banister, and with a crack it snaps. "Sorry." They are out the kitchen door and into the back of the ambulance faster than you might think.

George is in the kitchen drinking a cup of coffee. There's blood on his hands and flecks of something on his face, pieces of the lamp—shards. "No parking on the grass," he says to the first police officer who arrives. "Please inform your troops."

"Which one of you is Mr. Silver?" the cop asks. I assume he must be a detective because he is not wearing a uniform.

We both raise our hands, simultaneously: "I am."

"Let's see some identification."

George fumbles as if looking for his, flapping the hospital gown.

"We're brothers," I say. "I'm the elder."

"So—who did what to whom?" He's got his notebook out.

George sips his coffee.

I say nothing.

"It's not a complicated question; either way we'll dust the lamp for prints. Dust," the detective calls out. "Get a full evidence team." He coughs. "So—is there anyone else home, anyone else we should be looking for? If it wasn't one of you that clocked her with the lamp, maybe the person who did it is still in the house, maybe there's another victim to be found." He pauses, waiting for someone to say something.

The only sound is the tick-tock of the kitchen clock. I almost lose it when the cuckoo pops out—cuckoo, cuckoo, cuckoo, six times. "Rake the house," the detective shouts to his men. "Make sure there's nobody else. Any evidence—bag it. That includes the lamp."

He turns his attention back to us. "It's Monday morning, I got out of bed to come here. My wife gives it to me every Monday morning, no questions asked, she likes me to start the week happy, so I'm not exactly feeling fondly towards you."

"What the fucking fuck are you fucking thinking, you fuck," George blurts.

Two large cops move to block the kitchen door. Suddenly there is no exit.

"Cuff him," the detective says.

"I wasn't talking to you," George says, "I was talking to my brother." George looks at me. "And those are my pajamas," he says. "Now you've gone and done it."

"I'm not going to be able to help you this time," I say.

"Have I committed a crime?" George asks.

"Hard to know, isn't it," one of the cops says, cuffing him.

"Where are you taking him?" I ask.

"Is there a particular place you'd like him to go?"

"He was in the hospital. He must have walked out last night—notice the gown under his clothes?"

"So he eloped?"

I nod.

"And how did he get home?"

"I don't know."

"I fucking walked, in the fucking dark. Pussy Licker."

The ambulance takes Jane, the cops take George, I'm left behind with an officer waiting for the evidence team. I start to go upstairs, the cop stops me: "Crime scene," he says.

"Clothing," I say, flapping my pajama legs—actually George's pajama legs.

He escorts me up to the bedroom, which looks like a tornado hit, the lamp in pieces on the floor, blood, the bed undone. I change out of my brother's pajamas, and without a word to the wise, I borrow George's clean clothes, still in the dry cleaner's plastic bag hanging off the closet door.

"Leave the dirties in the room," the cop says. "You never know what'll come into play."

"You're right," I say, and we go back downstairs.

As the cop follows me down, I feel strangely like a suspect. It occurs to me that it would be smart to call George's lawyer and update him on the turn of events, but I can't remember his name. I'm also wondering if the cop is somehow watching me, if I should be worried about making fast moves, reaching for anything and so on. Also, how do I get away from him in order to make a private phone call?

"I think I'll go put some laundry in the dryer."

"Wait," the cop says. "That you can do later. Wet clothes stay wet."

"Okey-dokey." I sit at the kitchen table and casually pick up the phone and go through the caller ID, thinking the lawyer's name is there and will ring a bell. Bingo—Rutkowsky.

"Okay if I use the phone?"

"It's your nickel."

"Okay if I step outside?"

He nods.

"Did I get you at a bad time?" I ask when Rutkowsky, the lawyer, answers.

"Who is this?"

"Silver, Harry Silver, George Silver's brother."

"I'm on my way into court," the lawyer says.

I'm standing in the front yard, barefoot in the wet grass. "There have been developments." I pause. "George walked out of the hospital last night, and Jane has been injured, a lamp got her on the head. The police are here, waiting for an evidence team, and . . ."

"How come you're there?"

"I was asked to keep Jane company while my brother was in the hospital."

"Where is Jane?"

"She's off to the hospital."

"And George?"

"They've taken him as well."

"Is there the sense that the crime is serious?"

"Yes."

"When the police come, follow them even if they ask you to leave, you go wherever they go. Don't allow them to move anything, and if they ask you to touch or move anything, keep your hands in your pockets. They can take photos, they can pick up things with tweezers and put them in baggies."

"The neighbors are watching out their windows."

"I'll meet you at the house at four-thirty; until then, don't disturb the scene."

"I'll leave a key under the fake rock by the front door, in case I'm not back."

"Where are you going?"

"The hospital."

"Let me have your cell in case I need you."

I give him the number and he hangs up. In my head I hear Jane's voice: "Condoms?"

Yes. And where are they now? Gone, used, finished, dropped in the kitchen trash, loaded with jism.

I go back into the house. "Mind if I make a fresh pot of joe?"

"I won't stop you," the cop says. "Was that dog always here?" The cop points to Tessie, who is licking the water from my feet. Her bowl is dry. "That's Tessie."

I give the dog fresh water and kibble.

The evidence team suits up on the front lawn, laying out white Tyvek onesies and then climbing into them as if mounting a hazmat operation, complete with booties and latex gloves. "No, really, it's okay," I say. "We're not contagious and the carpet's already wrecked." They don't respond. "Coffee anyone?" I ask, holding up my mug. Usually I don't drink coffee, but this morning I'm already on my fourth cup; I've got my reasons. As directed, I follow them from room to room. "So you use film and digital?"

"Yep," the photographer says, snapping away.

"That's really interesting. And how do you know what to photograph?"

"Sir, if you could please stand back."

Before they leave, the cop takes out his notebook. "A couple of queries before I go. There are some blank spots, holes in the story."

"Like what?"

"Were you having sex with her when your brother came home?"

"I was sleeping."

"Have you been having a relationship with your brother's wife?"

"I am here because my brother has been in the hospital."

"And your wife?"

"She's in China. It was my wife's suggestion that I stay with my brother's wife."

"How would you describe your relationship with your brother?"

"Close. I remember when they bought the house. I remember helping them pick things out—the kitchen tiles. After the accident, I comforted Jane."

The cop slaps his notebook closed. "All right, then, we know where to find you."

When the cop leaves, I discover Jane's purse on the front hall table and go through it, pocketing her cell phone, house keys, and, inexplicably—lipstick. Before I put her lipstick in my pocket, I open it, sweeping "Sweet Fuchsia" across my lips.

From the car, I call Claire in China. "There's been an accident; Jane has been injured."

"Should I come home tomorrow?"

In China tomorrow is today, and where we are today is tomorrow there. "Stay where you are," I say. "It's too complicated."

Why was Claire so willing to let me go? Why did she send me into Jane's arms? Was she testing me? Did she really trust me that much?

"I'm going to the hospital now and will call again when I know more." A pause. "How's work?"

"Fine. I've been feeling punk, I ate something strange."

"Maybe a worm?"

"Call me later."

When I get to the hospital, they tell me Jane is in surgery and George is still in the Emergency Room, shackled to a gurney in the rear.

"You stupid fuck," he says when I part the curtain.

"What happened to your face?" I point to a row of fresh stitches above his eye.

"Call it a welcome-back present."

"I fed the dog and stayed until the cops were finished, and then I called your lawyer—he's coming later."

"They don't want me back on account of how I 'ran away.' It's not like anyone told me what the checkout policy was and that I needed some sort of permission to go."

A hospital housekeeper passes through with a metal mop and bucket.

"Is he contagious?"

"No, just violent; come in," I say.

A young male doctor wheels in with an enormous lighted magnifying glass. "I am Chin Chow and I am here to pluck your face." The doctor leans over him, plucking shards from his face. "You've got no tits," George tells the doctor.

"And that is a good thing," Chin Chow says.

I go to the nurses' station. "My brother has stitches in his head—they weren't there when he left the house this morning."

"I'll make a note that you'd like the doctor to speak with you."

I go back to George, his face now a polka-dotted canvas of bloody red spots. "Chow Fun fucking plucked me, trying to get me to confess: 'Oh, so what bring you here today? You have rough night at home?' He fucking dug holes in my face with no anesthesia. 'Stop,' I said a hundred times. 'Stop. Stop. Stop.' 'Oh, you a big baby, cry, cry, cry. You a big boy now, act like a man.' That was no doctor, that was an undercover agent, trying to pry a confession out of me."

"Really? I think he was making conversation. I doubt he knows why you're here."

"Yes he does, he said he was going to read all about me in the *New York Post*." And with that George starts to cry.

"Aw, come on, don't start that."

He sputters a little longer and then, snorting and snuffling, he stops. "Are you going to tell Mom?"

"Your wife is having brain surgery and you're worried I'm going to tell your mother?"

"Are you?"

"What do you think?"

He doesn't answer.

"When did you last see Mom?" I ask.

"A few weeks ago."

"A few weeks?"

"Maybe a month?"

"How many months?"

"I don't fucking know. Are you telling her?"

"Why would I? Half the time she doesn't even know who she is. How about this: if she asks about you, I'll say you were transferred overseas. I'll send her tea from Fortnum and Mason and let her think you're still a big macher."

He wriggles on the gurney. "Scratch my ass, will you? I can't reach. You're a pal," he says, breathing deep with relief. "A pal when you're not a complete son of a bitch."

An orderly brings George a lunch tray, and, arms and legs bound, he manages to contort himself sufficiently that with his knees he bounces it off the tray table and onto the floor.

"One per customer," the lunch lady says, "try again tomorrow."

"Start an IV on him so he doesn't get dehydrated," I hear the nurse say without missing a beat.

"They're not fucking around," I tell him, when she pulls back the curtain, needle in hand, with four guys singing backup behind her. "Speaking of lunch, I'm going to the cafeteria."

"You may not die today," he says, "but I will unwind you like a spool of thread."

"Can I bring you anything?" I ask, cutting him off.

"Chocolate-chip cookies," he says.

I go through the cafeteria line, circling steaming trays of mixed vegetables, stuffed shells, meat loaf, cold sandwiches made to order, pizza, doughnuts, cereal; I go around and at the end my tray is empty. I circle again and get the tomato-rice soup, a bag of Goldfish crackers, and a carton of milk.

When I tear the package open, orange crackers take flight, littering the table and the floor around me. I collect what I can. They are different from what I remember; I'm not sure if it's the Goldfish in general or the flaw of the hundred-calorie pack—they're smaller and flatter and now with facial expressions. They float on their sides, looking up at me with one eye and a demented half-smile.

I eat thinking of the "worm" in the Chinese food, of the way the man at the deli near my apartment says "tomato lice." I eat picturing the pot of soup on my mother's stove, soup that formed a membranous skin across the top as it cooled, and how she would obliviously serve me that stringy clot, which I always ate imagining that it was really blood.

I eat the soup, pretending it is blood, pretending that I am transfusing myself while Jane is upstairs having a "craniotomy and evacuation"—those are the words they used. I imagine a surgical stainless dust-buster sucking out the porcelain and bone. I imagine her coming out of it all with steel plates like armor and required to wear a football helmet twenty-four hours a day.

Did she even know it was happening? Did she wake up thinking, This isn't real, this is a terrible dream—and then, when it was over, did she have a pounding headache? Did she think my hair was a mess?

She is in surgery, my spilled seed loose inside her, swimming furiously—as much as we did it with protection, we also did it without. Will anyone discover me swimming there? Do I need a lawyer of my own?

The soup warms me, reminding me that I've not eaten since last night. A man with two black eyes passes, lunch tray in hand, and I think of how my father once knocked my brother out, flattened him, for not much of a reason. "Don't be confused who's the boss."

I think of George: the dent in the Sheetrock from his foot "slipping," the coffee cup inexplicably flying out of his hand and smashing against the wall. I think of a story Jane once told me about heading out for Sunday brunch and

George hitting a trash can as he backed out of the driveway and then getting so angry that he went back and forth over the can, rocking the gears from forward to reverse and back again, hurling the children this way and that, stopping only when Ashley threw up. Do outbursts against inanimate objects signal that someday you're going to kill your wife? Is it really so shocking?

In the hospital men's room, as I'm washing my hands, I glance in the mirror. The man I see is not so much me as my father. When did he show up? There is no soap; I rub hand sanitizer into my face—it burns. I nearly drown myself in the sink trying to rinse it off.

My face is dripping, my shirt is wet, and the paper-towel dispenser is empty. Waiting to dry, I carve Jane's name into the cinder-block wall with the car key.

A hospital worker almost catches me, but I head him off with a confrontation: "Why no paper towels?"

"We don't use them anymore—sustainability."

"But my face is wet."

"Try toilet paper."

I do—and it catches in the stubble of unshaven beard and I look like I've been out in a toilet-paper snowstorm.

Monday, in the late afternoon, Jane comes out of surgery; they bring her down the hall attached to a huge mechanical ventilator, her head wrapped like a mummy, her eyes black and blue. Her face looks like a meatball. There is a hose coming out from under the blanket, a urine bag at the end of the bed.

I kissed her down there last night. She said no one had ever done that before, and then I kissed her again, deeply. I made out with her down there. I used my tongue—no one will ever know that.

I am telling myself that I did what I was told. Claire told me to stay. Jane wanted me—she pulled me towards her. Why am I being so weak? Why am I looking for someone else to blame? I ask myself, Did you ever think you should stop yourself, but in the moment you couldn't or didn't? Now I understand the meaning of "It just happened." An accident.

The doctor tells me that if Jane survives she will never be the same. "Even in the short time she's been with us, there has been a decline. She is retreating, folding into herself. We cleaned the wound and drilled holes to accommodate the swelling. The prognosis is poor. Does her family know? The children?"

"No," I say. "They're away at boarding school."

"Let them know," the doctor says, leaving me.

Do I call the children directly or do I call their schools first? Do I phone their respective headmasters and explain, Their mother is in a coma and their father is in shackles and perhaps you could interrupt study hall and suggest they pack a bag? And do I come right out and tell them how awful it really is—do I interrupt the children in the middle of their day to let them know that life as they know it is over?

I reach the girl first. "Ashley," I say.

"Is it Tessie?" she asks before I can say more.

"Your parents," I say stumbling.

"A divorce?" She collapses into tears before I say more, and another girl calmly takes the phone.

"Ashley is not available right now."

To the boy I say, "Your father has gone insane. Maybe you should come home, or maybe you don't want to come home, maybe you never want to come home again. I remember when your parents bought the house, I remember picking out things."

"I'm not sure I understand."

"Your mother has had an accident," I say, wondering if I should tell him how bad it really is.

"Was it Dad?" he asks.

I'm caught off guard by the directness of his question. "Yes," I say. "Your father struck your mother with a lamp. I tried to tell your sister, but I didn't get very far."

"I'll call her," he says. I am grateful for not having to go through that again.

I am standing in an empty hallway washed with stale fluorescent light. A man in a white coat comes towards me; he smiles. I imagine him like a wicked wizard whipping off his white coat, revealing a judge's robe. Is it possible that your brother knew you were shtupping his wife and so he got up out of his sickbed and got himself home?

"I am going to limit my comments for now. I feel bad enough about the whole thing," I say aloud in the hallway though no one is listening.

I move to the Family Waiting Room. Again, I dial. "George hit Jane with a lamp," I say to Jane's mother.

"That's awful," she says, not realizing the gravity of what I've told her. "When did that happen?"

"Last night. Is your husband home?"

"Sure," she says, sounding a little vague.

In the background I hear him ask, "Who is it?"

"It's your daughter's husband's brother," she says. "Something happened to Jane."

"What happened to Jane?" he asks, taking the phone.

"George hit her on the head with a lamp."

"Is she going to press charges?"

"Most likely she is going to die."

"That's not the kind of thing you say to be funny."

"I'm not joking."

"Son of a bitch," he says.

I want to go home. I want my life back. I had a life of my own. I was in the middle of something when all of this happened, wasn't I? What was happening? I don't have my date book, but there had to be something, a dentist appointment, dinner with friends, faculty meeting. What day is it? I check my watch. In five minutes I am teaching a class. Twenty-five undergraduates will file into a classroom and sit nervously in their chairs, knowing they have not prepared, knowing they have not done the reading. The course, Nixon: The Ghost in the Machine, a close examination of the unexamined. They sit like idiots waiting for me to tell them what everything means, to spoon-feed them an education. And while they numbly perch, they compose letters to the Dean; one complained that he was being asked to write in class, another calculated the cost per session of each of the twenty-two sessions in the semester and made a list of things he could have bought for the same or less money.

I have yet to put a dollar cost on the stress of having them stare blankly at me for ninety minutes two times a week and showing up during my office hours, asking me, "What's new?" like we're old friends and then sitting down as though they own the place and telling me how they can't get "an angle on things." And before they go, wanting me to pat them on the head and say,

"You're a good kid," for nothing, for no reason. There is about them a kind of casual entitlement, the sort of thing that when I was growing up would have gotten you a lecture for bad attitude and a week of detention.

In all the years, I've never failed to show up, have only twice had to reschedule a class, once for a root canal and the other a gallbladder attack.

I call the university, I call my department, I call the secretary of the Dean of the school to which I am affiliated—voice mail everywhere. I cannot find a real person to talk to. What will happen if I don't show up, how long will they sit there? I phone the security office. "This is Professor Silver. I have an emergency."

"Do you need a paramedic?"

"I am already in the hospital, but I am supposed to teach a class in two minutes; could someone go and put a note on the door telling the students that I have canceled?"

"One of our men, an officer?"

"Yes."

"That's not what we do."

I try another tactic. "But of course it's exactly what you do. If no one shows up, if no one of authority takes charge, there could be rioting. This is a course on politics, and you know what that means—radical ideas are loosened, the students feel empowered, mark my words."

"What should the note say?"

"Professor Silver has had a family emergency and will not be in class. He is sorry and will make it up to you."

"All right, then, and what building and room?"

"Can you look it up for me? I never pay attention to the names and numbers."

"Hold," he says. "Silver, there is no class today. You're in the School of Arts and Sciences, your people are on vacation. Party on the beach . . ."

"Oh," I say. "I forgot. I simply forgot. Thank you."

I had a life. I was doing something.

I meet the lawyer later at the house. He arrives in one car, his men in another. They carry heavy cases and remind me of exterminators.

"Top of the stairs on the right," I say, sending them up.

"What the fuck happened here?"

"What do you mean, what happened?"

"The place is a mess."

"You told me not to touch anything," I yell up the stairs.

"It fucking stinks."

Tessie follows me up. Halfway, the smell hits me.

"Fucking shit," the lawyer says.

The dog looks guilty.

Tessie, home alone, did a kind of clean and purge: she licked Jane's blood off the floor, made bloody pink tracks across the floor, and then had diarrhea on the bed.

Tessie looks at me as if to say, "It's been crazy around here. Something had to happen."

"S'okay, girl," I say, going downstairs and getting a box of Hefty bags. The dog has done me a favor. Whatever evidence might have remained on the sheets has been obliterated. I stuff the sheets into two Heftys, open the windows, and fire off a can of Lysol.

The trash has been taken out. The lawyer and his men are leaving. "The situation is less than satisfactory," one of the men says to another as they make their exit.

"No shit, Sherlock."

I stand in the kitchen, obsessing about the sheets: Is in the garbage good enough? Would it arouse suspicion if I took them to the dump? What would happen if I tried to burn them? Would it send shit smoke signals for miles?

I dial Speedy Mattress Service. "How quickly can I get a new mattress?"

"Where's it going?"

"To 64 Sycamore."

"And what are you looking for? Do you have something specific in mind: Serta, Simmons, plush, pillow-top?"

"I'm open to suggestions, it's got to be a king, soft but not too soft, firm but not too firm, something just right."

"You're looking at twenty-eight hundred—that's mattress and box spring."

"Seems high?"

"I can do twenty-six fifty delivered, and if you buy our mattress cover you get a ten-year guarantee. It's usually one twenty-five, but I can give it to you for a hundy."

"And will you take away the old one?"

"Yes."

"Even if it has stains?"

"They all have stains."

"When?"

"Hold on."

I dig Jane's credit card out of my pocket.

"Between six and ten tonight."

I get a bucket of hot water, scrub brush, roll of paper towels, Mr. Clean, Comet, a bottle of vinegar, and Jane's latex gloves from Thanksgiving. I weep as I pull the gloves on.

I am on my hands and knees, scrubbing. The blood is dark, dry, and flaky. Wet, it softens to a swirling pink, spreading like beet juice through the paper towels. I slice my finger open on shrapnel, a shard of porcelain that tears the skin, and my blood mixes with the mess. Later, I use a tube of Krazy Glue to seal the wound. As I am working I have the sensation of being watched, spied upon. I feel something pass over, brushing against my leg. When I turn to look, something sails over my body, leaping. I spin. I slip on the wet floor, landing on my ass. There is a cat, sitting on the dresser, staring, his tail flicking this way and that.

"Motherfucker," I say. "You scared me."

He blinks and looks at me, hot green eyes like emeralds shining.

A creature of habit, I stop only when the job is done, the bloody water bucket emptied, the rags thrown away. I work, and then I look to see what's for dinner. Standing inside the open door of the refrigerator, I pick at the leftovers, at what we had the night before. I eat random bites of things, thinking of Jane, of our evening snack, of our lovemaking. I make a plate and lie on the sofa in front of the television.

The echo of gunfire wakes me. I come to thinking George has once again escaped and has come to kill me.

Bang. Bang. Bang.

A heavy knocking on the door.

Tessie barks.

The mattress has arrived.

"Nice thing is, mattresses aren't breakable," one of the men says, as they wrestle it up the stairs. "I used to do plasma-screen televisions—that was a nightmare."

They take the old mattress and box spring without comment.

As they exit, a flash goes off in the yard.

"What the . . ." Flash, flash-flash.

One of the men drops his end of the outgoing mattress and plunges into the darkness. I hear scuffling sounds from within the bushes. The mattress man comes up, holding an expensive camera.

"Give me the camera," a stranger says, pulling himself out of the flower bed.

"Who are you?" I ask.

"That's my camera," the stranger says.

"Not anymore," the mattress man says, hurling it towards the street.

I have to go home. It's almost 11 p.m. I lock up the house, lead Tessie to the car, give her a boost up, and head for the highway. Tessie shakes.

"No shots," I say. "No vet. We're going to the city, Tessie."

The dog passes toxic gases. I pull to the side of the road, and Tessie explodes onto the edge of the highway.

"Did you have a good trip?" the night doorman asks. I don't answer. "Your mail, your packages," he says, filling my arms, "your laundry." He hooks the hangers over my crooked finger.

"Thank you."

He says nothing about the dog, whose leash I've lashed around my wrist.

The apartment has a certain smell, familiar yet stale. How long have I been gone? It's as though everything is frozen in time, has been frozen, not only for the days I've been away, but maybe the entire decade preceding. What once was modern, sophisticated, looks like the set of a period piece, Edward Albee circa 1983. The phone is a push-button trim-line, rarely used. The sofa arms are worn. The carpet pile is uneven along a certain path, a well-traveled route from room to room. The piles of magazines are dated eighteen months back.

And still I am grateful to be in a place where everything is familiar, where I could go blind and still find my way. I sink into it, want to roll in it, I want none of what's happened to be true.

The orchid is still in bloom. I water it, and, as if I were watching a time-lapse sequence, within the hour the petals fall off, as if suddenly released, springing to certain death on the cabinet below. By morning, only the bare stick will remain.

The refrigerator seeps the curdled scent of sour milk, half of a dry grapefruit, a jar of ageless peanut butter, some brown bread white and furry on the edges, old rice pudding brewing a green bull's-eye center in a plastic deli container. In a frenzy I open every cabinet and throw out what's expired. I wonder, does everyone do it the same way—glasses here, dishes there, dry foods and cans together? Where do you learn it, the grouping of like things? I take the trash down the hall and order Chinese. The man recognizes my phone number and says, "You call late tonight, long time no see; hot-sour soup, fried chicken rice, moo-shu pork?"

While waiting, I take the elevator to the basement, unlock the storage bin, and wrestle out an enormous ancient blue suitcase. Upstairs, I open the bag on the bed and begin to fill it. Unsure of exactly what I am thinking, I pack as if to consolidate, to minimize myself. I assume that when Claire returns I will no longer be welcome. Pulling open the drawers, the closet, the medicine cabinet, I am impressed with the gentility with which things coexist, how they hang, nestle, rest side by side without tension or judgment. Her floss, toothbrush, Nair, mascara, my gargle, nose spray, nail clipper. All of it intimate, all of it human, all of it divided his and hers—there is little overlap.

We married late; Claire had already been married once, briefly. It was two years before I took her to meet my parents. The first thing she told them was "It was a small wedding, just friends."

"Why did you keep her from us for so long?" my mother asked. "She's beautiful and has a good job. You thought we wouldn't approve?"

My mother took her hands. "We thought there must be something wrong with you—a reason he wouldn't bring you, like you had a cleft palate, or a penis or something?" she said, raising her eyebrows as if to say, How 'bout it?

What is the take-away? There is no logic to what goes in the bag—a few photos, trinkets from my childhood, a couple of suits, shoes, the canvas bag with the most recent draft of my unfinished manuscript on Nixon, the small black clock from her side of the bed. I don't want much, don't want to be obvious; I purposely leave my favorite things—I don't want to be accused of abandoning ship.

—————

Long after midnight, the doorbell rings. I tip the deliveryman heavily and sit at the table eating straight from the boxes, eating like it's been days since I was fed. The flavor is amazing, hot, spicy, the textures a treat, everything from slimy mushrooms and tofu to hard cubes of pork. I paste plum sauce on the pancakes and douse it all in soy sauce—the extreme sodium and glutamate breathe life back into me.

Tessie sits patiently at my feet. I give her a bowl of plain white rice—the starch will be good for her stomach. She eats quickly. I give her more, and then she again passes toxic gases.

I think of looking it up on the computer, Googling "Ill effects of drinking blood," but don't want to leave an electronic record of my visit.

"Tessie, how old are you? Are you twelve? That makes you over a hundred in human years—you're someone Willard Scott should celebrate. Who was that cat? Do you know him from somewhere? You didn't seem to mind that he was there." I continue: "Here's what I'm thinking: we'll stay here tonight, and we'll go back in the morning, in the full light of day."

I'm talking to a dog.

I call Claire in China, figuring to give it one last go.

"I'm in a meeting," she says.

"We can talk later."

"Is Jane better?"

"She's on a ventilator."

"I'm glad she's feeling much better," Claire says.

The rhythm of the line is the same; the rest has been lost in translation.

In bed, I pull a pillow from her side, close, against my chest, missing her in a routine kind of way, Claire standing over my shoulder while I balance the checkbook, insisting that we have his/hers accounts as well as one joint. Claire in the bathroom, using a squeegee stolen from a gas station to rake the shower door dry, Claire at the kitchen sink taking a glass of water and then washing and drying her glass and putting it away. Claire, who leaves nothing out of place, nothing to chance, always on it. What I liked about her, of course, became the problem—she wasn't there. She asked very little of me. And that meant she wasn't there and gave very little back.

Tessie walks around, looking confused. I take a towel from the bathroom and make a place for her by the side of the bed. She is an old setter, bought as a pup at a time when there was hope and promise, when it still seemed like things might turn out okay.

W̲e sleep.

She comes at me, whacking me with a pillow. "Get out of my house, get out of my house," she repeats. A man in a suit stands behind her. "That's enough for now. We'll get him again later," he says. I rush for the door; a man is there, changing the tumbler.

I wake. Who was she—was it Claire, was it Jane?

T̲he dog wants to go out. The dog wants breakfast. The dog wants to go back to her own home.

T̲he children are coming, arrangements have been made, cars have been hired to chauffeur them home. There have been phone calls behind their backs.

"What about the children? Where should the children go?" Jane's parents ask on a conference call.

I don't like the children, I'm thinking to myself, but remain silent.

"They can stay with me," Jane's sister, Susan, says. "We have an extra room."

"An office," Susan's husband says.

"There's a bed," Susan says.

And twins on leashes looking for trouble. I am thinking of Susan's toddler terrorists, who are in constant motion, often running towards a precipice. I imagine Susan and her husband on vacation with the children, having contests on the beach where they let the twins loose and see who can catch one first.

"They have a dog," I say.

"You're allergic," the mother reminds Susan.

"Well, it's too much for my parents," Susan says. "Two mentally disturbed teenagers."

It's too much for the children as well. They would be driven crazy governed by grandparents who spend most of their time discussing the consistency of their bowel movements and whether or not they should drink more prune juice.

I ignore the reference to mental disturbance—they are no more or less disturbed than the rest of us.

"The children need to be in their own home," I say.

"We have lives," Susan says. "We can't give up everything, and besides, I don't even like that house, I never liked it."

"It's not about the house," I say.

As we're talking, I climb the stairs to the master bedroom. I've already made the bed, and moved the "matching" lamp from George's side of the bed into the closet. As much as anything can look normal, it does. I take a plant from the kitchen windowsill and put it on the night table on Jane's side of the bed.

Nathaniel gets home first; the car pulls into the driveway, and he climbs out, dragging an enormous duffel bag behind him.

With one hand on Tessie's collar, I hold the kitchen door open. The dog is relieved to see the boy.

"Hi," I say.

He doesn't answer. He puts his bag down and talks to the dog. "What is going on around here, Tessie?" he says, mussing her ears. "What is it, girl? It's madness!"

He turns to me. "Can I give her a biscuit?"

"Sure," I say, not expecting to be asked. "Give her a cookie, give her two. Are you hungry? Do you want a sandwich?"

Without waiting for an answer, I take things out of the refrigerator and pile them on the table: bread, cheese, turkey, mustard, mayo, tomatoes, cornichons, the same things Jane and I were snacking on all last week. I get him a plate, a knife and fork and napkin.

"Aren't you having anything?" he asks, after he's built his sandwich and is about to sink in.

"I'm not hungry."

"Do we have any cream soda?" he asks. It seems odd at a time like this to ask for something so specific. Digging around in the fridge, I find, on the bottom shelf, in the back, a six-pack of Dr. Brown's. I take out two.

Ashley arrives with only a small My Little Pony rolling suitcase that's clearly a holdover from her childhood.

She is immediately down on her knees with the dog. "Tessie," she says. "Oh, Tessie."

"Would you like a sandwich?"

"A glass of milk," she says.

I pour one for her.

She sips. "It's on the edge," she says.

I nod.

"The milk, it's going bad," she says.

"Oh," I say. "We'll get some more."

There is silence.

"Is Dad coming home?" Ashley asks, and I don't quite know what to say.

"No," I offer.

"Where is our car?" Nate asks.

"I don't know if your mother mentioned it, but this whole thing started when your father had an accident. The car is in the shop, but I've got mine. Do you want to go to the hospital?"

The children nod. They've not gone upstairs. They've done nothing but pet the dog.

As we head out, I feel a flash of childhood memory, my uncle Leon pushing me out the door, his knuckles digging into my back, my bones taking the knuckle with a great impression, fear and dependency. It still hurts.

I hold the door for the children. "Take your time," I say.

At the hospital, walking from the car across the parking lot, Ashley slips her hand into mine.

"What is it going to be like?" Nate asks.

"Your mother is in Intensive Care, so it's very bright. She's hooked up to a lot of equipment; there's a machine helping her to breathe, and she's got an IV in her arm which gives her medicines and food. Her head is bandaged from the surgery, and she looks a little like a raccoon—she's got two black eyes."

"My father punched her in the eyes?" Nathaniel asks.

"It's bruising from the surgery."

In the elevator Ashley squeezes my hand so hard it hurts; she squeezes the whole way down the hall and into the ICU.

Jane's mother bursts into tears when the children come in.

"Stop, you're scaring them," her husband says.

"Too many, too many, too many," the nurse says, shooing people out.

The children are left alone with their mother

Jane's parents stand in the hall, glaring at me. "Son of a bitch," the father says.

"Let's get some coffee," he says to his wife.

I press myself to the glass. Ashley takes her mother's hand. I imagine it warm, even though it is limp; she rubs her cheek and face with it, stroking herself, giving herself her mother's affection. Nathaniel stands next to her, crying and then stopping himself from crying. A little later, when Ashley's head is on her mother's stomach, she looks up smiling and points to her mother's stomach. "It gurgled," she says, through the glass, as though a gurgle is a sign of improvement.

When the nurse needs to do something to Jane, I take the children to the cafeteria.

"What happens next?" Nathaniel asks, as he's eating a second lunch.

"You should spend as much time with your mom as you want, let her know you love her, and know how much she loves you."

When Ashley excuses herself to go to the bathroom, Nathaniel leans over.

"Did you fuck my mother?"

I don't answer.

"She was into you; she used to tease my father by talking about you."

Again, I say nothing.

"Where is Dad?" Ashley asks when she gets back to the table.

"He's here."

"This hospital?" Nate asks.

I nod. "Do you want to see him?"

"Should we see him?" Ashley asks.

"Entirely up to you."

"I need to think he's dead," Nate says. "That's the only way I can make sense of it. He did this and then turned the gun on himself."

"There was no gun," I say.

"You know what I mean. Why didn't you stop him, why didn't you kill him?" Nate asks.

Why didn't I?

All too familiar with the hospital layout, I lead the children to the Emergency Room. George is parked in a back hallway, bound to a chair, slumped like he's been sleeping for days, his face roughened with stubble.

"Either we sedate him or he's out of control," the nurse remarks, spotting me.

"These are the children," I say, "Ashley and Nathaniel."

"He ate a good lunch, and we're awaiting his disposition," the nurse says, slightly more chipper.

"Is that like his mood?" Ashley asks.

"It's paperwork telling us where he'll go from here," the nurse says.

George opens his eyes.

"The children are here," I say.

"Hi, Dad," Ashley says. Nathaniel says nothing.

"Sorry," George says.

There is an awkward silence. We all stare at the floor, at the patterns in the linoleum.

"George, I've been meaning to ask you, there's a cat who scratches at the kitchen door, gray, with green eyes and a dab of white on the tail. It's gotten into the house a couple of times. And it looks like no one feeds it, so I bought some kibble."

"That's Muffin," George says. "Our cat."

"Since when do you have a cat?"

"Years. Her litter box is in the guest bathroom—you'd better clean it."

"She likes canned food," Ashley says, softly.

"What were you thinking?" Nathaniel asks his father.

"No idea," George says. "What day is it?"

We go back to Intensive Care. The doctor is there. "She's recovering well from the procedure itself," he says.

"Of course she is, she's a good girl," her father says.

"There's still no sign of activity. Have you thought about organ donation?" the doctor asks.

"Would that help her? A donation?" Jane's father asks.

"He means Mom being a donor," Nate clarifies.

"Don't you have to be dead to do that?" Jane's mother asks.

"Something to keep in mind. We'll know more soon," the doctor says.

"We can stay if you want, or we can go and come back after dinner," I say to the children.

"Let's take a break," Ashley says.

I take them to the mall. "Is this where you usually go? Is this what you do with your mother?" I buy them sneakers and frozen yogurt. The mall is uncomfortably empty; it's a weekday, no one is there.

"Why are you being so nice?" Nathaniel asks.

I say nothing.

"It sucks. It all sucks," he says. Back in the car, Nate asks, "Can you take me for a ride?"

"Where?"

"I want to get out of here."

"Do you have a bike? Maybe when we get home you can go for a ride. It's certainly warm enough out."

"I'm not asking if I can go for a ride," he says. "I'm asking you to take me on a ride." There's a pause. "I took some pills."

"What do you mean, 'pills'?"

"Not too many, but enough."

"Enough to kill yourself?"

"No, to calm down. I'm a wreck."

"Where did you get them?"

"From the medicine cabinet at home."

"How did you know which ones to take?"

Nate stares at me as if to say, I may be dumb but I'm not stupid.

"Okay, so where do you want to go?" I ask.

"Amusement park."

"You're kidding, right?"

Apparently not.

At Nate's insistence I phone the amusement park and find that due to the odd and unseasonably warm winter, they haven't closed for the season. "The owner thought it was better to keep folks employed and have a snow day if needed—which so far hasn't happened," the guy says. Nate goes on ride after ride, roller coaster, Zipper, Bungee Rocket, Tower of Terror, Gravitron, which spins so fast he's plastered to the side with an expression on his face like he's been whipped through a wind tunnel.

"Do you think it's weird?" he asks as we walk to the next ride.

"Who am I to judge?"

"I carry a diagnosis," he says.

"Like what?"

"Like supposedly there's something wrong with me."

"What's your point?"

"Do you think it's true?" he asks.

"Do you?" I ask.

He shrugs.

"Do you want to go on a ride?" I ask Ashley, who at eleven is holding my hand and seeming more like six. She shakes her head no. "Are you sure? I'll go with you." She shrugs.

"I miss the snow," she says, shaking her head sadly. "When I was young it used to snow in the winter."

"It will snow again," I say.

"When?" she asks.

"When you least expect it," I say.

We leave Nate at the roller coaster. He seems relieved by the spinning, by hurling through the air again and again. Ashley picks out something called the Wave Swinger; it seems innocent enough.

Like the mall, the amusement park is empty. Nate and Ashley both have their own attendants, ride operators who are like mechanical tour guides. They walk with us from ride to ride, turning each one on and giving it a test spin before letting the kids board.

"Isn't it hard to spend your days in an empty amusement park?" I ask one of the operators.

"Beats sitting home with my wife," the guy says, shrugging like I'm the idiot.

"My mother's in the hospital," Ashley tells the operator as he's turning on the chair swing. "We were sent home from school. Our father hit her in the head."

"Rough," the operator says, and it vaguely sounds like he's saying "Ruff," as in barking more than talking.

The Wave Swinger lifts gently off the ground. I am in the chair ahead of Ashley, suspended by twenty feet of galvanized chain. It makes a couple of graceful spins in a wide circle, rising higher each time, and then it takes off, spinning faster and faster. The chair swings out wide, it tilts, now we're flying up high and then swooping down low. I am dizzy, nauseous, trying to find one thing to fix on, one thing that is not moving. I stare at the empty chairs in front of me, the blue sky overhead. I am losing my sense of balance; I fear I will pass out and somehow slip out of the chair and fall to the ground.

Nate is waiting for us when we land. I stumble getting off the ride and knock my head into the chains.

We head for the Haunted House, all hopping into our own cars, and the train bangs through the double doors and into the darkness. It's warm inside and smells like sweat socks. Overhead there are howls and ear-piercing screeches from the dead, timbers crack, and ghosts fall from the sky, stopping inches short of our faces before being snatched away again. The mechanical soundtrack is punctuated by a frightful choking sound.

"What is that?" I ask.

"It's Ashley," Nate says.

"Are you choking?" I ask, unfastening my seat belt and trying to turn and look at her.

"She's crying," Nate says. "That's the way she cries."

As lightning is crashing around me and we're climbing a hill into a dark castle, I'm turning and trying to crawl out of my car and into hers. Suddenly strobe lights are flashing and, as in some slow-motion Marx Brothers movie, I'm on my hands and knees on top of the train car. The train is heading straight for the closed door of the castle, and right before it hits, the train turns sharply and I am thrown overboard, banging into a wall, reaching out and grabbing at anything for balance, worried about landing on the third rail—if there is such a thing in a haunted house. And then it all stops. It's pitch-dark. "Don't move," we hear a voice overhead. Ashley is still crying, sobbing in the dark. A minute later, the Haunted House is flooded with bright fluorescent light; every secret of the night is revealed—the lousy papier-mâché walls, the cheaply strung-together skeletons suspended on wire hangers, the yellow and purple glow-in-the-dark paint on everything.

"What the fuck," the ride operator says, coming down the tracks.

"Sorry," I say.

"Sorry, shmorry," he says to me.

"The little girl was crying."

"Are you all right, sweetheart?" the operator asks Ashley, genuinely concerned. "Is anybody injured?"

We all shake our heads. "We're all right."

The operator grabs a tow rope at the front of the train and pulls us all down the tracks, bending his head at the front doors, and we bang out into the daylight.

"You sure you're all okay?"

"As okay as we can be, given the circumstances," I say. I hand the guy twenty bucks. I'm not exactly sure why, but it feels necessary.

"Let's go home," I say to the children, herding them to the parking lot.

"It was all good until we got to the Haunted House," Nate says.

"It was good," I say.

For dinner we have Jane's spaghetti sauce from the freezer.

"I love Mom's spaghetti," Ashley says.

"Great," I say, worried that there are only two more containers in the freezer and they're going to have to last a lifetime. I'm wondering if spaghetti sauce can be cloned. If we save a sample or take a swab of Jane's sauce, can someone make more?

Spaghetti and frozen broccoli and cream soda and Sara Lee pound cake. You would almost think things are under control.

The cat walks by, flicking her tail at my ankles under the table. Ashley gets up and shows me the cabinet where forty cans of cat food are stacked in neat order.

"She likes the salmon the best," Ashley says.

After dinner I take the children back to the hospital. Everything is slightly more hushed; the ICU has a dimmed glow-in-the-dark quality. The large space is divided into eight glass-walled rooms, of which six are occupied.

"Anything?" I ask the nurse.

She shakes her head. "Nothing."

The children visit with their mother. Nathaniel has brought a paper he wrote for school. He reads it aloud to her and then asks if she thinks it needs something more. He waits for an answer. The ventilator breathes its mechanical breath. After he reads the paper, he tells her about the amusement park, he tells her about a boy at school that apparently she already knows a lot about, he tells her that he's calculated that by the time he's ready to start college it will cost about seventy-five thousand dollars a year and that by the time Ashley is ready to start it will be more than eighty. He tells her he loves her.

Ashley rubs her mother's feet. "Does that feel good?" she asks, smoothing cream over her toes and up her ankles. "Maybe tomorrow I can bring polish from home and do your nails."

Later, I walk through the house, turning out lights. It's nearly midnight. Ashley is in her room, playing with her old toys; all the dolls from her shelves are down on the floor, and she's in the middle.

"Time for bed," I say.

"In a minute," she says.

Nate is down the hall, in his parents' room, splayed out on their bed asleep and fully clothed. Tessie is with him, her head on the pillow, filling in for Jane.

In the morning, a van pulls up outside. A man gets out, unloads six boxes. From inside I watch him carry them one by one to the front door. At first I'm thinking it's a box bomb delivered by the surviving relatives of the family George killed. But there's something so methodical, so painstaking about the way this guy works that clearly he's a professional of another sort. The last thing out of the van is the enormous plant. He's got everything all lined up before he rings the bell.

Tessie barks.

I open the door carefully.

"Delivery," he says. "Can you sign for these?"

"Sure. What is it?"

"Your property."

"My property?"

"Office supplies," the guy says, turning to leave. "How the fuck would I know? I'm just the messenger. Eight o'clock in the morning and people are already asking questions. When is enough enough?" He walks back to the van, yelling the whole way.

I drag the boxes into the house. It's the contents of George's office.

"Did you order something?" Ashley asks.

"It's for your dad," I say, and the three of us drag it all into his office and close the door.

"Can I have the plant?" Nate asks.

The decision is made to take Jane off life support, to donate her organs. "I didn't sleep all night," her mother says. "I made up my mind and then I changed my mind and then I made up my mind and I changed my mind."

"Who will tell the children?" someone asks.

"You should," Jane's father says, stabbing his finger towards me. "It's all on you."

Nate and Ashley are taken to a conference room; they ask me to come with them. We sit, waiting and waiting, and then, finally, the doctor comes in. He's got scans, charts, and graphs.

"Your mom is very sick," he says.

The children nod.

"The damage to her brain can't be fixed. So we're going to let her body help other people whose bodies can get better. Her heart can help someone whose heart isn't working. Does that make sense?"

"Daddy killed Mommy," Ashley says.

There isn't much more to say.

"When are you going to pull the plug?" Nate asks.

The doctor braces. "We'll take her to the operating room and remove the parts that can be transplanted."

"When?" Nate wants to know.

"Tomorrow," the doctor says. "Today all the people who are going to be helped by your mom will get phone calls, and they'll go to the hospitals near where they live, and their doctors will start to get ready."

"Can we see her?" Ashley asks.

"Yes," the doctor says. "You can see her today, and again in the morning."

Somehow the police are notified and a cop shows up with a photographer, and they ask us all to leave the room, and they pull the curtains around her bed and start taking pictures. The white flash explodes again and again behind the curtain, lighting up the silhouettes of the cop and the photographer. I can't help but wonder: Are they taking close-ups, are they pulling back the blankets? Are they photographing her nude? The flashes of light attract attention; the other families look at us strangely but silently. Stroke, heart attack, burn—MURDER—we are known to each other by ailment and not by name.

When the cops finish, we go back in. I look at the blanket. If they pulled it back, what did they see? What does a brain-dead woman look like? I fear I know the answer: like a dead woman.

Rutkowsky the lawyer and I meet in the hospital parking lot and go in together to talk to George. "He's never asked how she is," I tell the lawyer.

"Let's assume he's out of his mind," the lawyer says.

"George," Rutkowsky and I say simultaneously, as the nurse pulls the curtain back. George is in a bed, curled into a ball.

"Your wife, Jane, has been declared brain-dead; she'll be taken off life support, and the charges against you will be raised to murder, or manslaughter, or whatever we can get them to agree to," the lawyer says. "The point being, once this happens, wheels will be put into motion and your options become more limited. I am negotiating to have you sent someplace, to a facility I have worked with in the past. When you arrive, there will be a period of detoxification and then, hopefully, they'll be able to address your underlying psychosis. Do you see what I'm saying, do you hear the direction I'm going in?" The lawyer pauses.

"She was sucking my brother's cock," George says.

And nothing more is said for a few minutes.

"What will she look like?" George asks, and I'm not sure exactly what the question means. "Well, no matter, I'm sure they can make a nice hat for her."

The nurse tells us she needs a moment alone with George. We take the cue and leave.

"Have you got a minute?" the lawyer asks me.

In the lobby of the hospital, the lawyer asks me to take a seat. He places his enormous bag on the small table next to me and proceeds to unpack a series of documents. "Due to the physical and mental conditions of both Jane and George, you are now the legal guardian of the two minor children, Ashley and Nathaniel. Further, you are temporary guardian and the medical proxy for George. With these roles comes a responsibility that is both fiduciary and moral. Do you feel able to accept that responsibility?" He looks at me— waiting.

"I do."

"You are conservator of assets, real-estate holdings, and other items that transfer to the children upon their majority. You have power of attorney over all transactions, assets, and holdings." He hands me a small skeleton key; it's like being indoctrinated into a secret society. "It's the key to their safe-deposit box—I have no idea what's in the box, but I suggest you familiarize yourself with the contents." And then he hands me a new bank card. "Activate this from the home phone at George and Jane's house. The accountant Mr. Moody also has access to the accounts and will monitor your usage. It's a system of checks and balances: Moody checks on you, you check on Moody, and I check on the two of you. Got it?"

"I do," I repeat.

He hands me a manila envelope. "Copies of all the related paperwork, in case anyone should ask." And then, weirdly, the lawyer takes out a little bag of gold chocolate coins and dangles them in front of my eyes.

"Gelt?" I ask.

"You look pale," he says. "My wife bought a hundred of these, and somehow it's fallen to me to get rid of them."

I take the small bag of chocolate coins. "Thank you," I say. "For everything."

"It's my job," he says, as he's leaving. "My occupation."

Where is Claire?

She has been lost in transit, was heading home and then rerouted. Along the way, she started hearing from her friends. I get a hostile call from Hawaii, where the aircraft has mechanical trouble. Accusatory.

"What are your comments based on? Hearsay?" I ask.

"The *New York Post*," she says.

"And that's the new paper of record?"

"Fuck you," she says. "Fuck you. Fuck you, fuck you." And she smashes her phone into the wall. "You hear that, that's the sound of me smashing my BlackBerry into a wall. Fucking asshole."

"I've got you on speakerphone," I say, even though I don't. "We're all here at the hospital, the kids, Jane's parents, the doctor. I'm sorry you're so upset." I'm lying. I'm alone in what used to be a phone booth that's now been stripped of its equipment; it's a denuded glass booth—powerless.

"FUCK YOU!"

The day of limbo. There is the oddity of knowing tomorrow Jane will be dead. When the phone in the house rings, Jane's voice answers: "Hi, we can't come to the phone right now, but if you leave your name and number we'll call you back. If you're trying to reach George at the office, the number is 212 . . ."

She is here, still in the house; I run into her coming around the corner, unloading the dishwasher, running the vacuum, folding laundry. She was just here—wait, she'll be back in a minute.

The next day, at the hospital, Jane's mother collapses at her bedside and everything is delayed until she is revived. "Can you imagine having to make a decision like this about your child?" she asks as they take her down the hall in a wheelchair.

"I can't imagine, which is why I don't have children. Correction, I can imagine, which is why I don't have children." I say this thinking I am talking to myself, silently in my head, not realizing that in fact I'm talking to everyone.

"We thought you couldn't have children," Jane's sister says.

"We didn't even try," I say, even though that's not exactly the truth.

The family takes turns saying goodbye to Jane privately. I am the last. On her forehead there is a mark from her mother's lipstick, like the blood-and-earth dot of a Hindu. I kiss her; Jane's skin is warm but uninhabited.

Ashley walks with the stretcher down the hall. As they wait for the elevator, she whispers something in her mother's ear.

We stay, even though there is nothing to stay for. We sit in the ICU Family Waiting Room. Through the glass I see a housekeeper stripping the bed, washing the floor, preparing for the next patient.

"Let's go to the cafeteria," I say.

In the hallways, people hurry past. They carry Igloo coolers marked "Human Tissue" or "Organ for Transplant—Human Eye." They come and they go. Through the large glass window of the cafeteria, I see a helicopter flying in, landing in the parking lot, and then taking off again.

Her heart has left the building.

On one end it's like time has stopped, and on the other, time is of the essence, people are gearing up. Where do you go when it is over, when it is done? With every hour, with every part taken, she is a little further gone. There is no going back. It's over. Really.

"It's good she can help others, she'd like that," her mother says.

"Her heart and lungs shouldn't go to waste," her father says. "Her eyes were good, so beautiful, maybe someone can use them; maybe someone can have a good life even if hers turned to shit."

"Don't talk like that in front of the children," her mother says.

"I'm hardly talking at all. If anyone wanted to hear what I'd really like to say, I could give them an earful."

"I'm listening," I say.

"I'm not talking to you. You are a shmuck, as much responsible for this as your son-of-a-bitch brother. Slime balls."

And he's right—it's unfathomable that this is how it ends.

The sister's husband is going to pick out a coffin. He wants me to ask Nate if Nate wants to come along, to help make the arrangements. I ask, but he doesn't hear me, he's got his headphones on. I tap his shoulder. "Do you want to be part of the arrangements?"

He looks at me blankly.

"Arrangements. It's another word for funeral plans. Susan's husband is going to the funeral home to pick out the coffin—do you want to go? I did it for my grandmother," I offer, as if to say it's not so bad.

"What do you do?"

"You look at coffins, you pick one, and you think about what your mother should wear as her final outfit."

Nate shakes his head no. "Ask Ashley," he says. "She likes to pick out things."

That night Nate comes to visit me on the sofa. "Have you Googled Dad?"

"No."

"He didn't just kill Mom, he killed a whole family."

"He had an accident. That's what started this whole thing."

"Everyone hates him. There are postings about how he ruined the network, about what a bully he was at the office—especially to women. It says that there were numerous claims settled quietly with regard to harassment of female employees."

"It's not new," I say to Nate. "People have always had strong feelings about your father."

"It's hard for me to read about it," Nate says, almost hysterical. "It's one thing when I think he's a jerk, but another when strangers say mean things."

"Do you want some ice cream?" I ask. "There's half a Carvel cake in the freezer."

"It's from Ashley's birthday."

"Does that mean it can't be eaten?"

Nate shrugs.

"Would you like some?"

"Yes."

Using an enormous serrated knife, I saw off chunks; the ice cream is old and gummy and hard as a rock, but as it melts it gets better, and by the time we're done, it's delicious. When we're finished, Tessie licks our plates clean.

"She's the prewash," Nate says.

Nate lies with me on the sofa, his head on the opposite end, his stinky feet near my face. When he's asleep, I turn off the television and put the dishes in the washer. Tessie follows; I give her a biscuit.

A long black limo pulls up to the curb outside the house. The children gather, dressed in their best. I stuff my pockets with Kleenex and snacks.

"I've never been to a funeral," Ashley says.

"I went once, when the kid of someone Dad worked with killed himself," Nate adds.

At the funeral home, two men hold the doors open for us. "The immediate family is receiving to the left," one says.

"We are the immediate family," Nate says.

The man leads us down the hall. Jane's parents are there, the sister and her husband.

There's something excruciating about this part. Strangers, or, even worse, friends, crouch at the children's knees, touching them, hugging them, stressed faces one after another pressing into theirs, faces like caricatures. There is the awkwardness of people feeling the need to say something when there is nothing to say. Nothing.

I'm sorry for your loss. Oh, you poor babies. What will become of you?

Your mother was such a wonderful woman. What does your father have to say for himself? I can only imagine. Is your dad going to get the electric chair?

They feel the liberty or the obligation to say whatever the hell comes to mind.

"I'm sorry, I am sorry, so, so sorry," people keep telling the children.

"That's okay," Ashley says to them.

"It's not okay," Nate says to Ashley. "Quit saying it's okay—it's not."

"When people say they're sorry you can just say thank you," I say.

We are led into the chapel for the service and sit in pews like at a wedding, Jane's family on one side, us on the other. Behind us are people who know Jane's family, people who the kids went to nursery school with, people who knew Jane from the gym, friends and neighbors. The anchorman from Thanksgiving is there, as is George's assistant, a gay guy who did favors for the kids. He was the one who got them good tickets, backstage passes.

The coffin is at the front of the room.

"Is she really in there?" Ashley asks, nodding towards the coffin.

"Yes," I say.

"How do you know they put the right clothes on her?" Ashley asks.

"It's a question of trust."

Susan's husband comes up to me. "Do you like the coffin?" he asks. "It's top-of-the-line. In a situation like this it seems cruel to be cheap."

"Are you asking for my approval?"

I think of Nixon's funeral. He had the stroke at home in New Jersey on a Monday night, right before dinner. His housekeeper called an ambulance, and they drove him into New York City, paralyzed but conscious. The initial prognosis was good, but then his brain swelled; he went into a coma and died. Nixon's coffin was flown from New York to Yorba Linda, where people wound through the quiet streets on a chilly night, waiting for hours to see him. I was going to go, make a kind of pilgrimage the way Mormons flock to the mountain or groupies to a Grateful Dead concert.

Instead, I watched on TV.

Forty-two thousand people viewed Nixon's coffin over a twenty-hour period. The fact that I was not among them is something I regret. I watched on television, but I felt nothing. I didn't have the actual experience, the shared night out in the cold. I only made it to Yorba Linda once, years after Nixon's death.

"How do I tell people at school?" Ashley asks.

"They probably already know," Nate says.

"That's not fair," Ashley says.

I pass Ashley some Gummi Bears.

Jane's sister sees and hurries over from their side of the room. She sits in the pew right behind me, leans forward, and whispers.

"Since when do you know about things like snacks?"

"I don't," I say without even turning around.

I don't like kids, but I feel guilty; worse than guilty, I feel responsible; worse than that, I think their lives are ruined.

And me, under stress I reminisce about the stories of a life that is not my own. I suck on a sweet; I pop a couple of Gummis into my mouth, without offering any to Susan.

"Where are the twins?" I ask Susan.

"With a sitter," she says, her Botox so fresh her face doesn't move.

An older woman leans in and tugs on Ashley's hair. "You poor children and your beautiful hair."

Music begins to play.

The rabbi appears. "Friends, family, parents of Jane, her sister, Susan, and her children, Nathaniel and Ash."

"No one calls her Ash," Nate says flatly.

"How does one make sense of a death such as this, a life interrupted? Jane was a mother, a daughter, a sister, and a friend—and she was also the victim of a crime, denied the natural course of life."

"I never liked George," her mother says loudly during the service. "George was an asshole from the first date."

The rabbi continues: "Out of Jane's death comes a break with tradition; when a Jew dies, no one questions if there will be a ritual washing or a funeral, but what of the body? Jane's family chose organ donation, so that the parts of Jane which remained strong, viable, could save the lives of others—they did the mitzvah of giving Jane to others. One of the purposes of the funeral ceremony is to help the friends and family adjust to the finality of their loss. And while the circumstances of Jane's death leave us searching for logic, we celebrate her life and the life she will now give others. *HaMakom yinachaim etchem batoch shar avlai Zion v'Yerushlayim.* May God comfort you together with all the other mourners of Zion and Jerusalem," the rabbi offers. "This is the traditional Jewish expression of condolence."

"Are we orphans?" Ashley asks.

"Kind of."

"Yit-gadal v'yit-kadash sh'mey raba, b'alma di v'ra hirutey, vyam-lih mal-hutey b'ha-yey-hon uv'yomey-hon uv'ha-yey d'hol beyt yisrael ba-agala u-vizman kariv, v'imru amen." the rabbi intones.

"Were we always Jewish?" Ashley asks.

"Yes."

The ceremony concludes, and one of the guests turns to me and says, "Given the circumstances, I think the rabbi did a very good job. What did you think?"

"It's my policy not to review funerals."

"If the guests would stay in their places until the family has had a chance to exit it would be appreciated," the rabbi says.

Jane's casket is rolled past us; the anchorman from Thanksgiving is one of the pallbearers.

Jane's parents exit with Susan between them. I notice that when she cries her expression doesn't change—tears of a clown.

Nate, Ashley, and I follow after the coffin, climbing into the limo as Jane is lifted into the hearse.

"I hope I never have to do this again," Nate says.

"Can we go home now?" Ashley asks.

"No," Nate says. "There's like an after-party thing?"

"From here we go to the cemetery. At the graveside, a few words are said and the coffin is lowered into the ground." I wonder if I should tell them the part about shoveling some dirt on your mother, or if some things are better left unsaid. "And after the cemetery we sit shiva at Susan's house. People who knew your mom will come and visit, and there will be food for lunch."

"I want to be alone," Nate says.

"It's not an option."

"Who sends these cars? And do they work other jobs?" Nate asks.

"Like what?"

"Like driving rock stars, or do they just do funerals?"

I lean forward and ask the driver, "Do you just do funerals, or funerals and rock stars?"

The driver glances at us in his rearview mirror. "Me, I do funerals and airports. I don't like rock and roll. They'll sign you up for a two-hour job, and four days later you're still parked outside of some hotel, waiting for the guy to decide if he wants to go out for a burger. I like regularity and a schedule." He pauses. "You got lucky with the weather. Hope you don't mind me saying but there's nothing worse than working a funeral when the weather is crap. Puts everyone in a bad mood."

In the limo en route to the cemetery, the children are on their electronic devices. On the one hand, it's not appropriate to play computer games while driving to bury your mother; on the other, who can blame them? They want to be anywhere but here.

Jane's plot is between her aunt and her grandmother, between ovarian cancer and stroke. She is with her people. They have died of illness and old age, but never has there been the victim of domestic violence. It's different— it's worse.

The children sit on folding chairs behind their grandparents. Despite its being a nice day, it's chilly, so everyone keeps their coats on, hands in pockets. As the casket is being lowered, a hushed set of whispers, a current of surprise, sweeps through the group.

"Daddy's here," Ashley says.

We all turn to look, and, sure enough, he's getting out of the back of a car, with two burly black men in scrubs on either side of him.

"That takes a lot of nerve," Jane's mother says.

All around us people are whispering, rustling, turning.

"She was his wife."

"Until death did them part."

"He should at least have waited until we left," Susan says.

"He still has rights," someone says.

"Until he is found guilty."

The timing is off. George should have stayed in the car, hidden until everyone was gone. He stays in the distance, until the graveside service is done.

"Should we go talk to him?" Nate asks.

"Not right now," I say. "We'll see him soon."

As the funeral procession is pulling out of the cemetery, we pass George on his knees at the grave, sunglasses on, his handcuffed hands in front of him. I see him pushing dirt barehanded into the grave, both hands at once, joined at the wrist.

There is someone with a long lens taking photos.

"Grandma and Grandpa hate us," Nate says.

"They're upset."

"They're acting like it's our fault."

The shiva is at Susan's house. It's far, an hour from the cemetery. After we've been driving for about forty-five minutes, the kids start to complain. I ask the driver if we can make a pit stop. The long limo drops out of the procession, waits until all the cars have passed; then we slip into a McDonald's.

"My treat," I say to everyone, including the driver.

"I thought they were serving lunch at the shiva," Nate says.

"What would you rather have, a hamburger or egg salad?"

"I'll toss the evidence," the driver says when we get to Susan's house.

"I'm assuming you'll wait?" I say.

"You don't have a car?" the driver asks.

"My car is back at the house where you picked us up."

"Usually we just drop the people off. But I'll wait. I'll make it a time call; the hourly rate is seventy-five, with a four-hour minimum."

"We won't be that long."

The driver shrugs.

The twins are on the loose. They're running through the house, chased by a small dog that seems like a trip hazard for old people. The front hall is mirrored tile with gold veins running through. Just glancing at it makes me nervous; my reflection splits into many pieces, and I wonder if it's a "magic mirror" somehow empowered to display my internal state.

Susan is leading a tour of her remodeled split-level, showing Jane's friends how she "blew out" the ceiling and "pushed back" the rear wall so she'd have a great room and a dining room, and how they "recaptured" the garage and made a den/breakfast room with French doors and added decks "everywhere."

"We did everything we could think of and more," Susan says, proudly.

And it shows.

The visitors are the same people from the funeral, friends, neighbors, do-gooders, and curious assholes who have no business being there. Despite having eaten a double cheeseburger, I circle the dining-room table, where lunch is laid out. Pitted black olives and cherry tomatoes stare at me, expressionless. Avocados and artichokes, deviled eggs with paprika, smoked salmon, bagels, and macaroni salad; I'm looking at it all, and suddenly it turns into body parts, organs: the Jell-O mold is like a liver; the macaroni salad, cranial matter. I pour myself a Diet Coke.

An older man comes up to me with a look of purpose and extends his hand.

"Hiram P. Moody," he says, shaking my hand, "your brother's accountant. No doubt you've got a lot on your mind, but what I want you to know, fiduciarily speaking, you're going to be okay."

I must have given him an odd look. "You've got nothing to worry about," he says. "Financially—you're in good shape. George was a bit of a player, he took some chances, made a gamble here and there, but let's just say he had a good sense of timing."

"I'm sorry?" I say, finding Hiram P. hard to follow.

He nods. "Let me be blunt. You and the children will be well cared for. I pay the bills; whatever you need, you let me know. I'm much more than a 'see you in mid-April' tax guy. I'm your go-to guy—the one who holds the purse strings—and now so do you. I've got some papers that you'll need to sign—no rush," he says. "I assume you know that you're the legal guardian for the children, as well as guardian and medical proxy for your brother, and Jane specifically wanted you as executor of any estate—she was concerned that her sister didn't share her values."

I nod. My head is bobbing up and down as if I were a puppet on a weight.

Hiram P. slips a business card into my palm. "We'll talk soon," he says. And as I turn to go, he calls after me, "Wait, I've got something better. Put out your hand." I do, and he slaps something into it. "Refrigerator magnet," he says. "My wife had them made—it's got all the info, even my cell—for emergencies."

"Thanks," I say.

Hiram P. takes me by the shoulders and gives a combo shake/squeeze. "I'm here for you and the children," he says.

Inexplicably, my eyes fill with tears. Hiram P. moves to hug me as I'm bringing my hand up to blot my eyes. Maybe it wasn't a hand, maybe it was my fist; maybe I wasn't going to blot my eyes so much as rub them with a closed fist. My fist connects with the underside of Hiram P.'s chin in a small but swift uppercut that knocks him against the wall. The picture hanging behind him slips on its hook, tilts.

Hiram P. laughs. "That's what I love about you guys, you're fucking nuts. So—call me," he says. "Whenever you're ready."

I sit next to Ashley and Nate on Susan's sectional leather sofa. An older woman sits next to us. "I knew your mother. I did her nails—she had beautiful nails. She talked about you a lot, very proud of both of you. Very proud."

"Thank you," Ashley says.

Nate gets up and goes to get something to eat. He comes back with a plate of berries for Ashley.

"You're a good brother," I say to him.

A woman bends towards the children, revealing loose, wrinkled cleavage. I look away. She extends her hand. No one takes it. The hand, with its big diamond, lands on Nate's knee. "I was her hygienist. We used to have wonderful talks—well, mostly I talked, she had the saliva sucker on, but she was a good listener. She was good."

"Do you have anything?" Nate asks me.

"Anything like what?"

"Like a Valium, an Ativan, maybe codeine."

"No," I say, surprised. "Why would I be carrying that?"

"I don't know. You had snacks—Gummi Bears—and Kleenex. I thought maybe you'd have some medication."

"Is there something you normally take for upset? Something that a doctor gives you?"

"I just take stuff from Mom and Dad's medicine cabinet."

"Great."

"Okay, never mind, just thought I'd ask." Nate walks away.

"Where are you going?"

"Bathroom."

I follow him.

"You're following me?"

"Are you going to look in the medicine cabinet?"

"I have to pee," Nate says.

"If you are, I'm going to do it with you. We'll look together."

"That's so fucked up."

"Any more or less so than you doing it alone?"

I follow him into the bathroom, locking the door behind us.

"I really do have to pee."

"So pee."

"Not with you standing there."

"I'll turn my back."

"Can't," he says.

"I don't trust you."

"When I'm back at school you won't be following me into the bathroom. There has to be a measure of trust. Just let me pee."

"You're right, but the minute you blow it, you are so fucked," I say, opening the medicine cabinet.

"His Prilosec, her birth control, her Prozac; acyclovir—that's nice, they must have herpes—oxycodone for his back."

"Oxycodone would be okay," Nate says. "Oxy is nice."

"Here, take this," I say, plucking out a pink-and-white capsule and handing it to him.

"What is it?"

"Benadryl."

"That's not even prescription."

"That doesn't mean it doesn't work; it's very sedating."

"What else is there? Diazepam, that's generic Valium—let me have two of those."

"No."

"How about one? That's what you'd take for fear of flying."

"How about four? That's what you need for a colonoscopy," I suggest.

"You're funny," Nate says, taking one pill and pocketing the bottle.

"Put the bottle back. For all you know they have a camera in here, and they'll blame me."

As we're coming down the hall, Jane's father catches my arm. "You should cut your dick off. You should have to live without something precious to you."

The father gives me a little shove and walks off to speak with the caterer. I see the caterer's big burly boyfriend coming towards me, and I'm thinking they're going to ask me to leave, and so I start weaving through the crowd, trying to avoid the guy, thinking I better get Ashley, I better tell the kids that it's time to go. The caterer's boyfriend gets to me before I reach the children.

"Did you try the tuna?" he asks.

"Uh, no," I say. "No, I didn't try it yet."

"Be sure you do," he says. "I make it myself from fresh tuna."

"Sure," I say. "Will do." I'm shaken. "I have to go," I tell Nate.

"Okay," Nate says. "I'll get Ashley."

"Where are we going?" Ashley asks.

"I don't know," I say. "I'm not used to telling anyone what I'm doing. I'm not used to going with anyone."

"You can't leave us here," Nate says.

I pause. "I'm going to see my mother."

"Are you going to tell her about all this?"

"No," I say.

We leave without saying goodbye. I tell the limo driver the name of the nursing home and he looks it up on his GPS and we take off.

"Should we bring her something?" Nate asks.

"Like what?"

"A plant."

"Sure."

"I think it's good to bring something you can leave behind, so it looks like someone cares about her," Ashley says.

When the limo driver passes a florist, I ask him to stop. We spend twenty minutes debating what to bring—finally picking out an African violet, assuming it to be most suited to the hot, dry air of the nursing home.

The nursing home smells like shit.

"Someone must have had an accident," I say.

The farther we get from the front door, the less it smells like shit and the more like chemicals and old people.

"We moved your mother into a semi-private room. She needed more companionship," the nurse tells me.

I knock on her door—no one answers. "Hi, Mom," I say, pushing the door open.

"Hello there."

"It's me," I say. "And I've brought someone with me."

"Come in, come in." We step into the room, and it's the woman in the other bed, thinking we're there for her. "Come closer," she says. "I can't see very well."

I go to the edge of her bed. "I'm Harry. I'm here for your neighbor. I'm her son."

"How do you know?"

"Because she was in the house when I was growing up," I say. "What's your name?"

"I don't know," she says. "What's in a name?"

"Do you know where my mother, your neighbor, is?"

"They're having an ice-cream social, make your own sundae, down the hall in the dining room, but the diabetics are forbidden, they make us wear this vulgar bracelet." She holds up her arm; on her wrist is a yellow bracelet with "DIABETIC" in caps written on it, and on her other arm is an orange bracelet that says "Do Not Resuscitate." "That's why my eyes are lousy—it's the sugar that got them."

As she's talking, my mother is wheeled back into the room, holding an enormous sundae in two hands. "I heard I had company," she says. I notice she too has bracelets, a blue one that says "Demented" and the same orange "Do Not Resuscitate."

"I was talking to your roommate."

"Blind as a bat," Mother says.

"But not deaf," the roommate says.

"It's about time the two of you came," Mother says to Nate and Ashley. "How are the children?"

"She thinks you're George and Jane."

"Does she know about Mom?" Ashley asks.

"Don't talk behind our backs in front of our faces, it's rude," the woman in the other bed says.

"It's nice to see you," Nate says, hugging Mother.

Ashley hands her the plant, which she places in her lap but otherwise ignores.

"Are you working hard?" Mother asks Nate. "Filling the airwaves with crap? Are the children in school, is the one with problems feeling better?"

"The children are amazing," Nate says. "Both brilliant in their own ways."

"Wonder where it comes from?" the roommate says. "Are they adopted?"

"Okay, Mom," I say. "We wanted to have a little visit; we'll come back again soon. Is there anything you need?"

"Like what?"

"I don't know, you tell me," I say.

"Next time you come, you could bring me something," the roommate says.

"Bring something sugar-free; because I'm diabetic doesn't mean I should be punished. Look at me, I'm not fat, I didn't overeat. And look at her, she's eating ice cream."

"With whipped cream, hot fudge, and a cherry on top," Mother says, and briefly chokes. "I ate the stem," she says. "Forgot to spit it out."

"Serves you right," the roommate says. "I could tie a cherry stem in a knot with my tongue."

"Bet you can't anymore," Mother says.

"Of course I can," the roommate says. "Girl, go get me one and I'll show you all."

"Should I?" Ashley asks.

"No reason not to," I say.

Ashley goes to the dining room and comes back with a maraschino cherry. She hands it to the roommate, its red juice dripping like blood on the white coverlet. The old woman pops the cherry into her mouth; we see it vaguely going around and around.

"Harder with dentures," she says, taking a break, "but I'm making progress."

And *voilà,* she spits the cherry into her hand, the stem tied into a knot.

"How'd you do it?" Ashley wants to know.

"Practice," she says.

"Okay, Mom, we have to go now."

"So soon," the roommate says. "You just got here."

"The car is waiting outside; it's a long story."

"All right, then," she says. "You'll tell me next time."

Early Monday morning, the children are driven back to school with lunches I make from what remains in the refrigerator.

With the children gone, the tick-tock of the kitchen clock is deafeningly loud. "Was that clock always there?" I ask Tessie. "Was it always so loud?"

I load the dishes into the dishwasher, give Tessie and the cat fresh water, putter and put things away until there is nothing more to do.

I walk around the house in circles.

Where does one go from here? I imagine leaving—walking out and never coming back. The dog looks at me. Okay, then, walking out and leaving a note for the mailman instructing him to have the pets sent to George at the nuthouse—animals are very therapeutic.

Before this happened, I had a life, or at least I thought I did; the quality, the successfulness of it had not been called into question. I was about to do something. . . .

The book. Now is the time to finish the book. I feel instant relief at having remembered that in fact there was something, a mission—the book. I drag the canvas bag with the thirteen-hundred-page manuscript, covered with an elaborate system of Post-its and flags that seems entirely undecipherable, over to the kitchen table.

I sit. Sweat trickles down my back even though I am not warm. My heart beats faster and faster, the world is coming to an end, the house is about to explode. I hurry to the medicine cabinet and take the pill marked "As Needed for Anxiety." I am taking George's medication, thinking of George. I have to get out of the house. It's cold in the house, bitterly cold. As quick as I can, I gather my things, my manuscript, my empty pads of paper. If I don't leave immediately, something will happen. I grab my things and run out the door.

Outside, the sky is bright, the air is even. I stand there.

The book. I am going to work. I am going to the library in town and I'm going to write my book. I am going. I get in the car; I have no keys. I have George's pants on. I run back into the house, grab the car keys, my phone. Tessie is wagging her tail, as though she thinks I've come back for her. "I'm going to the library, Tessie, I have to write my book. Be a good girl."

Last renovated in 1972, the library is perfect for my mission. Its modern look is along the lines of a Unitarian church or community center. The entry vestibule features a floor-to-ceiling pin board covered with community-service announcements for "coffee and conversation," "Mommy and me" programs, and a table stacked with voter-registration information along with pamphlets about *Disaster Preparation*. All I can think of is the wailing of the Thunderbolt civil-defense siren that went off once a month for three minutes at 11 a.m. all through my school years. Once inside, I spread the contents of my bag over a long table and begin reading what I have written so far, trying to be both critical and generous—an impossible combination. I skip ahead, picking up where I left off. When did I last work on this? I have legal pads, and a pen that's gone unused for so long it doesn't work—I borrow a stumpy half-pencil, a "golf" pencil, from the reference desk and return to my seat, thinking perhaps I should review what's new in the world of Nixonology before continuing the book. Nixon himself wrote ten books, the last, *Beyond Peace,* finished weeks before he died. Titles like that, *Beyond Peace,* make me nervous, like maybe some part of him knew the end was near—the first volume of Ronald Reagan's autobiography, published in the early 1960s, had the prophetic title *Where's the Rest of Me?* Is there room for another book about Nixon? People often ask me, and I say, Well, you heard about Nixon's trip to China, but what about his passion for real estate in New Jersey? What about his interest in animal welfare? I search the library's collection and find a few items that bear rereading. I have copies of the books in the apartment in New York—in what I call the Nixon Library, which Claire calls *your* Nixon Library as opposed to *the* Nixon Library.

I fill my arms with books and march to the checkout desk.

In retrospect, I wish I'd held off. I wish I'd sat down with the books, read through them, and left them right there on the table, where they belonged. I was wanting to check them out to be on the safe side, to leave no stone unturned.

I put the books on the counter and hand the woman the library card.

"It's not your card," the librarian says.

"It came out of my pocket," I say, pulling everything else from the pocket.

"It's not yours."

"You're right," I say. "It's my brother's. And these are my brother's pants, and this is his driver's license. I'm taking the material out for him."

"Your brother killed his wife," she says.

I take a breath. "My brother isn't able to come in and check out books himself, so I'm getting these for him."

"I'm going to mark the card as stolen—charges could be filed against you."

"For what?"

"It doesn't so much matter what," the librarian says. "We live in a litigious society, it's how people express their anger. And it would be a blot on your record."

"Give me the card back."

"Oh no," the librarian says. "It says right here on the back that the use of the library is a privilege that can be revoked."

"If it's not my card, how can it be revoked?"

"Lack of use," she says.

"Is it my subject matter? Is there something about Nixon that you don't like?"

"No," the librarian says. "It's you. It's you that I don't like."

"You don't even know me."

"And I never will," she says. "Go. Leave before I press charges."

"For what?"

"Harassment."

Outside, I trip over a crack in the sidewalk, my bag goes flying, my manuscript—Post-its and all—spills. On hands and knees I pick up the pages. Bent, glancing up into the sunlight, I spot the overnight book depository. I make a mental note of a thing or two I might deposit some night after closing. I have the thought and then immediately think of the Texas Book Depository. A phone rings. I feel my pockets and first pull out George's and then mine— it's flashing "Claire" on the caller ID.

"Hello," I say, still on the ground.

"Who knows the real story?" she asks.

"You're home."

"Who knows?" she repeats.

"I don't know who knows," I say as I finish collecting my papers.

"You know what I'm saying."

"If you're asking who I've spoken to, I've talked to no one."

"People know," Claire says. "It's all over the *New York Post,* and there are photos of a bloody mattress being taken out of the house and you standing there looking like an idiot."

"I must have missed a day."

"It was on the inside. On the cover, in the lower right corner, was a photo of your brother pushing dirt into the grave with handcuffs on."

"Do you think his lawyer staged that?" I ask.

"Speaking of lawyers," she says, "you're gonna need one. Also, I called a moving company."

"Where are you going? You don't have to move, Claire; the apartment is yours."

"I'm not going anywhere. It's for you. Where do you want your stuff to go?"

"Here, just send it to George and Jane's."

"Fine," she says.

And she's gone. I pull myself up, swing the canvas bag over my shoulder, and head down the street, slightly tilted to one side. I walk past the tennis store and the dry cleaner's and stop at the Starbucks. I'm trying to start a routine. I'm trying to do things that other people do.

"Medium coffee," I say.

"Grande?"

"Medium."

"Grande," the girl says again.

"*Non parlo italiano*," I say, pointing to the medium-sized cup.

She hands me the coffee, burning hot, and I take a table. I unpack the pages of the manuscript and shuffle them back into order. A group of women are staring at me; one actually points.

"What?" I say loudly, looking back at them.

"You look like the guy," a boy says as he's wiping tables with a rag that smells like vomit.

"What guy?"

"The guy who killed his wife? She used to come in here with them, after exercise. They come here a lot," he says. "You're new."

He starts wiping my table, as if to make the point that I should go.

"Okay," I say, getting up and taking the coffee with me—after all, it was four dollars. I don't even want the coffee. There's a guy outside who looks homeless, and I try to hand it to him.

"Are you giving me your coffee?" he asks.

"I am."

"Did you drink it?"

"No," I say.

"Why would I want your coffee? Maybe you doped it?"

I'm looking at the guy thinking he looks familiar, a cross between a guy who might change your flat and Clint Eastwood.

"You know," he says, "the thing is, I don't drink coffee."

"Oh," I say, accidentally splashing my wrist with the hot java.

"I come for the lemon pound cake and a cup of tea."

I nod, still thinking I know this guy from somewhere. "All right, then," I say, feeling the canvas bag slipping down my shoulder. "Enjoy."

"And you as well. I hope you find a taker for your coffee."

I put the coffee on the roof of the car and unlock the door and throw the canvas bag in. DeLillo, I think as I slam the door. DeLillo, as I start the engine. That was goddamned Don DeLillo. I would have loved to talk to him about Nixon. I put the car into gear and go. The back windshield is instantly doused in black coffee. In the rearview mirror I watch the cup bouncing down the street behind me.

Back to school. Am I ready for class? I've been teaching the same course for ten years. Of course I'm ready—I'm more than ready, I'm on autopilot.

I get lost driving to school. I've never come from this direction. I usually go from home, I know the route by heart. I'm late. In the car the phone rings. I scrape against a guardrail trying to wrestle the cell phone from my pocket. Again, it's Claire. She says nothing.

"Claire," I say. "Hello, are you there? Can you hear me? I'm in the car, Claire, driving to school. Let's try again later."

I rush to pick up my mail in the department office. There's very little in my box: A postcard from a student saying she's sorry but she'll miss the next two classes because her grandmother in Maine is very ill. The postmark is from Daytona, Florida. Unfortunately, the signature is a blur, so I don't even know who to demerit for that one. The only other mail is an interdepartmental letter. "The Chair of your department would like to schedule a time to speak with you." I poke my head into the department secretary's office. "Excuse me, I'm not sure if this is meant for me?"

"Yes," she says. "He does want to talk with you."

"Should we schedule something?"

She ducks into the Chair's office and returns almost instantaneously. "A week from Wednesday for lunch, your annual event. He says you already know all the details, you have years of experience."

"Great," I say. "Thanks."

I unlock the door of my shared space—Professor Spivak's on Tuesday, Thursday, and Friday, mine on Monday and Wednesday from 2 to 3 p.m. I wait. No one comes. I extract the manuscript that's become my travel companion and go at it, wildly jotting notes, suggesting revisions to myself, a teacher correcting his own work. Five minutes before class, I lock the office. Midway across campus, I am nearly decapitated by a Frisbee, which hits me on the back of the head. No one says sorry, or asks if I'm okay. I tuck the Frisbee into my bag and continue on.

In Room 304 of Donziger Hall, I stand welcoming each student—they barely glance up as they meander in. "Good afternoon, I hope you had a pleasant and productive vacation. Your papers are due. Pass them forward, and then we'll get right into our conversation about Nixon, Kissinger, and the Paris Peace Talks."

A handful of papers come towards me. One title catches my attention: "BLOW JOB or WAR: The Testosterone Paradigm." Another one looks promising: "Checkers and Buddy and the Role of the White House Dog in Shaping Public Opinion."

"I've only got a dozen papers here—who hasn't turned one in?"

My phone rings. I answer only because for some goddamned reason I can't turn the phone off without answering. "Oh, hi, Larry, I'm in class, literally right in the middle; can I call you later?" "My lawyer," I say. "Family emergency." And one of the students snickers. A plus—at least one of them keeps up with the news.

For ninety minutes I wax poetic about the complexities of the peace process that started in 1968, after a variety of delays including debate about "seating." North Vietnam wanted the conference to be held at a circular table at which all parties would appear equal, whereas South Vietnam felt only a rectangular table physically illustrating two sides of the conflict would do. They resolved it by having North and South sitting at the circular table while all other relevant parties sat at individual square tables around them. I go on to present details about Nixon, Henry Kissinger, and the role of Anna Chennault, who brokered the backroom sabotage of the 1968 Paris Peace Talks. The South Vietnamese withdrew from the talks on the eve of the election, helping Nixon win and paving the way for the continuation of the war. Kissinger received a Nobel Peace Prize for his "efforts" in 1973 along with the North Vietnamese Le Duc Tho, who refused to accept.

From there, a flight of ideas leads me to digress; I regale the students with stories about Martha Mitchell—not Margaret Mitchell, the author of *Gone with the Wind*, who ditched her proper suitor, John Marsh, and married Red Upshaw, a bootlegger who beat her up, and then left him and went back to Marsh. No, I am talking about Martha Mitchell, wife of former Attorney General John Mitchell, aka "The Mouth of the South," who was a drinker, known for calling folks in the middle of the night and saying things like "My husband is the fucking Attorney General of the United States." It is the alcohol-fueled Mrs. Mitchell that I find compelling. Her allegations that the White House was involved in illegal activity were described as symptoms of mental illness and dismissed. She was ultimately vindicated, and her experience was deemed a legitimate syndrome, given the moniker "the Martha Mitchell Effect," and described as the process by which a mental-health professional mistakes the patient's perception of seemingly improbable events as delusional when in fact they're real.

I spin, I whirl, I thoroughly unspool. It's the best class I've taught in years. "Thoughts? Questions?" I ask. The students sit unblinking in a stupor. "Okay, then, until next week."

I leave energized, loving Nixon all the more. I drive back to George's, struggling to remember which road leads where. As I pull into town, everything is closing for the night—the luncheonette, the ladies' clothing shop. There's a sticky family dripping chocolate outside the 31 Flavors. I park near the Chinese restaurant. The red neon Chinese letters could spell out anything. For all I know, it says "Eat Shit and Die" in Mandarin. I bring the students' papers in with me. The place is run by a family who cluck madly while serving steaming bowls of soup and perfect hills of white rice. Again my phone rings. "Claire, what's the point of calling me again and again if you're not going to say anything. Talk to me. I know I'm a shit, but I can listen. I can take whatever it is you want to say. I'm in a Chinese restaurant. I ordered scallion pancakes, which you hate, and hot-and-sour shrimp, and, yes, I know you're allergic to shrimp, but I'm not."

The house is dark. Tessie seems nervous; I let her out for a pee and give her some kibble. The cat rubs against my leg, flicking her tail.

"I didn't forget you," I say. "Have I ever forgotten you?"

Only when he calls again do I remember that I forgot to call Larry back. "Sorry, it's been a strange time." I laugh. "Very strange."

I sit on the sofa, remote control in hand, flipping channels, noticing how the television is so big that the lighting in the room changes profoundly with each click of the remote. I like the old black-and-white televisions better— easier on the eyes.

"It's Larry," he repeats.

"I—" I start to say something.

"Don't talk, listen," he says. "I've got news for you; Claire has asked me to represent her."

"But you're happily married."

"Represent her, not marry her. I'm going to be her lawyer."

I turn the television off. "Larry, we're friends; we've known each other since fourth grade."

"Exactly," Larry says.

"I don't get it."

"I've been waiting for this moment. I never forgot the way you and your brother treated me. I was the new kid, from Newark."

"Oh," I say, not really remembering.

"You did a 'new Jew' dance, and then your brother said I had to pay him three dollars a week if I wanted to live."

"You got off easy," I said. "I had to give him five."

"Irrelevant," Larry says. "Claire feels she has grounds. Do you have a lawyer, someone I should talk to?"

"You're my lawyer."

"Not anymore."

"Does Claire want to make a time to sit down and talk about our shared property, retirement and health-care benefits, who gets what, and all that kind of thing?"

"No. She's left all that to me."

"Isn't this a conflict of interest?"

"Not for me," Larry says.

"Well, if you're going to be her lawyer, who's going to be mine?"

"Don't you know anyone else?"

"No, it's not like I pal around with 'the law.' "

"I'm sure George has a lawyer. Also, I have to ask you to stop calling Claire. She says you keep calling her cell phone and leaving messages."

"I don't. Her cell phone keeps calling me, and I answer but she doesn't speak."

"I'm not going to engage in a 'he said, she said.' It has to stop."

I say nothing.

"Okay, then," Larry says. "There's one other thing—the clock. She says you took the clock from her side of the bed. It was a four-by-four-inch square black Braun travel clock."

"I'll buy her a new clock," I say.

"She doesn't want a new clock," Larry says. "She wants her clock." A long silence passes. "She's not asking for anything else, no alimony, no support of any kind. I'm authorized to offer you two hundred thousand dollars to never speak to her again."

"That hurts," I say.

"I could push it to two fifty," Larry says.

"It's not the money, it's that Claire never wants to speak to me again, with the added insult that, in order to accomplish that, she thinks she's got to pay me off."

"So, you'll take the two hundred?"

"Two fifty," I say.

"And you'll send her the clock."

"Fine," I say. And we are done.

I need air. I clip on Tessie's leash. She is hesitant to leave the yard, and as we get closer to the sidewalk, I have to really pull on her.

"Come on, Tessie," I say. "I know you like your house, but dogs need to go for walks. I need to go for a walk; once around the block and we can call it a night?" The dog sits down at the edge of the grass and won't budge. "Well, I can't very well go without you," I say. "A man walking on his own is suspicious. A man walking with a dog is someone doing his duty." I give the leash a strong yank, and Tessie yelps as she comes across the sidewalk.

"Are you okay? Did I pull too hard?"

I've never walked these streets at night. It's kind of thrilling, kind of terrifying. There's a sense of false calm, long driveways, houses at the end—lights on, emanating a pleasant kind of melancholy—the distant sounds of children playing, dogs barking.

Along the way, Tessie stops to eat strange things, dark lumps. I use my cell phone to get a better look. I'm thinking horseshit, but it seems odd, you don't see many horses around here.

The next morning, George's lawyer's secretary calls. "Do you have a pen?" she asks.

"Yes."

"I have information for you. Your brother has been moved to The Lodge, Mohonk Pavilion, Room B. They want a list of medications in the home medicine cabinet: date, dose, pharmacy, doctor. And any info regarding personal physician and psychiatrist would be helpful. Go through his credit-card receipts; anything unusual in the last six months, we want to hear about it. Meanwhile, charges have been filed." At first I'm thinking she's saying that George's credit card has been used to charge something, like when they suddenly cancel you because someone tries to buy a tractor online with your card number. But she goes on: "The district attorney is saying he left the hospital with the intent to do harm."

"Oh, I really don't think so," I say, surprised.

Something out the window catches my attention: a woman in full riding gear, crop in hand, strolls by atop a gigantic and very expensive-looking horse. It's cold out, and as the horse goes by I see steamy breath billowing out of its enormous nostrils.

"They're looking at murder or voluntary manslaughter, the bottom line being that, in their view, it wasn't an accident."

"Maybe he came home because he missed the dog. He's very close to the dog."

"Like he just needed to leave the hospital in the middle of the night and give her a cookie?" the secretary says.

"Yes, like that," I say.

"Lots of luck, mister," she says. "I'll fax you directions to The Lodge."

While waiting for the fax, I find a duffel in the closet and fill it with polo shirts, sweatpants, khakis. I grab socks, underwear, his toothbrush, toothpaste, shaving kit, sneakers, and bathing trunks—you never know. The dog barks—the mail slot clinks—a handwritten note slides across the floor. "We have something for you." I open the door—

The street is empty.

It's a beautiful day for a car ride. That said, I'm still surprised at how far The Lodge is upstate, deep in the hills, a rustic Adirondack mansion with a gatehouse.

A man comes out and asks me to pop the trunk. He uses a mirror to look under the car, waves a metal detector over me and the bag. "Mind if I hold this?" He's got the tire jack in his hand. "We won't let you leave without it. We're very careful," he says.

At the top of the hill a valet takes the car, and I walk in holding the duffel for George.

There's a large reception desk—more like a hotel than a mental hospital.

"I'm here to see my brother?"

"What's his name?"

"George Silver."

"No visitors."

I hold up the duffel bag. "I was told to bring his things."

She takes the duffel and unpacks it, sloppily piling clothing and underwear on the reception counter.

"Hey, I folded all that."

"We're a mental hospital, not a fashion show," she says, handing me his electric toothbrush, his deodorant, his toothpaste. "Unopened products only, and no electronics."

"When can I see him?"

"New admissions, five days no visitors."

She puts the rejected products back into the bag. "Do you want to take them, or shall I throw them away?"

"I'll take them. So—what happens next? Is there a Coke machine, or a place I could get a cup of coffee?"

"In town you'll find a full selection of places to eat."

"Look," I say. "His wife died, and we haven't had a chance to talk about it." The woman nods. "I'm finding this foray into mental health is anything but. I drive for three hours to—what—drop off clean underwear?"

"Enough," the woman barks. And then she settles down again. "I can give you a copy of our promotional film." She reaches under the counter and slips me a flat package. "It has all our information, a description of the program. We can't take you on an actual tour: we're very protective of our clients' privacy. I'll make a note that you'd like the doctor to call you. Family visits are scheduled in advance. We don't do drop-ins—too disruptive."

"I drove a very long way."

"Yes, you did," the woman says. "Would you like to write the note yourself?"

"Fuck the note," I mutter, turning to leave.

From a pay phone at Burger King, I call the lawyer; the cell is useless up here—no signal. I pour coins into the pay phone. "You're getting me out of court to complain that they didn't accept your toothpaste and that your feelings are hurt?"

"That's correct. I drove all the way the hell up here to see him. I could have FedExed his clothing. They didn't even accept his toothbrush, which he's not going to be happy about."

"I'm sure they'll tell him that you were there. Showing up counts for something," the lawyer says. "I gotta go." He hangs up without further explanation.

At the thruway gas station, the cell phone once again has a signal, but my bank card stops working.

"Yes," the bank representative says, talking to me from India and not Paterson, New Jersey. "It's been cut off."

"By who?"

"Fraud Protection. Do you know your password?"

"Jesus is coming," I shout. Everyone in the gas station stares at me.

"No abusive language," the man on the phone says.

"I'm not swearing, that's the password."

There is silence except for the clack of computer keys. "Fifteen dollars in a hospital cafeteria; a purchase from a garden store?"

"I made those charges. Who canceled the card?"

"I wouldn't be able to tell you that, but new cards are being mailed out; you should have them in seven to ten days."

"Can you send the card to where I'm staying, since I'm not in the city?"

"Unfortunately, we can only send them to the address on file."

"No cell phones," someone is yelling at me.

"Are you trying to kill us all?" another guy says.

"Step away from your car, fuckwad."

One hand on the gas nozzle, the other on the phone, I look at them all indignantly.

"Can't you fucking read, moron?" one of the guys yells, and points to a sign on the pumps—"Sparks from cell phones and other handheld electronics can ignite gas fumes. Do not pump and text or talk."

I take my hand off the pump; the nozzle slips out of the tank, and gas splashes on my shoes. I step away from the car and scream louder. "I'm at a gas station hundreds of miles from my branch," I say, shouting into the phone. "And I'd ask you your name, but you'll tell me it's John or Tom or some made-up name that 'sounds' American but really it's something like Abimanyu."

"Would you like to speak to a supervisor?"

"Please."

I get back in my car and start the engine, bracing myself for an explosion, which doesn't happen. The supervisor comes on the line, and I repeat the story, ending with the fact that I have no cash and am in a gas station hundreds of miles from home.

"It appears the account has been frozen due to pending legal action," the supervisor says.

"You froze my bank account; I didn't freeze the account."

"Do you need money?" she asks.

"Yes."

"There's a home-equity line attached to these accounts that, for whatever reason, has not been blocked; you can withdraw from that. The available amount is sixty thousand dollars, and that can be drawn down from a cash machine at one thousand dollars per day, excluding transaction fees."

From the snack shop of the gas station I make a withdrawal, and pocket the cash.

It's late afternoon when I pull back into George's town—the slow part of the day, when everything seems to hang unfinished in midair, until cocktails can be poured. If we were cats, we'd be asleep.

Instead of going to the house, I head for the synagogue. I'm in need of counsel. I park. I turn off the engine, but can't get out of the car. It's like I'm stuck. Do you think the rabbi would come out and talk to me—is there a drive-thru temple? I dial Directory Assistance and get the number. The temple's phone system is automated. "For Hebrew school press two, for a schedule of temple events press one, for Rabbi Scharfenberger's office press three." I press three. A woman answers, *"Ni hao."*

"I'd like to speak with the rabbi."

"Rabbi is very busy."

"I have suffered a recent loss. The rabbi spoke at the funeral. We shook hands."

"Are you a member of the congregation?"

"My brother is a member; my nephew was bar mitzvahed there."

"Maybe you join and then we talk."

"I don't live here."

"You make donation."

There's something about this woman's voice that's very odd—it's like she's speaking in translation. "I don't mean to be rude, but your accent is unusual: where are you from?"

"I am Chinese Jew. Big adopted woman."

"How old were you when you were adopted?"

"Twenty-three. Family came to get baby but did not like baby offered and so they take me instead. I am like a baby. I have no education. I know nothing. Good deal for all. We joke—I am big new baby—not so funny to me. I love being a Jew, nice holidays, good soup." She pauses. "So how much donation you make?"

"Are you telling me I have to buy the rabbi's time?"

"The Jewish community needs many things, hard hit by pony scream."

"Ponzi scam?"

"Yes, money up in smoke. How much you give?"

"A hundred dollars."

"That's not so good, you do better than that."

"What do you suggest?"

"Five hundred minimum."

"Fine, and how much time with the rabbi for five hundred?"

"Twenty minutes."

"You are a good Jew," I say. "Good businessman."

"Woman," she says.

I read her the number of my credit card, she puts me on hold for a minute. I hear ancient music, the sounds of the Jews crossing the desert.

"Card decline."

"Why?"

"They don't say. You call credit card and then call me back. Bye-bye, shlepper."

Did she really say "shlepper"?

Pulling out of the temple parking lot, I am nearly broadsided by a delivery truck.

Back at the house, there's another note resting on the floor under the mail slot.

"I have job to do on you. You need to be home."

"Tessie, who leaves these notes? Do you see them come, or does some anonymous hand feed them through the slot? What does the hand look like, what does it want from me?"

Tessie looks at me, as if to say, "Look, buddy, I know you're trying hard, but I hardly know you, and there's been so much weird shit lately, I don't even know how to begin to explain."

Something is different: nothing major, but just that odd sense that things have been moved, like when I left was the newspaper outside or inside? And the pile of mail I'd been keeping by the front door doesn't look the same. There's a can of cream soda on the counter. I touch it—the can is cold.

My heart kicks into a higher gear.

I look at Tessie. Her tail thumps.

"Hello?" I call out. "Anybody home?" Too weird. "Hel-lo . . ."

A noise from upstairs.

"Who's there—Nathaniel, Ashley? Identify yourself."

My heart is slamming around in my chest like it's broken loose. Cupping my hands together, I deepen my voice. "This is Sergeant Spiro Agnew from the police department. We know you are in the house. Come out with your hands over your head."

There's a big thud, like something falling. "Shit," someone says.

"All right, then, I'm coming up. I'm drawing my gun, I don't like having to pull out this enormously heavy, powerful weapon. Wallace, step back. . . ."

I slam my foot down on the bottom of the stairs four times—as if to imitate the sound of feet climbing. Tessie looks at me like I'm nuts. "This is your last warning. Wallace, call the station and have them send the SWAT truck." Tessie looks at me sideways, as if to say, "Who the hell is Wallace?" I take Nate's baseball bat from the umbrella stand and head up the stairs.

"Don't shoot," a woman's voice says.

"Where are you?"

"In the bedroom."

I walk in with the bat up, ready to swing. Susan is there, arms filled with Jane's clothing, clothing on hangers piled high. "You're not going to kill me, are you?"

"I didn't realize you had a key."

"I used the one under the fake rock."

I look at the clothing in her arms. "Did you find what you were looking for?"

"I wanted some of Jane's things. Is that weird?"

I shrug.

"Can I take them?"

"Take whatever you want. Take a TV—there's one in every room. You want some silver, there's a lot downstairs, in little velvet pouches."

"Should I look at it?"

"Your call. She was your sister; at this point you're stealing from your niece and nephew." I stand aside so she can go down the stairs.

"Where's your gun?"

"What gun?"

"You said you had a big powerful gun; all I see is Nate's bat."

"I lied." I put the bat down and help Susan carry things to the car. "She sure had a lot of shoes," I say.

"She had good feet," Susan says. "Easy to fit."

"Good feet and a mink coat," I say.

"Where do you think the coat is?" Susan asks.

"Did you look in the front hall closet?"

"The bastard killed my sister, I should at least get the coat." Susan goes back into the house, opens the front hall closet, and rummages. Susan finds the coat, puts it on, and walks towards the door, pausing to look at me, as if to ask, "Are you going to stop me?"

"Like I said, whatever you want, it's yours." I hand her the can of soda. "This yours too?"

"You can have it," she says.

I take a sip. "Do you know anything about the mail? Someone keeps leaving me weird notes mixed in with the mail."

"Like what?"

I show her one of the notes.

"You're screwed," she says.

"How so?"

"It's probably the family of the people George killed, looking for revenge."

"Should I show it to the police?"

"I'm not the one to advise you," she says, getting into her car. She backs out.

I go to the hardware store to look at burglar alarms and to buy night-lights and timers for the upstairs lights. Between Susan coming in with no warning, the notes being dropped through the mail slot, and the fact that for the last twenty-two years I've lived in a one-bedroom apartment eighteen floors above ground, the stress of being alone in the house is getting to me.

There's a woman in the battery aisle with something hidden in a pillowcase that she's desperately trying to work with. I don't mean to stare, but I do. I watch, mesmerized, as she keeps dipping her hands into the pillowcase and trying to do something.

"So what's in the bag? Bunny need a battery?"

She looks at me. "Is it that obvious?"

I shrug. "No."

She hands me the pillowcase, and I peek inside. It's an enormous pink dildo with a nut sack filled with ball bearings and oddly long rabbit ears.

"It just ground to a halt," she says. "Go ahead, push the button."

I do, and it spins a half-circle and sounds like a car that won't turn over, like a starter not kicking in. "Maybe it got burned out," I say.

"Ha-ha," she says.

"Seriously, the problem may be more than the battery," I say. I take the pillowcase from her, and discreetly working inside the bag, I get the battery compartment open, slide four cells in, and—*voilà*—the bunny is good to go. I turn it on and from the outside watch it spinning and dancing. "She's a real disco bunny," I say, handing the pillowcase back to the woman.

"It bends too," the woman says. "You can change the angle and also the vibration."

"Great," I say. Inside the pillowcase the bunny is still dancing; from all the writhing and flip-flopping, it almost looks like there's a snake in there.

"FYI, this never happened," she says. "Like, if I ever see you again, I don't know you."

"Likewise," I say, leaving her in the battery aisle and going to the home-intrusion section. I find a do-it-yourself alarm system that can be "trained." I buy one, even though I'm not quite sure what that means. It turns out by "trained" they mean "programmed to speak." You can elect for your unit to say, "BURGLAR, BURGLAR" or "TRESPASSER, LEAVE NOW" in a loud voice, or produce a loud piercing alarm, or record a message of your own, like a whiny voice saying, "Honey, I got the restraining order for a reason. . . ."

I put my bag in the car and go to the Chinese restaurant. They are starting to know me.

"You want same, you want different?" they ask.

"Same," I say.

"You a lonely man," the waiter says, bringing me my cup of soup.

Back at George's, I feed and walk the dog, and then I plug in the timers, setting the lamps in Nate's and Ashley's rooms to turn on at half past six in the evening and off at ten o'clock. The rooms are neat, empty, like rooms from a catalogue rather than rooms that are lived in. I think of children's rooms as overstuffed monuments to experience, collections that define their lives so far: a rock from a beach, a pennant from a game, a souvenir hat from a family trip. Here it's all been edited down to what fits neatly on a shelf. Everything is fixed, as though life has been suspended or otherwise delayed. The stillness leaves me depressed. I think of Nixon and his note keeping, Nixon and his endless legal pads, his tapes, his extensive and alas incriminating library of recordings. I think of Richard M. Nixon, named after Richard the Lionheart, son of King Henry II, brave soldier and lyricist, and realize that I don't know enough about Nixon and his relationship to stuff. I make a mental note to revisit the subject.

I go back downstairs and phone the children at school. "Is this an okay time to talk?" I ask Nate.

"Yeah," Nate says.

"I'm not interrupting study hall or football practice?"

"It's okay," Nate says.

"Ummm," I say. "So I just wanted to say hi and see how you're doing."

"Okay," he says.

"You're doing okay—that's great," I say.

"I'm not doing anything," he says, and then there is a pause. "Except that she doesn't call, except that it's all too quiet, I keep forgetting that Mom is dead, and I kind of like it that way. It's better when I forget; better with her not dead. When I remember I feel sick."

"I can imagine," I say, and then pause. "When did your parents usually call? Was there a set schedule, once or twice a week?"

"Mom called every night before dinner, between five-forty-five and five-fifty-five. I don't remember Dad calling."

"It must be very strange," I say, and pause again. "Tessie is getting along well. I take her for walks—I kind of get the sense no one ever did, she doesn't like to leave the yard, but once I get her past the end of the driveway she's okay."

"There's an invisible fence," Nate says.

"Must be—she's very well trained. Only goes out of the yard if I pull on her. Like I have to fight her to leave."

"That's because the fence gives her a shock."

"What fence?"

"The invisible fucking fence," Nate says.

"An invisible fence is a real thing?"

Nate sighs, painfully. "There's a small box on the dog's collar, that's the transmitter; if you take her out of the yard, take that off; otherwise she gets a shock. Even if you go out in the car with her, you have to take the box off."

I look at the dog's collar; the box is there, totally obvious.

Nate continues, "There's a bigger box mounted on the wall in the laundry room, next to the burglar alarm, that controls the invisible fence—the instructions for everything are in the drawer under the microwave."

"It's amazing that you know all that."

"I'm not retarded, I've lived in that house my whole life."

"There's a burglar alarm? I just bought a home security system."

"We hardly use it, because once it went off and scared everyone too much."

I fish through my pocket for the hardware-store receipt. "Is there a code or something you need to know to turn the system on and off?"

"It's all in the book," Nate says. "Read the book."

"All right, then," I say.

"I better go," Nate says.

And I make a mental note to call again soon, like tomorrow at five-forty-five.

Ashley can't talk. That's what her roommate says. She's in the school infirmary with strep throat. I call the nurse.

"Why didn't the school call me?" I demand to know.

"Who are you?" the nurse asks.

"I'm the uncle," I say, incredulous.

"We don't call uncles, we call parents."

"Well," I say, preparing to deliver an earful, "clearly you're a page or two behind. . . ."

And with that the cat hocks up a hairball, and I simply say to the nurse that I will call again tomorrow expecting to speak with Ashley, and that for now she should give Ashley my love.

"Are you on the call list?" she asks, but I am already hanging up.

I almost vomit cleaning up the hairball. Both the dog and cat look at me rather pathetically as I'm down on my knees scrubbing the carpet with seltzer and a sponge.

When I'm finished, I go into Jane's Amazon account and send Ashley some books. It's super-easy: Jane made a list of gifts in the computer. I pick a couple and click "send to Ashley." I spring for the extra bucks for gift wrap. "Feel Better Soon," I type. "Lots of Love, Tessie (Your Dog) And Your Cat, aka The Hairballer."

A little while later, the sharp clink of the mail slot catches Tessie off guard. She barks frantically as another note slides onto the floor.

"Tomorrow will come."

"Yes," I say to Tessie, "tomorrow will come, and I should be prepared." My cell phone rings, startling me. "Hello?"

"Is this the brother of George Silver?"

"Who's this?" I ask.

"Dr. Rosenblatt calling from The Lodge," he says, pronouncing "The Lodge" like it's supposed to mean something special, like the words themselves are encoded.

"You called my cell phone."

"Is this a good time to talk?"

"I can hardly hear you. Call me on the landline, I'm at George's house." I hurry into George's office and pick up the phone on his desk as it starts to ring.

I'm standing on the "wrong" side of the desk, looking at George's chair, at the bookcase behind his desk, at the price tags still on the backs of his picture frames.

"Should I sit down?" I ask.

"Whatever is comfortable for you."

I circle around the desk and settle into George's chair, facing photos of

George's kids; Jane; George, Jane, and the kids; Tessie; Tessie, George, Jane, and the kids.

"As far as you know, has your brother ever suffered any head injuries, concussions, comas, any previous accidents other than the most recent one, which I have some notes on?"

"Not that I know of," I say.

"Any illnesses such as meningitis, rheumatic fever, malaria, untreated syphilis?"

"Not to my knowledge."

"Drug use?"

"What does he say about that?"

There's an awkward pause. The doctor begins again: "In your experience, does your brother use drugs?"

"He self-medicates, medicine for this, medicine for that."

"Is your brother a sex addict?"

"The thing is this," I say. "As much as you think you know somebody, there are some things that one never knows."

"How about his early life? He doesn't seem to remember much about his childhood. Were you punished, spanked, or beaten?"

Unexpectedly, I laugh.

"What's so funny?" the doctor asks.

"I have no idea," I say, still laughing.

"There are rules," the doctor says. "Boundaries that exist for a reason."

I stop laughing. "We weren't spanked, screwed, or otherwise taken advantage of. If anyone was beaten, it was George who was beating them—he's a bully."

"So you experienced your brother as a bully?"

"Not only me, others as well, many others. I could give you names and numbers—the effects are still being felt."

The psychiatrist grunts.

"How would you describe your brother?"

"Large," I say. "Inescapable," I say. "Actually, he is small, medium, and large, it fluctuates. He is a person whose size fluctuates, whose mood fluctuates. He can be very intolerant of others."

"Your experience of him is one of intolerance?"

I pause for a moment. "What about you?" I ask. "How do you describe yourself and what you do?"

He doesn't take the bait—maybe he doesn't even know it was bait.

"Our approach is to treat the whole person, the family, the community in which we live. Mental health begins with each individual, but mental illness unchecked spreads exponentially." As he speaks his enthusiasm swells, as though the idea of an entire mentally ill country is amazing, a perfect storm of challenge. He takes a calming breath and shifts back to a more modulated voice. "We've run a battery of tests on your brother—blood, brain scan, standardized intelligence panels—and are wondering if you'd consent to have the same tests done, for comparative purposes."

"I'm not so sure I want my head examined."

"You don't have to decide tonight." He pauses. "Let me ask you another question: beyond your mother are there any relatives of your parents' generation still with us?"

"My father's sister."

"Would you be willing to pay a visit and ask some questions?"

"Perhaps," I say, unwilling to admit my own curiosity about why no one in the family has spoken of Aunt Lillian in years—was there a falling out?

While the doctor is talking, I'm on George's computer. Like a reflex, I automatically start Googling. First I check the ten-day forecast on the Weather Underground and then without thinking I type in "Sex+Suburbs+NYC," and a thousand sites pop up, as though the computer itself goes into hyperdrive. I put in the ZIP code, and am filling out the quick search. I am a MAN looking for a WOMAN between 35 and 55.

What's my e-mail? the computer wants to know. My e-mail address, Mihous13@aol.com, feels like something left behind, like it belongs to another person in another time. I craft a new one, AtGeodesHouse@gmail.com, certify that I am over eighteen, and *voilà*. It's surprising how fast you can find naked women online.

The doctor is asking about food allergies: peanuts, wheat, gluten . . . "Was George a picky eater? Did he have issues with his clothing, finding tags irritating? Did he rock or spin?"

"He threw rocks," I say, "right at people's heads."

"Again," the doctor says, "that's your opinion."

"He frequently threw rocks that hit people in the head," I rephrase.

"Bad aim," the doctor says. "And what about food?"

"He didn't throw food."

"Did he eat it happily?"

"In our generation there wasn't an option not to like something, you either ate it or you didn't. You wore the clothes your parents bought you—or you wore the ones your cousin wore before you—there wasn't a lot of choice."

"Did he have trouble in school?"

"He liked school. He was big for his age, and there were a lot of people he could pick on. At home, funny enough, my father thought of himself as the boss, which didn't go over so well with George."

I'm seeing breasts, lots of breasts. Apparently, women photograph their breasts and post them online and, depending on how far you're willing to drive, you can date a woman who is large, small, ginormous, subtle or not.

I'm filling out forms, describing myself, my hobbies, my income, eye color, hair pattern, all in haste to locate a woman who might want to meet me, who might want to do more than meet me.

"So—it was only the two of you growing up?"

"Uh-huh."

"And George and his former wife had two children?"

"She wasn't his former wife, she was his wife."

"They had two children?"

"Correct."

"And the children, where are they now?"

"Away at school. Nate is doing okay, and Ashley is in the infirmary with strep throat."

My mind wanders to what's on-screen; I am glad to be doing this under professional supervision, able to devote only a portion of my attention to what's before me, and equally glad that my "professional supervisor"—aka George's shrink—has no idea. If I were left alone with these sites, I would be overwhelmed. It's all more than I'd ever imagined. Why have I never done this before?

The doctor senses my distraction. "How do the children deal with their father?"

"Well, since he killed their mother, I think that changes things. I don't think it's clear yet to what degree. The last time they saw him was at the cemetery when they were burying their mother."

I am going through photo after photo, a veritable fleshy catalogue of human anatomy. Who knew that people would advertise themselves so explicitly, by showing their bare bits, it's so . . . animal kingdom.

The doctor is still speaking: "We'd like to encourage you to come up. Could you stay overnight, spend some time with us?"

"I can't," I say, not really listening. "I'm staying at George's and I've got his pets to care for."

"Perhaps you could bring them—George misses the dog."

Online, someone has posted: "Are your breasts filled with milk? I j'adore breast milk and would like to meet a lactating or pregnant woman for daytime feedings. If you like I will also bury my face between your legs and tongue you to orgasm after orgasm till you tell me to stop. No reciprocation required. I'm a professional MWM, D/D free, nonsmoker, gentle & respectful. Would like to do this on a regular basis at your place."

"Do you think you might come up sometime?" the doctor asks again.

The ads are so specific, so uncomfortably arousing, that I have to look away from the computer for a moment.

"I've been there," I say, distracted. "Just the other day, I drove all the way the hell up there with his stuff and didn't exactly have what I'd call a good experience."

"Yes. The hope would be that a scheduled visit would go better."

"We will see," I say; I am a million miles away.

"We'll talk again soon," the doctor says.

"Sure," I say. "Call anytime. I'm always here."

I am in the glow of the computer, bent like an old man hunkered down for the duration. The cat and the dog come to check on me.

"Suburban Mom seeks friends for lunch, NSA."

I mistake "NSA" for "NASA" and wonder what the hell the space program has to do with women in suburbia making dates. I Google "NSA" and find it to be an acronym for everything from the National Sawmilling Association to No Significant Abnormalities and No Strings Attached—which is apparently the most modern and intended meaning.

Somewhere between two-thirty and three in the morning, I fall asleep at the computer in mid-chat, and the woman I'm talking with asks, "Are you texting while driving?"

"No," I type, "not asleep at the wheel but at the desk." The woman I was chatting to was (or said she was) the wife of a cop, waiting for her husband to come home—she says she manages her anxiety about her husband's work by Internet-sexting.

The next night I am at it again, craving something, thinking it would be nice to have someone to share my wonton soup with.

I post a listing of my own. There is a corporate headshot of George on his computer, taken a few years ago, when his hair was better, when he was thinner. I upload it as my own. "Home Alone—Westchester Man Seeks Play Mate; tired soul craving nourishment—meet me for a smoothie, my treat. NSA."

A minute after I post it, a woman e-mails, "I know you."

"Doubtful."

"No, really," she says.

"Happy to chat, but trust me no one knows me."

"Photo for photo," she says.

"Okay," I say, and it feels like a game of cards—Go Fish. I search George's computer and find a photo of him on vacation, fishing pole in hand. I upload it.

She sends a photo of her shaved crotch.

"I don't think we're on the same page," I type back.

"George," she writes, terrifying me.

"?," I type.

"I used to work for you. I heard about the accident."

"I don't follow," I type, full well knowing exactly what she's talking about.

"I'm Daddy's little girl. We pretend Mommy's gone out. You ask to check my homework. I bring it to your office 18th Floor 30 Rockefeller Plaza. I do whatever you tell me to—I never disobey Daddy. You ask me to suck your cock, tell me it tastes like cookie dough. You're right. And then I bend over your desk, my breasts sweeping pens off your blotter while you have me from behind. The office door is open, you like the possibility that someone might walk in."

"Tell me more," I type.

"Oh come on George, it's okay. I'm not with the network anymore. I quit. I got a better job. My new boss is a lesbian."

"I'm not George," I type.

"Your photo," she writes.

"I'm the brother."

"You don't have a brother, you're an only child," she types. "That's what you told everyone, you were an only child, the apple of your mother's eye."

"Not true."

"Whatever," she types. "Goodbye and good luck, George."

In George's home office, I find a small digital camera, shoot some pictures of myself, upload them, and see how bad I look—I had no idea. Retreating to the upstairs bathroom, I give myself an ersatz makeover, combing, shaving, trimming, using Jane's hair gel to coif my chest hair, which has recently turned a kind of steel gray. I put on one of George's pressed shirts and take photos again, progressively undressing myself, shirt unbuttoned, shirt off, pants unbuttoned, unzipped, naked to the underwear line. I upload the photos—create a profile, "Ever heard of the Lonely Professor?"

In the morning, I wonder if any of it really happened or if it's all some warped wet dream. I shower, make breakfast, walk the dog. I stay away from George's office until nine-thirty.

I've got mail: "In the interest of full disclosure, I am someone in the process of transitioning." I'm thinking it's from a woman who lost her job, or is getting a divorce, but no. "For thirty-five years I lived as a man, but for the last three I've been a woman. I think of myself as a regular girl looking to meet a regular guy. If you're not interested—a polite no thanks will do."

"Soccer mom with time between games. Lets meet in my minivan. I'll cum to you."

"I'm miserable," the next one writes. "Don't even ask for details. Last week I increased my medication which gave me the energy to write this. Now, I'd like to get laid. Happy to host or meet for a BLT. Lets have lunch!"

I e-mail back, "What's a BLT?"

"Bacon lettuce tomato? Duh."

"Sorry, all the online acronyms are getting to me."

"What do you like for lunch?"

"I'm easy," I type. "A can of soup is fine."

She sends directions. "Don't be weird, okay."

"Okay," I write back. I can't believe I'm doing this. The woman lives seven miles from George's house. I get there, nervously park behind her car in the driveway, ring the bell. A perfectly normal woman answers. "Are you you?" I ask.

"Come in," she says. We sit in her kitchen. She pours me a glass of wine. We chat as she's taking things out of the refrigerator. I find myself staring at a large dry-erase board with a multicolored chart/schedule. The names Brad, Tad, Lad, Ed, and ME are written down the left side, and Monday, Tuesday . . . across the top. Each name has its schedule—football, tutoring, class trip, yoga, potluck—in a matching color, Ed in red, ME in yellow.

"Do you run a small business?"

"Just the family," she says.

"Cheryl, is that your real name?"

"Yes," she says

"Not like your online name?"

"I only have one name," she says. "More than that and I'd get confused. Is Harold your real name, or code for Hairy Old Codger?"

"I was named after my father's father," I offer. "He walked here from Russia."

"Shall we go into the dining room?" Cheryl leads me to her dining room, where the table is set. She brings out dish after dish, canapé, beef stew, salmon tart.

"I didn't make it just for you," she says. "My friend is a caterer, and I helped her with an event last night—these were leftovers."

"This is really good," I say, stuffing my mouth. "It's been a long time since I had anything other than Chinese food." Part of me wants to ask, "Do you do this often?" but if she says yes, I'll feel disgusting and compelled to leave, and the thing is, I don't want to go, so I don't ask.

"Should I feel sorry for you?" she wants to know.

"No," I say.

"You have kids?" I ask, to distract from my second helping of the stew.

"Three boys; Tad, Brad, Lad. Sixteen, fifteen, fourteen. Can you imagine? Do I look like I had three babies?" She lifts up her shirt, flashing me her flat stomach, the curve of the bottom of her breasts.

"You look very nice," I say, suddenly breathless.

"Would you like coffee?" she asks.

"Please," I say.

She goes into the kitchen. I hear the usual coffee-making sounds. She returns, coffee cup in hand—nude.

"Oh," I say. "I really just came to meet you, to talk, we don't have to, you know . . ."

"But I want to."

"Yes, but . . ."

"But what? I've never heard of a man who doesn't want free sex," she says, indignant. She hands me the coffee. I drink quickly, scalding my throat.

"I'm just not . . ."

"Not what? You better figure it out, buster, or there's going to be some hurty feelings around here."

"I've never done this before."

She softens. "Well, there's a first time for everything." She takes my hand and leads me upstairs. "Would you like me to tie you up? Some people can't relax unless they're restrained."

"Thanks, I'm okay," I say. "I prefer to be free."

Upstairs, she asks if I want a dough job; I'm thinking money, but then she's got both hands greased up and on either side of my cock and she's telling me that she's going to knead it like dough. It's vaguely medical at first but not unpleasant and then she's got my cock in her mouth and honestly I never thought it could be this easy. Claire never wanted to suck my cock, she said my balls smelled damp.

And then—the front door slams. "Hi, Mom."

Her mouth comes off my cock, but her hand clutches me firmly, as if refusing to let the blood recede.

"Tad?" she calls out.

"Brad," the kid answers, slightly put out.

"Hi there, kiddo, everything okay?" she calls downstairs.

"Yeah, I forgot my hockey stick."

"Okay, see you later," she says. "I made brownies—they're on the counter, help yourself."

"Bye, Mom."

And the door slams closed.

For a moment I think I may have a heart attack, but when her good work resumes, the feeling quickly passes.

I go home, take a long nap, and start thinking about tomorrow. I finally have a calling, a way to spend my time. I am going to do this every day. I'll get up early, work on Nixon from 6 a.m. until noon, go out for lunch with a different woman each day, get home, take Tessie for a walk, and get a good night's sleep.

A single session, once a day. I contemplate trying for two times a day, a lunch and a dinner, on the days I'm not teaching, but it seems too much— better to pace myself, to manage it like an athlete in training.

"How far will you go?" a woman asks.

"In what way?"

"Mileage," she writes.

It's a delicate balance—on the one hand, I don't want to stay too close to the house, in case I run into someone; on the other, I am suddenly mindful of time—I have things to do and don't want to spend the day driving. It's fascinating, everything from the real estate involved to the women themselves, the variations in décor and desire. Twenty-five miles at most; that seems reasonable. As I'm leaving, one woman tries to pay me. "Oh no," I say. "It was my pleasure."

"I insist," she says.

"I can't. That makes it like a work for hire, like . . ."

"Prostitution," she says. "That's what I'm looking for, a man who can accept money for it, who can feel both the pleasure and the degradation."

"I can't," I say. "I did it for myself, for my pleasure."

"Yes," she says, "but for my pleasure I need to pay you."

Twenty bucks is forced on me. Twenty bucks—is that all I'm worth? I would have thought more. Maybe that's her point?

After that, from each house, each woman, I take something. Nothing big, nothing of value, but like a trinket, something as small as a single sock, a little something that catches my eye.

On one particular Wednesday, I am especially looking forward to an early lunch because my pen pal is so spirited and funny. "What is this all about? Why do you do these things?" she writes.

"God knows," I write back. "But I'm looking forward to meeting you."

I arrive at the house, a modern glass-walled structure from the early 1960s nestled in the curve of a cul-de-sac. I can see into the house—highly stylized, like a film set, a place that people pass through, more along the lines of an airport or a museum than a cozy family home. I ring the doorbell and watch as a young girl of about nine or ten unexpectedly appears at the far end of the house and then crosses from room to room, window to window, carpet to carpet, until she reaches the front door.

"Is your mother home?" I ask as she opens the door.

"What's it to you?" she asks.

"She and I were going to have an early lunch?"

"Oh, you're the guy. Come in."

I step into the house. "Everything okay—shouldn't you be in school or something?"

"I should be but I'm not."

The foyer is a cube within the cube—I can see into the kitchen, the living room, dining room, and out into the backyard.

"So is your mom here? Maybe I should leave; tell her John came by, John Mitchell."

"I can make you lunch," the girl says, "like a grilled cheese or something."

"No offense, but I don't think you should be using the stove if your mom's not home."

The girl puts her hands on her hips. "You want the truth?"

"Yes."

"My mom's in the city. She and my dad are having lunch to see if they can work it out."

"Okay, then," I say, backing up, preparing to go.

"And so"—she pauses for effect—"my brother and I decided to play our version of that TV show *Predator*. My dad says it's amazing how dumb people can be. And we knew my mom was up to something, but didn't know what."

And with that the little brother comes out of the powder room, where he's been hiding, and gets my hands behind my back—slapping the cuffs on.

"Look," I say, "first off, you're doing it wrong, I've committed no crime. And, secondly, you've got the handcuffs on incorrectly—if you cut off my circulation, you've got nothing. You've got to make them looser." The kid doesn't blink.

I wiggle my hands. "The cuffs are too tight, they hurt."

"I think that's a good thing," the kid says. "They should hurt."

"Looser, please," I say. And the kid shakes his head. "Looser."

He doesn't budge.

I consider falling to my knees, pretending to foam at the mouth, or simulating a heart attack. I wonder how much it would be dramatic play and how much would be real, because I'm actually having a panic attack. I consider falling, but look down at the hard slate floor and calculate the possibility of broken kneecaps as too great a risk.

"How old are you?" I ask, attempting to distract myself.

"Thirteen," the girl says. "And he's almost eleven."

"Didn't your parents tell you not to let strangers in—how do you know I'm not some monstrous, dangerous person?"

"My mom wouldn't have lunch with a dangerous person," the boy says.

"I don't know your mom very well."

"Look at you," the girl says. "You're not exactly scary."

"Do we need more restraints?" the boy asks his sister. "Should I tie up his legs? I have bungee cords."

"No," she says. "He's not going anywhere."

The boy yanks my arm, hard. "Sit down," he says, pushing me, and I'm surprised by his strength.

"Hey," I say. "Go easy."

Once I'm seated on the living-room couch, if you can call it seated with your arms locked behind your body, the two kids stand in front of me, as if expecting me to say something. I take the cue.

"Okay," I say, "so how's this gonna work? Is there, like, a hidden camera?"

"We have a camera," the boy says. "But no battery."

The living room is all white—white sofa, white walls, the only color two bright-red womb chairs.

"So—what's the story?" I ask.

"Basically, our life sucks," the boy says. "Our parents pay no attention to us, Dad works all the time, Mom's entirely electronic, and I can't remember when we last did anything fun with them."

"We think he's having an affair," the girl says.

"What's an affair again?" the boy asks his sister. She whispers in his ear, and he makes a disgusted face.

"What makes you think he's having an affair?" I ask.

"Whenever his cell phone rings, he runs out of the room. And my mom yells at him, 'If it's work, how come you can't answer it in here?'"

"We logged into Mom's computer. She's also doing weird stuff, and we think our father knows, but aren't sure."

"How many times have you done it with her?" the boy asks, cutting his sister off.

"Done it?" I say. And then I realize what he's asking and blush. "Never," I say. "I've never met your mother. We chatted online and she invited me to lunch."

"That simple?" the girl asks.

"Yes."

"Do you have a wife?" the girl asks.

"I'm divorced."

"Kids?" the boy wants to know.

"No."

"Okay, but she does," the girl says.

"Yeah," the boy says.

"I understand," I say. "Have you tried talking to your mother, asking her what it's all about?"

"You can't talk to her," the boy says. "She doesn't talk. All she does is this." He makes weird repeating motions with his thumbs.

"My mother only talks to her BlackBerry. All day, all night. In the middle of the night she wakes up to BlackBerry people around the world. I hear her in the bathroom, typing and typing," the girl says. "My father once got so mad he flushed it down the toilet. It got stuck in the pipe, and the plumber had to come."

"Not a good idea," the boy says.

"*Very* expensive," the girl says.

We sit for a while. The kids make snacks: pineapple juice, maraschino cherries, white bread with slices of American cheese. They have to feed them to me on account of the handcuffs.

"Try not to crumb," the girl says.

I almost choke on a cherry. "You might want to check the expiration date on those," I say.

"What's tea-bagging?" the girl asks, while feeding me another piece of crustless white bread.

"I don't know," I say honestly.

She dabs the corners of my mouth with a napkin and lets me sip from a juice box.

"It's something grown-ups do; it was in one of my mom's e-mails," the boy says.

"It's not good to read someone else's e-mail, e-mail is private," I say.

"Whatever," the girl says. "I'll Google it later." She takes the juice box away.

"Do you have any pets?" I ask.

"I was in charge of the class fish over school vacation," the boy says.

"Do you like school?"

Both kids look at me blankly. "Do you have friends?"

"It's more like we know people. We're not friends but we know them. Like, if we're out somewhere or something and see them, we might wave or nod but we don't talk or anything."

"Do you have a babysitter?"

"Mom let her go. She decided she didn't like having someone around all the time," the boy says.

"We have an electronic minder. Every day at three p.m. we have to check in; if we don't it beeps us, and if we don't respond it calls a list of names, and if no one can find us it calls the police."

"How do you check in?"

"You dial a number and type in your code."

"I always forget mine," the boy says. "So I write it on my hand." He holds up his hand; "1 2 3 4" is written in ink on his palm.

"We have chips," the boy says, standing up.

"Thanks, but I'm trying to watch what I eat," I say.

"Not chips you eat—chips implanted under our skin so they can track us," he says.

"Like, if anyone wanted to know where we were right now, they'd know we're at home. I keep thinking maybe they never installed the software," the girl says. "Or they don't care."

"Look, kids, I hope this doesn't sound bad, but, despite the fact that you kidnapped me and held me against my will, you seem like good kids—you made nice snacks, you both worry about your parents and wish they showed the same concern for you, and that's really not asking too much. What about offering your parents a Get Out of Jail Free card? Offer them their freedom and ask them to give you up for adoption? Do you know how many people would love to have housebroken—I mean potty-trained—white, English-speaking children?"

"Wow, I never thought of that," the girl says.

"You could find a nice family where they'd make sure you went to school, did your homework, and flossed your teeth."

"Maybe you could adopt us," the boy says.

I shake my head. "Clearly I've got Stockholm Syndrome," I say.

"What's that?" the girl asks.

"You'll Google it later," I say. "I've got a lot on my plate—my brother's kids, and I'm trying to finish a book on Richard Nixon—do you know who he was?"

"No."

"He was the thirty-seventh President of the United States, born in the small town of Yorba Linda, California, in a house that his father built with his bare hands. Nixon was the only President in United States history to resign the office."

"What does 'resign' mean?" the boy asks.

"It means he quit in the middle," the sister says.

"His father must have been really mad," the boy says.

"What time is it?" I ask.

"Why?"

"I have to teach this afternoon. Do you mind if I use your bathroom?" I ask.

"It's over there," the boy says pointing.

"It's a half-bath," the girl says.

I slide myself to the front of the sofa and wiggle my arms. "Can't exactly use the bathroom with my hands behind my back," I say.

"Obviously," the girl says.

"Right," the boy says, coming to unlock me. The kid struggles with the key.

"Do your best," I say. And somehow encouraging them to do their best calms the kids, and within seconds the cuffs are off and I'm heading towards the bathroom.

"I've got news for the two of you," I say as I come out the bathroom door, fully prepared to fight them if I must. "I'm leaving now, but I urge you to talk to your parents—you deserve better. And I want you to know that what happened here today was a success, you did a good job convincing me never to do this again, no more Internet dates—it's not safe. This experience was like a Scared Straight program for adults."

"What's Scared Straight?"

"It's something for gay people," the older girl says.

I don't have the energy to correct her. "All right, then," I say, opening the door.

The girl looks tearful. "I fear it's hopeless," she says.

"You've got your whole life ahead of you. Next time they leave you home alone, call your school, explain how you're underachieving, how you're tracked like lost dogs. You may be young, but it's your life, you need to take charge of it."

"He's got a point," the boy says.

"You're very convincing," the girl says.

"Goodbye." I walk to my car, knowing their eyes are on me.

I imagine them moving from room to room, window to window, as they watch me cross the well-landscaped front yard, trampling the perfectly trimmed grass, which reeks of prosperity and the vigilant use of pest-control products. It's midday, midweek, and apart from the fact that the plants are thriving, there are no other signs of life.

I drive away thinking they could have really hurt me. They could have tied me up, chained me to a radiator—were there radiators?—or kept me in the basement like some science experiment. They could have buzz-sawed me into pieces and put me in the abandoned extra freezer. If what they said about their parents was true, it would be forever, or at least the Fourth of July, before I'd be found. My head is spinning. I was held hostage; I am an Internet idiot; I am a wreck. Something is vibrating as I drive; at first I think it's the car, but when stopped at a red light I look down and see my legs trembling wildly.

I drive straight to school. The department secretary looks at me with concern. "I hope you got my message?"

I have no idea what she's talking about.

"Your lunch today?"

I begin to sweat. "I didn't have lunch," I say, feeling the maraschino cherry rising in my throat.

"You were scheduled for your annual with Dr. Schwartz?"

I completely forgot.

"He had a dental emergency; I left you a message at home. Professor Schwartz cracked a tooth this morning at the faculty breakfast, and it looks like a root canal is in his future. He does want to see you sooner rather than later, so let's reschedule for tomorrow—noon."

"I'll be there," I say.

Office hour. It has to stop. Whatever it is I am doing or thinking I am doing with these "ladies who lunch," it needs to end. Today I got off easy; next time, it could be far worse. I check my date book. Tomorrow I'm scheduled to meet a woman—the only thing I can remember about her is that in our chat exchanges she made repeated references to the 1960s television show *Bewitched*. My sense, or maybe it was my fantasy, was that she had something quasi-magical in mind and needed a guy to play out the scenario. On the other hand, my experience of this morning leads me to add a darker spin to it—now I'm thinking that perhaps she is some kind of a suburban witch practicing her dark arts on dumb dogs of men who take the bait.

I attempt to log into my e-mail from the school's computer. I can't get online. Somewhat frantic, I feel like I need to cancel it now, right now—not ten minutes from now, but right this second, while I am strong and resolved and before I lose my will. I go charging up to the department secretary. "Is there a reason I can't get online?" I ask.

"The server is down," she says.

"All over campus?" I ask, thinking perhaps I can run to the library and do it from there.

"Yes, the whole system is down. If you need to check your e-mail, I'd let you log in from my phone." She holds up her phone—one of those twenty-first-century oddities with a slide-out keyboard.

Crumbs. If I log into my e-mail from her Android or whatever the hell it is, I will leave a trail of electronic crumbs, the same crumbs that I would also leave logging into my personal e-mail from the school's computer. With a little work—the equivalent of a small electronic mop—they could trace my steps directly to "Bewitched101."

"That's okay," I say, with everything suddenly less urgent. And in fact I'm glad the server is down—it just saved me from myself.

I head into class, prepared to discuss the origins of the moniker "Tricky Dick." I begin by introducing the figure of Helen Gahagan Douglas, actress and wife of actor Melvyn Douglas, who served Congress for three terms in the 1940s—including while having an affair with then Congressman and future President Lyndon B. Johnson. In 1950, Douglas ran for the United States Senate, against Nixon. Nixon took advantage of anti-communist sentiment, alluding to Gahagan Douglas's "red" sympathies, and launched a smear campaign, circulating anti-Douglas pamphlets printed on pink paper. Helen Gahagan Douglas lost the election, but coined the nickname that Nixon never lived down, "Tricky Dick."

"Tricky Dick" was later used to refer to various Nixon behaviors, ranging from personal use of campaign funds to the spying, stealing, wiretapping, plotting to overthrow, and likely worse. When Nixon was down he got mean, and when he lost or failed he got even meaner. His confidence in himself went a bit too far. In Nixon's famous 1977 interview with David Frost, when asked about the legality of some of his actions, Nixon said, with full conviction, "Well, when the President does it, that means that it is not illegal."

The class continues to stare. I repeat myself: "When the President does it, that means that it is not illegal." They nod. "Is it true?" I ask. And they look confused. "Think about it," I say. "Rent the film." I close my books and exit.

"I forgot my meeting with Schwartz," I tell Tessie as soon as I'm in the door of the house. "I had such a totally strange day, and I totally forgot." I get down on my knees and look the dog in the eye. "Tessie, even if I told you, you wouldn't believe what I've been through." I log on to the computer and cancel my lunch "date" for tomorrow.

"What do you mean you're canceling?" the woman writes back.

"I mean I have to cancel," I write.

"Do you want to reschedule?"

"Not at this time."

"You cancel on me and you get no more," she writes.

"I have no choice, it's my annual review at work."

"Your dick will die," the woman types.

"Your hostility leaves me at a loss for words."

"Fuck you."

"Be nice," I type. "I know where you live, you gave me your address, remember?"

"Is that a threat? My husband will kick your ass. . . ."

"Your husband? You said you were never married."

"Oops. Well, have a nice day and good luck with your meeting. You know I'm kidding right, like if you want to reschedule, e-mail me and we'll work something out."

I unplug the computer. I need to more than turn it off. I need the screen not just to go to sleep but to go black.

The annual review. I prepare myself for lunch with Schwartz. I look up all things Nixon and refresh my knowledge on recent and forthcoming books in the field. I review my class list and try to match names to faces in case he mentions the child of a friend of a friend. I study the school's annual report and gather my thoughts on the state of higher education. I depart, reminding myself that I am a player in the field and I am unique, I am a Nixon specialist.

Schwartz. On the one hand, I've known him for years; on the other, he took a turn, he teaches less, talks on TV more. His area of expertise, the history of war, makes him a go-to guy for a comment on almost anything. I'm thinking he's going to ask me to take on more, that he's going to say, Enough screwing around with this one class per semester, you have so much to say, so much valued experience, we need you more than ever—can you pick up another class or two?

Our lunch has been changed from the usual restaurant, where I always get Wiener schnitzel and he gets liver and onions and we joke about our parents and how when we were younger we never ate these things, but now that we're the age our parents once were we enjoy them enormously. At the diner, all I can think of is my mother and her friends going out for lunch and having cottage cheese and cling peaches.

"Are we here because of your tooth?" I ask Schwartz

"My tooth is fine," he says. "We're here because of the times. I'll have the soup," he tells the waitress.

"Cup or bowl?"

"Cup," he says.

And what else?

"A seltzer," he says.

"And for you?"

I'm backpedaling, I was thinking turkey club with fries; instead, I say, "Greek omelet."

"Home fries or French fries?"

"Whatever," I say, suddenly nervous. "Home fries."

"So—how's tricks?" Schwartz asks.

"Tricky," I say.

"Are you ever going to write that novel?"

"I'm taking notes, it's really more a nonfiction."

"You've been taking notes since he left office."

"I'm not done," I say. "The story is still unfolding; it's an ongoing situation, more is slowly being revealed."

"I'll keep it short, then—you've got a lot to deal with," he says.

The waitress hasn't even poured the water yet.

"You have been with us for a long time, but times are changing. . . ."

"Is there another course you're thinking I might teach? Contrasting Presidencies, George Bush Jr. vs. Richard Nixon, Who's the Sneakier Worm?"

"Actually, we're going to go with something else. We've got this fellow who has a new way of teaching history, it's future-forward."

"What does that mean, future-forward?" I ask, sounding more indignant than intended.

"Instead of studying the past, the students will be exploring the future—a world of possibility. We think it will be less depressing than watching reruns of the Zapruder films."

"Oh," I say. "Oh." And nothing else.

"You'll finish out the semester, of course."

I nod—of course.

The food arrives.

"I hope you won't fight us. Nixon's dead; your students weren't even born when Nixon was in office."

"Are you suggesting we no longer teach history?"

"I'm saying your class has no relevance."

"I beg to differ," I say.

"Don't," he says. "You have no idea. We filled your class with overflow kids who had to take one history to fulfill the requirement and the Internet and Americana class was full. Trust me, they don't care about Nixon."

"But some of their papers were pretty good."

"They buy them on the Internet. They get papers about other people and change the names—because, honestly, at this point they're not even selling papers about Nixon, so they buy a Clinton paper and tweak it accordingly."

"No," I say, genuinely surprised.

"Yes. In fact, we did a test case in your class, retitling 'The Morals of Monica Lewinsky' as 'Breaking Faith at the Watergate.' You gave a paper that wasn't about a break-in, but about a blow job, a B+."

"Was I grading on a curve?"

"You're out of touch," he says.

"I'm a professor. We're supposed to be out of touch. Remember elbow patches and pipes?"

"Not in this century."

"How about I teach a class in murder, in memoir, in my murderous brother, in the American downfall," I suggest; given the timing, I can't help but think this has something to do with what happened with George.

Schwartz is unmoved. "I can't save you now anyway—we have no money. Write your book, write a couple of books, and then we'll talk." He raises his hand and signals to the waitress for the check. "You know," he says, "there are all these schools that now run programs on the Internet; maybe you could pick up an Internet class or two and keep your hand in."

"That's it?" I say. "After all these years? I get half a lunch and a goodbye?"

"I don't meant to rush you," Schwartz says, "but there's nothing more to say."

Seeking counsel. In a local church there are late-afternoon meetings. I drive by, see cars parked outside, lights on in the old building. A feeling of warmth and welcome emanates. I park and enter, wandering through the upstairs chapel.

"Meeting's downstairs," the janitor tells me.

The meeting is already under way when I slip into the room and take a seat in the back. The men and women gathered have the posture of familiarity; I sense that not only do they all know each other, they've known each other for a long time. I am the odd man out. I feel them gently shifting in their seats so they can get a look at me. Finally, my moment comes.

"Hi, my name is Nit."

"Hi, Nit," they say in unison. The echo of their voices causes me to draw a deep breath; it is the echo of acceptance and welcome.

"What brings you here today?" someone asks.

"I got fired," I say. I pause and then begin again, "I fucked my brother's wife, and then my brother came home and killed her. My wife is filing for divorce. And now, today, after having taught at the same college for many years, they said this semester is my last. I am living in my brother's house while he's in the bin. I'm taking care of the dog and the cat, and recently I started using his computer—you know, going online, visiting various sites.

I've been making lots of lunch dates with women—mostly we don't have lunch, it's just sex. A lot of sex."

"Were you drunk?" someone asks.

"No," I say. "Not a bit."

"Do you have a drinking problem?"

"I hardly drink. I guess I could drink more. I've been watching you all from outside. You looked warm and friendly and welcoming."

"Sorry, Nit," the group says in unison.

"You have to go," the leader adds, and I feel like I've been kicked off the island. I get up from my folding chair and exit, passing the old aluminum coffeepot with its ready light, the quart of whole milk, the sugar, the dough-nuts, all the things I was looking forward to. I am tempted to take myself to a bar to become an alcoholic overnight so I can go back.

"There are other places, for people like you," one of the men says.

"There's a place for everyone," one woman calls after me.

I sit in the parking lot, imagining the meeting going on without me, all of them talking about me behind me back—or do they simply carry on?

As I'm pulling out of the lot, Claire calls on my cell phone. "We should sell the parking space," she says.

"Sure," I say. "We can if you want. Are you sure you don't want it?"

"I don't drive, remember? I'm selling the parking space to the people upstairs."

"The ones with the screaming kids who run up and down on our heads all day and all night."

"Yes," she says. "They have a minivan, and they offered twenty-six thou-sand dollars."

"Twenty-six thousand?"

"It went into a bidding war, since there are so few spots."

"Wow."

"They're paying in cash."

"Great, so we'll split it fifty-fifty."

"Actually, I'm the one who paid for the parking place," she reminds me.

"Then why are you telling me?"

"Just wanted you to know," she says, and then is gone.

I dream of Nixon. Nixon, the Night Stories. The idea being that he had a confidant; that every night, when Nixon couldn't sleep, he'd call this friend and they'd talk and sometimes the friend would read to him from books like *Moby-Dick* and *Notes from the Underground* and Paul Johnson's *Journey into Chaos* or *Enemies of Society,* and sometimes they would watch television together. Nixon liked the idea that his confidant was up when he was and that he was never really alone. Being alone frightened him.

Friday evening, as she's finishing up, having put the mop and bucket away and gone into the powder room to change back into her street clothes, Maria the cleaning lady says, "Mister, I can no work here no more. I miss Mrs. Jane too much. It makes me unhappy to come here. I am here working and you are sitting here all day. I don't know you. I know your brother killed Mrs. Jane. And what about those beautiful children, who no more have a mother? Please you tell them Maria said hello to them, but to you I say goodbye."

I reach for my wallet. I give her five hundred bucks. She takes three and gives me back two. "I have no debt," she says. And I don't know what she means.

"I'll tell the children," I say.

"Good," she says. "Also, you need Mr. Clean and Windex."

"Thank you, Maria."

Monday morning, a truck pulls up outside the house, a white truck with a giant insect mounted on the roof. Two guys in white suits get out, unload large stainless-steel spray canisters, put masks over their nose and mouth, and walk towards the front door. Before they come to the door, one breaks right, the other breaks left, and they circle the house, spraying. Tessie's bark and the sickening scent both prompt me to open the front door and call, "Can I help you?"

With the first breath I draw, I feel my lungs shrink back; my eyes start to burn. The guys pull their masks off.

"It smells horrible," I say.

"Who are you?" the second guy asks.

"I was about to ask you the same thing."

"We're under contract. Twice a year we come; the date was set months ago."

"Things have changed," I say.

"Too late now, we already started. Not the kind of thing you want to stop once you start. Breeds resistant bugs, *bigger* bugs—very bad things can happen." Tessie barks.

"Jesus, is the dog home too? Where's the lady of the house? She always got the dog and the cat packed in the car. They take off for the day. This stuff is noxious; it'll kill you if you sit in there with it."

"Well, what do you want me to do?"

"I don't know—you're not supposed to be here. You're supposed to take your dogs and your cats and be gone for eight hours, longer if you have asthma."

"Well, can you at least pause? Can you give me a few minutes to get it together?"

"Fuck, fuck, fuck," one of the guys says. "It's not even nine-thirty and now we're screwed for the day. Late. Late. Late." He turns to me. "Well, don't just stand there, get it together!"

I put Tessie on her leash and some biscuits in my pocket. I catch the cat. I can't find a carrier for her, and so somehow wrestle her into a canvas bag and run out to the car with her howling. I bring her litter box out and set it up on the passenger seat, let the cat out of the bag, set up water, food, crack the windows, and go back for Tessie. I figure we'll walk around for a while, and if need be I'll come back and drive both the cat and the dog somewhere later. It's not like a lot of planning went into it.

Tessie and I set off down the street; it's a bright, clear morning, unseasonably warm for a winter day, a day full of promise, of hope, of possibility.

The park is empty. It's a place that exists simply to contain the trees, to oxygenate the village, a green expanse to drive past while gesturing to visitors: Don't we have a lovely park, a beautiful village green? At the far edge there is a parking lot, tennis and basketball courts, a set of swings, a climber. I run Tessie across the park; on the other side, I tether her leash to the swings and then, to prove I still have the possibility of play left in me, I jump on the swing, the thick rubber seat matching my childhood memories. I rock back and forth, back and forth, climbing higher and higher, and then, at the peak of both height and motion, I throw my head back, the sky opens up, filling my vision, blue, rich bright super-blue with thick white clouds, clouds of perfection, and for a moment all is beyond perfect, it is divine. And then, as I sail forward, the velocity is overwhelming, my stomach rises to my throat. I am whirling. I close my eyes—worse. I open my eyes—worse again. I throw myself forward, tumbling off the swing, landing in the dirt on hands and knees. The swing slams me in the back—as if to say, "Take that, you idiot." A vestibular impossibility? I go for the slide, climb the ladder; the smooth curl of the handrails feels the same now as it did forty years ago. At the top I push off and glide down to the bottom. As I get up, the button on my pocket catches, tugs, rips. Despite the allure, the echoing memory of swinging from bar to bar, of hanging from my knees, I don't attempt the climber or the monkey bars. I firmly believe I still could do anything and everything and want to keep it that way.

I'm thinking of days that never were, the perfect childhood that existed only in my imagination. When I was growing up, the playground wasn't so much a well-coiffed green as an empty lot. Our families had no desire for us to have a safe, clean place to play—as far as they were concerned, playing was a waste of time. Supplies were limited; one guy might have a mitt, another guy a bat, and the rest of us caught barehanded, sucking up the incredible sting, hands smarting not only with pain but with the thrill of success at having plucked the ball out of the sky, having interrupted the trajectory and likely spared someone the cost of replacing a window. The bottom line was, if you had time to play, you didn't tell anyone, because if your parents knew, they would find something for you to do.

So we played quietly and out of sight, making toys out of whatever happened to be nearby—my father's shoes made a most excellent navy, his size-nine wing tips gliding in formation across the carpet, the smell of leather and foot sweat. And what did I use as the aircraft carrier? A silver platter that I borrowed from the dining room. And when my mother discovered the platter surrounded by shoes, she accused me of having mental problems. Why wasn't it obvious to her that the carpet was the ocean, the battleground? She called me a nogoodnik, and I remember crying and George thinking it was all so funny.

Two women in spandex walk in circles around the outside perimeter of the park, waddling as fast as they can without breaking into a run. They stare at me. They actually point, as if asking each other to confirm that I am really there. I wave. They don't respond.

Near the tennis court I find an old ball and throw it for Tessie; she takes off running, and I have to chase her to get it back. She seems thrilled with the game, the enormous expanse of open space, and runs in endless circles before digging a bed in the dirt and settling in to shred the yellow fuzz. It's out of season; half the trees are bare, the others are a dull evergreen, the grass is an uneven mix of zoysia and ryegrass.

I sit. I sit in the park on a perfectly nice winter day—alone. The place is so goddamned empty that I feel nervous, afraid to be in the middle of the open field alone. Something comes over me. It's not exactly an anxiety attack but more a cloud, a heavy, dark cloud, all the more threatening because the sky is perfectly clear. Everything is fine, or should be fine, except I've been kicked out of my brother's house by an execution squad. I'm sunk. Flat out in the grass, feeling the depth of it all, and maybe it's always been there. If pressed, I'd say I know that: I know I did all kinds of tricks and turns and fancy maneuvers to buffer myself, to puff myself up, to simply fucking survive. But now I'm feeling it, I'm feeling what it was like a thousand years ago in my parents' house—maybe my five minutes on the swing loosened something, but it's all coming back like a kind of psychic tidal wave, and there's a bad taste in my mouth, metallic and steely, and I'm feeling how much everyone in my family hated each other, how little we actually cared for or respected anyone but ourselves. I'm feeling how profoundly my family disappointed me and in the end how I retreated, how I became nothing, because that was much less risky than attempting to be something, to be anything in the face of such contempt.

Look at me. Look what has happened. Look what I have done. Take notice. At the moment I am not even talking to you, I am talking to myself. *Look at me,* homeless in a public park. I curl into a ball, a fucking human ball in the far corner of the park. I can't look at myself—there is nothing to see.

I am sobbing, wailing, crying so deep, so hard, it is the cry of a lifetime; I am bellowing. The dog comes to me, licks my face, my ears, tries to get me to stop, but I can't stop, I have just begun. It is as though I will cry like this for years—look what I have done. And, god-fucking-damn it, I'm not even an alcoholic, I'm nothing, just a guy, a truly average Joe—which is probably the worst part of it all, knowing that I am not in any way exceptional or distinguished. Except for and until what happened with Jane, I was entirely regular, normal; since my wedding I hadn't slept with anyone except my wife. . . .

Look at me—even though no one's come out and said it, you know it as well as I do, I'm as much a murderer as my brother, no more, no less.

I say it to myself—and I am undone.

A young cop shows up, "You okay?"

I nod.

"We got a call about a crying man?"

"Is that illegal?"

"No, but you don't see much of that around here, especially this time of year. Home from work?"

"Laid off, and the exterminator is in the house today, and they asked me to leave. Park seemed like the place to go."

"Most people go shopping," the cop says.

"Really?"

"Yeah, when people don't know what to do with themselves, they go to the mall, walk up and down, and spend money."

"I never thought of it," I say. "I'm not much of a shopper."

"It's what they do."

"Even with a dog?"

"Yep, you've got your outdoor malls and your indoor."

The cop stands there.

"I don't mean to be rude, but this is a public park and I'm minding my own business."

"No camping," the cop says. "No loitering."

"How can you tell if someone is loitering versus just enjoying the park? The sign says it's open from seven a.m. to dusk. I walked here with the dog so we could enjoy being outside. Apparently that's not okay, apparently in this town going into the park is considered weird. And you know what, you're right—it must be, because there's no one here; the whole park is empty except for you and me, so I apologize."

With both the cat and the dog in the car, I go off to teach. I drive to school, park in a shady spot—leave each animal a bowl of water on the floor, crack the windows, the air temperature is in the low fifties. I leave them knowing they're no better or worse off than parked outside the house.

"Today we are scheduled to discuss the Bay of Pigs. . . ."

Several students raise their hands and announce that they feel uncomfortable with the subject matter.

"Why?"

"I'm vegetarian," one student says.

"It's unpatriotic," a foreign student suggests.

"While I appreciate your concerns, I'll carry on as planned. And, indeed, the action was patriotic, if flawed—inspired by love of our country from within the government. The Bay of Pigs is not a restaurant or a food group but refers to an unsuccessful attempt in 1961 by CIA-trained operatives to overthrow the government of Fidel Castro. The plan was Nixon's idea and developed with Eisenhower's support but wasn't launched until after Kennedy took office. In retrospect, the idea of a new administration assuming the responsibility for the execution of a covert action planned by another 'team' seems problematic. Nixon's responsibility for the training of the Cuban exiles by the CIA was significant and is discussed in Nixon's book *Six Crises*. And yet it is safe to assume that many activities of our government are passed from administration to administration—one sees this retrospectively in the history of the Vietnam War and, more recently, in Iraq. The 1961 failure of Kennedy to overthrow Castro, and the mess made of the carefully laid and then abruptly changed plans, aggravated Nixon and his 'colleagues' to no end. It's interesting to note that several of the CIA players in this event make a return appearance with Watergate."

The students look at me empty-eyed. "Is any of this familiar?" I ask.

"Nope," the vegetarian says.

I let the rope out a little bit. I allow the conversation to wander. I talk about history's knack for repeating itself, the importance of knowing who you are, where you come from. We talk about history as a narrative, a true story writ both large and small. We talk about how one learns, researches—what it means to investigate, to explore. We talk about the value of historical documents and how that's changing in the age of the Internet and the hard drive. I ask what materials they hold on to.

"Texts," they say. "Like, when I'm dating someone—or have a fight with someone—I save the texts."

"We don't print out," another says. "It's not environmental."

I ask what their first memories were, when they knew there was a larger world, and who they think the most powerful person in the country is. It's usually either a sports figure or a movie star—not the President.

I remind them they are supposed to be working on a paper in which they have been asked to define and describe their own political views and compare and contrast their positions to the views held by leading political figures.

"That's hard," one of the students says.

"For some," I say, bringing the class to an abrupt close.

I go back to the car—the dog and cat are fine, though the stink is enormous. The cat, in a fit of anxiety, has shredded the passenger seat and used it as a bathroom. I drive home breathing only through my mouth.

Back at the house, there's a note on the floor. "Big surprise coming for you." The house still stinks of bug killer. I get cleaning supplies and go back to the car. I take the cat out of the car and put her back into the house—hoping she's not asthmatic—and clean the shit and shredded interior as best I can.

From the basement I drag an old webbed lounge chair and set it up in the backyard. I find an old arctic sleeping bag and make myself a bed of sorts and fall asleep, waking only when Tessie barks. Coming around the corner of the house, I spot a white van parked at the curb.

The passenger door opens, and an Asian man gets out carrying a small white square of paper—a note!

"Can I help you?" I ask.

"I very annoyed with the man who live here, you know him?"

"Which man?"

"His name is Silver."

"I'm Silver."

"Where have you been? I leave you one hundred notes like long-lost lover."

"What is this in reference to?"

"I have big delivery for you. For weeks I drive around with your stuff. I should charge you extra."

"What stuff?"

"Your life boxes are in my truck. Where you want it?"

"My life boxes?"

"The shit from your apartment," the other guy says, opening the back of the truck.

The man and his partner carry box after box up to the house. They build a wall of boxes across the back of the living room, and then, as they bring more, it becomes an installation of sorts, a cave. What's amazing is that each box is exactly the same—they are all unmarked white cardboard, fourteen by fourteen by fourteen. Whatever I might have owned that didn't fit isn't coming back. I accept delivery and give them each twenty bucks as a tip.

"After so much, that all we get?"

"I lost my job," I say. "I have no life."

I cannot begin to unpack. It is all that I can do to simply go on. I go back into the yard. After dark, I go back into the house, make myself a sandwich, get a blanket and pillow, and head out again. Tessie doesn't want to go—she curls up on her bed and refuses to budge.

Alone, I sleep in the lounge chair out back. I've never slept outside at night before. It's something I always wanted to do, but honestly I was scared. At this point I think, what's the problem? I have nothing to fear—in fact, I have become the guy they're scared of.

In the early morning, as I'm walking Tessie, still wearing the same clothes as the day before, now dirty and damp with dew, the cop from the day before spots me. He pulls his squad car over and asks what I'm doing.

"Walking the dog," I say.

"Where do you live?"

"Over there," I say.

He escorts me home and seems unhappy when I take the spare key from under the fake rock to let myself in.

"Most people don't use the spare key," he says.

I shrug and open the door. There is a note on the floor. "You suck, cheapskate. You need pay more."

I show the officer the white box installation of "My Life," I take him on a tour of the house, the upstairs bedroom, and explain why there are no bedside lamps. I point in the direction of George's office, where there are lots of family photos, from when "times were better," whatever that means.

"Looks like you're in the right place," the cop says as he's leaving. "Stay safe."

It happens a little while later, when I'm brushing my teeth, a creeping sensation, like water is rushing in, like I'm going under. I brush, I rinse, I look at myself in the mirror. There is a pain in my head, in my eye, and as I'm looking, my face divides, half of it falls, as if about to cry. It just drops. I try to make a face, I grin, a sloppy half-smile. It's as though I am mocking myself, as though I have been hit with novocaine. Using the butt of my toothbrush, I poke at my face, almost stabbing, and feel nothing. As I am standing there, I realize I am sort of slouching, like a tipped marionette. I am using only one arm. I walk out of the room, stumble. There is the sensation of plastic wrapping around my head, not exactly pain but a kind of liquefaction, as though I am melting and trickling down my own neck. I'm watching as my face continues to fall; it goes entirely slack—I have aged a hundred years. I want to change my expression but can't.

I assume it will pass. I assume I've got something in my eye, soap, and it will wash itself out. I come out of the bathroom and finish dressing—it seems to take hours. I'm exhausted. I don't know whether to lie down or to keep moving. It occurs to me that I need help. The dog is looking at me strangely. "Did something happen?" I ask. "I can't understand what I'm saying, can you?"

My right leg is like a rubber band, springing, firing unsteadily under me. I want to call my doctor, but besides the fact that I can't remember his number, I can't seem to work the phone. Fine, I think, I'll drive myself to the hospital.

I make my way out of the house and into the car. I put the car into reverse, and then realize that I don't have the key and the engine is not running. I take my foot off the brake and get out.

The car rolls down the driveway.

I vomit where I am standing.

The car rolls into the street and into the path of an oncoming car. An accident happens.

Somehow I am still standing in the driveway, next to the puddle of sick.

The cop who arrives is the same one who knows me from the park. "How can you be drinking so early?" he asks.

I can't answer.

"He wasn't in the car," the woman from next door says. "He was just standing there."

I try and say the word "hospital" but can't; I try "ambulance," but it is long and soupy; finally, "MORON" comes spurting out, perfectly clear.

I make a gesture, the same gesture I would use in a restaurant when asking for the check, please. I make the sign of writing, and someone hands me paper and pen.

"Something is wrong," I write in large wobbly letters. The effort does me in, I am knocked to the ground, leveled. I hear someone say, "We can water you," and I wonder if I've turned into a plant.

Ambulance. Too loud. It is all too much, an assault, an insult. Too fast, too slow, nauseating, I have never felt so nauseated, and I wonder, have I been poisoned? Maybe that's it, maybe it's something about that spray, maybe it's the box cave in the living room, maybe it's off gassing toxic fumes, my previous life is rotting in those boxes and giving off toxic fumes. And as I'm thinking it, I'm worried there's something about my logic that's not right.

An interruption, a clot, a stroke, a little leak in the head. An X-ray, an MRI, some blood work, tissue plasminogen activator, arrhythmia, interventional radiology, cerebral angioplasty, carotid endarterectomy, stent.

I blame George: George and his desk, George and high-speed Internet. I am blaming what's happening on everything from sitting at that desk for too many hours each day to the activities I've recently engaged in, both the physical exertion of suddenly having so much sex, and also the tension, the trauma. I'm blaming it on George and George's fucking medicine cabinet. As a "news" man, George believed he needed to know about everything. So his medicine cabinet was stocked with everything from Viagra to Levitra, Cialis, Tadalis, Revatio, etc. The combination of his computer, his medicine cabinet, and the events of the last few weeks—namely, what happened to Jane—caused a kind of mania, a sexual insanity that comes to an abrupt halt with me lying on a gurney in the ER.

Was this the big one or was this the small tremor, the warning? Does it get better—does the sensation of being in a dream underwater go away?

A nurse is standing over my gurney. "Mr. Silver. There's a problem with your insurance. It appears you've been canceled. Do you have the actual insurance card?"

"Tessie." I try to explain that there is no one to feed and walk Tessie. No one pays attention, no one does anything until I pull out the IV line. "Someone needs to walk the goddamned dog." They're trying to get me to lie back down and asking if it's a real dog and explaining that there is a volunteer pet-minder program.

"Call my lawyer," I say.

I am brought a phone.

I don't know why Larry's number is embossed like caller ID in front of my eyes—Train and Traub, 212-677-3575.

"Larry," I say. "Tell Claire that I am having a stroke." I say it, and I hear myself saying something that sounds like "Tell dare I'm outside having a smoke."

"What?" Larry says.

I try harder: "Can you please tell Claire that I am having a stroke?"

"Is this you?"

"Who else would it be?"

"Are you crank-calling me?"

"No," I say. I hear myself talking and it sounds like I've got rocks in my mouth.

"I can't tell her," he says. "It's manipulative. And, further, how do I know you're really having a stroke and aren't smashed?"

"I'm in the Emergency Room, Larry; they're asking for my insurance card, and I keep saying, 'Don't worry, I have insurance.'"

"You have no insurance," Larry says. "Claire dropped you. She asked me to drop you."

I throw up again, spreading sick over my gurney and across the EKG wires.

"Because you're still legally married, you may have some recourse. You can fight it."

"I can't fight anything—I can barely talk."

"Maybe they have a patient advocate at the hospital."

"Larry, can you please ask Claire to fax me a copy of the insurance card," I say, and the nurse takes the phone.

"Mr. Silver really shouldn't get agitated—he's had a cerebral incident. Agitation is definitely not a good thing."

Larry says something to the nurse and she hands me back the phone. "He wants a final word," she says.

"Fine," Larry says. "I'll take care of it, I'll fix this one. Consider it a favor, consider it the last favor I'll do for you." Did Nixon have to deal with shit like this, or did he hunker down with a bowl of SpaghettiOs?

I think of Nixon's phlebitis; was the first attack in his left leg in 1965 during a trip to Japan? I think of him during the autumn of 1974, just after his resignation, when again his left leg swelled and he also had a clot in his right lung. He had surgery in October, then a bleed, and remained hospitalized until mid-November, and when Judge John Sirica subpoenaed the former President, he was medically unable to testify.

As I lie waiting for my turn in the CAT scanner, which I'm thinking is like a cerebral lie-detector test, I am all the more sure there's a link between Nixon's clots and Watergate. And, not to put myself in the same league, but I'm sure the episode with George followed by Jane's death has caused my brain to blow.

During the CAT scan to comfort myself I review Nixon's enemies list.

1. Arnold M. Picker
2. Alexander E. Barkan
3. Ed Guthman
4. Maxwell Dane
5. Charles Dyson
6. Howard Stein
7. Allard Lowenstein
8. Morton Halperin
9. Leonard Woodcock
10. S. Sterling Munro Jr.
11. Bernard T. Feld
12. Sidney Davidoff
13. John Conyers
14. Samuel M. Lambert
15. Stewart Rawlings Mott
16. Ronald Dellums
17. Daniel Schorr
18. S. Harrison Dogole
19. Paul Newman
20. Mary McGrory

I am admitted to a semi-private room on a monitored floor. It occurs to me to call my "regular" doctor. Every word is a struggle. I do my best to explain my situation. The doctor's office manager tells me it's in God's hands, and besides that, the doctor doesn't practice outside of the city, and, more to the point, he's on vacation. She asks if I would like to be transferred to Death Israel when the doctor is back.

"What is Death Israel?"

"The hospital where the doctor is affiliated," the office manager says.

"Sounds anti-Semitic," my roommate says, having heard it all.

"I hope I'll be home before . . ." I say, my speech sounding slightly more coherent and familiar.

"If you change your mind, let us know," the office manager says.

"There's nothing worse than actually needing a doctor," my roommate says.

"What are you in for?" I ask, though I think it comes out sounding more like "Why you here?"

"The show is over," he says. "Clock's ticking down. Have you noticed I'm not moving? I'm stuck—all that's still going is my brain, or what's left of my brain. By the way, are you blurry or is it me?"

Before I can answer, the dog volunteer comes in. "I'm a Furry Friends Companion Consultant." She pulls up a chair and takes out an information packet and forms. "Do you have a cat or a dog?"

"Both."

"If a stranger opens the door, would they attack? Where is the food, and how much do they each get? Is the dog all right overnight—or do you need a nighttime companion? We have students who occasionally will do sleepovers."

"How long am I going to be here?" I ask.

"That's a question for your doctor. Adoption is also an option in some cases."

"Someone would adopt me?"

"Someone might adopt the pets—if, say, you weren't going to be going home. . . ."

"Where would I go?"

"To a skilled nursing facility, for example, or onward. . . ."

"Dead. She means dead," the guy in the next bed says. "They don't like to come out and say it, but I can, because, as I mentioned, I'm heading there soon."

"You don't seem so sick," I said to the guy. "You're perfectly coherent."

I wipe drool from my own mouth.

"That's what makes it so rough," the guy says. "Totally compos mentis, aware of everything, but that won't last for long."

"Did you consider hospice?" the furry friend asks my roommate.

"What's the difference—the art on the wall? They all smell like shit." His hand comes up to his face. "Was that me or someone else?" he asks, and no one says anything. "My hand or yours?"

"It was yours," I say.

"Oh," he says.

"I don't mean to interrupt," the furry volunteer says, "but you two will have all day and I've got things to do."

"All day, or not," the dying man says.

"About the pets—their names, ages? Do you have the house key with you?"

"Tessie is the dog, I don't know how old, and Muffin is the cat. There's a spare key under the fake rock on the left before the front door—a fake key and ten bucks."

The dying man hums to drown out the conversation. "Too much information," he says. "More than I should know."

"Like, what, you're going to get out of bed and steal my house?"

"Can you take dictation?" the dying man asks.

"I can try." I push the call button and ask for paper and pencil.

"It'll be a while," the nurse says.

"I've got a dying man who wants to confess."

"We all have needs," she says.

I nap. In my sleep I hear gunshots. I wake up thinking my brother is trying to kill me.

"It's not you," the guy in the bed next to me says. "It's on TV. While you were sleeping, a cop came to see you. He said he'll be back later."

I don't say anything.

"Can I ask you a question? Are you the guy who killed his wife?"

"What makes you ask?"

"I overheard someone talking about a guy who killed his wife."

I shrug. "My wife is divorcing me. She canceled my health insurance."

Someone comes in and says, "Which one of you asked for a priest?"

"We asked for paper."

"Oh," the guy says. He goes out and comes back with a yellow legal pad and a pen.

"Where to begin?" the dying man says. "For certain, there are questions that will go unanswered. The difficulty is that there is not an answer for everything—some things cannot be known."

He begins to spin a story, a complicated narrative about a woman—how they came together and then apart.

His story is beautiful and eloquent, Salingeresque; they didn't speak the same language, she wore a beautiful red scarf, and she got pregnant.

I try to get it down. As I'm looking at what I'm writing, I see that it's not making sense. I'm not writing in English. Whatever marks I'm making on this paper are not anything that another person could read. I focus on catch-phrases, I draw pictures, I try to make a map—I am all over the page, hoping I can clean it up later. He's going on and on, and right when we get to what I think would be the end, the dénouement, the guy sits bolt upright. "I'm not breathing," he says.

I push the call button. "He's not breathing," I shout. "He's going from pale pink to deep red, kind of purple."

Soon the room is filled with people. "We were in the middle of a conversation, he was coming to the punch line, and then, suddenly, he sat up and said, 'I'm not breathing.'"

Now he's sputtering, choking, in trouble, and more people come, and it's like an audience. They're all standing there watching the guy.

"Are you going to just watch or are you going to do something?" I ask.

"There's nothing we can do," the nurses say.

"Of course there is," I say.

"He's DNR. Do Not Resuscitate."

He wanted to die a good death. But look at him. He's struggling like he's choking to death.

"We know not when or how we will be called home," one of them says, and then they whip the curtain between the beds closed.

"That is not okay," I say, hauling my damaged self out of the goddamned bed and peeling the curtain open.

He's bucking and heaving and seems to be begging for someone to do something. Despite the tangle of EKG wires hanging off my chest and my double IVs, I get close to him, my exposed ass edging the nurses out of the way. And in my mind he's telling me to sock it to him, so I do. I give him one hell of an uppercut, slamming him in the gut with all I've got.

His mouth drops open, his teeth come flying out, and he gasps for breath. "Fucking dentures almost killed me," he says.

"You said you didn't want to be resuscitated," the nurse says, indignantly.

"I didn't say I wanted to choke on my own goddamned teeth."

"I thought it was an embolism. Did you think it was an embolism?" one nurse says to another.

"Do me a favor, send me home, where at least I can shoot myself when I'm ready."

"Would you like me to call someone?" the nurse asks.

"Like who?"

"A representative of the hospital? Case-management personnel, the patient advocates? A doctor? You tell me."

"Start at the top and work your way down," he says. "And change my forms immediately. Clearly you don't know the meaning of DNR."

Half an hour later, a woman comes with the forms rescinding the DNR order. "It can take a while before the change makes its way into the system, so how about I put a sign on your door."

"Do what's necessary," the man says.

"PLEASE SAVE THIS MAN," the woman writes on the dry-erase board mounted on the door that already lists our names and that we're IN DANGER OF FALLING/USE PRECAUTIONS.

In the middle of the afternoon, the pet person comes back, with photos of Tessie and the cat sitting on George and Jane's sofa next to some nice-looking young fellow. "You're squared away," she says happily.

The cop from the park comes—he's in uniform and carrying an FTD Big Hug bouquet—flowers with a stuffed bear clinging to the side of the vase. "Listen, I want to apologize—I treated you badly, you deserved better."

"Okay," I say.

The cop sits on the edge of my bed, and we make small talk, and then, when there's really nothing more to say, he tells me that he'll come back again another day.

"That was painful to watch. He must be in the program," the roommate says when the cop is gone.

"What program?"

"One of the twelve steps—This-Anon, That-Anon, Everything-Anon-Anon. Step number nine is making amends for the harm you caused."

"Interesting," I say. I'm tempted to tell him my story of crashing the AA meeting, but, given how much he knows about these steps, some things are better left unsaid.

When dinner arrives, there's nothing for him.

"Nothing?"

"I don't have you down for any meals, but I might be able to get you a liquid tray," the delivery woman says.

I lift the insulated cover off my plate and find the main dish unrecognizable.

"What is it?" I ask.

The delivery woman peers over. "That would be our chicken Marsala."

"I'm dying," my roommate says. "I have got no intention of drinking my last meal unless it's very good Scotch."

"How about some carry-out menus from the nurses' station? They're always ordering in."

"That would be great." He's suddenly pleased; more than pleased— inspired.

I put the cover back on my plate to keep the fumes from escaping and wait to see what happens next.

"What do you want for dinner?" he asks as he's going through the menus.

"Anything but Chinese."

Excited, he pulls his cell phone out from where it's been hidden under the covers and starts dialing. His ability to move is limited, but he's on a mission. First he calls the burger place and orders two cheeseburger deluxes with fries and extra pickles, then the pizza place for a medium pepperoni pie, the deli for some rice pudding and cream soda. I ask him to have them throw in a couple of Hershey bars with almonds. And when the deli guy says it's a minimum of twenty dollars to deliver, he tells the guy that he'll give him a fifty-dollar tip if he also stops at the liquor store for a very specific bottle of Scotch. The man says he'll do the job himself.

"So what if I order more than I can eat? I'm dying, I don't have to worry about leftovers. Is there anything special I can get you, something you've been dying for, no pun intended?" the roommate asks me.

I used to like caviar, fresh-made cheese blintzes, chocolate éclairs, and there was that doughnut I ate maybe forty years ago that I can't ever forget, an orange cruller on a cold morning outside a polling place during the 1972 presidential election that was as close to perfection as any food can be. But the fact is, I'm lying in a hospital bed and am not exactly feeling any kind of culinary craving. "Thanks," I say, "but I'm good with whatever you choose."

We wait. Will they remember to bring ketchup and mustard? Should we call back for mayo? We share a reverie about our love of mayonnaise, and he asks, Have I ever had Belgian French fries and dipping sauce, well done, salted and piping hot? Yes, I have, and his description of them is enough.

It takes longer than you'd think. There's a hospital to be navigated, security procedures downstairs—do they make them open the cheeseburgers?—elevators, corridors.

"Can you get my pants out of the closet?" the roommate asks. I get up slowly and make my way to his closet, dragging my IV pole and wires and my left foot, which doesn't seem to be fully functional. "Look in my pocket."

His pockets are loaded with cash, wads of twenties and a wallet filled with travelers' checks, euros, and English pounds.

"Looks like you're going for broke," I say, trying to make a joke.

"The last few times I left the house, I made sure I went to the cash machine. You never know what's going to happen and the worst thing would be to have no cash. We live in an economy and we die in an economy—wherever you go, you have to tip. No point being on a downward spiral and getting lousy service as you're sinking. I prepaid my funeral years ago. You want the euros, take them."

"I'm not going anywhere," I say, putting the foreign currency back in his pants.

We bet on how long it will take each of the delivery boys to find us. I am the winner at thirty-eight minutes, and the roommate gives me a hundred bucks in "bonus points" when the cheeseburgers arrive. The pizza is a close second. "I've never delivered to a patient before, it's cool," the guy says. "I mean, as long as you're not contagious." The deli guy is the last to arrive. "Sorry it took me so long, I had to find someone to cover the register." He hands over the bag of goodies along with the Scotch. My roommate peels off another hundred to cover the debt and offers him a drink.

"I'm gonna pass," the guy says. "I have to get back to work. But I'm curious what's wrong with you, that you're lying in bed ordering rice pudding and Scotch."

"I'm dying," the man says, "and you know what's amazing? Today I really did almost die once, they were about to let me go, and now that I lived, I feel great, not like I'll live forever, but I'm okay with dying." He pauses. "I'm dying," he says. "I've said it more today than ever before, and suddenly it's a fact, something that's out there, like a coming attraction at the movies."

"I guess we're all dying," the deli guy says. "I mean, sooner or later we gotta go."

The woman who delivered the hospital meals comes to collect my tray. She stays for a slice of pizza and a few fries.

I'm enjoying the cheeseburger; it's a perfectly gummy, gristly combination, cut by the salty fries and the sour snap of the pickles. I am well past my fill line when I take a tumbler of rice pudding and fill both of our hospital-issue blue plastic cups with Scotch.

"You want me to get some ice?" I ask.

"A straw," he says, "a straw would be good."

We've propped up the head of his bed, and now he's happily sucking down the Scotch.

"I wouldn't mind a square of chocolate," he says.

I give him a whole bar. "Live it up."

Bloated, belching French fries and pickle juice, and trailing the IV pole behind me, I take the trash down the hall and stuff it in a can on the other side of the floor. The nurses seem pleased at how well I'm getting around, dragging my sluggish side, sporting one gown worn forward, another worn in reverse, the chic way of shielding the butt.

We watch one of the cop shows on TV, and sometime between ten and eleven, he feels restless, uncomfortable, and buzzes the nurse asking for Maalox. They tell him there's no order for Maalox on his chart. He asks if his papers have otherwise been updated.

"Yes," she says.

"Good," he says.

"Just because I lived earlier doesn't mean I'm not dying now," he reminds me.

Sometime after midnight, a frightful sound wakes me up. The roommate is pitched forward, eyes bugged out as if a terrifying nightmare has grabbed him. I buzz the nurse. "Hurry" is all I can say. Before they get there, he's already slumped back in the bed, limp.

First one nurse comes and then a roomful and the red crash cart. They're rushing, shouting, cracking vials of drugs, shooting him full of this and that. It's brutal and terrifying, and at some point it's clear that, despite how hard they're trying, it's not going to turn out for the best. After they've shocked him twice and his body literally bounced up off the bed—and while they're still upon him like vultures—I walk out of the room. I pace, dragging my weak leg behind me, up and down the hall and finally back into the room, where I'm standing pressed into a corner when they "call it" at twelve-forty-eight. They cover him with a clean sheet and leave, taking their magic cart with them. There is debris everywhere, syringe parts, gauze, plastic bits. He lies under the sheet. I come closer, never having seen a body not breathing. The creases of the fresh sheet relax over him. I hold his hand, touch his face, his leg. His body is still warm, human, but vacant, the muscles dropping away from the bone, all tension dissipated. They leave us alone, and about an hour later, two security guards come with a gurney and take him away. Something about it, the here and gone of it all, is too strange.

The room still smells like French fries.

I need to talk. If I call the house, what will happen? Will the machine with Jane's voice pick up? If I speak, if I beg, if I prattle on long enough, the dog minder may answer. If I bark, maybe Tessie will bark back. I want to call Tessie. Tessie and Jane.

I am about to dial when a nurse comes in to offer me a sleeping pill.

"It's not easy," she says.

I accept the pill. She pours water into my cup, not realizing she's mixing it with Scotch. I say nothing and swallow it all, the sleeping pill, the Scotch.

She stays until I sleep.

———

In the morning, the bed next to mine is stripped, the floor washed, the debris swept away.

Not a word is said about the night before.

Midmorning, someone from the hospital comes with a plastic bag and cleans out his closet, his drawer, and asks me, "Is there anything else?"

"Like what?"

"Like you don't know? Like you were here all night with his stuff, maybe you took something?"

"There's a bottle of Scotch; you want it, it's yours," I say. "But if you're randomly accusing me of theft because I happened to be in the next bed—you are so far over the line. . . ."

"He may have had something else, like a watch, like a ring?"

"I have no idea what he did or didn't have."

The guy looks at me like he's the hospital heavy, the goon squad sent to shake down patients.

"I don't have to put up with this." I lift the phone, dial "9" for an outside line and then "911."

The guy fights me for the phone. "Give it a rest," he says, grabbing the receiver and slamming it down.

A moment later, while the guy is still there, the phone rings, I answer. It's the 911 operator calling back. I explain the situation. She tells me that because I hung up they have to send someone to make sure I'm not being held hostage, not being forced to give statements against my will. The goon squad is looking at me in disbelief. "You fuck," he says. "You fucking fuck."

"What are you going to do now, beat me up?"

He looks at me again, shaking his head. "You got no sense of humor," he says, leaving.

An hour later, the cops arrive—thank God it wasn't an actual emergency.

"You doin' all right?" they ask me.

"As best as can be expected given the circumstances," I say.

One of them gives me his card in case I continue to have trouble. "You'd be surprised," he says, "the number of calls we get from people in hospitals, old-age homes, trapped in their children's houses, elder abuse; it's a problem."

I never thought of myself as elder. A few minutes ago, I was a guy in the middle of his life; now, suddenly, I'm elder.

———

Today is a school day. I realize it when the nurse comes in and tears two pages off the calendar. "Sometimes we run late," she says.

I phone the school and tell them that I've got to cancel class due to a death in the family.

It's a relief when a volunteer from the physical-therapy department comes to get me.

In physical therapy I am given a walker—mine to keep—fitted with green tennis balls to make it slide easier. The physical therapist tells me it's her job to get me ready for discharge. "Usually after an event such as yours, a person goes to rehab for a week or so, but with your insurance an open question, they're not going to take you, so you'll have to do it yourself at home. The good news is that in the grand scheme of things what happened to you is relatively minor."

"Felt major to me," I say.

"On a scale of one to ten, yours was a two," she says. "Trust me, you got off easy."

She tries to get me to play a game with buttons and zippers, which at first seems idiotic, but when I try I'm surprised at how my fingers no longer seem to belong to me. I try the buttons again, and finally she gives me another, larger set and this time I can do it. "Great," I say, "so what am I supposed to do, have all my shirts retrofitted with clown buttons?"

"It's a look," the therapist says.

"Am I going to get better?" I ask. "Or is this the way it's going to be?" Who thought getting dressed and walking up four stairs would be so difficult?

"Don't panic. It takes time," the therapist says.

After an hour of therapy I'm exhausted, and return to my room feeling very alone, with an open invitation to come back again in a couple of hours if I want to try again.

Lunch is waiting. Tomato-rice soup, the same tomato-rice soup I had in the cafeteria while waiting for news about Jane. I can't help but think that if I eat it I will never get out of here, I will be in an endless loop of tomato soup and hospitals, and so I simply leave it.

A young woman comes into the room. "Papa?"

"You have the wrong room."

"No," she says, "I've been waiting. I was here and you were gone. I'm here for Bed A, but there's no one in Bed A."

"I'm sorry."

"Did he go home?"

I notice she is wearing a red scarf. "Where did you get that scarf?"

"It was a gift from my mother—why?"

Why do I have to be the one?

"He died," I say.

"When?"

"Last night."

"Can you tell me about him?" she says. "We never actually met."

"There was something your father wanted me to tell you." I take out the sheets of paper and attempt to decode my marks, filling in blank spots with fragments I remember but couldn't write down fast enough.

"My mother died two years ago. In her papers were letters from him. I wrote and he never answered, until very recently."

"He was lovely," I say. "One hell of an interesting guy. Complex and very human, with all that entails. I'm sure he felt bad about whatever happened, and no doubt it was more complex than we'll ever know."

A priest comes into the room. "I got a call that someone had a confession to make."

"He died," I say. "Do you have a rabbi?"

He pulls a yarmulke out of his pocket and puts it on his head.

I find it confusing, the yarmulke and the collar.

In the midst of all this, the doctor comes in. "How are we doing, Mr. . . ." He pauses to check the name on my chart. ". . . Silver."

"Have we met before?" I ask.

"No," he says.

The young woman stands, excusing herself. "It'll be a few minutes," I explain, "the doctors never stay long."

"I'll get a coffee and come back," she says, leaving.

"There's just one of us now," I tell the doctor, "the other guy died."

"Sometimes it can't be helped," the doctor says. "But you're okay. You'll be going home soon. Are there any questions?"

"Can I fuck?"

There's a loud pause.

"I worry that taking my brother's Viagra is what caused this 'incident.'"

"How so?"

"I was taking a good amount of the stuff and, well, I worry I blew a fuse, so to speak."

"I don't think so, but it's an interesting idea. I'll make a note of it."

"And so can I fuck? Can I take Viagra? Or Levitra, or whatever the hell comes next?"

"I'd give it a rest," the doctor says.

"How long of a rest?"

"Let's say, if you are able to get an erection on your own, with no assistance, fine, but if you get a headache or feel ill, stop. If you can't get an erection, which you may not be able to after an event such as this—not permanently, but for the short term—I'd lay off the hard stuff—no pun intended. It's about how much risk you're willing to tolerate. I've known men who after an event like this were terrified, they couldn't even think of trying to have sex. Others try again right here in the hospital—they say it's a 'safe' environment, but you didn't hear that from me. That's off the record, of course."

"Of course," I say. "And of course the question is hypothetical. The truth is, I'm terrified, I'm suddenly terrified of everything. I can't imagine taking the pills again, I can't imagine ever wanting to have sex."

"That's more like it," the doctor says. "Men need to stop feeling pressure to perform. Let yourself off the hook."

"What I really want to know," I say, trying again, "is was this *it* or was this just a warning? Is there more to come? Should I prepare myself for the worst?"

"We make no promises," the doctor says, shaking his head. "Your arteries look good, there's no hidden clot waiting to break off and play marble run through your veins. You're in good shape for the shape you're in. I expect you'll make a full recovery, you'll be back to work next week. Gotta go," he says, checking his watch.

The girl comes back, coffee in hand.

"You're tired," she says, looking at me kindly.

"Yes."

"It's been a difficult time," she says, and I can't tell if she's being sarcastic or not.

"Yes," I say. How is it that she found her father on the day after he died—where was she yesterday?

I think of Nathaniel and Ashley, wondering where I left off, if they're curious why they haven't heard from me, if they're all right. I'd call them right now, before I forget, but can't remember exactly where they are: what are the names of their schools?

I'm guessing I should feel fortunate I haven't forgotten them entirely.

In the middle of the afternoon, with no warning, I am released.

"Okay, Mr. Silver, you are free to go," the nurse says. I feel less like I'm being released than kicked out. "I had a stroke and you're already sending me home?"

"You lived, you get to go home, be happy. We have people sicker than you stacked up in the Emergency Room, waiting for a place to go. There's a taxi waiting downstairs."

I don't know how or why, but my pockets are loaded with cash—my roommate's cash. I didn't do this, but someone did—quite intentionally. I only discover it when I reach for my wallet and find wads of twenties. "It's your lucky day, pal," I tell the taxi driver, giving him two twenties for a twelve-dollar job.

"I'm not going to ask," he says.

The dog minder is gone, but has left a note: "Hope you're feeling better. I'll come by around 5 to walk Tessie. P.S. I'm also happy to keep working as needed—the card with my fees is below." I glance at the card, which is decorated with paw prints. Fifteen dollars a walk, fifty dollars a night for sleepover—seems reasonable.

I fall asleep on the sofa. The dog and cat curl around me. No one is paged overhead, no code red or blue, there's no antiseptic smell, no hint of steamed broccoli, simply the silence of the house, the clink of the mail dropping through the slot, the comfort that Tessie is on duty. I am still sleeping when the pet friend comes at 5 p.m. He covers me with a blanket, walks the dog, and then tells me he'll be back in the morning.

"I don't know how to thank you," I say.

"You don't have to."

I nod; my eyelids feel heavy.

"Until tomorrow," he says.

As it gets dark, a kind of cold fear sweeps through me. I turn on every light and the television and find myself wondering, how do I figure out what's for dinner? I go into the kitchen, I open and close the refrigerator and then I go back to the sofa.

Among my discharge papers is a sheet about Meals On Wheels. I call the number; they're closed for the day, so I leave a message.

Recalling a commercial for Domino's Pizza thirty-minute delivery guarantee, I call, order pizza and a couple of Cokes.

While I'm waiting for the pizza to arrive, someone calls back from Meals On Wheels.

"Look," she says, "your message sounded pathetic: you just got home from the hospital; you're living at your brother's house while he's 'away,' whatever that means. But we're not a turn-on/turn-off service like cable television, there's a process, one must qualify for the program."

As she's talking, something about the tone of her voice has me regretting the call. I tear the Meals On Wheels flyer into a thousand pieces. She goes on: "My point is," she pauses, "the reason I called you back is that if you've got no food in the house I can drop a little something by."

"I'm fine, thank you," I say, wanting to end our conversation.

"Are you sure?"

"I'm positive."

"You know, there are other options for people with resources. A lot of the new diet plans offer home delivery: The Zone, Home Bistro, Smart Food, Carb Conscious. If you're all right for tonight, how about I have someone call you tomorrow and they can talk you through an application?"

The doorbell rings—the pizza!

I hang up on the woman as she's still talking and use my walker to go to the door. Tessie and I do a strange dance, related to the tennis balls on the bottom and our mutual insistence to be first to the door.

The pizza is like salty cardboard with melted rubber on top. I eat the whole thing.

My first night home, George's psychiatrist calls. "Sorry to have been out of touch," he says.

"Me too." I take a breath and am about to tell him about the hospital, about the man who died, about everything, and then stop myself. A personal caution light goes on.

"I had a small event," I say.

"I hope it was pleasant," he says.

"It wasn't a wedding," I say, and say no more.

"I was hoping to talk about your family."

"I was in the hospital." Despite my desire not to say it, it slips out like a leak, like a thing sneaking away; it comes out on an inhale, a swallowing of the words.

"Pardon?" he says, not having heard.

I say nothing.

He continues: "As you recall, we spoke about the need for a more complete family history. I have some forms I'd like to e-mail you. They ask for information about your family, where they were born, how they lived, illnesses, hospitalizations, incarcerations, death."

"All right," I say.

"Have you given further thought to visiting with some of the older relatives? We'd like to know more."

Call it the wake-up call of mortality. "I'd like to know more as well," I tell the doctor. "Go ahead, send the forms and I'll get on it."

"Wonderful," the doctor says. "Once we complete this process, we'll think about a second stage, about bringing you up for a day or two, but we're not quite there yet."

"Is there any further news regarding his legal situation?"

"It's not my area. Perhaps the case coordinator can help you with that."

The call is aggravating enough that it gives me a strange rush of energy. Off the phone, I think of my mother, realizing it's been weeks since I visited.

I call the nurses' station on her unit. I ask if I might speak with her.

"She's not available right now," the nurse says.

"What does that mean, 'not available'? Shouldn't she be in her room, it's almost bedtime."

"She's at a dance class."

I am incredulous. "Not only is it nine-thirty at night, my mother is bed-bound."

"Not anymore."

"Really," I say, genuinely surprised.

"Yes. It's a combination of factors. One, we got a new therapist, and your mother has taken a shine to her, and so we put her in a wheelchair and brought her down the hall; and then a young doctor has been with us doing some research, and your mother elected to participate in a study, so we're giving her a new cocktail, and while she's not exactly flying around, she's doing much better."

"Is she walking?"

"Crawling," the nurse says, with pleasure. "She's down on the floor, crawling everywhere, and seems to be loving it. We have to be careful not to trip over her . . . and I've put some of my son's hockey pads on her knees and elbows. I can send you a photo if you like?"

She e-mails me a photo and, sure enough, it's Mom, on the floor, crawling down the hall, like a crab scurrying.

I call Lillian, my father's youngest sister, and she grudgingly agrees to allow me to visit her.

"Is there anything I can bring you?"

"Some borscht from that place on Second Avenue."

I don't tell her that I'm an hour and fifteen minutes from Second Avenue. "How much do you want?" I ask.

"One of the large," she says. "Actually, make it two—I'll put one in the freezer."

"Anything else?"

"Well, if you're going, just get me whatever else looks good."

My mother phones back. "The woman at the reservation desk helped me make the call," she says. "She told me you were hunting me down."

"I called to say hello and she told me you were at a dance class—is everything okay?"

"Everything is great, I'm getting my moves back," she says.

"I'm going to go visit Lillian," I say, and before I can explain she cuts me off.

"Is she not well?" my mother asks, filled with concern.

"I just want to see her. I have some questions."

"Yeah, well, I have a question or two as well," my mother says, snapping back to her usual self. "Where are my pearl earrings? And the matching bracelet that your grandmother gave me, which Lillian borrowed to wear to a party, and then decided it all belonged to her?"

"I can certainly ask her about the jewelry," I say.

"Don't ask," my mother says. "Just do what she did, go into her jewelry box and take it. Then tell her later, when you're safe at home."

"I'll see what I can find out."

"And while you're looking, see if there's a little necklace with a ruby in the center and some diamonds—I never can remember if I lost that one or if your father hocked it to go to the track."

"Did Dad do things like that?"

"All men do things like that," she says.

Nervous about driving since the stroke, I call the driver who took us to Jane's funeral and ask if he'd be willing to take me to Lillian's, wait, and then bring me home. He tells me it's what's called a "time job," seventy-five bucks an hour, four-hour minimum—I sign him up. He picks me up right on time; we swing by the 2nd Avenue Deli, which is now no longer on Second Avenue, and head out to Lillian's on Long Island. I have the guy park a couple of houses away, hoping to avoid having to discuss my circumstances with Lillian.

Walking slowly up her driveway, I have flashbacks to summer birthday parties, Fourth of July sparklers, hot dogs. The houses on her street used to be uniform, split-level brick, every house the same, distinguished only by what year Pontiac or Buick was parked in the driveway. The houses now are bastardized versions of their former selves. Some have had additions, renovations, making them look like they grew room-sized tumors; others were leveled to make room for postmodernist steroid monsters. Double-height living rooms and grand entry parlors have replaced the beloved bay windows that gave every home of the 1950s and '60s a unique fishbowl effect. I unpack the groceries at Lillian's kitchen table, wondering, could the ancient, almost crispy oilcloth table covering be the same one she's had for thirty years? Lillian puts things away like a scurrying mouse. She's tiny, maybe four feet tall, and shrinking fast.

"What happened to you?" she asks. "You're all banged up."

"Car accident," I say. I can't bring myself to tell her about the stroke; it makes me feel old. "Beautiful flowers," I say, nodding towards the vase on the table.

"I've had them for years," she says. "They're plastic; I wash them once a week with Ivory. This you should keep." She hands me back a container of kasha. "I won't eat it. This too," she says. "Can't have poppy seeds, no seeds, nuts, or small kernels—that means no popcorn at the movies, no pistachios. I've got trouble with my gut."

The way she says it, I'm tempted to make some crack about "hardly makes life worth living," but, given my recent experiences with how precarious life is, it's starting to seem like something I shouldn't joke about.

"Your brother should be ashamed," she says.

"Yes," I say.

"Is he?"

"No. I don't think so."

We sit at her dining-room table. She makes me a cup of tea, Lipton, strong and incredibly good. "Do you take sugar or do you want Splender?"

"Sugar is fine," I say. It's sugar that's been in the bowl so long it's lumpy, sugar that many generations of wet spoons have touched, celebratory sugar, infected sugar—old sugar. Lillian comes out of the kitchen carrying an artifact, the blue metal tin marked Danish Butter Cookies that if I didn't know better I would swear had been in the family for generations—when the Jews left Egypt, they took with them the tins of Danish Butter Cookies. And tins, which as best I could tell never included Danish Butter Cookies, traveled from house to house, but always, always, found their way back to Lillian. In every family or tribe there is a keeper of the tin, whose job it is to intone annoyingly, "Don't forget my tin," or "How could you forget my tin? No more for you. I don't bake without the tin. What's the point, the cookies will rot."

Aunt Lillian's long, thin gnarled fingers twist and turn the thin metal top; the contents knock around inside—trapped. Lillian's hands are leopard-spotted with age; her fine-gauge hair, dyed a deep unnatural red, is fixed high on her head like rusted steel wool.

She finally gets the tin open; there are only about ten cookies left. "I don't bake as much as I used to," she says.

I take one, bite into it: hard as a rock, like Jewish biscotti. "Good," I say, with my mouth full.

"The last time I saw you was at your father's funeral," she says.

I dip the cookie into my tea; the second bite is better. I finish the cookie, and when I move to take another, Lillian yanks the tin away from me and puts the top back on. "I have to ration them," she says. "I don't bake often; in fact, this may be the last batch ever."

"Tell me about my father," I ask, and it's as though, after exhaling the word "father," on the next breath I inhale the look and smell of him, five suits hanging in the closet after he died, his hair tonic some kind of oily, spicy-scented stuff that he splashed on his hands, ran through his hair, and combed back. It left stains my mother called "fat" on the pillowcases, the sofa, the living-room chairs, anywhere he rested his head.

"Middle management," Aunt Lillian blurts, "that's all he ever was. There was always someone above him who he hated, and someone below that he took it out on. He sold insurance. He worked the congregation temple. Then, later, he went into investments. If you ever questioned something your father did he'd explode—he managed to do things his way by making everyone afraid."

I nod. What she's saying fits with my own, dimmer recollection.

She goes on: "Now, my husband, he didn't like the family, felt they were too judgmental and undereducated. And he was right. Your father would argue with Morty and wouldn't give up until Morty crumbled—didn't matter if he was right or wrong."

I shake my head.

"And then Morty was gone. I never said it, but to a large degree I blame your father for that," she says with a sound of disgust, a kind of sputtering spit, as though she's revealed a deeply held secret. "Your father was like that, always needed all of the attention and acted like a child if he didn't get it. That's why he and your brother never got along—they were the same. And you," she says, wagging a gnarled finger at me, "you stood there like a little retard."

I say nothing—as far as I can remember, no one's ever referred to me as a "little retard."

"Was there something specific that happened, a reason that we stopped seeing your family?" I ask, jotting down the comment about my being a retard in the margin of the legal pad I'm using to write notes on.

"I had a falling out with your mother."

"My mother?"

"I know what you're thinking—she was the one who was easy to get along with—but she picked up a trick or two from your father."

"What was the falling out about?"

"Matzoh balls."

I glance up to see if she's kidding. Lillian looks at me as if to say, Isn't it obvious?

"A matzoh-ball war," she says. "Do you make them in the soup or separately? What is the ideal consistency, fluffy or chewy?"

I look at her, waiting for more, waiting for the answer. "Your mother seemed to think whatever her answer was had to be the right answer and also meant she was a better Jew. And, frankly, between that and your father, I couldn't be bothered to stay in touch. Just because we don't talk to you doesn't mean we don't talk amongst ourselves."

I'm about to ask who from the family is still alive when she abruptly cuts me off.

"And then there was the incident with you kids in the recreation room." Again she gives me the look. "Are you playing dumb or are you actually dumb?"

Not knowing what she's talking about, I decline to answer.

"Your brother performed surgery on my son," she says, as though offering me a clue, a little something to jog my memory.

"What kind of surgery?"

"He recircumcised him, using a compass and a protractor and Elmer's glue."

I vaguely remember something. It was one of the Jewish holidays, and all of the children were downstairs playing. I have a thirty-watt memory of being down on the floor, on the rug with the cousins, and there being an intense Monopoly game going on with some off-site buying and selling of property and hotels, and while we were playing, my brother and my cousin Jason were doing something at my father's desk that seemed strange. I remember thinking how like George it was, getting someone to do something they shouldn't for his pleasure. The recreation room was part playroom, part office, with the office area blocked off by file cabinets and white shag carpeting, so it wasn't like I could actually see what he was doing, but I knew it was weird.

"Was Jason all right?"

"Yes, there was very little physical damage—a small cut, a lot of blood, and a visit to a plastic surgeon—but now he's gay."

"Are you saying that George made Jason gay?"

"Something did—I don't think you're born gay, do you? Something happens, a trauma that turns you that way."

"Aunt Lillian, there are lots of gay people who would say that's the way they came, and in fact some theories about intrauterine hormonal levels . . ." I go on, wondering how I even know this; must have been an article I read. Whatever I'm saying is clearly irrelevant to what Lillian believes. "What did my parents say about the incident?"

"I never told them. Jason swore me to secrecy; he was so humiliated," she says. "George only stopped because someone went downstairs to check on you kids."

"Who came down?"

"Aunt Florence."

"And what did she see?"

"She saw nothing, but it frightened George and he stopped."

"And what did your husband say?"

"He wasn't there," she says, "which only made matters worse."

"Where was he?"

"Good question," she says, and says no more. "There was no excuse," she says.

"None," I say.

"The last time I saw you was at your father's funeral," she repeats her line from earlier.

"Can you help me with something?" I pull out the family tree. "We need to fill this out."

"Fill out a family tree—are you going to pay me for my time? Should I be compensated in some way?"

"I brought you borscht," I say. She makes a dismissive gesture and moves her chair closer to mine, so she can see the forms and my yellow legal pad of notes.

"How old are you, Aunt Lillian?"

"Older than I look; I'm eighty-eight but am told I pass for mid-seventies."

Together we fill out the family tree. At one point she brings over a couple of old family photo albums, the physical evidence, and goes from page to page, spilling the beans about everyone. "Your father had a lot of issues about masculinity."

"Are you saying you think he was a closet case?"

She lifts her shoulders and makes a face. "Who knows what anyone is or isn't."

"Were there any criminals in the family?" I ask.

"Oh sure," she says. "Plenty. There was Uncle Bernie, who got stabbed to death in a card game."

"By who?"

"No one ever wanted to say."

"And what happened to Aunt Bea?"

"Dead," she says. "And you know she had three children, none of them ever lived to be more than four years old; they called it crib death, but your mother and I weren't so sure—we never left any of you alone with her."

"Really, that seems unlikely; Jews don't kill their children, just drive them crazy."

"Trouble runs in the family," she says.

"What are you talking about?"

"Your father's temper. Are you such a goody-goody? You thought your mother had a nose job; your father punched her."

I know exactly what she's talking about, and she's entirely right—my mother broke her nose, but I thought she'd been in some kind of accident.

"Why?"

"Who knows," Lillian says. "Sometimes he just exploded."

"This is not what I expected."

"Your parents protected you and your brother. Your uncle Louie was another one, a nogoodnik always trying to make a deal. And his wife, what did she know, carrying on with the accountant from the temple."

"The guy with the bumps—like blisters or warts?" I say, again dimly recalling.

"They were fatty tumors, and he was a very nice man, nicer than your Louie, but that doesn't make it right. He was married. His wife was a clubfoot mute; he won her in a poker game."

I can't help but laugh.

"I fail to see the humor. He loved her, took very good care of her, and they had four children."

"Do you remember that we used to celebrate the High Holy Days together, Rosh Hashanah and Yom Kippur, and then, suddenly, we didn't?" I ask.

"Yes," she says. "Of course. It's all about matzoh balls." Lillian pauses and then looks at me, filled with pity, frustration, contempt. "Why can't you take responsibility for what your family did? I was hoping you were coming to apologize."

"I'm sorry."

"For what?"

"For whatever it was that you felt happened that wronged you—I am sorry. Very sorry."

"I'm not sure you mean it."

"Well, I'm not sure I understand exactly what happened, but the fact that you're hurt—I'm very sorry for. I came with an open heart. I can't exactly apologize for something I didn't do."

"You came because you had nowhere else to go. If things were going great, we never would have heard from you."

I am not feeling very well. Her accusations, the tension, the whole damn day with the trip into the city to get the soup, the drive out here, the fatigue, the finding out, all of it has been a lot—too much. "Aunt Lillian, I should go now, but if you'd like, I'll come again."

"It's not necessary," Lillian says. "Give your mother my best. Where is she?" she asks as though it's slipped her mind.

"She's in a home."

"And what condition is she in?"

"She seems to be improving."

"Tell her I'm sorry about the soup; cooking the balls in water first or in the soup is fine—in the end, what the hell does it matter?"

"Thank you," I say. "I'll tell her. By the way, she wanted me to ask you about a pair of earrings. . . ."

Lillian throws up her arms. "Not that crap again. Is that what this was all about? You came all the way out here to make nice, you bring me some soup, and then, just as we're about to say goodbye, you come in for the kill? I should have known. . . ."

She storms out of the room. "Aunt Lillian," I call after her. "I wasn't trying to give you a hard time, I just asked because my mother wanted me to."

She comes back carrying her ancient jewelry box. "And you do everything your mother asks."

She puts the box down on the table, opens it, and extracts the pearl earrings, the bracelet, and the necklace with the ruby.

"She wondered if that one was lost."

"Your father sold it to me," she says. "Can you imagine, he sold me his wife's jewelry. He wanted to keep it in the family."

Lillian gives me what my mother was looking for and more. "Some of it your mother gave me, some she wanted me to hold for safekeeping, but I don't want it, I don't want it on my conscience, I want nothing to do with any of it, I never did."

She grabs my head with both hands, pulls me down to her level, and gives me a wet kiss. "You're still a little retard," she says, pushing me towards the door.

When I speak to Nate a few days later he asks, "Are you coming for our Winter Field Day?"

"Am I?" I'm just beginning to feel back to normal, or not really normal, but whatever it is that's filled in for normal for the last month or so. I can't say I feel like myself at all; in fact, I can't actually remember what I ever felt like, and what "myself" might mean.

"My parents always came for Field Day," Nate says.

"When is it?"

"This weekend. It starts Saturday morning and ends after church on Sunday."

"Do Jews go to church?"

"It's nondenominational," he says.

"Church means that it's Christian."

"I like it," he says.

"Do I bring the dog?" I ask.

"No, someone stays with the dog."

"Does Ashley come?"

"Didn't they leave you a manual or any kind of instructions?"

"None," I say. "I'm flying blind. I'll figure it out—just need to know the parameters. Anything you need me to bring you—something you want from home?"

"Like what?"

"A favorite sweater, your copy of *Catcher in the Rye*?"

"No," he says, as though the question is stressful. "I've got what I need."

A weekend in the country sounds good—permission to get the hell out of here. I don't know how it happened, but I'm totally trapped in George's world, worried that if I leave for a moment, whatever is left will all fall down.

While Nate and I are talking, I'm Googling the school; it's far more prestigious than I was imagining. Among the alumni are several of Nixon's former Cabinet and staff members.

"Do you know anyone at the school named Shultz?"

"As in *Peanuts* Schulz?"

"No," I say. "What about Blount? Or Dent?"

"Who are they?"

"Historical footnotes."

"Not ringing any bells," Nate says.

"No worries. I'll see you on Saturday," I say, signing off.

The school's Web site has a list of local accommodations; I start calling, but all the hotels and B&Bs are booked. By the time I speak to the woman at the Wind Song, I'm imagining sleeping in the car. It's fine, I'll bring some pillows, the arctic sleeping bag, extra blankets, some Ambien, and find a safe place right on campus.

"Is there anything you can do to help me?" I beg. "I can't let this kid down, I'm all he's got, his mother died, his father is under lock and key—do you have any ideas?"

"My daughter's room," the woman says. "We don't usually rent it, but there's a twin bed, I can let you have it—a hundred and fifty a night, breakfast included, shared bathroom."

"Perfect," I say.

"Actually," she says, pausing—and in the background I hear voices—"I was wrong, it's a hundred and eighty a night. Like I said, we don't usually rent it, but my husband is reminding me that last time we did, it was one eighty. There's a new mattress."

"Can I give you my credit card?" I say, fearing another uptick in the price if I don't act fast.

Determined to do a good job playing the parental substitute, I borrow a tie, shoes, and a sport coat from George's closet and depart promptly at 6 a.m. on Saturday. It takes two hours and twenty minutes to crawl to the edge of Massachusetts. At the gates of the academy, parents in their Mercedes wagons and weekend toy sports cars are directed to the main building, where coffee and Danish are being served. Young men with names like Scooter and Biff greet their parents, gruffly hugging their corduroy fathers and politely pecking the boiled-wool mothers. They all have the same heart-shaped faces, deeply American, impenetrable. There are four Asians, three blacks, and that's it for diversity.

The school is laid out like an olde English village and makes the college where I teach look like an urban vocational school buried in one of the five boroughs that at best would teach men and women how to change oil and fix TV sets. The main building is a mansion, grand, imposing, with enormous oil portraits of the school's founding fathers hung high, large flower arrangements on ancient wooden cabinets. Everything is dark—there's a lot of deep, dark wood paneling, secret passageways, old leather sofas and chairs. On long tables dressed in starched white tablecloths they've laid out quite a spread. Nate finds me in the coffee line; I'm grateful to spot a familiar face.

"The Danish are really good, you should have one," I say, unsure of the protocol regarding my hugging him or not—I assume not.

"I already did," he says. "They bake them every weekend. There's a pastry chef on staff."

"How did you end up at this school?" I whisper.

"You mean, what's a loser like me doing in a place like this?" He pauses. "I test really well, and Dad used to be 'someone.' The Chairman of the Board of the network is a very active alum."

"You have friends here?"

"Yes," he says. "I'm happy here, happier here than at home."

"And Ash is at a place like this too?" I ask, chewing through a cinnamon bun.

"Hers is different. The girls live in small houses, not dorms. It's a bit less competitive, more homey."

"Your mom did a great job finding the right places for you guys." I slip a bagel with cream cheese, wrapped in a cloth napkin, into the pocket of my sport coat. My hand bumps into something. "Tessie sent this," I say, pulling a well-chewed rawhide from my pocket and handing it to Nate. He smiles. As we walk out of the building, Nate points out the library: "We have approximately one-point-five million volumes and an active interlibrary loan system."

"Better than most small colleges and where I teach," I say.

"Wait until you see the pool," Nate says.

Outside the field house, a man dressed like a court jester hands out parchment scrolls tied with a ribbon, like something they would have passed out in Rome long ago.

"It's the program for today's events," Nate says. "It begins with the dedication—used to be the firing of the first arrow, now it's the Headmaster's cannon. He's from Scotland."

Moments later, there's a droning of bagpipes, and a pair of pipers slowly crosses the hill opposite us, followed by the Headmaster, marching in his plaid kilt, pumping his scepter up and down, keeping time. "He's naked under there," Nate whispers, "that's the tradition. And he's hung like a horse and makes sure everyone knows it." From the grassy knoll, the cannon is fired, and reflexively I duck. "Let the games begin," the Headmaster declares.

"Do you have a sport?" it suddenly occurs to me to ask.

"Sure," Nate says, "ice hockey, lacrosse, tennis, I'm on the inter-school fencing team, and swimming—we'll do both of those today. I also do hurdles and the pommel horse. And I signed us up for father/son rock climbing."

"I didn't even know you liked sports," I say. I really only ever saw the kid playing video games.

In the field house, the coaches remind us that "these games are intended as demonstrations of our programs rather than competitive events. Within the school we work to build teams so our boys can bond." The coaches spew catchphrases such as "environment of success" and "a prize for every player, medals for all who participate." But, despite the coaches' talk, everyone is clearly keeping track of who wins and loses.

"Which one is yours?" one of the parents asks me, nodding towards the cluster of boys.

"I'm with Nate," I say.

And I feel the theoretically imperceptible recoil. "Of course," he says, and nothing more; they all know what happened.

I look at Nate—tall, tousled. The other boys are a range of shapes and sizes and pimple patterns. Nate is among the better-looking, attractive in a way that the others are not. In sport he is neither the best nor the worst; what is clear is that he is the one they all want on their team. He's a reliable performer, steady, true, with no need to sacrifice the team for personal gratification. I feel an unfamiliar sensation of pride, a rising in the chest, a pleasant reflux as I watch Nate butterfly-stroke across the pool. I cringe, during the fencing exhibition, when the other boy lunges forward, "stabbing" Nate, and the "assault" is called to an end.

At lunch, various boys and their mothers stop by our table. "If you ever need a place to go during the holidays, you can always come ski with us," one mom says. Another squeezes his shoulder and asks, "Are you holding up?"

"I'm doing well," Nate says.

"Of course you are," she says.

I'm eating my second piece of cake, simply because it is there, because there were four kinds of cake to choose from and two seemed reasonable. I am eating cake when Nate fills me in about the father/son rock climbing.

"It's right after lunch," he says, clearly looking forward to it.

"It's a tradition," I say sarcastically as I'm pushing my plate away. Too late, one whole piece of cheesecake is gone and half of the chocolate layer.

"Yes," Nate says. "It's on a man-made indoor wall three stories tall. The fathers aren't expected to go all the way up, but some will—even if it kills them, some will always exceed expectations."

"I'm not that man," I say bluntly. "How about I stand at the bottom and watch you."

"Can't," Nate says. "It's a hundred percent participation."

"I recently had a minor stroke and am supposed to avoid overexertion," I say.

Nate looks at me, worried, suddenly fragile.

"I'm fine," I say. "I just have to be a little careful."

"You're pretty much just managing your own weight," he says. "Would that be okay? There's a harness and a lock, so you can't really fall."

"I never was much of an athlete," I say.

"Trust me, these guys aren't either—they're blowhards."

It's turning into a standoff—my dread of sports, of having to show off or, worse, failing to show off, in front of all these children and their parents, is making me cranky. "Dad would never do it either," Nate says, annoyed.

"Why not?" I ask; I'm surprised.

"No real reason. Every year I signed up for it, it always happened that he didn't have to do it—a call he had to take, a pulled this, sprained that."

"I'll do it," I say, finding inspiration in the fact that George never would.

———

The climbing teacher fits each of us with a harness. We're given a lesson on how the ropes work. He makes it sound simple, effortless—I'm sweating. The other men look no more or less capable; a last-minute addition is a chunky guy wearing dark sunglasses and dressed like he's left the house in his black long underwear—or someone else's long underwear, because it's way too tight. He's wearing nothing beneath it—his cock and balls are pancaked, all too explicitly. I can't help but stare, and then wonder, is this kind of full-on peacock display standard around here?

By the time I get four feet off the ground, I'm praying that Nate, who's holding my line, is stronger than he looks, and that when I plummet, he doesn't go flying through the air like some seesaw gone wrong. I'm both defying gravity and entirely aware of gravity's pull.

"Use your feet," Nate says, coaching from below.

I feel around for the lumps of faux rock to use for leverage; they're like doorstops. Pushing off, I rise a few feet and then grab at the holds just above my head.

"Push," he says, "push yourself up, don't pull. It's easier."

For sixty-five thousand dollars a year in tuition, according to the school's Web site, I'm glad he's learning something about physics.

I push up and belch; acrid coffee and cake fill my mouth. I swallow, get my footing, and push again. There are other men above and below me; the air is filled with a gamy scent of men under pressure. I go higher, determined, really fucking determined.

While I'm on the wall, the Headmaster comes around, working the crowd on the ground, shaking hands. I'm two stories up and hoping that Nate doesn't get distracted by his "boss" in a skirt. I shift my weight and look down below; suddenly my testicles are trapped under the harness, which has slipped. It's excruciating, and now I'm almost dancing, trying to address the situation.

"What are you doing?" Nate screams.

I hug the wall, use both hands, and adjust accordingly.

I notice some men have special climbing shoes on—I've got George's fucking slip-ons. One falls off, bouncing against the wall, tumbling to the floor.

"I can throw it back up to you," Nate says.

"Never mind," I say, pushing higher, my sock foot slipping.

"Is this Dad's shoe?" Nate shouts up to me.

"Yes," I call down.

"Weird."

I turn and focus on the wall. Fuck, yes, I tell myself as I fight my way to the top.

And guess what's there? A goddamned GOLDEN EGG. I'm not joking: there's a golden egg, a porcelain fucking piggy bank at the top. The problem is—how do you bring it down? How do you carry something fragile when you need both hands and feet? I stuff it down my pants. Hung like a horse, fucking the golden egg, I rappel down. Nate is at the bottom with tears in his eyes, and I've got no option other than to unzip my pants, extract the egg, and give it to him—a kind of offering. He's hugging me and crying. I taste victory and sweat and think this is amazing. For one shining moment I am HIGH!

Twenty minutes later, my head is throbbing. I'm walking like a broken cowboy and I have a distinct absence of sensation in three fingers. When I sit on the toilet I can barely get up. I ask Nate if he's got any Tylenol, and he says I should go see the school nurse.

"Forget it," I grouch, and we head back into the main building for afternoon sherry and cheese cubes.

I drink too much—honestly, drinking any sherry constitutes drinking too much. The headache is getting worse.

"Have a Coke," Nate suggests, and he's right.

I have two Cokes and a half-pound of cheese, and show off my medal to anyone who will listen to the story of my stroke and miraculous recovery.

"What now?" I ask as the cocktail hour winds down.

"We go to dinner at the Ravaged Fowl," Nate says, as though it's obvious. "You made the reservation?"

I look blank.

"We always go there, but you have to have a reservation." The way he says it, there is no way out, it's definitive.

"Not a problem," I say. "All taken care of."

From the stall of the men's bathroom I call the Ravaged Fowl; there's a embarrassing echo.

"Sold out," the woman says. "Fully booked. No tables until Monday."

I don't tell Nate—some things are best addressed in person—but as we're heading there, my already fragile constitution is taking on a kind of anticipatory stress, wondering what is going to happen.

We arrive, I play dumb, I give the hostess our name. "Let me check," the girl says. I get nervous. "We have a reservation. Every year we come here. How many years now?" I turn to Nate.

"Four," the boy says, looking at his shoes.

"For the last four years we've been coming here, this same day every year. I always make the reservation." I become indignant. The girl doesn't care. She is busy answering the phone; I talk right over her: "I thought we could rely on you." She holds her finger up, as if putting me on hold—my voice is getting louder. My mood turns.

"Your face looks like Dad's," Nate says.

"Always, or just right now?"

"Right now," he says.

"I'm in a lousy mood."

"Do you want to leave me here? You can go deal with your headache, I'll join another table."

"That's not an option," I say. "Can't I be in a bad mood for a minute? It's a lot for me." I can't begin to explain how or why, but the opulence, the success, the beauty of this bright and shining day is getting me down. It has all been so wonderful that it's made me sick—I can't tell Nate and his buddies that the threat, the creeping encroachment of their youthful, excellent promising future, is for me a giant fucking depressant.

"Yeah, sure, whatever," he says, and I feel him retreat, vacate, leaving an empty shell.

The hostess hangs up the phone and walks away. I am tempted to chase after her—you can't walk away from me, you can't leave me standing there, having made a fool of myself in front of the kid.

My anger is intense. Without speaking, I am tearing her apart, surprised at the ugly clarity of my thoughts. She is singularly unattractive—grotesque. All too proud of what some would call a good figure, she's wearing an emerald-green dress that's too tight with a scoop neck and her boobies spilling out. She looks less like a hostess than a hooker, or a homely drag queen. Her lips are thick and wide, smeared with cheap frosted pink goo. Her pores are large and black, each like an individual cesspool, each blackhead a black hole. There's a thing or two I have half a mind to say: Don't tell me you can't manage a reservation that I made months ago; what's the point of my making a reservation if you can't keep track of it? And then I remember that I never made a reservation, and I imagine turning over her little bowl of crème mints, tipping her toothpicks, telling her to shove her creamed spinach up her cunt, and then whisking the kid off to some lousy diner twenty-five miles from here.

I imagine doing it, then hear Nate say, "You're disgusting, just like my dad." It stings, hurts deeply. I don't want him to think George and I are demented doppelgängers, I don't want him to have a clue about what goes on in my head.

"Are you all right?" Nate asks.

"I think so. Why—am I doing something?" I can't help but wonder if perhaps I've been talking out loud.

"You seem distracted."

"I didn't get my nap. Ever since the stroke I need a nap every day. As the doctor explained it to me, my brain has been insulted and needs time to recover."

The hostess comes back with a short, mustached man who shakes my hand. "Sorry for the delay; we weren't sure you were coming. I have your table, of course; right this way."

It couldn't have been easier.

I dig around in my pocket and find twenty bucks to slip the man as he settles us into a prized banquette.

"Did you really make a reservation?" Nate asks.

"Your mother must have made it long ago," I say. "She was very organized."

Before the waitress comes to take the drink order, Nate leans forward.

"FYI," he says, "it's a tradition that you order me a beer."

"You're underage."

"It's the tradition," he says. "You order it, I drink it."

I look around; none of the other tables have kids drinking beer.

"You're working me," I say.

He says nothing.

"Why don't you be honest with me? It's better all around."

"Fine, I want a beer," he says.

"Fine, have a beer; you're not driving, you put in a good day's work, what do I care. Is there one you prefer?"

"A Guinness if they've got it . . ."

"Really?"

"It's like a meal in a glass. I got used to it last summer, when I was at Oxford."

I order one Guinness and a root beer, and when the beer comes I take a sip and then put it down in front of the kid. "Do you want a straw with that?"

He drinks, closes his eyes, happy. Clearly this is not a first.

"I saw you checking out the hostess," he says when he comes up for air. "Maybe you should ask her out? You are single now, aren't you?"

If only he knew what I really thought of the hostess. "I had no idea you were such an athlete," I say, changing the subject. "No one in our family has ever been an athlete."

"It doesn't all come from your family. Mom's grandmother was a great swimmer, she was the first woman to swim around the island of Manhattan."

"Really?"

"Yep. And her husband, my great-grandfather, was a fire-eater—apparently he had enormous lung capacity."

"I never knew."

"You can't assume everything is all about you," Nate says.

"What can I bring you boys?" the waitress asks. I notice the Headmaster, still in his skirt, walking in, his pleats flouncing on his hairy, very white knees.

"How are the crab cakes?" Nate asks.

"Perfect," the waitress says. "One hundred percent lump meat."

"I'm not sure crab is in season," I say.

"I get them every year," Nate says. "I'll start with the iceberg and blue cheese, and then have the crab cakes."

Why am I picturing vomit everywhere? Beer, blue cheese, crab cakes?

"I'll have the iceberg and blue cheese as well and the steak special," I say.

"Baked or fried?" the waitress asks.

"Grilled," I say.

"Your potato—baked or fried?"

"Baked, please."

I sip the kid's root beer. The Headmaster is coming in our direction. "What's that you're drinking, son?" he asks Nate.

"Just having a sip of my uncle's beer—he thought it tasted funny. Does this taste bad to you?" He holds the beer glass up to the Headmaster.

"All beer tastes like piss water to me. I only drink bourbon, but not while I'm on duty."

The man with the mustache hurries over. "Everything all right?"

"Bring this man a fresh beer, and the young fella looks like he could use a refill too—what was that son, a Coke?" the Headmaster bellows.

"Root beer, actually," Nate says.

"I like your sporran," I say, unable to help myself. "Is it sealskin?" And I'm wondering, where the hell did I pull the word "sporran" from?

"It is sealskin," he says. "You've got a good eye. It was my grandfather's," he says, affecting a full Scottish accent.

"And so it was," I say.

He nods. "Have a good dinner, and congratulations on your climb. I'm glad to finally see where Nathaniel's prowess comes from."

The Headmaster saunters off to another table.

"What were you talking about—spawning salmon?" Nate asks.

"Sporran. His purse. I complimented him on his purse. That's what that chain-belted thingy is—no pockets with a kilt."

Nate is, for a moment, impressed.

I pull out my packet of pills (and the page of directions) and line up the dinner series, before, during, and after.

"So what else about you, Nate, should I know?"

"I have a school in South Africa," Nate says. "I'm pretty proud of that."

"You mean you raised money to help build a school?—I think your mom mentioned something about that."

"I built it," he says, flatly.

"With your hands?"

"Yes, with my hands, and with the villagers who live there, and some wood and nails and sheets of metal—all the things you build a school with. And I set up a water-filtration system for the town. It's named for me. It used to have another name, but everyone who lives there calls it Nateville."

Is he telling the truth? "How were you able to do this all by yourself?"

"It's not as hard as you think," Nate says. "It's kind of like a big Lego. I had these Sunset books of plans for small structures that I was going to use to build myself something in the backyard, and we used those for inspiration. The real question is, if a kid can do it, why can't others? There's no reason the world is in as bad shape as it is, except that people are so fucking passive and immobile and focused on what can't happen instead of what can."

Nate goes on. Everything he says is not only true, it is logical, well considered, articulate, persuasive. He's explaining himself and the world around him, and all I can think is that it's shocking that George didn't kill him too.

I am falling in love with Nate; he's the boy I wish I had been, the boy I wish I was even now. I'm in awe of him and terrified. He's more capable than any of the rest of us and yet he's still a kid.

"Does your dad know you can do all this?"

"I doubt it," he says.

"Did you ever tell him?"

"I don't know how to say this politely, but when Dad came up here, he was basically shaking a lot of hands and didn't exactly notice anything. And I'd like to keep it that way. He never noticed me, thought I was some lump of a loser sucking up air and resources—that's what he called it, resources."

"He's a pretty tough customer," I say.

"I don't want to talk about it," Nate says.

"Not a problem," I say. "What can we talk about?"

"Why didn't you and Claire have kids?"

I take the beer from Nate and drink too much, too quickly; it tickles my nose and I choke, spitting Guinness across the table.

"Pretty," Nate says as I wipe it up.

"We almost had a baby. Claire got pregnant once and something happened."

"She lost the baby?" Nate presses for clarity.

I nod. That's the polite version of it. The truth is, the baby was stillborn and got stuck and actually came apart as they were pulling it out. I saw the whole thing. I'd been on Claire's side of the drape, and then, when they were pulling the baby out, the doctor made a painful sound, and so I stood up and looked over and saw pieces. It must have been dead for a while. Claire lifted her head. "Can I see the baby?" she asked. "No," I said, too abruptly. And I never told her the rest.

"The baby has passed," the doctor said, and I was never sure if he was trying to tell her that it was all out or that it was born dead.

"Claire was depressed for a long time. 'It's hard to say goodbye to someone you never met,' she'd say. And I didn't know what to say. We didn't talk about trying again, it was too painful, too traumatic."

"Did you like my mother?" Nate asks, pulling me back into the present.

The waitress puts my plate down in front of me; steam rises from the potato, and the meat, like smelling salts, revives me.

"Did you?" he asks again.

"Yes," I say easily.

"Did you love her?"

"It's all a bit complicated," I say.

"Do you miss her?"

"Enormously," I say.

"I like to think she died for a reason," Nate says. "To die for love is a reason."

"Has anyone asked if you want to see your dad?" I ask.

"Yes," he says. "And no." He pauses.

"How often do you talk to Ashley?"

He looks surprised. "I call her every day."

"Did you always?"

"No," he says, and then pauses again. "You grow up thinking your family is normal enough, and then, all of a sudden, something happens and it's so not normal, and you have no idea how it got that way, and there's really nowhere to go from here—it will never be anywhere near normal again. It's not even like an accident when someone is killed because a tree falls on their head, it's not like you can be mad at someone else, some stranger . . ." He trails off. "What ever happened to the boy?"

"What boy?"

"The boy who survived the car accident?"

"He's living with his family—an aunt, I think."

"We should do something for him," Nate says.

"Maybe we could set up a fund to make sure he has what he needs," I suggest.

"We could take him with us on vacation," Nate says. "I really love amusement parks; I bet he does too."

"I can certainly look into it. Is that what you'd like to do, take the boy somewhere on a vacation?"

"It's the least we can do," he says, and he's right.

We eat. There is truly nothing better than an iceberg-lettuce wedge with blue-cheese dressing, steak, and a baked potato. I heap cold sour cream into the steaming potato jacket, reminding myself that sour cream is not on my doctor's list of recommended foods. Fuck it. I grind salt and pepper across the top—it's sublime.

After dinner I take Nate back to school, slowly snaking up the driveway as part of a long line of parental vehicles returning the boys for safekeeping.

One can imagine how and why humans, young men in particular, form special clubs, develop rituals, habits that are repeated and passed on. There is great comfort in these things, refuge in being one of many, part of a group, a pack—apart from the family.

"Do adults ever sneak in and stay over?" I ask, longing for an intimate view of dormitory life.

"No," he says.

I take my foot off the brake, and the car gently coasts up the hill. One by one, in front of the main building, the boys are welcomed back, checked in for the night. "Church begins promptly at nine a.m., coffee and continental breakfast at eight a.m.," the Headmaster says, and I'm sent on my way.

"Thanks for climbing the wall," Nate says. "It was awesome."

As he's closing the car door I blurt, "I love you." The slamming door crunches my words. Nate opens the door again.

"Sorry, did you say something?"

"See you in the morning."

"Will do," he says, slamming the door a second time.

I head over to the bed and breakfast. It is as though I am the child and I left the grown-up—Nate—in the big house on the hill. My room at the B&B is tiny—it's what would commonly be known as a maid's room—and has a pleasant cedar smell. When I arrive, the lady of the house asks if I mind the resident child's hamster remaining in my room overnight. She explains that they can relocate him if need be, but if at all possible it's better he stay put. "He gets confused if we move the cage. I think he has Alzheimer's, although I'm not sure what the symptoms are in a hamster."

I look at the hamster, the hamster looks at me. I don't think he has Alzheimer's—he seems far too "conscious." I turn away and undress, an alien among the white faux–Queen Anne furniture decorated with Hello Kitty stickers. Who is this Hello Kitty? From what I gather, she's no Janis Joplin or Grace Slick. I pick up the small pile of rough towels off the bed, throw one over my shoulder, and go down the hall to the bathroom.

I ablute (my word for it), and finish with the filling of a plastic water glass, which I spill half of on the carpet en route back to my room. I close the door, put the chair in front of it—there's no lock—and lay out my nighttime pills. I never thought I'd be using a day-of-the-week pill minder with compartments for morning, afternoon, and evening. It's like a big book of pills that I carry with me with rubber bands wrapped around it to keep it from an impromptu opening.

I take my pills, sit on the bed. It's ten-thirty.

I decide to call Jason, Aunt Lillian's son. He's been on my mind since the visit. I dig out my cell phone, flip it open—good signal here in the bedroom— and find the scrap of paper with Jason's number. I dial.

"Hello," a man answers.

"Jason, this is your cousin Harry calling."

A silence.

"I visited your mom."

Still silence.

"We had a good talk."

Through the wall, I hear the wife, the co-owner of the B&B, say, "What?"

"Nothing," the husband says.

"You called my name."

"I didn't," he says. "The guy in Laurie's room is talking to someone."

"Someone in the room?" the wife asks.

"On the phone," the husband says.

"Does he seem weird to you?" she asks.

"No," the husband says, "he doesn't seem weird. You're the one who's weird—every day you ask me, does someone seem weird. You're so suspicious, I can't imagine why you ever wanted to open a B&B."

"Jason?" I say. "I'm calling from my cell phone, can you hear me?"

"Yes," Jason says. And again there is silence.

What does Jason think the call is about? Did his mother tell him I came to visit? Does he think I'm calling to tell him his mom has too many outdated jars in the fridge, that the famous cookie tin is near empty and there's great concern about its ever being refilled?

"Jason, I'm calling to apologize on behalf of my family. Whatever happened to you in the basement, I'm really sorry."

"I don't remember it," he says.

"How could you not remember it? Your mother says it made you gay."

"She needs to think something 'happened' to make me gay, that life with her wasn't enough. The family is filled with gays."

"Who's gay?"

"Aunt Florence," he says.

"No!"

"Yes. And Great-Uncle Henry and his friend Thomas. And, in our generation, Warren and Christian, who wants to become Christina."

"Who names a Jew Christian?" I ask, and then pause. I'm getting swept up in the revelations. "Jason, did he harm you?"

"I don't know," he says.

"Would you be willing to tell someone?" I ask, putting the phone on speaker, sparing myself the burned-ear effect.

"Like who?" Jason asks.

"I'm not sure. I don't know if you heard. . . ."

"Of course I heard. The whole world heard; it was the front page of the *New York Post*. What's the point of this?" he demands, now fully annoyed.

"Who's yelling?" the wife and co-owner of the B&B asks her husband. "Is he sitting in Laurie's room yelling at someone?"

"He's being yelled at," the husband says.

"Why did you call?" Jason says.

"I don't know," I say. "George's doctor asked me to gather information about the family. I went to visit your mother, to understand what the falling out was about. . . ."

"Matzoh balls," Jason says, as though it was a well-known fact.

"Yes, I know that now. And while I was visiting, your mother told me about what happened in the basement."

"You were there when it happened," he says. "Were you totally oblivious?"

"Apparently," I say. "Anyway, I want to apologize for my family." I take a deep breath and start again, speaking more softly. "Can I ask you a question?"

There's a long pause. "You may," Jason finally says.

"Is your father dead? Your mother mentioned your father being 'gone'?"

"My father left."

"What do you mean, 'left'?"

"He left for a business trip and never came back, never called, never wrote."

"Did she report it to the police?"

"No, she just let it go."

"Did you search for him?"

"Many years later."

"And?"

"He was hiding. He said he needed to get away. He said Mother wanted more from him than he had to give. He didn't seem to notice that it affected me as well."

"Jason," I say, repeating myself, "I'm really sorry. If you ever want to get together, for a drink, for the holidays, for some lousy Chinese food on a Friday night, give me a call—do you have my number?"

"Yes, it came up on my caller ID," he says.

"I'll hope to hear from you," I say. "Good night, Jason."

"I don't hear anything," the wife says after a minute.

"Maybe he's sleeping," the husband says.

"You don't just suddenly talk and then sleep," she says.

"Okay, so maybe he's reading."

"I don't think so," she says.

"What does it matter, can't there be a moment's peace? Maybe he's thinking."

In this tiny bed, this tiny room, I have a moment of clarity. I am a grown man who has hardly grown. I am like Oskar in *The Tin Drum*, refusing to grow.

I am up in the night. There are light scratching sounds, and then it begins, an e-awh, e-awh, like a loose bedspring, like people having sex. At first I think that's what it is—motel springs! The rhythmic squeaking of cheap, well-worn bedsprings. I listen at the wall—nothing. The other wall—the husband and wife talking. I listen to the floor—a television.

I glance at the hamster. He crouches, frozen, caught in the act, his beady black eyes meeting mine. The round chrome wheel is no longer spinning, but still gently rocking back and forth, its motion slowing.

"You?" I ask.

The hamster wiggles his nose. "Me?" he seems to ask, equally surprised.

In the morning, I wake feeling like I've been on a long journey and still tasting the steak from last night—not an unpleasant flavor, just not breakfasty.

My headache is gone.

I go to church with Nate. The academy chapel, built from enormous old stones—hauled all the way from England—is perfect. The Tiffany-glass windows illustrate various Biblical narratives. The school chaplain introduces a woman rabbi, who speaks as though she has been elected to remind us of what we already know: that we are human, flawed, and that with our humanity, our consciousness, come expectations of compassion, of kindness and acceptance. Something about her seems to be questioning rather than lecturing—she is asking us to ask ourselves what we think, as though she wants our opinion. "What does it mean to be of service?" she asks. "Is it something you undertake to put on your résumé, to get into college? What do you actually care about? Are you someone working within your culture or tradition, or are you someone who feels outside of it, left behind? The important part is to be part of the questions, to be engaged," she continues. By the time church ends, we all feel lifted up, spiritually motivated, prepared to start the week anew. I understand what Nate likes about it: the quality of talk, the parental good counsel he's not otherwise getting. On the way out, the young rabbi, the school's chaplain, and the Headmaster, now in pants, form an ersatz reception line. It's hard to get by without shaking hands. I don't know why, but I'm tempted to say something stupid, like "Good Shabbos" or "May the Force Be with You," but manage to keep silent.

We exit onto the lawn. Everyone in their Sunday best, bundled in winter coats, looks up at the blue sky, the high white clouds. In the center of the lawn, an enormous box is being opened, a thick old rope is being extracted, laid out. I see people digging into their pockets for gloves, others passing rolls of duct tape, people horridly taping their hands, tearing at the tape with bared teeth and passing it along. One woman wraps Ace bandages around both hands— like wounded paws. Everyone seems to have something on their hands: driving gloves, oven mitts, golf gloves, a piece of felt in each palm, a ski glove on one hand only.

"What's going on?" I ask Nate.

The rope is now fully extended. It is heavy, old, the kind of rope you see when visiting ancient shipyards—not anything made today, not anything you could buy.

"It's the tradition," Nate says. "The weekend concludes with a tug-of-war, parents versus students. The rope dates back to the ship our Founding Fathers came to America on. It's wildly old, and no one knows why it's never broken. In theory it should just snap."

"What's the deal with the hands?"

"The rope hurts the hell out of your hands—it burns."

And they've got cleats, golf shoes, soccer shoes, high heels that can dig in the dirt, snow chains—clearly this is serious business and they've planned ahead. Many of them take off their coats. "Better range of motion," one fellow says. The men and women take positions along the rope, five men up front and then male, female, male, female, until the end, which is again all male. There are some who sheepishly stand off to the side and repeat their excuses— knee replacement, two hips, a shoulder eight weeks ago, quadruple bypass. There are a few boys in casts, on crutches, one in a wheelchair, and I wonder, was he in the chair before he came to the school or did it happen here?

I am watching and suddenly remember George and me playing tug-of-war, me pulling with all my might and then George suddenly letting go and me flying backwards, crashing through a window—ending up essentially sitting in the broken glass. "I'm still a mess from yesterday," I say to Nate. "So I'm going to pass on this one."

"No worries," Nate says, hurrying off to secure his spot on the line.

A shot is fired—I glance up and see the Headmaster holding an ancient pistol. The air stinks of gunpowder, and his hand is singed black and appears to be smoking.

The contest has begun. I become fixated on a woman in a boiled-wool jacket, her hair band pulling dyed blond locks out of her face, her lips rolled back, teeth clenched, pulling on the rope like her life depends on it.

"I notice you keep staring at my wife. Do you know her?" the man side-lined with an amputated half-leg asks.

"She looks familiar," I say, not because it's true but because I have nothing else to say.

"She's a Middlebranch," he says. "The family goes back a very long way— one of them was Ben Franklin's roommate in France in 1753—kept one hell of a journal."

"How did you meet?" I ask.

"I was a student here, and she and two gals from Emma Willard came over to visit her brother. Odd that you marry someone that you meet at fourteen, don't ya think?" he says.

"Might be the best thing, there's great clarity in youth," I say.

"Why aren't you pulling?" he asks.

"Stroke," I say. "You?"

"Goddamned colostomy," he says, patting his stomach through his coat. "Had cancer the size of a grapefruit and they rerouted everything. They swear they're going to reconnect the pipes, but I'm not so sure how."

A groaning sound from the line distracts us. Someone splits his pants, a woman grinding down breaks a tooth. The adults pull and pull and pull, digging in as intractably as toddlers. Each side is so determined, so sure not only that they will win, but that in winning, in defeating the other, there is some greater gain.

"Pull," the man on the parent side calls.

"Pull," the boy on the student side calls.

"Pant," one of the women calls, "remember your Lamaze."

The seams of the Middlebranch boiled wool are pulling, stretching—white fibers, threads, are showing. It is truly a power struggle, and I get the feeling the parents are the ones desperate to prove something, what or why I'm not sure. And then, suddenly, as it all seems about to explode, the boys have the rope and are doing a strange improvisational victory dance across the lawn— Martha Graham gone wrong.

The parents gather themselves up and dust themselves off, and the weekend is suddenly over. Within minutes, the fathers and mothers are hugging their sons, bidding them adieu.

Nate gives me a powerful squeeze and thanks me for coming. "Let me know you get home safe," he says.

"Will do," I say.

As I'm walking to the car, the man married to the Middlebranch tells me this is the way it goes—the adults rarely win. And the academy likes to keep the parting short and sweet: the boys will finish the weekend with study hall and a suckling pig for dinner, that's the tradition. Tomorrow is Monday, a school day, and these future captains of industry, titans of banking, orthopedic surgeons, and accountants to the stars all have homework to do.

I quickly settle back into the routine at George's house, and on Thursday evening, as I'm relaxing, rereading John Ehrlichman's *Witness to Power*, George's psychiatrist telephones.

"We've reached a second stage. The team thinks it would be useful for you to come and spend some time with us."

"In what capacity?" I ask, fearing that I'll have to somehow "enroll."

"Think of it as a supervised playdate," he says.

"Can I leave if I'm not having a good time?"

"In theory, yes," he says.

"In theory?"

"There's really nowhere to go, but we're not going to hold you hostage."

"All right, then," I say.

"And you'll bring the dog?" the doctor asks.

"I could do that," I say—noting that the one thing missing from my otherwise great time last weekend was Tessie.

I pack a bag for myself and one for the dog. In Tessie's I put a giant Ziploc of kibble, a smaller bag of dog biscuits, treats, toys, some poop bags, and an old towel to sleep on. In my bag, a change of clothes, pajamas, toothbrush, and a Ziploc of my new "medications," along with the instructions, which I have to reread daily; otherwise I can't remember in what order they are to be taken.

It feels like months since I drove George's clothes up to the "facility." It's far, much farther than Nate's school. Driving there is like taffy pulling: with every hour, the place gets farther away. Halfway, I pull off into one of those odd wooded places marked "Rest Area." There are a couple of long-haul trucks and port-a-johns at the edge of the parking lot. I recline my seat, close my eyes, and am dreaming of Nixon's creation of the Environmental Protection Agency in 1970, his passage of the Clean Air Act, the Marine Mammal Act, the Safe Water Drinking Act, the Endangered Species Act—the Magna Carta of the environmental movement—only to be woken by a tapping on the window and Tessie's startled bark.

A man stands by the car, his fly unzipped, his anxious swollen gray underwear poking through at eye level. "Looking for love," he says through the glass, voice muffled, hips wiggling. I look up at his face, unshaven, wild-eyed. I lunge for the key, grind the ignition, and floor it out of the parking lot. Tessie lurches forward, losing her balance, and bangs into the dash. I slow, let her get her footing, and am back onto the highway, trying to maneuver my seat upright while gunning the gas pedal.

As I am driving, speeding farther and farther upstate, I keep having flashbacks. . . . The guy was erect, bulging out of his pants, and wanted me to what?

"How could he have thought that was appealing?" I ask Tessie.

It's late afternoon when I make the left at the mailbox marked "The Lodge." Tessie growls at the man at the gatehouse, who ignores her and asks me to open the trunk, which I do. Cleared to enter, I park and let Tessie out. She bounds towards the main building, wanders into the flower beds, and immediately lets loose with a load of diarrhea.

"What's the dog's name?" a burly man carrying a walkie-talkie asks.

"Tessie," I say.

He crouches, failing to notice the beastly smell. "Are you a good dog, Tessie? A soft, fluffy dog, Tessie? A kind dog, Tessie, not a big mean bitey dog, not a growly-wowly dog?" The dog licks his face. "I knew it," the guy says. "You are a kissy-wissy dog."

With Tessie's name and mine officially on the list, the staff are friendlier this time around, although, admittedly, I do approach the front desk expecting trouble. I drop my bags on the counter, and practically demand, "Search me." The receptionist all too willingly unzips the bag, pulls my big baggie of medications right off the top, and calls for a supervisor, announcing over the intercom, "We have a drug check at the front desk."

"I'm not sure you'd call prescription medicine a bag of drugs."

"We speak our own language," the receptionist says. "Would you like a cookie and a cup of tea? The supervisor may be a few minutes." She points to a hot-water pot and a tin of Danish Butter Cookies. I accept a cookie for myself and one for Tessie.

"Is that a therapy pet?" the woman asks.

"No, just a dog," I say.

The supervisor appears and lifts the Ziploc bag high, holding it up against the glare of the fluorescent bulbs in the ceiling as though it's a kind of X-ray machine. She gives the bag a shake, a kind of jingle bells, and hands it back to me. "In your room there is a lockbox like a hotel safe. You keep your medications in there at all times. Do you have any metal, cameras, recording devices, or weapons?"

"Nothing beyond whatever the CIA planted in my head," I say.

"Humor is easily misconstrued," the supervisor says.

"I'm nervous," I say. "I've never been in a mental hospital before."

"Nothing to be nervous about—you're just visiting, right?"

A young man appears; he looks like a high-school student, but introduces himself as Dr. Rosenblatt.

"We spoke on the phone," he says, shaking my hand. "I know that last time you were here you didn't get much of a sense of the place, so I thought we'd start with a tour. The grounds were laid out by the same fellow who designed Central Park and Paris," Rosenblatt says, leading me through the main "pavilion" and out the back door.

"Nice," I say, noticing the dappled afternoon light on the rolling hills. "It's like a national park."

"We call it a campus," Rosenblatt says.

A "campus" complete with a bowling alley, golf, and tennis. All of it enough to make insanity look appealing. Tessie loves the tour; she pees and poops multiple times. Rosenblatt ends the tour at a part of the estate slightly off the grid—a long, low building that looks like an old upstate hunters' motel. "We use this building for a variety of purposes, including as housing for our guests. If security seems a little high, you're not seeing things. We currently have a former presidential hopeful in-house. We need to be extra cautious: paparazzi have been known to sneak through the woods and so on."

"Interesting," I say.

"We treat a full range of issues."

"Is losing an election an issue?"

"It's very stressful," Rosenblatt says. "We're known for our ability to manage high-profile clients: our remote location, low staff turnover, private airport fifteen minutes away are all on our side. A few years ago, we had a major movie star who had a face lift that got infected, ended up looking like an entirely other person, almost lost his mind."

"How'd you treat that?"

"Encouraging him to grow a beard until he felt comfortable," he says, as though it was obvious.

Rosenblatt unlocks the door, ushering me into a room that could have been designed by a Martian who read books in translation about American history:

everything is red, white, or blue—or brown. All of it conspiring to seem entirely Yankee, Norman Rockwell, and good for one's health. The furniture is Ethan Allen, wooden, 100 percent made in America, a style I guess best described as Colonial—I think I'd nickname it "safe" and "timeless." The hangers don't come off the rod in the closet, there is a battery-operated electric clock, the lamps all have very short cords. On top of the dresser there's a small basket with two bottles of water, a protein bar, and some dried cranberries, in case you have to go into survival mode. And as an ironic antidote to the faux-homey approach, a large red-and-white glowing EXIT sign hovers over the door. It's all like a flashback to an America that never existed, America as it was dreamed by Ozzie and Harriet. On the night table next to the bed, there's a notepad featuring the logo of this place—an excellent souvenir if you're into the ephemera of insanity.

I think of Nixon's furniture: The beloved brown velvet lounger that he used to nap in after lunch in his "private" office in the Old Executive Office Building, around the corner from the White House. I think of the "Wilson" desk Nixon requested for the Oval Office thinking it was the one used by President Woodrow Wilson, but instead receiving the desk that belonged to former Vice-President Harry Wilson, within which, in 1971, Nixon had five recording devices installed. The desk, now back in its original location, the Vice-President's Office within the United States Capitol, has since been used by Walter Mondale, George Bush, Dan Quayle, Al Gore, Dick Cheney, and Joe Biden. I have no idea what happened to the "bugs" Nixon had wired from the desk down to an old locker room in the White House basement. I look around the motel room and wonder about bugs of all kinds, electronic and bed—there's been extensive news coverage about epidemic levels of bedbugs.

"Are conjugal visits allowed?" I ask Rosenblatt.

"Up to the doctor," Rosenblatt says, forgetting that he is a doctor.

Noting that there is no television in this room, I ask, "Does George have a TV?"

"No television on campus, but we have movie nights on Fridays."

"At home, he has a television in every room. He can't bear to be alone. Even when he's peeing he needs someone to be talking to him. You do know he ran a network?"

Rosenblatt nods.

I go on, waxing poetic about George. "He changed the face of television.

George was singularly responsible for shows such as *Your Life Sucks* and *Refrigerator Wars, My Way or the Highway, Doctors in the Off Hours.*" Rosenblatt doesn't seem to be listening. I throw in a couple of titles that I make up myself as a kind of test, like *Better Dead Than in My Wife's Bed,* and Rosenblatt's head bobs along. "Not much of a TV guy, are you?" I ask.

"Don't own one," Rosenblatt says. "Never have. Would you like a glass of water?" he asks Tessie.

"She's more of a bowl dog than a glass half empty," I say, still on a roll. As I'm unzipping Tessie's bag and digging out her bowl, she finds the bathroom and has a nice long drink from the toilet.

"So—where did you do your medical training?"

"Harvard," he says.

"And how'd you end up here?"

"I'm an expert on electroshock," he says. "As a teenager I treated my cat for extreme anxiety with a home electroshock system, which has since been adapted for use in third-world countries."

"A lot of pet anxiety in the third world?"

"Human use," he says.

"I didn't know anyone still did electroshock."

"It's very popular," he says. "Made a real comeback as one of the few successful treatments for drug-resistant depression."

Something about the way Rosenblatt says "treatment for drug-resistant depression" makes me think of those commercials for detergent that show the detergent lifting grass stains right out of the khaki knee and washing them away. I now have electroshock and Tide inexorably bound in my mind.

"I had no idea," I say. I honestly thought it had been banned as inhumane and perhaps cruel. "By the way, what does this place cost?" I ask.

"Your brother has very good insurance."

"How good?"

"As good as it gets."

"Where do people go from here, you know, when they 'graduate'?"

"Some go to other residential programs, others to a transitional facility, and some go home."

"How about jail?"

"You sound angry at your brother," Rosenblatt notes.

"Just a little," I say.

"You'd like him to be punished."

"I don't think he can be punished—at least, that's what my mother used to say."

"Really?"

"Yes, she often said, it's funny about your brother, he can do whatever he wants, because if you try to punish him he doesn't care."

"Interesting. Do you think it's true?" Rosenblatt asks.

I nod. "It's hard to make much of an impression on him," I say. "Speaking of which, when will I be seeing George?" I check my watch; it's five-thirty.

"Dr. Gerwin, who is taking the lead in your brother's care, would like to speak with you briefly, and then we'll take you to George." He pulls out a typed schedule and hands it to me. And then he hands me a second sheet—a feedback report. "If you could complete this before you depart and leave it with the front desk. The reports are graded, and we earn points, like miles that can be used for travel, shopping, or other services, depending on the grade.

"I'm about to go for a jog," he says, looking at Tessie. "I'd be happy to take the dog."

I think of Rosenblatt and his cat experiment. "Thanks, but I'll keep her with me."

B ack in the main building, Dr. Gerwin and I meet in a small room like the kind of place you'd go to sign up for a gym membership or apply to join the navy—generic, antiseptic. We shake hands, and then immediately he pumps foaming Purell onto his hands.

"Perhaps I should as well," I say, trying to make light of it. Gerwin pushes the Purell towards me; I fill my hands with foam and rapidly rub them together. "What fun."

Gerwin looks like the actor Steve Martin; his features are somewhat rubbery, but his facial expression remains fixed, as though he has studied himself in the mirror and decided this one—a kind of tolerant but uncommitted half-smile—works best. He pulls out a manila folder and makes himself comfortable behind the small desk.

"When did you first see a psychiatrist?" he asks.

"Me?"

"Yes," he says.

"I didn't. Or I should say I don't. I've never seen a psychiatrist."

"Does it seem strange to you, to have come this far in your life without getting help?"

"No," I say.

"Moving on," Gerwin says, "your sex life." And I'm not sure if it's a declarative statement or a question.

"Yes," I say.

"How would you describe it? The flavor?"

"Vanilla," I say.

"Any sex outside of your primary relationship?"

"No," I say, wondering how much he knows about the events that have brought us to this moment.

"Prostitutes?"

"Is this about me or George?" I ask. "Feel free to write down 'defensive' there, in that box. I want to help my brother, but, that said, I do feel I am entitled to have a private life."

"Yes, we all have a private life," Gerwin says, echoing my sentiment. "Prostitutes?" he asks again.

"No prostitutes. A private life—by that I mean one not discussed with you."

"From our perspective, given the circumstances, it would be useful to discuss certain things."

"Better for you than for me," I say.

"How do you describe your emotional life?"

"I don't have one," I say honestly. In this arena I am actually jealous of Nixon—he was a good crier, you might even call him a crybaby. He often wept, or more like sobbed, openly. "I avoid emotion."

"We all have our strategies," he says. "If something happens that you don't like, if someone treats you poorly, what do you do?"

"I pretend it never happened," I say.

We find George on the tennis court, with the ball machine firing balls at him and a coach shouting at him to swing, flatten out, follow through.

"He's got a strong backhand," the doctor says, watching through a window.

"Always did," I say.

At the end of George's lesson, I'm invited to meet him in the locker room. Gerwin takes Tessie, and I go in to find George naked in the shower, talking to me through the soap and water.

"Is Tessie with you?" he asks.

"Just outside. I didn't bring her in; she doesn't like tile. Your backhand looks good," I say, trying to make conversation. I'm not sure what the hell I'm supposed to talk about.

"They say I'm making progress."

"That's great," I say, and I'm half wondering if he thinks he's on some sort of executive retreat and not an inpatient in a lunatic asylum.

"Almost time for dinner," he says. "You staying?"

"Yes," I say. "I'll be here tonight and tomorrow." It's all a bit strange, out of body. I've been sent by his doctors into the locker room to reunite with him while he's naked and floating in what would appear to be a heavily medicated, post-game high.

"I'll let you get dressed," I say, preparing to leave. I exit and find Gerwin, who hands me the leash, with Rosenblatt and the tennis coach, all standing around talking about how good it is that George is "back in the game."

When George comes out of the locker room, Tessie sees him and pulls hard on the leash. George gets down on his knees, in front of her, butt in the air, arms extended—play position. The dog is excited but suspicious. George rolls onto his back, puts his hands and feet in the air. The dog acts like she's pleased to see him but knows he's nuts. I feel the same way myself—cautiously optimistic.

"Smart girl," I say.

As we go into the dining room, one of the staff takes Tessie, leading her off "while you have dinner."

George turns to me and says, "You look old."

"I had a little incident," I say.

"Didn't we all," he says.

"I had another one," I say. "After that one."

Rosenblatt, Gerwin, and the tennis coach follow us into the dining room.

We sit. I tuck the accordion file of papers I brought from home and have been carrying everywhere under my thighs. A waiter asks how many of us would like a "berry blast." They all raise their hands.

"Are you in or out?" the coach says, looking at me.

"What's a berry blast?"

"A green-and-red smoothie, antioxidant-rich, with added omega-3," he says, as though it's obvious.

"Fine," I say, "I'm in."

"What's the candy bar?" George asks.

"A Toffee-Mocha Musketeer."

I'm wishing I knew what language they were speaking. "I'll have the steak," I say.

"We're vegetarian," the waiter says. "I can bring you seitan piccata. It's a mock meat; people say it tastes like veal."

"Can't wait."

The waiter takes the rest of the orders and lets us know that the salad bar is open. I look at the other guests. It's hard to tell who's on staff and who's a patient; everyone looks like they're dressed to play golf. On the other side of the salad bar, there's a door leading to what looks like a private dining room. Suddenly there's a burst of commotion as an entourage sweeps across the main dining room and into that small dining room. In the middle of it all, surrounded, I see the back of the head of an older man with thick white hair—the former hopeful.

"You're a historian?" Gerwin asks, attempting polite conversation.

"Professor and author; I'm working on a book at the moment."

"My kid brother thinks he knows a thing or two about Nixon," George adds.

"I'm older, actually, by eleven months. I'm older," I repeat.

"What is it about Nixon that interests you?" Gerwin asks.

"What isn't interesting? He's fascinating, the story is still unfolding," I say.

"The fact is, my brother is in love with Nixon, he finds him compelling despite his flaws. Kind of like me, a regular laugh riot," George says.

"Speaking of you, will George go to jail for the rest of his life?"

"We're not the ones who make those decisions," Gerwin says, as if protecting George.

"We're not legal types," the coach says.

"Nothing like cutting to the chase," George says.

"George, have you told these guys the story of how Dad once knocked you out and how you saw stars for a week?"

"Remind me," George says. "How does that one go?"

"You were giving the old man a hard time about something and he asked you to come closer and you did and then he said, 'I don't ever want you to be confused about who's the boss,' and he popped you one. Pop was like a Mafia man, always bullying and berating, a very primitive man."

"You're saying bad things about him because he liked me better," George says.

"I'm okay with how much he liked me or not," I say. "When I look back at you, George, I think we should have read the writing on the wall: the coffee cup smashed against the kitchen cabinet, the body-sized dent in the Sheet-rock, the trash-can lid bent."

"Outbursts against inanimate objects don't always signal that you're going to kill your wife," Rosenblatt says.

"You're right. George, do you remember the time a psychiatrist asked you, 'Have you ever hit a woman,' and you said, 'Only on the ass'?"

George laughs heartily. "I do, I do," he says.

"What about target games?" I ask George's team. "What about when you're playing carnival games on a boardwalk, shooting a straw of pellets at Mr. Magoo, only you turn your rifle away from Mr. Magoo and aim right at your brother?"

"Out of context, it's hard to evaluate," Rosenblatt says.

"Did he tell you about how he ran me down with the car?"

"There you go, dragging out that old chestnut, your favorite of them all. And I didn't run you down, I bumped you."

"On purpose."

George shrugs. "I won't deny it."

"His nickname in high school was Vanquisher."

"Enough," Gerwin says. "The point of this dinner was to talk about mind-less things, and simply get along."

"Yeah," George says. "Put a cork in it."

I dig into my seitan piccata, which tastes like breaded cardboard with a kind of gummy lemon-caper-cornstarch gravy. During the meal, I ask Rosen-blatt about when I might have a few minutes with George alone to go over some private family business, house repairs, the children, pets, financials.

"It's not on the schedule?" he asks, perplexed.

I shake my head. "It's why I'm here; I need to speak with him. How about tonight, after dinner?" I suggest.

Rosenblatt looks at me like the thought never occurred to him. "Could do," he says, taking out a pen and scribbling it in on the schedule.

And so, after Tofutti with fake hot fudge and pots of green tea that taste like fish water, Gerwin, the coach, and Rosenblatt stand. "We bid you adieu," Gerwin says, "for tonight."

The coach slaps George on the back. "Proud of you," he says. "You're really working hard."

They are so fucking encouraging that it's nauseating. "Are all the patients treated like this?"

"Yes," Gerwin says. "We're about creating a safe environment—much difficulty comes from fear."

"I'll be over there"—Rosenblatt points to a table near the door—"if you need me."

"Fuckin' freak show," George says when they're all gone.

"And you're the star," I say.

"How's my dog and kitty?"

"Fine," I say. "It would have been nice to know about the invisible fence, but we figured it out."

"Are you giving Tessie the vitamins and the anti-inflammatory?"

"Which ones are hers?"

"In the kitchen cabinet, the big jar."

"I thought they were yours," I say. "I've been taking them daily."

"You're a moron," George declares.

I pull the accordion file out from under my ass. "There are some things I have to ask you. I'll start with the small stuff: How does the outdoor light for the front yard work? Also, I met Hiram P. Moody, he came to the funeral—does he pay all the bills? Is there anything I need to know or keep an eye on, about the accounts or how Moody gets paid? What's your PIN number? Also, I tried to use one credit card but it was password-protected; they asked for your mother's maiden name, I typed in Greenberg, but it didn't work."

"Dandridge," George says.

"Whose name is that?"

"It's Martha Washington's maiden name," he says, like I should know.

"Funny enough, that had never occurred to me; I thought they meant *your* mother's maiden name, not like the mother of America."

"Sometimes I forget the actual family, but I never forget Martha," George says. "I'm surprised you didn't know, you call yourself a historian."

"Speaking of history, I tried to enter your place of birth as New York, but again I was wrong."

"I use Washington, D.C.," George says. "It's really a question of what I can keep in mind."

"Exactly," I say. "And before I forget," I say, triggered because the word "mind" rhymes with the word "online," "I met a friend of yours."

"Oh," he says, surprised.

"She says your dick tastes like cookie dough and says you know her better from the back than the front."

The face George makes is priceless. "I'm not sure what this is all about," he says, flustered. "You said you wanted to ask me about some things in the house, and now this bombshell. Are you sure you're not working for the enemy?"

"How would I know? Who is the enemy, and do they identify themselves? And while we're sailing down the slippery slope, does your lawyer visit you? Are they preparing any kind of a defense? Do you receive any calls or letters?"

"Nothing," George says. "I have been forsaken, like Christ on the cross."

I am amused by the grandiosity of George's comparison of his situation to Christ on the cross. "Are you making friends here?"

"No," he says, getting up from the table, "they're all wack jobs."

"Where are you going?"

"I have to take a leak," he says.

"Are you allowed to go by yourself?" I ask, genuinely concerned.

"I may be insane, but I'm not an infant, you asshole," he says, and exits the dining room.

Rosenblatt, sitting up front writing in his charts, shoots me a look—all okay?

I give him the thumbs-up.

The dining room is empty except for one guy setting tables for tomorrow and another working the carpet sweeper.

When George comes back, it's as though we start fresh. He smells like rubbing alcohol. "I Purelled," he says. "I did my hands and face; it felt so good, I took my shirt off and did my pits too. I love the smell, very refreshing. Gerwin's got me hooked on the stuff. All day long I see him washing himself—can't help but wonder what's going on there, what makes him feel so dirty." George winks at me.

I ignore the wink and tell him about the trip to school for Field Day. "I stayed in a B&B for a hundred eighty a night—everything was sold out, the woman rented me her kid's room. I had a Hello Kitty mobile spinning over my head all fucking night."

"I have a room at the Sheraton; it's booked and paid in full for the next five years."

"How would I know?" I ask.

"You wouldn't," he says.

"So that's why I'm here: there are things I need to know. Do you think the children should see you, should they come for a weekend?"

"I don't think children are popular here," he says. "I've never seen any." George looks wistful, lost in time. "Do you remember the day—a long time ago, we might have been eight or nine—when I punched a random stranger, some guy who was walking down the street?"

I nod: who could forget?

"It was fantastic," George says, clearly still getting pleasure, if that's the word for it, from the incident. "I saw him double down and wonder what the hell, and I felt fantastic—high." He shakes his head, as if clearing the memory and coming back into the present time. "We were lucky little shits who got what we needed."

I shrug. "Speaking of oddities," I say, "there's a particular memory that keeps coming back to me." I pause. "Did we screw Mrs. Johannson?"

"What do you mean, we?" George asks.

"I have a memory of the two of us screwing the neighbor lady: you giving it to her on the king-sized bed, me cheering you on, bursting with pride—go, go, go. Then, when you were done, she still wanted more, and I gave it to her."

"I screwed her and maybe I told you about it," George says. "I used to mow their lawn, and then sometimes she'd invite me in for lemonade, and then she started inviting me upstairs."

Is that what happened, did George screw her, tell me about it, and I came up with a fantasy that put me right there in the room? My mental footage is so vivid, I can see George's purple prick, sliding in and out of her, her dress hiked up, her dark mother-cave gaping open, like a raw wound.

I am quiet for a moment, suddenly drained.

"You asshole," George says, as I'm packing up the accordion file, getting ready to go. "The one thing you haven't told me about is Mom. How is Mom? Does she ask about me?"

I remind George of my own recent incident and tell him that I've not seen Mom lately, but that the home says she's doing well. I tell him about the crawling, and he looks disturbed.

"She's crawling like a roach along the floor?"

"That's what they say. They have photos, if you want to see them."

"You need to go see her," George says. "The minute you get out of here, you go see her and find out for yourself."

"It's on my list," I say. "Is there anything else I should know?"

"Take care of my roses," he says. "Feed them frequently, spray them, don't let them get aphids or thrips, black spot, canker, or any other plague. My favorite is the pink Gertrude Jekyll near the front door."

"I'll do my best," I say. "Do you have any kind of a list of who fixes things, your plumber, electrician, grass cutter, et cetera?"

"No idea; ask Jane," he says briskly, and then we are silent.

"Time for bed," Rosenblatt says, coming to claim us. He's got Tessie with him, and George reaches for the leash at the same time I do.

"She's coming with me," George says.

"George wants her," Rosenblatt says.

"She's my dog," George says.

"I've been taking care of her," I say. "We're bonded."

"I could be the punishing parent and say Tessie sleeps with neither of you, but I won't. George gets the dog tonight, because you have the dog all the other nights."

"I win," George says, yanking the leash from Rosenblatt's hand.

I am escorted through a back door, out into the cold night, and taken on a shortcut back to my room. I am buzzed through doors, led through double-bolted locked areas, wondering what happens if, God forbid, I need to get out in the night. "I know what you're thinking," Rosenblatt says. "Don't worry, they're only locked in one direction, you can exit from your side."

At the door to my room Rosenblatt says, "We're very glad you're here. It's a good thing." And I have the feeling he's going to hug me.

"All right, then, see you tomorrow," I say, and quickly dart into the room and close the door. I prop the chair under the doorknob; not only can I not get out, but no one can come in.

The sight of Tessie's bag on the luggage rack next to mine makes me aware of how alone I am. Can I fall asleep without the dog, without TV, with nothing to distract me from this nightmare? I unlock the safe, take out my medication, read the directions, realizing that I forgot to take the dinner pills with dinner and hoping it's all right if I take them now, along with the night pills. I swallow eight various capsules and tablets, put on my pajamas, get into bed, and wait.

The room makes the Hello Kitty room at the B&B look like a fucking Four Seasons. I find myself actually missing the hamster, craving the black beady eyes, the unrelenting squeak of his wheel. All I've got is cinderblock silence.

To quiet my thoughts, I think of Nixon, his love of bowling, his favorite candy, Skittles, his approach to life: "A man is not finished when he is defeated. He is finished when he quits." And, "I don't think that a leader can control, to any great extent, his destiny. Very seldom can he step in and change the situation if the forces of history are running in another direction." "I can take it. The tougher it gets, the cooler I get."

I think of my book and what I want to do with it next. I think of my mother crawling like a roach, of George, imagining him coming to the nurses' station at night—in enormous one-piece footed pajamas, saying, "Want milk."

"The kitchen is closed, go back to bed."

"I want milk!"

And the nonplussed nurse pushes the button under the counter, and there are large men coming from every side, with batons and a Taser gun, and they zap him. George crashes to the floor and is taken back to bed riding on what looks like a luggage cart.

I hear what sounds like a thousand feet running and crashing into a wall and realize that my room is next to an ice machine and it's just dumped a load into the bin.

I begin to panic, to feel there is no air in this place. I obsess about what's behind the blue velvet curtains. I peel them back with one urgent yank. Worse than nothing, there is an ugly cinderblock wall. I search for a window and find only a tiny vent in the bathroom. Pressing close to it, I suck up air, convinced that there is something poisonous about this place and that I am about to die. I hurry back to the lockbox and break out my supply of Ambien as though it's the antidote. I almost never take a sleeping pill, but tonight I take two, suck up a few more breaths from the vent, and then force myself to lie back down in the bed.

An enormous banging wakes me up. The chair tucked up and under the doorknob is moving, jumping, and I hear a muffled voice: "Are you awake? Are you all right?"

It takes more than a moment to get my mouth working. "Arhggymmby," I call out and the chair stops moving.

"You missed breakfast," the voice says—it's Rosenblatt.

"Onanasshchclllp," which I think is me saying I overslept.

"Can you be ready in twenty minutes?"

"Yemmmina." I take myself into the bathroom, feeling like now I know what it would be like to live two hundred and fifty years, and take a cold shower, talking aloud to myself, carefully enunciating my words. Twenty minutes later, I am dressed, sitting on the chair that I had jammed in front of the door, eating the protein bar from the basket, and wondering what the day will bring.

"You scared the crap out of me," Rosenblatt says when he comes knocking for the second time. "I thought maybe you killed yourself."

"That would be too easy," I say. "I couldn't sleep, I missed the dog, I took a giant sleeping pill."

"Guess it worked. How about some coffee?"

"Please," I say.

I am given a large cup of coffee, and then Rosenblatt says, "We'd better get on with it. George is working with the coach right now, and I've got something to show you."

We go to a conference room where a machine, a pair of wired goggles, and a screen have been set up. "We ask you to put the goggles on—they simply track eye movement," Rosenblatt says. "And on this screen a series of words will come up." He hands me a little clicker that is wired to the same machine as the goggles. "We'd like you to click this when a word resonates for you in the context of your relationship to your brother. Are you ready?"

"Yes."

The first word comes up. "Flower." I click.

"Did you mean to click?" Rosenblatt asks.

"I did, George loves flowers."

The second word, "Benign." No click.

"Sympathetic." My finger is at rest.

"Wrath." Click.

"Antagonism." Click. Click.

"Did you mean to click twice?"

"I don't know."

"Hostility." "Spite." "Rancor." Click, click, click.

"Benevolent." Trigger-happy, I almost click.

"Gentle." I rest, take a breath.

"Openhearted." My fingers are numb from inaction.

"Wound." "Annihilate." "Bully." This seems too obvious: click, click, click. "Attached." Click.

The screen goes off.

"Are you familiar with intermittent explosive disorder—IED?" Rosenblatt asks.

"Sounds like bowel trouble," I say.

"It's often described as 'partial insanity.' It's more common than you think, the inability to resist the aggressive impulse, extreme expression of anger, uncontrollable rage. That's what I'm thinking is at play here."

Why am I waiting for him to say "devil's work"?

Rosenblatt goes on. "In a situation like this, it's clearly not one thing, but many—chemistry, stress, drugs, mood, and other mental instability. We're going for a multifaceted diagnosis and a prolonged treatment approach."

"Are you going to give him electroshock?"

"No, but I personally think he may be a candidate for some of our newer psychosurgical techniques, such as gamma knife irradiation or, more likely, deep brain stimulation. We implant something like a pacemaker in the brain— drill a hole, place three leads, implant a battery-powered neurostimulator, calibrate the stimulation. It's not without side effects—some decline in executive function—and of course we're aware of what the court might say if we present your brother as having agreed to undergo experimental brain surgery."

I'm shocked by what he's saying. I thought they might have something weird up their sleeves, but the old ice pick in the melon ball had never occurred to me. "So what you're saying is something akin to a lobotomy?"

"I wouldn't call it that, but it does fall within the same rubric."

"And with the courts, do you think having brain surgery is a plus or a minus?"

"It certainly says we took an aggressive approach. I'd say it's a plus."

"And what does George say?"

"He doesn't know it yet; no one does. I haven't even told Gerwin. I'm doing some research, and then I'll make my case."

"Would you have psychosurgery?" I ask, knowing I never would.

"In a heartbeat," he says, "no pun intended. I wouldn't even mind performing it on myself."

"Interesting," I say, and that's an understatement. Fucking crazy, is what I'm thinking. "Okay, so what else is on the docket, and how's Tessie?"

"Good. She had breakfast in the kitchen and has gone out for a walk. Our plan is to have you and George do some structured play, geared towards bonding and team building."

"Like what?"

"Fun stuff."

I'm suspicious. George comes in from his morning session, stinking of sweat, his clothes plastered onto his body.

"How are you?" I ask.

"Fantastic," he says.

"Glad to hear it," Gerwin says, following him into the room, carrying what looks like a cardboard treasure box. "So today I thought we'd play some games."

George's eyes brighten, "Risk? Monopoly? Trivial Pursuit? Mafia? As kids we played murderball: you throw the big red rubber ball as hard as you can right at someone's face and you murder them."

I can still remember the sting of the ball. "You weren't supposed to aim for the face."

"Let's start with a balloon," Gerwin says, pulling a limp yellow balloon from his pocket, stretching it a couple of times, and blowing it up.

"I'm not exactly the playful type," I say, dreading whatever is coming next.

"I can assure you we know that and have taken it into consideration," Gerwin says, tying a knot in the end of the balloon. "I would now like the two of you to stand face to face."

We dutifully do.

"I am going to place this balloon between you," Gerwin says, fitting the balloon into the space between our bodies. The balloon slowly falls to the floor. "Let's try again. Can the two of you move closer, more nose to nose?"

George steps closer; reflexively, I step back—he's out of focus. George steps closer again, and again I step back—like a dance.

"Ahh," Gerwin says.

"The fact is, I can't see him so close up, he becomes a big blur."

"Perhaps focus on a point beyond George," Gerwin suggests.

I do. And we stand with the balloon lodged between us, and I feel George's hot breath on my face, I smell his sweat.

"Are you bathing regularly?"

"I think so," he says, as though he doesn't know.

"Enough," Gerwin says, and we are quiet.

"The goal of this game is for the two of you, working together, to move the balloon from here to there"—he points to the far side of the room—"without letting the balloon touch the floor. *Capisce?*"

"*Capisce,*" George says, and he starts to walk south, towards the far wall. I take a couple of sideways steps to catch up with him. The balloon slides from our sternums to our diaphragms.

"Should we make a plan?" I ask George. "Do you want to call out each step before you go?"

"Step. Step. Step."

We make good progress, and then George seems distracted and heading not straight across the room but towards me. "We're going more north—we need to head south," he says. The balloon slips lower, we're about to lose it, George knees me in the groin—to push the balloon up. I double over and the balloon falls farther still.

"Can't you do one thing right?" George asks.

I don't answer. I wriggle one thigh and then the other, pressing the balloon against George's body, working the balloon up higher, I get it from his knees up to his crotch.

"Your turn," I say.

"Step. Step. Step."

We do it, we get the balloon across the room. "Yes!" I say, giving George a high-five. "Yes!" It is only when we are safe on the other side that it occurs to me that perhaps there are people who don't make it to the other side—not making it wasn't something I thought of as an option.

"You may pick a prize," Gerwin says, holding the treasure chest. "One per customer."

I stick my hand in and pull out a paper glider, similar to the ones I used to get as a child for being good at the dentist's office. George gets a sheriff's badge—with a sharp pin, so they make him switch it for something else, and he picks a rubber snake.

"Our next game is . . ." Gerwin starts, and as he's saying it, George jumps on the yellow balloon, popping it. Rosenblatt swoops down and picks up the shards of balloon, and Gerwin repeats, "Our next game is . . ." And so it goes: we play game after game, collecting prize after prize. And then Gerwin brings out the hand puppets.

I put one on and turn to George. "I am not a crook," I say.

George puts one on and aims it at himself: "Good night and good luck." He slips a puppet onto his other hand. "Thank you, Edward R. Murrow."

"No, thank you, Mr. Cronkite. How about we go over to Toots Shor's and get ourselves a steak."

"Let's start this somewhere else," Gerwin says.

"Fine," George says, pointing to me. "I'll be F. Scott Fitzgerald, you can be Hemingway and kill yourself."

"Why don't you be William Burroughs and shoot your wife?" I say.

"Stop, stop, stop!" Gerwin is jumping up and down between us. We're loading our hands with puppets and sometimes throwing them across the room, hurling puppets like epithets.

"Winston Churchill," George says.

"Charles de Gaulle," I say.

"Nikita Khrushchev," he says.

"Barry Goldwater and Roy Cohn," I say.

"Herbert Hoover," he says.

"Willy fucking Loman," I say.

Gerwin picks up something that looks like a can of deodorant, holds it high in the air, and sprays—a deafeningly loud BLAST, an air horn, like from an eighteen-wheeler.

"TIME OUT!" Gerwin shouts. Both George and I start to say something, but Gerwin interrupts: "Silence! We are going outside now." We stuff our prizes in our pockets, leave the puppets behind, and follow Gerwin, who carries the treasure chest, mumbling to himself that now we can't play the blindfold trust walk, and why can't it be easier.

We get out onto the rolling hills behind the main building, and I have a moment of supreme understanding of how the Founding Fathers could have fought for this land. It is spectacular, majestic. Gerwin throws me a football; I catch it. We are all tossing the ball around. It's idyllic, the blue sky, and the smell of fresh-cut grass, stains on our knees. The ball goes around and around, there is talk of teams, of us against them, but Gerwin keeps saying, Keep it going, keep it going. And at some point he pulls a camera out of his pocket and starts shooting pictures. George camps it up for the camera, acting heroic, fierce. I'm not sure why Gerwin is taking pictures, but it seems impossible to break the reverie and ask.

Rosenblatt throws the ball to me; I catch it, look up, and see George bearing down on me, hurtling forward like a human bowling ball, a torpedo. He slams me to the ground and is pummeling me. We are rolling down the hill, spinning on a spit of brotherly rage. I see Gerwin and Rosenblatt in the distance, and then Rosenblatt runs off. I am struggling to get out from under. At the bottom of the hill, we stop rolling. George is pounding me, whaling away, fists pumping. Gerwin comes closer, but does nothing to stop him. "You fucker, you stinking little fucker, this is only half of what you deserve, you useless piece of shit, you motherfucking . . ."

I am trying as best I can to guard my face, my ribs, and my balls. From wherever she's been kept, Tessie is let loose; she runs down to where we are, barking heavily, trying to stop the mayhem, she's barking at George's face and therefore in my ear, and, "accidentally or not," George smacks her in the muzzle; she yelps and slinks away. The heavies pull George off me.

I lie on the grass, bloodied, bruised, struggling to catch my breath. No one moves to help me. No one does anything. I am lying there, and my first thought is not of myself but of the children. I have to protect Nate and Ashley; whatever happens or doesn't, I cannot let this monster anywhere near his children. I glance at George, huffing and puffing, clearly wanting more, held back by a team of four enormous men. I roll over and slowly, limb by limb, pull myself together. Tessie comes and licks my face.

Our prizes have escaped our pockets and are sprinkled across the lawn—a yo-yo, the glider (now bent), a rubber snake, a Chinese finger-catcher.

Hobbling back to the main building, I am looking at Gerwin, expecting something. "I am at a loss for words," he finally says.

"Minimally, if you can't protect me from physical harm, I cannot be part of your process. You'll be damned lucky if I don't sue you for not having your patient under control. And some ice, I need ice packs."

Someone brings me several ice packs—black trash bags filled with ice, knotted at the top.

"Would you like a doctor to take a look at you?" Gerwin asks.

"No," I say, "I want the dog and I want to go home."

"I don't suppose you want to say goodbye to George?" Gerwin asks.

"Very funny," I say. "So he can deliver the knockout punch?" And while I'm waiting for them to get the car, I overhear one of them say, "We're actually very pleased. It was a good visit, we saw a side of George that we've not seen before. It'll give us something to work with."

Tessie is already in the car when they bring it around, as is my bag, and Tessie's, all packed. I am in incredible pain, and it's only getting worse—every part of me, the parts that bend and the parts that don't. I lower myself into the driver's seat, wincing. As I adjust the seat, I notice a brown paper bag with my name on it—two bottles of water, peanut-butter-and-jelly sandwiches, and a Ziploc filled with carrot sticks. Who the hell serves an adult peanut butter and jelly? I eat the sandwiches, wondering if it's meant to be patronizing.

At a rest stop along the way, I go into the men's room, lift my shirt, and in the chipped mirror look at my side—it's the color of raw meat. Annoyed with myself for not pushing back, not putting up a better fight, I go into the convenience store and grab some Advil. When some woman tries to cut in front of me I say, "Hey, I was first," and she says, "Clearly you weren't or I wouldn't be here now." Tired of being the wimp, I throw her an elbow, I literally push her out of the way. The man behind the counter whips out some kind of enormous long black umbrella, pops it open in my face, and tells me to leave the store, using the metal end to poke at me.

"I'm injured," I shout, "I'm trying to pay you for this Advil."

"You are a bully," the man shouts from behind the umbrella with a strong Indian accent. "I sell nothing to bullies. You go away now and don't come back."

"I am taking the Advil," I say. "And I am leaving ten bucks here on top of the Fig Newtons."

I back out of the store, tripping over a step and falling into a pool of grease and gasoline. Stinking, I get back to the car, take my shirt off in the parking lot, put my shirt from yesterday back on, swallow four Advil, and start the car. As I'm barreling towards home, thinking that it's all too weird and that I'm never going back to that place, my cell phone rings. It's George's lawyer.

"The hospital asked me to inform you that you are not to visit again; they said you were threatening to the patient and the staff."

"I was physically attacked by George."

"They saw things differently. In their eyes you provoked him, you wouldn't throw the ball to him, you spoke only to the doctors and not to him, you belittled him and made him feel left out and like there is something wrong with him."

"Oh my God, that is so crazy. They're nuts. It's a freak show up there; I've never seen a crazier group of mental-health professionals. Do you know that one of them is planning on doing brain surgery on George, but hasn't told him yet? It's like a horror movie. How did you find that place anyway?"

"My brother-in-law," the lawyer says.

"He was a patient?"

"The medical director," the lawyer says. As he's speaking, the reception gets crackly, and then the connection crumbles out from under before becoming a void.

"Hello?" I say. There is nothing. "Hello."

It's Monday, and I'm back at the house, the literal scene of the crime. I have this horrible sinking sensation; the house has some kind of force or electromagnetic charge, it's an incredible weight taking me down.

Returning from the visit to George, as I approach the door, I lose power. I come in and cease to function. Like in Michael Crichton's *The Andromeda Strain*, my bone marrow has turned to dust. I imagine being found days from now dead on the floor, my blood reduced to a fine green powder that pours on the floor like Lik-M-Aid when they inexplicably slit my wrist. Inexplicable because why would someone slit a person's wrist? The cat will be sitting next to me, unfazed, cleaning herself, rubbing her eyes, licking. I imagine the men in the white suits trying to pick her up as a specimen of what survived.

I am sitting on the floor weeping. What happened? What is happening now? I sit on the floor hating everything, hating myself most of all—that's the truth of it, more than anything else I am so fucking disappointed in *me*. How's that for the Me Generation coming to a crashing halt?

It's as though I've been waiting for my life to rev up and get going for years. Sometimes I thought I was making progress, getting closer; other times it was like I was simply waiting to be discovered—by who? Looking at myself, my half-spent life, I find it unbearable that this is where I have ended up. Is my life over? Did it ever begin?

I have done nothing—or, more specifically, the one thing I have done, the one big thing of consequence, was essentially a crime that led to Jane's murder. My accomplishment is as an adulterer, an accomplice to murder, like that's something to be proud of. . . .

My mind leaps to my theory about presidents—that there are two kinds, ones who have a lot of sex and the others who start wars. In short—and don't quote me, because this is an incomplete expression of a more complex premise—I believe blow jobs prevent war.

And I can't help but wonder, did George want to kill me too? I have no doubt that the only thing that stopped him was narcissism—to kill me was also to kill some part of himself, which might also explain why Nate and Ashley survived.

I urge myself to gather my green-and-blue Lik-M-Aid veins and leave the house and see what is outside. Things are only odd by comparison; in the absence of anything else, the odd can seem normal. My mind hops to John Ehrlichman, a Jew, a Christian Scientist, and the only figure from Watergate to serve jail time. Ehrlichman went to jail before his appeal process was completed. He offered himself up.

Like a drunk who has stumbled into the wrong house, I go back outside, reminding myself that the prior weekend, Field Day with Nate, was good, it was filled with promise, hopes for the future—it was a thousand times better than the horrific visit with George.

In the backyard, I open George's garden cabinet and take out the trowel and split-fork weeder and get down on my hands and knees. It's like a goddamned premature spring awakening. The yard is heavily planted, everything is thriving. I dig in the dirt. I think about my class this afternoon. I've told no one about being fired—who would I tell? What the hell kind of job could I get now? I'm digging, hurling clumps of weedy earth over my shoulder, and imagining the faces of my students, idiots who sit there waiting for me to spoon-feed it to them, waiting for me to inform them that there is such a thing as history and that it matters.

I crawl on my hands and knees, obsessively plucking errant growth, weed stumps, clover, various things that seed, blow, spread. I am diddling in the dirt looking like every other asshole who mucks in the backyard as though we can rekindle our ancient energy by sinking our hands into the soil.

The pet minder appears at the edge of the yard. "Are you okay?" he asks. "Should you be bent over like that? Isn't it too much pressure on your head?"

"No one mentioned not bending."

"Might be too much," the minder says. "My aunt had a stroke and they told her no forward bending."

I lift my head. "No longer bent," I say.

"Perhaps take a rest," he says. "I got Tessie a pizzle stick. And I gave the cat a catnip mouse—she loves them."

"I never thought of giving the pets toys," I mumble.

"They get bored and need something new—same as us," he says, walking down the drive. "Call me if you need me. I'm fish-sitting not far from here."

Tessie smells the overturned dirt. She lies on her back in the center of the yard and rolls on my pile of fresh-plucked weeds.

A minute after the minder is gone, I accidentally flip a massive clot of rich black dirt into my eye, blinding myself. I paw at my face, trying to clear it. I use my shirt, get up too fast, and step on the trowel, throwing myself off balance. I crash into the barbecue and rebound—mentally writing the headline: Idiot Kills Self in Garden Accident. It's Tessie who guides me to the stair, with me holding on to her collar, saying, "Cookie, cookie, let's go find a cookie." In the downstairs half-bath I let myself have it. "Shit face," I say, looking at myself in the mirror, thinking it is really possible that I didn't flip dirt into my eye but shit of some sort: Tessie shit, kitty shit, raccoon or deer shit—whatever it is has a funky smell, like fancy cheese, cheese so rare and ripe that they keep it in its own cave and bring it out only for royal holidays. I have one eye open and am looking at myself in the mirror, giving myself a talking to, remembering another time when I looked in the mirror, I literally dissolved—the stroke.

"Don't stare," I say to myself. "You have that dumb look like you don't even know what I'm talking about, like it's all a big surprise. How could it be? Just because you're hearing this out loud for the first time doesn't mean it's new information. I've been talking to you for weeks, really more like years, or the entirety of your whole goddamned life, you fucking idiot."

"Why are you talking to me this way?" I ask.

"Because you don't hear it any other way, you want it to be all touchy-feely. You fucked up, your sister-in-law is dead, your brother is in an insane asylum, and you want me to make you feel good about yourself? Wake the fuck up—you are a disaster. You're even more dangerous than your brother; the fact that he's in there and you're out here, on the loose, proves it."

My head slams into the wall. Slam. As though somehow it is just happening, as though someone else is doing it. Slam. Slam.

"Why did Jane call me when she wanted to know where the light bulbs were, why was I like the other half, the functional half of my brother?"

"Are you blaming her?"

"No," I say.

And now my head is not in the sink anymore, not slamming into the wall, it's in the toilet, and there is pressure at the back of my neck; at first I think it's a hand pushing me down, but then I realize my head is stuck under the rim of the seat.

"Are you going to throw up? Are you sick of yourself now?"

I don't answer.

The toilet flushes, soaking me, drowning me. I am waterboarding myself.

Coughing, sputtering, I pull my head out of the toilet. I vomit. I am on the floor of the bathroom, wet, sour—silent.

"Pouting?"

I don't answer.

"Not talking to me? Should I stop?"

"Say whatever you want, give me what you've got, bring it on. Clearly you've been sitting on it for a long time."

"Okay. Number one—how could you spend so many years writing a book on Nixon? It's boring, it's beyond boring, and it's pathetic. I wouldn't even care if you fucking failed, it's the fact that you've done nothing that's sent me over the edge."

"Is my book really that bad?"

"It's shit. You are shit. Your personality is necrotic, dying; it eats away at everything. Look at me, would I lie to you? I'm like a ghost from within trying to knock some sense into you."

"What do you want from me?" I ask, fearing this is all hurtling towards some inevitable end.

"I want your life," he says.

And there is nothing more to say.

The telephone is ringing.

"Hello," I say.

"Is this you?"

"Yes," I say.

"It's me," she says.

"Claire?"

"Who's Claire?" she asks, her voice suddenly strict, as though insulted, as though I should have known.

I go deeper into my own darkness, "Jane?"

"How many are there?" she wants to know.

"How many of what?"

"Girls," she says, "women, fuck buddies."

"Who is this?" I ask, frightened.

"Why don't you run down your list, and when you get to me I'll call out, 'Bingo.'"

"You have the wrong number."

"Oh no," she says. "I have the right number. I double-checked before I dialed."

"Maybe it's my brother you're looking for," I suggest.

"Does he have a heart-shaped mole over his left nipple?" she asks.

Deep silence. "Who is this?"

"Crap," she says, sighing. "You don't remember me. I fed you lunch and then some." She pauses. "Look, I didn't mean to catch you off guard. Can we roll back and try this again? Push the restart button."

"Sure," I say, still not knowing who I am talking to.

The line goes dead. I hang up. Immediately the phone rings again.

"Hi, it's Cheryl calling. Is Harry there?"

"Speaking," I say.

"How are you?" she asks.

"Good," I say. "And you?"

"I'm sorry I never called you," she says. "I mean before now, I mean after we had our moment and before now."

"Oh," I say, still unable to make sense of it, "that's okay."

"I want to be honest with you about the whole Internet thing."

"Sure," I say; the pieces are coming together.

"I thought I was okay, doing really well, so I stopped taking my medication and I was working in a friend's catering company and then business got slow and I had all this extra time and I started surfing and then making these 'dates' like the one I had with you. It got out of control and I crashed," she says. "Hard landing. I had to be hospitalized—briefly."

We are silent. I take my shirt off and let it fall to the floor. Stripped down wet, stinking of vomit, I sit at the kitchen table.

"Actually," she says, "I'm not being entirely honest. I stopped taking my medication and then I started self-medicating. I was completely out of control; our meeting was one of many. I put myself and my family at risk. My son, you may recall, he came home when we were in the middle of . . . Well, it wasn't good."

It's suddenly clear to me. "Of course," I say, enthusiastically.

"And you," she says, unnerved by my burst of enthusiasm and needing to change the subject, "what have you been up to?"

"If we're doing full disclosure," I say, "I was hospitalized as well. I had a stroke."

"Perfect," she says.

"What do you mean, 'perfect'?"

"I mean, I'm glad we both had something happen, some sort of event interrupted us."

"I suspect it was the Viagra," I say. "I was taking too much of it."

"Amazing, isn't it," she says, "how easily we slip right off the rails. Are you okay now?"

"I'm fine," I say. "Really good. And you?" I am looking around the room; everything is blurry. I am at least half blind and have no idea if it's permanent or not.

"You've been on my mind," she says. "A lot. But I needed to wait to call you. I needed to be in better shape."

I make an agreeable if innocuous sound.

"Forgive me if now I've forgotten the details. But who was it you're interested in, Richard Nixon or Larry Flynt?"

"Nixon," I say. "Nixon died of a stroke, and I don't know why, but when I was having mine I kept thinking of him, feeling like I always knew we had something in common but was never quite sure what until that moment; it was like a psychic connection. It wasn't about belief or political philosophy, but on a human, emotional level. I think the guy got a raw deal."

"I'm wondering if I might run an idea past you," she says, cutting me off.

"I'm all ears," I say—and it might be true, considering the condition of my eye.

"You should talk with Julie," she says with enthusiasm, like it's a done deal.

"Julie?"

"Julie Eisenhower."

"Julie Nixon Eisenhower?" I ask, vaguely skeptical.

"Yes," she says.

"Really?" I say, suddenly gleeful, as though an entire tide could turn on three names, Julie Nixon Eisenhower, as Humbert Humbert once liltingly tripped over three syllables in *Lo-lee-ta*.

"Yes," she says.

I laugh out loud and then, coming to my senses, ask, "How is that possible?"

"Don't ask," she says. And then pauses. "Okay, full disclosure, she's my husband's cousin by marriage. Can I have her call you?"

"Please," I say.

"I don't know how current you are, but in recent years there were some issues with the library."

"Yes," I say, recalling various articles detailing Bebe Rebozo's nineteen-million-dollar bequest and tension between Julie and Trisha with regard to how the library would be run.

"So now here's the other thing." She pauses. "I want to see you. I want to talk to you, to have lunch."

"Sure," I say. "I don't see why not."

"Just lunch," she says.

"Of course," I say.

"When?" she says.

"Whenever works for you; I have nothing on my plate."

"Okay," she says. "Let's give it a couple of days, in case you change your mind, or in case it turns out I've gone off again."

"How about Friday?" I suggest.

"Friday," she says. "And, not just because I like the name, there's Jerk Q'zine—it's crazy cheap."

"Think of someplace nice," I say, "someplace you actually want to go."

"Have you ever been to Quarry Tavern?"

"No," I say. "I'm not really from around here."

"It's really good," she says. "They make wonderful meatball pizza. I've been known to eat it in my car. I'll meet you there," she says. "And I'll give Julie your number."

"I'll look forward to it," I say.

She pauses. "If Julie asks how we know each other, say we met at a barbecue. No, wait, say kids and sports and don't go further."

"Got it."

"Okay, then," she says, "I'm glad we talked. Like I said, you've been on my mind."

"Friday at noon," I say.

"Friday at noon," she repeats.

"See you then," I say, coming down, crashing. I'm all at once up and down, both extremes simultaneously, and, well, it's hard to keep talking.

Is it possible that a woman I don't remember holds the key to my future?

I'm giddy, light-headed—actually, my head is pounding. I tell myself not to get too excited, not to buy into my own enthusiasm; it could all be for naught.

I hold myself in check, and then I am laughing out loud. Check! Checkers, the Nixons' famous cocker spaniel. I play with my mental footnotes—like catalogue cards. Checkers died in 1964 and is buried at the Bide-a-Wee Pet Cemetery, not far from where Aunt Lillian lives. Perhaps next time I'm out I'll visit.

Maybe this is the moment, the big break, the swift kick-start that I've been waiting for. Julie Nixon Eisenhower and me!

Tessie is in the bathroom licking the floor, cleaning up my mess.

"Good dog," I say, aware that my mood is all too subject to the winds of change. I go upstairs to shower and get ready for class. My eye looks bad, red, bulging. I put in some kind of drops from the medicine cabinet which burn like crazy—makes sense, they are ear drops—and rinse the eye again. I shower, dress, and leave for school, proud of myself for remembering to bring some empty boxes. Today is packing day; years of class plans, student evaluations, examples of good and bad papers will be edited—the highlights crammed into well-worn liquor boxes. Anticipating the end, I want to be out long before it is officially over. On my final day I simply want to be done—teach and go.

As I'm walking into the department, the secretary stops me. "The Chair would like a word," she says.

As nonchalantly as possible, I stick my head into the Chair's office, hovering at the edge of the doorway. "You looking for me?"

The Chair, my former friend Ben Schwartz, looks up. "How are you doing?"

"On what level?"

The Chair doesn't answer right away; then he says, "I've known you for years, we're old friends."

"That's right," I say. "And not so long ago you took me out to lunch, ordered a cup of soup and half a sandwich, and told me my career was over. You said, 'We've got this fellow who has a new way of teaching history, it's future-forward. Instead of studying the past, the students will explore the future—it's all about possibility. We think it will be less depressing than watching reruns of the Zapruder films.'"

"I didn't have the sandwich," the Chair says. "Just the soup. And the decision wasn't entirely mine. I like to think I'm your friend. I'm the one who hired you."

"You didn't hire me. We were colleagues, you told me there was a job opening, but you didn't hire me. Frankly, I think if you could have ordered the soup by the spoon, you'd have had two spoons and left it at that."

He says nothing.

"What is it you want?" I ask, wondering if he wants my pardon, my forgiveness.

"Take a walk with me," the Chair says, putting on his jacket.

We exit the building and walk to his car.

The parking lot is filled with compact cars of various ages. The reflection of the sun off the endless sea of chrome is blinding. Ours is a commuter school. We used to think we were special because faculty got numbered parking places, hot until a graduate engineering student intentionally blew up the car in Spot 454 and the administration decided that it was better for parking to be random, democratic, with the exception of those with handicapped plates.

The boss unlocks the doors of his Toyota. The song of the automatic lock echoes off the other cars in the outdoor lot. I imagine someday cars will actually answer each other's chirps in a postmodern reenactment of call and response. Hybrids, where are you? Chirp-chirp, we're everywhere. He pulls out an envelope from under the seat, a standard white #10, and he hands it to me.

"Take it," he says.

My hands remain in my pockets.

"Take it," he repeats more urgently.

"What is it?"

"What does it look like?"

"One might assume it's money," I say.

He pushes the envelope towards me. "You idiot," he says. "I'm trying to help you. I feel bad, I should have handled things differently, and you," he says, "you should have finished your book."

"Blame the victim," I say, hands still in my pockets.

"I couldn't protect you—I had nothing to use to support my argument." Again he pushes the envelope towards me.

"No thanks," I say.

"On what grounds?" he asks.

"On the grounds that I don't take envelopes of money from anyone. For all I know, you're setting me up, having your secretary witness, call me in, making me walk out to your car, where you have the envelope hidden; for all I know, there are cameras everywhere, recording this—the car is miked."

"You are a paranoid motherfucker," he says.

"I am a *Nixon* scholar," I shout. "I know whereof I speak," I say, as I turn on my heel to march across the parking lot and back to the building.

"Where are you going?" he calls.

"Office hours," I say.

I hear the chirp-chirp sound of him relocking his car, and his hot breath as he jogs to catch up with me. "Look, it's not about the money," he says.

"But you are offering me money, hush money to go gently into the night."

"It's my own money," he says. "Not the department's."

"That makes it even more perverted."

"I hope you'll reconsider," he says when we get back to the department. "Think of it as a research grant."

I pick up the boxes that I left outside his office door, one of which someone has inexplicably filled with balled-up sheets of paper—all I can think of is target practice.

There is someone in my office, sitting in the guest chair. His back is to the door, a yarmulke bobby-pinned to the back of his head.

"Can I help you?"

"Are you Professor Silver?"

"I am." Does he know what just happened in the parking lot? Is he sitting here ready to receive my confession of temptation—is it like some Scared Straight program, or is he part of the setup? "Are you interested in Richard Nixon?" I ask, taking my seat.

"Not so much," he says. "I am a rabbinical student."

"You get to dress like that even though you're still a student?" I ask.

"Dress like what?" he says, looking down at himself. "This is the way I dress."

"Are you working for the Chair?" I ask.

"Pardon?"

"Schwartz, the Chair of the department, just tried to get me to take an envelope of money from him."

"And what did you do?"

"What do you think I did?" I ask. "I told him to go fuck himself."

"I'm interested in your brother," he says.

"Drumming up business?"

"Exploring the Jewish relationship to crime. With the exception of gambling, Jews aren't much engaged in criminal activity." He gives me an amused look, like he's stumbled on a treasure chest of goodies and is trying desperately not to show how excited he is.

"How did you decide to become a rabbi?"

"I didn't decide," he says. "In my family we are all rabbis. My father is a rabbi, my uncle is a rabbi. My sister is a car mechanic; she felt to be a woman rabbi had too many restrictions."

"My brother, George, had a bar mitzvah because he wanted the savings bonds, the clock radio from my aunt, the Cross pen from the temple Sisterhood, and a free trip to Florida from my grandparents. He got lucky down there, met some girl who gave him his first, um, oral experience. His affinity has nothing to do with God and everything to do with sex."

"I want to study him," the rabbinical student says, and then corrects himself. "I am studying him, but I want to study up closer."

"What is your premise?" I ask. "Jews gone bad?"

"May I sit in on your class?" he asks, not even acknowledging my question.

"No," I say quickly.

There is silence.

"Jews don't kill their wives," he says.

"Are you talking with anyone else?" I ask.

"Lefkowitz," he says.

"The Ponzi who stuffed Rolexes and his wife's jewelry up his dog's ass and then took the pup for a walk while under house arrest? The dog would crap, and then some shmo would come along and pick up the poop. He cleaned the watches, sold them, kept fifty percent of the profits. The feds used to call him Shitty Fingers."

"That's the guy," the student says.

"Who else?"

"Hernandez and Kwon."

"They're both converts," I say. The rabbinical student is surprised that I've heard of them, but why wouldn't I? I am after all in the business of knowing about things.

He pauses. "Can I ask you, what is your relationship to God?"

"Limited," I say. "Limited with the exception of spontaneous prayer in times of acute distress."

"I'd like to learn more about your family."

"I'm a very private person," I say. "My brother and I, we're not the same person. Different sides of the coin."

"But you have much in common. What do you do when you get angry?"

"I don't get angry," I say. "Mostly I don't have any feelings." I check my watch. "We're going to have to stop for now," I say. "I have to prepare for class."

"I'd like to see you again," he says.

"During office hours, my door is open."

"Next week?" he says.

"Sure," I say. "If you feel compelled. May I ask your name?"

"Ryan," he says.

"Interesting," I say. "I never met a Jew named Ryan."

"We are few and far between," he says, leaving. "See you next week."

My office shelves are filled with Nixonalia; I purposely packed the place with fat historical volumes, wanting the students to see my office as a historical repository. I also have some rare political posters—McGovern/Eagleton, Humphrey, Geraldine Ferraro. I carefully take things down and roll them up. Apart from Nixon, my second favorite is LBJ. I think it has to do with when I came to political consciousness, when I realized there was a world outside my parents' living room.

En route to class, I take the boxes to the car; the envelope is on the front seat. The door is locked but I see it right there, on the seat. Did Schwartz plant it? Am I being set up? I take the envelope and try to put it back in Schwartz's car; the doors are locked. I try stuffing it through the top of the window; I get the edge of the envelope in, but the fatter part (the bills) won't go in. I hurry back up to the office. Schwartz's door is closed; the department secretary is gone. Shit! I put the envelope back on the seat of my car, relock the door, and hurry to class. I don't want it with me. I don't want a confrontation in the classroom.

"Good afternoon," I say as I enter. The room is only a third full. I give them a few minutes' grace period and then begin with a series of announcements about exams, last dates to make changes with the registrar. "As you know, your assignment was to write a paper, which is due today. Would you please pass those forward?" I wait as twelve papers are passed forward. "I'm wondering when I might hear from the rest of you?" No one says a word. I glance down; the paper on top is titled "Richard Nixon as Villain: A Story in Pictures." I flip through. The student has made a comic book in lieu of writing a paper; I should be annoyed but I find the idea promising. His drawings are distortions of Nixon, Haldeman, and Kissinger with exaggerated features, an elaboration on "See no evil, hear no evil, speak no evil." There is intentional blurring, such as "Let me be perfectly clear."

My eye is throbbing. I feel it starting to close, and the other narrowing to a thin slit as though in sympathy. "Okay, so where are we?"

"Watergate," someone says.

"Very good. And what do we know about Watergate?"

"It was the first of the 'gates,'" one of the students says. And a few others laugh.

A student's phone rings. It rings and rings while she digs through her bag—everyone watches. She answers: "Hello." I stare, amazed that she actually answered her phone during class.

"Who is it?" I ask.

"My mother," she whispers loudly.

"Pass the phone forward," I instruct, and the phone comes to the front of the room. "Hello," I say.

"Who is this?" the mother asks.

"This is Professor Silver. And who am I speaking with?"

"Malina Garcia."

"How many children do you have, Mrs. Garcia?"

"Four."

"That's lovely," I say. "You must be so proud; but right now we're in the middle of class."

"Oh," she says. "Is it yoga? My daughters love yoga."

"No, Mrs. Garcia, it's not yoga. Does the name Richard Nixon ring a bell?"

"Yes," she says, "the president who died of the forgetting disease. Such a shame, a beautiful man."

In the classroom, her daughter blushes.

"Yes, Mrs. Garcia, he was a beautiful man. It was a pleasure talking with you. Your daughter's paper was due today. Did she mention that to you?"

"No, I don't think so."

"Any idea what she might be writing about?"

"Not really."

"Does she typically discuss her schoolwork with you?"

"Not so much; mostly we talk about the family and her friends and things like that."

"Thank you, Mrs. Garcia," I say, hanging up and passing the phone back to the girl. "Anyone else have a call they'd like me to make?" There is no response. "Isn't it interesting that during Nixon's time there were no cell phones, no texting, no BlackBerrys. Imagine how things might have unfolded differently if Nixon had been more of a future-forward president, instead of running an old-fashioned tape recorder with big bulky buttons that could get confusing—so that his secretary could accidentally push the wrong one and then, while answering the phone, put her foot on the remote pedal and erase all the good stuff."

The class stares at me, blankly.

"Okay, well, let's get back to it. Where were we . . . ? Can one of you refresh us about what Watergate was?"

A single hand goes up. " 'Gate' is a suffix applied to a word to modify that word into a scandal, as in 'Watergate,' which was also named as such because it took place at a complex in Washington known as the Watergate. But in the years since then, any big blowup is called Whatevergate. So in fact it was the first of the 'gates.' "

"Interesting, and thank you. Do I have your paper?"

"Yes, you do," he says. "I am here from far away, and I must have very good grade in order to stay in this country. My family will cut my head off if I do not do well."

The class laughs. "You mean your family will cut you off if you do not do well."

"I mean what I say," the student says.

"I will take you at your word," I say, and carry on, quoting from Nixon's memoirs:

> *The factual truth [about Watergate] could probably never be completely reconstructed, because each of us had become involved in different ways and no one's knowledge at any given time exactly duplicated anyone else's.*

I explain that at the time the scandal unfolded it was the most public example of political dirty tricks in American history and prompted the only resignation of a United States president and the indictment of the Watergate Seven (with Nixon named as co-conspirator—again a historical first). John Mitchell, H. R. Haldeman, John Ehrlichman, and Charles Colson all served time; Gordon C. Strachan, Robert Mardian, and Kenneth Parkinson were never jailed. Among the others who served time related to Watergate were John Dean, E. Howard Hunt, G. Gordon Liddy, James McCord, Fred LaRue. . . . As is my habit, I digress, laying out the evolution of Nixon's Special Investigations Unit, dubbed "the Plumbers." Their first job was to break into the office of Daniel Ellsberg's psychiatrist and get the scoop on the former RAND employee who felt it his civic duty to leak the Pentagon Papers. Nixon felt this leak was a "conspiracy" against his administration and wanted to discredit Ellsberg. He ordered his Plumbers to get everything they could find out to the media and "try him in the press . . . leak it out." The attempted burglary is a comedy of errors: the burglars wait until the cleaning lady leaves, then find the door locked and have to break through a window. There are three burglars, Bernard Baker, Felipe de Diego, and Eugenio Martinez, and two lookouts, E. Howard Hunt and G. Gordon Liddy. Oddly enough, several of these "Plumbers" are CIA and ex-CIA and can be traced back to the Bay of Pigs and forward to Watergate. . . .

My eye is killing me; after class I go to the Student Health Center. They have an actual eyewash station built right into the sink. The "nurse" on duty, who turns on the faucets, makes a point of saying, "Just so you know, I'm not really a nurse, I'm a health aide; they cut the nurse a couple of years ago, during a budget crunch; there is no nurse . . ." and then asks, "Are you sure you didn't get some kind of chemical in there that might have burned your cornea?"

"It was just dirt," I say, thinking, for all I know, I could have gotten a chemical in there; maybe there was one of those toilet fresheners in the bathroom, maybe I waterboarded myself with fucking Ty-D-Bowl.

The not-a-nurse gives me some ointment for my eye. It's so thick everything becomes blurry. "It's a lubricant," she says, handing me the tube. "Put more in tonight, and if it's still sore tomorrow you'll have to see a doctor."

"Thank you."

Half blind, I walk to the parking lot, the voice of the Indian student calmly saying they'd cut off his head echoing in my mind. The goddamned envelope is still in my car. I sit on it and drive to Schwartz's house. His wife answers the door. I hand it to her. "This is for Schwartz," I say.

"He's not home," his wife says. "He's at a department cocktail party."

"Take it," I say, pushing the envelope slightly aggressively towards her.

"It's really not necessary," she says.

"I am returning it to him," I explain. "The envelope and its contents belong to him."

"What is it?" she asks.

"I don't know," I say. "I didn't open it, he left it in my car."

She takes the envelope. "It was very good of you to return it."

I shrug.

"What happened to your eye?"

"Spider bite," I say, without knowing why.

"Maybe take something for it," she suggests. "It doesn't look good."

"Will do," I say, turning to leave.

"I look forward to reading your book," she calls after me. "My husband speaks of it often."

Without stopping or turning back, I say goodbye: "Goodbye and good luck."

As I'm cooking, the phone rings, I grab it, thinking it's her—Julie Nixon Eisenhower.

"Hi," Nate says. "I tried you earlier and you weren't home."

"Teaching day," I say.

"Might want to change that outgoing message," Nate says, his voice tight. "It's still Mom."

I haven't been able to bring myself to change it—I can't erase Jane, but I can imagine how hard it is for him to hear.

"I'll get a new machine tomorrow," I say, though I've secretly liked hearing Jane's occasional "Hello, we're not home right now. . . ."

"I keep thinking about the boy from the car accident," he says. "We have to take care of the boy."

"I know you're concerned about him," I say. "I'll talk with your father's lawyer about what's being done."

Meanwhile, as glad as I am to hear his voice, I'm also wondering, does George have call waiting? What if Julie Nixon Eisenhower phones and gets a busy signal? As he's talking, I simply blurt, "Does this phone have call waiting?"

"Why?" Nate asks. "Are you beeping?"

"I'm not sure," I say.

"Well, there's beeping that's call waiting, and then there's beeping if someone is recording the call."

"Are you recording the call?" I ask.

"No," he says, "I know about it because we studied wiretaps in my Twentieth-Century Political Scandal course—it's a history elective. If you want to tape a call you must first ask permission, record the granting of permission, and acknowledge that the call is being taped."

"Interesting. In what context did that come up?"

"We were studying Watergate. I wrote a paper on Aunt Rose."

"Who?"

"Rose Mary Woods, she was Nixon's secretary."

"Of course," I say, proudly. "You do know that Nixon is my area."

"I know," Nate says. "The Nixon children called her 'Aunt Rose.' She was fiercely loyal," Nate says. "I'm very interested in loyalty, even if the person to whom one is loyal is flawed, criminal, or otherwise in the wrong. I'm also studying the evolution of the Dictabelt, which came out in 1947, preceded by the Ediphone, and followed, of course, by the reel-to-reel, and on and on to some pretty fantastic items, including the eight-track tape, which my father still has—he kept his copy of *Iron Butterfly Live*—it's red, and he keeps it in his sock drawer. . . ." Nate stops himself, having perhaps revealed more than he intended to. "How's Tessie?"

"Good, except she has diarrhea. She got into the garbage."

"She loves garbage," Nate says. "Well, I better go, lots more homework to do."

"All right," I say. "I'll ask about the boy, but my bet is there's nothing we can do before the trial—it would seem like we were trying to influence the outcome."

"I hadn't thought of that," Nate says. "I was just thinking about the boy."

The next morning, bright and early—the phone rings.

"Sorry it took so long, busy day here," Julie Nixon Eisenhower says.

"I saw your father once at a distance," I blurt, so excited that I start sweating. "I was in junior high, and they took the class to Washington. We went to the White House; your dad was welcoming a foreign dignitary—I saw him far across the lawn. And then we went to the Smithsonian, we saw Foucault's Pendulum and the flag made for Fort Henry by Mary Young Pickersgill, that's the flag that Francis Scott Key spotted and which prompted him to write 'The Star-Spangled Banner.' We went to the U.S. Mint, the Bureau of Engraving, and the National Archive to visit the Declaration of Independence." It's all coming back to me, spilling out of me; I didn't even remember any of this until the phone rang, and then it was like a door in some old part of my brain opened and stuff came tumbling out. "I love Washington. When I was younger, all I wanted to do was grow up and live in Washington and drive to work down Independence Avenue, past the Smithsonian, to the United States Capitol. . . ."

"My," she says when I pause for breath, "you are a true patriot."

"Thank you," I say. "It's a thrill to be speaking with you."

"I'm not sure how up-to-date you are," she says, "so forgive me if I'm telling you what you already know. As of 2007, the library became part of the federal system of presidential libraries; prior to that it was a private library housing my father's pre- and post-presidential material."

"If I remember correctly," I say, putting my foot in my mouth, "there was some family tension."

She says nothing for a moment and then goes on. "The move into the U.S. Archives and Records Administration prompted us to do some reorganizing. Long story short, we came across a few boxes, materials that had been kept apart."

"What kind of materials?"

"My sense is that they were somewhat personal to my father, writings that the rest of us aren't familiar with, previously unknown documents. What I'm trying to say is, we discovered something. . . ."

"Really?" I say, rather surprised. "Something like what?"

She pauses. The line is silent, almost dead.

"I'm listening."

"Writing that we didn't know about," she says in a clipped voice.

"Journals?"

"Perhaps. Or something else."

"Love letters?"

She says nothing.

"Memoir?"

Again silence and then, finally, "Stories," she says, "short stories."

"Like the kind of thing you'd see in *The New Yorker*?" I offer.

"Darker," she says.

"Fascinating."

"In looking for someone to work with the material, we wanted to go outside the box, away from the usual suspects, well-known scholars whose opinions with regard to my father are perhaps a bit too codified, and Cheryl thought you might be interested."

I almost ask, "Who's Cheryl?" but catch myself and cough. "I'm interested," I say, "very interested. Did you know your father wrote fiction?"

"No one knew," she says. "I'd like you to take a look, and then perhaps we can talk further. Where are you?" she asks.

"In the kitchen," I say.

She waits.

"In Westchester."

"David and I are near Philadelphia. I could arrange to have the materials available at an attorney's office in Manhattan."

"I'm available," I say. "Mondays and Wednesdays I teach, and this Friday I've got a meeting scheduled, but other than that—wide open."

"Let me see what I can arrange, and I'll call you back," she says.

"Looking forward to it," I say. I hang up so excited, it's like being given the key to a kingdom. I throw Milk Bones to Tessie and litter the floor with cat treats. I open the fridge, which remains empty and sour-smelling, and remind myself to go to the grocery store for food and something to clean the fridge.

I owe Cheryl big-time and start thinking of what I can do to thank her.

(

I can't exactly send flowers; maybe a box of steaks? What can you send that remains a secret? I could have supplies sent to Nateville. "In your honor a hundred, make it two hundred, jars of fortified peanut butter for starving children have been sent to Nateville, South Africa." Maybe I should buy her spa certificates—women love having their feet rubbed without the football game on in the background.

Meanwhile, I go back to the hardware store, hoping that I might run into the woman who needed new batteries again, and buy a new answering machine for the house. "I love this hardware store, it has everything you need and even things you didn't realize that you need," I announce to the old guy at the cash register, who looks at me blankly.

I put the old answering machine in Jane's closet and set up the new one—I let it speak for itself with a mechanical voice, "Hel-lo we are un-able to take your call, please leave a message."

In the late afternoon, the phone rings; I let the machine pick up as a test. It's Ashley, in tears. "Is this my house? Did I call the wrong number? I need Mom," she sobs.

"What happened?" I say, picking up. The machine automatically turns off.

"I just need my mom," she says.

"Tell me."

She sniffles. "I need to talk to Mom."

"I know, but she's not here," I say as tactfully as possible. "What happened?"

"I'm going through some, um, changes, and I need her advice."

"Changes?"

"You know, like, growing up."

"Did you get your period?"

She sniffles and doesn't say anything.

"Is there a school nurse or someone there you could talk to?"

"I tried. She gave me a big biology lecture and some pads and Tampax and said if I was religious I should discuss with my priest before using them, and then said, 'Actually, I take that back—use whatever you feel most comfortable with.' I found it all very confusing."

"What do your friends do?"

"They talk to their moms or their older sisters." She sobs. "I don't know anything about this stuff. The only thing Mom ever told me was some story about when she was in junior high and the school nurse gave her a giant sanitary pad. She said it was like a diaper, and she put it between her legs and waddled down the hall, sure that everyone knew she had her period. She was so embarrassed, she asked to be excused from gym, took a scissors into the bathroom, cut the pad into four pieces, and used masking tape to attach it to her underwear."

"Your mom was always right out there on the cutting edge," I say, finding myself not exactly excited about the story but happy to be talking about Jane. "I tried to use the Tampax," Ashley says, bursting into tears again. "I put it in the wrong hole."

I am trying to imagine what she's talking about. I say nothing. "You know how there are two holes down there?"

"I think so," I say.

"I put it in the wrong one."

"How do you know?"

"It doesn't feel right."

"You put it in your tush?" I don't know what else to call it—I don't want to say "behind" because everything we're talking about is behind, and I don't want to say "ass" or "butt" or "bung hole" because it's all too crude when talking to an eleven-year-old.

"Yes. It hurts a lot. It was really hard to feel what was going on down there, and the first hole seemed too small, and so I kept going."

"Does it have a string?" I only know about the string because once I was trying to have sex with a girl and she said, I have my period, and I said, I don't mind, and she said, But I'm plugged—and I looked confused. Pull the string, she said, and I did, and out popped a clotted wad of cotton and blood, and, thinking I was going to drop it on the floor, I kind of let go and sent it flying harder than I thought—it slapped against the wall, slid down, and landed at the molding, leaving a bloody trail.

"It had a string," Ashley says.

"Can you get a mirror and take a look?"

I feel like someone trying to land a plane who's only ever ridden on one.

"It's so gross down there," she says.

"I'll stay on the phone with you," I say. "Where are you now?"

"In my room."

"Do you have phones in the room?"

"No, I talked someone into loaning me her secret cell, we're not allowed to have them."

"Turn on the radio so no one can overhear you," I suggest.

She turns on some music in the background.

"Okay, now take a look with the mirror and tell me what you see," I say, thinking I could get arrested for this.

"I don't know."

"Can you put your finger in the place where you think you put the Tampax in—can you feel it in there?"

"I can feel it, but I can't reach it."

"Which hole is it in?"

"The back hole," she says.

"The farthest-back hole?"

"Yes," she says, exasperated and embarrassed.

"It's okay, I'm sure it's happened to lots of other people. You can't be the only person who's made this mistake. Are you sitting or standing?"

"I'm just standing here."

"Okay, well, squat down. Can you feel it now?"

"Yes, but I still can't grab it," she says, her frustration evident.

"We're going to get it," I say. "Don't worry. So, while you're squatting down, I want you to push, like you're trying really hard to go to the bathroom, and see if you can get it out at the same time as you're pushing."

"Oh my God, that's so gross," she says. And the phone drops.

"What happened? Did you get it?"

"I pooped on the floor," she says. "It's disgusting."

"Did you get the Tampax?"

"Yes," she says. "Oh God, how am I going to clean this up?"

"Pretend it's a Tessie poop; use a plastic bag and carry it down the hall to the bathroom."

"I gotta go," she says, hanging up.

I am left shaken, but, oddly, I feel like a rock star, like I am a NASA engineer having given the directions that saved the space lab from an uncertain end.

In the evening, when the phone rings again, I answer ahead of the machine.

"It's Julie," she says, reminding me of another Julie, Amtrak Julie: "Hi, I'm Julie, Amtrak's automated agent. Let's see if I can help you. Are you calling about a reservation? I think you said that you'd like to speak with someone; one moment and I'll connect you."

"Are you there?" she asks. "Can you hear me okay? I'm on a mobile."

"Loud and clear," I say.

"Good. I've arranged for you to view the materials. Thursday at ten a.m. at the firm of Herzog, Henderson and March." She gives me the address and closes by saying, "Ask for Wanda, she'll take care of you."

"Is there anything in particular you want me to be looking at or looking for?"

"I'm sure you have questions, but at this point the less said the better. Take a good look, and then we'll talk further. And just so we're clear, this is not an invitation for ongoing access, it's a first step; if it goes well, we'll take it from there." She pauses. "By the way, do you know anyone at Random House?"

"No one comes to mind," I say.

"At one point an editor named Joe Fox asked my father if he had an interest in writing fiction. Does that name ring a bell?"

"He's gone on," I say.

"To another company?"

"Dead, collapsed at his desk," I say, wondering how it is I know this. "He was Truman Capote's editor."

"That explains it," she says. "My father kept the letter but jotted 'Never in a million' in the margin. He hated Capote, loathed him, said he was among the worst of them."

"Them?"

"Homosexuals. Daddy did not like homosexuals." She pauses. "Thursday at ten, Wanda will show you the way."

"Thank you," I say. "I am intrigued."

"As it should be," she says.

At 6 a.m. on Thursday morning, I am showered, wearing one of George's suits fresh from the dry-cleaning bag, and online looking up "cheapparking .com" to find an inexpensive garage near the law office. I pack one of George's old briefcases with legal pads and pens and set off.

I park half a block from Claire's office; did I not know that, or did I know and choose to forget? The streets are teeming with well-dressed men and women. I feel like an out-of-towner, like everything about me is all wrong.

Overcome with déjà vu, I know that I have been here before, under other circumstances; it is as though I now live in an alternate reality and I can't help but worry there might have been more damage from the stroke than I realized.

My excitement turns to anger.

In the lobby of the building a guard asks me for my identification. I put my hand in my pocket: I find two twenties and a fifty rolled together—funny money—and realize that when I put on George's suit I forgot to "repack" my pockets. Anxious, I begin to sweat; I confess to the guard that I have no identification.

He throws me a bone, offering to phone upstairs and ask Wanda to come down and collect me.

Wanda is tall, black, efficient. She handles me like I am a specimen—the confused professor.

"Apologies for making you come all the way down," I say in the elevator.

"Not a problem," she says as the elevator door opens on the twenty-seventh floor. "The firm is located on this floor and the one above."

The firm is silent; telephones don't ring, they blink, and people glide soundlessly across the carpet. The only noise is the shussshing of their clothing. Wanda leads me down a corridor, unlocks a door, and ushers me into a conference room filled with innocuous, if expensive, furniture. In the middle of the table sits something that looks like a UFO, a telephone pod for conference calls. On the far end of the table are two battered cardboard boxes with "R.M.N." written in block letters on the side. My heart races.

"You'll have to leave your backpack with me," Wanda says.

"My backpack?"

"Your bag." She points to what I am carrying in my right hand.

"George's briefcase?"

"Yes."

"It's for taking notes"—I pat the briefcase—"paper and pens."

"No outside materials," she says. "We have supplies"—pointing to legal pads and pencils on the table. "And, please, no quoting more than seven words in a sequence."

I nod and hand her my briefcase. She hands me a three-page confidentiality agreement. I sign the document without reading it.

"How much time have I got?" I ask.

"I'm here until five."

"Thanks."

She moves to leave and turns back. "You're under constant surveillance; that means no funny business."

"Am I allowed to unpack the boxes?"

"Yes," she says.

"And handle the material?"

"There are gloves on the table. You're not allergic to latex, are you?"

"Latex is fine," I say. "Perfect."

I put the gloves on, imagining myself as a physician and RMN as my patient. With enormous excitement, I open the old box. The sight of Nixon's handwriting makes me blush. My cheeks are warm, my palms sweating inside the gloves. I'm glad to be alone, because, frankly, I'm a little overexcited, like a twelve-year-old with his first girlie magazine.

I am touching the paper that he touched—this is not a reproduction, this is 100 percent real. The legal pads are embossed with Nixon's rich blue cursive, with cross-outs and fresh starts, numbers, underlines—often a page has several headings, things numbered 1, 2, 3, 4.

He quite literally breathed on these pages; these are his thoughts, his ideas. "Eat less salt. Try pepper instead" is scribbled in the margins. "Or cinnamon. I hate cinnamon," he writes in response to himself. "It's like dirt."

Holding these well-used legal pads, I am overwhelmed with pleasure. I hear Julie's voice in my head, "Take a look, and then we can talk." I think of Julie marrying David Eisenhower, grandson of the general and former President, in December 1968, only weeks after Nixon won the presidency, the ceremony officiated by none other than the Reverend Norman Vincent Peale—Mr. Power of Positive Thinking.

Pondering the high hopes, the promise, the great aspiration of RMN, I start thinking of myself. I trip over a psychic speed bump, tumble down, and am deep into my own family history. The irony is that, though my parents expected George and me to grow up and be president, they didn't believe we were actually even capable of crossing the street on our own. It was the mixed message, simultaneous extremes of expectation and reminders that we weren't worth crap, that in retrospect seems abusive. I am sure it was "unintentional" and was born from their own deprivation and the sense that we should be lucky for anything we got. I always had the feeling that my family was some-how "defective" and that it was those well-matched flaws—the ability to love and loathe all at once—that kept my parents together. Basically, they were lousy with bitterness. We were supposed to become president ruling from the children's table while never daring to dream of going beyond where our parents had been; never transcending.

My heart sinks—here I am with these legal pads, the literal hand of my subject in mine, and I'm losing time, digressing.

I begin again, staying focused on Nixon and his contemporaries and a period of enormous change in this country—the bridge between our prewar Depression-era culture and the postwar prosperous-American-dream America.

FROM R.M.N. BOX 345 LEGAL PAD #4 NOTES MARKED; GOOD AMERICAN PEOPLE.

Wilson Grady is a man alone. Each morning Grady wakes with pride swelling in the center of his chest—he is filled with possibility, the hope that each day will be better than the last. He is a lucky fella, a fella of good fortune, crossing the plains, mile for mile, trailing a cloud of dust, his holey muffler so loud people think it's a crop duster flying low. He sees folks in the distance looking on as he's coming in—he jokes about it when he gets out of the car. "No surprises here," he says. "She may be loud, but she's what got me to you folks and I'm countin' on her to get me back home at the end of the week."

The lady of the house steps off the front porch and comes towards him—a woman home alone will never invite him in—that's understood.

"Wilson Grady," he says, extending his hand. "Thank you in advance for your time."

If she likes him at all, she'll offer him a cup of coffee.

"That would be nice," he says, whether or not he had another cup two miles down the road.

"How do you take it?" she asks and then before he can answer she adds, "We're low on milk."

"Black with sugar would be fine."

He waits while she goes back inside. You can tell a lot about folks from their porch—Is it painted? Are there chairs, flowers? Curtains in the windows? Crocheted doilies under the lamps in the parlor? He has made himself a kind of a mental checklist.

The coffee is hot—the thick ceramic cup nearly burning Grady's hands.

"You mentioned your children; how old are they?"

"*William, the oldest, is eleven, Robert is nine, Caroline is eight, and Raymond is six.*"

"*One of the things I've got with me is an encyclopedia set, packed full of information, history, maps, things each and every one of us should know.*" He leads the woman towards his car—carefully opening the trunk, which is outfitted like a traveling five-and-dime. "*What I can tell you about these books is that every night when I have my supper I myself sit down with another letter of the alphabet—there is so much to learn. I'm on the letter 'H' right now—and getting a good education.*"

"*How much is it?*"

"*I'll be honest with you,*" he says. "*It's not cheap. The 26 letters of the alphabet are combined into 13 volumes and it comes along with an atlas of the world. Makes a heck of a Christmas gift and it's something all the kids can use—even the little fella will be reading soon.*"

"*Do you have children, mister?*"

"*Not yet—but someday. I've got my eye on the girl I want to marry, she just doesn't know it yet.*"

The woman smiles.

"*I could let you have the full set for forty dollars.*"

She nods. "*That's quite a lot.*"

"*It is,*" he says. "*It's an investment, a lifetime of knowledge.*"

"*Do you by chance have an iron?*"

"*I do*"—*taking a moment to find it.* "*Steam electric,*" he says, carefully taking it out of the box to show her. "*I got one of these for my mother and she says it does a beautiful job.*"

"*How much does that go for?*"

"*Six dollars and forty-nine cents.*"

"*And what about penny candy?*" she asks shyly.

He laughs. "*Don't think you're the first person this week who's asked—I have peppermint balls, lemon drops, red and black licorice, and, if you're looking for something fancy, I've got a couple of boxes of See's chocolates.*"

"*I had one of those once,*" she says, "*it was heaven on earth.*"

"*Chocolatiers to the stars,*" he says.

She laughs and reaches into her dress pocket. "*How about I take the iron and fifty cents' worth of candy.*"

Grady works door to door 9 a.m. to 5 p.m. If the husband is home, Grady makes it a point to seem interested in whatever it is the fella wants to show him—it's always something—a project he's got going in the barn out back or in his basement workshop. Grady finds it sad—all the fellas want is a pat on the back and someone to tell them they're doing fine. He listens, lets the man go on longer than he ought to, and then, before starting his pitch, he sobers the fella up with the story of how he never saw his father in a suit until the day he died. And then he goes for the sale—anything less than fifty bucks he considers a failure. It's a success if he can get them to buy the encyclopedia for the kids and a box of candy for the wife—and near the holidays he also keeps a supply of toy trucks with working headlights, and dolls whose eyes open and close for the girls.

For Wilson Grady, a good day ends in a diner. With the exception of his mother's pies, he's had the best meals of his life tucked into a window booth under the glow of the neon sign and with a letter from his encyclopedia as good company.

"I'll start with a cup of the chowder and then I'll have the special."

His plate, with two thick slices of meat loaf, well-cooked green beans, a warm biscuit, and a scoop of mashed potatoes mounded like hills with a well of brown gravy in the center, is so perfect it almost makes him cry—he loves America.

At night a wind sweeps across and the temperature drops down. Even though it's been a good day, Wilson Grady is achingly cold. He keeps a couple of old wool blankets in the car, along with a pillow that belonged to his brother as a young boy. He parks on a side street and hunkers down for the night—most of the time no one notices him, and if they do he apologizes and drives off into the night, thinking of the waitress with her apron tied neatly around her waist like a chastity belt, as he vanishes down a darkened road.

I finish and I'm almost in tears—it's a side of Nixon that I've never seen before but always suspected existed beneath the surface. There's a humanity, a desperation to this Nixon, which is early Nixon, not presidential Nixon, but Nixon as he knows himself. This Nixon is a man with burgeoning ambition, an idealized, if clichéd, everyman, crisscrossing the country laying the groundwork for the great moment to come. Wilson Grady is a man who wants something but doesn't quite know how to get it.

I find a short p̶…
tion to it is how Nixo…
across the top two inches of the …
a vignette of a man being attacked b̶y̶
arrives late, having been delayed by train tr̶…
soaked. His socks are wet. He comes into his office, t̶a̶…
off and lays them on the radiator, puts his damp leather b̶r̶… —
noticing that it actually smells like a barnyard—takes out his i̶m̶…nt
papers, and sits in his chair, which promptly spins him in endless circles before
tipping him forward onto the floor. He remounts the chair and leans forward
to turn on the desk lamp, which delivers a surprising shock. He then picks up
his ink pen, which leaks all over his fingers, and then, finally, in a rage, as he's
looking for a handkerchief to clean himself, he slams the pencil drawer shut,
pinching his fingers.

> *"Christ."*
> *"What the hell?"*
> *"Damn it."*
> *"Son of a bitch."*
> *"Cocksucker."*

From there I find another story; scrawled across the top in parentheses is a
note, "no names, because I actually once had a drink with this fella."

An Apartment on the Avenue
  Arthur comes home late, having had one or two more than is good for
him. He finds his wife in the bedroom, undressing; he watches her thinking
she still looks good, sexy, he'd be in the mood for getting frisky, but as soon
as she speaks, his hopes . . .

...uy you were standing there that

...ning."

...wanna know what it is, Blanche? The truth of it all . . . I never loved you—I married you because I thought it would be good for me."

"I already know that, Arthur."

"And if I didn't think it would cost me in more ways than one, I would have been out of here long ago."

"You're not the only one who feels that way," she says.

"When was the last time you wanted me?" he says. "In the way that a woman should want her man."

"I've never liked sex, you know that," she says, looking at him in the mirror of her dressing table.

"Exactly," he says, talking to her reflection. "But imagine how that makes a fella feel? The thing is, I like it and it would be nice to do it once in a while with someone who didn't think it was disgusting."

"It is my understanding that you certainly have found places to 'do it.'"

"It always comes back to that, doesn't it?"

"Doesn't it?" she says. "Well, Arthur, when you talk about things that could hurt you, having relations with your boss's secretary can't be good for you, can it?"

"Men don't see it the same as women," he says.

"I'm sure," she says.

He comes close to her, close to the dressing table where she's sitting, putting cream on her face.

"Put some on me," he says, almost begging for it. She's not interested.

"You know how to take care of yourself," she says, getting up and walking away.

He reaches out to pull her towards him, but everything goes wrong, and his hand connects with her face, like he's taking a swing at her. It's not the first time something like this has happened.

She has no reaction, she just takes it, and somehow it's the lack of a reaction, the absence of anything human, that prompts him to do it again—this time with clear intention. Fingers rolled into a fist, he lays one on her, hitting her cheek.

She doesn't fall; she stands there, barely swaying. "Are we done for the
night?" she says and then spits—a single tooth lands on the carpet.

With nothing left to say, he goes down the hall, takes the blanket they
used to use for summer picnics in the park out of the closet, and sets himself
up on the sofa. Alone among the side tables, lamps, and wing chair, he sobs.
Heavy tears like marbles running down his face as he talks out loud to
himself, in a rambling incantation that stops only when he plugs his mouth
with his thumb—sucking until sleep comes.

At noon, Wanda comes into the conference room, puncturing the reverie.
"Time for lunch," she says.

"That's okay," I say, "I'll work straight through."

"We break for lunch," Wanda says. And I look at her. "There's no one available to monitor you, so you need to come out for an hour. You may leave your
materials as they are; we'll lock the room."

I ride down in the elevator with Wanda. As we're getting out, I glance at
her; she looks at me, concerned. "Do you need money for lunch?" she asks.

"Oh no," I say. "I've got plenty of money, just no identification. Not to
worry. Is there someplace you'd recommend?"

"There's a salad bar in the deli across the street, and restaurants up and
down," she says, relieved.

I walk out of the building and into the light, realize Claire could be out
there, and furtively duck into the deli, where I slip into the rotation of people
walking in slow circles around the salad bar, vaguely mumbling like they're
meditating. There's chopped lettuce, cherry tomatoes, hard-boiled eggs, steamy
trays of meat in mysterious sauce, brilliant orange macaroni and cheese.

I think of Nixon's short story about the diner and find myself putting meat
loaf and mashed potatoes into my container, and then a large scoop of hot,
heavy macaroni that softens the Styrofoam. I pay and go to the back of the
deli, where I see a few guys sitting on empty plastic pickle barrels. "Mind if I
join?" I ask, and they simply look at me and go back to eating. The food is
delicious—beyond delicious, it is divine, a mélange of flavors like nothing I've
ever had before.

"You look busy," the Chinese woman from the deli says to me while I'm
perched on the pickle barrel.

"I've had a very big day," I say.

"You go to work, you win, win, win."

I nod. She brings me a cup of tea.

"Do you know Richard Nixon?" I ask.

"Of course," she says. "Without Nixon I'd be nowhere."

"I'm working on Nixon."

"Pick something," she says. "Before you go, you pick for yourself for later."

"That's okay," I say, not sure what she wants me to do.

She slaps a Hershey bar into my hand. "You like with almond?"

"This is great," I say, looking down—almond.

"You do good work," she says, nodding. "I know you from before, long time ago, you buy cookies for your wife."

I'm confused.

"You don't remember?" she asks, holding up a box of cookies. LU Petit Écolier. "You buy these."

"Yes," I say. "That's right, I did. I used to buy those for Claire."

"Of course you did," she says.

"Was that here?"

"One block down," she says. "We move, this much better location, big building right on top, big bankers, crunching numbers, need something to chew on."

"I'm surprised that you remembered me."

"I never forget," she says, and then pauses. "I sorry for your life. I see you in the newspaper—one big mess."

"It's more my brother than me."

"It's you too," she says. "You are your brother."

"I'm okay," I say. "Things are looking up."

"See you later, alligator," she says, walking me out the door.

In the lobby, after lunch, while waiting for Wanda, I peel open the chocolate bar and take a bite. I am amazed that the deli lady remembered me. It's so strange that she knew who I was. She knew me and Claire and all about my brother. She felt sorry for me and gave me a chocolate bar. No one just gives anyone anything anymore. I take another bite, no longer worried what my suit looks like or that Claire is "out there" somewhere in her tight work skirt, her heels a little too high to be respectable. In the lobby I watch people come and go, thinking of Nixon, a man of his own time, wondering what he would make of the new technology for spying, for gathering information. I'm wondering if he'd still write longhand, wondering if he'd be surfing porn sites on his iPad while kicking back in that beloved brown velvet chaise longue in his secret Executive Office Building retreat, wondering what he'd think of all the women in power these days. After all, he was the one who said he didn't think women should be in any government job—he thought of them as erratic and emotional.

The afternoon is spent reading multiple drafts of a chillingly grim novella, *Of Brotherly Love,* set in a small California town, in which a failed lemon-farmer and his wife conspire to murder their three sons, convinced that the Lord has bigger plans for them in the next world. After the youngest son dies, the middle boy catches on and tries to tell his older brother, who treats him as though he's gone insane—violated the very word of God. When the middle boy comes home at the end of that day and his parents tell him that the oldest boy has gone to the Lord, the boy becomes terrified. Fearing for his life, he collapses and tells his parents that there must be a reason that the Lord, having taken two of his brothers thus far, has spared him. The Lord must have a plan for him. The parents, grief-stricken, nod and urge him to go up to bed. He says his prayers, then feigns sleep. He rises after midnight and slays first his father and then his mother, all the while fearing the hand of God. He murders his parents, then sets the house and barn afire and rides off in the family car, hoping to get across the border before the authorities find him.

The story is filled with paranoia, questions of faith, and the fear that the parents didn't take good enough care of the children, that God himself was not pleased. The expectation is that the surviving brother should do something more, something heroic—he is obligated to make up for their loss.

I read these incomplete fragments as Nixon's attempt to process the early death of his two brothers, Arthur and Harold, and his own crisis of faith. Despite the unnerving morning, the afternoon brings a new comfort level. I ask for the key to the men's room and am given a programmed card, like a hotel-room key, and told that it will expire in ten minutes. The bathrooms are deluxe; the urinal is filled with ice—which snaps, crackles, pops as my stream hits it. They say it keeps bathrooms cleaner if men have something to aim for. The card gives me the excuse to walk the halls, wondering how the Nixon documents found their way here. What is the "firm's" relationship with the Nixon family? Someone knows someone who knows someone; it's all about who you know, who you went to school with, who you grew up with in the backyard. After a couple of laps around the firm, I go back into the conference room. Moments later I sneeze, and a young man appears with a box of Kleenex.

"Thank you," I say, reminded that I am being watched.

At four-thirty Wanda appears. "Thirty minutes until closing," she says. And at four-fifty, "Ten minutes." At four-fifty-five, I put my pencil down. Wanda appears, and I show her the few pages of pencil notes I've scratched out on their legal pads.

"Do you think you'll be returning?" she asks.

"I hope so, it's a very exciting discovery, I barely made a dent."

"I'll let Mrs. Eisenhower know you were pleased."

"Thank you. And thank you for your help as well. Have a good evening." She smiles.

I drive home loving Nixon all the more, marveling at his range, his subtlety, his facility with describing human behavior. I stop to pick up Chinese food, go home, set myself up at the dining-room table, and tell Tessie everything. I'm talking to the dog, spooning hot-and-sour soup into my mouth, and simultaneously writing as fast and furiously as I can. I'm transcribing everything I can remember, marveling at the nuance of Nixon's thinking, the depth of character, the humor, so dark, so wry, revealing a much greater self-awareness than most would imagine Nixon capable of. I'm thinking about how these stories will redefine Nixon, alter the shape of scholarship—my book in particular. I write nonstop for an hour and a half, then remember the confidentiality agreement and tell myself that whatever I write now is just for me, a first draft, initial impressions. As I go deeper, I find myself wanting to describe the characters, the text in detail. I feel silenced, screwed, used, baited, and start plotting a way around it. If the family denies that the materials exist, if they've not been catalogued, it's going to be hard to prove, hard to get anywhere. I am hoping the Nixons are reasonable people. I am hoping that they are willing to let him be known as he was, in his glory and his complexity. I am wondering what the next step is; do I have Julie's phone number? I go back through caller ID. Be patient, I tell myself, let events take their natural course. The phone rings. "Good evening, is this Mr. Silver?"

"Perhaps. Who may I ask is calling?"

"Geoffrey Ordy Jr., from Wurlitzer, Pulitzer and Ordy."

"Which Mr. Silver are you calling for?"

"How do you mean?"

"George or Harold?"

"Given where things stand, I'm assuming George is unavailable at the moment," the guy says, annoyed.

"Correct."

"I'm sorry to phone so late."

"Not a problem. I was out all day," I say.

"I'll cut to the chase. There's a hearing tomorrow at eleven a.m. in White Plains in regard to your brother's car accident—we forgot to tell you. They're bringing George down for it, first public appearance. The press will be all over it."

"Tomorrow?"

"Like I said, someone who should have known better forgot to tell you."

"I have a lunch tomorrow, a lunch of great importance with someone I can't afford to disappoint."

"I'm just relaying the information."

"It sounds both important and something that in the greater scheme of things could be skipped—it's a first appearance, no doubt there will be others."

"Correct."

"Eleven a.m. in White Plains."

"That's the news."

"George will be there."

"Confirmed at the County Court House."

"I'll work around it. Next time a little advance warning would be appreciated."

"Noted, and good night."

That night I dream of Richard Nixon lying on the floor in a charcoal-gray suit and white shirt, his head on a tufted sofa pillow, his torso writhing from side to side as though he's trying to work out a kink. Pat is there, walking back and forth across the room, repeatedly stepping over him in a tight red dress. In the dream Nixon is trying to peek under her dress. "Stockings, no panties?" he asks, surprised. "Is that comfortable?"

"Yes," she says.

The phone is ringing.

"Listen, you son of a bitch . . ." a disembodied voice is yelling at me.

I'm terrified, thinking it's him—Richard Nixon calling me.

"You have one hell of a nerve," he says, continuing to shout as I come to consciousness. I realize it's not Nixon, it's Jane's father. "I think about you and your lousy brother and I'm disgusted."

She seduced me, I think to myself, but say nothing.

"I want you should never forget what you've done."

"I think about it constantly," I say, knowing that's of little comfort.

"We hear things are coming to a head, the ball's rolling, there's a hearing, and the proverbial ax is going to fall, and, well, we're worried about the children," he says.

"The children are at school."

"It's enough already. We think they shouldn't be a part of this."

"They're doing very well."

"We think you should take them somewhere."

"I saw Nate a couple of weekends ago, at Field Day—he's quite the athlete."

"They don't need to be exposed to the brouhaha that's going to surround this whole thing."

"And Ashley called a couple of days ago. We had a wonderful phone call—really bonding, it was like we went through something together."

"Shmuck," he says. "Are you hearing anything I'm saying? We think it would be good if the children were out of the country."

"Where?"

"You could take them to Israel."

"They don't speak Hebrew. They barely know they're Jewish."

There is silence. "Look, you giant creep," Jane's father says. "I was kidding when I said Israel."

"It was a joke? What Jew makes a joke about Israel?"

"Who sleeps with his brother's wife while his brother is in the nuthouse? I meant you should take them somewhere, get their minds off all this crap, I don't care where."

"I don't know what to say."

"Listen, asshole, I will pay you to take the children someplace."

"They're at school," I say. "But, more to the point, if you want to take them someplace, why don't you plan a little vacation and let me know the dates."

"At the moment it's all I can do to care for my wife and myself," he says. I hear him cry out, a single deep, bellowing sob, and then he hangs up.

I walk the dog; the morning sky is a rich benevolent blue, filled with promise and opportunity. It's overwhelmingly optimistic—in other words, it makes me nervous, sets the bar too high.

I dress for court and lunch in one of George's charcoal-gray suits, a white shirt, and a blue tie. Blue seems more about justice than red, which signals aggression. An impending sense of doom is gnawing at me from the inside. I dress as best I can, putting deodorant not just in my armpits but in a thick line down the center of my chest, a ring around my lower back, as far up each side as I can reach. I'm a sweater—under duress I drip raindrops of stress; I can soak a shirt in two minutes.

In White Plains, I circle the Court House; there are "No Parking Anytime" signs posted everywhere. I end up parking at the Galleria shopping mall and walking through the mall.

Like all modern courthouses, this one is a characterless fortress, testament to paper pushing, bureaucracy, and the incipient insanity of our system. Going postal is no longer reserved for those who pledge that "Neither rain nor snow nor gloom of night would deter its couriers from their appointed rounds." It's become a kind of rite of passage: disgruntled employee returns and shoots boss, disgruntled wife kills kids, disgruntled husband wrecks car, kills strangers, and then kills wife. Hard not to be surprised, when the bulk of public conversation goes like this: "Paper or plastic?" The loss of the human touch scares me.

I approach expecting a media circus, TV trucks, satellite dishes—this is America, everything is a circus. The fact that it is not a "scene," no red carpet, just business as usual, is all the more unnerving. Is it still "real" if it's not documented and delivered back to us in the media? Does anything have meaning if it's not covered? And what does it say about me that I feel these events are not legitimate without a camera crew? Inside the building, an anonymous recording plays: "Welcome, please empty your pockets into the bins provided and pass through our screening process."

Reflexively, the man ahead of me takes off his shoes.

The guard says nothing and simply ushers him through the metal detector, ignoring that he's clutching his well-worn lugs close to his chest. Looking at the heels, I see he walks on the outsides of his feet—is that pronation or supination?

My turn. I dig deep into my pocket and throw my handful into the basket; it misses, splatters, nickels and dimes hitting the floor like shattering glass and rolling this way and that.

"Sir, please step to the side."

"Is there a problem?" I ask

"Is there?" the guard repeats.

"I worry that I was too enthusiastic," I say. "I'm a little nervous. My brother is coming today."

"How exciting," he says, giving me both the wand and the pat-down. "Do you want your money back?" he asks when he's done; another guard has been walking in circles collecting my nickels, dimes, and quarters.

"Keep it," I say.

"I can't," he says. "Either you take it or it goes in the bucket." He tips his head towards an unmanned Salvation Army cauldron, like the kind Santa minds in season.

"Bucket," I say. And then, as I'm repacking my pockets, I ask. "Am I being treated specially?"

"We treat everyone specially."

I'm taking all of this far too personally, as though I'm the one who's on trial. I locate the courtroom, which I mistakenly call a classroom when asking for directions. It's half empty, with activity of a low-key preparatory sort, papers changing hands, people milling about. It's like watching stagehands getting ready for a scene. The system is a bastardized construction, vaguely English, surreal, and reeking of American culture, fast food, and an absence of style—the clerks and officers of the court are fat and poorly dressed. The room itself is ugly and not well maintained; you get the feeling no one is feeling any love for this place—it's more like a bus station than a place you'd hold in high esteem.

So there I am, expecting media, press, people fighting to get in, and instead it's a big nothing. A man with a beer belly takes notes on what we used to call a steno pad, and a woman wearing what Mother would call a shmatte is doing the same. When the case is finally called, George and his lawyer enter through a side door and take their places. I am in the third row, looking at George from the back. George turns and glances at me; he looks dull, puffy, medicated. Various formalities are run through, a kind of recap of where we are and how we got to this point. In the middle of it all, George makes a sound, like the grunt of a rhinoceros about to charge; it's disconcerting, but no one says anything. The lawyers continue. I drift in and out, perking up when I hear someone from the DA's office say, "Long story short—we're dropping the charges with respect to the fatal traffic accident." He reads from a prepared statement: "Independent investigation corroborates defense assertion of known manufacturer fault. Manufacturer is documented to have failed to notify consumers in a timely fashion. In the twelve months prior to this accident, manufacturer received numerous claims about failure, hesitation, and issues relating to the brakes, including inconsistency of brake application. Evidence obtained confirms that in fact the brakes on the defendant's car were of the same type as those found to be faulty and that the defendant at the time of the accident stated to officers on the scene that he, quote, 'tried to stop but the car kept going.' Defendant has a clean driving record, and in the end it is our belief that the accident was the fault of the vehicle and not the operator. We feel our resources are best spent pursuing the manufacturer, and to that end papers have been filed."

Am I hearing what I think I'm hearing—George is off the hook for the car accident?

"So, with regard to the accident, you're dropping all charges against Mr. Silver?" the judge asks for clarification.

"Yes, sir, we are dropping all charges related to the car accident, noting insufficient evidence to proceed."

The only people who seem surprised are George and me.

"This is ridiculous," George says loudly. "I am a guilty man, more guilty than you can possibly imagine. I want to be punished."

"I second the motion," I call loudly from the audience.

"Order in the court," the judge demands, banging his gavel. "What you want is irrelevant, Mr. Silver. This is a court of justice. Until further notice and or any change in condition or circumstance that would warrant a revisiting of the placement, Mr. Silver is to be returned to the custody of The Lodge."

George turns to face me. "Thanks for backing me up," he says, as one of the "staff"—bullies from The Lodge—leads him out of the room.

I find one of George's lawyers by the water fountain. "I'm Ordy," he says, shaking my hand, "we spoke last night."

"It's all so strange," I say. "Did you see this coming?"

"If we did, we'd be psychics, not lawyers. There are reasons people hire us: we did good investigative work on this."

"But he did it, it was his fault. I was there; I talked to him the night of the accident."

"It doesn't really matter what George said. The brakes were faulty and the manufacturer had knowledge."

"I picked him up at the jail; he was not himself that night."

"He is who he is—the fingerprints match."

"He killed his wife."

"About some things only time will tell," he says, wiping his lips with the back of his hand.

"I have no doubt," I say. "I saw it happen; he hit her on the head with a lamp."

"Is that so?" The lawyer looks at me. "Maybe it was really you—maybe you hit his wife on the head and are blaming him?"

"I don't think he ever denied doing it," I say.

"For all we know, he's trying to protect you; you are the younger brother, after all."

"Actually, I'm older."

The lawyer shrugs. "Whatever."

"Is there going to be a trial for Jane's murder—because I'd like to be here for that," I say.

"Remains to be seen," the lawyer says. "We're still negotiating."

I change my tactics. "Nate wants to do something for the boy, the surviving child."

"Who's Nate?"

"George's son?"

"And what would he like to do?"

"He's interested in adopting, or at least taking the kid out for a day."

"Because why?"

"Because why? Because he feels bad that his father killed the kid's family. Why are you asking why—isn't it obvious?"

"Obvious is meaningless. It's not up to me," the lawyer says. "The boy is living with his aunt."

"Could you give her my phone number and let her know that we'd like to do something? More than something, we'd like to do a lot."

"Are you seeking to avoid a civil suit?"

"This is about one kid who lost his family wanting to help another kid who also lost his family, but if you want to make it ugly you can," I say.

"Just asking," he says.

"How about you get me the aunt's phone number and I'll do it myself," I say.

"Whatever floats your boat," Ordy says, taking a drink from the fountain and wiping his lips on the back of his hand.

I don't have a boat.

I'm late for lunch. I arrive and tell the maître d' that I'm meeting someone. "A lady alone?" he asks.

"Yes," I say, suddenly nervous, trying to remember what Cheryl looks like. The only thing that comes to mind—a striking but odd detail which is not useful in this situation—I'm remembering that her pubic area was groomed in such a way that instead of a vertical landing strip (that is, a strip of hair running from top to bottom) she had what she called a "flight path," which was a wider patch running from side to side, and which had been dyed hot pink. Hard to forget that. I'm blushing as the maître d' leads me to a table where a woman sits alone.

"Are you you?" I ask.

"It is I," she says.

"Sorry I'm late," I say, sitting down.

"Not a problem," she says.

I look at her more closely. If I were being honest, I'd say she looks entirely unfamiliar, which prompts me to think that it's all a setup, that some guy will pop out from behind the grill and announce himself as "Stoned Pauley from peepingtoms.com." Maybe it's my obsession with media, with a camera crew, with the idea that everything has to be documented in order to be real. Whatever it is, it's making me nervous. She seems to intuit my concern.

"I changed my hair," she says.

"It looks nice," I say, with no commitment.

"I play with my hair a lot," she says. "It's a way of being expressive—you may recall the pink?"

I blush but am relieved.

"What happened to your eye?" she asks.

"Gardening accident."

"It looks like you've been crying," she says.

"Sweating, not crying. The salt water may have aggravated it."

"So—how are you?" she asks, struggling to make conversation.

"Weird," I say. "And you?"

"Were you always weird, or is it only now a thing?"

"I was in court for my brother this morning—he's in a bit of trouble and, oddly enough, today the charges were dropped."

"That's fantastic," she says, raising her water glass. "Cheers."

"He's guilty," I say, indignantly. "I was ripped off. I was counting on justice being served."

"You mentioned that you'd had a stroke?" she says, changing the subject. "How did it affect you?"

"What makes you ask? Is my face falling? That's what it did, it slipped and fell while I was watching in the bathroom mirror."

"No reason, just trying to find out more about you."

I nod.

The waiter brings some olives and bread and tells us about the specials and offers us "a moment to think."

I tell her about Nate and Field Day weekend.

"Aren't kids great?" she says, beaming. "But, look," she says, leaning forward and forgetting that Nate is not my child, "this isn't about our kids, this is about us. I've been there," she says, "the soccer mom, standing out in the warm afternoon rain with the coach whose corporate-lawyer wife just got breast cancer and he's so sad and lonely and wants a little action on the side. 'Could you just touch it, right now, right here, under my poncho? It would feel so good to have someone touch it. Come on, I've got it out, feel, it wants to do a little dance for you.'"

The way she tells it is both terrifying and a turn-on.

The waiter comes back. "Come to any conclusions?"

"No," I say, "we haven't had a chance to think."

"Should we share something?" she asks.

"Whatever you desire," I say, and she seems pleased with that.

She looks up at the waiter. "The meatball pizza with no onions, and a large salad." The waiter nods and then leaves.

"So—what happened with you? You mentioned you'd come unraveled."

"I went off my medication. I'd been on it so long I couldn't remember why I was taking it. They gave it to me for postpartum blues sixteen years ago and I stayed on it, but recently I thought it made no sense. I'm happy, I said to myself, I have all the stuff I'm supposed to have, I can do whatever I want. So I stopped taking the medication, I weaned myself off, and everything seemed good."

"And?"

"And then, a few months later, a girl I knew since nursery school dropped dead, and something shifted. Slowly, it all got away from me."

"How did it start?"

"Flirting," she says. "I would go online and send flirty little e-mails. And then I had some phone calls—very innocent, but fun. And then someone dared me to meet him in the Dunkin' Donuts parking lot—said he'd be wearing a jelly doughnut—and, well, I took him up on it." She takes a sip of her drink. "I really don't know you very well," she says.

"Why sex instead of shopping, for example?"

"Are you calling me a slut?" Her voice gets sharp.

I lean forward. "I'm trying to understand what it means to you and why you wanted to see me today."

The waiter puts the salad between us.

She throws her head back and shakes out her hair. It's the kind of move that looked good when Farrah Fawcett did it, but here it looks odd, like a health hazard. She sheds coarse blond threads into the salad.

"Ugghh," she says, plucking them out. "They say not to dye your hair more often than once every six weeks, but I can't wait that long—when I need a change I need it now." She's blinking and seems to have a lash in her eye, which is reminding me that she wore glasses when I met her for lunch at her house—she had glasses on, glasses on a string around her neck, glasses that hung down in front of her like odd breast-magnifiers tapping against her chest again and again, as if to remind her of something, as I had her from the back.

"Do you wear glasses?" I ask.

"Yes, but I broke them. I'm flying blind," she says, putting a bite of hairy salad in her mouth.

She slowly extracts the long thread and calls the waiter over. "There's hair in the salad," she says.

"How unusual," he says in a deadpan tone. "Would you like another?"

"We'll wait for the pizza," I say.

"Enough about me," she says. "Let's talk about you. So you're teaching?"

"Yes," I say, and nothing more.

"Well, I was thinking about you and couldn't remember if it was Larry Flynt, Nixon, or, for some reason, that guy George Wallace; he sticks in my head because wasn't he shot?"

"Wallace and Flynt were both shot; Wallace in 1972 while campaigning for president in Laurel, Maryland, by a guy called Arthur Bremer—whose diary prompted the film *Taxi Driver*, which prompted John Hinckley to aim for Ronald Reagan. Larry Flynt was shot in 1978 in Georgia by a sniper while he was on trial for obscenity. These days he rolls around in a gold-plated wheelchair."

"I love that you know all that," she says.

"I'm a historian," I say. "It's actually more layered than that. People wondered, was Bremer working for someone? Whose side was he on? Did Nixon succeed in planting McGovern campaign materials in Bremer's apartment—if so, was it propaganda or cover-up?" I pause and look at Cheryl. I find myself wondering: how many men did she have "lunch" with during her period of insanity, and does her husband know?

"He doesn't know," she says, as though reading my mind. "In theory, in the rules of 'recovery' I should tell him. But while I may have gone nuts, I'm not crazy—he knows I lost my mind, the details aren't relevant."

The pizza lands, hot, gooey, truly exceptional. I burn the roof of my mouth on the first bite and manage to peel it off with the third—after that I taste nothing except my own flesh.

"And what about Julie Eisenhower—are you close?" I ask, still peeling cheese off my palate.

"She's very nice, but I wouldn't say we're close. I wouldn't even know her except that we're distantly related. Me, I'm not at all political, I'm more social, a people person. But I guess you found that out."

"Has anything like this happened to you before?"

"Anything like what?"

"Any of this."

"I had depression in college; no one knew about it. I stayed in bed for a month and then I got up."

"Did you miss classes?"

"No, I got up for classes and meals, and then I went back to bed."

"So you weren't really paralyzed by the depression?"

"I felt like I was dying," she says, looking me in the eye.

"And then it passed?"

"I was able to do what was expected." Her voice is tight, sad, like something was lost and never recovered.

"On the phone you mentioned something about 'our moment'?"

"Yes," she says, licking her lips. "You struck me as someone who hadn't had his moment yet."

"A late bloomer?" I ask.

"Big-time," she says. "I find it charming, it's like you're still waiting for something to happen."

"Good fortune to fall upon me," I add.

"Something like that," she says. "And you're so charmingly out of it, it's like you're from another era—sweet. All I know about is what sixteen-year-old boys are interested in, and my husband talking about boats and cars and vacations and what toys he wants to get, remote-control this and that." She looks at me guiltily. "I have a real problem," she says.

"And what's that?"

"Well, after I recovered, I remembered that I liked you—that's what made me call. But now I have a real problem." She signals for the waiter. "Could I have a glass of wine?"

"How about an Arnold Palmer?" I suggest.

"White," she says. "A big pour of white."

"How about a bottle?" the waiter says.

"Just a glass, thanks," she says. And the waiter is gone. "In a nutshell—no pun intended—I still like you. I don't know why. It's ridiculous, but I do, and I know I shouldn't. And I'm back on medication and I am myself, or my 'better' self, but the thing is—I still want you. And, weirder yet, if you want to hear weird, I once met this guy, a young guy who collects masks of presidents, he has like forty famous faces and likes to role-play with women who maybe fantasize about getting banged by JFK, or done doggy-style by Abe Lincoln.

Or how about being tied to a lectern and being made to submit by a leather-bound Jimmy Carter? His scenarios were endless, but the thing was . . . is . . . he's not you. He's like a fake historian and you're the real deal. So what do I do?" she asks.

I don't know what to say, and so I adopt what I call the "Thumper pose," one hand on the chin and brow furrowed. In *Bambi*, Thumper says, "If you can't say something nice, then don't say anything at all." Good advice, dating back to 1942. She's still looking at me, waiting for something. "I don't quite know what to say."

"Say you want me too," she says.

I do a couple of presidential imitations to spin off the stress.

Her glass of wine arrives; she downs it in a couple of gulps and orders another.

"Look," I say, trying to be compassionate, "I don't think we should do anything that puts you at risk. I don't want to do anything that would be unhealthy for you or that puts your marriage and family in peril. For now, let's sit with it. This isn't something that we have to solve right now." I raise my hand and signal for the check.

"We can have lunch again in the next few weeks."

"I want more than lunch," she says.

"Really, I don't know what to say."

"Say you want me," she repeats herself.

I say nothing. The check comes, I pass the waiter my credit card without even looking at the bill—I need to get out of here.

Her eyes fill with tears.

"Don't cry—this was nice, we had fun, the pizza was delicious."

"You're so sweet," she says.

"Really I'm not," I say.

Together we walk to the parking lot. As I'm bidding her farewell, she pushes me between two parked cars, throws her purse over her shoulder, and gropes my crotch. "You need me," she says, giving the goods a hard pump. "I am your future."

Monday's class was described in my syllabus as "Nixon in China: The Week That Changed the World." The line is a direct quote from the great man himself, describing his 1972 trip to China. The trip was actually an eight-day, carefully orchestrated, made-for-television view behind the Bamboo Curtain. An incredibly unlikely diplomatic achievement pulled off by a staunch anti-communist—in fact, when Nixon first presented the idea to his own men, they thought he'd lost his chips. In classic Nixon fashion, the President appeared to back off but instead worked through diplomatic back channels via Poland and Yugoslavia, taking advantage of a fissure in Soviet-Sino relations, and mindful that the country with the world's largest population was "living in angry isolation." The payoff of his daring détente increased U.S. leverage with Russia, prompting the SALT II talks and the slow unwinding of Cold War tensions. My favorite bit of the script—Kissinger's July 1971 stop in Pakistan, during which he feigned illness at a dinner, left, and flew to China for secret meetings with Zhou Enlai that laid the groundwork for Nixon's trip. The presidential visit itself was replete with the stuff of burgeoning friendship, an excursion to the Great Wall, displays of Ping-Pong and gymnastics, and of course the First Lady, indelible Pat, in her bright-red coat.

And at the infamous February 21, 1972, banquet in Peking, President Nixon raised a glass to Chairman Mao, and said,

> *What legacy shall we leave our children? Are they destined to die for the hatreds which have plagued the old world, or are they destined to live because we had the vision to build a new world? There is no reason for us to be enemies. Neither of us seeks the territory of the other; neither of us seeks domination over the other; neither of us seeks to stretch out our hands and rule the world. Chairman Mao has written, "So many deeds cry out to be done, and always urgently. The world rolls on. Time passes. Ten thousand years are too long. Seize the day, seize the hour." This is the hour, this is the day for our two peoples to rise to the heights of greatness which can build a new and a better world.*

A few days later, the telephone rings. I don't hear the ring, only the voice on the machine.

"I trust you realize that, however we decide to proceed, our work must remain in confidence."

I pick up. "Of course," I say, without a clue to whom I'm speaking.

She continues. "At some point we'll spend some time together, but for the moment I'd like to get a sense of what you think might be there. . . ."

"Where?" I ask, hoping for a clue.

"In the pages," she says.

"I'm sorry," I say, "but I picked up as you were speaking, may I ask who's calling?"

"Julie Eisenhower," she says.

"Of course, my apologies." I take a breath.

"What was it like?" she asks.

"Amazing—a dream come true. I felt like a kid in a candy store—up close and personal. It was a thrill to hold the pages he wrote on, to feel the weight of his hand, the pressure of his pen, the urgency with which he needed to express himself. It was"—I draw a long breath—"transcendent."

"And what about the material itself—what do you make of the content?"

"Well, there's a freedom to the work, a lack of self-consciousness—the stories are surprisingly candid. And there's a depth of imagination and feeling, perhaps call it pathos, which people don't often associate with your father. And more: the stories are illustrative of a kind of knowing about the common man, about an everyday Joe, in a way that humanizes your father, giving the reader a sense of his history, his values, his own progression and development as a person. These writings add dimensionality. I guess what I'm saying is that these could help reframe how history characterizes him. . . . Your father is a classic of his time, aspiring, striving, and desperate, capturing the moment where America turned, and summing up the darkness in the American soul, the change in who were pre– and post–World War II."

"So you think there may be a book in it?"

"As you know, I'm not a literary scholar, but I was enthralled, I saw a side of your father that I never knew existed, a description of a hard worker who felt unappreciated and, damn it, wanted someone to notice. I was reminded of Arthur Miller's Willy Loman." I say "Willy Loman" and stop short—smacked down by a historical flashback. Miller was called up to the House Un-American Activities Committee, and of course Nixon played a key role on that committee. Miller refused to name names and was cited for contempt of Congress. As soon as I say Miller's name, I'm horrified that somehow I "forgot," which proves every idea I ever had about the importance of knowing one's history and not forgetting. I fall silent.

"Am I right in thinking there's a Miller play on Broadway right now? I can't recall which one it is, but David and I were planning to go. . . ."

I sputter to restart: "There may have been a mention in *The New Yorker*.

Anyway, the stories echo the work of some classic American authors—Sherwood Anderson, Richard Yates, Raymond Carver. . . . They're not about politics as much as they are about people, about men and women. And you know what, it's always been a narrow line between us and them—between right and left, blue and red, personal and politic—"

She cuts me off.

"I am not afraid of Democrats, Mr. Silver," Julie says. "I know you have a deep affection for my father that goes beyond politics. We're hoping something can be done with this body of work, and we're interested in having you begin to give it a shape." She goes on to say that she'd like my thoughts about whether or not there might be a book or two in the boxes and that she'll arrange for further access, and reminds me to bring some identification next time, and then laughs. . . .

"Clearly Wanda delivered a full report," I say, embarrassed.

"It's all right," she says. "My mother always did things like that—left the house without her purse. And we'd get these calls about a woman down at Garfinkel's in Tenley insisting she was Mrs. Richard Nixon and trying to use the 'house charge.' She didn't go out all that often on her own—usually Trish or I went with her."

We wrap up with Julie proposing a fee of seven thousand five hundred dollars to start and a contract that provides for either the termination or continuation dependent on a review in eight weeks.

"Sounds good," I say.

"We'll speak soon," she says, hanging up.

As soon as we're off, the phone rings again.

"I hope you realize that I don't give up easily," a woman says.

I say nothing.

Is it Julie calling again or is it *her*? I wait for another clue.

"Are you there?" she asks. "Are you ready for me? I am ready for you . . . ready and waiting."

"We are supposed to be working on building a friendship."

"I don't want to be friends," she says. "I want you to pound my pussy, I want to come hard, fast, and frequently. I want you to do me and then do me again."

"Do you do this with other fellas as well or am I the lucky one?"

"I cut back, you're it. You and my husband."

"And what does he think about all this?"

"He wants me to pretend I'm a hooker and negotiate with him for my services. He likes to pay me after the deed in front of the kids, who have no idea what he thinks is so funny. So when am I seeing you? Seriously, how about I come to your place this afternoon?"

"Not possible."

"I thought you lived alone?"

"I have animals," I say.

"Like what, a jealous monkey?"

"It's not my house, I'm just a guest here; complicated story."

"What about a motel?"

"How about we meet at a diner, like for lunch or coffee."

"I want your cock in my hole."

"Look, if you keep talking to me like that we're not going to be able to continue. . . ."

"You're kidding, right?"

"Am I?"

"I met you on an Internet site. If you don't do what I want, I could claim you raped me; I still have the underwear I wore the day you came over—no pun intended."

"What do you mean?"

"I save my underwear from every encounter, just in case . . ."

"In case you feel the need to extort?"

"How about you do me on the phone—I'll talk you through it."

She somehow forces me to engage in phone sex with her, and even though I don't want to be excited by it, I am slowly drawn in.

"I keep thinking I'm supposed to be helping you—not enabling you," I say as I unzip my pants.

"I'm already so wet," she says. "My hand is way up my pussy and I'm dripping—all I need is your cum gun to nail it. I want you to bang me. I want to feel your balls slapping my ass. I want you to do it to me doggy-style. Pinch my titty, pinch it hard." And then she starts whooping—that's the only word I can think of for it—kind of a charging, galloping sound like a rodeo cowboy, and I can tell she's not faking. It's kind of grotesque and kind of inescapably hot. As she's coming I get more and more excited, and then it's like I can't stop myself—I'm sitting in George's desk chair and just before I erupt I turn away from the desk, spinning in the swivel chair, and explode, shooting onto his bookcase, his volumes of American history and the silver-framed family photos. I immediately grab a tissue and try and clean up. "I have to go," I say. "I've made quite the mess over here."

She laughs. "I knew you'd crack."

I've been had.

Moments later, when Nate calls, I feel as though I've been caught with my pants down. I pick up the phone on George's desk, clear my throat, and bleat hello.

"You okay?"

"Fine," I bleat, clearing again.

Nate is filled with energy and thoughts going about a hundred miles a minute—by comparison, I feel stoned.

"Where are you?" he asks.

"At your father's desk, I was doing a little work."

"We can video-chat," he says, excited. "I don't know why I didn't think of it before. There's a camera right there on Dad's computer, it's all set up. You just push the blue button at the bottom of the dock—it looks like a word bubble. Wait," he says, "I'll call you." And seconds later, the computer makes a ringing sound. "Click 'accept,'" he says, and without thinking I do.

Nate is there, waving at me. "I can see you," he says.

"And I can see you too," I say into the phone.

"We can hang up the phones," he says. And I do.

"Can you hear me?"

I can. A video camera mounted in the computer—it's terrifying. What if someone has been watching me? "What do you call this?"

"Facetime, iChat, or Skype," he says. "It just depends on the program—the end result is pretty much the same thing."

"Skype," he says, and all I can think of is Ella Fitzgerald singing skat.

"What can you see?" I ask Nate, wondering how fine the resolution is.

"I see Dad's whole office, his bookcases, his prizes. Everything that's behind you. I don't know why I didn't think of this before—we could have been talking face to face this whole time. . . ."

"Yes, we could have been talking like this all along," I say, all the while obsessing about my earlier encounter, wondering if there's any evidence left behind on the bookshelf—some missed bit of something. . . .

Video chat is like talking NASA-style; there's an ever-so-slight delay to the sound and images that reminds me of pictures sent from outer space, pixelated, like some weird postmodern animation.

"Helloooo out there," I call out.

"You don't have to yell," Nate says. "I'm in the library; a normal voice is sufficient."

"Okay, then," I whisper.

"Where are we going over break?" Nate wants to know.

"What do you mean?"

"There's a school break coming up, and I'm wondering where we're going."

"Do you always go somewhere?"

"Yes," he says in an almost patronizing tone.

"Does Ashley's school have break at the same time?"

"Yep."

"It seems excessive to take a trip for no reason," I say.

"Sometimes people need a break, a little time off."

"Where do you usually go?"

"Skiing in Aspen, sometimes the Caribbean, or on an educational exploration, like to visit a turtle habitat in the Galapagos."

"And what about the summer, what happens then?"

"Camp, summer school, travel, some time at the Vineyard. Mom has it all figured out. I'm sure there's already a plan for this year."

"Good to know. So, about this upcoming holiday vacation, is there a plan? Something you've got in mind?"

"Not really. If you can't think of anything, we can always go to Disney World."

"How does a kid who has his own town in South Africa want to go to Disney World?"

Nate is silent for a moment. "I'm human," he finally offers. "You think the kids in Nateville don't know Mickey Mouse? They wear Mickey Mouse T-shirts. All those clothes that we stuff in charity bins in the parking lot of the mall are sold—not given—to poor people in foreign countries."

"I had no idea."

"No one does, but that's why whenever you see a documentary about impoverished parts of the world the kids are all wearing U.S. character or slogan T-shirts. Meanwhile, what about the boy, the orphan—can we take him with us?"

"It's certainly something to think about," I say, stalling. I've never traveled with children, much less two children, much less two children and an orphan.

"What's his name?"

"I don't know," I say.

"How could you not know? Didn't you go see him in the hospital?"

"I stopped in and dropped off some gifts," I say, wondering if I did at one point know his name and have since forgotten. I agree with Nate, it seems odd. "I'll find out his name," I say. "While I have you on the phone—do you want an update on your father?"

"No," says Nate.

"Okay," I say. I'm not going to force it on him, but I don't exactly like being the only one sitting with information.

"So—can we plan a conference call with Ash to talk about the trip?" Nate asks.

"Of course. Should we Skype with Ash?" I ask, more softly.

"Can't," Nate says. "Her school doesn't allow video chat—they're worried about predators and stuff."

"Okay, then, we'll set up a regular call for later this week."

A few nights later, with both kids on the phone, I begin by saying, "The purpose of this call is to come up with a plan for the holidays."

"Something fun," Nate says.

"Like what?" I ask.

"Roller-coaster rides," Nate says.

"Room service," Ashley says. And then she adds, "Nowhere too hot, or too cold, and not entirely indoors."

I don't know how, but we decide on Williamsburg—credit goes to Nate, who Googled his way through the conference call like a travel agent, sifting wants, needs, demands.

"It's historic, it has room service, and it's near Busch Gardens Amusement Park and a water park called Great Wolf Lodge. If we wanted to, we could stay at Great Wolf in a room that's, like, got bunk beds and a built-in log cabin. There's also a go-cart track nearby."

I look up the place he's talking about and am reminded that he's a child. What we're talking about looks like a bacterial nightmare, a summer camp run amok, a child's fantasy—water slides and French fries. I feel the chlorine singeing my sinuses as I'm picturing sheets made of 100 percent polyester, chairs with vinyl-wrapped cushions. I think of my weekend visit with George, and by comparison even that looks better than this. I say nothing—some cards are best held tight.

"Shall we take a vote?" Nate asks.

"Sure," I say.

"All in favor of Williamsburg and the surrounding area?"

"Yay," we all say.

And so it is decided—and as soon as it is decided, Nate starts gunning for me to take the orphan.

As we're about to hang up, the boy's name comes back to me—it's really the memory of George and some crappy comment he made about the boy's mother crying out his name—"Ricky," I say. "His name is either Ricky or Ricardo."

"And what do they call him?" Ash asks.

"Ricky or Ricardo," Nate says.

"Nice," Ashley says. "Let's invite him."

I agree to call, even though I fear injecting our family further into the lives of these people who we've already harmed so profoundly. And then I think of Nate and Ashley and their youthful belief in the possibility of repair, and so it is with that that I push myself to make the call.

"Is Christina Menendez there?" I say her name slowly—because in my head I've inexplicably started calling her Carmen Miranda and am convinced I'm going to actually say it to her face.

"She no home," the man says.

I am about to ask if I can leave my name, but he hangs up.

I try again in the evening. "Is Carmen there?" I ask.

"Wrong number."

"I'm trying to reach Carmen. It's about the boy?"

"You got it wrong, her name is not Carmen, it's Christina. She's not back yet."

"I'm sorry," I say, not even realizing that I in fact said it. "When will she be home?"

I'm noticing things in the kitchen, photos of the kids that have been on the fridge for years, things that have been stuck there and now are almost shellacked on with age and coatings of orange juice, milk, splashed spaghetti sauce.

"Can I give her a message?"

"I'd really like to speak with her," I say, picking at the edge of an old sticker for the newspaper delivery guy. It's deeply stuck on; my picking makes it worse—it really needs to be scraped with a razor blade.

"Hold on."

"Hello," a woman says suspiciously.

"Hi," I say. "I'm . . ."

"I know who you are."

"No," I say, "I'm the brother, the uncle of the children."

She says nothing.

I speak, I spill my guts, I say all the things that are so difficult to say. "The children of the man who killed your family feel bad, they are very worried about the boy, they want to help him. . . ." It's awkward, I really don't know what to say. "I'm taking the children to Williamsburg and they'd like to invite the boy."

"What's that?"

"Williamsburg? It's a place in Virginia, an old town, a former plantation. It was the state capital after a fire in Yorktown; I guess it's where the American Revolution gathered momentum. It's a place you go when you're studying American history." And then I jump to "There are amusement parks nearby. The kids thought the boy might like it—and you too, of course."

"I work," she says.

"If you can take time off, we could cover your lost salary," I say. "We're going for a couple of days, a long weekend."

"He is a big pain," she says without affect, so it's hard to know what she's getting at.

"Still in pain from the accident?"

"No," she says, "he is a big pain, he has learning disability, ADD, DDD, BPI spectrum, et cetera. I have to give him medication."

"Oh," I say. "Well, the kids would like to get to know him better, and as I said, you're invited as well."

She seems unmoved, or like she doesn't understand what I'm saying.

"I will talk to my husband," she says.

"Okay," I say. "Thank you."

A little too proud of myself, I call Jane's father. "I took your suggestion," I say.

"You couldn't have," he says.

"I did," I say.

"Trust me," he says.

"I'm taking the kids away—we're going to historic Williamsburg."

"I get it," he says, pauses, and then comes back: "My suggestion is that you goddamned rot in hell, you and your piece-of-shit brother. You took my beautiful daughter, God knows what you're doing to those children."

I collect my thoughts. "You're right," I offer. "What happened was unforgivable, and I wanted you to know I heard what you said; I'm trying to do my best for these children."

"Shmuck," he says—and then there's a pause. "So why are you calling?"

"You suggested I take the children somewhere; I wanted you to know we're going to Williamsburg."

"And you're expecting me to pay for that? You think Williamsburg is like Israel? Not a penny, asshole, not a penny."

"I wasn't asking for money—I just wanted you to know. We'll send a postcard," I say, hanging up.

The next time we talk, I tell Nate that I called the boy's aunt.

"What's today?" Nate asks.

"In what sense?"

"The date?"

I give him today's date.

"I know," he says. "Mom's birthday."

"Right," I say, not having realized.

"Are we supposed to do something—have a cake with an unlit candle, something symbolic?"

"You could do that," I say.

"Yeah," he says, "I could ask the kitchen for a birthday cake for my dead mother, with an unlit candle. . . ."

"I'll go to the cemetery," I say.

"And do what?"

"Check on things, talk to her. . . ." The more I say the worse it seems—I picture myself standing at her grave singing "Happy Birthday."

Silence . . .

"So what did the boy's family say?" Nate asks.

"They're thinking about it," I say.

"I hope he comes with us."

"How come?"

"This whole thing has been so bad," Nate says, "we have to make something go right, and this is something we can do."

"I hope so too," I say, surprising myself.

I go to the cemetery and drive in circles—it all looks the same, a few scattered cars, gravediggers, and a funeral in progress. This one allows no markers aboveground, so there's something apocalyptically flat about it. There's not a stray baby tree springing up, a lone elm taking root.

I can't remember where Jane's grave is and have to check in at the office. "Please sign our Visitor Book," the woman at the desk urges, but I don't.

I would have brought flowers, but the cemetery doesn't allow them: no live flowers also means no dead flowers that have to be collected and thrown away.

I get the directions, and as soon as I'm out of the car and up the small rise of land I see her—Jane's mother, Sylvia. I see her and am tempted to leave, to turn and go back to the car, to respect her privacy, to avoid a confrontation. But, really, there is nowhere to go, nothing I can do except go forward.

"Hello," I say.

She nods at me.

We both look at the grave. A few rocks have been placed, indicating that Jane has not been forgotten, others have been here.

"It's a place," she says.

It's hard to know how to respond. "Yes," I say, "it is. It's her birthday."

"Yes," she says, brightening. "I remember the day she was born—vividly— like it was yesterday, but yesterday I don't remember so well. Pardon me," she says, as if begging forgiveness. "I'm on medication, I needed something to calm me down—but now I'm like the walking dead."

"I can imagine it's difficult." I pause. "Nate called—he was wondering what to do about today—I told him I was coming here." I give her a few details about each of the kids and then stop: she's not listening.

"I knew about the affair," she says.

I nod.

"Jane and I talked. . . ."

I don't say anything, because what is there to say.

"I had an affair as well," her mother says. "When she told me about you, I told her about me."

"Whom did you have the affair with?"

"Goldblatt," she says, "the dentist. And Troshinksy, the girls' piano teacher. He had beautiful hands. I also had a moment, but not an affair, with Gural-nick, who was for a time working in my husband's office. Of course, my husband knows nothing of it."

"Of course."

"Jane liked you very much."

"I liked her."

"Was it worth all this? A moment of . . . whatever you want to call it, cost my girl her life," she says, as though she can't believe it.

"What happened is very unusual."

"The affair?" She looks at me incredulously.

"The murder," I say.

She pauses. "Your wife was a foreigner," she says. "She married you to become legit."

"My ex-wife," I say, "is Chinese-American. She was born in this country and graduated Phi Beta Kappa from Stanford and her father was considered a strong candidate for the Nobel Peace Prize."

"I never knew," she says. And it means so many things. She puts a little blue box from Tiffany down on the dirt where next year the marker will be.

"You bought her a gift?"

"I'm not foolish," she says. "The box is empty. She always liked the little blue boxes."

In the car, on the way home, I debate calling George. I imagine the conversation in my head: "It's Jane's birthday. I didn't know if you'd remember, but I thought I should check in on you."

"You fucked her," he says.

"That's not why I'm calling. . . ." The thought of it stops me from going further.

The boy's aunt Christina calls back, says she's got a couple of questions—she wants to make sure it's not going to cost them anything.

"It's all on us," I say.

And then she says, "My husband wants to know if we have to bring a tent?"

I'm not sure where the tent idea comes from, but it makes me nervous.

"No need for a tent," I say. "We'll be staying indoors. A couple changes of clothes and a toothbrush."

"Okay," she says, "we'll go."

We pick them up at the aunt's house. The husband comes out with them, carrying two enormous suitcases, a knapsack, and a bag of groceries. The aunt is dressed up, wearing her good jeans, a nice blouse, high heels; and Ricardo looks doughy, tense, and overexcited all at once—I instantly don't like him. He's wearing bright-yellow soccer shorts and an enormous blue Yankees T-shirt, all of it conspiring to make him look like a giant molten blob. By Trenton, I'm having second thoughts. The noise level of Ricardo's video game seems to drive only me crazy, it's like no one else can hear it. "Can you turn it down? Can you please turn it down? How about off? How about turning it off for a little bit? Just take a rest. Please. I'm asking you nicely. Okay, I'm begging you, I can't keep driving if that noise persists." And then he starts kicking the back of my seat and opening and closing the electric windows— changing the air pressure in the car. Nate and Ash speak to the kid in Spanish, he laughs, he puts the game away. The kid has a really odd, almost animal laugh that's off-putting, and yet totally genuine and charming.

I ask the aunt where she's from—I'm assuming Colombia or Nicaragua.

"The Bronx," she says.

"And where were you from originally?"

"The Bronx," she repeats. "My father is the super for a group of buildings, and my mother owns a store."

Jealous, or worried she's leaving him for the murderer's brother and two kids, the aunt's husband calls every twenty minutes.

Meanwhile, despite the great laugh, Ricardo is hyper—he never stops moving, except when he's eating smelly papaya and blowing explosive farts.

On the Delaware Memorial Bridge, after the fifth phone call from her husband, the aunt breaks down: "It's too much for me, I can do no good for anyone. Everyone wants my attention—I don't know why men can't take care of themselves, why they can't cook something to eat. . . . He works in a restaurant, you would think he could cook. . . . I am only one person. I cannot be there for everybody all the time. There is nothing left of me. I work for someone else, and then I come home and work for him, and then my parents need my help, and my husband says I'm not fun anymore. I used to laugh and go to the beach and play with him—or watch him and his friends race remote-control cars. . . ." I nod, hoping she'll keep talking as I cross the bridge. I don't know why, but I worry she's going to jump out of the car and throw herself over the guardrail—I wouldn't blame her if she did.

"He can't share me with anyone. In my dreams I run away, I get a job taking care of a very old man who likes to sleep all day and have oatmeal for dinner and oatmeal for breakfast. He has no teeth, so he can't bite me. The man falls in love with me and his family is glad—okay, not really glad, but I pretend they are. We have a wheelchair wedding and he takes me to a spa that I already have the T-shirt for—Canyon Ranch. I got it from my cousin who cleans houses, who got it from the lady she works for, who was doing 'spring cleaning.' He takes me to Canyon Ranch for our honeymoon and says, 'I knew you would be happy here, because your T-shirt told me so.'"

She goes on and on. I'm nodding and listening, occasionally offering a compassionate "uh-huh," or "I can imagine that would be difficult."

Somehow, in the back seat, the kids know better than to interrupt; it's like a curtain of quiet has fallen over them, and they play video games with the boy.

We go from Delaware into Maryland, slip past Baltimore, and then are in downtown Washington, D.C. I take them on a quick tour of the Capitol, the World War II Memorial, Jefferson Memorial, Vietnam Veterans Memorial, Lincoln Monument, Iwo Jima Memorial, and the White House.

As we go from place to place, I fill everyone in on the history. At one point the aunt stops me and says, "Why do you think my history is different from your history? I was born here."

"But your family came from somewhere else," I say, lamely.

"So did yours," she says, and she's right.

The husband calls a half-dozen more times, and just before we're about to get back on the road towards Virginia, the aunt announces she's decided to go home; she gives me Ricardo's medication and writes out the instructions on how and when to give it.

"What exactly is it for?" I ask.

"It's to help him think at school," she says. "But when it wears off, he's cranky and bouncing off the walls—I like to send him outside."

We say goodbye and put her on a train in Union Station with a souvenir FBI baseball hat from the terminal gift shop. The aunt seems relieved to be dismissed, and the boy happy to be with Ash and Nate.

We continue on to Williamsburg, arriving just before supper. The children quickly get into the program. Ash wants to dress in a costume of the time period. While I'm in the process of renting her one at the Visitor Center, Nate leans in and says, "Save yourself the trouble, buy new and avoid lice; besides, she won't want to give it back." And so I do. I buy her the dress, and then she wants the Pilgrim shoes—which in the old days were neither left nor right—and so we buy those, and the boys want tricornered hats and wooden guns, which seem safe enough until they start using them as bats and fencing foils. We visit Tarpley's Store and the post office, where Nate buys old newspapers and various legal documents and proclamations, while Ash collects quill pens and powdered ink and I play the role of human cash machine. Every time I buy something for one of the kids, I have to buy something for the others as well. Whenever I take my wallet out, they come running like ducklings, but, curiously, Nate wants very little. Instead of stuff, he repeatedly says, "I'll take the cash," and I give him ten or twenty bucks. For Ashley it's something from the silversmith, and then something from the pottery place, and then a candle for her art teacher, and, and, and. I find myself wondering what a period cash machine would look like—someone posted in the center of town squatting on sacks of gold coin?

I have my own dim memories of coming here long ago, recalling that at Yorktown I got a black wooden spear with a rubber arrowhead end and later used it as a fishing rod. We have dinner at Ye Olde Pub and attend an evening performance in which we're all taught to dance the Virginia Reel.

"Usually we have one room and our parents have the other," Ashley says as she surveys our very large room at the lodge.

"Well, this time we're bunking together," I say, and no one says anything more.

I'm less stressed staying in a hotel than I would be at home. I don't have to worry about cooking and cleaning, and it feels as though I've got backup: housekeepers armed with extra pillows and towels, and the elderly concierge who never comes out from behind his desk but does a decent job of getting us tickets to everything from dance performances to farm tours and munitions experiences.

Ricardo is fascinated by the breakfast buffet. "It's like a breakfast party," he says, "like potluck at the church, you go around and take whatever you want and then you go around again and again." I give him his medication, and he washes it down with ten pieces of bacon, four pancakes, one half-bowl of cereal, a large scoop of scrambled eggs, and some kind of cinnamon-swirl Danish. Nate and Ashley, used to cafeteria dining from school, stick to cereal and fruit, and I admire their moderation.

Ashley decides we should more fully live in the time period and wants us to move around the hotel room by candlelight. Nervous about fire, I agree to flashlights only after dark. With quill pen and ink, we write each other letters and messages, seal them with wax, and deliver either via express mail, folding them into paper airplanes and throwing them across the room, or by the slower pony express, Ricardo riding his wooden gun-pony, which runs only every fifteen minutes.

Each kid seems to gravitate naturally to a part of our quarters, carving out his or her own turf. For Ashley, the bathroom is "her office," Nate claims the actual desk in the room, Ricardo operates out of the minibar, which I ask housekeeping to empty—later, I find soldiers stationed in each of the little spaces where the liquor used to be. My personal zone seems to be half of the queen-sized bed which I share with Nate. In the middle of the night, I wake to find us face to face, his night breath sweet, his expression open.

Ashley is quiet, often in her "office" texting or having long late-night conversations with a school friend. I find her asleep on the floor, still holding the phone, her head resting on the bath mat.

"I must have taken a catnap," she says when I wake her up.

"While you were talking?" I ask.

"A friend was reading me a story," she says.

"Don't your friend's parents have rules about how late she can stay up?" Ashley shrugs. "What about all the long distance?"

"It's okay," Ashley says. "I called her; you don't pay for long distance, it's included."

While the kids are at breakfast, I check with the man at the front desk, who tells me she's racked up a four-hundred-dollar phone bill.

"We're not paying that," I say, and ask to speak to the manager.

"Okay," the manager says, "how about two hundred?"

"A hundred and fifty and no more," I say, and the manager accepts.

I say nothing to Ashley. I can't exactly give the kid a hard time; I'm glad she has a friend to talk to.

Every time I look at Ricardo, I blank on his name. It's further complicated by the fact that he had a name tag on his coat, clearly there for a long time, that says "Hello My Name Is" and "CAMERON" is written in faded black Magic Marker.

"Who is Cameron?" I ask.

"What do you mean?"

"Hello My Name Is CAMERON?"

"I guess it was the name of the guy who had the jacket before me," he says.

"Why do you keep it on there?"

"I like it," he says. "I call the coat Cameron."

And then there's a pause.

While we're outside the Williamsburg Courthouse, waiting for Ash and Nate, who wanted to watch a speech given by an actor playing George Washington, Ricardo asks, "Why did you kill my mommy and daddy?"

"I didn't kill them, my brother did—George killed your mommy and daddy," I say, taken aback by both his directness and my own defensive tone.

"Who is George?" he asks.

"George is my brother. He's Nate and Ashley's father."

"Was he trying to kill me too?"

"No, he wasn't trying to kill anyone, it was an accident, a big huge accident. I'm really sorry."

"You brought me the balloon."

"That's right—I wanted to see how you were," I say.

"How do I know it wasn't you who did it?"

"Well, because I wasn't there when it happened. I came later. And George is in a special hospital now. He lost his mind."

"He killed my mommy and daddy," the boy says.

"Accidentally," I say. "And then he killed Nate and Ashley's mother." I'm not sure the kid knows that, not sure I should be the one to tell him, but somehow I want to get the message across that he's not the only one who lost his family.

The boy shakes his head. "He was a rich guy with a big TV, he didn't need to kill anybody."

"It's true," I say. "He didn't need to kill anybody."

I panic. Perhaps I didn't give him his medication—his sudden rise to the surface, his clarity is because he's unmedicated—and I worry what will happen next. Will he turn into the Incredible Hulk?

"Did you take your medicine today?" I ask.

"Yes," he says. "You gave it to me this morning."

Nate and Ash come out of the Courthouse, and we head for a demonstration of ice-cream making in the colonial kitchen and then to lunch. I keep waiting for something more to happen—but nothing does—and we carry on.

In the late afternoon, the pet minder calls to ask, "Did you see the cat before you left?"

It feels like a trick question. "Is she missing?"

"She had kittens," the pet minder says. "Six survived; one didn't make it, and I buried it under the rosebushes out back."

"I didn't know she was pregnant; she never mentioned it."

"I'm thinking I should take them all in for a checkup."

"Yes," I say. "That makes sense. And Tessie?"

"Out of her element," the minder says. "Oh, and she had them in the master bedroom; I threw the bedding out, hope that was okay?"

"Fine, all fine."

"I'll let you know if there's more news," he says, and hangs up.

I must look surprised, because the children all ask, "What?"

"Tessie had kittens," I say, and they look more confused.

"Tessie is a dog," Ashley says.

"You're right," I say.

And then in the morning, as though everyone but me got the memo, the kids show up to breakfast dressed normally and Nate announces we're going to Busch Gardens. I'm the last to know.

Busch Gardens is not your "average" amusement park—it's like a fiberglass steroid extravaganza with a European theme: rides with German names—Der Autobahn, Der Katapult, Der Wirbelwind.

Ricardo is deeply excited but scared to go on the rides, so Nate and Ash go off together, and I take Ricardo on some of the smaller-kid stuff, the Kinder Karussel, Der Roto Baron, and so on. He loves it, and soon we meet up with the big kids and he's off and running—as long as I hold his hand, which means that I too am hurled through the air, twisted, turned, left and right, spun speechless and stupid, until, of course, I throw up.

"Ewwwww," Ashley says as I throw up in front of the three of them. Ever since we arrived, I've been finishing their junk food, hot dogs, curly onion rings, chicken fingers, half-eaten ice creams.

"That's not good," Nate says as I empty myself again and again into a trash can modeled to look like a dwarf. I try to vomit into the hole, the dwarfy gnome's mouth—but it's futile. I let loose all over his head, on the ground in front and in back. And then, suddenly, as though the bottom has come out from under, I can't hold myself up. I am compelled to lie down—or fall down—at the curb of the yellow brick road, my head on a pile of their jackets.

"I need a minute," I say, wiping bitter spittle off my chin.

Moments later, as though we've been spotted on some sort of central-office Webcam, the super-sized park nurse comes by in her extra-large golf cart and takes me to her office. The kids ride on the back. As we're driving, she says, "Officially, and for no additional charge, I can give you smelling salts, ginger ale, a saltine, Bactine, and a Band-Aid, and we do have a defibrillator. I bought it at Staples and told them it was toner for the copy machine. Everyone should have one." She pauses as we pull up outside the first-aid trailer. The kids follow me in. There are fiberglass boat-shaped cots—two of them—and a couple of chairs. The nurse goes on to tell me that for a hundred bucks she can hook me up to an IV bag of vitamins and minerals. A shot of B12 is another seventy-five. "Think about it," she says, as the kids sit down. I stand, wondering if I should wait in the bathroom, claim my moment there.

"Would you like a cookie?" she asks the children. "I have Thin Mints and Samoas. My daughter is a Girl Scout—I buy fifty boxes a year." The kids each take a cookie. "It's important to have something you can offer your guests, considering I get the lost kids as well—and whether it's a skinned knee or separated from the pack, you need a little something to perk 'em up, josh them out of their pain. . . ."

Just the smell of the Thin Mints and the sound of the kids crunching away makes me sick—I run for the bathroom.

"Ice," she says, "I can give you ice. I see a lot of heat- and food-related ill-ness, also inner-ear issues—people who literally feel topsy-turvy."

With me in the bathroom, she directs her attention to the children, who are working their way through boxes of cookies. "Don't worry, this happens to lots of older folks who aren't used to having to keep up with the kids full-time, so I am well prepared."

I come out of the bathroom as she's showing them her "crash cart," a giant yellow plastic toolbox, like what you'd find at Home Depot, filled with supplies.

Ashley gives me a piece of gum. "Your breath," she says.

"Thanks."

"So what'll it be?" the nurse asks.

"Have you got some Tums?" I ask.

"Used the last one this morning for myself," she says. "It's on the list." She taps a long, narrow shopping list on her desk. "What about a couple of boxes of cookies to go?"

"Sure," I say. I pull out twenty bucks, and the kids pick out cookies from her enormous supply cabinet. The nurse hands me a mini-can of ginger ale and a straw and tells me to take it with me and drink slowly.

"We're here all day and half the night, same as park hours," she says. "So if you need us just call, or ask someone else to call—they know where to find me."

I reach out to shake her hand, but she demurs. "Can't," she says, pumping herself a giant handful of Purell and urging the rest of us to as well. We wash our hands, take our cookies, and bid the nurse adieu. At a roadside gas station I buy a large, out-of-date, overpriced bottle of Tums and pop them frequently. "Like Gummi Bears," Ashley says.

"Chalky bears," I say.

In the middle of the night, Nate wakes up with a stomachache and asks me to come into the bathroom with him, as he's stinking up the place with explosive diarrhea.

"Flush," I say after he fires off a round, and he does. I am looking for matches to light, but apparently there are no more ashtrays or matchbooks in hotel rooms anymore.

"There are some in my bag," he says, "in the outside pocket." I don't even ask why; I light the whole pack up. A few minutes later, the phone rings. Nate picks up the receiver by the toilet and hands it to me.

"Can I help you?"

"We have a smoke alert coming from your bathroom," someone from the front desk says.

"We're not smoking, we're pooping," I say, wondering if we've been poisoned, felled by colonial-era cuisine?

"Apologies for the intrusion," the front desk says.

"You think you have a normal family," Nate says, as he's straining on the toilet. I am breathing through my mouth and trying to listen attentively. "And then something like this happens, that's not so normal." An enormous explosion escapes him. "I don't mean this," he says tapping the bowl, "I mean Mom and Dad. . . . In just a phone call, your life changes. . . ." An enormous bellowing belch from his behind fills the air with fumes. "Sorry," he says. "You don't have to stay in here with me." I shrug. And then, as he's sitting there, he suddenly says, "I'm gonna barf." I pass him the trash can, which luckily has a plastic bag in it. And he barfs and expels at the same time, and I feel bad for the kid. "Do you think we need a doctor?" He shakes his head. "No, this has happened before, I'll be okay," and he throws up again.

"I think we've been had," I say, trying to make light of the situation.

"In what sense?" Nate asks.

"First me, then you; let's hope Ash and the boy don't get it."

"Fuckin' Thin Mints," Nate says, spitting into the trash can.

"What do you think of the kid?" Nate asks.

I say nothing.

"I think he's very funny," Nate says. "He reminds me of Charlie Chaplin."

"How so?"

"The way he walks, like he's waddling, and his facial expressions are very rubbery."

"Do you think he's smart?" I ask.

"Why is that the criteria?" Nate defensively replies.

"Good question."

We go back to bed. I dream that I am going to South Africa. At the airport I'm told the only way to get there is as luggage dropped out of a plane, wearing a parachute. The airline informs me that my mother has sent my old trunk from sleepaway camp and it's already on the plane. I consent, and when the plane is at fifteen thousand feet I crawl into my old camp trunk. Once in the trunk, I am pushed into the rear bathroom and told that on signal someone will push the flush button and there will be a large whooshing sound and I will be vacuum-ejected.

When I try to ask questions, they shrug and say, "That's just how it's done."

It's a cross between something Curious George would dream up and some kind of terrorist situation. Clearly I must have known this was going to happen, because I'm wearing a giant parachute, which I notice only as I'm falling. Just before I wake up, I pull the rip cord and float, catching an invisible breeze high above the plains as a herd of giraffe runs below. I wake up at 3 a.m. with my arms above my head, as if still clutching the parachute, and find Nate sitting up, knitting.

"What?" he says, defensively.

"Nothing," I say.

"I do it when I can't sleep," he says. "It's very relaxing."

I'm still half in the world of the dream, half watching Nate as he's turning out a long striped scarf. "Don't," he says.

"Don't what?"

"Don't ask if I'm gay. . . ."

"Okay," I say. "How's your stomach?"

"Noisy, but otherwise stable," Nate says. And I go back to sleep.

In the car on the way home, everyone crumbles; there's some kind of tension about returning to our "normal" lives. I wonder if we've spent too much time together—or maybe it wasn't enough?

The kids ply Ricardo with treats, like life is all about getting a giant booty bag from a birthday party. "It's not about stuff," I keep saying. They know I'm right but don't stop. Nate asks the kid if he has an e-mail account—he doesn't. At a rest stop, Nate takes me aside and asks if we can buy Ricardo's family a computer so they can Skype.

"No," I say, perhaps too firmly.

"Transitions are difficult for everybody," the woman working the register in the gift shop says. "I used to be a teacher, and it broke my heart to watch what the children went through. One boy ripped his mom's skirt off, crying,

'Don't leave me here.' We turned it into a teaching moment and duct-taped the mom's skirt back together."

And that prompted you to get a job in a rest-stop gift shop? I wonder.

Ashley is trolling the aisles—trying to buy a present for her friend. Everywhere we go she buys something, and then, later, decides it's not the right thing—it's starting to seem a little strange.

"I keep picking out things that I like, but I'm not sure she and I have the same taste." Ashley's knapsack is full of stuffed animals, lockets from the rest stop, small shot glasses.

"Well, what kind of things have you seen her wearing?"

"You know," Ashley says, "grown-up stuff, the stuff that comes in the little blue boxes, like what Dad used to give Mom when he didn't know what else to get her."

"Tiffany?"

"Yeah, that," Ashley says. "And she hated it. Mom always liked that other store better—the one that was kind of horsey—started with an 'H'? What is the name of it?"

"Hermès?"

"Yeah, that's the kind of thing she'd like."

"Uh, Ash," Nate interjects, "there's a big difference between a souvenir from your trip and, like, a five-hundred-dollar present from Tiffany or Hermès."

I stay out of it. I have no idea what to say. Clearly boarding-school friendships go above and beyond the usual standard for a little gift from the trip.

"What is she going to give you?" Nate asks.

"It's not a competition; I wanted to bring her something nice. You don't have to make a big thing out of it; you don't have to turn it into something gross."

"I was only trying to help you think of what to get her," Nate says.

"Drop it," Ashley says in a particularly sharp and adult tone.

When we bring Ricardo back to his family, both the aunt and uncle come out to greet him. They seem glad to have had some time alone. The uncle hauls the boy's giant suitcase out of the trunk, and the aunt winks at me, or maybe she doesn't wink, maybe some debris blows in her eye and she blinks to get it out. Either way, Ricardo has a lot to tell them, and gifts for everyone.

Nate and Ash give him lots of hugs and tell him they'll see him soon.

The car is painfully quiet as we head home until Nate manages a near-perfect imitation of Ricardo's laugh, and then we all crack up, trying our own versions of it.

At home, the kittens are a major distraction; they are tiny, helpless, and almost terrifying. We watch as the mama cat feeds and cleans them—literally licking their private parts to get them to "go."

I overpay the pet minder—"hazardous duty"—and he updates us on what will happen next: their eyes should open within the next few days, but it'll be a while before they can really see or do much.

Tessie is looking at me as if to ask, What were you thinking when you left the whole place in my command? Can you imagine what it's been like for me—the stress, the responsibility? Promise me you won't try it again. . . . And, by the way, can I have a cookie?

"I think the kittens are deaf," Nate says. "I talk to them and they don't seem to hear."

"They're born deaf," the pet minder says. "It's a defense mechanism. Soon their hearing will improve. See you soon—call if you need me," he says as he's leaving.

"I miss him," Ashley says at dinner.

"Yep," Nate says.

"What are you going to do about it?" Ashley asks.

"Well, both of you are heading back to school tomorrow," I say, thinking that at least buys me some time.

"He needs us more than just once in a while," Nate says.

"We want him in our family," Ash says. "We talked about it."

"Behind my back?"

"Yes," Nate says.

"But you realize I'm the one who'd be taking care of him?"

"We think you can do it," Ash says.

"He could be our little brother, like a phoenix rising out of the ashes . . ." Nate says.

"Didn't Ricardo say that he's allergic to cats?" I ask.

"We'll get rid of the cat," Ashley says. "I never liked the cat."

"How can you say that? She's your cat, she just had kittens. . . ."

"I like the cat," Nate says.

"Maybe we can get Ricardo made unallergic, "Ash says.

"Maybe the cat could stay out of his room," Nate says.

"Which room is his room?" I ask.

"His room is my room," Nate says, like it's obvious.

"I don't think I'm ready for a full-time live-at-home child," I say.

"Send him away to school," Ashley says.

"We kill his parents, take him from his family, and send him away to school—it's starting to sound like an old English novel."

"Is that a bad thing?" Ash asks.

"Plus, you two can't adopt him, you're underage. . . ."

"But you can," Ash says, nonplussed.

"I am in the middle of a divorce and recently unemployed."

"You quit your job?" Nate asks.

"I got fired."

"You got fired?"

"Well, not exactly fired. I'll finish teaching the semester, but, basically, yes."

"And you didn't tell us?" Nate is shaken.

"I didn't think you needed to know."

"Well, that sucks," Nate says. "Talk about a lack of trust. What's the point if you don't think you can tell us anything? It's not all about you babysitting us, this is supposed to be some kind of relationship—a two-way street."

"It's true," Ash says. "You should tell us things. No one ever told us anything except Mom." She bursts into tears. "I love the cat," she says. "I shouldn't have said I didn't—I really do." And she gets up and runs from the table.

"Good work," Nate says, leaving, disgusted.

I have no idea of what happened, except that I feel like shit.

The next morning, the kids go back to school. After breakfast, a minivan comes for Ashley, and I drive Nate to a collection point about twenty minutes away.

"I'll call you tonight," I say as he's getting out of the car. He slams the door—I don't know if he heard me or not. I beep. His shoulders tighten, but he doesn't turn around; he adjusts the straps of his knapsack and keeps walking towards the bus.

I wait to leave until after the bus pulls out and then go home and sit with the kittens, who are doing well; their eyes are open, they're standing—it's amazing.

Cheryl calls. "Don't you think it's weird that you vanished without telling me? Who did I hear about it from? Julie. And how did that make me feel? She said you went to Williamsburg on a school trip."

"Something like that," I say.

"A little colonial action? A happy ending over a keg of gunpowder? A wank in the stockade?"

I say nothing.

"Oh, please," she says, "I've been there, done that."

"If that's what it was like when you went, then I went someplace else—the other Williamsburg. Were your kids on break last week as well?"

"Tad did a community-service project, Brad went to football camp, and Lad stayed home. So—when can we meet—does Friday work?"

"Trust me, now is not a good time."

"In what sense?"

"I came home with a parasite, they're not sure which one yet. It could have come from undercooked venison, or from the volunteer firemen's breakfast we went to. I've got to bring a stool sample to the doctor this afternoon."

"TMI," she shouts, like a referee calling for a time-out.

"You seem to want to know everything." I continue: "It's very contagious. I have to wash my hands constantly, and my clothes."

"I'll give you ten days," she says.

"And after that?"

"I'm not prepared to discuss that yet."

"Do me a favor," I say. "Don't tell Julie."

"Of course not," she says. "Some things are private. Meanwhile, I've been doing some reading on Richard Nixon. I'm not sure I think he was such a good guy."

"He wasn't a good guy."

"Well, then, what do you see in him?"

"So much. His was an intractable personality; he believed rules didn't apply to him. I find it fascinating."

"It's interesting," she says. "I would have imagined you going for someone either more conventional, a Truman or an Eisenhower, or perhaps even more modern and heroic, you know, like JFK. But Nixon—it's almost kind of kinky."

"Almost," I say.

"I'll call you in a few days; if you're feeling better we can make a plan."

Something is missing. I feel like I've fallen into a space between spaces, like I don't really exist—I'm always out of context. Searching for clarity, I visit my mother.

In the lobby of the home, there's a large dry-erase board. "Feeling bored? Need a lift? Join us and Make Your Own Smoothie, 10–11 a.m. and 3–4 p.m. (We have fresh fruit, fiber, probiotics, and frozen yogurt.)"

"She's not here," the woman at the front desk tells me. "She's gone out with the others, they've got a new hobby."

"What's that?" I ask.

"Swimming," she says. "Eleven of them went off in the minivan to the local YMCA. They've all got floaties on their arms, and some of them are inside inflatable kids' rings—like ducks and frogs—and they're all wearing bathing caps. Big babies, we call them—because they all wear diapers. We get them dressed before they leave. It's great for their mobility."

"Since when does she swim?" I ask.

"We got lucky with this new therapist who also works with the psycho-pharmacologist; this place is hoppin'. More work in some ways, but very exciting. Sometimes we joke that we're bringing back the dead. And they all seem so happy—well, almost all." She nods towards an older man heading down the hall, seeming quite purposeful; he approaches us.

"What the fuck is going on around here? That's all I want to know. What the fuck? Who is that man in my office? Did you fuckin' replace me behind my back? I'm the goddamned boss around here, or at least that's what I thought. We'll see what you're thinking when Friday comes, see if I'm signing your check. Who the hell are you?" he asks, looking at me.

"Silver," I say.

"Good job," he says. "Keep up the good work."

"Now, where the fuck is my secretary? She said she was going to lunch, and I swear that was ten years ago. . . ." The man wanders off.

"Like I said, it's been good for most people, and it's nice to see him up and around," the woman says.

"What are they giving him?"

"I'm not at liberty to discuss the patients—in fact, perhaps I've said too much already. It's a little of this, a little of that—there are advances being made every day. It's a lot about movement—getting them up and out. Short of true paralysis, there's no reason a person should be in bed or sitting down all day . . . and for those who are too weak, we start them off just hanging up." She leads me down the hall to a room and opens the door. Dozens of long springs hang from the ceiling, and each pair of springs is attached to a modified straitjacket/canvas lace-up vest, and laced into the vests are old people. They hang like limp puppets, half standing, half bouncing, half dancing to music, as physical therapists make their way from person to person. "They seem to like it," the woman says. "We invented the units here—weighted standing-assist devices. It cuts down on the respiratory illnesses—better lung function."

"They seem pleased," I say, unable to get over the sight of a roomful of "suspended" elderly.

"Enough show-and-tell for one day," the woman says, closing the door. "Are you going to go down to the YMCA and look for your mother? They just left, so you should be able to catch them."

I have to pay fifteen dollars and fill out a liability waiver before I can enter the pool area of the YMCA, and the fact that I am not going swimming seems irrelevant to the person at the desk.

I enter through the men's locker room, an unappealing old green tile space dotted with male flesh and the smell of sneakers.

As soon as I enter the pool area, I am sent back—told that I must take off my shoes and socks and wash my feet in the shower before entering.

"Hi, Mom," I call out when I get into the pool area, my voice echoing off the tile walls and then absorbed into the chloramide fumes rising off the pool's surface. "Hi, Mom," I repeat.

The entire class turns to face me. "Hi," all the ladies in the pool answer.

My mother is wearing a latex cap, the same kind she used to wear thirty years ago—white with large rubbery flowers in full bloom bursting off the top. Could it be the same bathing cap she's had all along? She swims towards me and, considering that not so long ago she was bedridden, it's disorienting to watch her kicking, swinging her arms through the water's surface. She breast-strokes to the edge of the pool, where I find myself staring down into an oddly open face—framed by the latex flowers—and a deep, wrinkled cleavage.

"You look great," I say. "How are you?"

"Fantastic," she says.

A barrel-chested man swims to her side.

"Hello, son," he says.

"Hello," I say.

"Good to see you," he says.

"You too," I say, going along with it.

"How's your sister?" he asks.

"Good," I say, even though I have no sister.

"I'm very worried about your mother," he says. "I can't find her anywhere." He speaks in a booming voice, like a former radio announcer.

"You can't find her because she's gone," my mother reminds him. "But you've got me now."

"You have each other?" I ask.

"Yes," they say.

"And what about Dad?" I am confused, suddenly a child again.

"Your father's been dead for years—I'm entitled to have a life," my mother says.

"Would you two like to come back to class?" the instructor asks, and they turn around and swim back to class, their diapers poking out from under their suits.

On the way home, I stop at the A&P. It's not my regular store, I just happened to go there. A woman seems to be following me through the store, everywhere I go.

"Are you following me?"

"Am I?"

"Are you?"

"Hard to know," she says. "Most people go up and down the aisles," she says, "they go row by row; unless you have a system of your own, you're bound to see the same people twice."

"Sorry," I say. "Have we met before?"

She shrugs, as though it's irrelevant. "What kind of cake do you like?" she asks. We're in the frozen-foods section, stopped by the desserts. "Plain pound cake, or something with frosting?"

"I've never bought cake," I say, and it's true. "If I wanted cake, I think I'd go to a bakery, but I'm not really a cake person."

"I think young people like frosting, old people like plain," she says, putting a plain Sara Lee pound cake into her cart.

"You don't look old," I say.

"I am, inside," she says.

"So how old are you?" I notice that her body is thin, sinewy, more like that of a child than a grown woman. Her hair is long, thin, almost stringy—dirty blond.

"Guess," she says.

"Twenty-seven," I say.

"I'm thirty-one," she says. "You have a lousy sense of what's what."

I push my cart onward—perhaps I should be grateful for her attention, but at the moment I'm not, I'm distracted—dog biscuits, cat litter . . .

She intercepts me again: "You're an animal lover?"

"The cat had kittens," I say.

"I always wanted pets," she says, "but my parents hated the idea: 'They track in dirt,' my father would say. 'It's all I can do to manage you and your sister,' my mother would say."

"Well, you're thirty-one now," I say, "so I guess it's up to you."

"I recently had a cat," she says. And then pauses. "Can I meet your kittens? Can I? How about I come to your place for hors d'oeuvres?" She throws some frozen cheese puffs into her cart.

I don't really know what to say—or, more precisely, I don't know how to say no.

And so, when I pull out of the A&P parking lot, she is behind me, following me—almost bumper to bumper. Her car is as nondescript as her person—a white compact of indeterminate age—one of a million. As I'm driving, I'm realizing that I didn't pick her up, she picked me up, and it makes me nervous. Why is she following me? There's a reason people used to be "introduced," a reason why polite society is called polite and why it evolved the way it did—with great castle balls and formal letters of introduction.

She parks behind me in the driveway and comes in carrying a bag of her frozen things, asking if she can put it in the freezer for the moment, and suddenly it's entirely awkward. It's not like she's stopping by to borrow a roasting pan, or so I can show her how to make tarte tatin.

Tessie barks.

"Who is this big bad doggy?" she asks, in a babyish voice.

"It's okay, Tessie, it's a woman from the produce section who wanted to come home with me," I say.

"You invited me over," she says, still bent and talking to Tessie. "He said, 'Do you want to come to my house and play with the pussy cats?'"

"I don't think so."

"Um-hummm," she says to the dog, who wags her tail, grateful for attention.

I put away my groceries and ask if she'd like some coffee or tea.

"How about a glass of wine?" she says.

"Sure." I go into George's wine closet, feeling like I'm raiding the supply chest; I go in hoping to find something unremarkable—i.e., cheap. "You know," I say as I'm digging around, "it's not really my house."

"Oh," she says. "You seem to know where everything is."

"It's my brother's; I'm long-term house-sitting." I find a Long Island Chardonnay that looks like a gift someone brought to a cookout rather than something George got from his "wine dealer." "So do you do things like this frequently?" I ask.

"Like what?"

"Meet men in the grocery store and follow them home?"

"No," she says. "I'm just killing time."

"Until what—the five o'clock movie at the Yonkers cinema?"

"Where are the kittens?" she asks.

"Upstairs," I say, taking her to the master bedroom, which has been not so much converted as taken over as the cat nursery.

"Oh my God," she says, getting down on her hands and knees and crawling towards the kitten pen. "They're adorable." The kittens are in fact adorable; they're now walking around a bit and playing, and the queen seems willing to allow me to play with them. . . . I change the towels in their box.

"Lots of laundry," I say.

She picks one up and rubs it against her face—the queen mother seems unhappy.

"Best not to pick them up," I say.

"Sorry."

I am watching her down on her hands and knees in the rather smelly "cat room."

"Do you have a husband?"

She shakes her head no.

"A boyfriend?"

"Former, not current," she says.

We play with the kittens for a few minutes and then go back downstairs. Reflexively, I turn the television on. It's as though I need backup, more voices, the simulation of a cocktail party. A soon as I push the button, I think of George, who always had the television on.

I look at the woman. "There's a reason your mother said not to talk to strangers," I say.

"Can we change the channel?" she asks.

I'm thinking she means change the subject. "Sure," I say, pretending to push a button on my stomach—bing, channel changed. "Are you hungry?"

"No, I mean really, can we change the channel? I need to, like, clear my head. Can we put on something different, like not Headline News but a real show, you know, like *Two and a Half Men*? You know—cheerful?"

The show that starred a cokehead hooker-abuser—cheerful? I think, but say nothing. "Yeah, sure." And I change the channel. "You know it's not real people laughing," I say.

"It was once," she says, and there's nothing more to say. "It's kind of cold in here."

"Would you like a sweater?" In the front hall closet there are still some of Jane's things—I give the girl a soft magenta sweater.

"So you're married," she says.

"My brother's wife's. She passed away—keep it."

"It's cashmere," she says, as though obligated to disclose the value of what I'm giving away.

When she puts it on, I remember Jane wearing it, and I remember noticing the curve of her breast and feeling compelled to touch it, wondering if it felt as good as it looked, delicate, sexy. Now, on this other girl, the look is different, but it still has a special effect.

"Hors d'oeuvres?" she asks.

"You want me to make your cheese puffs?"

"What else have you got?" she asks in a way that makes me wonder what she bought the cheese puffs for—like she's saving them for something better.

I dig around in the freezer and find some old pigs-in-blankets and pop them into the toaster oven.

"Piping hot," I announce when I bring them out eleven minutes later—at the third commercial break.

"I didn't know they made these for home use," she says.

"Sorry," I say, not understanding her point.

"I thought pigs-in-blankets was, like, something only a caterer could get."

She dips the hot dog into the Dijon mustard and pops it in her mouth. "Wow, I like it. Quite a kick. What is that?"

"Dijon mustard?" And all I'm thinking is, how can you never have tasted Dijon mustard?

When the snacks are gone, we watch a little more TV, and then she declares she's still hungry. "Who delivers around here?"

"No idea," I say.

"I know there's pizza," she says.

"Had it for lunch," I say. "Chinese?"

"Do they deliver?"

I call my usual place. "It's me," I say, "Mr. Half Hot and Sour/Half Egg Drop. Do you by any chance deliver?"

"You sick, you can't come in?"

"Something like that."

"Okay, so what you want?"

I look at the woman. "A double order of my usual soup, a couple of egg rolls, an order of moo-shu pork, and sweet-and-sour shrimp. Anything else?" I ask the woman.

"Extra fortune cookies," she says, loud enough for the man taking the order to hear.

"How many you want?"

"Six," she says.

I give them the address and phone number and turn on the outside light. And then, a few minutes later, out of small talk and worried they won't find the house, I suggest we wait outside. We sit on the front stoop. There's something wonderfully melancholic about being outside on a spring evening watching the vanishing sunset against the deepening blue; the outlines of the old thick trees, full with bright fresh leaves, the surprising, gentle tickle of a breeze, and it somehow feels so good to be alive.

I breathe deeply.

"It's like when we were kids," she says. "We'd eat dinner early, before Dad came home, and then sit outside and wait for the Good Humor truck—my favorites were Strawberry Shortcake or Chocolate Éclair."

"We weren't allowed ice cream from the truck," I say, suddenly remembering. "My mother thought that was how children got polio."

Tessie is working the yard, sniffing everything, bushes, the daffodils, lilies that are pushing up through the dirt; she pees a little here and a little there.

"She's really well trained," the woman says. "She doesn't seem the least bit interested in going in the street."

"She hates the street."

Mr. Gao, the owner of the Chinese restaurant, pulls up to the curb in a Honda SUV with the name of the restaurant on the side.

I go down to the car. Mr. Gao is at the wheel, and his wife sits beside him, holding the heavy brown paper bag filled with dinner—the inside of the car smells delicious.

Even though she could easily hand me the bag through the window, the wife gets out of the car. She is wearing her Chinese hostess dress. "Ding-dong, delivery," she says, pretending to ring an invisible doorbell.

"How have you been?" I ask.

"Good," she says. "We no see you in long time."

"I've been busy. Who is minding the store?"

"Mr. Foo, the headwaiter. He has been with us a long time." She glances up at the house. "Nice place."

"Thank you," I say, as I take money out of my wallet.

I pay her, and she hands me the bag and then dips both hands in her side pockets and pulls them out, fists clenched.

"Pick a hand," she says.

I tap her right hand; she turns it over and opens. Her palm is filled with the white mints with the jelly center that they have at the cash register. "Trick-or-treat for you," she says.

"Thanks," I say, popping one in my mouth. She pours the rest into my hand—they are kind of sweaty-sticky.

The woman is hanging back, high up on the lawn, near the door, as though she doesn't want to be seen.

"Come visit soon," the woman from the restaurant says.

"I will, and thank you."

I watch as they drive off, and then turn back towards the house. The woman has already gone inside and is in the kitchen, looking for plates and silverware.

While we're eating, she asks if I've ever stolen anything.

"Like what?"

"Like anything?"

"No, but it sounds as though perhaps you have."

She nods.

"Okay, so what's the biggest thing you've ever stolen?"

She stops to think for a moment and takes a bite of her moo-shu roll-up; cabbage and soy sauce squirt out. "A thirty-seven-inch plasma TV," she says, still chewing.

"Under your coat?"

"No, in a rented car; I had to have it; I'd lived with a thirteen-inch for so long—no remote. It was time to get with the program."

"Do I need to worry that the real reason you came here is because you're casing the joint and you and your boyfriend are going to come back later with a U-Haul and clean me out?"

She looks up. "Oh no, I don't steal from people, only stores. I would never take something from someone I know."

"Do you know me?"

"You know what I mean, an individual as opposed to a corporation."

We finish eating, and then she neatly packs up the leftovers, puts them back in the brown bag, and tucks it into the fridge.

"Time for cookies," she says.

"Would you like some tea?" I ask.

"More wine," she says, cracking a fortune cookie. She opens one and then another and another, each time apparently not pleased with the result, until, finally, the fourth fortune reads, "Your Good Fortune Starts Now."

She feeds cookie bits to Tessie until I say no more: otherwise she'll get a tummy ache.

We retreat back to the sofa and watch more television, and I find myself thinking that I now understand what the perfect use for TV is—it gives people who have nothing in common something they can do together and talk about: it gives us familiar territory. I have a new respect for what George used to do, how television binds us as Americans—we are what we watch.

"Soon I have to go," she says.

I nod. I'm not thinking about sex, but apparently that's part of the deal—on the menu, right after orange sections and fortune cookies. Without warning, she dive-bombs me on the sofa with heavy wet kisses, her mouth open and oddly gifted: I can't help but respond. She's thrusting her tongue into me and then pulls back for a moment, lifts her shirt over her head—and essentially gifts me with herself. Her breasts are bigger, fuller than I would have expected— she wears a bra that is dark blue and lacy, which sets off her pale skin. Rather deftly she's down on me, wrestling my stiffening situation from its hiding place, but when I reach for the button of her jeans—she shakes her head no. I obey. The rest is frenetic, urgent, with a lot of grappling and sliding off the leather cushions and onto the floor. And then I come and it's over. I am left, spilled, my dick shrinking back in my lap like messy melted ice cream, and she is up, putting her shirt back on like this is just the way it goes. She walks into the kitchen, collects her frozen stuff from the freezer, and pops back into the living room, where I'm still on the floor. "See ya," she says, like it's all so easy.

"Do you want to give me your phone number?"

"I know where you live," she says.

When she's gone, I clean myself up, straighten the sofa cushions, and try not to think about how really strange it all was. I don't even know her name.

The next morning, via certified mail, I am informed that I am officially divorced. The mailman rings the bell, Tessie barks, I sign for the letter, and, *voilà,* I have the divorce in hand. It wasn't as hard as I thought it might be.

I remember as a kid overhearing conversations about marriages that had failed and how the wife had to prove the husband had been cheating, had to "catch him in the act," and other cases where one or the other of the couple would have to go live in another state for at least a year or two until things could be resolved.

Now it literally comes in the mail, along with discount coupons for pizza and a thank-you note from Ashley, written on her "official" stationery, embossed "A.S.S."

Ashley Sarah Silver.

Why didn't anyone think this might someday look odd when they named her—ASS?

"Thank you for the trip to Williamsburg, it was really fun, I learned a lot. Thank you for the dress, the shoes, the quill pens, the powdered ink, the writing paper, the sealing wax and seal, the book about Pocahontas, and anything else I forgot to write here. Your friend—Ashley Silver. P.S. I know you're not really my 'friend' but I didn't know what else to write—it seemed queer to write 'Love.' . . ."

Also in the mail is a letter from The Lodge.

> Dear Family Member,
>
> At a recent meeting The Board of Directors voted to approve the proposal to transition THE LODGE INC. from an inpatient mental health center to an executive conferencing and seminar site. This vote represents a change in direction for the organization from therapeutic environment to motivational and organizational meeting facility.
>
> As you know, The Lodge Inc. has served its patients, their families, and our surrounding community for almost fifty years. This change in focus represents a significant shift in the direction of mental health and associated health care services, not just at this facility but across the country, as the therapeutic model moves from inpatient to more outpatient, community-based services.
>
> We will work closely with all of our patients and their families to facilitate a smooth transition either back to the home community or to an appropriate facility for your family member. We hope to complete the transition process by the end of August and we will be in touch with you on an individual basis as to how best to proceed. We realize that receiving a letter such as this can prompt a spectrum of emotions and questions and would like you to feel free to call the director of our medical staff or our communications office with any questions you might have.
>
> As this news was somewhat unexpected, we apologize for the mass mailing—but wanted to be in touch with you before the news breaks in the media.
>
> Our deepest thanks for allowing us into your hearts, homes, and minds.
>
> Sincerely,
> John Trevertani
> CEO, The Lodge Inc.

I call.

"We tried to reach you about ten days ago," Rosenblatt says—clearly he's the designated 'responder'—"but someone else answered the phone and said you'd gone colonial, and then said he needed to get off the line—something about helping the kittens 'go.' He suggested I call back and leave a detailed message on the machine, but in the interest of privacy I thought I'd just give it a week or so and try you again."

"It was the pet minder—I was out of town, and the cat had kittens."

"Ahhh," he says. "Well, anyway, I see you've received the letter. We've already been in touch with George's lawyer as well as some folks from the state prosecutor's office to talk about what the appropriate setting for George might be. Given that the first set of charges was dismissed and that he remains pretrial on the murder charge, you could move him to another 'hospital'-type setting. My sense from his lawyer is that they'd like to keep him out of a traditional prison setting as long as possible—perhaps try something 'nontraditional.' But I must also add that I've spoken with George and I think, quite honestly, he's bored with the inpatient setting, and I worry that his resistance to participating in activities like group therapy, occupational therapy, crafting, and so on could end up reflected as noncompliance in the reports—and that won't fare well when the case goes to trial."

"You mean he's going to flunk pot-holder weaving?"

"Something like that—he doesn't play well with others."

"Never did. You mentioned a nontraditional program."

"Yes," he says, "I'm talking with some people at the state level about whether they might consider him for a pilot program they're running—it's rather unusual, and I'm hesitant to say more until I have a better sense of things. Perhaps we can talk again soon."

"I'm here," I say.

"As am I, until August," the man says. "Then all bets are off."

All bets are off—an understatement.

I find myself craving the normal, the repetitious, the everyday, the banal. I crave the comfort of what might seem to others to be exceedingly boring. For years, every Monday through Friday, I ate the same thing for breakfast— two slices of rye toast, one with butter, the other with orange marmalade; the same brand of bread, the same jam, the same butter. On Saturdays I had an egg along with the bread, and on Sundays either pancakes or French toast.

Dutiful regularity was something Claire and I actually found exciting. We took pleasure in going out to dinner on Friday, staying home on Saturday, making a habit of a matinee movie and Chinese carry-out on Sunday. If we added something new or different, it was discussed, regarding what it meant to the routine, the schedule.

But now it's like I'm in an endless free fall, the plummeting slowed only by the interruption of being summoned to do something for someone else. If it weren't for the children, the dog, the cat, the kittens, the plants, I would come completely undone.

Out of curiosity, I call the County Department of Social Services and ask what's involved in being a foster parent. Among my questions: Do you have to take whatever kid they give you, or can you pick?

"We're very careful where we place all the children," the woman says.

"Of course you are. . . ." That's why the coverage on TV about foster parents is so uplifting. "I guess what I'm asking is, what if the relative of a child needs a break and wants me to take the child for a while—is there a way to officially do that, to get certified or whatever it would be?"

"To accept what we call a directed placement, you would need to be an approved foster parent."

"And what does that entail?"

"A letter of intent, an application, a legal clearance, letters of recommendation, a home study, a medical form, proof of immunization, a letter from a lawyer, financials that would make clear you're not doing this for personal gain."

"All the foster parents in your system have passed these requirements?"

"Yes, sir, they have."

I go on to describe myself as a retired professor and author who does consulting work for the family of former President Nixon.

She cuts me off. "Do you have children?"

"I am the guardian for my brother's two children—my brother is disabled."

"You should see a psychiatrist," she says.

"Pardon?"

"Fancy people like you, that's what they do. Part of the application is a mental-health evaluation. It will move more quickly if you don't resist."

I am tempted to ask if the lousy foster parents I see on the evening news all have psychiatrists; but I restrain myself. "It's certainly something to think on," I say. "Can you send me more information?"

"Oh, we don't send anything anymore—always a budget crunch around here. It's all online."

"Right," I say. "I'll look online. Thank you."

Fuck it.

I call Ricardo's aunt and ask if she'd like me to take the boy out on Sunday.

"Can you pick him up early?" she asks.

"Is eight-thirty too early?"

"Eight-thirty is good," she says.

Part of building my relationship with the kids is talking with them more often and more honestly, as though they're real people.

Nate has been distant since the Williamsburg trip, I'm not sure why, but it seems smarter not to draw attention to it and simply to wait it out. I ask for his advice about what to do with Ricardo on Sunday.

"Well, there's an indoor rock-climbing place, or bowling, or the video arcade." Nate pauses. "You could just take him out and play catch. I didn't get the sense that anyone plays with him. My glove is in my bedroom closet. And if you want to give it to him, that's okay—it's my old glove, I've got a newer one."

"Very generous of you, Nate."

"What made you call him?"

"The truth, I missed the kid, and I miss you and Ash even more. I had a really good time on our trip." There's an awkward silence, but I don't mind, I'm glad I said what I did. "What about you, how's it going there?"

"Going," Nate says, and then goes quiet. "I wrote memoirs in our English class."

"I can imagine that would be difficult."

"I wrote about Dad—about something I remembered."

A long pause. "Maybe I could read it sometime?"

"I don't know," he says. It's as though what happened with George and Jane is just beginning to dawn on Nate; the initial trauma has now quieted, and he's beginning to put it all together. "I've been having trouble sleeping, and so I went to the school counselor, who suggested I join some kind of meditation group two nights a week."

"Might just give it a try," I say. "It's been a pretty difficult few months."

"We'll see," he says.

After talking with Nate, I call Ashley. "I just want to thank you for your note," I say.

"Did you get it?" she asks

"I did," I say. "And I was very impressed."

"When I was younger, I had a teacher who made us practice writing thank-you notes for everything. Like 'Dear God, Much thanks for the sunrise this morning. It was very beautiful and I look forward to seeing it again tomorrow. Your Friend, Ashley Silver.'"

"Amazing."

"She said if we had nothing else at least we'd have manners."

"She may have been right. What else is going on up there?"

"Science," she says. "We're doing a lot of cooking. There's a new teacher who is trying to use household chemistry as the basis for a cookbook, and the chemistry lab is functioning as a kind of test kitchen."

"Sounds flavorful," I say.

"Not really. I think it may actually be dangerous."

In preparation for my return to the New York law firm to begin working with the stories, I replay my Nixon tapes—videotaped interviews he did with Frank Gannon in which he talks about Pat, about his family. I think of it as "the official version." In all families we have the official version, the tacitly agreed-upon narrative that we tell about who we are and where we come from. I listen carefully, wanting to get Nixon's cadence, his phrasing into my head, so that tomorrow, when I'm looking at the stories, I can hear his voice.

The next morning, Wanda introduces me to Ching Lan, who will do the transcribing.

Tall and thin, like a hand-pulled noodle, she shakes my hand vigorously. "Pleased to be working with you," she says. "Just so you know, I read okay, I speak not so good."

"Where are you from?"

"Downstairs," she says. "I am the daughter of the deli owner."

"I know your mother from a long time ago," I say, laughing.

The woman nods. "She told me you are Mr. Cookie. I am so lucky," she says. "They discover me; I type really fast; I can read Chinese, so any bad handwriting looks good to me; I can read like the wind—so I read and I type for them. I have no idea what I type, but they don't care. It's good I see my parents at lunch. We go to work together. And if I no know something, I ask," she says happily.

"Where were you born?"

"Lenox Hill," she says. "I am twenty-one years old. I play professional volleyball part-time."

"You are a lucky woman," I say. "Transcendent."

Before we jump in, I explain a bit about my interest in Nixon to Ching Lan. "No worry. I study," she says. "Wanda told me what you are doing and I go on Wikipedia and learn so much."

I nod. "I am most interested in his personality and the ways in which his actions and reactions were of a particular era and culture—the era that built and defined the American Dream. I'm not sure how familiar you are with the subject; the phrase 'American Dream' was coined in 1931 by James Truslow Adams, who wrote, 'Life should be better and richer and fuller for everyone, with opportunity for each according to ability or achievement regardless of social class or circumstances of birth.' In 1931, Richard Nixon was eighteen years old, just coming into himself and when he resigned he was sixty years old, signaling the end of an era and perhaps the unacknowledged death of the dream, though some people feel it has just gone underground."

Something about Ching Lan inspires me to talk, to digress, to keep elucidating. It feels liberating, inspiring. And she seems to follow what I'm saying.

We work side by side. I explain how I want the documents transcribed and let her know that if she comes across anything that doesn't make sense she should bring it to my attention.

Every hour, Ching Lan takes a brief exercise break; as she stands, she encourages me to do the same. "Do what I do," she says, and I echo her movements, flowing like an ancient dance brought forward.

"What is it called?" I ask.

"Qigong," she says. "I do it every day—it brings blood to mind, awakens the true nature."

I follow along until she breaks away—leaning backwards so far that her hands are on the ground behind her. She then lifts one leg, and then the other into the air. Ching Lan is standing on her head—holding the position. "So good," she says. "So right." And then she is upright and back in her chair, and we carry on.

S unday at 8:30 a.m. I pick up the boy. His aunt has packed a large grocery bag full of food, Tupperware containers, metal forks, knives, spoons, napkins, and a change of clothes.

"He spills all the time," she says.

Ricardo shrugs.

"How many meals did you pack?"

"Not so much," she says. "He's got a good appetite."

"Okay, then," I say. "I'll plan to have him back by six—I know it's a school night. And here's my cell number if you need to reach us, and if you want me to we'll check in during the day."

"My husband is taking me on a day trip," she says. "You go have fun."

On the way to the car, I ask Ricardo if he's had breakfast. "Yes," he says, "but I could have more."

"How about we wait a couple of hours; meantime, we can go to the park and play a little ball."

At the park, Ricardo spots a group of boys kicking a soccer ball. I can tell he wants to join in, so I encourage him to go.

"I don't know them," he says sadly.

I walk with him, inject myself into the group of fathers on the side, and ask if Ricardo can join in—one of the men blows a whistle and yells, "New man comin' in." I give Ricardo a shove and he's in the game. The fathers stand around talking about their hot-water heaters, their zoned heat, and other manly things like gutter cleaning. I nod along as part of the chorus. I also watch Ricardo. He's not very coordinated—tripping over the ball, falling on his ass after he kicks it—but the other boys seem to tolerate having him in the game.

When the game dissolves, Ricardo and I sit on the benches; I suggest that perhaps he and I could do some practicing with a ball—I think there's one in the basement.

Ricardo breathes deeply, red-faced, trying to catch his breath while digging through his grocery bag.

"Do you want to have a picnic?"

"Maybe you could eat this and I could get McDonald's," he suggests. "My aunt is a really good cook, but I eat it every day."

He hands me something that looks like an empanada—it's filled with beef, onions, spices that are hard to name. Despite the fact that it's at room temperature, it's delicious.

"Okay," I say, "I'll trade, but for what?"

"Double cheeseburger, large fries, and a shake?" Ricardo suggests.

"Cheeseburger, small fries, and no shake."

"Fine," he says, grudgingly.

We go to McDonald's and then to a movie—it's some kind of 3D kid thing—and after I get used to the glasses and my nausea passes, it's kind of great. Ricardo laughs so many times in his funny, strange way that he wins me over—pounding me on the arm when he likes something.

"I have to run a quick errand—do you like hardware stores?"

"I guess," the kid says.

The upstairs toilet needs a new handle. I find the part and then notice the kid poking around. From a couple of rows away I watch as he digs through bins of this and that, and then I see him digging through his pockets. At first I worry he's shoplifting, but then realize he's counting out change.

"How much have you got?" I ask, coming closer.

"Two dollars and sixty-seven cents."

"How much do you need?"

"Two dollars ninety-nine cents."

"Plus tax," I say. "What is it you want?"

Ricardo points to a green frog-shaped flashlight that makes a sound like ribbit-ribbit. I give him a dollar.

There among the nuts and bolts, a slightly older guy says to me, "Nice boy."

I smile. "He's a good kid."

And then the man bends and pointedly asks Ricardo, "Where's your other daddy?"

Ricardo looks confused.

"What are you doing?" I ask the guy, immediately protective of Ricardo.

"Sorry, I didn't mean to offend, I just assumed you were from a two-daddy family; usually straight families get the white kids and they give the leftovers to the queers."

I pin the guy to a shelf. "You have no idea what you're talking about; you don't even have a clue." I've got a fiery knot in my gut, and what I really want to do is punch the guy in the nose. All my life I've never punched anyone in the nose, but now would be the perfect moment.

"My father's dead," Ricardo says, frightened.

Realizing my behavior is actually freaking Ricardo out, I let go of the guy.

"Cocksucker," the guy says, shaking me off.

I flip him the bird—another thing I haven't done in years. Disgusted, the guy walks away.

"What does that mean?" Ricardo asks, mimicking the gesture.

"Please don't do that," I say quickly.

"You just did it," he says.

"I know, but I shouldn't have. It's the kind of thing that can get a fella in a lot of trouble." We go to the register, and while the clerk rings things up, I grab a couple of glow sticks from the bin at the counter, the kind you keep in your glove compartment for emergencies. I buy one for myself and one for the kid—spending nervous energy.

"So what does it really mean?" Ricardo asks as we're leaving the store.

"What does what mean?"

"That thing I'm not supposed to do again."

"It just means a person is very frustrated. . . ."

"I was hoping it was like sign language or like an ancient Indian gesture," Ricardo says.

When we're outside, I snap the light sticks; they spring to life, glowing like alien sabers against the waning afternoon light.

"Cool," Ricardo says.

I hand him one. We pretend to duel—it's fun. I haven't played like that in . . . forever.

And later, when I drop him off at his aunt's house, I say, "Hey, I'm sorry about what happened in the hardware store."

Ricardo shrugs. "It's cool," he says. "You protected me." And then he gives me a kind of a hug, like how maybe he once saw a kid on a TV show hug a grown-up, or like something from *Two and a Half Men* that would be punctuated by a guffaw from the laugh track. "Let's do it again soon," he says, exiting.

That evening, while looking for something, I find myself in the basement. It's like a multigenerational storehouse of stuff, skis, golf clubs, tennis racquets, sprinklers, old garden hoses, boxes of glass Mason jars, a good amount of which I suspect was left here by the previous owners and somehow memorialized by George and Jane as ephemera from another era.

I decide to get rid of it all.

Four hours later, with a dozen giant green plastic bags dragged to the curb and an overflowing blue recycle bin, I feel as though I've mucked out a stall. Someone had to do it.

Why did George have four sets of golf clubs? Why were there tennis racquets galore and skis so long, bindings and boots so old, all of it caked with a kind of crusty residue, perhaps toxic?

Finished and filled with a master's sense of virtue, I microwave myself a late dinner and call Nate.

"How was Ricardo?" he asks.

"Good. I accidentally taught him to flip the bird."

"Accidentally?"

I explain, and Nate says, "Sounds like you're off to a good start."

"In the long run I like to think it's a minor offense." I pause. "I never know what to tell you or not—about your father."

"Yeah," Nate says, not exactly giving me a clue, "it's hard to know."

"The place where he's been is closing."

"What kind of a place is it?"

"Therapeutic," I say, for lack of a better word.

"Do you know what he used to do with me?" Nate asks. "He'd turn me upside down and swing me around. It was half fun, half terrifying; sometimes he would crash me into things, like a table, chairs, or a wall. I didn't know if he just got so distracted or if he really had no idea, but it was a fine line. It might have been different if I was another kid—another kid might have liked it more."

"Or less," I say. "It sounds like you were a pretty good sport about it. Why take on what some other kids would have tolerated? It's okay to say it scared you, or that you just hated it for whatever reason."

"I always thought he wanted me to be another kid, he thought I was a wuss." Nate pauses. "Are you eating while we're talking?"

"Yeah, sorry, I'm starving; somehow I didn't eat with Ricardo. I was setting an example about moderation, and then, when I got home, I went on a tear and cleaned out the whole basement. There was so much shit down there."

Nate gets very quiet. Worse than quiet—serious. "Like what?"

"Skis, tennis racquets, boxes of old glass jars . . ."

"My award-winning science experiment on remaking antibiotics from home-grown sources such as ginger, horseradish, mustard, and nasturtiums?"

"I don't think so," I say, worriedly remembering that some of the jars did in fact have dirt and something growing inside—I thought it was simply mold. . . . "It was just a lot of junk, your dad's old golf clubs."

"And my clubs?" Nate asks.

"Which ones are yours?" I quiz, likely sounding as nervous as I am.

"Mine were in a wheely plaid bag, and I have a second set as well with blue knit toppers."

"You know what," I say, stumbling, knowing full well they're in a bag at the curb, "I'll take a look, I'll double-check on that, just to be sure."

"Damn it," Nate says, "can't you leave anything alone? Do you have to put your mark on everything? It's not your stuff. It's my house—that's where I live. . . . Are you going to make it so I don't have a home, so there's no place left to go?"

"Nate," I venture, trying to repair what's been done. "Nate . . ."

"No. I have been so fucking calm, so goddamned decent through this whole thing—I think I gave you the wrong impression. You fucked my mother, my father killed my mother, and now you're in charge of me? I am not going down this road—I am not going to be another one of you. I will not let you drag me down." And he hangs up.

I am taken aback—not only is he right, but it's surprising that this moment hasn't come sooner. I run down to the curb and reclaim his golf clubs along with any other equipment that looks reasonably current, and "reinstall" the goods in the basement in what I hope is a user-friendly sort of way.

A couple of hours later, Nate sends me an e-mail.

"Apologies—one of the guys gave me some of his medication telling me it would help me concentrate and I think I had a bad reaction. P.S. My school may call you about the broken desk but I can assure you that was really an accident—it had been in precarious condition from the year before when Billy butthead landed on it during an attempt to fly."

I write back: "No worries, your point well taken. Your clubs and all else— safe and sound."

Tuesday morning, just after eight, the phone rings.

"There's someplace I need you to go with me," Cheryl says.

"What happened to 'hi, hello, how are you'?"

"Is that necessary?" she says. "I'm trying to ask you for a favor."

"It's customary," I say. "It's the way most things begin. Where is it you'd like to go?"

"Is that important? Isn't it enough just that I'm asking you to go?"

I wait.

"A club," she says.

"What about your husband, can't you get him to take you?"

"I can't even get him to go to a movie. So—will you go?"

"What is it?"

"Like-minded people?" she suggests.

"A political group?"

"Not exactly, more like a social gathering."

"When is it?"

"Tonight."

"This evening?"

"Like you're so busy? It's eight to eleven—I figure to go around nine."

"Does it have a name?"

She sighs. "It's a friends-and-neighbors party. Do you want me to pick you up?"

"I'll meet you there. Have you got an address?"

"It's at the laser-tag place called Night Vision, in the mini-mall. . . ."

"The one with the CVS?"

"That's the one. Can we meet in the parking lot?"

"Sure," I say. "What's the dress code?"

"Casual," she says.

Sitting in the car outside of CVS, waiting, I consider telling Cheryl about the woman from the A&P. I'm not sure why I feel guilty about letting the grocery-store woman "service" me—like I'm somehow cheating on a woman who is cheating on her husband—or why I feel compelled to tell all to a woman who I have absolutely no relationship or commitment to, and yet I am equally or more uncomfortable keeping it to myself. I am lost in this peculiar reverie about confession when she taps on my car window—scaring the hell out of me.

I get out. "I'm not usually up and out at this hour," I say, half kidding—I used to like to go and listen to jazz in the evenings when I lived in New York.

"I went to the grocery store to kill time," she says, somewhat nervous.

"I spent a hundred seventy-eight dollars. I'm assuming the perishables will be fine for a couple of hours."

"As long as you didn't buy anything melty."

"Meat and milk," she says.

"You changed your hair," I say, realizing that every time I see her she looks different. Today it's in more of a wedge, like Dorothy Hamill, the ice-skater.

"It's a wig," she says.

As we're crossing the parking lot, I begin, "In the interest of full disclosure. . . ."

"Don't," she says, and I stop. "Is it really important?" she then asks.

"Not really," I say.

"It can wait," she says, half a question.

I nod—it can.

"I'm a little nervous," she says.

"What about?"

"I've never been to one of these things before." She pauses. "In the interest of full disclosure," she says, almost mocking me, "I probably should have told you over the phone, but . . ."

"What?"

"I'm not sure if everyone will be clothed," she says, not missing a beat.

"What?" I stop; a car pulling in brushes past me, nearly taking me down.

"I'm just saying . . ."

"That it's, like, a nudist party? And somehow you didn't want to tell me until now?"

"I didn't want you to be nervous," she lies.

"You didn't want me to say no."

She says nothing.

"Is nudity required?" I ask.

"Optional."

"Are you going to get naked?" I ask.

She shrugs. "First I want to see what it's like."

There's a handwritten sign taped to the door—"Closed for Private Party." A table in front of the ticket booth is decorated with a banner that reads "Welcome OurFriendsandNeighbors.org."

"May I help you?" a guy in polo shirt and khakis asks.

"I signed up for the event," Cheryl says.

"May I have your name?"

"Cheryl Stevens."

He finds her name on the list, smiles, and says, "And I see you've brought a friend."

"Is that all right?"

"Of course, the more the merrier," he says, handing me forms to fill out.

"We are a private membership club—ten dollars to join and thirty for tonight's event." I take the papers.

"While you're working on those, I'll go over the parameters and give you some information on our upcoming potluck."

Working on the form, I initially skip the name and address parts and fill out my e-mail and cell-phone number.

The man in the polo shirt notices the blanks.

"Not sure who you want to be tonight?" he asks.

I say nothing.

"Come as yourself," he says, "it keeps things simple. Once, we had a guy who bumped his head at a roller rink, and it took three days to figure out who he was."

I leave the blanks open.

"Okay, the parameters . . . As you know, this is a public facility that we've rented for the occasion, so we want to reiterate that, while we are a clothing-optional gathering, it's not a free-for-all," he says, winking. "And . . ." He pauses. "This one we take seriously: no means no. We're rigorous about that. We may be a private club, but there's basic mutual respect—take your lead from the ladies." And then he looks up at me. "Our privacy statement—we are highly confidential—I urge you to use first names only. We do not sell, give, or tell any of our membership list or use it for anything other than to provide discreet invitations to our events."

I nod.

"Have you ever played laser tag before?"

"Nope," we both say.

"There are small lockers just inside the entryway for any personal items, and referees who will review the rules of the game and instruct you on use of the vests and the guns. It's open bar—your thirty dollars covers that—and if you need to take a rest, there are a few private rooms to the back of the facility: make a left in front of the mirrored mountain. We also have private parties every other week—that's when the fun stuff happens, but it's behind closed doors, private houses, invitation only. Tonight is more of a meet-and-greet, a good opportunity to get to know us and have us get to know you." He smiles. "How did you hear of us?"

"A woman in my Pilates class kept saying she thought I was ripe for adventure and hinting at something."

"Was it Doreen?"

"It was. How did you know?"

"My wife," the guy says happily. "She's not here tonight—the little one had an ear infection. I'll tell her you were here; she'll be thrilled. We always need more women. Lots of guys, never enough girls." He laughs. "But that's just my perspective."

As we're walking down the black-lit hallway into the "chamber," Cheryl says, "I took my son here for a couple of birthday parties—he liked it."

"You brought him here?"

"Not this event," she says, "this place. What Doreen told me is that once a month they rent it out—they pay double the asking rate and provide their own staff. The volunteer decorating team comes in midafternoon and makes some special changes.

"I think we should suit up in laser gear," she says. "It'll help us relax and blend in."

We don the outfit—a chest pack with gun attached on a kind of stretchy leash. One of the referees explains, "Your gun won't fire for fifteen seconds after you've been hit—a hit in effect turns you off. Twenty-five hits and you're off for five minutes." He goes on to illustrate how you can use the mirrors to ricochet a shot towards someone—so you don't always have to stalk your prey. "You guys are good to go. Just remember, no running, no pushing."

As we're heading in, we pass the bar, where a woman in a yellow sports bra with laser gear on top is drinking white wine from a paper cup while two shirtless men, one with a shaved chest, chug an assortment of hard and soft beverages.

I am expecting both more and less. I have in my mind's eye images from 1970s sex clubs where half-bald or toupeed men fondle sexually liberated women right, left, and center. By comparison, this seems hairier, fleshier, and more juvenile—it may be the laser tag that brings it down. Here sweaty men run around in BVDs with toy guns, in a cracked reenactment of games played at home when they were nine, ten, and eleven, but now the games have been pushed to a newly awkward edge. The men range from late thirties to mid-fifties, and their behavior is made creepier by a plethora of body hair, fat, and the occasional tattoo. Not that I came here as a critic, but I am amazed at how unattractive the people are, and how unashamed—one somehow thinks of only those who have the body to do it as exposing themselves like this. And, further, it would seem as though the men gave no forethought to the idea that they'd be running around half naked—they've made no effort in the fashion department and are wearing the most standard white BVDs and semi-saggy boxers, their plump junk visibly flipping from side to side as they scurry around shooting at each other. The women have tried a little harder. Some of them wear arty lingerie or some version of hooker-hostess costumes; others look like they're about to take off on a bike ride—sports bras and tight shorts, one with the ass cheeks cut away. All of it reads like porn gone wrong and gives me a new appreciation for the professionals versus the amateurs.

"I see someone I know," Cheryl says.

"Where?"

"Over there, at the three o'clock position, the guy and his wife."

I look. At the two-thirty spot I see a group of men watching two women kiss. I've never entirely understood why men like watching two women, or having two women at once. To me it just seems potentially confusing: four breasts, two whoosits, a lot of work to do. . . . I imagine blacking out from overload.

"I remember hearing about them," Cheryl says.

"Hearing what?"

"Something like this—that they did things like this—but I didn't think it was true. I thought I was the only one."

"Clearly there's never just one—there's always some sort of a need."

At nine-thirty the referees announce a five-minute break, to be followed by a round of strip tag—every time you're hit you have to take something off. Whoopee!

I head for the bar, stopping en route to peek into the private rooms. It's a lot of what we used to call dry humping—but would I do it in a mini-mall with people from the "neighborhood"?

I hug the bar, drinking more than usual. Topless women with laser packs make themselves wine spritzers while men run around with semi-stiffies—and I can't tell what's got them more jazzed, the naked girls or the thrill of the game.

"May I?" I overhear a woman ask Cheryl.

"I guess," Cheryl says.

I look away—even in this place, people are entitled to their privacy. Out of the corner of my eye, like slow motion, I see the woman's hand, her long thin fingers, the glint of her wedding ring as it extends towards Cheryl's breast. The woman brushes Cheryl with her fingers, lightly, almost as if dusting the breast—touching without touching. And then she leans forward and kisses her. Cheryl kisses back. And then the woman is gone—vaporized by the experience.

"I don't want to rain on your parade, but I have to go to the city tomorrow morning and want to be home at a decent hour," I say to Cheryl.

"I let a woman touch me," she says, apparently unaware that I was standing right next to her when it happened.

"Was it your first time?"

"Yes." She pauses. "She touched me so lightly—it tickled."

"It sounds like maybe you liked it."

"I didn't not like it."

"That's what you call a double negative—do you mean that you liked it?"

"I wouldn't go that far. I've felt a woman's hands before—but always, like, in a doctor's office—like, raise your arm, and they take your breast and smoosh it into the mammo machine—but I never had someone touch me just for fun. I had no idea a woman's lips felt that soft. What about you? Any action?"

"Yeah, a guy rubbed against me," I say. "But I think he was just trying to get by. He rubbed me, then said sorry. It was the 'sorry' that made me uncomfortable. The rub was kind of interesting, but when he apologized I felt like a creep because I actually liked it."

"I think you're reading too much into it," she says.

"Wouldn't be the first time," I say. "I've got to go," I say, "it's getting late."

"Do you have time for a coffee?" she asks. "We could debrief?"

She laughs at her own joke. As we're crossing the parking lot she says: "Can you believe such a place exists, right here, right next to the drugstore, the hospital supply, and the card shop? I buy cards for my mother-in-law in there."

Stinking of sweat, some of it other people's, we go to Friendly's.

"I don't think you were very into it," she says as we're sitting down.

"Frankly, I was surprised by how depressing it was."

"Me too," she says.

"What can I get you?" the waitress asks.

"Coffee," I say.

"Is that all?"

"Coffee and apple pie?"

"À la mode?" she asks.

"Yes, please."

"Coffee and apple pie," Cheryl says. "That's what Grandfather used to order."

"Fine," I say. "Eighty-six the apple pie, and I'll have a clown sundae—with chocolate ice cream."

When the waitress leaves, I lean forward. "Why did you want to do this?" I ask Cheryl, who looks tearful.

"I'm just really curious," she says. "I would think you already know that about me. I want something different, something more."

My ice cream arrives, and she digs in.

"You need a job," I suggest, "maybe get a real-estate license, or go back to school and become a social worker."

"I got the real-estate license," she says. "It just means you fuck strangers in other people's houses." Impromptu, she belches; the scents of white wine and chocolate ice cream blast across the table. "Apologies," she says. "I don't think I'm supposed to drink while I'm on this new medication."

"I didn't know you were on new medication," I say, sobering up.

"Yeah—a whole new regimen."

"Do you think maybe the new medication prompted this whole thing tonight? How do you know it's what you actually want to do and not some strange side effect?"

"I don't think the desire to explore a swingers' club is listed under side effects. Like I said, I'm curious; is that a bad thing? And, honestly, I like the idea of having sex with some guy and not having to do his laundry and make his lunch and shop for his socks. . . ."

"Can I get you anything else?" the waitress asks.

"Just the check," I say, noticing that now several other "couples" from the party have come into Friendly's, pink-cheeked and laughing too loud.

I dress for my last class, solemnly. I wear a suit and tie; there is a seriousness of purpose, like for a funeral, I suppose. I enter with my head held high, having checked my underlying grief and sense of betrayal, carrying only an old oversized cassette recorder. "Today's class marks the closing of a chapter of my life," I say as I'm setting up. "In honor and memory of Richard Milhous Nixon, I am going to record my comments." I set the recorder down on the hollow lectern, thumping it several times to get their attention. The thumping on the hollow wood is amplified, thump, thump, like the pounding of a gavel—hear ye, hear ye. I press "play" and "record" simultaneously and clear my throat. "Testing, one, two, three . . . testing, testing." I hit "stop," then "rewind." I play back the test; the tone is as expected—classically metallic.

"I come before you on this, our final meeting together, with the power of history foremost in my mind, the awareness that if we live only in the present, without consciousness of the past, we will have no future. Imagine, if you will, an America without Richard Nixon, a country without a past, a world in which it is truly every man for himself and there is no building of trusts, alliances between men and countries. Think of your own moment in time. Your history—your culture, your behavior—is perhaps more documented, scrutinized, than any previous generation. Your image is captured dozens if not hundreds of times per day, and the line you are expected to walk is thin and unforgiving. Consider for a moment the Internet posting that doesn't go away—remains perpetually present, doesn't allow for a kind of growth, progression, or forgiveness."

I pause for breath.

"Today's class marks a passage in my life: my last performance on the academic stage, a curtain call of sorts. I thought I'd take the opportunity to simply share my thoughts with you.

"But first I am going to ask you to turn off all your electronic equipment and imagine a morning meeting in the Nixon White House—the President, his Chief of Staff, Haldeman, Haig, Henry Kissinger, and a select handful of others—and imagine each of them holding in one hand a cup of Starbucks coffee with his name and the contents annotated on the side and in the other hand brandishing some kind of electronic device on which he is e-mailing, tweeting away, texting, whatever. Would Nixon think they weren't listening? And instead of writing his thoughts, his middle of the night musings, in ink on legal pads, would Dick Nixon break out his smartphone and tweet away or text himself volumes of digression on the devolving state of the union?

"Think about it as you power down your devices—this is my last stand, and I want your full attention."

I pause for an extended moment; assorted electronic goodbyes chirp around the room. "This is the nineteenth time I have stood before you—in a place that has been a center of learning for so many years, shaping minds and lives for generations. In all of my decisions, in the materials that I presented to you, I have tried to do what is best. I felt it was my duty to make every effort to introduce you to your history and the history of this country and to make every effort to educate you as to the relevance, the value of both knowing and questioning the past. Today is in some ways a resignation. In order to teach, one must have students, eager learners. I am aware that many of you took this class to fulfill a requirement that you take a history class. I know, via scuttlebutt, that this class is rumored to be "a fluff." I am equally aware that many of you are the first in your family to even go to college, and that, instead of taking that privilege as a mandate to educate yourselves, you use it as time to hang out with friends and party. I have always thought of myself as a professor, a teacher, a mentor to the young. With no children of my own, I have perhaps wrongly allowed my students to act as surrogates. I have rallied for you, shown up for your football games, cheered you on. I believed in you. And despite shifts in the winds of academia, in the tides of the study of history, despite waning interest, I have always felt it was my duty to persevere. And let me make this perfectly clear . . . I would have preferred to carry on despite the personal hardship, the fact that a teaching obligation cuts into my hours of research and writing as a historian. I have never been a quitter, but, given the direction this institution feels the study of history is moving in, it would seem my effectiveness is coming to its conclusion. My own view of things is a long one. Here I note the contrast of the Nixon White House to that of Bush Senior and Dick Cheney, who makes Richard Nixon seem simplistic by contrast.

"It is my sense that Nixon was besieged with a guilt about his family, particularly the two brothers he lost early in life. And in the dark days of my own recent family drama, I think of my relationship to my own blood and the meaning of being thy brother's keeper—literally. I think of my own marriage failing in this public debacle. I consider Dick and Pat and their fortitude in the face of all that we knew and didn't know about them. I think of my rage at being trapped in this life, inexorably of my own making."

I pause for breath.

"Pardon the digression.

"There are paths, forks in the road, journeys we must take. Sometimes it's not a choice, but about what we do with what we are given. Today it is with

mixed emotions, marking a beginning and an end, that I am leaving the university and will be working full-time on the Nixon Project and am looking
forward to deepening my relationship with my subject matter. For those who
have come to bid me adieus, our special guests: a young rabbinical student
exploring the relationship of Jews to crime, Ryan, good luck to you; to the
Chairman of this department, Ben Schwartz, whom I have known for many
years, and who knows the depth of my feeling for him, I need not say more.
Today I speak to you not only as students, but as men and women—citizens,
I hope. Further, I pledge to you today that, as long as I have a breath of life in
my body, I shall continue in that spirit. I shall continue to work for the great
causes to which I have been dedicated throughout my years. There is one cause
above all to which I have been devoted, and to which I shall always be devoted,
for as long as I live. When I first took the oath, I made this sacred commitment, to 'consecrate my office, my energies, and all the wisdom I can summon
to the cause of peace among nations.' I have done my very best in all the days
since to be true to that pledge. As a result of these efforts, I am confident that
the world is a safer place today, not only for the people of America but for the
people of all nations, and that all of our children have a better chance than
before of living in peace rather than dying in war. This, more than anything,
is what I hoped to achieve. This, more than anything, is what I hope will be
my legacy to you."

Again I pause, and look around to see if anyone has caught on vis-à-vis the
degree to which I have "quoted" or "sampled" some of Nixon's most famous
speeches, including of course his resignation. There is not a glimmer of recog-
nition in the room. I conclude, as did the master, "May God's grace be with
you in all the days ahead." The room explodes with applause. I nod, I bow, I
almost fucking curtsy. Near the back of the room a hand goes up. Authorial
guilt overwhelms me. "Before I take your questions, I must footnote that my
comments were drawn quite extensively from speeches delivered by Richard
Nixon—namely, his resignation broadcast live on television at nine p.m. on
August 8, 1974."

A girl in the front row laughs. "Nineteen seventy-four, I wasn't even born
yet," she says.

"My point exactly. And now to the question from the rear."

"Can you tell us, without being able to factor in a final exam, what you will
grade us on?"

"I will be grading on a U-turn," I say, smiling at my own wit. They look perplexed. "If you turned in your papers and participated in class discussions, you will pass the course."

The clock strikes five, the students cheer; I'm not sure if it's because this is the last class or because they know I will finally stop talking. Whatever it is, I choose to take it for myself. I leave victorious, holding my cassette recorder high above my head, and thinking aloud, "You never even knew me."

A few days later, I am summoned to The Lodge for a "placement" meeting regarding George. When the administrative secretary calls to confirm, she advises me to bring extra clothing for George. "Think outdoorsy," she says. "Jeans, heavy socks, wool sweaters."

"It's a done deal?"

"No idea," she says. "I'm just reading what's written on the Post-it. Also, I'm supposed to ask you if you're planning to stay the night."

"I'm not," I say curtly. "Do you know who else will be there?"

"I have the attendants listed as you, your brother's lawyer or a representative from their firm, the medical director, and someone from the State Corrections Office."

"Does the person from the state have a name?"

"Walter Penny."

While we're talking, I Google Walter Penny and get photos of a superskinny college track star from Gambier, Ohio. Do we live in a world where there are multiple Walter Pennys?

The pet minder comes to take care of Tessie and the kittens.

I pack for George, emptying his drawers into an enormous suitcase—more like an armoire than something you'd attempt to travel with. I figure what he doesn't want can be donated.

At The Lodge, they remove the suitcase from the car and carry it in for me.

"Checking in?" the fellow asks.

"You're new," I say.

"Is it that obvious?" he asks.

"Yes."

They're running late. I sit in the waiting area outside the director's office, eating from a blue tin of Danish Butter Cookies and drinking tea poured from a pot that I suspect has a higher-than-normal bacterial count. I hold the tin on my lap to catch crumbs.

"Manny," the guy sitting opposite me says, jutting his hand forward, "from the firm—Wurlitzer, Pulitzer and Ordy."

"Have we met before?"

"I came along for the ride with Ordy in White Plains. Rutkowsky isn't going to be here today—he's in the middle of a trial."

"Any idea how formal or informal the meeting will be?" I ask.

Manny shrugs. I offer him a cookie; he declines.

"I was under the impression that it was going to be a discussion of what should happen next—but then they asked me to bring George's extra clothing. I get the sense that decisions have already been made."

"Nothing is definite," Manny says. "But, in the interest of conserving energies and expenditures, we have a plan that I think will serve George well."

I must have scowled or made some other face.

Manny anxiously adjusts the large shopping bag he's got parked between his feet and says, "Why don't we wait for the official meeting."

A few minutes later, we're summoned into Dr. Crawley, the medical director's office. Walter Penny is already there. Clearly there was a pre-meeting to which we were not invited.

"Come in, come in," Dr. Crawley says. He's a plump, balding man of indeterminate age. Walter Penny introduces himself, shaking hands with a strong up-and-down pump. He's young, rail-thin, and wearing a cheap suit, which looks good on him only because there is nothing to him. His hair is close-cropped into a fuzzy buzz cut. He could pass for eighteen. Scratching behind his ear, Walter Penny makes a repetitive gesture reminding me of Tessie scratching herself with her back foot.

I look at him, wondering if he is in fact the Walter Penny of Gambier, Ohio, who ran track a couple of years ago, and curious what he could possibly know about people, or justice.

He hands me his business card. Dr. Walter Penny, with a Ph.D. in criminal justice.

"Walter, how'd you get interested in criminal justice?" I ask.

"My family was in the military, and we're hunters," he says as though that explains it.

I nod. "What part of the world are you from?"

"Ohio," he says.

Manny hands over the shopping bag, and the director extracts from it an enormous tin of Garrett's of Chicago caramel corn.

"It's from my brother-in-law," Dr. Crawley says. "The infamous Rut-kowsky."

"A bribe?" I suggest.

"My wife loves the stuff," Crawley says. "She grew up on it." He pulls him-self together. "Okay, so Walter here is going to tell us a bit about the program he's been working on—and I can tell you that, while we've not placed anyone in it before, I've been talking with lots of folks about options for George, and short of either a classic loony bin or jail, there's not a lot out there. And I hon-estly don't think either of those would be right for George."

"May I?" Walter asks.

"Please," Dr. Crawley says.

"We're always exploring new concepts in criminal justice, everything from the architecture of prison structures to the psychological experience of punish-ment. The Woodsman is an experiment that can be boiled down to a low-cost survival-of-the-fittest model. And while George isn't the typical candidate, we think he's a viable candidate and this could be a strong placement option."

"Who is your typical candidate?" I ask.

"Someone with more of a criminal history, rural as opposed to urban expe-rience, not much white-collar, more robbery, grand theft, a little murder. A man good with his hands who needs physical challenge. We've found that violent men are less likely to behave violently in a natural setting. When they're up against the elements, they train themselves, they self-regulate—they see it as man versus the land, instead of man versus man. We have no serial killers—we think of that as a very different profile, and as much as we have a legal mandate to punish, we also have to respect the inalienable rights of our prisoners and not put them at undue risk. Essentially, The Woodsman is designed as an inexpensive self-policing penal colony. As you may know, there is a long history for a self-sustaining prison farm, as well as the Quaker model. They built the first penitentiary, which included the need to look towards the sky." Walter in fact looks up as he speaks. "In essence, see the light, be with God, and repent!"

"You sound almost like a minister when you say that," the medical director notes.

"Thank you," Walter Penny says.

"Could you be a little more specific? The way you've described it so far, it sounds like an episode of *Mutual of Omaha's Wild Kingdom*," I say.

"Show him the PowerPoint," Crawley urges.

"Of course," Walter says, tilting the screen of his laptop towards me. "A quick bit of background to keep in mind: the cost per prisoner in New York is more than fifty thousand dollars per year, the cost per prisoner in our program is less than ten thousand per man." He pushes the start button. A macho logo comes on-screen, "THE WOODSMAN," followed by intense heavy-metal music and a highly produced video rollout that looks like a commercial for joining the army or the National Guard. The "sample" inmates—"Tough, Strong, Willful, Resistant"—are shown climbing trees, fishing for their own food in a river, rappelling off a rock wall. All using the carefully selected supplies provided in their Woodsman pack, which is given to them upon launch into the program and replaced annually. It closes with the disclaimer that "The Woodsman is a back-to-basics model for human management using the Physics 300a or 300b microchip, tracked by satellite, with the 300b chip also providing a constant read of vital signs. Should there be any kind of uprising or behavior problem, it can be neutralized either temporarily or permanently by drone or computer-assisted power shot within one to five minutes."

"That's pretty much it," Walter Penny says. "The prisoners are micro-chipped and released onto a forty-five-hundred-acre parcel, a former military testing facility. There are no live munitions there, but enough infrastructure so that we can run some back-office activities from the underground bunker and so on. There are shelters for sleep, the prisoners farm and forage, and there is a central structure above the bunker where they can come and do laundry, bathe, and restock their supplies—we have government cheese, surplus foods including peanut butter and milk, and water on hand. We're testing a new doc-in-a-box system by which routine medications can be dispensed and medical conditions can be tracked via a robotic field medic who can take temperature, blood pressure, EKG, and draw blood if needed. In the winter—each man has a solar yurt."

"So it's like a tag-and-release wildlife refuge—only the wildlife is human?" I ask.

"Yep," Walter says. "This is a highly monitored safe zone—we have it under twenty-four-hour observation."

"What if one of the guys goes after another?"

"We know where they are and what they're doing at all times—we monitor them around the clock. And discipline, if needed, is swift and unforgiving."

"From above," the medical director says, like he's drunk the Kool-Aid.

"That's right—a drone is launched, and that's all she wrote."

"What if they manage to leave the chip behind and escape?"

"They're chipped at the back of the neck; there's no way to remove it without losing cerebral function. If one kills another, we know exactly who did it and how and, zippity-boom-bah, here comes the predator drone."

"And do these men eventually graduate from your program?"

"And do what?" Walter Penny asks, caught off guard.

I shrug. "Become park rangers?"

"These are bad men," Walter says, like I've missed the point all along.

"Do they escape?"

"The men and their representatives sign a contract going in which says we can Taser, shock, or execute as needed. We're judicious re discipline; mostly we haven't had to."

"And do the men make friends?"

Walter shakes his head like it's all been lost on me. "This isn't exactly your campfire, 'Kumbaya,' and melted-marshmallow crowd."

"So—why do you think this would be a good place for George?"

"I'll take that one," the medical director says. "George has a lot of anger and excess energy, and he very much likes to be the boss."

"I just want to jump in for a moment," Manny says, "and color things in a bit for you. As per what we were talking about earlier, if we settle on this program, if we agree that this is the place for George, the placement would be considered a deal. A deal mitigates the need for George going to trial, which would be a lengthy, expensive, and very public process."

"You're saying that if we send George off into the woods—there's no trial?"

"Correct," Walter Penny says.

"How long would he have to stay in the woods?"

"Hard to tell, but any subsequent placement would be covered under this agreement—it's not like he'd come out of the woods and have to go to trial," Manny says.

"Let me be honest with you," Walter Penny says. "It would be good for us to have a few higher-profile cases. It keeps us on the map—we got the initial funding, and while the cost is amazingly low per prisoner as compared with a traditional facility, we need some good PR to stay up and running."

"It certainly looks like a lot of money was spent on your logo and presentation."

"Branding is everything these days," Walter says. "We had a couple of really nice grants to get us going—but now we're on our own."

"Just to review," Manny jumps in, cutting off what I think is a fascinating conversation about who gave them a grant to come up with the wood-grained/green logo. "The terms of the placement are as follows: We accept the placement in The Woodsman as a one-time-only offer; the offer and acceptance are not precedential, and any further placement following the first forty-eight hours at The Woodsman facility is to be considered under the umbrella of this agreement and is not subject to revocation. It is understood that time spent in The Woodsman program is covered by the laws of the state in which the facility is based and the laws of the United States and subject to due process, et cetera. Further, the costs of the move from the private facility, The Lodge, to a public facility, The Woodsman, will be borne by The Lodge as a 'give' due to the closure of the facility."

"When would this happen?" I ask.

"Sooner rather than later," Walter Penny says.

"I'd also like to note that I presented this package to the parents of Jane, George's now deceased wife. Their response was 'Good riddance'—they were more than happy to send him deep into the woods."

"When?" I ask again.

"By the end of the week," the medical director says. "In case something backfires or we have to rethink—we want to be there as backup."

"Is that the forty-eight-hour clause that I heard a moment ago?"

"The first forty-eight hours are the most telling," Walter Penny says. "If a man makes it through two days, chances are he'll do well. We've only had to pull one man out."

"Does George know about all of this?"

"Yes," the medical director says. "We've talked it through."

"I showed him the photos," Walter Penny says.

"We met privately and discussed the legal ramifications earlier this morning."

"What does he think?" I ask.

"To be fair," the medical director says, "there are some mixed emotions."

"Which would seem reasonable," Manny adds.

"Does he know that I'm here now?"

"Yes," the medical director says. "Would you like to see him, or are you afraid?"

I say nothing and just stare at the man.

"It's a question, isn't it?" he says.

———

The meeting ends with Walter Penny once again shaking hands, and, oddly, I congratulate him on his innovative project, his spirit, and his drive.

"We get the job done," he says.

I couldn't be more different from Walter Penny, but, inexplicably, I like him; he's the kind of guy you want to have on your team when your car breaks down in the middle of nowhere, when your plane crashes into a snowy mountain. . . .

George is in his room, alone. "I'm fucked, aren't I?"

I sit at the edge of his bed.

"I'm fucked," he says again, loudly. "And I'm not medicated. Over the last month, they've been cutting me back, taking me down, so now it's just me, au naturel. I'm fucked," he repeats.

"Maybe there's another way to look at it?"

He glares at me.

"Kind of like a Get Out of Jail Free card?" I suggest.

"You're an idiot," George says.

"Well, it's not jail and it's not a nuthouse."

"They're fucking feeding me to the wolves," George says.

"I'm not sure now's the moment to say it, but I never trusted your lawyer. He's in bed with the medical director of this place."

"They're not in bed—they're related, you idiot," George says.

"I'm just not sure they have your best interests in mind."

"So now, at the eleventh hour, I should get a new lawyer."

"It would buy you some time."

"I'm fucked," he says, panicking. "They're sending me out into the wilderness, into the cold night, to live among men worse than animals."

"It's spring, George. Every day it's going to be warmer and warmer, and every night it'll be warmer too—it's getting on to summer, George. Think of how you always wanted to go camping. Remember you loved Yogi Bear and all that—and hated that we didn't have a real backyard."

"This isn't fucking Jellystone Park we're talking about. They shot a chip into the back of my neck and gave me a tetanus shot—my arm is hot like a baseball—tomorrow I get a rabies vaccine."

"Well, George, your options are limited. Try it—if you don't like it, we'll see what else there is."

"Were you always this stupid?" George says, looking me in the eye. "I remember you as dim-witted, but not so moronic."

"I don't know what to say. Do you want to hear a bit about my life, about the kids, Tessie, and the kittens?"

"Who the fuck is Tessie?"

"Your dog."

"Oh," he says—like now it makes sense.

"She's doing well."

George nods.

"And the children seem to be finding their way." Again he nods. "Look, George, I know this isn't easy. It's an odd situation, with this place closing and the idea of this nontraditional program, but, seriously, maybe you can make something of it. You have done things that none of these guys have ever done. Okay, so maybe they stole stuff, you've certainly done that; they've murdered, so have you. But how many of them held a job for years, how many of them ever ran a television network?"

It's like I'm giving him a pep talk, convincing him that he can get back in the ring, he can go another round—it's not all over yet. "You're as big and bad as any of the men out there—remember when you bit me?"

"By accident," he says.

"It wasn't an accident, you tore off flesh."

George shrugs.

"My point is, you can do this. Remember when we used to wear Dad's old army uniforms and play in the basement? You are Colonel Robert E. Hogan."

George quotes a line from *Hogan's Heroes*.

"That's it."

George quotes another line.

"That's the spirit. You can do this. Don't think long-term—think about it like an Outward Bound summer camp. And we'll take it from there. Okay?"

He nods and speaks in German.

As I'm getting ready to go, I stand, and George hugs me hard—almost too hard. I reach into my pocket.

"I brought you something," I say, handing him a Hershey bar with almonds.

Tears well up in his eyes. Our grandmother always used to give us each a Hershey bar with almonds—she'd open her enormous purse, reach in, and extract one for each.

"Thank you," he says. And then hugs me again.

"We can write to each other, and I'll come visit you in a couple of months—you'll be okay."

He sniffles and pushes me away. "You are such a fucking asshole," he says.

I nod. "Okay, then, George, we'll be in touch." And I am gone. "Such a fucking asshole"—what did he mean by that, and do I even want to know? I am such a fucking asshole that I come when called, I mop up after him, I take care of his wife—a bit too well—I water his flowers, feed his dog, care for his children—I am such a fucking asshole.

The kittens are ready. Ashley and I have agreed that we'll keep one for ourselves. I e-mail photos of the kittens to her, but the school computer system doesn't allow her to open them, and so I print them out and FedEx the pictures before we confer—deciding on "Romeo," small; black, white, and gray; deeply mischievous; and clearly one the mama thinks she needs to keep an eye on.

"How are you going to find homes for the others?" Ashley wants to know.

"The good old-fashioned way," I say. "I'm going to set myself up somewhere with a big box marked 'Free Kittens.'"

The truth is, I feel like a giant bully taking the kittens from the mother cat. For a couple days, I practice separating the mother and her kittens by taking the kittens away and then bringing them back a few hours later—thinking it's somehow less stressful than a sudden and permanent absence.

When the day comes, I bring the plastic cat-crate up from the basement and line it with old towels. I find an old card table in the basement, which still has a sign on it from a lemonade stand Ashley must have had. I flip the poster board over and write "Free Kittenz" in large artful letters. I've prepared paperwork—eight-by-ten photos of each kitten, information on the mother, the date of birth, and what vaccinations they've had so far. I also prepare starter kits for each cat, with samples of their current food and litter.

If you're wondering what this newfound energy is all about, all I can say is that I've gotten particularly attached to a bottle of small round blue pills I found in George's bathroom, the bottle marked "1–2 daily upon awakening." I take a couple, and for about five hours I'm amazingly organized. In an effort to identify what it is I'm taking, I repeatedly Google "little blue pill," but all I get is ads for Viagra, which is not round but diamond-shaped.

As I put the kittens in the carrier, they start making noise, the mama cat is pacing, and Tessie looks up at me from the floor as if to say, God help you now.

I head for the A&P where I met the woman, both on the off chance she might show up again and because I feel self-conscious setting up outside my regular grocery, the one that was Jane and George's. More than once people have given me strange looks; I'm never sure if they know it's me or think I'm him, but either way I'm a sitting duck.

I set up just outside the pet store. I have brought the carrier, my pictures, some tape, the samples, and a large cardboard box where someone can put a kitten to play with it—that way, there's no danger of its scampering off into the street. Open for business. My first customer comes out of the pet store, wearing a tag that reads "Brad—Assistant Manager."

"What are you doing?" Brad asks.

"Giving away kittens," I say, even though it's obvious.

"We sell kittens," he says.

I say nothing.

"You're going to have to move your pop-up shop," Brad says.

"Sorry."

"You're competing with our interests."

"But the ASPCA has a pet adoption stand right here every weekend."

"Are you a nonprofit?" Brad wants to know.

"I'm giving them away."

"You're small potatoes," Brad says.

"I beg to differ," I say. "Whoever takes these kittens is going to need supplies. How about just thinking of these five as a loss leader?"

"Loss leader?"

"The things a store is willing to lose money on in order to get people who will buy other things in the store. Milk, for example, is a common loss leader," I say.

"Move," Brad says. "Take your act over to the A&P. I'll help you. . . ." He picks up the edge of the table, and the carrier starts to slide.

I grab the carrier. "Take your hands off my table or I will call the police, and then corporate pet whatever, and have your dumb ass fired."

"I'm a witness," an old woman says. "I will testify."

"It was an accident," Brad says, and I sort of believe him.

"Tell it to the judge," the old woman says as she helps me carry the table closer to the A&P.

"Do you want a kitten?" I ask her.

"Absolutely not," she says. "I dislike pets almost as much as I dislike people. My husband says I should only shop online—that the world is a better place with me safe at home. He thinks I'm bad." She shrugs. "I think he's worse."

"How long have you been married?" I ask, laying out my flyers and supplies.

"Since the beginning of time," she says, and heads off.

An unseasonably overdressed young woman in a heavy coat and scarf, with multiple bags of groceries hanging from both arms, approaches and puts her bags down.

"Can I hold one?" she asks.

I reach into the carrier and take out the closest kitten and hand it to her. The woman puts the kitten up to her face—rubbing its body over her cheeks, her nose, her mouth. "Yum-yum-yum," she says, making lip-smacking sounds. The kitten looks stressed. "So fragile," she says, "like a baby bird."

I reach for the kitten. "Let's keep it in the box; you can pet it there."

She dutifully follows directions and puts the kitten in the box, then asks if she can try another one. I put the first one away and take another out.

"Do you have any pets?" I ask the woman.

"No," she says. "No pets. Pets are against the rules."

"Aggie," a woman calls, spotting her from a distance. "We've been looking for you everywhere. Remember we said we'd meet in the produce section? And whose groceries have you got?"

"Mine," Agatha says, putting the second kitten down.

"Where did you get the money to buy all that?"

"My parents sent it to me."

"I think they meant for you to use a little bit each week, not spend it all at once."

Agatha shrugs. She doesn't seem to mind. "The man has kitties," Agatha says. "They taste good."

"That's nice," the woman, who is clearly younger than Agatha, says. "Now, come along, and let's catch up with the others." I track Agatha with my eye, watching as she joins the others and, hand in hand, they walk across the parking lot like a twisted rope of Arbus imagery.

"Are the kittens returnable?"

"Pardon?" Someone is standing in front of me. Her enormous purse, the size of a lawn-and-leaf bag, is blocking my view.

"If I take one and am not happy, can I bring it back?" she asks.

"Not happy in what way?"

"Like, if our dog, or cat, or my husband, or the kids don't like it—can I bring it back?"

"Sounds like you've got a full house," I say.

She nods. "I love a new baby."

I don't like her; I don't like how she's just planted herself in front of me; I am anxious for her to leave. "Why don't you think on it while you do your shopping, and then you can come back and see me? I'll be here for a while."

The A&P and surrounding shopping mall is a whole other world. Conspicuously absent are men between twenty-five and sixty, and there is an abundance of older couples, women with babies and toddlers, and the straggling unemployed shopping the sale flyer. A woman with twins approaches.

"Can we get a kitty?" the little girl asks.

"Can we?" the boy seconds.

The children are fascinated and stare into the cat carrier.

"How many are in there?" the boy asks.

"Five," I say.

"They have enough," the girl tells her mother.

"What will your father say?"

"He's never home anyway," the boy says.

"Maybe we don't have to tell him," the girl says. "We can just keep them in our room."

I put two kittens in the box, so they can each play with one.

"Let me check with Daddy," the mother says as she uses her long nails to peck out a text. Seconds later she gets a reply—which she holds up for me to read. It says, "Use your best judgment." "I think it's an automated response," the mother says. "He's got a smartphone—you can program auto-responses to anything. Watch," she says, texting back. "Do you want chicken or steak for dinner?" And again, "Use your best judgment" comes back. "See what I mean?" she says. "He's probably having an affair."

"Why do you always say that?" the daughter asks.

"I'm no dummy," she says. "I went to Yale." She turns to me. "We'll take two. There's no point in having one of anything anymore."

"Can we go into the pet store and buy them a carrier like his?" the girl asks.

"Yes," the mother says.

"And some food and some toys?" the boy asks.

"And maybe some clothing, so I can dress them up?" the girl asks.

"We'll be right back," the mother says. "If you could just put those two on hold for us . . ."

She is true to her word: about ten minutes later, bearing shopping bags of cat products and fancy carrying cases, they return. I put both kittens in one case.

"Enjoy," I say.

"We already are," the boy says.

Something is happening; the mood is shifting, like a sea change, like the quickening of the breeze before a spring storm. I begin to hear snippets, bits and pieces of conversations, as everyone anxiously comes and goes a little faster. "I know the mother. . . ." "She went to camp with my kids." "Regular people—just like us." "You never know what's on someone's mind." Apparently, a girl has gone missing.

An old man and his wife stop at my table; their stooped shoulders and curved spines fit together like a pair of salt and pepper shakers.

"This might be the day," the man says to his wife.

They smile. Their faces are open and cheerful, good-natured despite the effects of time.

"That would be nice," she says.

"Ours died," she tells me. "She was nineteen years old."

I nod, half thinking we're talking cat, half thinking about the missing girl.

"Do you have one who is mature for its age?" the man asks.

"Playful, independent, and wise," the wife adds.

I look into the carrier and take out the one I would describe as thoughtful.

"He's beautiful," the wife says, stroking him as I put him into the box.

"I can give you some samples of the food and litter they've been getting—they're very healthy, been to the vet, and have their first shots."

"We got the last one from a little girl who had a stand like this—she was selling Girl Scout cookies and giving away kittens."

"An entrepreneur. We gave her twenty bucks," the husband says.

"I think you'll like the kitten," I say.

"I think so," the husband says, excusing himself to go back into the store to get a cardboard box. "Just something we can put him in for the ride home."

Across the parking lot, a woman is putting up posters on light posts, on the cement parking stanchions—"MISSING PERSON."

"It's worrisome," I say to the woman.

"Where do you think she's gone?" the old woman asks.

The husband comes back with an empty banana box, and we slip the kitten in. I give them food, litter samples, and my phone number, and then, remembering my promise to Ashley, I ask, "Could I trouble you for your name, address, and phone, just in case we need to be in touch?"

"What a good idea," the old woman says, and she writes her name and information in glorious script.

Brad comes out of the pet store and walks towards me. "On my break," he says, as though that means "truce."

"How many do you have left?"

"Two."

"Can I see?"

I take the kittens out.

"I know we had a little altercation," Brad says. "But if you can get over it—I'd like to adopt these two."

"But you sell kittens," I say. "And I'm sure you get a discount."

"The kittens we sell are from animal mills, but this is a real kitten, raised with love." He extends his hand as though we've not met before. "I'm Brad," he says. And I'm compelled to shake his hand. "What do you think? Is there room for second chances?"

"I hope so," I say.

"I've always loved animals."

"Why else would you be working in a pet store?"

"When we lived in Arizona, I worked in my uncle's pet store—mostly lizard sales. I myself have a bearded dragon," he says, "but I don't think it contradicts a cat. The dragon lives in a large heated tank. Very sensitive, dragons."

"I didn't know there was such a thing as a domesticated dragon," I say.

"Oh, sure there is," Brad says. "So what do you say?"

"They're yours," I say, giving him the kittens, the cardboard box, and what I've got left of my samples.

"I'll spoil them silly," Brad says.

Doing my due diligence, I collect his full name, address, and phone and tell him that I'll check in next week and I expect to see a photo.

"I really appreciate it," Brad says. "And if there's something I can do for you, let me know."

"Thanks," I say, painfully pinching my finger as I fold the card table down, but otherwise happy to close on an up note.

A cop car crawls through the parking lot. In the distance, I spot a school crossing guard working the intersection. She uses her body, her orange vest, her meter-reader hat like the elements of a human shield, spreading her arms wide as she blocks the crosswalk; the children spill forth, truly oblivious.

I keep thinking about the missing girl. I'm not sure why, but I feel guilty, like I'm somehow a participant. It's not a sensation I've had before—but this one crawls under my skin. Because of the woman I met at the A&P, because of Ashley, because of Jane, because I am now more awake than ever before, because I can't stop thinking . . .

There is a world out there, so new, so random and disassociated that it puts us all in danger. We talk online, we "friend" each other when we don't know who we are really talking to—we fuck strangers. We mistake almost anything for a relationship, a community of sorts, and yet, when we are with our families, in our communities, we are clueless, we short-circuit and immediately dive back into the digitized version—it is easier, because we can be both our truer selves and our fantasy selves all at once, with each carrying equal weight.

I stop at Starbucks. I take a good look at the poster taped to the phone pole outside. Is it the woman from the A&P? I don't think it's her, but I don't really know. I try to remember what the girl I met looks like. I remember the dirty-blond hair—which the missing girl also has. I remember her breasts, larger than I expected, pale with beautiful blue veins, like an ancient river under the surface of the skin. I remember that her face was plain, blank—her eyes blue-gray.

And I wonder—how does a person take another person? A news truck is setting up on the corner, cranking its satellite up high.

Inside Starbucks, the girls behind the counter are in tears; apparently, the missing girl worked there last summer part-time; they all know her. I leave without coffee—it's too upsetting.

Pulling into the driveway, I'm really depressed. I carry the empty carrier to the house, the metal door of the cat box swinging open and closed repeatedly, slamming my finger. I've done a terrible thing; I've taken something that's not mine, the mama cat's children, and given them away. I enter empty-handed. The cat approaches, sniffs me, checks the carrier, and seems to have gotten the news. She goes under the sofa. Tessie doesn't bother getting up until I put her dinner down.

The 6 p.m. news begins with "Breaking Local News"—the story of the missing girl. Heather Ryan is twenty years old and was home visiting her parents for the weekend. "Ryan reportedly went for a run last night and never returned. According to police, her family is especially concerned as she had been having some personal problems and was on a new medication following a basketball injury to the head. We hear a lot about the guys and football or soccer injuries, but as girls' sports have become more competitive, we're seeing some of the same injuries. Last fall, while playing a regular-season game at Leduc College, she was struck . . ."

The reporter prattles on as they replay footage of the ball bouncing off the side of Heather's head, her head slamming to the left as another girl mows her down, knocking her to the gym floor. "It's repeated incidents of brain shears that worry us," says the doctor they've brought in to comment, "the banging of the brain against the inside of the head." The reporter closes by saying, "If anyone has seen Heather or has any information, please call the special hotline."

Great. So the missing girl has problems. What kind of problems? Problems like she can't say who she is? Like she's living in some kind of fugue state? Who is or was the woman from the A&P? There was something odd about her, about that whole encounter, something she made a point of not telling me. Should I inform someone, call that special number and leave my lame confession? I consider it, but then decide that it's all in my head—that the girl I met looks nothing like the missing girl. I attempt to make a sketch, a re-creation of what I remember about the woman. I draw a kind of an oval for her head; I draw her neck, which I remember was long, her chest—the fact is, her breasts are the only part I remember well. I draw them over and over again, and then go back, trying to find her neck, her head, her face. I wonder if there's a DNA sample from her in the Dijon-mustard jar. There must have been one on my cock, but I've showered multiple times since then. I go over everything she said and did; I think about the stolen TV, the items in her grocery cart, her comments about frosted cake versus plain. I wonder—did she look lost? I wonder if perhaps they could come in and dust for fingerprints. I take Tessie for a walk, circling the house, the yard, wondering whether someone might be there, hiding out.

I'm stuck on how a girl could be there one moment and missing the next—how someone steals another person. Is it sheer physical force? A psycho-logical game? Is it that women, girls, boys are all weaker than adult men, who can simply pick them up and move them from one end of the earth to another? And this happens in a dark vortex, a break from reality; it's like some door opens to a dark underside and one of us is dragged down under.

By eight o'clock, I've worked myself into a frenzy, worried not only about the missing girl and every girl everywhere, but also about the kittens. Are they all right—are they in their new homes weeping, clawing, wishing more than anything to get back to the safety of Mama?

How do any of us survive?

By eight-fifteen, I can't tolerate my anxiety any longer—I call Ashley at school, just to check in.

There seems to be confusion—she's not there. I ask for her roommate, who hands me over to the housemother, who tells me that the school made a change in her living accommodations. "I thought you knew," she says.

"I had no idea."

"She's been staying with one of the teachers. Let me get you that number."

I call that number, get a machine, leave a message; a few minutes later, a very nervous-sounding Ashley calls back.

"What's wrong?" she asks.

"Nothing's wrong," I say. "I was just checking in."

"You don't usually make unscheduled calls," she says.

"Surprise," I say.

There's something in Ashley's voice that's not right.

"I didn't get you away from something important, did I?"

"No," she says. "I was just doing my homework."

She is a bad liar—but I say nothing. "What was for dinner tonight?"

"I think it was fish," she says.

"What kind of fish?"

"White, with a kind of yellow-orange-colored sauce," she says.

"Did you eat it?"

"No," she says.

"What did you have?"

"There was a vegetarian option—stuffed shells and salad."

"Everything else okay?" I ask.

"Yeah, I guess," she says.

"Okay, then, I'll say good night—talk to you tomorrow, the usual time."

"Thanks," she says.

I hang up feeling awkward, like I stepped in something I don't quite know what.

The 11 p.m. news has live coverage from a candlelight vigil being held in the park where the girl was last seen—the same park where I take Tessie, the one where I had my sobbing meltdown. Women in packs are running through the park in a Take Back the Night rally and throwing their running shoes over the telephone wires. The police are following up on multiple leads but have no new information as of this hour.

I open a can of salmon for the cat; she shows no interest. I leave it on the counter as a peace offering and go up to bed. None of the animals join me.

Life goes on—a lie. I think of volunteering, joining one of the search groups that are combing the nearby woods, but I worry someone will figure out who I am—someone will make something of it.

The next day, I try and distract myself with the book. I work for an hour or two. I move paragraphs here and there and then back again.

I get in the car and drive in circles and ask myself: What am I doing? Do I think I'm looking for her?

I think of where people might congregate, might meet to worry as a group. I can't go to the Starbucks—it's too close, like a ground zero. I think of an excuse—light bulb—and go to the hardware store.

Men are gathered there, doing what men do, pretending they're not worried, pretending they're not human, but wanting to be together nonetheless.

"I was out with them last night—going through the woods. I let 'em use my truck."

"It's a damn shame."

"They'll find her; girls do this, they run off. . . ."

"They don't do it anymore. That was before; now they stay close to home, it's no longer safe."

"What do you know?"

"I raised three of my own."

Life continues, but I don't really know how anyone can carry on when someone is missing. Life is suspended; worse than suspended, it is a living hell, it's impossible not to be driven mad with worry, fear, lack of information. The brain loops, cannot let go, cannot take a breath, because to let go even for a second might mean to forget; to stop sending the search signal might let her fall through the cracks.

Out of the corner of my eye I see DeLillo at the register. I can't tell if he's listening in on the conversation or not. He's buying duct tape and dust masks and a flashlight.

"Putting together your disaster kit?" the guy behind the register asks.

"Spring cleaning," DeLillo says. He glances up at me, blankly, expectantly returning my glance. We make eye contact, but then I quickly look away.

I buy my light bulbs. Somehow I want to scream at them: You're wrong, you're all wrong, the world has changed, something evil has risen, like a serpent hand of Hades, has slithered its ugly head up from below, out from within, and snatched something fresh off the shelf.

The way they talk about it is so suburban, so brainlessly parochial, that it is unbearable. I leave, almost running out of the store, gasping for air.

A panic attack, as though my familiarity with a kind of darkness, my less-than-oblivious musings, has caught me off guard.

I remind myself that I did not do this, and yet just knowing, just feeling, just being the little bit more familiar than most with the impulses that allow such things to happen makes me uncomfortable. I think of myself as an outsider—a suspect. My devolution, my despicable descent into adultery and murderous familial fellowship, has welled up and undone me.

And then she is there, on my doorstep, waiting, as though nothing has happened. "I've been terrified you were gone," I say.

"Gone where?"

"Missing."

"What are you talking about?"

"That girl."

"What girl?" she asks.

"Are you blind? Don't you see the posters all over town or watch TV?"

She says nothing—she knows but doesn't want to talk about it.

"I saw you," she says. "Outside the store, giving away the kittens."

"You were there?"

"It's my grocery store."

"How come you didn't say anything?"

"I liked watching you."

"What was I doing?"

"Giving away kittens."

"Are you stalking me?"

She changes the subject: "Did you give all the kittens to good homes?"

"I had to keep one."

"For your daughter?"

"I don't have children."

"Right," she says, like I'm lying. "You just borrow them. . . ."

"You want the truth?"

She says nothing.

"My brother, the owner of this house, is insane."

"There's one in every family—no biggie," she says.

"There was a murder in this house," I say, wondering if I am being provocative because I'm annoyed with her.

"Really?"

I nod ever so slightly, as though realizing the enormity of what I'm saying.

"Was this before you bought the house?" she asks.

"Like I said, it's not my house."

"Oh, right," she says, "I spaced." And then she crosses her legs and shifts, preparing herself, bracing for information. "Okay, I'm ready."

And all that comes out is so short, as though the story has sucked itself back into the deep ether, like a tragic genie racing back into the bottle—my own guilt, my awareness that I've not actually discussed this with anyone.

"My brother killed his wife."

A long pause.

"On purpose?" she asks.

"Hard to know," I say.

"That's terrible," she says.

"Awful," I say, and realize that, except for the calls I made when it happened, I haven't told anyone.

"It's really kind of a downer," she says. "You're making this up, right? This is like one of those weird urban legends?"

"Why would I make it up? Does it make me more attractive? That's my big secret, what's yours?"

I try to get a careful look at her. What color are her eyes? Why does nothing about her stay in my mind? I think of taking a picture with my phone—her and the kitten, something to hold on to, to analyze, and submit as evidence if need be. She is wearing casual clothing, which makes her look young. Her hair is neither blond nor brown, neither thick nor thin; it frames a face that is like so many faces. She looks like everyone and like no one. Her hands are the only giveaway: the skin is a little loose on the fingers, which are thin and nimble, almost monkeylike. There are a few light-tan freckled pigment spots on the tops of her hands—age. I return to her face. She is and is not similar to the missing girl, whose photo I have printed out and placed in the center of George's desk.

"Is there anything you want to tell me?" I ask.

"Can you stop?" she says. "You're freaking me out." She takes a breath. "Why did you ask people if they had other pets, and if the cat would live indoors or out, and if the new owner would be so kind as to e-mail photos of the kitty to you?"

"How close did you get?"

"You're in a bad mood. Maybe I should go," she says, but makes no move to leave. "I saw the part where you got into an argument with the guy from the pet store and had to move your stand."

"And you saw that we made up and I gave him the last two kittens?"

She shakes her head no. "I guess I left before that happened."

"I need to know something about you," I say.

"I play the flute," she says.

"More," I say.

"I majored in French literature, with a minor in library science."

I nod.

"I wanted to grow up and be a spy," she offers.

"What side would you spy for—us or them?"

"Them," she says, without a pause. "I never felt like one of us."

"What prompted you to come here now?"

"Last time I saw you, you had one of those really cool rain showers, and I thought maybe I could try it, and I brought you a little gift."

"What?" I ask.

"I ate it," she says. "There was a bake sale; I bought two seven-layer bars, and then I stopped at McDonald's and got a coffee, and on my way over here I just powered right through both of them."

"Maybe you didn't need to tell me that you brought me a present."

"I was just being honest. So I'm here all sugared up and ready to go—almost a little hyper."

"Okay, the shower is yours. I'll get you a clean towel."

I sit on the bed watching as she undresses—that seems to be part of it, she wants me to watch. "We don't have to have sex," I say. "I don't need you to use your body to get a shower."

"What if I want to have sex?" she asks.

"I'm not sure I want to. I've had a lot on my mind—I don't even know if I could."

She makes a face. "I've never heard a guy say that ahead of time—usually it's after the fact, usually it's after a lot of hemming and hawing and it turns out they've got a wife."

"I'm divorced," I say, getting up off the bed, leaving her to shower alone.

I take advantage of the moment to rummage through her bag—looking for clues. I find an enormous old wallet with almost nothing in it, and in the bottom of her bag, a driver's license. I panic at the sight of the name, immediately put it back, and close the bag. Heather Ann Ryan. Is that the name of the missing girl? I'm confused.

When she comes out of the shower I ask, "Do you have any sports injuries?"

"I'm not very athletic," she says.

She comes towards me, still damp from the shower.

Is it her? Is she the missing person? Is she having some kind of psychotic break and amnesic state? All of her answers are so vague, so nonspecific.

"Who are you?" I ask.

"Who would you like me to be?" she asks, dropping the towel.

And she is upon me.

There is a lot of noise, labored breathing, the dog begins to bark, the cat jumps onto the nightstand, looks at us, arches, pounces onto my back, claws out, I scream.

"I better go," she says when we are done.

"You sure you don't want another shower?"

"No, I'm okay," she says, "but it was nice, I like the rain shower."

"So how about a number?" I ask while she's dressing.

She shakes her head no.

"How am I going to know you're okay? It was very uncomfortable worrying that something happened to you."

"I am not someone that things happen to," she says.

"I don't think I can do this," I say. "I can't have some nameless person appear at my house and have me."

"It's not your house," she says, zipping up.

"Are we ever going to have a real conversation?"

She puts her shoes on and stands up. "I don't know what to say."

"You're scaring me," I say.

"Men aren't scared," she says. "Can we not do this? I hear your stress—but I really have to go."

"Go where?"

"Back to where I came from."

"Am I making any progress?"

"We'll talk," she says, "just not now."

"Take something," I tell her.

She looks at me. "What?"

"Take the television."

"Not funny."

Her cell phone rings; she looks at it.

"Boyfriend?" I ask.

"No."

When she leaves, I lock the door. I walk around the house putting down the shades—I'm overexposed.

At ten the next morning, the telephone rings.

"Mr. Silver?"

"May I ask who's calling?"

"This is Sara Singer from the Annandale Academy."

"Yes."

"Is this a good time to speak?"

"It's a fine time, but, just to be clear, I'm Silver the uncle, not Silver the father."

"I am aware." There is silence, and then she begins again: "Mr. Silver, this is a bit awkward. . . ."

I hadn't been worried but suddenly I am—profoundly. "Is Ashley all right?"

Sara Singer doesn't answer.

"Do you know where Ashley is?" All I can think about is the missing girl.

"Mr. Silver, if you would just hear me out. . . ."

"Is she alive?" I scream into the phone.

"Of course she's alive. I didn't mean to frighten you. She's in English class until eleven-twenty, and then she has science at eleven-thirty until twelve-thirty." Again she pauses.

"Perhaps you're not aware of what's going on here," I say. "A local girl has gone missing—it's been very stressful."

"My apologies," Mrs. Singer says. "This has to be hard for someone such as yourself."

"Which version of myself?"

"A man with no children suddenly playing daddy."

"I like to think I've made the adjustment very well."

"As I was saying, I'm afraid this is one of those situations that no school likes to be put in. Mr. Silver, were you aware that during the spring break Ashley was on the phone?"

"Yes," I say. "Ashley has had a hard time sleeping and found it useful to talk with someone."

"Do you know to whom she was speaking?"

"She said she was talking with a friend."

"I'm afraid it's more than that."

"More than what?"

"More than a friend. What's the right word? Pardon me, I'm struggling here." She stops for a moment. "Mr. Silver, Ashley has a lover."

Given all else, I'm relieved. "She's very young, but in many ways this could be a healthy development," I suggest.

"It's a woman."

"That shouldn't come as a surprise at a girls' school; don't many young girls pass through a lesbian phase?"

"She's screwing the head of the lower school."

"Oh."

"I can appreciate that Ashley has had a very difficult year, but this is not okay."

"Of course not."

"I'm glad you agree," she says, relieved, but there's something in her tone that suggests she's blaming Ashley—the victim.

"What does the head of the lower school have to say for herself?"

"I'm not at liberty to share that with you." She pauses.

"Do you want to tell me exactly how this happened?"

"When Ashley returned to school following her mother's death, we suggested she stay with the head of the lower school."

"You allowed her to move in with this woman?"

"It was intended as a temporary measure. At the time we thought it might be helpful for Ashley to have twenty-four-hour access to someone, in case she had bad dreams, or needed to talk."

"So Ashley is screwing the head of the lower school, and is the head of the lower school screwing her? Who is the adult, Mrs. Singer, and who is the child? It's a rhetorical question, Mrs. Singer—who is the person with a big problem?"

"The head of the lower school has a long-term contract with us."

"Child abuse would be seen by most as valid grounds for termination or breach of contract."

"I'm afraid no one beyond Ashley will tell that story," Mrs. Singer says. "That said, I would like to assure you of how seriously I take the situation, and that we are in fact dealing with the matter internally."

"We are charged with an enormous responsibility, Mrs. Singer. We are like superheroes who cannot fail our children."

"Of course, Mr. Silver, that's why I'm calling you."

"How was the situation uncovered?" I ask, no pun intended.

"It was brought to our attention by someone who wishes to remain anonymous."

"May I speak with Ashley?"

"As I said at the top of our conversation, she's not available right now—she has English and then science and lunch."

"Will you have her call me?"

"This goes without saying, but I'm hoping you'll keep it confidential."

"I have not said that I would or wouldn't—but suffice to say I am concerned. As the guardian of a girl going through so much at home, I had hoped that school would be a safe place for her."

"Mr. Silver, times have changed. The world is not what it once was."

"Quick question, Mrs. Singer—do the other students know?"

"It is my belief that they do not."

She takes a long breath; I suspect she's actually sneaking a cigarette. "Against the advice of counsel—my ex-husband was a lawyer, so he taught me to say that—I'd like to give you my home and cell numbers, in case you need to reach me."

As I'm writing her numbers down, I'm simultaneously texting Cheryl.

"Urgent," I text.

"Motel?" she texts back quickly.

"More like soup and sandwich," I type.

"I have errands," she answers slowly.

"I need help."

"What kind?"

"Kid stuff."

"Fine—meet me at the food court in the mall at one. I'll be near the frozen yogurt."

"Thx," I type. She's squeezing me in.

"You have to be really cool about it," Cheryl says, as she feeds me crunchy noodles and cold chicken from her Chinese chicken salad.

Today her hair is in a blond pageboy. "Is that a wig?"

"No," she says. "I got a haircut. Listen, if you freak Ashley out, she's going to clam up and you'll get nothing. It's not clear-cut abuse, but more of a Lolita kind of thing."

"Do I take it to the police? Does that make it worse?"

She shakes her head. "Keep it under the radar unless the kid wants the authorities involved. If she doesn't, and she's the only one talking, it could get ugly and be worse for your niece in the long run. You need to talk to her, let her know that you know, and make a safe place for her to share her feelings—or not. . . . And ask her how she feels about reporting it—some people feel like it's not taken seriously unless it's reported; others would rather die than have to keep talking about it."

"Maybe it's all a big false alarm," I suggest. "Maybe Ashley got a crush on the head of the school and it was more of a mother thing, a platonic emotional affair. I doubt much happened of a truly sexual nature—I don't think Ashley even knows about that 'stuff.'"

"What planet are you on?" Cheryl asks. "These kids are sharp; they're not going to let on what they're up to. You can bet the teacher put it all in the guise of being parental or teacherly—giving her lessons. Ask if they used any fruit."

"Fruit?"

She looks at me like I'm an idiot. "My husband taught my son about condoms with a banana, and when my friend's daughter asked her mom what it felt like to have a penis inside her, her mother directed her to the vegetable bin and said, 'Male genitalia are like vegetables, they come in all shapes and sizes, there are carrots and zucchini and hothouse cucumbers.' She was fond of telling her girls that in a pinch they could use the free hotel shower caps as a birth-control device. 'And whatever you do, you never want to get any of "it" in you or on you. Think of "it" like Krazy Glue, hard to get out of your clothes, of your hair—and disrespectful. Any man who respects you leaves his "discharge" in a receptacle other than you, and any man who doesn't should take his interest elsewhere.'"

"Do parents really talk with their children that explicitly?"

"Kids are curious, they find out—it's better they find out from you. Also, given that your niece is almost a teenager and she doesn't have a mother, you should find her a female doctor who practices adolescent medicine."

"I didn't know there was such a thing."

"It's better; she doesn't need to be talking to Dr. Faustus about her period."

"How did you know she goes to Faustus?"

She rolls her eyes. "Because that's where everyone goes," she says, and then asks me to go get her a nonfat frozen yogurt with rainbow sprinkles. "Bet you wonder why I can't get it for myself?"

I wasn't going to ask.

"The girl behind the register was my son Brad's first girlfriend. I made him dump her. I think she puts Visine in the yogurt when I order from her."

"Why Visine?"

"It gives you diarrhea—they say stewardesses put a few drops of it in the drinks of assholes on the airplane."

"That's a total urban legend."

"So you say," she says, urging me to get up and get her the yogurt.

"You probably get diarrhea because you're lactose-intolerant."

She pauses. "I hadn't thought of that. Will you please just go get it for me?"

"Of course."

I return with a heavily sprinkled yogurt and a spoon. "Aren't you having one?" she asks.

"I was going to, but the girl behind the counter was a total bitch."

"I told you—that's why I made Brad break up with her. Do you want some?" She offers me a spoonful of yogurt; I open my mouth and let her feed me.

"Don't you worry about someone seeing us?"

She shakes her head.

"Why not?"

"I'll just tell them you're a stroke patient and I'm doing volunteer work." She feeds me another spoonful of yogurt.

"So—about the missing girl," Cheryl says.

I wipe yogurt from my face—her aim sucks.

"I think they know who did it," Cheryl says.

"Could you be more specific?"

"They—i.e., the police—know more than they're telling the public—i.e., us."

"Is that based on fact or your own independent conclusion?"

"I'm just saying. . . . We all know how these things work. I watch a lot of TV, reality and otherwise, and I'm telling you—they're waiting for the guy to come to them, for him to make a little screw-up, to give himself away."

"So you're thinking they've already got him pegged and are watching him?"

"I'm sure of it. Nothing is as random as it seems."

"Except that which is totally random, such as this . . ." I say.

"What's this?"

"This—whatever this is between us," I say. I can't help but notice that I've become close to Cheryl, that I share things with her, that I'm starting to think of her as a friend, a confidante.

"Honey, if you were doing the math, it's not all that random—it's common as hell," she says.

There's something brash about her voice that prompts me to ask, "Have you been drinking?"

"I had a Bloody Mary this morning—kind of a little celee-bration."

"On a weekday?"

"Yes," she says. "They all got out early, and I spotted the tomato juice and some celery in the fridge and thought, Why the hell not."

"You scare me," I say.

"No, I don't," she says.

"Yes, you do," I say.

I debate telling her about the A&P woman. I don't like feeling sneaky, but what is my obligation to this married woman? I can't exactly ask for help and then say, "Oh, by the way, I'm seeing someone. . . ." All the same, it slips out:

"I'm seeing someone."

"What's her name?"

"I don't know."

"You're seeing someone and you don't know her name?"

"Yes."

"Since when?"

"A few weeks."

"Where'd you meet her? Is she from online?"

"We met at the A&P."

"How often have you seen her?"

"I've seen her twice," I say, and she seems relieved.

"And what have you done on those occasions?" she asks, like she's trying to get to the bottom of it.

"I'm not sure it's fair for you to ask me to elaborate—it's kind of private."

"Since when is life fair, mister? If you're going to put your poker into someone else's pookie, I think I have a right to know—minimally, for security purposes, so I can make an informed decision."

"And vice versa?" I ask.

"What do you mean?"

"Well, if you should know what I'm doing, should your husband know what you're doing?"

She looks down for a moment as if contemplating her next move—as if.

"I told him," she says.

"Really?" I ask, genuinely surprised.

"Really," she says.

"When?"

"After the night at Friendly's."

"Why?"

"I panicked."

"About what?"

"I thought maybe someone he knew was there and had seen me."

"Wouldn't they be outing themselves if they told your husband?"

She shrugs. "They might have assumed that he knew, and, more to the point, I felt the need. I'm not deceitful by nature."

"What did he say?"

She looks down again. "He said he was glad to have someone to share the burden with. And was I seeking a divorce or just entertainment?"

"And?"

"I said entertainment, and he said, 'Well, then, I won't worry unless you tell me there's something to worry about.'"

"It's nice he trusts you to use your own judgment about when he should be worried."

"I'm very trustable," she says, and then is quiet. "He asked if you pay me; he always wants to pay someone. And I asked if he'd ever 'strayed,' and he said no."

"Why not?"

"Scared," she says.

"Of what?" I ask

She shrugs. "I told him that if he wanted to he should. He's got hooker fantasies. I said, 'Do it'; he said, 'I can't.' And then I asked him, 'Do you want me to do it with you?' 'Like, you would participate?' he asked. 'No, like I would just go with you,' I said. 'That's very nice of you,' he said. 'Since when am I not nice?' I asked him."

"So?" I ask, surprised by all of it—wanting more.

"So I went with him."

"When?"

"Last Tuesday, after work."

"To whom did you go?"

"He got a number from a guy he knows."

"And you didn't tell me?" I ask.

"You were busy."

"How was it?"

"I have no idea. I sat in the girl's living room and read a magazine—my own that I brought with me—and I kept my coat on, and then I washed it when we went home. I was careful not to touch things."

"Did your husband have a good time?"

"He was glad to get it out of his system—but it was weird."

"In what way?"

"He said her breasts were enormous. I met her before he went in; they looked big but not that big. He said they were hard like basketballs. And she wouldn't kiss him."

"Anything else?"

"Her pookie was completely waxed, from front to back. He'd never seen such a thing—he used the word 'industrial.' In the middle of it all, her roommate came home and said she needed to get something from the bedroom. She acted innocent enough, but I whipped out the kitchen knife I'd brought from home, figuring it was all part of the plan: the roommate comes home and they hold the guy hostage for more money. I don't think she was planning on seeing me there. I told her, My husband is in the other room having private time with the roommate, and if you scream or ruin it for him, I'll kill you. She and I sat quietly on the sofa. I told her it wouldn't be long—it's always quick with him. When he came out and saw me there, defending his . . . his . . . whatever you want to call it, I think he was very impressed. It was good for our marriage."

"Really?" I ask, somewhat skeptical.

"It opened things up," she says, "took us to a whole new level."

I'm stunned.

"He wants to meet you," she says.

"For sex?"

"No, just to say hello, maybe dinner." She smiles. "And you thought you were the only one with news."

"So you're not upset about the A&P woman?"

"Of course I'm upset," she says. "You're shtupping some chick you met at your grocer's dairy case who doesn't even have a name. What exactly is it that you like about her?"

"It's hard to put a finger on—she's kind of mysterious."

"It sounds like you don't know her very well."

"You're not being nice."

"You don't even know her name," she reminds me.

"You know what I like about her?" I say. "She demands nothing of me."

Cheryl scrapes the last drops out of the yogurt cup; the Styrofoam squeaks. She checks her phone. "Gotta go," she says, getting up abruptly.

"Are you dumping me?" I ask, suddenly vulnerable.

She looks at me like I'm crazy. "Which part of my-husband-wants-to-meet-you-for-dinner sounded like I was dumping you?"

"Sorry," I say, "it's been a very weird day."

That evening, I finally speak to Ashley. "Are you okay?"

She doesn't say anything.

"Was that an invisible shrug? It's not a video phone."

"Uh-huh."

"Is there anything you want to tell me?"

"Not really."

"Are you alone? I mean, are you somewhere where you are at liberty to speak?"

"There's no one here," she says.

"You sound sad," I observe.

I can hear her clothing shrug.

"Scared?"

She says nothing.

"Ash, if it's okay, I'm just going to talk for a couple of minutes, but I want you to feel free to interrupt at any point. Okay?"

"Uh-huh."

"Okay. So the woman who runs your school called me. I know what happened. And the first thing I want you to know is, it's okay. I want you to know that you're not in trouble. And that I understand and don't think it's weird or anything. I also want you to know that you can talk to me, tell me whatever you want or not tell me, I just want you to be okay. The thing that I care most about is your well-being."

"Can I ask a question?"

"Of course."

"Do I have to move back into my old house?"

"Your old house?"

"It's officially called Rose Hill, but everyone calls it Patchouli."

"Is there a reason you shouldn't live in your old house?"

"Well, where I am now there's a TV, and I really like watching TV. It helps me calm down. Like at night, if I can't sleep, I just put it on and Miss Renee doesn't mind."

"Miss Renee? The head of the lower school?"

"Yeah, and then, like, if I'm really stressed, sometimes I come back in the middle of the day and watch, like, *All My Children, General Hospital, One Life to Live*, and then all is good again—it's like they really help me understand the world and get some perspective. Also, my life is more like the people on the soaps than most of the people around here."

"Interesting," I say. "I need to think about that."

"I really can't go back to the old house," she says. "I'm not okay with that."

"I hear you."

She starts to cry. "I want to come home."

"We can do that," I say.

She sniffles. "I have a project due. . . ."

"How about you come home for the weekend?"

"Okay," she says, sniffling.

"Can you manage until then? We don't have to decide about the house issue right now. I think Mrs. Singer said you could stay with *her*—I bet she has a television."

"Not as many channels," Ashley says, still sniffling.

I pick her up on Friday afternoon. The entire way up to the school, I marvel at the scenery; the trees have sprung into bloom.

Ashley babbles the whole way home—going on and on about soap operas. I can't tell if it's an anxiety response, an odd verbal downloading of daytime drama, or some kind of hypomanic state—I simply let her roll.

"*All My Children* is set in Pine Valley, it has the Tylers, the Kanes, and the Martins; it's been on for, like, forty years, that's more than ten thousand episodes. . . ." She details a bit about Erica and the Cortlandts.

"And then, this week . . ." She lays out the story lines—the past history, who was married to who, who fathered what child, what secrets have not yet been revealed.

"Ash, how long have you been watching these shows?"

"A long time," she says. "I started when I was, like, seven and was home with mono for a month and Mom let me watch them with her."

"Your mom watched them?"

"She loved them. She'd been watching the exact same shows since she was in junior high and stuck at home with a broken leg. And once, at an airport, she actually saw Mrs. Tyler, Mrs. Phoebe Tyler! Mom saw her at the airport and ran over and helped her with her bag. Her 'real' name was Ruth Warrick. She died a few years ago. Mom said something about having seen it in the newspaper."

"You really miss your mom," I say.

"I have no one," she says.

"Well, I'm very glad to see you, and Tessie and Romeo will be happy to see you—you're gonna love Romeo."

"Could we go to the cemetery?" she asks. "Would that be weird?"

"We can go—I'm not sure how it would be."

"What's it like there?"

"We were there for the funeral; do you remember?"

"Not really."

"It's like a big park and there are some trees and the graves are flat."

"Why?"

"Because that's the Jewish tradition, to have flat graves, and a year after the funeral there's what's called an unveiling, and the plaque with your mom's name will be there. And whenever you visit you leave a small stone on the marker, which indicates that you were there and the person is not forgotten."

"Why does it take a year?"

"That's the tradition. We could go visit your grandmother—would that be fun?"

"Can we take her out?"

"Like where?"

"I don't know. Just out—it's like she's one of those fragile dolls in a box that you can just kind of look at, and maybe she'd like to get out and go somewhere."

"We can certainly ask her; my sense is, she's pretty happy where she is— but, like I said, we can ask. So what do you think? Visit Grandma? Bake cookies? Clean your closets?"

"We could bake cookies and bring them to Grandma," she says.

"We could."

"Okay, so tonight, when we get home, we'll make cookies."

"Tonight, when we get home, we'll have dinner and go to bed."

"Okay, so tomorrow morning we'll bake the cookies and go see Grandma," she says, pleased to have a plan.

"When you bake cookies, what do you do?" I ask a couple of minutes later.

"What do I do?"

"Like, how do you make them?"

"We either do slice-and-bake or we mix together all the things that are listed on the back of the chocolate chips—they call that 'from scratch.'"

"And you know how to do that?"

"Yes," she says, like now I'm the idiot. "Have you never made cookies?"

"Never," I say.

"We better stop at the store," she says, and we do. Ashley makes a beeline for the chocolate chips, and we buy everything as directed on the back of the bag, plus extra milk.

"You have to have really fresh milk," she says. "Otherwise there's no point."

And then she looks around, smiling at the rows and rows of groceries. "I really miss grocery stores," she says in a way that reminds me of the oddity of her existence, and how boarding school is an isolated kind of social/educational incubator.

We make the cookies, and when the kitchen starts to fill with a wonderful warm chocolaty smell I feel deeply accomplished. We immediately eat too many and drink the milk, and Ash was entirely right when she said it was all about the milk's being fresh. It's amazing—a truly sublime experience. We start laughing for no reason, and the cat comes out and rubs my leg for the first time since I gave away the kittens—I pour her a saucer of milk.

And when the cookies are cool, we go to the nursing home. On the way there, I explain about Grandma's progress and Grandma's boyfriend.

"I don't get it, are they married or not?"

"Not officially."

"And what's the deal with her crawling and swimming?"

"Remember how she was in bed last time we saw her?"

"Uh-huh."

"Well, she's out of bed now. We're not sure if it's a new medicine or perhaps she forgot why she was in bed. I myself can't remember exactly what happened. I know that we put her in the nursing home because she was bedridden—I'm not sure anyone ever knew why."

"Well, so that's cool, she's getting better."

"That's one way to describe it."

"Hi, Mom," I say as we walk into her room.

"So you say," she says.

"What's wrong?"

"They're here," she says with a particular expression of annoyance, as though long-awaited aliens have finally made themselves known.

"They are?" I say.

"Yes," she says, definitively. "They came this morning and they haven't left yet."

She looks up at Ashley. "You look less Chinese—did you have work done?"

"Mom, this is Ashley—not Claire."

"Who are your people?"

"You are my people," Ashley says, kissing her.

"Mom, Ashley is your granddaughter, she is one of us."

"It's a pleasure to meet you," she says, shaking Ashley's hand.

"Mom, I've been meaning to tell you—when I visited Aunt Lillian, I got your jewelry back."

"The diamond engagement ring?" my mother asks.

"No, some pearl earrings, a bracelet, the necklace with the ruby, and a few other little things, a pin, and a little necklace. She was very happy to give them back—seemed to want it off her chest."

"I'm sure," my mother says. "Did you look at her hand? Is she still wearing the engagement ring your father bought for me?"

"I have no idea, Ma," I said. "It really seems like something the two of you should work out together. When you told me to ask her for the jewelry you didn't mention a diamond engagement ring."

"I wanted to see what she would fess up to—before I really put the screws on her," my mother says.

Time for lunch—in the dining room. The floor assistant comes to take her to the dining room.

"I'm not going," she says.

"Why not?" I ask

"A protest," she says.

"I don't think they're going to bring your lunch," the aide says, shaking her head.

"They used to," my mother says.

"That was before," I say.

"Well, it's not like I'd miss much," she says.

"Don't be too sure," the aide says. "It's chicken and pasta."

"Damn," my mother says.

"What?"

"I really like the chicken and pasta, it has lemon and broccoli, and I get one of the girls from the kitchen to slip me some olives and capers. It's almost like real food."

"I brought dessert," Ashley says holding up the cookie tin. "Homemade."

"Fine," she says, "we'll go." And up she gets, and as she leads us down the hall I notice she's walking with a certain jounce or bounce in her step.

"Mom, you're walking really well," I say.

"It's the dancing," she says. "If you think of dancing, then you can walk; it's just like stroke patients who sing in order to talk."

"Fantastic," I say.

"I was always a very physical person," my mother says. "I'm not sure your father knew that."

When we get to the door of the dining room, she signals to one of the aides as though he's a maître d' in a fancy restaurant. "Table for three," she says.

"Anywhere you see a vacancy," he says.

"Do you want iced green tea or bug juice?" my mother asks Ashley.

"Bug juice?"

"Fruity punch," my mother says, "only here it's laced with vitamin C and Metamucil."

"Just water," Ashley says. "Is the water plain?"

"As far as I know," my mother says, and then she gazes into Ashley's eyes and says, "I'm so glad to see you."

"Me too, Grandma," Ashley says.

"How's college?"

"I'm in fifth grade, Grandma," Ashley says.

"Well, don't be discouraged," my mother says.

"So where's your friend?" I ask, unsure what exactly to call him.

"What do you mean where—he's right there across the room, with his people. That's why I didn't want to come to lunch. Didn't you see them glare at us?"

"I missed it."

"You're a moron," she says to me.

"Did you two have a falling out?" I ask.

"Of course not," she says, defensive.

"Then what's the problem?"

"His people hate me, they actually ignore me. If we're sitting next to each other, they speak only to him, never to me."

"That doesn't sound right," I say.

"Are you saying I'm lying? That's why I never tell you anything, because you never think I'm telling the truth. I never should have married you."

"Ma, it's me, Harold, not Dad."

"Well, then, you're just like your father."

"Grandma, what was Pop-Pop like? When did he die? Did I ever know him?"

"Why are you trying to distract me with all this talk about the past when what I care about is that my man, my living and breathing man, is being kept from me by his ungrateful little bitches?"

"Can you be more specific?"

"Those are his daughters," she says.

"Should I go over and break the ice?" I ask.

"Between him and me there is no ice. We knew each other before."

"Before what?" Ashley says.

"We went to the same junior high," my mother says. "I was friendly with his sister, a lovely woman, who died on a cruise ship. She was thrown overboard and eaten by sharks, and they never figured out who did it."

"Her husband?" I suggest.

"She never married," my mother says.

As the dishes are cleared, Ashley pulls out the cookie tin and is wrestling the top open when nursing-home staff surround us. "You can't open that here—no outside food," they say.

"It has no nuts or seeds," Ashley says.

"It was made at home with love," one of the attendants says.

"Yes," Ashley says.

"Can't allow it—everyone here has to be treated the same. We can't have people who have no visitors getting depressed just because your mama has someone who cares about her."

"How about if we share?" Ashley says.

"How many cookies you got?" the worker asks skeptically.

"How many patients do you have?" Ashley asks.

The worker checks with another aide. "The lunch census is thirty-eight, and that doesn't include folks eating in their rooms."

Ashley puts the cookie tin down and starts dutifully counting. "I have forty cookies."

"You go, girl," the worker says.

Ashley goes from table to table, person to person, offering her cookies. Some people don't want any, others try to take two, and Ashley has to stop them: "One per customer," she says.

After the cookies are distributed, I urge my mother to go and say hello to her boyfriend and his family.

"No," she says, shaking her head and making a face. "They don't like me."

"Well, I'm going to introduce myself; if he's someone you care about, we should be polite."

"I'll stay here with Grandma," Ashley says, and then she whispers to my mother, "They wouldn't let him have a cookie."

His family is not polite.

"I thought I would just say hello," I say, extending a hand. Only the man in question reaches for my hand.

"Nice to see you, son," he says.

We exchange small talk until one of the daughters pulls me aside.

"We're not happy," she says.

"Why not?"

"Your mother is a nursing-home slut. She persuaded him to cheat on our mother, who took care of him night and day for fifty-three years."

"I didn't realize," I say.

"Of course you 'didn't realize.' We know who you are. . . . I repeat, your mother seduced our father. We heard that happens in places like this—so few men, so many women."

"I think my mother knew your father from before," I venture.

"She tried to steal my father from my mother," the girl says.

"That was in junior high," my mother calls across the room. "These new hearing aids are really good. At the time I didn't think their relationship was so serious—excuse me, it was junior high."

"If I may ask, where is your mother now?"

"She's at Mount Sinai—that's what landed him here. They went out for dinner, she fell, knocked him down—he broke a hip, she hit her head. She's been in a coma, and we're trying to make some decisions."

"I didn't realize."

"Do us all a favor—keep your hooker mother away from our father."

"Look," I say, "I don't think name calling is useful here."

"There you go, being all 'reasonable,'" his daughter says. "What part of 'stay the fuck away' are you not hearing?" she shouts at me.

"I think everyone has heard you now," one of the aides says, shooting the daughter a look.

I excuse myself and go back to my mother and Ashley. "Did you know his wife is still alive?"

"Of course," my mother says. "I know her from before also—we used to play pinochle. He talks about her constantly. He tries to call the hospital. I dial the phone for him. She's a vegetable," my mother says. "The nurse holds the phone to her ear, or at least says that's what she does, and he talks to her. He tells her stories about what they used to do. He remembers what they ate on their honeymoon." She shrugs. "And then, when he hangs up, he sobs, he just wants to go home. And those girls, they're the worst—you'd think they'd take him in, take care of him, take him to see his wife. Selfish little bitches they are, but I don't say that to him, no, I tell him they have lives of their own, they must be so busy." She shakes her head. "But look at you, you make time to see me. That's the way it goes—if you were doing well, you'd have no time for your mother. You're a shlep, you show up, you can be counted on—but you're so boring."

"He's actually very nice," Ashley says, coming to my defense.

"It's fine," I tell Ashley. "We've always had a complicated relationship."

"Grandma, could we take you out sometime?" Ashley asks. "Take you out somewhere?"

"Like where?" my mother wants to know.

"I don't know, like maybe to our house for dinner?"

She shakes her head. "I don't think so. I've been to your house before—the food is lousy."

"Well," Ashley says, not the least bit fazed, "I've been doing a lot of cooking; my whole science class is about the kitchen as a laboratory."

"Why don't you come see me again sometime, sweetie," my mother says. She stands up, blows us each a kiss, and heads off down the hall.

Ashley and I just look at each other. "Our family isn't like others," Ashley says.

"None of them are quite what they seem," I say.

We drive back to the house quietly, then take the dog for a long walk and talk about what we might make for dinner.

"I'm thinking pizza," she says.

"There's a pretty good place that delivers."

She shakes her head. "We'll make it ourselves."

"From what?"

"Dough, sauce, cheese," she says.

"You really do like to cook," I say.

"I guess," she says. "Miss Renee and I made dinner almost every night."

"You didn't eat with the others?"

She shakes her head. "We made dinner and watched TV," she says. "After I did my homework."

I nod.

"She said she loved me," Ashley says, in a multilayered tone—both defending and questioning.

"I'm sure she did." There's a pause. "Can I ask you, were the trinkets from Williamsburg for her?"

"Yes," she says. "That's why they had to be good."

"Right," I say. And then we don't say anything more until we've fed the animals and are mixing up some pizza dough.

"She kissed me," Ashley says, looking at me for a response. I give her a recently rehearsed blank face. "So I kissed her back. It was soft, and I don't know how to describe it."

"You don't have to," I say, and then regret having said it—I don't mean to cut her off.

"It felt good. It was comforting—like Mom," she says, and then she just wails. "She said I could sleep in her bed," she says through her tears. "And you know how they, like, say, don't get in strangers' cars, don't 'friend' someone you don't know in reality and all that—it was Miss Renee, I've known her for years."

"Ash, it's not you, you did nothing wrong," I say as her tears literally fall into the pizza dough. We both notice and can't help but laugh. "Salt," I say. "Adds flavor."

"When I was little, I always used to sneeze into the pancake batter," she says. "Not on purpose, but, like, by accident. I'd be helping Mom stir it and I guess maybe a little bit went up my nose and I'd always sneeze right into the bowl." She sniffles.

"Do you know who outed you?"

She looks perplexed.

"Who told on you?"

"Britney," she says, without missing a beat. "Britney got jealous because she has a crush on Miss Renee, which I think is because Britney's mom thinks Miss Renee is so great. Anyway, she started snooping—she's got nothing better to do—I think her father is some kind of spy who works for the government. So one night she asked Miss Renee if she could come over after dinner, and so she did, and I was there doing my homework, and she said she needed to talk with both of us, and she laid out her evidence—which was some pictures and a videotape she made by hiding a camera on Miss Renee's windowsill. She offered to forget it all if we could have a ménage à trois—which I didn't even know what that meant and still don't really. Miss Renee got very pale and said to both of us, 'This is very serious.' Britney repeated the ménage-à-trois idea a few more times, but my French sucks, so all I could think of was, like, the play *The Glass Menagerie*, which I saw last spring. I'm still not sure I get it. And when Miss Renee said she was going to have to call 'the authorities,' Britney freaked out and went back to her room and took an overdose of some kind of medicine, or really a combination of medicines, because it turns out she has a weird problem where whenever she goes to someone's house for a weekend she steals drugs from everyone's medicine cabinets. She actually has a prescription bottle for sleeping pills that belonged to George Bush—her father stole that one for her, it says 'Bush, George' and then has the name of the medicine and how often to take it for sleep. Apparently, a lot of people knew she has this 'habit'; that's why no one invites her anywhere anymore. I guess she's stolen other stuff too, and then the girls have gotten blamed for it. And so she took, like, every pill she had and then ended up passing out in the bathroom after throwing up everywhere—and the cats found her. . . ."

"What cats?"

"Are you kidding? All of the houses have cats, on account of all the mice that are there, on account of the crumbs, on account of how all of us are always nibbling on something in our rooms at night. It's like that book—*If You Give a Mouse a Cookie*."

"I'm not familiar with it. So is Britney still at school?"

She nods. "Her mother is an alum and is also on the board." She pauses. "Can I ask you a question?"

"Sure."

"Did you do it with my mom?"

I don't say anything.

"Nate says you did."

I am still not sure how to proceed.

"You said we all need to be honest with each other."

I nod. "It's true we need to be honest. I just don't really feel comfortable talking about my relationship with your mother."

"I didn't ask you to talk about it—I just asked if you did it." She crosses her arms in front of her chest.

"Yes," I say, and I start sweating profusely.

"Did you love my mom?"

I nod.

"I'm asking because when you're a kid it's really hard to know anything. Maybe I don't even know what I'm talking about—I feel so weird . . ." She trails off.

"Do you need to see the doctor while you're home—maybe we should just make an appointment with the pediatrician?"

"This is so beyond Dr. Faustus."

"You know, it's normal to have feelings for other girls."

"It was so gross," she says, catching me off guard.

I worry what will come next. . . . I am imagining Miss Renee making Ash go down on her. I am thinking of how terrifying I personally find putting my head down there and can only imagine what it's like to a kid—a kid who only likes plain pasta.

"She would just lie there playing with my hair, and then she'd kiss me and ask me to lie on top of her."

"And did you?"

"Yes," Ashley says, as though it's obvious and she shouldn't have to come out and say it.

"Did you kiss anywhere besides on the mouth?"

"Yes," she says, like, again, I am so dumb.

"Where?"

"On the arm to the elbow—we played that game, except that instead of tickling her I'd kiss her."

I shake my head; I have no idea what she's talking about.

Ashley takes my arm and I'm terrified she's going to kiss it, fearing that this is exactly how trauma begets trauma begets trauma, how the seduced becomes the seductress. I yank my arm away. Overreactive?

"Arm," Ashley says, firmly.

I return my arm to the table and lay it out.

"Close your eyes."

"Don't kiss me," I say.

"I'm not going to kiss you. Why would I kiss you? That's creepy."

Thank God.

She tickles my arm with her fingers. "Tell me when I get to your elbow," she says. Her fingers dance up and down my arm, teasing; the thin hairs stand on edge, my skin turns to gooseflesh—it's tickly and weird, and quickly I have no idea where my elbow is, but after a few minutes, just wanting to put it to an end, I call out "ELBOW" and open my eyes.

"We call it 'spider,'" she says. "Didn't you ever play that game with anyone?"

"No," I say.

The phone rings, splitting the air, terrifying me. The machine picks up; the caller waits and hangs up only after the beep. I am sure it's her, Ms. A&P.

Ashley looks at me suspiciously.

"Who?" she asks.

I shrug.

"I think you have a friend," she says. "The person you keep texting is trying to call you."

"What makes you think it's the same person?"

She says nothing, then offers, "It's okay to have a friend—it's not like you have to hide her."

"Thanks," I say.

We play Monopoly. The phone rings again and again, no message.

"Just so you know: The person I text is a friend. The person who keeps calling I'm not so sure about."

On Sunday afternoon I take Ashley back to school. We bring Tessie along for the ride—Ashley wants to bring the kitten too, but I tell her it would be hard on the kitten's mama. I give her a new watch that I found in the "gift" section of George and Jane's closet. We talk about cutting back on watching television and reading more; I make some suggestions of books that might replace her television habit—Charles Dickens, Jane Austen, George Eliot, the Brontës.

"All men," Ashley says.

I shake my head no. "George Eliot was a woman, as was Austen, and the Brontës." I promise to send her some. "I think you'll like them; they're classics, and a lot like soap operas—in fact, that's where the soap-opera writers get their ideas from."

"Don't push it," she says.

"Look at Shakespeare, look at *Romeo and Juliet,* it's all right there . . ." I tell her.

She takes her bag and gets out of the car, planting a foggy kiss on the closed window. I beep and wave.

Two days later, the missing girl is found in a garbage bag.

Dead.

I vomit.

The newscaster pronounces "a tragic end to this story."

I know it is not about me, but I feel guilty; perhaps it is my feelings about Jane, about Claire, my Internet escapades, and the woman from the A&P, who may or may not be the dead girl. It may not be logical, but the depth to which I see myself as criminal, despite my recent best efforts to rehabilitate myself, is real. It is only a matter of time before the cops are at my door. Hours pass. Days. If I had no other responsibilities, I would consider suicide. This may strike you as an overreaction, but what I am trying to say is that I feel guilt, shame, and responsibility on a profound level. Clearly it's not just about the dead girl. I am aware of the damage to everyone—it's as though this girl and Nate and Ashley weren't real, as though nothing was real—except the stirrings below—until all this—until I got to know them. Before this I was detached. The depth to which I now feel everything, when it is not paralyzing, is terrifying. Again, I vomit.

That evening, just before dusk, the doorbell rings. She is standing impatiently on the flagstone step. "I thought you were dead," I say.

"May I come in?" she asks.

I am alternately angry and relieved. My tolerance for not knowing, for obliviousness, is gone.

"Who are you?" I ask.

She says nothing.

"Your ID belongs to a dead girl."

"I found it," she says.

"Where?"

"In a trash can."

"You have to call the police."

"I can't do that."

"I am not going to continue this conversation until you give me your real name and address." I hand her a Post-it and a pen. She writes down the information and hands the paper back to me: Amanda Johnson. "I'm Googling you," I say, walking away—leaving the front door open.

"You might also use my father's name—Cyrus or Cy."

"I will," I say, yelling from deep within the house. According to the Internet, her father, Cyrus, now in his late seventies, was the top dog of a large insurance agency and was forced out following a corporate scandal.

"He stole money," she yells a moment later.

"Apparently," I say. "And you were the maid of honor at your younger sister Samantha's wedding and played the flute at the reception, 'a once-promising flautist.' . . . Are you still playing the flute?"

"Fuck you," she says, coming into the house and finding me at George's desk. "I told you I played the flute."

"So how does it happen that you've got a dead girl's ID?" I ask.

"Like I said, I found it."

"Like I asked—where?"

"In a trash can in the parking lot of a church."

"And you didn't tell the police."

She shakes her head no.

"Why not?"

"It was a while before I put it all together, and because I go there and I don't want to have to stop going there."

"To the church?"

She nods.

"On Sundays?"

"During the week." She pauses. "I have a problem."

"You drink?"

She shakes her head no.

"Drugs?"

"No."

"Sex?" I ask, somewhat guiltily.

Again, she shakes her head no.

"Then what?"

She begins to cry.

"Is it so bad?"

She nods.

"Tell me," I say. "Really, Amanda, you can tell me."

"I can't," she says. "If I tell, you'll never trust me."

"It's not like I trust you now," I say.

She laughs and starts crying again.

"Shoplifting? Eating issues?"

"Quilting," she blurts. "I'm a quilter, okay?"

"We all feel like quitting sometimes. You mean you quit a lot?"

"QUILT," she shouts. "I MAKE FUCKING QUILTS. And if I tell the police, they won't believe me, and then the whole wretched story will come out, and it will all be an enormous mess, and I'll be more alone than I already am."

"Do you know who killed the girl?"

"No."

"Okay, well, that's a start."

She's still crying. "I'm a liar," she blurts.

"You do know who killed her?"

She shakes her head. "I'm a compulsive liar, I lie about everything. That's why I go to that group at the church, it's a group for liars; even just then I was lying. I don't fucking quilt, and if I tell the police, they'll think I'm lying, since that's what I'm there for. That's why, the other day, it was so important to me that I told you the truth about the seven-layer bar—the gift that I bought you and ate."

"Slow down," I say.

"What's the point of telling the police?" she says.

"It's a clue—like, maybe the woman was robbed, maybe the killer left something of his own in the same trash can, maybe his fingerprints are on the very same piece of ID you're using, maybe they're going to trace it all back to you and say you're the one who did it."

"Maybe I should just burn the ID," she says.

"Destroying evidence," I say. "How about just going to the police and saying, 'Hi there, I found these in a trash can and realized they belong to the girl in the garbage bag.'"

"It's kind of fascinating," she says, "what you find in the garbage."

"What made you look in there?"

"I don't know. Something caught my eye. I used to have a boyfriend who was into Dumpster diving."

"Why would you appropriate someone else's identification?"

"Haven't you ever just needed to be someone else?" she says.

I shrug no.

"I was working, I had a job, I lived in Brooklyn. I really liked it. I was dating this guy, flawed but a warm body; we had a cat. And then my mother fell and my father couldn't take care of her, and so I came home, and it's like sinking into quicksand. I had to give up my job, my boyfriend wasn't really into family. Let's be real, let's not drag it out, I said, but I'm coming back soon. He didn't believe me. He kept the cat, won't let me see or speak to her—says I'm an unfit mother."

"Your friends?"

"My boyfriend didn't like most of my friends, so I'd already dropped them. I lost my health insurance and stopped taking my medication and started taking my mother's, which is covered—but it's not really the same."

"I have lots of medication," I offer, wondering, is everyone on medication? She says nothing.

"It still feels like something's missing from the picture—you're taking care of your parents and you're pretending to be someone else? Amanda?" I repeat the name. "Amanda, was that always your name?"

"Are you picking on me? I feel like you're picking on me."

"I'm just trying to understand. When you're taking care of your parents, are you yourself, or this other person—the assumed identity?"

"When I'm taking care of my parents, I live in the bedroom where I grew up, with my same books and toys on the shelf, and it's like I'm still in junior high, like I just got home from school and happened to find them there, sitting on the living-room sofa, but maybe now my dad has wet his pants."

"Do they know what year it is?"

"Sometimes, and sometimes it changes many times in the course of a day. 'Do you have homework?' my mother will ask. 'Just a little,' I say. 'I may have to go to the library—so-and-so's mom is giving me a ride.' When I take them to the doctor, she asks, 'How did you learn to drive, and do your feet reach the pedals?' "

"And what do you say?"

"I'm tall for my age." She pauses. "This is my life for now," she says.

"And later?"

"I'm leaving and never coming back."

She says this and I'm frightened—I don't really know her, and I already feel abandoned. Racing thoughts: What about me? Take me with you—we'll go to Europe, we'll travel the globe.

She notes the shift in my expression. "Oh, come on," she says. "Really? You're living in your brother's house, wearing his clothes, and I'm living with my parents—you can't think this is a relationship?"

"We need to find the guy who put the girl in the garbage bag. I would feel a lot better if that was resolved."

She gathers herself to leave. "You've been watching too much TV."

In the morning, the phone again summons me. I answer quickly, thinking it might be her. "Is this Harold?" a woman asks.

"Yes."

"Good morning, Harold," she says, "this is Lauren Spektor, the director of celebrations here at the synagogue."

"I didn't know there was a director of celebrations."

"It's a new position," she says. "Formerly I worked in development at City Opera." Another pause, as though she's reviewing her script. "We were going over our calendar and I see that we've got Nathaniel down for a bar mitzvah on July 3." Another pause. "I was wondering where we are with that?"

"Good question."

"Does Nathaniel know his Hebrew? Has he been studying? No one here has heard a peep. . . ."

"Actually," I say, "I tried to make an appointment with the rabbi a while ago, but his assistant demanded a contribution of not less than five hundred dollars and I found that off-putting."

There is a long pause. "That issue has been addressed."

"Is the Chinese woman no longer working at the temple?"

"She's gone back to school," Lauren Spektor says.

"Good," I say. "Hopefully, she'll find something that's a good match."

"She's studying at the yeshiva."

A moment of contemplative silence passes between us.

"There are two ways we can go with this," Lauren says. "I can refer you to some party planners and our preferred vendors for catering, flowers, personalized yarmulkes, or we could consider a postponement—I hate to use the word 'cancellation.'"

There's something in her tone that gives me the sense that the temple would rather there not be a bar mitzvah on July 3.

"The temple is mindful of its image; between your brother and his wife and the Ponzi, we've been slightly higher-profile than some of the community is comfortable with."

I take a breath and start again. "Tell me, Lauren Spektor, is there still such a thing as the Sisterhood Luncheon?"

"Are you talking about egg salad, tuna, and cherry tomatoes galore?"

"That's the stuff."

"Long gone," she says. "Our current Sisterhood is mostly working women who don't have time to cook—but we have several caterers who can provide something similar." She pauses. "I don't mean to pressure you, but I'd like to know sooner rather than later. We've got a gay couple looking for a wedding that morning—they want to be done by eleven so they can get out to the Pines for the weekend and beat the traffic."

"Something to think on," I say, at a loss for words otherwise. "As you can imagine, I'm at a bit of a loss as to what the plans may have been."

"I would think Jane had a file—everyone has a file," Lauren says. "Also, she left a deposit. Typically, that's nonrefundable, but we're willing to work with you. We'd consider a partial."

"How much was the deposit?" I ask.

"Twenty-five hundred," she says. "So—how should we proceed?"

"Let me talk with Nate and get back to you."

"It's been a difficult time for everyone," she says.

"So it has."

When I raise the subject of the bar mitzvah with Nate, his voice cracks. I've been dreading this.

"I don't think I can do it—it makes me too sad. It was something Mom was working on."

"You could do it for her—in her honor?"

"I can't imagine everyone we ever knew just staring at me, somehow thinking I am a survivor. I can't imagine writing the thank-you notes for all the iPods and all the crap people give me that will mean more to them than to me, because the truth is, I don't want more stuff. I can't imagine that any 'god'

I believe in would think this is the thing to do." He stops to take a breath. "If I was being honest," Nate goes on, "I wouldn't want to do anything that would bring the whole family together again. People talk about the nuclear family as the perfect family, but they don't say much about meltdown." He stops. "Did you have a bar mitzvah?"

"I did," I say.

"And? Was it a good experience?"

"You want to know about my bar mitzvah?" I pause. "My parents didn't want me to get a swelled head—as though having any decent feelings about yourself caused something akin to encephalitis from which one might not recover—so I shared my bar mitzvah with Solomon Bernstein. It was pitched to me as a good deal, cheaper, and, with the Bernsteins further up the food chain, it put my parents in with the right people."

"Basically, it was all about your parents?"

"Yes." I pause. "After the ceremony there was what was called a Sisterhood Luncheon. All the ladies of the temple made egg salad and tuna fish. Some people got food poisoning—luckily, no one died. But there were new rules after that: all food for Sisterhood Luncheons had to be made at the temple, and they all used Hellmann's mayonnaise and not Miracle Whip—which was deemed a goy food and not to be trusted."

"Goy food?"

"According to my mother—your grandmother—all things, products, food, et cetera, can be divided into Jew and non-Jew."

"Such as?"

"Crest toothpaste—Jew; Colgate—non-Jew."

"Tom's?" Nate asks.

"Atheist or Unitarian. Gin is non-Jew, as is Belvedere, Ketel One, or any artisanal liquor with the exception of Manischewitz, which is Jewish. In any Jewish household you might find a single bottle of honey-colored liquor that no one can remember if it's Scotch or bourbon, rarely two—certainly not three. Crème de menthe on vanilla ice cream is assimilated Jewish. Mah-jongg and pinochle are Jewish."

"Back to the bar mitzvah," Nate says.

"There were two tables of gifts, one with my name, one with Solomon's, and all during the party I kept going over and checking to see whose pile was higher, whose looked better."

"And?"

"It was hard to tell—on account of how someone gave me a set of encyclopedias and wrapped each volume separately. The one thing I really liked was a pair of binoculars that were meant for Solomon but ended up with my gifts."

"How did you figure out it was for Solomon?"

"The card: 'For Solly, With Love from Auntie Estelle and Uncle Ruven.' My mother wanted me to give them back to Solomon, but I refused. I took the binoculars and hid them outside, under the house."

"Is it unreasonable to expect a rite of passage to feel good or be essentially positive?" Nate asks. "What about losing your virginity?"

"Look, Nate, I'm a lot older than you. I just don't want you to be disappointed."

"So you pop the bubble now?" he asks. "You make me feel as miserable as you?"

"No," I say definitively and then stop. "I just want to protect you."

"From what?"

"Life?" I suggest.

"Too late," he says. "Did you ever give the binoculars back to Solomon?"

"I spilled the whole story to him one day at school. 'Keep 'em,' he said, 'I already have binoculars.'" I pause. "I don't think I ever told anyone that story before."

"Not even Claire?"

"No."

There's a pause. "Why didn't you and Claire have children?" Nate asks.

"Claire was afraid she'd be too cold as a parent; she thought she had no capacity to really love and that a child would suffer."

"And?"

"I agreed."

There's a long pause. "I used to pray," Nate says. "Every night I said a prayer to cover my bases; I always believed there was something larger—some bigger idea. I'm not sure what I think now; my relationship to belief has changed."

"So—I get the feeling that you're thinking no bar?"

"I thought it was meant as a conversation."

"You're right. It's not something we have to resolve tonight."

After her cover is blown, Amanda of the A&P vanishes.

Half as a prank, half because I'm genuinely curious, it occurs to me not to wait for her to come to me, but to go to her. I round up the half-empty cartons of Chinese food from the fridge, pack it all into the brown paper bag it came out of several days ago—receipt still attached—and staple it shut. Wearing Nate's old white lab coat like a waiter's jacket, I drive to her house, upscale Tudor, and ring the bell.

"What are you doing here?" she asks, opening the door.

"I have half-order for you," I say in a bad Chinese accent as I hand her the bag. Peeking into the house behind her, I see nothing except a faded Oriental rug, a coat-and-hat rack, and a heavy dark wooden banister and stairs—carpeted. I imagine that on the left is the living room, on the right the parlor or dining room, and straight back under the stairs a half-bath, and then the kitchen across the back of the house—with perhaps a breakfast nook.

"You brought used Chinese food?"

"There's a lot of it," I say. "Fried rice, moo-shu pork."

She hands the bag back to me as her mother comes up behind her: thin, with basketball belly pushing at the waistband of her bright-green pull-on pants; formerly tall, now substantially reduced; her fluffy white hair neatly fixed in tight rolls around her head, mid–George Washington.

"We give to the Kidney Foundation regularly," the mother says. "My husband doesn't approve of door-to-door solicitations, but how about some of my pin money—do you take cash?" She clicks open a small wallet and digs out five dollars, which she moves to hand me.

"Mother, he's delivering food," Amanda says, pushing her mother's arm away. "And he has the wrong address. Better luck next time," she says, closing the door in my face.

Out of boredom I try again. In my mind, it's humorous and demonstrates my determination—I want something more, some better conclusion. I drive to the 7-Eleven and get a gallon of milk and some orange juice and pull up at the curb outside her house. After cutting across the dewy lawn on foot, I hop up onto the front step and ring the bell twice. BING-BONG, BING-BONG.

Her mother answers the door.

"I remember you," she says, and I'm suddenly nervous that I've been made—so much for my disguise. "You used to come around years ago; the milk was in a bottle."

"I'm not the one you remember," I say.

"Must have been your father, then," she says. The mother is elfin, playful, and very charming. She takes the milk from me with surprisingly strong arms.

"Put me down for half a gallon next week, and some of the powdered-sugar doughnuts if you've got them." She looks past me. "Crocuses are coming up," she says, and I turn around and see that I've trod across a good number of them. "Daffodils come soon."

"Is that man related to us?" I hear the father ask.

"No relation to you," the mother says, closing the door.

Amanda calls me that afternoon. "All right, then, Mr. Curious, you want to come for dinner?"

"I think your parents like me," I offer.

"They've conflated you into a milkman who needs a heart transplant. My mother said she gave you fifty bucks."

"She gave me five."

"Welcome to my world. She bragged to my father that it was fifty. 'Any man comes to the door, you give him fifty bucks?' 'Just the good-looking ones,' my mother said."

"What time is dinner?"

"Come at five-thirty."

"Can I bring anything?"

"Drugs?" she suggests.

"What kind?"

"Your choice."

I bring one of George's better bottles of wine. "You kids drink the grape juice, I'll stick to my usual, if you don't mind," her father says, making himself a drink and mumbling that soon they're going to have to let the cleaning lady go because clearly she's dipping into the spirits and watering it down to cover her tracks.

The décor throughout is stiff—chintz, toile, and Staffordshire bull terriers on the mantel, a clock that chimes every fifteen minutes. Honestly, I didn't realize that people lived that way: very non-Jew, very company man and proud of it, a chair with ottoman, and a sofa, all beyond formal and almost painful, with crocheted doilies under the lamps. Amanda brings out a plate of appetizers, Triscuits dotted with Cheez Whiz, sliced green olives with red pimiento centers.

The table is set with china, crystal, and silver, a small cup of soup at each of our places. "Cream of mushroom," Amanda announces. I dig in, and then see that no one is eating it. The mother has dipped her spoon in, and the father seems interested only in his drink and the remaining Triscuits. At first I think it's about grace—they're waiting for someone to say grace—and then I realize it's just the way it is.

Amanda looks at me. I move to help her clear the table, and she shakes her head no. She clears and returns with dinner plates—serving her father and me first, and then her mother and herself. Four fish sticks each for father and me, and two for Amanda and her mother; six Tater Tots for the men, four for the women; three spears of asparagus each; and a broiled half-tomato.

"So much," her mother says, "I'll never be able to eat it all."

"Do your best," her father says.

"The fish is nice," her mother says.

"Mrs. Paul's," Amanda mouths to me, as she takes a bite of a fish stick. Later, she tells me that the family's menus are based on what her elementary-school cafeteria used to serve—fish sticks, spaghetti and meatballs, tomato soup with grilled cheese sandwiches, snickerdoodles. "For some reason my mother saved all the mimeographed menus—she calls it her recipe book."

"What's for dessert?" her mother asks just after the fish is served.

"Pound cake with whipped cream and berries," Amanda says.

The berries prompt the father to talk about eating strawberries and cream at Wimbledon. "Back in the days when tennis was played with racquets."

No one says anything; I am assuming he means wooden racquets.

"Let me tell you a little bit about what I do," the father says, leaning in. "I'm the guy who would decide what your life is worth if you died right now. I'd evaluate who you were, what you might have become, and what your family counted on you for—a big responsibility. Everyone thinks they're more special than they are. Sometimes I just pick a person and think, what would we settle that life for?"

"Like who?" I ask.

"William F. Buckley," the father says.

"He's dead," Amanda says.

"When?"

"A few years ago."

"That's a shame—he was valuable. Mother Teresa, then," he suggests.

"Also dead," Amanda says.

"What would you pay for her?" I ask.

"Nothing. She had no family, no obligations, and no income; she's worth nothing. Interesting, isn't it?" he says enthusiastically. "Any ketchup or cocktail sauce? Sometimes I like to spice it up."

Amanda goes into the kitchen, and returns with condiments.

"I'll be sure to leave you a good tip," her father says, and I can't tell if he's kidding or not.

"Coffee or tea?" Amanda asks.

"I couldn't manage another bite," her mother says. The tomato is half gone, two asparagus, half a fish stick, and two Tots.

"My daughter tells me you like social studies. Ever read the report of the Warren Commission?" her father asks.

I nod.

"I can't put it down. I'm on my second copy—the first one fell into the tub. I just keep going through it. I'm not sure why, not sure what I'm looking for. It's like an Agatha Christie mystery. Off the record, a fellow in my field used to swear that what killed Jack Kennedy was his corset."

"Pardon?"

"Look at the film, you see that after the first shot Kennedy goes down but then he bounces back up; that's because he was wearing a corset for his back, which held him up. The second shot gets him in the bean," he says, tapping the side of his head. And then, as if speaking to himself, he asks, "How many bullets were there?"

"Three?"

"So—you think it was a conspiracy?"

Before I can answer, he continues, "The arrogance caught up with him; he was taking ladies upstairs during state dinners, leaving his wife right there at the table. I'd like to have had half the bad back he had—if you get my point. I'm telling you he had one too many of the ladies, and some Miami mafioso with a baby boy a little too Kennedy-looking wanted revenge."

"Interesting, I hadn't heard that one before," I say.

"Harrumph," he says, like I'm an idiot.

"Daddy," Amanda says, "Harry isn't so interested in Kennedy, he's a Nixon man."

Amanda clears the table; I get up and help her. In the kitchen, I press against her as she's rinsing dishes.

"No," she says. "Absolutely not."

"Why?"

"Not in my parents' house."

"Didn't you ever make out with a boy in here? Play spin the bottle in the recreation room?"

"Ours is an unfinished basement," she says, glaring at me defiantly.

When we come back, her mother is sitting in the living room with a book and her father is nowhere to be seen. Her mother looks up, "Do you remember that I used to call you and your sister Salamanda?" her mother asks. "Samantha and Amanda combined. I loved that. 'Come, Salamanda, time to get outta the wattah.'"

"I loved it too," Amanda says, her face softening for a rare moment. "Do you know where Daddy is?"

"No idea."

"I'll be right back," Amanda says, heading off to find her father.

"Nixon liked to put ketchup on his cottage cheese," I say to her mother in an attempt to make conversation. "His breakfast usually consisted of cottage cheese with ketchup or black pepper, fresh fruit, wheat germ, and a cup of coffee."

"You can bet that's not what his mother fed him growing up," she says. "Cyrus's mother always made shirred eggs and dry white toast. Took me years to get his breakfast right."

"Where was Daddy?" the mother asks when Amanda comes back.

"He's gone to bed. He said he thought we were done for the night."

"So much for game night," her mother says. "We were going to play Scrabble; your father is a very good strategist."

I'm home by seven-thirty; the sky is still light. The air is filled with the promise of spring; each day the light clings a little longer, the plants are plush with new growth. I hear crickets, distant dogs barking.

Ricardo's aunt is waiting on the front stoop. "Everything okay?" She shakes her head. "My husband is jealous of the time I spend with Ricardo," she says. "Maybe Ricardo could come live here for a while. I would do everything like I do now—I would cook and clean and do his laundry—but he could stay here with you."

"He has to go to school," I say.

"His school is not so far, the bus could come."

"What does Ricardo say?"

"Please, mister," she says. "You took my sister and left me with this boy who is too much. You have money; you can help him. I love my sister so much, but I am not prepared. Why does everyone's life have to be ruined? Please, you seem like a nice slob."

Nice slob—does she mean "slob" or "SOB"?

"You can't just give me Ricardo," I say.

"Why not?"

"I am not approved by the state."

"But he is a U.S. citizen," she says. "He was born here."

Rather than try and explain the social-service system, I say, "Let me see what I can do. Meanwhile, I can take him this weekend. We can have a sleepover."

"He was Mommy's baby," she says, and she's crying.

"Don't cry, please don't cry," I say, almost crying along with her. She sniffles to a stop. "What do you have to cry about? You are a big white guy with a big house," she says.

Out of the blue, a postcard arrives from George. The image on the front is of a hotel in Miami; the card itself is well worn, like it has been going around the globe at the bottom of a suitcase for years.

> *This place is everything I thought it might be. Around the fire at night the other guys teach me lock-picking and in arts and crafts I'm learning to make cement shoes from grass and dung. Don't forget to deadhead my perennials.*

The card, with no return address, prompts me to realize that I have no contact information for George—no address, no phone for emergencies. I put in a call to the director's office at The Lodge.

"Good morning and thank you for calling The Lodge, the new executive conference center in the heart of the Adirondacks."

I explain that I'm trying to reach the medical director.

"One moment, please."

My call is transferred.

"Human Resources—are you seeking employment?"

"No," I say crankily, and then repeat my story. "The medical director said he'd be staying on until August. And does anyone know where my brother, George, is?"

The head of HR comes on the line. "Sometimes things change faster than expected—a combo of a buyout, and vacation, and we booked a big conference for the end of July—but you didn't hear it from me. Let's see if someone can access that info and we'll give you a call back."

I phone George's lawyer, Rutkowsky, who, surprisingly, picks up on the first ring. "Do you know where George is?"

"Now that you mention it," the lawyer says, "no clue. Hang on." He makes noises like he's going through some files. "Apparently, we're still waiting on the paperwork; he may be lost in the system."

"Have you got an address? A way to send letters or packages? His birthday is coming up."

"I have a card for Walter Penny and there's an address on there. I'm sure you could put something in the mail addressed to George care of that address and it'll get to him."

I jot down the address he gives me. "When I called The Lodge, they said the medical director was gone. Isn't he part of your family?"

"Separated," Rutkowsky says. "We're not speaking to him at the moment. And in fact, I'm representing my sister against him, so, for conflict-of-interest reasons, I'm going to be passing George's file over to Ordy, another attorney at the firm."

I am at the mall with Cheryl; we are going from store to store. We've made progress. We're not meeting at one of the cheap motels where, fearing bedbugs, Cheryl pulls down the old chenille bedspread, puts a layer of green Hefty yard bags on the bed, and covers them with an old white sheet, and we fuck like drunk drivers sliding all over the place. Instead we're wandering aimlessly, fully clothed, in a skylight-topped faux-tropical paradise.

"Are we here for exercise, or is there something particular we're looking for?"

"A sofa and a nonstick pan," she says, giving equal value to both.

This time her hair is in short blond braided pigtails—something like what an eight-year-old might wear. I'm slightly embarrassed for her but say nothing.

"Are you still seeing her?" Cheryl asks.

"Apparently. But I feel uncomfortable having two sexual relationships at the same time."

"Why?"

"It's confusing."

"In what way? I mean, that one's like a mercy fuck, right?" she asks.

"I'm not sure. What's a mercy fuck?"

"Like you feel bad for her—so you do her."

"I don't feel bad for her," I say.

"Do you care about her?" she asks. "Does she know about me?"

"I think she knows," I suggest.

"Did you tell her?"

"She doesn't care. She doesn't want anything from me—zero involvement. She just wants me when she wants me. She says it's not personal, it's just the way it is."

In the middle of the mall there is a missing-persons kiosk shaped like a milk carton. The kiosk is plastered in posters of Heather Ryan, notices about the Safe Haven Baby Drop and a domestic Cool Out Zone. A large permanent sign reads: "Pregnant? For anonymous assistance pick up phone." An orange receiver waits at the ready.

"Was that always there?" I ask.

"Yes," she says, without looking.

Coming out of one of the stores, I spot Don DeLillo. Our eyes meet; he looks at me as if to ask, What are you staring at?

"I see you everywhere I go."

"I live here," he says.

"My apologies, I'm a big fan." He nods but says nothing. "Hey, can I ask you a question?" He doesn't say yes, he doesn't say no. "Do you think Nixon was in on the JFK assassination?" DeLillo looks at me with a grim snakelike grin. "Interesting question," he says, and walks away.

"You should dump her," Cheryl says, having entirely missed the preceding exchange. "Keep things simple."

I change the subject. "Are we looking for something in particular?"

"I already told you, sofa and nonstick pan. Oh, and here's what I want: we'll go to Macy's, I'll pick out some lingerie, and then you come into the dressing-room area and ask, 'What room are you in?' and . . ."

"And what?"

"You come in and do me—down on your knees, with your tongue—while I watch in the three-way mirror, and maybe I even shoot a little video with my phone. It would be the back of your head, so no one would recognize you."

"Clearly you've given this a lot of thought."

She shrugs.

"We'll get arrested."

"For what?"

My cell phone rings—Amanda. At first I don't answer, but when it rings again, Cheryl urges me to pick up. "Don't be rude on my account," she says.

"Hello?"

"They caught the guy—Heather Ryan's murderer. He was someone her parents had sold her old twin bed to—online. Turned out she'd sewn her diary into the mattress and the guy found it and got obsessed and had been stalking her. Her boyfriend, the one she'd recently broken up with, actually met the guy, who claimed that he was her new boyfriend and told him all kinds of personal stuff about her that he knew from the diary. And when the former boyfriend confronted Heather and she wouldn't admit that she was seeing someone new, the boyfriend said, 'He knows everything about you, he knows more than I know. And I've seen you with him, crossing campus. He's always right there next to you, and when I get close he walks away. . . .' Anyway, Heather and Adam broke up, and then the creep made his move, and let's just say it didn't work out. . . ." Her voice is so loud, its pitch so specific, that even though she's not on speaker, every word seeps out.

"Wow," I say. "Well, thank you for calling."

"Wow? That's all you have to say? You are so weird."

I look at Cheryl, who is clearly listening to the whole thing. "Well, I'm very relieved, and I look forward to hearing more. It's not that I don't believe you, but I want to check some other sources."

"Whatever," she says, hanging up.

"Well, that's a giant relief," Cheryl says. "I feel much better now."

"Why?" I ask.

"Because you're not the guy who did it," she says, smirking.

"Did you think I was?"

"No, but you thought you were."

"What makes you think that?" I ask, oddly exposed.

Cheryl rolls her eyes. "That's what I love about men—see-through," she says. "And by the way, you are so dating her," Cheryl says. "She may not think so and you may not think so, but I know so."

"You still want to go to Macy's?" I ask.

She shakes her head. "I'll take a rain check."

For his birthday, I buy George an iPad and load it with photos of the kids and music from home before sending it off, along with a solar charger, to the address on Walter Penny's card.

"Happy Birthday Brother."

I sign up for Spanish lessons at the local Casa Española. The other people in my class are a McDonald's manager, a guy who runs a landscape company, and a woman who "married well" and wants to communicate better with the "help."

The nurse from Ashley's school phones to say, "Nothing to worry about but . . . Ashley has a skin infection, and we've talked with Dr. Faustus and want to get your permission to go ahead and give her a course of antibiotics."

"Sure," I say. "Do I need to do anything else?"

"Not at the moment," the nurse says cryptically.

When Ashley and I speak, I don't ask about the infection; instead, we talk about *Romeo and Juliet* and her ongoing study of the soap operas.

"It's good," she says. "I watch from one to three in the afternoon, and take notes. I'm working on a paper about the narrative of the soap as modern theater, played in the public square—the TV square is like theater."

"Sounds pretty sophisticated," I say.

"Yeah," she says. "The thing is, they tailor assignments to each student's interests—and you know how, like, if you're really interested in something, you can really go far? I mean, this is, like, eighth-grade level."

Near the end of the conversation she says, "Okay, so there's a letter that's going to come in the mail; just so you have the real story, I better tell you a couple of things." She pauses. "It wasn't a tattoo 'club,' there were three of us, and we gave each other homemade tattoos—not a big deal—but then another group of girls went into town on the weekend and got real tattoos. So Georgia, from my group, decided that ours were supposed to be ugly on purpose and all about scarification. She looked up ancient scarification traditions, and the three of us had a ritual and all rubbed dirt from the compost onto the wounds, which is how I got the infection. It was so not my idea. Anyway, the parents who found out about the 'clubs' got all freaked out, and so this letter is being sent out saying, like, no new tattoos for both students and staff and blah, blah, blah."

"What was your tattoo of?" I ask.

"A unicorn," she says, like it's a given.

I spend the evening glued to the television set. Amanda's story about Heather Ryan's murderer checks out. Her parents have identified the guy who bought her bed, and her diary was found in the guy's car, along with chunks of Heather's hair.

Pretending to be a librarian following up on a book she's put on hold, I call Amanda. Her mother answers. "Good evening, I'm calling from the circulation desk for Amanda. Is she in?"

"One moment, please."

"Who is it?" I hear Amanda ask in the background.

"Your husband," her mother says, handing her the phone.

"Hello?" she asks, baffled.

"What was for dinner tonight?"

"I deviated," she says. "I served Wednesday on Tuesday, just to see if they would notice. Chicken fingers and macaroni and cheese. Not a peep except that when they sat down my father said, 'We want to confirm that there are snickerdoodles with this meal.' 'Of course,' I said, even though I'd planned to serve them angel-food cake. I'm flexible."

"I have an idea: let's put up a tent in your parents' backyard and have a sleepover."

"For my parents?"

"For ourselves—we could sleep together, in the tent."

"I've never slept outside," she says.

"Me either."

"I was always afraid to," she says.

"Even in the backyard?"

"My sister and I would start off brave with flashlights and mayonnaise jars filled with lightning bugs, but as soon as it was really dark, as soon as the lights in the houses all around us started to go out, I'd panic and we'd run inside."

"If we set up a tent, would they spot us outside?"

"Oh no," she says. "They never look out."

"Friday?" I suggest.

"I'll think about it," she says.

"It's a plan," I say. I hang up, excited.

I dig out the tent, the AeroBed and battery pump, some sleeping bags, new batteries for the flashlights. I fill a giant canvas tote bag with bug spray, pillows, an old black-and-white video baby monitor, so we can keep an eye on her parents.

We have dinner with her parents. I slip upstairs and set up the old baby monitor and then bid them good night and leave. I think I'm so clever and crafty, going out the front door and then slipping around back.

I wave to Amanda as she's in the kitchen; I have a melancholy split-second flash—her yellow gloves reminding me of Jane, of that Thanksgiving.

Amanda does the dishes and gets her parents settled for the night while I'm around back, decorating with a string of Christmas lights I found in George's basement. It's like being a kid again. I'm decorating and thinking about Amanda: Will I ever really know her? It's like she's one person inside the house and entirely another outside—an indoor/outdoor personality.

She comes out at about nine-thirty, offering herself to me. She stands before me in the lantern light, taking her clothes off, and then, in a panic, thinking she hears something that we can't see on the monitor, she puts them all back on and goes in to check on her parents.

In a reversal of the children being checked on by the parents, Amanda keeps thinking something is wrong, something is happening, and goes back inside every ten or fifteen minutes, worried they will fall and break their hips, there will be carbon-monoxide buildup, a gas leak that will cause the house to explode, they will wake up frightened of the dark, they will want a glass of water, a sip of Scotch, a little nightcap.

Despite my idea that it would be exciting, it's a lot less erotic than I'd hoped. The AeroBed is squishy, the ground beneath it cold and hard. At around eleven-thirty, when we've been going at it on and off with limited success on both sides, we see her father on the grainy black-and-white monitor, leaving his room. Seconds later, we watch him enter the mother's room, pull down the sleeping woman's blanket, push up her nightie, and mount her.

"It looks like he's hurting her," Amanda says, shocked.

"Hard to tell," I say.

On the small monitor, it looks like her mother is trying to fight him off in her sleep. She swats at him as though he is an oversized nuisance, an enormous fly, and he is holding her down, forcing himself on her.

Amanda stares at the small screen; you can see his equipment jutting out of his pajama bottom. "Is my father raping my mother?"

"Maybe," I say. "Let's see how they are in the morning."

"I can't believe how blasé you're being," she says

"I don't feel blasé, I just don't know what we should do about it. Go into the house and create a distraction? Do you want to confront them in the act? Maybe this is how they do it, the way they've always done it. Remember, you're spying on them; they may be senior citizens, but they have rights, and at least one of them still has feelings of a certain sort."

She is mad at me.

"If you feel so constantly worried and overburdened, why don't you put them in a retirement home?" I ask.

"Why don't you go to hell," she says sharply, turning off the monitor, then rolls away from me and feigns sleep.

I am in the office three days a week. I have my own ID card to get in and out of the building, the office, and the men's room. I have been given a small office with a narrow window—Ching Lan sits in a cubicle outside. Often I ask her to come into my office and read the stories out loud; she is practicing her English. It's interesting to hear Nixon's words with a strong Chinese accent.

Nine of the stories are in close to finished form. I review them, tease out the narrative thread, trim the digressive dross. For a man who didn't like a lot of small talk, Nixon was almost verbose in his fiction.

"What's the best way for me to contact Mrs. Eisenhower?" I ask Wanda. "There's a story I'd like her to consider sending to some magazines."

"I'll let her know," Wanda says. "Which magazines?"

"*The New Yorker, The Atlantic, Harper's, Vanity Fair.* What the hell, we could even try *The Paris Review.*"

"What about *McSweeney's?* or *One Story?*" Wanda asks. "They take risks."

"All right, let's go wide, send it everywhere," I say, not wanting her to know that I have no idea what she's talking about.

"I minored in creative writing," Wanda says, exiting deftly. "Mrs. E. is on the line," she says an hour later, when she rings the phone in my office, which never rang before. "Press the blinking light to take your call."

"Much thanks." After a minute of small talk, I make my proposal: "Ultimately, it will be easier to place the collection if a few have been published first. There is one which is ready to go out, but I'm wondering, under what name?"

"What do you mean?" she says rather aggressively, like she thinks I mean perhaps under my name.

"Richard Nixon? R. M. Nixon? R. Nixon? It depends on how 'out there' you want to be, how obvious or not."

"Interesting," she says. "Let me discuss that with my family and let you know. Can you send me the story?"

"Of course; do you want just the clean copy or all the revisions?"

"Both, if you don't mind," she says.

"I've read the story," Mrs. Eisenhower says in a measured tone the following Monday. "The original version was eleven hundred seventy words, and yours is less than eight hundred."

"Yes," I say. "I worked on that one pretty hard, took it down to a short-short, what folks call flash fiction."

"You cut a lot," she says.

"It shouldn't be so much about word count but about impact. This particular story had a limited vocabulary, and I wasn't sure how long readers would stick with it until they got to the punch line."

" 'Cocksucker,' " she says.

"Yes, that's the punch line."

She pauses. "My father wasn't given to spontaneous humor, but when he'd let himself go, it was quite something. He liked to bang out songs on the piano and it would drive my mother crazy. We would go to pieces, laughing. I still have the letters he wrote me as a kid—very formal, full of good counsel. He wanted things to go well, but often felt so isolated. Whatever it was he was after, he had to find his own path to it. A life like that takes its toll, more on my mother than on him," she says, ruminating aloud. And then, abruptly, she stops. "All right, then," she says, "send it out, let's go with Richard M. Nixon."

"Thank you," I say, and hang up.

I draft a cover letter:

Dear Ms. Treisman,

Enclosed, please find a short piece of fiction of great historical significance. In recent months I have had the pleasure and responsibility of bringing into the light the collected fiction of the notable R. M. Nixon. And while Nixon was long known to have made copious notes about all manner of things, it was only during a recent transfer of materials that a particular series of boxes was fully explored. You are the first to be reading this story, because I can't imagine a better place for it than in the pages of *The New Yorker*. I will hold my breath awaiting your response.

Thanks in advance,
Harold Silver

My phone rings again. "I'm not ready to go public," she says. "I want you to continue with your work, and we'll talk again when the collection is complete."

"Of course," I say; my balloon's been popped.

Ricardo comes for a week. I drive him to school; the bus brings him home. The house rules: no television during the week, no video games, no sugar.

"And what am I supposed to like about this?" he asks.

"That I care about you."

In the late afternoons we play, do homework, and walk the dog. I check his spelling, his math, make sure he bathes, takes his medication. I make his lunch and pack a snack for the bus trip home. By the end of the week, I would swear that Ricardo is doing better. I'm not sure if it's true, or if I've gotten used to him.

I call the Department of Social Services to see where we are regarding the foster-parent approval. "Your paperwork is in the system; that's all we can say," the woman tells me. "Have you got your references, your clearances, your letter from the bank, and the psychiatric evaluation?"

"I was waiting to hear from you about the next step."

"Never wait for us, just keep moving, and eventually we'll catch up."

"All right, then; is there a psychiatrist you recommend? Someone 'in the system'?"

"No idea. I'm new—I usually work in the Motor Vehicle Administration. Hold on, let me ask."

I am on hold for what seems like forever.

"I couldn't find anyone who knew, so I looked in some files of approved families; here are some names of who they used."

I write them down, Google each, and call the one whose office is closest.

Cousin Jason phones to say he's gotten an e-mail from George. "Does that seem weird? I thought he was in jail?"

I don't say that I got him an iPad for his birthday.

"He 'friended' me on Facebook and sent a message: 'I always knew you were gay, sorry if I embarrassed you at the family dinner.' I wondered if maybe he was in a twelve-step program and making amends. I wouldn't have taken it seriously, but he was so specific. I said thank you. Yesterday he wrote to say all my Facebook friends were so masculine and good-looking and he bet I was getting 'it' a lot. I didn't know what to say, so I didn't answer. Today I got another one, asking if I knew anyone in the 'holy land' with a bank account."

"What was the e-mail address?"

"Woodsman224@aol.com," Jason says.

I write it down.

"I wonder if maybe he's involved in a cult or some weird activity, or maybe his e-mail was hijacked. I had that happen, and all my friends got an e-mail saying I'd been robbed in London and they should wire me money—cost my buddies a couple of thousand bucks."

"I'll look into it," I say. "And you, are you doing well?"

"I'm fine."

"And your mother?"

"As well as can be expected."

"Jason, would you want to have dinner sometime?"

"In the city?"

"Yes," I say, "that would be nice."

"It doesn't have to be, like, a big long thing," he says.

"Of course not," I say.

"A quick bite somewhere," he says.

"A quick bite," I echo.

"I don't mean to be rude, but is it something specific?" Jason asks. "I mean, is there an agenda or some specific something that you want to talk about?"

"No, really nothing at all," I say.

"Fine," he says, "we could do that sometime; not right now, but sometime."

"Okay," I say, "let me know what works."

I hang up, wondering, do I e-mail George, do I somehow contact AOL and find out if this is really George's account? I'm not sure I want to be "in touch," so easily reachable. I continue to draw circles around the address until it looks like a Spirograph project. I pin it to the wall by the fridge just in case. . . .

Sara Singer, the head of Ashley's school, calls again. "I won't beat around the bush," she says. "It is my feeling that it is no longer in Ashley's best interests to remain here."

"You're kicking her out?"

"We are protecting her."

"From what, your staff?"

"And the other students. It's getting ugly. Ashley deserves a more accepting environment."

"Let's not throw out the baby with the bathwater. Are you pathologizing a child struggling with the death of her mother, the collapse of her family, who was preyed upon by a teacher—a figure of authority, who should have been a comfort, a moral compass?"

"She's been taken over by the gays and the bois."

"I didn't realize that there were gangs at the school."

"Not gangs—but preferences. She's been taken in by the gay students and the gender-confused. Frankly, I don't think it's the place for her. And it's become a bit of a stir—sort of 'who can feel sorrier for her,' like that experiment where kids carry around an egg for a week and have to take care of it like they would a baby. . . . In this case, the various factions are warring over who should take care of Ashley, and as you can imagine, the faculty has had to adopt a hands-off policy."

"No pun intended," I mutter.

"It's time to think about looking at different options. It would be nice if she left sooner rather than later—gave the other students a chance to begin to heal."

"When would you want her to leave school?"

"The sooner the better," she says. "I realize there's not much left to the school year but the lid is about to blow. I am prepared to offer you a full refund of the tuition along with the deposit for next year, that's a total of seventy-five thousand dollars, and we will give her a strong letter of recommendation and suggest an internship for the last part of the term. She can continue to explore her interest in soap opera. I've got someone who can set it up. Ashley mentioned wanting to work at ABC in New York, but my old college roommate runs a puppet theater in Scarsdale, called Higgledy Piggledy Pop: A Puppet Place. It's a local community theater, and I think it would be a good placement. Ashley can write a final paper about her experience, combining her interest in theater, puppetry, and the narrative of the soap operas."

"Sounds ambitious for an eleven-year-old," I say. "What does Ashley think?"

"She's in her room packing. The bois are helping her with the heavy stuff."

"Well, I don't think seventy-five thousand is going to do it," I say.

"What do you mean, 'do it'?"

"Considering the damage not only to her academic life, but to her emotional development, the violation of trust—"

"I can go to one fifty," she says, cutting me off.

"Two fifty is where the conversation starts," I say.

"I'll need to go to the board."

"Ashley is not leaving until there's a certified check in hand," I say.

"Can I call you back?"

"Please," I say, and hang up, pleased with myself for pushing hard on Ashley's behalf.

An hour later Sara Singer calls and says, "We'll have the check by noon tomorrow—I'm keeping Ashley with me tonight."

"Hostage taking?"

"Safekeeping," she says. "And we'll want you and Ashley to sign a non-disclose."

"I'll sign," I say. "She can't, she's a minor."

Before I can close such a substantial financial arrangement I feel an obligation to check in with Hiram P. Moody. I explain the situation as best I can, going on to say that I feel comfortable with the settlement—that I think I did a good job.

"They're just giving you a quarter of a million bucks?" he asks with a kind of joyous incredulity.

"Apparently," I say.

"On what condition?"

"I agreed to sign a non-disclose about the incident."

"I assume that means you won't press charges."

"I don't want to put the child through anything more."

"Do you know what really happened? I mean, if they were willing to go to two fifty, you can't help but wonder if there's something they're not telling you—like, the woman had a venereal disease?"

"If there's information they're intentionally not disclosing, it would be a bigger problem, but my sense is, they're embarrassed and concerned about their reputation. When I get the check, I'll forward it to you. Let me know what makes sense in terms of taxes, whether it should go into a trust, or what the best handling is."

"Of course," he says. "And forgive me. I didn't mean to be offensive regarding venereal disease."

"No offense taken," I say, even though the comment seemed weird. I hang up and breathe.

When I pick Ashley up, both her arms are wrapped in gauze. "Dramatic effect?"

She shakes her head. "Pus," she says.

"Your idea to wrap it?"

"Hardly," she says.

Sara Singer hugs Ashley goodbye as though everything is as it should be. As they are hugging, Ms. Singer hands me a thin white envelope.

"What's that?" Ashley asks.

"Information about your internship," Sara Singer says without missing a beat.

It occurs to me Ashley doesn't know she's been kicked out of school but simply thinks she's won an award of some sort—the privilege of leaving early and getting to work at a puppet theater. A few friends run across the quad and tearfully hug her goodbye.

"E-mail me." "Text." "Keep a journal." "Collect ephemera for eBay."

"Ashley, it has to stop," I say, when the car is all loaded up, when we're on our way home. "We have to get you back on track—lesbian love affairs, tribal warrior marks—it's all a little out of control."

"It's boarding school, what do you expect?"

"We should go see a doctor. Maybe you need to be taking some kind of medication?"

"I'm on an antibiotic."

"I mean something else: maybe the events of the last few months have just been too much to process without a little pharmaceutical support."

"I feel fine. I've been kind of freaked out since 'the accident,' which is what everyone calls it, since no one knows what to say. But apart from that, apart from how my life was going along perfectly normally and then my father killed my mother and Miss Renee got me all overexcited—and now I've got this oozing thing on my arm, and one on my hip that only you and the girls know about—apart from all that, I don't feel sick or anything."

I swerve to avoid hitting an enormous groundhog lumbering across the road. "Of course," I say, "that's my point. It's a heck of a lot to deal with on your own, and there are medicines that can sometimes help us feel better. You have lots of potential, and medication might make life a little easier."

"Is this about being smart? Everyone has always said I was dumb."

"You're not dumb. Who ever said you were dumb?"

"Dad," she says. And there's a long silence. "I don't want to be a drug attic," she says.

"I don't want you to be a drug addict either," I say.

"Isn't this how it starts? I'm only eleven," she says. "That's still pretty young."

We're quiet for a while.

"I do want to get my ears pierced," she says. "Mom said I could. Can I?"

"No."

"Please?"

"Maybe."

"This weekend?"

"We'll see. I'm not sure I should be rewarding behavior like this."

She twists my arm for the next three days: Can I, can I, can I? And on the weekend, I take her to the gift shop at the mall; it's a cross between what we used to call a head shop, selling rolling papers, bongs, and Jimi Hendrix T-shirts, and a Hallmark store, but with a section of erotic novelties. The girl who waits on us is pierced up and down, through the nose, eyebrow, lip, and tongue. It is hard to understand her when she talks: her speech sounds lumpy and a little slurred.

While we're waiting for her to find the ear-piercing gun, I whisper to Ashley: "See what you have to look forward to if you do all that self-decorating? When you grow up you can get a job working in a mall."

Ashley looks at me as if to say, I don't get it.

"I think it makes it hard to do other things, like get into college or have a real job, unless your application essay is about embracing your native culture and having a clitoridectomy."

"A what?"

"Never mind."

Walter Penny calls. "What the hell," he demands, unpleasantly.

"Who the what?" I ask.

"Penny," he says. "Walter Penny. Buddy, you have got yourself one big problem. I am about to crawl so far up your ass, you're going to feel like you had sinus surgery."

"I think you dialed the wrong number."

"Why the hell would I dial the wrong number?" he shouts. "I'm goddamned calling to scream at you—you academically impaired idiot."

"What seems to be the problem?"

"International arms dealing."

"I have no idea what you're talking about."

"Of course you have no idea, I wouldn't expect you to have an idea. Let me be blunt, did you or did you not send your brother an iPad?"

"I did, as a birthday gift. I thought it would be nice to send pictures of the kids, or so he could map his way if he got lost in the woods, or stream movies on a cold winter night. It's hard to think of what to get for a guy like George."

"You provided the hardware for illegal commerce on an international scale. We could throw you in jail and lose the key."

"That certainly wasn't my intention," I say.

"Open your e-mail—I sent you something."

I go to the desk and, as instructed, open the mail; it's a series of infrared aerial photos of George with the iPad in hand. There's another guy peering over George's shoulder.

"Is that your brother?"

"Sure looks like him. Who's the other guy?"

"The Israeli arms dealer," Walter Penny says.

"How did he get in the picture?"

"He's one of our inmates from New Jersey."

"But you said this program was only for hard-core types, not your average white-collar—"

"Quit whining. This guy is a former used-car dealer, Jersey Jewish mafioso, left his family for the Israeli army. When he came back, his wife had taken up with another man; he killed the guy point-blank at the dinner table, in front of everyone. Funny enough, we didn't want to put some Israeli commando in one of our standard facilities. What the fuck made you think you could send your brother 'presents'?"

"I didn't think it was a big deal to send a birthday gift."

"You opened a portal to the free world, asshole. These guys are on Amazon Prime and have stuff coming every day—food, clothing, pornography." He stops screaming and then takes a long, thin sucking breath. "Where to begin?" Walter says. "This is now a federal incident, the purview of the Secret Service, ATF, FBI, and the CIA—that's how big it gets. Can you imagine the number of eyes on my little pilot program that I worked so hard on, the one with the wood-grain logo, the one with the yellow, green, red, black—four-color print-ing! Can you imagine how fast they'd like to close me down? I'm disappointed in you, Silver. When we met, I thought you had some good ideas, a sense of justice. You presented yourself as a thinker, and it turns out you are just another idiot."

"What can I do to fix it?" I ask.

"We're gonna come up with a plan," Walter says.

"It's set up on auto-pay; I can cut it off. I'd be happy to do it right now, while we're on the phone."

"Don't do anything—we don't want to arouse suspicions. Let me liaise with the others and get back to you. But for now, one move without my approval and you will go to jail. Oh, and think of something George would like to have, something he can't get on Amazon."

Walter calls me again a few days later. "I have been in conversation with the related agencies: ATF, FBI, Secret Service, National Guard. We are going to use you as bait and bring the Israeli in."

"I am at your disposal," I say.

"You bet you are. E-mail George as per the address you got from Jason."

"You know about Jason?"

"He's a good boy," Walter says.

"Is he in on this?"

"We're using a range of assets."

"Have you been in my e-mail?"

"First stop on the tour," Walter says. "Tell George you're driving up Friday night to get his signature on some paperwork."

"But I've got company on Friday—Ricardo will be here for the weekend," I say.

Walter Penny doesn't even acknowledge what I'm saying. "Tell George you're able to meet anytime after six on Friday through six on Saturday."

I do as I'm told; George replies he can do it anytime before sundown on Friday or after sundown on Saturday. I call Walter.

"Crap," Walter says, "this confirms my suspicion. Your brother is practicing Judaism. He and Lenny are observing the Sabbath; that's what we've been seeing them doing on Friday nights. The feds couldn't figure it out—said they were lighting some kind of 'flares' and then sitting dormant—as if waiting for something. The feds couldn't crack it."

"A Jersey used-car dealer got George hooked on religion?"

"Strange things happen when men are left to themselves." In the background a phone rings. "That's the big boys—do nothing further until you hear from me."

Meanwhile, another message from George appears in my inbox: "When you come, bring my silk boxers—upstairs dresser on the left. And some cookware—pots, pans, a spatula, and a ladle—and maybe Mom's old candlesticks, not the silver ones—glass?"

A little while later, the phone rings. "So what's your special gift, something you can bring that he can't get from Amazon?"

"Aunt Lillian's chocolate-chip cookies," I say, not telling him that (a) I'm not in possession of her actual cookies and (b) I don't have the recipe to attempt re-creation.

"It's like the frontier; your brother and this Lenny character are running a general store up there. The bad boys bring them a dead duck and get Hershey bars in return. They've used the Amazon boxes to build themselves some sort of fort in a fort, which at the moment our camera can't penetrate—we're thinking it's made out of some kind of river mud."

"Dung," I say. "Grass and dung."

"Shit?" Penny asks.

"Yes."

Aunt Lillian's cookies. I make it my secret mission to replicate the cookies and the tin. I go to CVS, buy a tin of Danish Butter Cookies, come home, play kick-the-can with it while I walk Tessie, send it through the dishwasher, tumble it in the clothes dryer on hot with a bunch of towels, basically abuse the hell out of it, in a program to rapidly achieve the patina that would otherwise come with age. I buy the semi-sweet morsels, walnut halves, brown sugar, white sugar, vanilla, butter, flour, salt, baking soda, and remember the all-important tablespoon of warm water that Ashley told me about. Soon I am turning out Toll House hockey pucks that are equal in size, color, and lumpitude to Lillian's famous. I leave them out to air-dry. Each day, fewer cookies remain—I say nothing to the suspected culprits at home, except that I am counting and know exactly what I've got, and I offer them a two-for-one special on the "defective" batch, which is actually far better.

And then, when I've got all the details, I call Ricardo's aunt and tell her that I've got to work late in the city and ask if she can come and keep an eye on the kids.

"Of course," she says.

And then—the real craziness starts. Later, I will wonder if this part really happened or if I dreamed it.

I am directed to a location several hours from home, and then, once I'm there, I'm led by an unmarked car to a deserted airstrip lit like a film set. Parked on the dirt runway are a small private plane and two military helicopters. By the time I arrive, the sky is sinking from twilight to the flat black of a starless night. On the grass nearby are several unmarked black cars, four guys in ATF nylon jackets, a dozen or more National Guard in full gear, Secret Service men trying to look low-key in polo shirts and khakis, a couple of unidentified men, assumedly FBI or CIA, and Walter Penny with a clipboard and a whistle on a lanyard around his neck, looking like a coach, preparing for the big game. The field is lit with giant floodlights—there's even a quilted silver snack truck serving hot coffee and doughnuts.

I take out a nine-by-twelve envelope filled with papers for George to sign, permission slips from school, bank forms, health forms for summer camp for the kids, release of documents re the mortgage, etc.

"Are these for real?" Walter asks.

"Mostly," I say. "So what's the plan?" I ask.

"We need the iPad and the Israeli. Beyond that, the less you know the better."

I notice some guys are working on my car—the hood and trunk are open.

"I'm sending you in with two hundred pounds of halvah," Walter Penny says, with some difficulty pronouncing "halvah." He says it as though he's been practicing in a mirror.

It triggers an instant flashback—cultural insensitivity. "Here we go again. Don't you people ever learn?"

"What are you talking about?" Penny demands.

"Iran Contra," I say, "Oliver North, Robert McFarlane, and arms-for-hostages. They sent a Bible signed by Ronald Reagan and a chocolate cake shaped like a key—baked by an Israeli, no less."

"I still don't know what you are talking about," Penny says.

"You may not, but I do," I say. "What's the point of the halvah?"

"I figure it might appeal to this character; also high in fat, so good for these guys, and it's not something the government food bank can distribute easily, with all the rules about nuts and seeds. They can't use it in school lunches, hospitals, the VA, or old-age homes. And I was thinking the indigenous birds also like it. And if the men like it, we can get them more: apparently we've got tons—literally."

"At what point during this 'mission' am I supposed to say, 'Oh, and I have two hundred pounds of Middle Eastern sweets, aka Jew food, in the trunk if you're interested'?"

"Play it by ear," one of the unidentified men says.

"And why are so many agencies involved?"

"The transactions were international, with multiple money sources, and involved what would have been considered top-secret information that seemed too easily accessible to your brother and the Israeli," Walter says.

"Do you think he's a spy? A double agent?"

"I think it's time to shut up and do your job," the unidentified man says. "One pointer, when you're with your brother and this other guy, make sure to leave a space between you and any other man—you don't want to be collateral damage. Our soldiers are armed, the bullets are experimental pellets. We're testing a glycerin-based product, with kind of an entry dart, something that we'll be able to add an additional agent to if desired."

"Agent?"

"Like a nerve agent, or a bio agent, or a little sleeping medication. Nothing for you to worry about . . ."

Walter Penny resumes the lead: "Earlier this week, we dropped a marker that's sending a signal; that's the point you need to drive to. We put a GPS in your car that will lead you there. And we're using the same marker for the operational assistants."

I must have looked confused.

"The soldiers," he says. "Your car has now been wired, it's now miked inside and out. Do not talk with us or engage in any way en route in or out. It's two-point-five miles in, down a rutted old road, really less of a road than a path."

Suddenly things are moving quickly. I'm ushered back into my car—sent packing.

The road is beyond dark, it is like driving into a tunnel from which all hope has been removed. The car's headlights seem to frame things only a half-second before I am upon them. I keep driving blind towards the blinking light; a few times I am thrown off track by fallen trees and have to navigate around.

As I pull up to the spot, the GPS goes dark without my even turning it off. I flash the brights on and off a couple of times before getting out of the car.

I hear rustling in the bushes. George steps out into the headlights, looking pretty good in a kind of rough-hewn, Sunday-morning way.

"Hi, George, how are you doing?"

He moves to hug me, which seems uncharacteristic. "Are you hugging me or patting me down?" George doesn't answer. "Glad you got the birthday gift."

"Lousy reception," George says. "If there's cloud cover, I get nothing."

"What about Netflix?"

"Slow, very slow."

"Can I see? I've never seen one in person before." He unzips his jacket and takes it out. The iPad glows. "It really is a beautiful object, isn't it?" I tap around at the various applications.

"How do I get to the pictures?" I ask.

George taps something, and the photos of the kids open up, interspersed with images of guns and other military paraphernalia.

"What's that?"

"Just stuff," he says. "Remember how we used to play army and *Hogan's Heroes* and all that?"

"Yeah," I say.

"I got back into it—not much to do up here."

"Fun," I say. I tap on his mailbox—an e-mail in Hebrew pops up. "Hard to read without my glasses," I say, pretending not to realize it's in another language. Until I saw the photos of the missile launchers with Arabic writing, and the e-mails from Israel, I didn't really believe Walter Penny—I thought it was some crazy game. But now it makes sense. George always liked to be a big shot, to wheel and deal, and playing war was a childhood favorite.

"It's so fucking slow," George says, grabbing the iPad from me and shaking it like an Etch A Sketch.

"I'm sure there'll be a faster one soon," I say, taking out the envelope of papers I need him to sign. "Sorry to bother you with this stuff; I've not been able to get your lawyer on the line."

"Me either," George says. "He's not answering my e-mails."

"You want me to ask around about finding someone new?"

"Maybe," George says, using the car hood as a writing surface and scrawling his signature on one document after another.

I start to relax.

"You brought my underwear?" he asks.

"Yep."

"Good," he says. "The stuff they give us is crap. Government-issue Jockeys, chafes around the leg—so you're raw and can't run, and it's too damned binding. Big balls," he says.

"Yes—you've often said that about yourself."

"And the pots and pans?" he asks, still signing.

"Got 'em. You doing a lot of cooking?"

"It's not like I'm in the Domino Pizza thirty-minute delivery zone."

"What do you make?"

"Cheese sauce and peanut sauce; there's a lot of flour, butter, cheese, peanut butter, and pasta—not so much sugar—we need more sugar. Have you got any?"

I pull a couple of packets of Splenda out of my pockets. "If you'd asked I would have brought—"

He cuts me off, as though trying to keep it short. "Candlesticks?"

"This is what I could find," I say, handing them to him. "They were Jane's."

He takes the candlesticks like that's the most important part of all. "Matches?"

I open the passenger door of the car and dig around in the glove compartment; stuff falls out.

"Give me the flares," George says, "I might need those."

"This isn't fucking trick-or-treat," I grumble as I hand him the flares and the rest of the snacks I packed for the ride. George plucks a half-empty Coke from the cup holder and sucks it down.

"Amazing," he says. "The flavor, it's like the nectar of the gods. I wish they'd get a fucking Coke machine in this place."

"I brought you a gift," I say, pulling out the cookie tin. George immediately looks both excited and concerned.

"Is that Lillian's tin?"

I nod enthusiastically.

"What happened—she died?"

"It's on loan; she's fine," I say, suddenly panicked. I hadn't thought about this part—about how it would happen that I had Lillian's tin. I knew that Lillian's cookies were a good lure.

I proudly open the tin, having replicated the same old crinkly, rarely replaced circles of wax paper, the cookies vaguely pale but rich with lumps of chocolate chips and walnut halves.

"How many?" George asks, looking at me expectantly, like a child, not realizing that if he wanted it the whole box could be his.

"Two?" I suggest.

"Per person?" he asks.

I shrug, imagining he wants his two and my two as well.

"Are they kosher?" George asks. I'm caught off guard.

"I don't know if Lillian keeps kosher," I say, genuinely perplexed.

"I think she does," George says, wanting it to be true.

His friend Lenny steps out from behind a tree directly behind me and scares the hell out of me. "So you're the putz?"

"This is Lenny," George says. "He's part of the program."

I hold out the tin. "Would you like a cookie?" I ask.

And then they are upon us. Like fucking Spider-Man—they drop from the sky. The cookie tin flies out of my hand. There are men everywhere, their infrared goggles lit up with tiny red blinking lights like bug eyes. There is smoke and confusion. Something stabs me in the ass and throws me to my knees. My eyes are burning, I am facedown in the dirt. There is commotion all around me, and then silence. I see what look like blurry puffs of white being sucked upward and realize it's George's silk boxers blowing in the updraft of the chopper. I dimly see George just ahead, flat out and bleeding from the head.

As fast as it happened—it's over.

The Israeli is gone.

I crawl back to the car and into the front seat. "You blinded me, you fucking blinded me," I bellow, rubbing my eyes.

"You'll be fine—just stay put," Walter Penny's disembodied voice speaks to me. "And stop rubbing your eyes, you're only making it worse."

"Stay put for how long?"

"A few hours, maybe until morning."

"With these dead people?"

"They're not dead, they're sleeping."

"You can't just leave me here. What if he wakes up angry, what if there's one you missed, what if someone wants the car? I am a citizen, I have rights."

I hear multiple people talking in the background, someone saying, "The playmate is turning into a tuna melt and wants a ride home. Can we send someone in to drive him out?"

I start beeping the horn.

"Hold on."

"You're not coming to get me? Fuck it," I say. And I beep again. "Fuck it, fuck it, fuck it." A beep for every fuck it.

"Your microphone is in the area of the horn. If you don't stop beeping, I'm going to fucking unplug your ass. We'll have someone to you in two minutes. Don't beep again."

I hear the chopper coming in—dark. My eyes are stinging, blurry, as I watch them lower a man in full combat gear. He's clutching a bottle of spring water and looks like a demented commercial for managing your thirst during wartime. The soldier lands, unhooks his tether, and gives a yank; they pull up the rope. He comes to the driver's side like a gigantic glow-in-the-dark bug, opens the car door, twists the top off the water bottle, and squirts water directly into my face. "Feeling better?" he asks.

Drenched, I get out, go around, and get in on the passenger side of the car.

"You only have half a gallon of gas?" he says, starting the engine.

"It's not like I passed any gas stations on the way in."

He throws the car in gear, and we bump along the road. "Are you going the right way?" I ask. "Why haven't you turned?" I'm wiping my eyes with my shirt. It's not working: whatever is in my eyes is also on my shirt.

"Hey, shit-for-brains," Walter Penny's voice comes over the speaker, "the putz is right, you're going the wrong way."

"Sorry," the soldier says. "I'm kind of dyslexic." He turns the car around and steps on the gas, and there's a giant ka-thunk. It's not a sound but the weighty sensation of having struck something.

"What the fuck was that?" Walter Penny asks.

"I think I hit an animal," the soldier says.

"Let's hope it was an animal," Walter Penny says.

"I think we can keep going," the soldier says. Dented, we limp towards the finish line. At the road, we're met by two unmarked cars that escort us back to the deployment area.

I get out. Someone hands me a bottle of eyewash. The first thing I see when my eyes are clear is the dented hood, ripped fender, a crack in the windshield, and blood.

Walter Penny comes over to me, looks at the car, and takes a white claim form from his manila folder. "I always keep a few of these with me. It's a government claim form, same for an auto accident as if you're killed by friendly fire. The government is self-insured—one form for everything. But here's the thing," he says, dangling the form. "It only works if you were at the wheel. Did you drive yourself out?"

Confused, I look around. The soldier has vanished.

"Did you drive yourself out of the woods?" Walter asks again.

"Apparently," I say.

"Alone?"

"Guess so," I say, plucking the form from Walter's fingers.

"Then you can use it for your car and your person."

"You shot me," I say to no one in particular.

"The car, your person—put it all on the same invoice," Walter Penny says.

"Grazed," one of the unidentified men says. "I watched the playback."

"You look a lot like your brother," one of the soldiers says, like that explains it.

I don't even ask where the Israeli is but notice that one of the unmarked vans is gone. "Are we done here? Am I free to go?"

"Yes," Walter says. "And don't forget to get gas."

I am escorted to the thruway. There is an eerie absence of traffic. I fly towards home at eighty miles an hour. I would go faster, but anything over eighty elicits a disturbing rattle.

Shivering, I turn on the heat—nothing happens. I reach down; the car seat is damp. I flick on the map light and see the seat is dark with blood.

Outside, the sky is beginning to lighten. I'm not sure what time it is—the car's clock is frozen at three-forty-three. Just before my exit, I take a detour, pulling in at the local hospital. From the parking lot I text Ricardo's aunt to say it's all taking much longer than planned and notice six missed calls—messages from Ashley and Ricardo saying hello, telling me jokes, wondering when I'm coming home.

A security guard comes to the window. "No standing," he says. "Patient parking only." He points to a sign.

"My ass is bleeding," I announce, getting out of the car. The guard escorts me to the triage nurse.

"What happened?" the nurse asks.

"I've been shot," I say, and then faint, falling flat to the floor. I come to facedown on a gurney with my ass up in the air, and someone is taking photos. I overhear that they've already gotten an X-ray and that luckily there's no shrapnel to be found.

"We're going to clean it up," the doctor says. "There's really nothing to sew."

"I got a new digital camera for Christmas; I could bring the old one in," someone says.

"What's the resolution?" another guy asks.

"No idea, but it's better than this piece of crap."

They're talking supply chain while my ass is up in the air. The one guy bends down and speaks directly to me. "We're going to put some numbing medicine on your tushy and clean it up," he says. "The wound was deep."

"What happened?" a second asks, bending down.

"I don't really know," I say. "It was like *Deliverance* met *The Shining*."

"Do you want to file a police report?"

"No," I say, "I'd like to keep it private."

As soon as I say that, I can tell they're thinking it was some kind of sexual assignation gone wrong.

"There are a couple of questions we need to ask," one of the doctors says, bending down so we're eye to eye. "Are you safe in your home? Is anyone hurting you, or otherwise abusing you? You don't need to feel ashamed about answering these questions. . . ."

"Do I look ashamed? I really have nothing to say. I don't know who it was."

I am given a card for a men-only abuse hotline, a giant shot of antibiotics, and a tetanus shot, and, just like goddamned George, my arm swells: as I'm leaving the ER, I can already feel a hot baseball forming under the skin.

I take the car through a car wash and ask if there's anything they can do about the car seat—maybe steam-clean? "Hit a deer," I say, shaking my head.

"Guess so," the guy says, looking at me funny, noticing the blood all over my pants. "Was it inside the car?"

"It was enormous," I say.

When I get to the house, a large "WELCOME HOME" sign written in multicolored bubble letters is mounted on the front door. Ashley, Ricardo, and Christina have clearly been up most of the night and are looking at me with great concern.

"Was there an accident?" the aunt asks.

"Did you go see Dad? Did he beat you up?" Ashley wants to know.

"You look crazy," Ricardo offers.

"Let's just say it was quite an adventure." I excuse myself, take a shower, have some Tylenol, eat a giant breakfast, and promptly fall asleep.

"I called in sick," Christina says in the afternoon, when she comes to check on me. "I couldn't leave you and the children like this."

I nod and fall back asleep, facedown—arm throbbing, ass stinging.

I can't say I'm entirely surprised when a state trooper comes to the door that evening to ask me about a hit-and-run forty miles away. He comes right out and says it: "My brother-in-law works at the car wash and is really into these crime-solver shows. . . ."

"I get it," I say, handing him Walter Penny's card. He calls Walter, and despite the late hour Penny answers and explains that it was a special operation and, yes, there was damage to both the person and the vehicle, but in general it went well, and he has no further comment.

"You're like an operative—cool, very cool," the trooper says, hanging up. "I'm going to have a hard time not telling the brother-in-law."

"I'm really just a former professor who sometimes gets dragged in over my head."

"Are you coming to the wedding?" my mother asks, near the end of my visit.

"When are you getting married?"

"Soon," she says. "And why are you just standing there?" she asks. "You've been standing there for more than an hour with an awful expression on your face."

"I have an injury," I say. "Sitting is difficult at the moment."

"Hemorrhoids?" she asks.

"No," I say. "Is the wedding definite?"

"What kind of a question is that?"

"Are you really going to marry him?"

"Isn't that why I asked you?"

"I think so," I say. "But what do you two have in common?"

"We're old," she says. "And we both have a love of motion. We like to play catch—they give us these Nerf balls. We love to throw them back and forth. And bingo," she says. "I help him with his cards. He doesn't see so well—he lost an eye playing golf years ago—and he has a ringing sound in his head that he's had for years."

"That's what you like about him?"

"We want to move in together," she says.

"I have no problem with that. And, so you know, you and your friend are always welcome to come and live at home."

"With you?" she says. "You're a slob. I was so happy when you moved out of my house. Why should I leave my condo to come to you and have to cook and clean? I'm happy here."

"Marriage is something to take seriously."

"It's not such a big deal," my mother says nonchalantly. "I've done it before. So," she says, "I'll put you down as a yes?"

I say goodbye and hurry down the hall, hoping to catch someone from the nursing-home administration before they leave for the day. "Excuse me, who do I talk to about your policy on inter-patient marriage?" I get an old-fashioned runaround, lots of hemming and hawing, and finally someone comes out and says it: "We don't like unmarried couples to room together."

"That's the least of my worries," I say, wondering if my mother and her husband-to-be are in their right minds. "There are estate issues to be concerned about. Should there be a prenup? At their age, shouldn't this be more of a family decision?"

"Do you have power of attorney?" someone from the home asks. "Are you prepared to have her declared incompetent?"

"Look, I've only met the man in question twice, and he's already calling me 'son.' I'm not sure what I'm prepared to do."

"On occasion," the social worker chimes in, "we have facilitated commitment ceremonies complete with real flowers, cake, dress-up, and someone who does a little ceremony. That seems to do the trick. We tell the couple that the person performing the ceremony is not recognized by the state but that it costs less than an official wedding. I have the couple and their families sign a release stating that the ceremony is not binding and that, should the couple break up or either or both members die, there is no right of survivorship, no community property, and so on. The paralegal who does the DNR paperwork can help you with that."

"That sounds good," I say. "And then do you let them room together?"

"For as long as they are willing and able," the social worker says. "Meanwhile, your mother is up and walking. She's been dancing. She may not be the woman you remember, but whoever she is now—she's doing very well."

On the way home, I pull into the drive-thru at the Chick-Inn and order a whole bird to go. The woman shoves an enormous piping-hot roasted bird through a window that I think was built only for doughnuts and coffee. A second bag follows with sides of biscuits and potatoes.

As I'm coming in the door, I hear Walter Penny's voice on the answering machine: "I received your claim form: thirty-eight hundred dollars for damages to the car. We should be able to get this processed pretty quickly."

I put the bags down and let him go on for a while.

"Don't forget you've still got the halvah in the trunk; I think it worked for you as ballast when that nutcase was driving you out. No worries about bringing it back—once it's out of our hands, we can't take it back anyway. I wanted to remind you. It shouldn't stay in the trunk, probably too hot in there. And, by the way, you left your cookies up at the camp—they're very good. What's the trick?"

I can't resist any longer. I pick up the phone. "Tablespoon of warm water," I say.

"Just one tablespoon?" Penny asks.

I cut to the chase. "Where's George?"

"George complained of an injury, so we brought him in just after you left—didn't seem like we could leave him out there after what happened. As soon as he's feeling better, they'll transfer him to a more traditional facility."

"What about the agreement?" I ask.

"What agreement?" Walter says.

"The agreement we signed in the director's office at The Lodge that said George would never go to a regular jail?"

"Do you happen to have a copy? I don't think I have a copy."

I'm not sure what kind of game Walter is playing with me, but I make an excuse to get off the phone and immediately call George's lawyer.

"We never got a copy," he says.

I call Walter back in the afternoon. "So, if no one has a copy, I guess there is no agreement?" Walter says.

"How long is he in for?" I ask.

"Five to fifteen," Walter Penny says. "We compromised."

"No trial?"

"Trust me, it's better this way."

"When's the soonest he'll be out?"

"Figure three years. We had to give him some credit; the Israeli was a good catch."

Late one night, I drive to the temple and unload the halvah on the back steps. I leave a note: "This is good halvah—I am leaving it here for the community to enjoy as it's more than one man can manage."

As I'm unloading, the rabbi appears, sneaking out of a side door. He's clearly frightened when he sees me, as though I'm a religious terrorist—unpacking C-4 plastique explosives.

"It's just halvah," I call out.

"What?" he says, his tone the familiar annoyance of an old deaf Jew.

"Halvah," I shout as loudly as possible.

He comes closer, and I introduce myself as George's brother, and lie: "I was recently doing a job and received the halvah as partial payment," I say. "I thought perhaps the temple had a soup kitchen."

"We have a preschool, and a day camp for the elderly," the rabbi says.

Now is the moment. I have the rabbi's attention; this is the meeting that I called months ago to arrange. It's my chance to get good counsel.

"So," I say, "what do you think? Was Nixon really an anti-Semite?" I ask, surprising myself.

"Nixon?" the rabbi intones.

I nod.

"You want to know about Nixon?"

"I do."

"He was a son of a bitch, hated everyone but himself. The one who makes me nervous is Kissinger, who never stood up for himself—he sold us down the river."

A police car pulls into the parking lot. "You okay, Padre?" the cop asks.

"Fine, thank you," the rabbi says.

The cop looks at me like he knows me from somewhere. "Why don't you go home now, mister," he says. "Let the padre get a good night's sleep." He hovers until I say goodbye and then follows my car most of the way home.

As part of my quest to become a foster parent, I've made an appointment with Dr. Tuttle, a psychiatrist. Strange though it may seem, I've never been to a psychiatrist before, and so it is with some trepidation that I approach his office on the ground floor of a small strip mall. To the right of his "suite" is Smoothie King, to the left a dry cleaner's, and next to that a cell-phone store. The office windows are covered in wide metal vertical blinds circa 1977; the waiting room is dark, with a low acoustical-tile ceiling and oatmeal-colored wall-to-wall. Six chairs with caned seats that are starting to sag dot the room in pairs like couples. There's a little glass table with a precarious pile of magazines and a trash can so small it seems to say, Don't use me. Sitting down, I spot a lone Cheerio in the corner, and then more—a series of Cheerios tucked up against the molding, likely pushed there by a vacuum cleaner. There are numerous signs, handwritten and poorly laminated with Scotch tape.

If you need a bathroom, go to Smoothie King and ask for the key.

If you need your parking validated, please ask, 1 hour free.

The psychiatrist opens the door and calls me in. "Tuttle," he says, shaking my hand. His hand is wet, smelling of perfume and rubbing alcohol. I immediately spot a bottle of hand sanitizer on his desk—the sample from a drug company. Tuttle is a short, thin fellow, prematurely hunched—the top of his head comes to a kind of a shiny point, absent of hair but for a ring of yellow fringe that goes all the way around and is longer than the fashion. He wears horn-rimmed glasses, which he edges higher by repeatedly wrinkling his nose. The office has the same metal blinds as the waiting room and would be dark but for the afternoon sun reflecting off the cars parked outside.

"Have a seat," Tuttle says, directing me towards a worn sofa.

I look past Tuttle; clear plastic cups from Smoothie King are in an even row on the edge of his desk, each less than a quarter full, one yellow, one pink, one purple. Mango, strawberry, and berry-berry lined up like some kind of experiment. There's a half-empty old five-cent gumball machine filled with what look like greasy peanuts and piles of used legal pads. An air conditioner hums noisily.

"First let me get a little information: name, address, phone?"

I give him the details.

"Employer?"

"Self," I say for the first time.

"Insurance? I don't take insurance, but I'll give you a bill each time we meet and you can submit it. The initial meeting is five hundred and runs for an hour, and subsequent visits are forty-five minutes and the charge is two fifty. I am a psychiatrist, not a social worker, not a psychologist." He looks at me carefully. The glasses seem to be magnifiers—his eyes look enormous. "What medications do you currently take? Previous hospitalizations?"

I mention the stroke.

"Do you have a diagnosis that you are familiar with? And/or how has your condition been described to you? What was the referring agency?"

"A girl at Social Services gave me your name," I say, thinking that something here is not entirely on the mark.

"Do you require court-ordered drug testing—i.e., do I have to watch you pee?"

"No," I say.

"Good," he says. "When I watch someone else pee it makes me feel like I have to pee. In fact, I usually get one of the employees from Smoothie King to do the watching. I tap one of the guys to follow us into the toilet, and I tip him a few bucks to do the watching. I really don't want to see a patient's water works and then have to talk to him about what he's like with his wife. Plus, I happen to know the bathrooms are monitored—so there's very little chance of the patient trying to get away with anything. But I digress, and this isn't about me, and this isn't about Smoothies. What can I do for you?" He puts his pad down, crosses his legs, and looks at me, again wrinkling his nose and lifting the glasses up a little.

"I think I'd like to begin by asking, what kind of people do you typically work with?"

"Spans the gamut, from court-ordered counseling for boys who get into trouble, to anger-management issues with married men, a few middle-aged ladies who wished they'd done things differently, and a good number of teenage girls who want to be dead. What brings you here?"

"I've applied to be a foster parent and I need a psychiatric evaluation." I hand him the form. "You were among those recommended by the Department of Social Services."

He takes the form and looks at it as though he's never seen one before.

"It would be a directed placement of a little boy with some learning problems who was recently orphaned."

"Have you ever been arrested?"

"No."

"Do you enjoy pornography?"

"Not especially," I say. "But there is something," I say, laying the groundwork. I tell him about George. He listens carefully, appearing never to have heard any of it before. Either he doesn't read the papers or he's very good at concealing what he knows.

"Let him cast the first stone . . ." the doctor says, when I come clean about my part in the domestic debacle. "And so, before all this, before last Thanksgiving, you led a conventional life, no affairs, no relationships outside the marriage?"

"A most conventional life," I said.

"And the children?" he asks.

I tell him how I have come to know the children, how they are so much more interesting than I had expected, and that I love them. I share the details of our Williamsburg adventure.

"And are you in a sexual relationship now?" he asks.

"Yes, with a local girl, very nice family," I say, as if bragging.

He shrugs as if to say, How would you know? "Okay, so this boy Ricardo that you want to foster . . ."

"He survived the accident, and the kids want to help, and the aunt who was left in charge has been struggling, and . . ."

"And what makes you think you're qualified?"

"Good question," I say.

He nods.

"I care about the kid. I was a teacher for many years. I have the time and energy to focus on figuring out what he needs and how to get that for him. I feel very bad about what happened and would like to see him through."

"Would you send him to school?"

"Every day."

"What if he needed to go to a special school?"

"I'd find the best one and fight to have it covered by the state education system, which is legally obligated to educate every child regardless of disability; and, depending on the outcome, I'd see what I could do."

"Would you be doing this with an eye toward adoption?"

"The children would like me to adopt him. I'm not sure that's what his family wants. But, yes, I'm doing it with an eye towards the long term; this isn't something I take lightly."

"And what is your work as a self-employed person?" He says "self-employed" slowly, like it's a suspect notion.

"I was a professor of Nixon studies for many years, and as a Nixon scholar I am working on a book about him and also working with the Nixon family on a special project."

"Interesting. What drew you to Nixon?"

"Nixon is like someone from another time: old-fashioned to the point of being a bit backward, inescapably ugly whether he knew it or not, bitter, self-spiting, insecure and overly confident simultaneously."

The psychiatrist nods. "Not uncommon, to be both driven and conflicted."

"I find it fascinating—his sweat, his paranoia, his emotional lability. Even as President of the United States he didn't fit in."

"Do you have a title for your book?"

"While We Were Sleeping: The American Dream Turned Nightmare—Richard Nixon, Vietnam, and Watergate: The Psychogenic Melting Point."

"That's a lot of title."

"I've been thinking a lot about the drug that is the American Dream as the American entitlement, which gave way to the American downfall. Without Kennedy's assassination, we wouldn't have had Johnson, who paved the way for Nixon. The seeds of Nixon's 'success' were planted in a moment of failure—that hot, sweaty flop of a television debate and the lost election of 1960. Look at the Presidents all in a row and it makes sense: they are a psychological progression from one to another, all about the unspoken needs and desires and conflicts of the American people. I'm writing about Nixon as the container for all that was America at that moment in time and why we elected him and what we hoped he'd do. . . ." I'm digressing, and nearly aggressing, as I jump all over the place, hitting the highlights.

"You seem quite passionate on the subject," Tuttle says. "But what's your dream, what do you want for yourself?"

"Nothing," I say.

"Really?" Tuttle seems surprised.

"Really, I can't think of anything."

"Is it self-punishing to not want anything in a society that's all about desire?" Tuttle asks.

"Is it?" I ask.

"You have no desire?" he suggests.

"Limited," I say.

"Depression?"

I shrug. "I don't think so."

"Then what is it?"

"Contentment? Satisfaction?" I suggest.

"Is there such a thing?" Dr. Tuttle asks.

"You tell me. Is contentment death? Does one need to want in order to live? Can one aspire to that which is not material?"

"It would seem wise to aspire to objects more real and less fleeting than a feeling state which you can't bank on," Tuttle says. "You may feel good now, but say something happens and you don't feel so good later. In your model there's no backup: you can't say, 'Well, I feel like crap but at least I have a really nice car and a big television set.'"

"Why not say, I may feel bad now but I felt good before and chances are I'll feel good again?"

"Oh, that would be asking a lot of most people, a very lot," he says, pressing back in his chair, tapping his fingers rhythmically against each other. He glances at the clock, an early digital model with tiny number flaps that tumble forward as each minute passes. When it's quiet, you can hear the dull click as the digit drops.

"We're running out of time for today," he says. "Should we schedule another session?"

"I'm hoping you'll be able to fill out the form for me," I say, nodding towards the mint-green sheet of paper I gave him when I came in. "It's the psychiatric report for the Department of Social Services, asking if I'm fit to parent."

"Leave the form with me," he says. "I should be able to complete it by the end of our next session."

"So the total cost is seven hundred and fifty dollars to get the form filled out?"

"Is that a problem?" Tuttle asks.

"No, I just want to be sure I understand."

Tuttle nods. "Same time next week?"

During the day, when I'm not doing something for the kids, visiting my mother, working on the Nixon story project in Manhattan, or sitting at George's desk trying to finish the book, I see Amanda.

We meet in parking lots between errands. Amanda tells me what's new in the grocery store—an expanded aisle of "ethnic" foods, more heat-and-eats, and that one of the checkout ladies has a heavy thumb on the produce scale. Amanda is a puzzle. I tell her that I wish I knew her better.

Amanda says nothing.

As I start to elaborate on my mother's upcoming wedding, she cuts me off. "I'm really not interested in you as a person," she says.

As hurtful as it sounds, I don't take it personally. I think she's lying.

In the evening, while I'm repainting the upstairs bathroom, I talk with Nate on speakerphone.

"Any further thoughts about the bar mitzvah?"

"Yeah," he says. "Let's cancel it."

"No bar mitzvah?" I ask.

"Yeah, I can't go into the temple," he says.

"What about doing it somewhere else?" I dip the brush into the can of Benjamin Moore semi-gloss and sweep it across the wall.

"Like where?"

"Here at home?" I suggest. "I've been sprucing it up."

"She was killed at home," he says flatly.

"At a country club? Or hotel?" I dip the brush again.

"Over-the-top awkward," Nate says, "and besides, I think the rabbi is a jerk."

"Well, we should do something special. How about taking a trip?"

"Like to Disney World?" Nate asks, and I remember that I am talking to a twelve-year-old.

"I'm thinking something more substantive—a game changer."

"I don't know," Nate says. "The one place I'd like to go . . . is back to Nateville. I'm not sure I'll ever get there."

"You're twelve years old and worried you'll never go there again."

"Don't mock me," he says.

"So—you'd like to go to South Africa?"

"I think so."

"Just to Nateville, or on a more expanded trip, like on a safari?"

"A safari would be cool. We'd take Ashley?"

"Of course."

"And Ricardo?"

"If you like."

"Cool," Nate says, seeming genuinely pleased.

"Okay," I say, standing back to look at my work so far. "I'll see what I can find out." The call waiting beeps; I say good night to Nate and take the call.

"Your mother called my mother," Jason says.

"What happened to 'hello'?" I say, stepping off the ladder.

"It was all very pleasant until she invited my mother to her wedding and got upset when my mother said, 'I already went to your wedding. Don't you remember?' And your mother said, 'Of course I remember—I'm talking about now, I'm getting married again.' Long story short, my mother thinks your mother is out of her mind."

My brush slips out of my hand and bounces across multiple surfaces before landing in the toilet. "She's actually doing well; she met someone at the home," I tell Jason as I fish the brush out of the bowl and shake it off.

"Are you going to let her get married?"

"I'm not sure that it's entirely up to me." I pause—it occurs to me that Lillian might know the fiancé. "Hey, could you ask your mother if she knows Bob Goldman? They all went to the same junior high, so it might ring a bell."

"You mean Bobby Goldman, Yetta Goldman's baby brother?"

"Maybe."

"He's the one who was so bad as a kid; he flushed a rug down the toilet at the temple."

"I think he used to be into sports," I say, as though somehow rug flushing could be considered sporty.

"Goldman played professional ball for a season or two and then was a radio announcer under the name of Bob Gold, so no one would know he was Jewish."

"How do you know all that?"

"Because when our parents were sitting around talking I actually listened. You and your brother were always too busy trying to kill each other."

I stop—cold.

"We were trying to kill each other?"

"You were always fighting."

"Really? I don't remember that."

Ricardo has come for a week, gone home for two days, and then returned with a larger bag of clothes. My new life has an unrelenting schedule: 6 a.m., wake up; 6:15, wake Ashley; 6:30, wake Ricardo, feed and walk animals and children; 7:45, drop Ricardo at his school; 8:45, drop Ashley at the puppet theater, where she's working on their upcoming production of *Romeo and Juliet*. And then, if it's not a workday in the city, back to the house, clean, groceries, work, and get ready for Ricardo's return at 4:30. Tessie seems to have quickly learned the routine and anticipates the yellow school bus's arrival by about forty-five seconds, barking to tell me it's time. The bus stops, the narrow door peels open; Ricardo hops out and cuts across the grass, his enormous backpack kind of like a second person on top of him. We have a snack and catch up, and a little while later, the car service slides into the driveway and out comes Ashley, suddenly looking like a young woman, texting as she walks up the driveway. On the days I'm in the city, Ricardo stays late at school, or Christina or a friend of hers picks him up and then we collect him by 6:30 and go out for pizza.

The kitchen is filled with homework charts, an incentive-based program that I've started for both children. Ricardo is also now on a swim team and part of a soccer club. I buy a used Ping-Pong table at a yard sale and set it up in the living room. We play round-robins and mixed doubles. The speed and the eye-hand coordination are good for all of our mental acuity.

At the law firm, the infamous boxes are kept in a vault. Because the material has not been acknowledged or otherwise publicly recorded, they're vigilant about keeping it under lock and key. Each day we work, the enormous vault is opened and the vault minder takes the boxes off a shelf—puts them and our work computer and assorted printouts on a metal cart, which I push to my office along with a locked rolling file cabinet.

Ching Lan sits in my office and reads the rough drafts out loud. I mark them while she is reading. Her pronunciation is awkward, but that prompts me to listen carefully, to edit judiciously. She transcribes my corrections and prints the pages, and we go around again. I enjoy the sound of her voice; it makes me work hard to find the meaning in the story. Ching Lan has enrolled in a copyediting course, which she enjoys. "The marks are almost like writing in Chinese—almost." We have thirteen stories and twenty-eight fragments of varying lengths, from three hundred fifty words to an eighteen-thousand-word ramble that I find brilliant but quasi-psychotic, or certainly under the influence of something. The subjects range from the pastoral (sniffing of the butt of a melon to tell if it's ripe, and almost romantically lush descriptions of lightning storms sweeping across fields on summer nights) to elaborations on the value of a man's having a life of his own, apart from whatever life he has with his family, a private life that no one knows anything about, "a place he can be himself without concern of disappointment or rejection."

Every day, Ching Lan eats lunch with her parents in the deli. All morning they wait for her to come and restock the shelves beyond reach—she is the ladder. Not wanting to intrude, I stop going to the deli and start getting lunch from a place two blocks away, but I feel like a traitor and go back to the deli.

"We are good, clean place, we have letter 'A' from Board of Health," Ching Lan's mother says. "You get parasite if you eat somewhere else."

"I didn't want to intrude on your family time."

"You are part of our family," she says, ushering me behind the counter to sit where the family sits, on their pickle barrels, eating food brought from home in colorful Tupperware containers. "Pok ball?" she asks, lifting up a small round meatball with chopsticks.

"My sister works at dumpling house, she brings home leftovers," Ching Lan says.

I eat the pok ball, translating only after swallowing: pork ball.

"Good boy. You eat turtle?" the mother asks.

"No," I say.

"Not yet you don't. It is very good, like strong chicken. What about congee?"

"I never had it."

"You would love—rice gruel like cream of wheat."

I nod.

"Prawn?" she asks.

"Yes," of course.

"Bok choy?"

"Frequently," I say, if only to make conversation.

"My sister owns a restaurant in Los Angeles and my cousin has one in Westchester County—we are what you call foodies," she says, putting more rice in my bowl.

After lunch, the mother slips me another Hershey bar—it has quickly become our tradition. "Chocolate is keeping your spirits up," she says.

On the way back to the firm, I stop at a Super Store for office supplies. I go up and down the rows, admiring the plenty. I find tape flags in fluorescent colors that I can use to notate Nixon's use of language and theme so that it remains consistent but not overly repetitious or redundant.

Clutching my bag of goodies, like adult penny candy, I enter the elevator and push "16."

"Working hard?" a guy behind me asks. He's standing behind my left shoulder; I can't see him without turning around.

"You bet," I say, trying to turn in his direction. I see only the brim of a baseball cap, a blue windbreaker, dark pants and shoes, and what I assume to be a nondescript man between fifty and seventy, white, unremarkable.

"I'll keep it brief," he says, speaking without changing his tone. No one else in the elevator seems to be hearing him or is the least concerned.

"You really don't have a clue—you're like a love-struck kid. The whole thing goes deeper than you can imagine. For one, Chotiner had his fingers all over everything. And two, even if it was unconsummated, it was one hell of a love affair between Dick and Rebozo. Three, it's common knowledge that Nixon was in Dallas the morning of the assassination, and so were Howard Hunt and Frank Sturgis. Isn't it a little too convenient that they were also the Watergate burglers—take a look at the hoboes, or Secret Service agents, on the grassy knoll. And Ferrie's damned library card was in Oswald's wallet!" He laughs, and one woman in the elevator turns to look. His voice lowers to a whisper. "They were all in and out of Cuba, playing both sides—and the Mafia. Check out who was there and bingo—it's a triple play." A pause. "Did you know Jack Ruby worked for Nixon in 1947 under the name Jack Rubenstein? My point, buddy boy, is: you've got nothing, the big zippo."

A sound involuntarily escapes me, a cross between extreme excitement and gagging.

"It's nothing to laugh at. Let me be perfectly clear," he says, and his phrasing has a familiar ring. "It wasn't one guy in particular, but a group of guys. No one's hands are clean. Pawns, we're all pawns. There's no man that can't be bought and no man that can't be brought down. It was like a freak show." He stops for a moment. "Uncle Bebe bought your little Julie a house as a wedding gift. Do you think she registered for that at Tiffany's? I keep track of these things. I'm a history buff. The government used to be filled with guys like me, guys who think they know something, who are smart but not smart enough— sons of bitches. Watergate was a domestic incident, 'a bizarre comedy of errors,' as Nixon called it, that got blown out of proportion when you look at the rest of it. As Nixon himself said, 'You open that scab and there's a hell of a lot of things and we just feel that it would be very detrimental to have this thing go any further. This involves these Cubans, Hunt, and a lot of hanky-panky that we have nothing to do with ourselves.' " My man stops for a second, then starts again, this time doing the most uncanny imitation of Richard Nixon:

" 'Look, the problem is that this will open the whole, the whole Bay of Pigs thing, and the President just feels that ah, without going into the details . . . don't, don't lie to them to the extent to say there is no involvement, but just say this is sort of a comedy of errors, bizarre, without getting into it, the President believes that it is going to open the whole Bay of Pigs thing up again.' "

He stops, clears his throat. "So how are you liking the stories?"

"I like them," I say, forgetting for the moment that no one knows about the stories.

"Did you get to the one about the SOB?"

I nod.

"That one's all about me," he says, winking. The elevator opens and he steps out. "Double-check your homework, and good luck."

I ride all the way up and then back down to the lobby and ask the guard at the front desk if he could show me the video loop from the elevator. I see the guy standing in the one blurry spot, as if he knew exactly where to be. All you can see is the brim of his baseball cap—you can't even tell that he's talking to me, except that I appear increasingly agitated and am looking around as if to see if anyone else is hearing what I'm hearing and what it means to them.

Is it some kind of test? I don't want to make anyone nervous, but, on the other hand, if it's a test from the inside, it would be smart to report it. I ask Wanda if she might come into my office. She comes as far as the doorway and then stands there while I explain about the man, the baseball cap, and so on.

"He stood behind you," she says. "Seemed to know exactly who you were, told you things you hadn't heard before."

"Yes," I say, excited we're on to something.

"Nothing on the surveillance video?"

"Just a blur," I say.

Wanda nods. "He's been here on and off over the years," she says, unimpressed.

"Who is he? Like a crazy hanger-on?"

"Something like that," she says. "There used to be others, but there aren't too many left now—it's generational."

I'm still concerned.

"The world is filled with people," Wanda says.

I stand waiting to hear the rest—but Wanda says no more.

How many others? How much more is there to know? I get the sense that, once one begins to dig, the information stream is not only endless, but passed under the table from administration to administration, as though there is some much larger playbook that only the President and his men are privy to. And clearly, once you take a look at that playbook, not only are you forever changed, but the twists and turns of party politics braid the cord of information and deal making so much that true change becomes impossible.

Who wrote the playbook? And when? Is anyone in charge? It is all such a gnarly web that at best one can only pick at the knots.

"Everything okay?" Ching Lan asks when I get back to my desk. "You look discolored," she says.

"Sorry?"

"Erased," she says, "very white, like paper."

I nod. The man in the elevator was dropping a lot of little beads about things I didn't want to hear. The man he was talking about wasn't my Nixon, he wasn't Nixon as I wanted him to be. He wasn't the youthful RMN as a vice-presidential candidate, accused of using campaign funds for personal expenses, going on national television, and making sure the people knew that he was of modest means.

> *Pat and I have the satisfaction that every dime that we've got is honestly ours. I should say this—that Pat doesn't have a mink coat. But she does have a respectable Republican cloth coat. And I always tell her that she'd look good in anything.*

This man's Nixon was darker, more menacing than I ever allowed myself to imagine. Upset by my own naïveté, I wonder, Can I allow myself to know what I know and still love Nixon as deeply as I do? Can I accept how flawed, how unresolved he was, the enormous fissures in personality, in belief, in morality? Is there any politician who hasn't sold his soul ten times over before he even takes office? The mystery man in the elevator told me what I didn't want to hear, and on some level I know it all might be true. For some this might be a turnoff, but it draws me closer, makes RMN all the more human. He clearly wasn't the first or the last to have gotten confused with regard to the boundaries between executive power and imaginary superpowers—he just may have been that rare bird who documented himself more heavily.

I ask Ching Lan to pull up the "SOB" story so I can take another look. Quoting from "SOB":

"If people had a clue about what's been going on they'd be shocked, more than shocked, they'd want something to happen—the last thing anyone wants is for the truth to come out—that'd be detrimental to us all."

"Son of a bitch it would kill this country."

"Whatever it is you know or think you know or that anyone else you know thinks he knows—you make sure they forget it, make sure that it goes away. There's a way to do that, have things go quiet for a while—for as long as it takes."

"Son of a bitch who the hell does he think he is—Charlton Heston in the Ten Commandments. SOB . . ."

I glance up and see Wanda in the hall chatting with Marcel, who pushes the chrome mail basket around delivering mail. Later, I ask Marcel what he knows about Wanda. "Not much," he says. "Only that she's the granddaughter of Nelson Mandela—or Desmond Tutu, or someone like that . . ." He trails off. "Born in South Africa, sent to England for school, came here, sold her memoir for three-quarters of a million dollars," he adds as an afterthought.

"Why is she working here?"

"Going to law school in the fall," he says. "And she gave away the advance, donated to charity."

"Really," I say.

"Really," Marcel says, echoing my tone, as he pushes his cart down the carpeted hall.

Tapping the resources of what she calls "the sisters-are-doing-it-for-themselves network," Cheryl has arranged for a party planner and a travel agent to come to the house and discuss Project BM South Africa. Everywhere we go, Cheryl keeps saying "BM" loudly—it gives me flashbacks to my mother asking, "Did you make a nice BM?" "I can't talk right now, I have to make a BM." "Are your BMs regular?" and so on . . .

"Can we change the name?" I beg her. "Just call it what it is, a bar mitzvah."

"Too much to say," she says.

"Then let's just say 'bar,' as in 'We're planning a bar.' "

"Won't people be confused?"

"No more than they already are now."

Sofia, the party planner, arrives with a box of props marked "Bar Mitzvah." She slaps it down on the dining-room table. "I have boxes for every occasion— Communion, Bar-Bat, Sweet 16, Engagement, Baby Shower, Adoption Celebration, Family Reunion, Corporate Picnic, props for every event, everything from your yarmulkes to flight jackets and those magic pens with a photo of either the bride or groom, tilt it and their clothes fall off—very popular. Let's face it, people like free stuff. It's gotten so bad, you go to someone's house for dinner and you leave wondering, Where's my booty bag?"

"How did you become a party planner?" I ask.

"By accident," she says. "My mother was a wonderful hostess: flowers on the table, so many ways to fold a napkin. You'd be shocked to know the number of people who don't know the fork goes on the left, much less what to do if there's a salad fork and a dessert fork. . . . Okay," she says, catching herself, aware that she has a propensity to go on. "What's the time frame?"

"The temple date was July 3; Nate's actual birthday is the fifth."

She looks stricken.

"What?" I ask.

"We're beyond late—this is like sudden-death overtime." She takes a deep breath. "It is what it is—so we'll jump right in and get started. First the invites."

"The good news is, we don't need invites. It's going to be really small, and Nate has already told me, no gifts. We're going to make a donation to the village to help them improve the school."

Sofia looks at me like I'm an idiot. "You're having the bar mitzvah in July in South Africa—no one is going to come, so what you want to do is invite everyone. All the more if you want to raise money for the school. Invite his whole class and the faculty. Do you have a list of who came to the funeral? The family holiday-card list? The wife's relatives, who might hate you but still care for the boy? Invite everyone you can think of—it's halfway around the world and in the height of summer; they'll be thrilled to say no and send a gift. Figure you invite two hundred fifty people and they each spend fifty to a hundred bucks, you'll do very well. The cost of the invite is going to be a little high. We want it nice, lined envelope, reply card, stamped envelope. It's about three fifty per—plus some kind of a rush charge. Let's call it a start-up or opportunity cost. We want people to open the card, read the program, and be moved to send money. We'll have thank-you notes printed at the same time. Anyone who sees this is going to know the kid got lucky having an uncle like you."

This is the first compliment I've gotten about my new role, and I am surprised at how good it feels.

"Okay," she says, not giving me a second to revel in it. "Let's use our time wisely. For the invitation, thermography is fine. In this case, with the family history, to go full-on engraved would be excessive. And I strongly suggest you *not* invite people by e-mail. We'll have a nice invite, and people will feel obligated. . . . 'At Nate's request, all gifts will be directed to building a school in the village. . . .' They can make a PayPal donation—I'll find out how you do it. Meanwhile, can you get a quote from Nate about his visit there and why this place is important to him?"

"Sure."

"Write it down," she says, tapping the blank pad of paper in front of me: "This is your to-do list. 'Please Join Mr. Harold Silver and'—what's the sister's name?" she asks.

"Ashley."

"'Ashley Silver in celebrating the Bar Mitzvah of Nathaniel'—what's his middle name?"

"Ummm, Allan?"

"Nathaniel Allan Silver on, let's call it July 9 in—what's the name of the town?"

"Nateville."

"Nateville, how cute, South Africa. 'Bar Mitzvah at Noon, Followed by Ceremonial Feast and Dancing.' Do you know where in South Africa Nateville is?"

I shake my head no.

"What's the biggest city?"

"Durban"—I think.

"We're going to need a caterer, a rabbi, a band, and probably a refrigerated truck to get everything to the location, maybe a tent and air conditioning. What's the temperature there in July?"

"I think it's their winter."

"I'll find out." She jots a note to herself. "What are you thinking regarding food? Roast-beef carving station? Omelets made to order? And what about the band? A Jewey klezmer rock group imported from the big city—you know, top hits plus traditional Jewish songs to a danceable beat? And we need to talk budget. I can dream all day, but I have no idea what you're thinking."

"I'm thinking something a little more—what's the word?—not exactly low-key, but taking advantage of whatever we can arrange right there in the village."

"Rustic?" she suggests.

"Whatever we do should be in keeping with whatever the South African village traditions are and not too over-the-top."

"Is there, like, a hotel or a B&B in this village?" she asks.

"I don't know."

"You know," she says, "you and I are working at a disadvantage right now."

"What's that?"

"We have no idea what we're talking about. Have you ever been to South Africa?"

"No."

"Me either," she says. "But I have a couple of clues. Whenever I'm in slightly over my head, I ask myself, what would Lynne Tillman do?"

"Who is Lynne Tillman?"

She looks at me as if to say, you don't know? "You know how Oprah works with Colin Cowie?"

Again I have no idea what she's talking about.

"Colin is this amazing party planner who arranges events all over the world for Oprah, but Colin knows what he knows because he studied with Lynne Tillman."

"Also a party planner?"

"No, she's a writer, but filled with insight about why people do what they do, so Colin applies the aesthetic of Lynne Tillman to everything he does, which is what makes him so good. I was thinking I might reach out to Colin and see what he suggests—or I suppose I could call Lynne Tillman. It might help to get her opinion."

I nod, still not sure what it is she's talking about.

"Let's move on for the moment to the gifties. In the past I've suggested things like the personalized yarmulkes, sometimes a personalized iPod—but that's expensive, and most of the kids have them now. We do a lot of snow globes, baseball hats, T-shirts. . . . But in this case I'm thinking soccer balls that say 'Nate 13.'"

"That's brilliant," I say, genuinely excited for the first time.

She takes my enthusiasm and runs with it. "And jerseys, baby-blue and white with felt hot-press letters with each individual's name on them. Do they have electricity there? Is it the same alphabet?"

"How much are custom soccer balls?"

"We'll buy them by the dozen. Do you want just shirts? Or shirts, shorts, socks? It would be nice if we got everything. Sneakers in a variety of sizes? And a couple of umpire things? Maybe we should get two colors of jerseys, half and half, so they can have teams?"

"Better get it all," I say.

"For the girls too?"

"Of course, everything equal."

She hands me another to-do list, my homework for our next meeting: (1) Address books, preferably in electronic format. (2) Ideas regarding content of service. (3) Do I want her to find a rabbi or not? (4) Budget?

Cheryl comes in with a tray of coffee and cookies. We have a quick snack, during which Cecily, the travel agent, arrives. Sofia packs her box, leaving me with a pen and paper stamped with her info and logo: "Swa-Rei by Sofia."

Cecily has prepared a PowerPoint presentation featuring three scenarios, from least to most expensive. "I've done a little legwork; we're talking approximately nine thousand per person for airfare."

"No need to fly business—coach is fine," I say.

"That is coach. I may be able to get it down to about sixty-five hundred if there's a little leeway with your dates and flight times."

"Plenty of leeway."

"Don't forget," Sofia says as she's leaving, "the date is set—July 9 at noon."

"Right," the travel agent says. "So—how many days in the village?"

"Two? Maybe three?"

"Let's do two nights, three days. And then what, big-five game safari? You know—lion, elephant, buffalo, leopard, and rhino. And from the safari we go to a hot-air balloon ride, bungee jumping, ride over a waterfall?"

"Let's stick to nature and history—no bungee, no balloon, no ride over the waterfall," I say. "Did you always want to be a travel agent?"

"I was a stewardess," she says. "I met my husband on the plane—he was a frequent flier, married. The other girls said, 'They never leave their wives,' but he did. He came back and said, 'You gotta make an honest man out of me.'" She pauses. "So I guess the big question is, how luxe do you want to go?"

"I want it to be nice but not excessive. I care more about safety than luxury."

"You don't want to impress them?"

"I don't want to look like a jerk, going to some remote poor village for a couple of days and then saying '*Hasta la vista,* baby,' and heading off on a luxury safari. It would seem dissonant with the core idea—celebrating a rite of passage from boy to man."

Cheryl is beaming, pleased with herself and her resources.

"Who do they think I am to you?" I ask when Cecily is in the bathroom.

She laughs. "They know all about you," she says. "They call you my other husband. I think everyone should have one—even my husband thinks so. We are such a backward culture, too literal to survive."

"What about tutors for Ashley and Ricardo? Do you know any?"

"Of course," she says. "Between us we have an annotated list of who is good for what kind of kid and in what subject matter."

"Electrician?"

She looks at me. "I'll e-mail you the list."

On Sunday at noon, my mother marries Bob Gold. Ashley starts shooting video as the sliding glass doors to the home open with a sucking sound, like a pop, and the air lock is breached. She pans to the left. "Silver marries Gold at noon" is written on the dry-erase activity board by the front door of the home. The air conditioning in the home is on the blink—and the place stinks like old diapers. My mother is in her room, being tended to by her bridesmaids. Two large ladies block the door. "No boys," they say, allowing Ashley and her camera to slip between them. Ricardo and I wait in the dining room, which has been transformed into a chapel of sorts, with a three-storied wedding cake and flowers.

"Will you be giving your mother away?" someone asks, and I'm not sure what she means. "Down the aisle?" she says.

"Yes, of course, no problem."

A middle-aged man introduces himself as Bob Gold's son, Eli. "Apologies with regard to my sisters."

"I understand."

"He is still married to our mother, even though she's in a coma." I nod. "It's difficult for my sisters to see him move on. When Dad told us that he felt capable of loving more than one woman at a time, my sisters weren't ready to hear it." He pauses. "We have a mutual acquaintance," he says. "Your aunt Lillian's son, Jason. I used to date him—small world."

"Tiny," I say.

The dining room has begun to fill with old people dressed in their Sunday best, arriving in varying stages of mobility: some on their own, some with canes or walkers, others being pushed in wheelchairs. A caravan of three wheelchairs pushed by an aide makes its way into the room.

"Cake before dinner," one of the residents says, excitedly.

Ricardo is wearing a blazer of Nate's; his stocky build absorbs the excess.

"You look good, Ma," I say, kissing her cheek as she comes into the room.

"You're very tan," my mother says to Ricardo. "And you're shorter and fatter than you used to be."

"This is Ricardo, Grandma, not Nate. Ricardo is new," Ashley says, coming to his rescue.

"Oh," she says, "pleased to meet you."

"He's my brother," Ashley says.

"Welcome to the family," my mother says, distracted.

"Thank you," Ricardo says. "Congratulations on your wedding."

"Can Ricardo be the ring boy?" Ashley asks. "He wants to be in the wedding too."

Bob gives Ricardo the ring, and Ashley is given a basket of rose petals. The music begins, and Ashley starts off down the aisle, followed by Ricardo. I take my mother's arm and lead her down the aisle while one of the nurses takes Bob Gold's arm.

Bob Gold, I realize, is my new stepfather. Somehow this dawns on me when he and my mother are side by side facing Cynthia, the "energy worker" and former nurse who has agreed to perform the ceremony.

The ceremony itself is surprisingly moving, even though it's not legally binding. The words pronounced upon my mother and Bob stress companionship and good care, memories and history. I am on the verge of tears when my mother throws her bouquet and it's caught, or more like lands, in the lap of a woman with one leg, who smiles. "You never know," she says.

My mother and Bob cut the cake, and when Bob moves to feed her the first bite, his hand is shaking so badly that Mother takes his arm, guiding him towards her mouth.

I overhear two aides talking.

"Is he moving into her room?"

"Apparently," the aide says. "They'll put their beds side by side. Let's hope the wheels stay locked and they don't fall in the crack and break a hip."

When it is over, the residents are ushered back down the hallway for an afternoon nap, and we bid the newlyweds adieu.

We're all dressed up with nowhere to go. "Do you guys want to go out for an early dinner somewhere nice?" I ask, as we're walking out to the car.

"We could," Ashley says. "Or we could go home and have, like, a pajama-and-pizza TV party."

I look at Ricardo buckling himself into the back seat.

"I would like to try someplace new," he says.

"How about we go into the city?"

Both kids nod. "That would be inventive," Ashley says.

I take the kids to the Oak Room at the Plaza and we have Shirley Temples and club sandwiches; it's the most fun I've had in years.

"My cousin used to work in a hotel," Ricardo says, as he's digging into a thick slice of cheesecake. "He'd come home with his pockets full of chocolate coins that they put in the beds at night—can you imagine going to sleep in a bed filled with chocolate?"

I'm thinking all too well of myself when I tell Nate that I found some novelties to bring to South Africa—mini-solar chargers for cell phones.

"That's nice," he says. "But what they need is solar heat for the houses, solar hot-water heating, lights for the village at night—maybe think a little bigger."

"Okay," I say, "note taken. Is there someone in charge at Nateville, like a mayor or an elder?"

"Sakhile is the *induna,* the headman. His wife is Nobuhle. Mthobisi, Ayize, and Bhekiziziew—his top dogs."

"How do I contact them?"

"Usually I e-mail."

"They have e-mail?"

"They do now," he says.

"And how do you send money?"

"Lots of ways—through PayPal, or on Dad's credit card, or direct into a bank account. They also do a lot of banking via cell phone. And there's also, like, a corner deli near Nateville that processes the charge and gives them the cash."

"How much do you send?"

"A couple hundred dollars a month."

"Where do you get it?"

He's quiet for a minute. "You really want to know?"

"I do."

"Selling stuff."

"What kind of stuff?" I say slowly, hoping that by stretching it out I won't show that I'm panicking.

"School supplies?" Nate says like he's not sure himself.

"Nate, right now this story has so many holes, it's like Swiss cheese. Pony up."

"Okay, okay, so, like, when a kid here at school needs to buy something at the school store . . ."

"Yes?"

"I buy it for him on my account, which is linked to Dad's credit card, and the kids pay me in cash, and I send the cash to Nateville."

I'm relieved.

"No one minds," Nate says. "They think it's a good cause. They're very 'keep the change.' I did this thing last fall: whenever someone bought a school team shirt, I asked people to buy one for the school there."

"What does the head of your school think about that?"

"It's not exactly something he can complain about—after all, they were the ones who took us there. . . ."

I draft an e-mail to the village headman: "Good evening, I am the uncle of Nathaniel Silver, who has told me of his relationship to your village. This July we are celebrating Nathaniel's 13th birthday, a special occasion in the Jewish faith, marking the transformation from boy to man, and Nathaniel would very much like to have his bar mitzvah in your village. Could you let me know if this might be possible? And also the best route to your village from the East Coast of the United States. Yours sincerely, Harold Silver."

I hear back within minutes. "Fly to Durban and we will arrange car, 1–2 hour drive, leave time for flat tire. What day you come?"

"My thanks in advance," I write back. "I don't know what day yet. Meanwhile we have some supplies for the party that we'd like to send to the village. What is the best way to ship them?"

"Send to Durban and my Bro will pick them up."

"Do you have Internet?"

"Of course, that is how we are talking. Do you Skype? We boast to be the only village to have our own satellite—it fell from the sky one night and landed in the hills nearby. We thought it was an earthquake or space aliens. It gets good reception. Our phones have four bars all the time—very good signal." He pauses; a minute or two passes.

"How many people are in the village?" I write.

"We have a school with sixty children and we have another thirty or forty some of whom are old. Come to us. Our children love to party. Can you send money for supplies?"

Is there a polite way to ask, what will we get for the money? "I'll need you to get receipts—my accountant is very strict about receipts."

"What is an accountant?"

"The man who keeps track of the money," I type. "How much money should I send?" I ask. "Five hundred dollars?" I don't want to be cheap, but I don't know what things cost.

"For a full village party?" he writes back. "We may be a poor little village but we are living in twenty-first-century reality." A minute passes and then the man writes: "Can I ask a favor? Can you bring ibuprofen? We have some terrible aches."

"Sure," I say.

"Thank you."

"Okay, so let me know your ideas re: the party and how much you think it will cost and we'll go from there."

"Okay," he types. "I will talk to my Bro and get back to you."

I sign off, surprised that I was only a moment ago conversing with a stranger on the other side of the world—we were going back and forth like you would with someone you've known for years. I check to see what the time difference is: seven hours. Wow—it was two in the morning for him.

On Friday night, Ricardo's aunt's best friend comes to babysit, and I go out to dinner with Cheryl and her husband, Ed.

Ed is a totally affable, slap-on-the-back kind of a guy. We talk about everything except the fact that I'm sleeping with his wife.

"What line of work are you in?"

"Formerly an academic," I say, "now doing some writing and editing."

"Oh, yeah?" he says. "How does that work? How do you decide what to write about, or what to put in and what to take out?"

I shrug. "You have to get a feel for it. And what about you?"

"Family business—we vulcanize."

"Remind me how that works?"

He digresses into a long speech, combined science lesson/sales pitch.

"Fascinating," I say.

"Don't humor him, really . . ." Cheryl says.

"It's really interesting."

"It's just what we do," he says. "So are you married? Got kids?"

"Recently divorced," I say. "No kids."

"So how did you two meet?" Ed asks.

I signal for the waitress: "Check, please."

I am working methodically through Sofia's checklist for the bar mitzvah—and having a hard time locating Ryan Weissman, the young rabbi in training. The phone number on the business card he gave me when he appeared at office hours to discuss "The Jew as Outlaw" is no longer working. Ryan S. Weissman, Herschlag Fellow in Post-Judaic Studies. What are post-Judaic studies? I Google the Herschlag Fellowship. Double click.

> Binnie and Stanley Herschlag celebrated their lifelong love of learning with the creation of the Herschlag Fellowship on the occasion of their 50th Wedding Anniversary. They are so proud of their sons, Arthur and Abraham, "twin boys who became rabbis," says Binnie Herschlag.

"Who could ask for more?" says Stanley Herschlag. "I could," Binnie says. "And I did." The text is interrupted by a photo of Binnie holding her first grandchild. "Allen Steven Koenig Herschlag. I couldn't be more proud. Well, I could but . . ."

I locate Ryan by methodically searching the Web and little postings, like rabbit droppings along the way. His thumbs-up "like" of a site called "Embracing the Gap (Can Jews and Gentiles Really Be Friends?)" is what leads me to him.

"Did you finish your paper on Jews gone criminal?" I ask when I finally make contact by phone.

"I quit," he says.

"What do you mean, you quit?"

"I'm done," he says. "Dropped out of school."

"But you're from a family of rabbis, you're not allowed to quit."

"Can you imagine how hard it was?"

"What happened?"

"I got so depressed at how disingenuous people are, how fake leaders are, how full of shit everything is. I had a big spiritual and familial crisis and had to ask myself—do I want to be a rabbi?"

In the background there's a weird snuffling kind of honking sound. "What is that noise?"

"Pigs," he says. "I'm working upstate on an organic farm, and one of my jobs is to tend to the pigs. Isn't that ironic?"

"I guess."

"They're very intelligent animals," he says.

I ask for advice on bar-mitzvah essentials, what makes a bar mitzvah legal—are there rules, specific prayers you have to do or say to be sure you're officially a bar mitzvah?

"What they don't tell you is that nothing is required," Ryan says. "When you turn thirteen, you are a man—the ceremony is a public gesture. At thirteen you are obligated to observe the Torah's commandments, to be counted as part of a minyan, and you are liable for your misdoings, you can be punished. Usually the bar-mitzvah boy reads from that week's portion of the Torah, or he could deliver a paper on a particular topic."

I ask Ryan if he'd consider joining the trip as our official spiritual leader.

He loves the idea of bringing Jewish traditions to a remote village, loves what Nate has done, but . . . "I can't," he says. "I can't. I want to but I can't. The pigs need me, or maybe I need the pigs."

I'm at the office in Manhattan, making small talk with Wanda while waiting for the vault man to pull out the boxes.

"Just a heads-up that I'm going to be taking some time off this summer," I say. "I am taking my family to South Africa."

"Have a good time," she says.

"I'll be reachable on my cell in an emergency."

Wanda nods. "What kind of an emergency? Like a misplaced comma?"

"I'm just saying. It'll give Ching time to catch up on the transcriptions and copyediting."

"Okay," Wanda says.

"Any travel tips? Pointers about great places to go, fabulous restaurants?"

"Not a clue," she says.

"But aren't you the granddaughter of—?"

"The Nixons' old cleaning lady in Washington?" she says, cutting me off. "Marcel tells everyone that my mother worked for Mrs. Nixon."

"That's weird," I say and go no further. "What's Marcel's story?"

"Well, he's either the illegitimate son of Nelson Mandela who was sent to Harvard to get a divinity degree and flunked out, or he's a kid from New York City who does stand-up comedy at the Upright Citizens Brigade."

"I wonder where the truth lies," I say, knowing I've been had.

"It's an open question," she says.

As the days go by, everything becomes more urgent. I'm juggling passports, plane tickets, health forms for camp, iron-on name tags.

Cheryl and I are in the drugstore at the mall, shopping for supplies. "I thought it went well with Ed," she says.

"As well as could be expected," I say.

"What does that mean?"

"I can't picture the two of you together. What do you talk about?"

"We don't talk. That's why I'm here buying hand sanitizer with you," Cheryl says, annoyed.

"Are you mad about something in particular?"

"Sofia has a crush on you," she says.

"All she talks about is you and the bar mitzvah and how wouldn't it be so fun if she got to go with you and that she can't believe she's going to miss it."

"I'm not interested in her," I say. "Maybe she just wants whatever you're having. Women are like that: when they go to lunch they like to both order the same thing."

"She's after you," Cheryl says. "Her husband is dumping her for a new kind of trophy wife, a particle physicist who's a big skier."

"Not going to happen," I swear to Cheryl.

"Because you're already in a 'relationship' with Amanda?"

"Because I'm not interested in Sofia."

"Are you inviting Amanda on the trip?" Cheryl asks.

"I haven't yet," I say. "Are you asking because you want to go?"

"I'm not going," she says. "It would look weird. What would my kids say if I said I had to go to South Africa for your nephew's bar mitzvah? They've never even met you."

"That's what I was thinking, but didn't want to say it. Just so you know, it's an open invitation for you and your family, husband, kids, whoever. . . ."

"Sounds fun, like an adulterers' Brady bunch," she says.

"And," I say, like a TV game-show host heaping on the prizes, "I really would like to meet your kids sometime—it would make things more real."

"Meet them in what way? Like you come for dinner and I say, 'This is the guy Mommy plays with while Daddy's busy vulcanizing'?"

"Meet them like I'm a friend of yours," I suggest.

"I'll think on it," she says. "Married women don't have male friends."

"Times are changing," I say.

I'm loading my basket with travel sizes of toothpaste and shampoo while Cheryl is trying to get me to "do" her in the new grocery section—"grab and go," it's called. Her idea is that we should have a sexual adventure in every store in the mall. We've made our way approximately one-quarter of the way around the horseshoe-shaped structure, but I'm convinced store personnel, security guards, and others recognize us. I'm not sure if it's because we're regulars—like the old ladies who come to walk, doing exercise laps—or because they're trading some kind of hidden-camera videos.

I'm putting disposable toothbrushes in the basket when my cell phone starts to ring. I ignore it. After four rings it stops, and then it rings again. "It's her," Cheryl says. "Who else calls you twice in a row? You may as well answer it."

"Hello," I say.

"I can't find my father," Amanda says, panicked. "He's wandered off."

"Where are you?"

"Outside, in some fucking shopping center," she says, "near the parking area."

"What does your mother say?"

"I sent them into the Dairy Queen while I was taking the sofa cover into the dry cleaner's—I didn't want to embarrass them by explaining that there were feces on the sofa. . . ." Despite the fact that I'm not on speakerphone, every word is coming through loud and clear for Cheryl and anyone within ten feet to hear. "My mother told my father that he couldn't have chopped nuts on his sundae because it's bad for his diverticulosis, and he stormed out. I'm trying to look for him, but she can't walk fast enough to keep up."

"Maybe put her in the car while you look, or see if there's someone who can keep her for a few minutes."

"Ask her if there's a Home Depot," Cheryl whispers. "Men gravitate towards hardware."

"Is there a Home Depot?"

"Yes," she says.

"Check there. Find one of the people in an orange vest and tell them that you're with the missing person."

There's a bit of a delay, and then Amanda says: "The orange vests are on the lookout. Hang on—something's coming over the walkie-talkie. . . . They've spotted him in the plumbing section—he's peeing in one of the display toilets. I'm heading over there now. He sees me. He's heading the other way, he's running. My father is running away. I've got to go. I'll call you later," she says, hanging up.

While I'm talking, Cheryl has been adding things to my cart, things I don't notice until I'm in the checkout line: enemas, Tampax, adult diapers, duct tape, and now she's somewhere in the makeup aisle.

"What do you think of these?" Cheryl texts.

I turn my head; standing at the end of an aisle, Cheryl lifts her shirt and flashes me a bare breast wearing false eyelashes.

My heart beats fast—did anyone else see that?

"Is this yours?" the man at the register asks, taking a large tube of K-Y out of my basket.

"No," I say as I'm rapidly digging through and taking out the glycerin sup-positories. "All that's mine is the Purell and the travel sizes. Someone must have confused my cart for theirs." I take out a box of Midol and leave it on the counter.

She texts again: "I'm not the only one laughing."

"How do you confuse your cart when you've got diapers and a large milk of magnesia?" someone mumbles.

"He's just embarrassed," someone else says.

"I'm not embarrassed," I say. "I was buying travel sizes for a family trip."

The security guard comes towards me. "What's the problem?"

"These people keep saying that I'm embarrassed by what's in my basket—but my point is, someone put these items in my cart and no one believes me."

"Do you want to buy the things or not?"

"No," I say, putting my hands up, as though surrendering. "Forget it, I'll do it some other time."

"Look, mister, get what you need. Don't let people intimidate you."

"I'm not intimidated," I say, my pocket vibrating again.

"Sore loser," Cheryl texts.

I pay for my items, and the security guard follows me to the door. I buzz loudly as I leave, and I just stand there—knowing Cheryl is watching from somewhere laughing.

"Go," the guy says.

"But I'm making noise," I say.

"Did you steal anything?" he asks.

"Of course not."

"Then just go."

"I've got a falsie glued onto my nipple and no idea how to get it off—I wasn't thinking about how much more sensitive nipples are when I put it on," Cheryl says when I catch up with her.

"Try nail-polish remover," I say.

"I already did, on aisle three; that's why I was late."

"Well, then, you're going to have to keep it on until it falls off," I say, unmoved.

She sticks her hand into my back pocket and pulls out a bunch of metallic bar-code sensors. "You're free," she says.

"You're getting too weird," I say.

"I admit it," she says. "I'm jealous."

"Of what?"

"Of you and what's-her-name."

"Amanda," I say.

"Exactly," she says.

On Sunday, when I take Ricardo to Aunt Christina's house, I tell Christina and the uncle that I've been planning a South Africa bar mitzvah for Nate. I describe the trip, explaining that, as part of the celebration, we might slaughter and cook a goat, there will be dancing and people wearing traditional beaded costumes, old-fashioned drums, and feathers. I can tell they think it's weird.

Christina shakes her head. "I don't know why you want to go into the past when the future is right here in front of you."

"He is a historian," Ricardo explains. "He lives in the past. All day he reads books about things that already happened."

The uncle revs Ricardo's remote-control car and sends it speeding across the floor backwards and forwards—popping wheelies.

"Does Ricardo have a passport?" I ask.

"I don't think so," the aunt says.

"Is it okay with you if I find out what we need to do in order to get one?" She nods.

Ricardo dances around the room. "I'm goin' on safari," he says. "On safari, I'm gonna catch an ele-phant, an ele-phant."

The uncle crashes his car into Ricardo's foot—on purpose.

"Have a good time," he says.

The invites arrive. They are beautiful, substantive, serious. The envelope looks elegant with its blue tissue lining. I FedEx one to Nate.

"I got the invitation," he says—it sounds like he's crying.

"You don't like it?" I ask, heart sinking.

"No," he says. "I mean yes. It looks totally real."

"It is real," I say.

His crying sniffles to a stop. "I'm kind of amazed. Since everything went weird with Mom and Dad, I gave up on the normal stuff—it just didn't seem possible."

"So you think it's okay?"

"It's great," he says.

"All right, then, what kind of cake do you like?" I ask, figuring I should take care of a few things on my checklist while I've got him on the phone.

"Chocolate," he says.

"And what about the Torah—have you decided what you want to do in terms of a reading?"

"You know," he says, "I'm not really so into Hebrew as a language. I kind of want to write my own thing. . . ."

"Consisting of what?"

"Have you ever been to Burning Man?"

Sofia sends out the invites, each addressed in her beautiful calligraphic script. She gives me a computer spreadsheet to track the RSVPs. I know the invitations have landed when Cousin Jason starts e-mailing me bad press about South Africa, articles saying that car crashes are the leading cause of tourist death, and about how many people are mugged at the airports, and that there's been increased violence against white people and diseases like Ebola, and that if you're stopped at a red light at night, people will come and smash your windows and grab whatever is in your car, or hijack you.

"Thanks for all the advice," I write back. "I'll assume from the attachments that you'll be joining us in spirit but not in person."

Shopping heavily from both the Oriental Trading Company and the Lillian Vernon catalogue, Sofia has ordered pencils, notebooks, and backpacks for every kid in the village. She's packed giant plastic tubs with soccer jerseys, school supplies, musical instruments, sheet music, a cassette player, and a recorded copy of all the songs she wants them to learn, along with devil's-food cake mix, chocolate frosting, sprinkles, and candles.

Meanwhile, on the floor of George's office are four suitcases that I've been packing with clothing for the children—the same items for each kid but in different sizes and colors. I take Ricardo and Ashley to Dr. Faustus for shots, and arrange for Nate to get what he needs at school.

And as I prepare, I worry; I don't doubt that the villagers' affection for Nate is genuine, but without the money backing him up, they would be less enthusiastic. Not wanting to detract from his moment, I say nothing to Nate, but I am aware they are working us for our sympathies, for whatever we can give, as well they should—if ever there was a population entitled to reparations, this is it.

During an increasingly rare afternoon rendezvous, Amanda tells me there's more to know about the murdered girl, Heather Ryan.

"Like what?"

"Like when I found her wallet I found some other stuff too."

I look at her. "Like what?" I repeat.

"Gym clothes, notebooks from school—stuff."

"Do you ever think of giving it back to her family?"

"No," she says.

"Why not?"

"They have a whole lifetime of her stuff, but this is all I have," she says.

"But they are her family—"

"And she is me," Amanda says, cutting me off.

"So, when you said there's more to know about her, what did you mean?"

"Her cell phone still works."

"I guess her parents haven't turned it off yet. I'm sure it's not the first thing on their list."

"She gets messages. . . ."

"What kind of messages, and from who?"

"Voice mail from her best friend."

"Really?" I ask, surprised.

Amanda nods and hands me the phone. "The first one is from the day she went missing," she says, pushing the voice-mail button and putting it on speakerphone. "Where are you? Helloooo? Call me. Okay, seriously, why are you being so weird? Call. Should I be worried? If you don't call me in the next five minutes I'm going to call Adam. . . . Okay, so Adam doesn't know where you are either. FYI, you're officially a missing person. . . . Helloooo! Okay, so, the police told your parents that they found your body in a garbage bag. Your mom screamed and then vomited all over the kitchen floor. Your dad told me and Mrs. Gursky to stay with her, and he left with the police. Mrs. Gursky cleaned up the mess. I took your mom into the living room. I'm not sure what to think. I spent the night in your room with your sister. We just kind of sat up. I kept thinking you'd come home at any moment—and show everyone that this whole thing with search dogs and people canvasing was all a giant overreaction. Your dad got back at about five in the morning. They made him look at your dead body to make sure it was you. How could you be dead? Is it freaky that I'm calling a dead person? I guess I don't really believe it. It's like I won't believe it until you tell me it's true. You're the one who always tells me what is and what isn't, how weird is that? Who am I supposed to talk to now? I went home this afternoon, my parents kept asking if I was okay. I'm not okay, but I couldn't take the way they were looking at me, like I was a lost dog. I had to get out of the house, and then all these reporters were chasing after me and I went to your house and your family is a mess, which makes sense. The rest of us are, like, in shock. I met Adam at the park; he thinks that it's all his fault, on account of how he didn't believe you when you said you weren't going out with that guy, and that he fucked everything up. . . ."

"How many of these are there?" I ask Amanda.

"A lot," she says. They go on:

"Today was your funeral, you would have loved it. Everyone was there, even Mr. Krupatskini, who acted like he was in charge, and of course no one paid any attention to him, but your parents let him announce that there's now a scholarship in your name. And your mom invited me over and took me into your room and asked if there was something special of yours that I wanted; I took the bracelet you shoplifted in seventh grade. 'That was one of her favorites,' your mom said. 'I know,' I said. 'I have a matching.' And she gave my sister your old blue bike. Your dad looks like he's going to have a breakdown; he keeps doing that thing where he sweeps his hair back off his forehead, but since he's bald it looks freaky to see him sweeping invisible hair off his head over and over again.

"Meanwhile, you'll never guess who killed you: it was the guy with the bumps on his face who Adam thought you were going out with. The reason he knew so much about you was because he had your old journal, so he did kind of know you. Now I keep dreaming that he's following me. I know this is supposed to be about you, and in the dream it's like I'm second best.

"Do you think there's any chance you'll come back—is that too weird to ask?

"What's it like there? Is it a real place? Are there other people?

"Miss you."

_____

Amanda pushes the skip button a few times. "Sorry not to have called in a while. I hope you won't take this the wrong way, but Adam and I are sort of seeing each other. You're not mad, are you?"

"And then it stops," Amanda says. "The phone got turned off."

"Who is she to you?"

"I don't know. Like someone I never was. I feel very close to her. I'm assuming these will stay on here as long as I keep the phone charged—or do they, like, vanish over time?" she asks.

"I have no idea," I say, uncomfortably mesmerized.

We part company at the grocery store; she has shopping to do, and I need to get home in time to meet Ricardo's bus.

"Come for dinner on Friday," I say as I'm leaving. "Bring your parents."

"Are you sure?" she asks.

"Yes," I say. "Six-thirty. I'll make fish sticks and Tater Tots."

"I'll bring a pound cake," she says.

Friday night, the children help set the table. We lay out a beautiful tablecloth and use the good silver, the good dishes, all the things that have not been out of the closet since Jane died. I have bought fresh flowers and teach Ashley and Ricardo how to cut the stems and arrange them. Ashley makes the salad, Ricardo helps me prep the fish sticks and Tater Tots. When Amanda and her parents arrive, the children are fixed like little ambassadors at the front door.

"May I take your coat?" Ricardo asks, even though they have no coats.

"Would you like a drink?" Ashley says while they're still in the front hall.

"That would be lovely," Amanda's mother, Madeline, says.

I'm wildly proud.

"What a treat," Amanda's mother says, shaking Ricardo's hand.

"Your hands are very soft," Ricardo says. "Like velvet."

"Thank you," Madeline says.

As I'm finishing the preparations for dinner, I peek into the living room and see Madeline on the floor playing a game of jacks with Ashley, and Cy trying to explain the finer points of backgammon to Ricardo.

Amanda sits on the sofa, alone, arms crossed in front of her chest—looking pouty.

I call everyone to the table. The fish sticks and Tater Tots are a big hit. Waxing poetic during the meal, Madeline and Cy drift back in time and talk about great trips they went on, walking from vineyard to vineyard in France, adventures in Italy, how they found themselves hitchhiking through the mountains near Turin.

Amanda recalls being left at home with her sister and an unmarried neighbor woman who knew nothing about children.

Ricardo and Ashley share stories of the trip to Williamsburg, including some of the more "colorful" details—which cause Cy to laugh out loud.

"He's always loved scatological humor," Madeline whispers to me.

As dinner comes to an end, I find myself liking Amanda's parents better than Amanda herself.

After pound cake and berries with fresh whipped cream, Ashley, Ricardo, Amanda, and I are clearing, and when we come out of the kitchen, Amanda's parents are gone. I catch a glimpse of her father's back as he's heading up the stairs.

"Christ," Amanda says.

"I'll go," I say.

Her parents are standing in the master bedroom. "Could I trouble you for some tea?" her mother asks. "And I fear our luggage has not yet arrived."

"How do you take your tea?" I ask.

"Not too dark," she says.

"Two lumps," he says.

"Would you like some as well?"

"None for me—but she always complains that it's too dark and not sweet enough. Have you got a finger of Scotch?"

"I can certainly check," I say, and go back downstairs. "They seem to be settling in for the night," I say, putting on the kettle for tea.

"Are they having a sleepover?" Ashley asks.

"Not sure," I say.

Amanda marches up the steps and returns a few minutes later. "They said they're happy that I joined them on their trip and are so glad to be traveling again and that all of this reminds them of how much they like trying new places. And then they said I could have the rest of the night off and that they would see me again sometime soon."

I make tea for Amanda, for her mother, for Ashley, pour the Scotch, and go back upstairs.

"Well?" Amanda asks when I come down.

"Your parents are in bed—they're each wearing a pair of George's pajamas. Your mother is sitting up, reading the book I left by the side of the bed—wearing my reading glasses. 'I couldn't find my nightgown,' she said, smiling as I handed her the tea, 'so I put on one of his.' And your father was in the bathroom, brushing his teeth with what I assume is my toothbrush."

"Tell them to get dressed and come back down here right now; it's time to go home," Amanda says, stressed.

"They looked very comfortable," I say.

"Let them stay," Ashley begs.

"Fine with me," I say.

"As long as I don't have to share with the lady," Ricardo says.

Amanda looks at us like we're nuts.

"I can tell them that checkout time is noon tomorrow, or you can just leave them here. . . ."

"What do you mean, leave them?" Amanda asks.

"They said they were so happy to have their old room back, one big bed rather than separate rooms."

"Don't they know that they chose to have separate rooms?" she asks, agitated, as though she's being blamed.

"What I'm saying is that your parents are welcome to stay the night. You can have a few hours to yourself—go do an errand or two."

"There's not much I can do in one night," Amanda says grumpily.

"We can make breakfast for them," Ashley says. "Pancakes and eggs."

"With bacon," Ricardo says.

"You're welcome to join us," I say to Amanda.

"I'm going," she says, hastily picking up her purse. "A whole night off. I have no idea what I'll do."

The next day, around noon, Amanda calls to see how they're doing. I tell her that they're fine—we had breakfast, and now they're sitting in the living room, reading.

The more I tell her how much I like her parents, the less she talks to me.

"They're falling apart," she says.

"No more than any of the rest of us," I say. "They're spirited."

"Fine," she says. "Since you're all so comfortable together, maybe I should take the weekend and go somewhere?"

"Such as?"

"I don't know, go see my sister in Philly? Visit old friends in Boston? I can pack up their medications and some clean clothes and drop them off with you."

"Should I be sad that you don't want to go away with me?"

"It's not about you," she says, with a childish bitterness to her tone. "It's about me. There's almost nothing left of me—I have to preserve what I can."

It's not like you can call someone who has been caring for his or her aging parents selfish. "Okay," I say, "enjoy yourself."

She goes for the weekend and comes back. I know she's returned because while I'm out she leaves giant plastic bags filled with more clothing and refilled prescriptions hanging off the doorknob. She leaves me a message on the home phone saying she's off to run errands—bank, dry cleaner's. Her voice is charged with renewed enthusiasm.

She goes and comes back, and then, stopping by to visit, she leaves me with a bank card, house keys, and a list of names and numbers—all of their doctors, etc. She's here and gone, here and gone—and then gone.

Ashley is the one who tells me Amanda's not coming back. "Hit the road, Jack," Ashley says.

"Did she say that?"

Ashley shakes her head no. "Not in so many words."

I call Amanda's sister in Philadelphia. "I have your parents here and want you to know they're fine."

"Who is this?"

"Harold, I'm a friend of your sister's. How was your weekend?"

"In what respect?" she asks.

"Your weekend with Amanda?"

"I haven't seen Amanda in years. Is this some kind of a crank call? Are you trying to get something from me—because I'll tell you right now, buster . . ."

"Never mind," I say, hanging up and realizing that chances are high that Ashley is right—Amanda is gone.

I text Cheryl, who is less than sympathetic. "I told you it would come to no good end."

"Do I call the police? What if she's injured or dead?"

"She's gone," Ashley says, "you have to let go. . . ."

In a panic, I dial Amanda's cell phone. It goes right to voice mail. And then I notice she's left a message on mine:

"I made you trustee of my parents' accounts. You have power of attorney; there are a few papers that have all been signed by me that require a counter-signature—they are in a folder on your desk. I know you have questions. . . . I wouldn't have done it if I didn't think you were capable. This voice mail will be disconnected on the first of the month. I can't be who any of you or anyone else wants me to be. I need out from under. P.S. Don't bother calling my sister—she's useless. If you don't want them, just send them home. They'll figure it out—they always have."

"I thought she would stay because she liked me," I text Cheryl later that day. "I thought she would stay because I was nice to her parents, because I'm reliable—a good guy."

"That's why she left them with you," she says.

"Do I have to cancel the trip?" I ask Cheryl.

"Absolutely not," she says, and because she is so definitive I believe her.

"It's late to buy more plane tickets, and I'm not sure I can manage two adults and three children—much less wondering if they're up for the rigors of the trip."

Cheryl thinks I'm nuts. "They're not going anywhere," she says, firmly. "They've been here for a long time, and they'll be here when you get back."

"Good point."

I arrange for the pet minder to bring his sister, a practical nurse, and the two of them will take care of the animals and the old folks.

The school year is winding down. Ashley shows me the draft of her extended meditation on the death of the soap opera—interwoven with her thoughts on staging *Romeo and Juliet* at the puppet theater. In her paper, Ashley writes about seeing herself in the characters, how she gets involved in their lives and thinks about them between episodes. I'm surprised at Ashley's ability to find common ground between soap opera, Shakespeare, and the fine art of puppet theater. She's got good ideas, but my professorial self kicks in: has anyone ever discussed structure with her? Multiple revisions are required. I share my thoughts, prompting hissy fits that blow through like severe thunderstorms.

She storms off, and then ultimately the paper is revised, sometimes slipped under my door in the middle of the night. She wants to do well, and that is a good sign. I pretend I can manage the hysterics—but make a note to myself that, if/when I see Dr. Tuttle again, I need to ask him about the care and management of female adolescents.

Meanwhile, Ricardo is often staying late at school, rehearsing for his class play, in which he's featured as a young Benjamin Franklin, a busy man with something always up his sleeve—his almanac, his various inventions and proclamations. As part of his embrace of the character, Ricardo asks permission to take apart an old typewriter and attempt to make his own printing press; I say yes and am secretly pleased. His incentive chart is filled with check marks and gold stars—he's working his way towards tickets to a Yankees game.

And Nate—school ends the second week of June, but he's elected to stay a couple of weeks longer for what's called a mini-camp; this year's focus is math, more specifically micro-finance.

The truth is, despite how stressful it all is—not to mention the uncanny sensation that the minute you start to think it's all going well something is bound to fall apart—despite it all, I am pleased with how well the children are doing.

As we get closer to departure, my conversations with the village become more frequent, the list of things I need to bring grows longer. I take sweaters and shirts out of my bag to make room for instant Jell-O pudding, a twelve-inch wok, rechargeable batteries, acetaminophen, surgical cement, chocolate chips, Fleischmann's yeast, and effervescent vitamin C.

The expediter I hired to get Ricardo's passport asks for an extra two hundred and fifty dollars, because it too has required more explaining than usual.

Sofia has sent Sakhile, the South African village leader, a moment-by-moment breakdown of what should be happening while we're there. "I like to be organized," she says defensively, when I suggest we leave space for things to unfold naturally. "I realize that it can be difficult for others to see the value of this level of detail, but," she says, "I want it to go well, and I am aware that there may be cultural differences related not just to the bar-mitzvah event but to a sense of time and occasion, and so I wanted to make my expectations clear." Sakhile's face appears on the computer screen. "Do you have everything you need?" she asks Sakhile. "Any last-minute items you need me to slip into a suitcase?"

"We are good to go," Sakhile says. "I have your instructions in hand." Sakhile holds up a clipboard with many pages attached.

"We are very excited," Sofia tells Sakhile. "Harold will bring you a copy of the printed invitation."

"You have a very powerful wife," Sakhile says later, when Sofia is not there.

"Not my wife," I say, "a party planner."

"Like Colin Cowie?" he says. "He made a big event for Oprah."

"Exactly," I say. "Sakhile, I'm curious—how did Nate come to your village?"

"We built the school to save our village, and from that good things come," he says. "My generation had to leave to find work—most didn't return. We were shrinking smaller and smaller, and then I had an idea. With democracy comes money—we can apply and get money for a school which can support our village. So first I build a small school, and then I say we need money to build a bigger school where the children from villages nearby can come. Most of the children who come have only grandparents who cannot take care of them, and all the more important is that they have an education."

"Where did you go to school?"

"I went only to a missionary school for two years, but there are things I know. My family has been here for a very long time. I am all that remains."

"Noble," I say.

He shakes his head. "I am not so noble, I am practical. I don't want my village to die. There was nothing left, no more reason for anyone to be here except that we have always been here. That is how Nate came to us. 'If you build it they will come,'" he says, and laughs. "I am quoting from *Close Encounters of the Third Kind,* when Richard Dreyfuss builds a mountain of mashed potatoes. . . ." The way Sakhile says "potatoes," pronouncing each syllable like it was a word itself, makes potatoes sound delicious.

"I think that's from *Field of Dreams,* the baseball movie with Kevin Costner. In *Close Encounters,* Dreyfuss says, 'I guess you've noticed something a little strange with Dad. . . .'" I say the line without knowing how I even know it and make a mental note to watch the film again—clearly it had a big impact on me.

"Safe journey," Sakhile says. *"Ulale kahle."*

The night before we leave, everyone is outside playing Wiffle ball. Nate and Cy are coaching Ricardo. Madeline is cheerleading. It is twilight—the lightning bugs are blinking, and except for the mosquitoes, it is sublime. Ashley and Nate's embrace of Ricardo is unqualified—one never has a sense of the two of them apart from him or competing with him. He is their brother; he has been left to us and we to him.

I stand on the front steps, slightly apart, observing, as though I now hold knowledge that separates me from them—but I don't. They are simply engaged in what is before them, and I am thinking about what time we have to leave, about passports, currency, and suitcases, while they are thinking it is summer and the day is perfect and I'm making spaghetti and meatballs for dinner.

"Play with us," Ricardo calls to me. At first I don't respond. "Play," he demands.

"Where are the bases?" I ask.

"The azalea is first, rhododendron second, and the lilac by the driveway is third," Nate says.

I go up to bat. Ashley pounds her fist into her glove. "Sock it to me," she says.

I am 0 for 2 trying to read Cy's wobbly pitch when I connect—the hollow thwack of plastic on plastic sends the ball careening to the right, bouncing off the lamppost by the front door, skittering under the boxwood, and rolling down the hill inches ahead of Ashley, who pounces after it. I make it safely to third base. Madeline is up next; she bunts, and I slide into home (and gracefully excuse myself to ice what's left of my knees).

The next afternoon, the car for the airport comes early. Ricardo has never flown before and is baffled by the security process—taking off his shoes (and socks), his belt, emptying his pockets, which contain an inordinate amount of junk. On the other side the kids go to buy some gum; Ricardo's hunger for all things is immense—he wants comic books, soda, chocolate, pistachio nuts. His enthusiasm is so genuine that it's hard to say no. "Pick one," I say. "One of each?" he asks. "Just one," I say.

On board, he sits between Nate and me, with Ashley on my right—we are four in a row across the middle, holding hands for what Ricardo calls "blastoff." Whatever has been forgotten will remain forgotten until we are long gone. During the night, I wake up with his head resting on my chest like a bowling ball.

In Johannesburg, Cecily has arranged for a people minder, like an airport babysitter. She shuttles us around in a golf cart, letting the kids take turns beeping the horn, and off we go on a smaller plane to Durban.

The plane empties, we get off, we claim our bags, watch people come and go. Various people approach, asking if we need transportation.

"No," I say. "Someone is coming."

After twenty minutes, I call Sakhile.

"No one is there?" he asks. "You are kidding me? I'll call you back," he says. Minutes later, my phone rings. "Car trouble. We are making another plan. I will call you back with details."

We sit on our suitcases—conspicuously white in a sea that is everything but. I don't think I've been in a place that is so entirely other.

Thirty minutes later, a man arrives. "I am Manelisi, the cousin of Nobuhle. Please come." Manelisi leads us to his bakkie, a small pickup truck with an extra seating area. The children sit behind me; I share the front with Manelisi. "I am a gardener," he says. "That is why the truck smells like dung—I did a big job today."

The truck doesn't smell like dung so much as earth. We ride with the windows open; I ask the children if it is too much air.

"No," they say, glad to be out of the plane and out of the airport, "it's good."

"Right now," Manelisi says, "we are going to pick up some packages." He looks at a map, and in about ten minutes we pull up in front of a place called Esther's Kitchen. Manelisi runs in, then returns with two helpers and numerous boxes, which they load into the back of the truck. Only later do I realize this is food for tomorrow's lunch, packed in dry ice. The helpers speak a language that is unfamiliar but sounds rhythmic and joyous.

"Okay," Manelisi says. "Now we get on a good road."

The radio is on—a contemporary blend of rock and hip-hop; I am comforted by the disc jockey's speaking in English.

"Did you grow up in the village?" I don't know what it was called before "Nateville."

"No," he says. "We are from pineapple farmers in Hluhluwe."

As we are leaving Durban, we pass what look like slums—shacks with tin roofs, homes made of random scraps of wood, metal, and brick. Boys walk barefoot along the edge of the road.

"What direction are we traveling?" I ask.

"North," Manelisi says.

"And what time does it get dark?"

"In winter, between five and six."

Outside of Durban, the expanse of land seems infinite and undiscovered. The tires of the bakkie hum as they roll along the highway. In the distance, electric lines rise like giant twenty-first-century figures. Small bunkerlike houses dot the landscape.

"What is that?" Ricardo asks, pointing to an animal at the edge of the road.

"Baboon," Manelisi says, as he changes the radio station to one where the DJ speaks what I assume is Zulu.

The landscape is richly green and hilly in the late-afternoon light. I put down the sun visor and look at the children behind me in the small mirror. Ashley and Ricardo have been lulled to sleep by the ride and the wind in their faces. Nate, awake, seems unusually quiet.

"You okay?"

"What if it was all a fantasy, what if it's not like I remember?" he asks.

"It will be different," I tell him. "Things change, you've changed, but whatever it is—it will be."

And we lapse into a long silence.

"We're here," Nate shouts enthusiastically, as we turn onto a secondary road. As soon as the car stops beside a small group of buildings in the middle of nowhere, Nate jumps out.

"Ninjani," he says, greeting everyone. *"Ngikukhumbulile kangaka!* You have gotten so big," he says to the children.

"Ninjani," I say, getting out of the car and helping Ricardo and Ashley climb out of the back.

"I am Sakhile," a man says, putting his hand out to me—he looks younger in person. "Welcome."

"Thank you," I say.

"We will take you to your room," he says. "And then we must begin, we are off schedule." He waves the printout that Sofia sent him.

The village is smaller than I imagined, less a village and more a small grouping of about fifteen to twenty houses with dirt paths between buildings.

Sakhile leads us to the school; others walk behind us, carrying our bags and watching from a distance, as though wondering who we are, that we are being treated so differently.

"This is our school," Sakhile says proudly, showing me a low building that looks like a suburban recreation center. "We set you up in here because the toilet is good."

"Thank you."

"I do not mean to rush you, but we must go quickly or we will miss sundown."

I catch a glance of the sheet Sakhile is holding—various elements have been highlighted in yellow, green, or pink.

4:30 P.M. **ARRIVAL**

4:35 P.M. **GREETING OF THE VILLAGE OFFICIALS**

4:40 P.M. **FAMILY SHOWN TO QUARTERS**

4:45 P.M. **WASH UP**

5:00 P.M. **PREPARE FOR LIGHTING OF CANDLES (SEE ATTACHED)**

5:15 P.M. **SABBATH BLESSINGS**

6:00 P.M. **DINNER**

PLEASE PROVIDE BOTTLED WATER FOR THE FAMILY AND ENCOURAGE THEM TO DRINK.

I had no idea how deeply orchestrated all of this would be—we are being handled like rock stars or heads of state.

Ashley pulls a nice dress out of her carry-on bag and quickly changes. I go into the bathroom and wash my face and hands.

"Life here is simple," Ashley says. "I like it—it's like being on a camp-out."

"Yes, but this is the way it is all the time," I say. "The basic elements are the daily struggle. No one here is worrying about what college they're going to get into."

"That's good, right?" Ricardo asks.

"It's different," I say, ushering the kids down the hall.

At a table in one of the classrooms, they have set up silver candlesticks, a silver goblet, and a loaf of challah covered in a cloth.

The entire village is here, filling the room, eyes on Nate.

Ricardo and Nate take their places at the front of the room and begin to sing "Lekhah Dodi" as Ashley walks down the aisle—draped in a white lace shawl and matching kippah, which I have never seen before.

When the song is finished, Nate begins: "Thank you for inviting me and my family to celebrate this special occasion with you. My family doesn't have many traditions, we are not very religious, so these traditions are really those of my ancestors. What I take away from the Friday-night service is the importance of pausing to take notice of each other, to give thanks that the week has passed and that we are still here—and, in the middle of our busy lives, to make time to connect with our families and our heritage. Mostly, I want you to know how glad I am to be here. I would like to introduce you to my brother, Ricardo, and my sister, Ashley, who is now going to light the Sabbath candles."

Ashley steps forward. "On the Sabbath we say three prayers, one while lighting the candles, one for the bread, and one for the wine. Tonight, in the absence of my mother, I will light the candles."

Everyone pushes closer to the front. All eyes are on Ashley, as if she is going to perform a magic trick. She lights the candles, then covers her eyes and recites:

"Baruch atah Adonai, Eloheinu, melekh ha'olam, asher kid'shanu b'mitzvotav v'tzivanu l'hadlik ner shel Shabbat."

Ricardo says, "This is the blessing for the bread: Praised are You, Lord our God, King of the universe, Who brings bread from the Earth."

"And the blessing of the wine," Nate says: *"Baruch atah Adonai, Eloheinu, melech ha'olam borei p'ri hagafen."*

The service is turned over to Nate. "Since I was here two years ago, I have been through a lot. It is our tradition after a death for the immediate family to grieve for a year, and so, since my mother was killed this past year, I have gone every Friday evening to the chapel at my school and I have spoken to my mother. I have prayed for my mother, for my family, and for all of us. And while this may not be the traditional way, I always conclude with this prayer, which I think works well whether one is Christian or Jewish:

"The Lord is my shepherd; I shall not want. . . ."

As Nate begins to recite, the whole village joins in—those who don't know it by heart have cheat sheets. Goose bumps run up and down my spine.

"And in the Jewish religion there is a special memorial prayer we say, Av Harachamim—and I would like to ask Ashley and Ricardo, who also lost his family this year, to join me." The children solemnly recite the prayer in English.

And when they are done Nate says, "We would now like to invite you to come and taste the challah bread and have a sip of wine—grape juice for the children." Ashley and Ricardo break the challah, and the village children each come forward for a piece of the bread.

"Like candy floss," one of the children says, and Ricardo laughs, and the ice is broken. And as children can do so effortlessly, we instantly go from the most solemn to joyous.

There are small cups of wine for each of the adults. "Good stuff," one of the men says to me as he waits to get another cup. *"Thela iwayini."*

"One per customer," Nate says.

"Ubani iugama lakho?" the man asks me—I don't have a clue.

"He wants to know your name," Nate says, translating for me.

"My name is Harold."

"Igama lami ngiungu, Harold," Nate translates.

"Harry," the man says, "I thank you for the wine."

"When did you guys pull this together?" I ask Ashley and Ricardo.

"Sofia is very bossy," Ricardo says. "Whatever she tells you—you do." In the main room of the school, long tables have been set up. "We have some things from your world and some from ours," Sakhile says, motioning that I should sit next to him. The women of the village carry out bowls of matzoh-ball soup. I recognize the plates—they are ones that Sofia picked out, melamine, which the school will be able to keep and use for years to come. There is also fish in cream sauce and chopped liver from the caterer in Durban, with pieces of hard-boiled egg diced in just like my great-aunt Lena's. And for the children there is plain pasta with red sauce and grated cheese on the side; they seem deeply relieved to be eating something familiar. I am feeling very grateful to Sofia.

The broth is warm, and salty—the elixir of the ages. The matzoh ball is plump, soft on the outside, hard in the center. If George were here he'd make a crack about how Jewish women love to serve a man his balls. Either the fleeting thought of George or my sudden awareness that it is now completely dark outside floods me with anxiety. When it was still light, I could see my way out, but now we are trapped for the night, and I must surrender to the experience.

"And we have a traditional stew—*inyama yenkomo,*" Sakhile says, capturing my attention. "My wife made it, you must have some." I taste the stew; the meat has a stringy texture, the sauce is spicy and sweet. At first I do not like it, but then it grows on me. "And this," he says, filling my glass, "is homemade beer—*tshwala.*"

While we are still eating, the teacher stands up. "Nathaniel, I had not yet arrived when you visited two years ago, but we speak often of your generosity. The children have prepared a song for you." Each child pulls out a bright plastic recorder. Weee-dee de de deeee dee de deeee dee dee weeamumu-awahhhh. The notes climbing and falling—wee—ummm mummm awah . . .

Sakhile leans over and says, "*Eem boo beh* means 'lion.' It is an old South African song. Sofia suggested it—I did not know it was so popular for you."

"It's a classic," I say, singing along, ". . . mighty jungle, the lion sleeps tonight."

After dinner there is dancing with music from a boom box, and then some drum playing. One by one the villagers leave; Nate wants to stay up with his friends.

"No," I say. "Tomorrow is a big day, it's time for bed."

"You must listen to your father," Sakhile says. I'm not sure Sakhile notices his error, but Nate and I do. Nate says nothing, and I am pleased.

Before going to bed, I bring Sakhile the things he asked for. "Who is the wok for?"

"It is a surprise for my mother," he says. "In the house where she works she saw one on a cooking show on television, and she couldn't stop talking about it." He picks up the wok and turns it over. "How do you turn it on?"

I can't help but laugh. "You put it over a fire or an electric burner, and it gets very hot. . . ."

He nods. "Then what's so special about it?" he says, mystified.

"I think it's about the shape," I say.

"Thank you. *Lala kahle*," he says. "Sleep well."

Our beds are like pallets, a very thin mattress, and piles of blankets that smell like sweat and dirt; it is not unpleasant—it is musky, human, real. The mats have been draped with hotel sheets that have been borrowed (or stolen), as though someone told them that Americans need ironed sheets and fluffy fresh towels in order to feel comfortable. On top of our beds are rolls of toilet paper with fancy stickers on the ends. I have no idea what time or day it is— all I know is that tomorrow will come soon. The children are almost instantly asleep.

Just after sunrise, I smell coffee. I dress and go outside; on an open stove, three women are making eggs and pancakes—per Sofia's directions. Ricardo and Ashley eat the traditional porridge, and I have the anchovy paste on toast as well as everything else. There is also marmalade and tea, which Ashley declares the best ever. The village children taste the pancakes and maple syrup and call the syrup "good medicine."

Around the village, decorations are being put up, streamers in blue and white. At about eleven-thirty, we come back to our rooms to get dressed. I packed dress-up clothing, which now seems ridiculous, like putting on a costume, but because Ricardo and Ashley want to, we do. Nate thinks we're being weird and wears jeans and a green-and-yellow Bafana Bafana T-shirt Sakhile has given him.

We go to the center of the village, where there is a large circular open space. The village children open with a traditional Zulu song, which I think says something like "Here come our mothers, bringing us presents. . . ." Then the men of the village surround Nate, wearing whatever they have, bits and pieces of "traditional" Zulu gear—I'm no longer sure what is traditional and what are tourist props. They dance in an energetic circle around Nate, their song a call and response between Sakhile, the village men, and Nate—gathering momentum and ending suddenly with a loud shout.

Sakhile turns the podium over to me. I introduce myself and begin to talk about Nate and tell the story of when Nate was born, how proud his father was—he saw the child as an extension of himself—and that I then also saw Nate as an extension of my brother and brought to my relationship with this young boy all the complications of my relationship with my brother. I go on to say that it wasn't until this grievous family tragedy that I began to see Nate as a person in his own right. "Nate has pushed me to be a better version of myself, to expect more—to rise to an occasion and not run from it or sink beneath it," I say. "The circumstances of his life were not of his choice, but when I see Nate, and Ashley and Ricardo, I am impressed with their resiliency. What I have learned this year is that the job of parent is to help the child become the person he or she already is. I am not just Nate's uncle, I am his biggest fan, and I thank him for bringing me to you." And then, as though I'm introducing a performer, I say, "Ladies and gentlemen—Nathaniel Silver."

"Today I celebrate my bar mitzvah, which in the Jewish religion happens on your thirteenth birthday and marks the time when a boy officially becomes a man. I celebrate in the absence of my mother and father. I feel lucky to have survived.

"I have often thought of you and this village since my visit two years ago.

I have thought of hardships of economy, race, and illness and become aware of how privileged my life is. When things got difficult for me, I thought of you and felt an obligation to survive, not just for myself, but for others. And it is what you taught me two years ago that kept me alive. For this I come back and say thank you—you have given me my life."

While Nate is still talking, Ricardo leans over and tells me that when he's thirteen he wants to come back to this place for his bar mitzvah, and that he also needs to get his penis "fixed."

"I think it's better to just be the way you are," I say, trying to stay focused on Nate.

"How come you and Nate get to have a better penis than me?"

"Ricardo, I hear what you're saying, and I promise you it's something we can talk about when we get home, but it's not something we're going to deal with in South Africa. And there is no such thing as a better penis. . . . Have you noticed that the boys in South Africa have the same kind of penis as you?" I say, directing his attention back to Nate.

"Yeah," he says, "poor boys have bad penis," he mutters. "I want to have a rich man's cock." He looks down at his lap.

I am devastated by his reading of the situation and his use of the word "cock."

Nate concludes by reading a poem he wrote at school, and everyone applauds.

Sakhile takes the stage. "Nate and the family of Nate—you come to us to celebrate this rite of passage to go from boy to man—but also from friends and relatives to being a family. Your belief in our village reminded us to believe in ourselves and demanded that we do more for ourselves—that we work harder. That hard work made us stronger—we had gotten soft and we were sad and sorry for ourselves, we had seen many hard things. You came like fresh air that says, Think outside of yourself, think forward, and I am so happy now, and we are not alone—we have a big world. And our friend-ship showed me that black and white can come together, can be true friends. We lived a long time carrying a great weight, and it will take a long time to feel our lightness. Someone once told me there are people you do not know—strangers—who care very much about you. I did not understand what that could mean until now. I wanted to thank you." He pauses. "Your father's friend Sofia and I talked a long time about traditions. And for this bar-mitzvah day we decided to do something very American—a celebration of independence. So for lunch we will have a giant barbecue of hamburgers and hot dogs."

"An all-you-can-eat buffet," Ricardo says, "and it's free. . . ."

I see the village women scurrying around to indulge our very American fantasy and worry that it's wrong, and at the same time it's clear how much they are loving it, how much the images of American culture have become part of their dream. Sofia has thought of everything: ketchup, mustard, mayonnaise, dill pickles, helium balloons.

During lunch Nate asks me, "Does my father know we're here?"

"I don't think so," I say. "Do you want him to know?"

Nate shrugs and takes another hot dog.

As lunch is winding down, the village children vanish—I assume gone off to play, but they return wearing the blue-and-white soccer jerseys and carrying in the cake. They sing "Happy Birthday" and joyously add the verse "You look like a monkey and you live in a zoo," and they think it is so funny.

Nate cuts the cake. He leans over and says, "I always thought you were an asshole, just another one of them, someone who couldn't do anything, who couldn't be trusted. Now you're like a real person—it's cool."

Everyone is wearing a Nate shirt, everyone is playing soccer, even the old women. While the game is on, Sakhile says to me, "There is someone I want you to meet this afternoon, someone special to me, Londisizwe, the *inyanga*—medicine man—he is like my brother."

"What does he do?"

"A little of everything. He gives me powder for my feet to stop the itching. I am allergic to dirt—can you imagine the joke of that, living here and allergic to dirt?" Sakhile laughs and raises his pants to show me that he is wearing shoes and socks—tall white crew socks.

Londisizwe arrives during the soccer game; he looks older than Sakhile. He introduces himself. "I want to thank you for the supplies. Many of the things you brought are for my medicine bag. We are just enough in the twenty-first century that people believe everything can be fixed—I am no longer a medicine man, I am like a repairman, Mr. Maytag."

I laugh.

"It's not really so funny when you think about it," he says.

I nod. We watch the soccer game.

"You have a beautiful family."

"Thank you," I say.

Ashley runs over—she needs my help in putting her hair up. I introduce her to Londisizwe, and she shakes his hand.

"Are you enjoying your trip?" he asks.

"It's amazing," she says.

"I'm so glad," Londisizwe says, holding on to Ashley's hand. "What has been your favorite part?"

She pauses. "I liked lighting the candles on Friday night, and then when everyone sang 'Wimoweh.'"

"All good things," he says, nodding. Londisizwe lets go of her hand; she runs back into the game.

"She has been sad a long time," the medicine man says.

"She's okay," I say.

Londisizwe looks at me as though I am refusing to hear him. "Does she do well at school?"

"It's complicated," I say.

"She is afraid, she worries what will happen to her. And the heavy boy . . ."

"Ricardo," I say.

"Ricardo needs to be trained. He is overflowing with energy, which he controls by eating heavy foods to slow down. He should do karate or sword-fighting until he becomes himself."

"How do you know all that?"

"Some things you can see just by looking," he says.

"Tell me more."

"Nate needs to go more gently. He uses anger to push himself forward, but at some point he will collapse, he needs to find a food more nourishing than anger."

I nod, thinking this guy really does know something. And then he turns his eyes on me. He asks me to stick out my tongue, he sniffs my breath—which I imagine smells like hot dog and mustard. He nods, as if thinking about how best to say what he has seen.

"You almost died," Londisizwe says. "You may feel okay right now, but you are not okay inside. You are holding something foul—it needs to come out, and you are afraid to let it go. It is something from long ago; you have kept it like a companion so you don't feel so alone, but now you have a family, and in order to be healthy, it needs to come out."

I nod, knowing that he is right. My ability to describe my experience is limited, with the nuances unarticulated. How does anyone explain himself? It's as though all I can do is grunt and hope that, from the intonation, you might understand. I could blame the stroke, but I would be lying. How can I tell anyone that there has always lived within me a rusty sense of disgust—a dull, brackish water that I suspect is my soul?

"What is it that needs to come out?" I ask Londisizwe.

"That is my question to you," he says. "It is something that has kept you from life. I would like to give you something to clear out the old. We will start with a tea—it will give you strong dreams and wind, but you must continue with it for four days. You will feel much worse before you feel better."

The idea of feeling much worse before feeling better doesn't exactly make me jump up and down and say, Let's start now. "What do you mean by wind?" I ask.

"Clouds of smoke from your stomach," Londisizwe says. "But no matter how you feel you must keep drinking it until the smoke stops, and then you will feel notably lighter of spirit. We will start now," he says. "I will make the tea." Londisizwe leaves.

I focus on the soccer game.

Twenty minutes later, Londisizwe returns with a large mug. I drink the tea, which tastes earthy, heavy, like boiled peat moss and mushrooms. "What is it made of?" I ask, in part to stall for time between sips.

"I cannot tell you," Londisizwe says. "Because if I told you I would have to kill you." He smiles. I see that he has only four teeth in his mouth—the front four, and there are gaping holes on either side. He laughs. "Just kidding," he says.

Forty-five minutes later, I am overcome with exhaustion. I have no choice but to lie down; I am not sure if it is the tea or the fact that the bar mitzvah is over, but it feels like a lifetime of exhaustion, like something is draining out of me. I go back to the room and sleep for hours. My dreams are uncomfortable, vivid, in incredible color—as if supersaturated. They are so intense that while I am having them I'm sure I will never forget them. And then I wake, like I'm drunk, and I remember nothing—well, almost nothing. There are strange fragments: Like, I am at a meeting with a group of men; we are sitting in an office and as they are talking I realize that it is the 1960s and I am in a suite and the men who are talking are Nixon's men and I am working for Nixon, and the men all turn and look at me, waiting expectantly for something. And then there is one with my father dancing around the house in his undershorts and wearing my mother's bra while my mother chases after him, hitting him again and again with a dish towel saying, "Just fix the air conditioner."

I get up and stagger out to find the children. I have no idea how long I've been sleeping and am now having a paranoid anxiety attack—thinking they drugged me so they could take the children.

I find everyone not far from where I left them: Nate on a ladder, working with the villagers to fix a water heater; Ricardo playing with a group of boys; Ashley helping to cook dinner. It is about as wholesome and bucolic as you can imagine.

"You're sweating," Ashley says, and it is then that I see I am drenched in sweat, that during my nap I have soaked through my clothing.

I nod and retreat without saying anything. I return to the school, to our rooms, and take a shower. Londisizwe finds me there. "How is it going? Has my *umuthi* begun its work?"

I nod.

"Are you okay?"

I nod again.

For dinner, everyone else eats a beautiful feast. I am given a bowl of porridge and another cup of tea. This time it is a greener, grassier tea. I drink it quickly and almost immediately throw up.

"I must have been allergic to something in it," I say, apologizing to Londisizwe.

He shakes his head. "That tea makes everyone throw up."

I look at him as if to ask, then why would you give it to people to drink?

"If I told you you'd throw up after drinking the tea, would you have drunk it? In a little while, I will bring you another tea, and I promise it will not make you vomit."

After dinner, there are fireworks. Sofia has hired a pyrotechnic team to put on a show. The children's faces are filled with delight. Even the older people have rarely if ever seen fireworks. Londisizwe brings me a new cup of tea, and this one tastes sweet and pleasant, and I drink it quickly, in part because I am distracted and just want to get on with things.

Explosions fill the sky. Red peonies, blue rings, golden dome-shaped weeping willows, fire-hot chrysanthemums, spiders, heavy golden glittering Kamuros fire up into the night, like snowflakes, like a bouquet of fine flowers, like gems or shooting stars. I wonder how far away they can be seen, and even though it seems against the grain of the celebration, I wonder what it costs.

As the fireworks whistle and hum, crackle and bang, my stomach begins to rumble, flatus starring ancient archetypical gases, primitive evolutionary elements—carbon dioxide sulphur, methane, ammonia. Enormous bilious clouds that I imagine are colored blue and green and look like gigantic, unevenly formed iridescent soap bubbles rise up out of me, wobbling, expanding—exploding. Never as scatologically invested as some, I am impressed by what is coming out of me; at one point it feels timed to the fireworks.

The show ends with the traditional bright-white salute of fireworks, low to the ground, with an enormously loud report echoing off the hills. As the white smoke billows away, each child is given a fiery-hot sparkler to wave through the air. I watch vigilantly.

And then there is ice cream—enormous cardboard bins brought from Durban of vanilla, chocolate, and strawberry, which spent the night on dry ice. There are children here who have never had ice cream before, and again it is just an amazing thing to see children and adults enjoying themselves so much.

That night when we return to our quarters the children complain they can't bear to be around me: I smell disgusting. I drag my bed into the hallway of the school and debate going outside, and would except that I am afraid of the dark.

The next day after breakfast we give out the backpacks and pencils and all the things Sofia ordered as gifts. The children are polite, grateful, trained to curtsy to the white people. They are gentle, a little fragile, as though their right to life is still precarious. One of the boys gives Ricardo a tin truck he's made out of soda cans; the girls give Ashley a beaded necklace and a small basket; Sakhile gives Nate an old tribal headdress made of animal skin and beads; and then he hands me a small pouch that contains an old piece of rhino horn filled with a magical ingredient that gives warriors invincibility. "It is mixed with animal fat and rubbed into the wrists. It is good for sex, gives dogs a hard-on."

"Thank you," I say.

Londisizwe brings me a kit containing the supplies I will need for the next three days—teas labeled for breakfast, lunch, and dinner—and reminds me not to eat any animal flesh while I am taking the teas and to drink a lot of water. He also gives me some teas to bring back to America. "Drink this one the day you get back," he says, "it will help loosen what you are still holding. And then drink these once a day for three days—and then as needed when you start to feel like you are becoming your old version again. They will free you." Just before I go, he brings one more cup of tea, "for the road." This one tastes vile, like horseshit that has been soaked in beer and left for days—it is fermented, dark, foul; I have a very hard time drinking it.

"Perhaps I made a mistake," he says, taking the cup back when I am done. "I put some cinnamon in and tried to make it more pleasant—I should have left it as it was."

Two Land Rovers arrive to pick us up; there are white men at the wheel who introduce themselves as Dirk Kruger and Pieter Goosen, and two black men who are helpers are introduced only as Kopano and Josia and take our bags.

We go. The village recedes into the distance—we watch for as long as we can; I'm sure everyone there is still outside waving. The children begin to cry, first Nate, then Ash, and finally Ricardo, who says, "Why am I crying? I am happy and sad at the same time."

"It's like when it's raining and there's a rainbow," Ashley says.

What to do with the strange sense of having been there and gone so quickly? It feels as though we haven't done enough, and yet what more should we do? This is the life of the village; does it need to be fixed?

We spend hours talking about the village and about the people we met. Nate is thrilled to have shared this world, and that things went well. The guy driving the car is trying to participate by saying things like "So you had a good time, eh?"

We drive for a couple of hours before coming to the waterfall, which is truly spectacular. "This one breaks even the hardest of nuts," Pieter says as we get out of the car. "If you're game, we can go for a bit of a hike," he says. And on cue, Josia and Kopano open the back of the second Rover and get out walking sticks, ropes, and harnesses for the children.

Overcome with stomach cramps, I excuse myself and go into the woods.

I have diarrhea and then move to another spot and have more and then more. In the end, I am holding on to the branch of a tree, my pants completely off and wrapped around my neck and shoulders as I involuntarily projectile-squirt shit into the woods. My body empties and seizes and empties and seizes. "You all right in there?" one of the guides shouts every couple of minutes. "Make sure nothing comes up and bites you on the ass."

"I'm fine," I weakly call back, not because I am but because there is just nothing to say. "Why don't you go on ahead without me," I suggest.

"We'll take the kiddies for a walk and meet you back here in an hour," one of them says. "I'll leave the car unlocked. There's water—be sure you drink when you're finished in there."

When they come back, they are all glowing. "It was amazing, we did belaying and climbed up this amazing rock," Ricardo says.

"The waterfall was so beautiful, I could feel the spray on my face," Ashley says. "And I saw a rainbow—isn't that cool? Because I said the word 'rainbow' this morning, when we left the village, and there it was. . . ."

"Safe as kittens in their mother's mouth," Dirk, who Ricardo later refers to as Dirtik, says.

"And then there was a zip line and we went flying through the forest," Nate adds, as though I need to hear more. "Are you feeling better?"

"I hope so," I say, because, honestly, I can't imagine feeling worse.

"Likely something you ate," Pieter says. "Zulu cooking can kill you."

"Really?" Ashley asks.

"Not really," Pieter says for her benefit. There's something in his tone—call it racism—that I really don't like.

In the late afternoon, we arrive at camp. "Just in time for tea," Dirk says. We are shown to our tent, which is kind of Lawrence of Arabia, over the top. It is less like a "room" and more like a tented house—with a large wraparound porch, a living area with Oriental rugs, couches, comfortable chairs, old trunks as footstools, lamps, a campaign desk in case letters need to be written, a bathroom with an enormous old claw-footed tub that opens right out into the bush. There are bowls of Gummi snakes and small stuffed animals for the children. Two black servants bring in tea, lemonade, and biscuits—cookies filled with lemon crème—and peanut-butter-and-jelly sandwiches. I can't decide if this is the way things are always done or if Sofia asked for some kind of special treatment.

We rest for an hour, and then one of the guides comes in and talks with us about the safari drive we'll go on at dusk. The rules are reviewed—cameras are welcome, no loud talking, never any yelling since it could cause an animal to stampede, no getting out of the cars, no trying to feed or otherwise attract the animals closer, hands in the vehicles at all times.

I drink the tea and worry that while watching lions have their dinner I will once again have to relieve myself. I think of canceling, but the idea of sending the kids off into the twilight with Pieter and Dirk just isn't going to work.

We rest; I give the kids the safari packs Sofia made for them, cameras, hats each with a giant metal button, "NATE'S BIG BM."

Dirk brings me a special drink. "This will help you feel better," he says.

"What is it?"

"Gatorade," he says. "We keep it on hand for pregnant ladies."

I'm not sure if he's teasing or not, but I do feel better after drinking it.

In the car with us for our evening drive is an older couple from the Netherlands. "I've wanted to do this my whole life," the husband says. The wife, who speaks no English, nods along. "My grandfather came here years ago and brought home an elephant's skin."

"He killed an elephant?" Ricardo asks.

The man nods proudly. The rest of us say nothing.

"As you know, this is a photographic safari," Pieter says. "The only thing that will be shot is a camera."

The fellow from Amsterdam nods grimly, as though he's really wishing he signed up for more.

"We know that a pride of lions lives in this area; there are multiple females, a couple of males, and some cubs who are a few months old." The car slows down. Pieter whispers, "What we see here, across the road, are fresh paw prints from the pride: they're close by."

Suddenly one of the black guys points off to the side, and we see a male lion emerge from the bushes, followed by a female and a few younger cubs. The male lion appears to be stalking something; his tail twitches.

"I know this lion," Pieter says.

The lions come closer and we all begin taking pictures of the lioness and her cubs, and then another female lion approaches and we track them to an area where several lions are chewing on what is, thank God, an unrecognizable carcass.

"What are they eating?" the fellow from Amsterdam asks.

"Steenbok," Pieter says.

"Are the animals fenced in?" I ask. "Is there any chance of running into a wild lion along the road?"

"Very little," Pieter says. "Most of our big animals are in game parks and reserves. You might see monkey, baboon, or some antelope out and about, but highly unlikely that you'd spot elephant, lion, rhino, or buffalo. . . ."

"And do people still hunt those animals?"

"They do," Pieter says.

"In a fenced park, that seems kind of pathetic," Nate says.

And no one says any more, until Ricardo says, "So this is kind of like an indoor/outdoor zoo?"

"Sort of," Ashley says.

We spot a male lion having an argument with another male, and that's good for about a hundred pictures, and then we make our way back to the camp as the sun is setting. The sky is enormously big, and before we are back, the stars are all out and we're naming and, as a game, renaming constellations.

Our tent has been remade for the evening. Each of the three giant sofas surrounding the master king-sized bed has been turned into a bed, crisp white sheets, plumped pillows all draped with mosquito netting—at once opulent and rustic. We are given the choice of dining with the other guests or on our own terrace.

We choose the terrace. Each tent has its own "butler." Ours is Bongani, a lithe young man with rich black skin who radiates goodness. When the children ask him to sit at the table and share their macaroni and cheese, he shakes his head no. "I have already eaten," he says, "but it is good to see you enjoy." Bongani brings me more Gatorade, some toast, and a pot of hot water in which to make my tea. Opening the kit Londisizwe gave me, I see there are balls of tea, each one labeled with the time of day and day of week they are to be used. Tonight's ball is a dark purply black.

"Would you like cream and sugar?" Bongani asks me.

"Some honey if you have it," I say.

"At safari camp we have it all," he says. And it is uncomfortably true.

After dinner, I drink the tea, which is smooth and calming, and take a bath while the children watch movies—I overhear them talking. Ashley tells the boys that it's very hard to be a girl in South Africa—girls get no respect. The boys tell her they haven't noticed; I'm impressed that she did. "It's depressing," she tells them. "The women do all the work of cooking and cleaning but have no authority, no one cares about them."

"I'm sure people care about them," I say as I'm coming out of the bathroom. "But it may be that the fight for racial equality overtook the fight for women's equality."

"Basically," she says, flouncing off to her bed, "girls don't rank."

Bongani offers to make the children a bonfire at which they can roast marshmallows. Their faces light up.

Oiled with insect repellent, they go outside to make s'mores; from the tent I can see the firelight flickering across their faces.

I stay inside. I'm exhausted but feeling a bit better, almost high in a strange way. I count nine tea balls left.

Ricardo falls asleep by the fire; Bongani carries him inside. "Do you want me to change him into sleeping clothes?" Bongani asks.

"I've got it, but thank you," I say.

As Ashley and Nate get ready for bed, Bongani asks the children if they would like to hear a story.

"Yes," they say.

And we are lulled to sleep listening to the melodic rise and fall of Bongani's voice as he tells tales of heroic elephants and lions of long ago.

About an hour later, Ricardo wakes up and comes to the side of my bed. "I'm scared," he says, climbing into the big bed. A little while later, Ashley says, "I can't sleep," and crawls in next to Ricardo. At 2 a.m., Nate wordlessly joins us. We are like a pack of dogs, curled around each other, softly snoring, jockeying for pillows and blankets. It's the best night's sleep I've had all year.

At dawn, Bongani is already preparing breakfast. He notices that I am awake and brings me tea. When the children wake I have more tea and some plain toast and watch the children consume an enormous breakfast. While we are eating, I ask Bongani about his family. He says they are all well and that he has lived here his whole life.

We are told to pack bathing suits and a change of clothes, and take off on an early ride in pursuit of elephants. This time the couple from the Netherlands is in another car, and we are on our own. A child in one of the other cars has a temper tantrum and throws his stuffed animal overboard; the cars all come to a halt. Dirk approaches the little boy; I'm worried he's going to give him a talking to about breaking the rules. Instead, he gives the boy a lollipop to quiet him while Josia hops out to pick the teddy out of the brush, and we continue on.

At the next stop, while the others are shooting photos, I mention to Dirk how magical I find Bongani's presence. Dirk tells me that Bongani's father was murdered and that his mother became a prostitute in order to survive and later died of AIDS.

We have a feast of a picnic lunch at a picture-perfect spot under an enormous tree, which just happens to have several swings—strung from enormously long ropes that allow the children to sail through the air. The air smells deliciously like earth and grass. "Picnic" means cocktails and large comfortable chairs, as well as beautiful tables set with real dishes and food that materializes out of endless enormous wicker hampers. On the way back to the camp, we stop at a river where dressing "tents" have been set up and we're told we can swim, alligator-free, while a "lifeguard" with a gun stands watch. The children go in. I abstain, fearing parasites or anything that might aggravate my digestive tract.

That night, after dinner, there is no pretense about who is sleeping where; we all put on our pajamas, hop into the big bed, and sip warm cocoa as Bongani talks us to sleep.

What do you want? Tuttle asked me, what seems like months ago.

I want this, whatever this is, never to end.

The next morning, while the children are visiting a nearby crocodile farm, I'm busy stuffing everything we arrived with and everything we accumulated along the way back into our suitcases. Abruptly, I decide not to bring most of our clothing home, keeping only what I use to wrap fragile items.

The suitcases are laden with tourist memorabilia—hats, T-shirts that seemed so urgent and of the moment earlier in the week but which likely will never be worn again.

I put aside a giant pile of clothing, and when Bongani returns I ask him if he will keep it.

"Yes," Bongani says, taking the job very seriously. "I will hold them until you return."

"I want you to use the clothing," I say, "or give it to someone who will. I do not expect it back."

"Thank you," he says. "I will wear them well."

As we are leaving, I give him money and he gives some of it back to me. "It is no good for me to have too much money. If someone thinks I am rich, they will try and steal from me. I can only take so much. I enjoyed being with you and your family."

I think of bringing him to the United States—he could go to school and study. I write my name, address, phone number, and e-mail on a piece of paper and give it to him. "Do not hesitate to contact me," I say.

We hug goodbye.

"So long, it was good to know you," he says.

On the road to Durban, we make two stops for shopping. Ashley buys a painting for her room and some earrings. Determined to bring the right thing home for Madeline and Cy, she has been shopping for them, much like she shopped for the beloved Miss Renee. She buys something, and then finds something else and buys that too. Ashley and Ricardo zero in on a variety store and beg the driver to stop. Sensing a serious shopper, the owner encourages Ashley to take her time, which she does, settling on what she thinks is the most perfect gift—dark-black baby dolls, rather large, male and female, anatomically correct. I tell her it's fine if she wants to get one for herself but I don't think it's the right gift for Amanda's parents.

"You're wrong," she says, point-blank. I then have to decide between asserting that I am not only the adult in charge but am footing the bill, or just sucking it up and letting her have her way. "All right," I say. "But this is it, this is the last perfect gift."

"I actually know what I'm doing," she says. "I saw it on one of my favorite shows, and then I looked it up for real life—fact checking, we call it at school. There was a study done in which demented old people were given dolls to care for and it made them much happier." She takes the dolls to the cash register.

"It made them feel closer and needed." At the last minute, as the shop owner is about to swipe my credit card, Ashley adds a blanket for each one. I say nothing and sign the charge. Ashley immediately takes the dolls out of the packaging, swaddles them, and calls them her twins.

Ricardo says he wants an all-too-real-looking toy gun—the kind that the police see and accidentally shoot you for.

"Absolutely not," I say.

"What are the twins' names?" Nate asks when we are out of the store and the owner is pulling the metal gate closed behind us.

"We'll have to wait and see," Ashley says.

We get back in the car, and are on the outskirts of Durban when things start to go wrong. The driver seems nervous: he's stepping on the gas, passing cars on a road that is for the most part lightly trafficked.

"Everything okay?" I ask.

"They are on my tail," he says.

"Who is on your tail?"

"A car," he says, pulling into oncoming traffic, attempting to pass a slow truck. Another car is heading right for us, and before we are able to pass, the driver has to cut back into our lane. As we approach a red light, the driver pauses, checks the intersection, but doesn't stop.

"Hey," I say, "we've got kids in the car."

"Trust me," he says. "Sometimes it is better not to stop."

I glance out the back; the other car did not stop either. There are three men in the car. Soon they are next to us, pushing us off the road. Ashley screams. Our driver keeps going, pushing the pedal to the floor; great clouds of dust rise up. The white car is beside us still, urging us farther off the road.

"Maybe we should just stop," I say.

"No," the driver says. "No good can come of it."

It goes on like this for what feels like a couple of minutes—maybe it's only thirty seconds—and then there is an enormous sound like a bang, and the car jerks to the right. The driver struggles to maintain control; slowly we roll to a stop, and the dust settles around us.

"Are we in an accident?" Ricardo asks.

"Flat tire," the driver says.

The three men stop behind us, get out of their car, and approach. As soon as they're within striking distance, they start banging on the car, rocking it from side to side—it's terrifying.

"Hijacking," Nate whispers. "Just give them your money."

"My babies, my babies," Ashley suddenly screams. "My babies aren't breathing."

I throw open the car door—knocking over one of the men, who'd been leaning against it. Ricardo, Nate, and Ashley jump out, carrying the brown babies wrapped in their blankets.

Ashley is on the side of the road, wailing, "My babies, my babies are not breathing."

Nate is hunched over the babies, pressing his ear to their chests, his mouth to the plastic baby mouths. Nate shouts—"Do you know CPR?"

Ricardo and I are on our knees at the side of the road, hunched over the brown baby boy, while Nate is compressing the baby girl's chest—shouting, "Breathe. Breathe."

"He's not doing well," Ricardo says. "Does anyone have a de-frigerator?"

The driver is still in the car, paralyzed by fear.

Ashley's scream has now turned from a piercing shriek into a high-pitched wail—as though she's summoned all the pain, the grief of Jane's death. She's on the side of the road, keening, truly hysterical, and I'm not sure what to attend to first. "You killed my babies," she wails again and again.

The hijackers are thoroughly perplexed; they get back into their car and speed away. We wait until they are far gone, and then Nate and I pick up the babies and go to Ashley, who is having a hard time calming down. Nate shows her the dolls. "Look," he says. "They're all right. Here, hold them." He puts the dolls in her arms. Ashley's breathing is shallow; she's wild-eyed, like she doesn't quite know where she is. I get the paper bag that the dolls came in. "Breathe into this," I say, crumpling the opening into a mouthpiece and putting it to her lips.

"That was amazing," Ricardo says, "and really scary."

We all nod. And when Ashley has caught her breath, we go back to the car. Our driver is still at the wheel, silent tears streaming down his face.

"Do you have a spare tire?" I ask.

He nods. We quickly change the tire and drive off—shaken.

"It's very common," Nate says. "Hijacking. Sometimes they take the car, sometimes they just want money."

"You were very lucky," the driver says. "Sometimes they want rich white people too."

"Are you okay?" I ask Ashley.

She nods but says nothing.

"What you did was pretty amazing. Where did that idea come from?"

"TV," she says. "You know how the TV was always on in our house."

"Yes," I say.

"Well, I always used to see these crying ladies, mamas and aunts, and it made me feel so sad and scared. They'd be standing in their doorways sobbing while a reporter tried to push his way in, or they'd be at some candlelight vigil where they'd fall to the ground. I don't know," she says. "It just kind of came over me."

"You did a very good job," I say.

"Like Academy Award–winning," Nate says.

"I can't believe that happened," Ricardo says. "And we all just leapt to action, like superheroes, like guys in the movies." He smiles broadly. "Did you like when I asked for the de-frigerator?"

I keep replaying the event in my head; the more I think about it, the more traumatized I am. I look at the children—they seem fine, as though they don't fully realize how wrong that could have gone. I think about what might have happened and know that in a blink I would have done anything to protect the children. For the first time I'm aware of how bonded to them I've become, how attached.

At the airport, my mood starts to sink. I am still upset about the attempted kidnapping and worried about going home. How do we maintain the sense of hope and possibility, the feeling of not holding back that infused our trip up until now? I'm suddenly filled with dread and wondering if it's just me. We have done so well outside of our home—outside of ourselves, up against a world so much bigger than we are. We banded together, working as a team, and I worry what will happen when we get home, when all bets and expectations are off.

The flight from Durban to Johannesburg is fine, and as we prepare to board our plane home, the children, still riding high, rush to buy last-minute things: Simba chips, sparkling lemonade, as though they will never see South Africa again. Johannesburg is like a transfer station for all humanity; fortunately, once again Sofia arranged for a people minder to shuttle us from one plane to the other.

I think of the house, of George and Jane. I know I am overtired, but it's like I am seeing it, feeling it all again, or maybe more like feeling it for the first time. Suddenly it is all alive for me, it is all right there, in gory detail, to be touched. It seems unreal—I can't believe it happened, I can't believe it was earlier this year and that we are now in a South African airport, waiting.

I think of what Londisizwe said about releasing what lives inside and realize that I did not drink my noontime tea. I will ask for hot water as soon as we're on board the plane. I think of Londisizwe, of the foul smell that escaped—the children laughing as I writhed in pain. "Very good," Londisizwe said the morning after the first dose, when I told him how ill I felt. "It is good that you feel sick—that is just the beginning of what is inside of you. . . . But you felt it," he says, happily slapping my shoulder. "That means you are not dead."

I am feeling it again at the airport; bile rises in my throat, tasting like a combo of fermented leaves and animal shit. I swallow it; it burns hot and sour going back down.

"Whose child is this?" A customs agent points to Ricardo.

"Ours," Nate says.

"I am their brother," Ricardo says.

I take out the letter from his aunt and give it to the agent, who calls another agent over. They ask me if I have a phone with international calling. I say yes and hand it to them so they can call the aunt, who says that Ricardo has not been kidnapped. Satisfied, the officer asks Ricardo if he had a good time in South Africa. "Did you ride on an elephant?"

"No."

"Bungee off a cliff?"

"No."

"What did you do?"

"I played soccer," he says.

"Good on you," the agent says, smiling, flashing loose tobacco bits in his teeth, as he hands back our passports and gives each of the children a small piece of hard candy, just the size you could choke on, which I immediately confiscate.

Our arrival in New York is delayed by thunderstorms; we circle the airport for what seems like hours and then land in Boston for gas and fly back to Kennedy. I text the pet minder from the tarmac at Logan to say we're delayed. He writes back, oddly chipper, "We are ready and waiting, looking forward to welcoming you." Something about his tone makes me nervous. "Everything okay?" I ask. "Just dandy," he texts back. Oh no. . . .

Landing in New York, I feel a kind of flat-footed relief that we are back in the land of Mets and Yankees, of traffic and abrasive people.

The United States Customs agent asks me to open my suitcase.

"Where are your clothes?" he asks.

"I gave them away," I say.

"Are you opening a business?" he quizzes, looking through all the merchandise acquired.

"No, I took three kids on a trip, and this is the stuff they got; there was no room for clothing."

"Why didn't you just buy another suitcase?"

"Didn't want another suitcase."

"You want to hold my babies?" Ashley asks the agent.

"Did you know that in South Africa they sell the clothing that we put in the recycle bins in church parking lots?" Nate says. "You think you're donating your old clothes to needy people in this country, but your clothing is being sold to impoverished people for profit."

"Guess it was like an educational trip," the customs man says, closing my bag and pushing it towards me for a zip-up.

"Fact-finding mission," Ashley says.

"I almost got circumcised," Ricardo offers. "I still want to but he said no." Ricardo gestures to me like I'm the bad guy.

"TMI," the man says, stamping our passports and urging us on.

"What does TMI mean?" Ricardo asks.

"It means some things are private," Nate says.

We walk outside, the heat smacks us down. The transition from the oxygen-less chill of the airplane to an eggs-on-the-sidewalk broiler is too abrupt, we are instantly sticky and cranky.

"You're late," says a rumpled guy holding a placard with "Silver" scrawled on it in grease pen.

"Weather delay," I say. "And we had to stop for gas."

The padded ride of the big black car gives me the uncomfortable sensation of floating, of being divorced from reality. I find myself craving the bumpy ride of the old Land Rover, with its homemade seat-belt contraption for the kids, harnessed like a backyard rocket ship.

We pull up at the house. The rosebushes by the front door are in bloom—a deep bloody red. A climbing White Dawn rose stretches up the front of the house, wrapping around the windows. Ashley picks a low pink rose and puts it to my nose. "Abraham Darby," she says. "They make perfume out of them."

I draw a deep breath; the heavy scent catches in my lungs—I breathe again, a little less deeply.

"Nice."

Ricardo insists on going to the front door and ringing the bell. Tessie barks excitedly.

Cheryl opens the door—she smiles.

It's hard to describe, but what I've been dreading instantly falls away. I don't think I've ever had that sensation before—a kind of darkness lifting, like sun coming out from behind a cloud—as literal and elusive as all that.

There are balloons, brightly colored streamers, and an enormous chocolate cake with "Congratulations on the Big BM" written in baby-blue script.

Cheryl, Sofia, Cecily, the pet minder and his sister, Madeline and Cy, Tessie and the cats, and a few people I've never seen before stand in a reception line.

"The house looks different," I say, pleasantly surprised.

"You bet it does," Cheryl says. "We gave you a makeover—painted the kitchen, living room, and dining room, rearranged the furniture, got a few new things like chairs that are easy for Cy and Madeline." I follow Cheryl through the house with my hand over my mouth, awed, saying, "I can't believe it. I just can't believe it," over and over again.

"The look on your face is priceless," Cecily says.

Yesterday, in Durban, I was dreading coming back to the house, falling into the same routines, but this is incredible, a wonderful welcome home. For the first time I'm part of a community. I stand there, eyes watering, and raise a giant glass of diet orange soda. "My heart is full."

There is pizza, soda, and cake so teeth-curdlingly sweet and richly American that I can't stop eating it. I have one slice and another and another until I am high. I cut the high with coffee and am shaking and dizzy.

"We got hijacked," Ricardo tells everyone. "Run off the road by some crazy men."

"Ashley and Ricardo saved us by pretending the dolls were her children and that they were injured," Nate says.

"What made you think to do that?" Cheryl asks.

"At my school they taught us," Ashley says.

"Taught you what?" I ask.

"In gym class there was a unit on self-protection. They taught us to go for the eyeballs and the ball balls and that if we were ever approached by someone who wanted us to get into a car or tried to hurt us in any way, we should act crazy. Or roll under a parked car. They said bad guys don't want to get down on their knees and try and pull you out from under a parked car, and that crazy people made them nervous. When I was younger I would always be thinking about what I'd do."

"Brilliant," Madeline says.

Terrifying—my thought repeats.

I make the tea Londisizwe sent home with me; it tastes of the South African ground, the dirt, and the air. I swirl the muslin bag in my cup and would swear that I see blue, green, and purple colors like an ersatz rainbow floating.

Later, I overhear Cheryl talking to Nate.

"What happened to your mom could have happened to any of us," she says.

"I doubt it," he says, not believing her.

"Trust me," she says, "I've lived longer than you."

"Do you really think it could have happened to anyone?" I ask Cheryl after everyone else has gone and she and I are in the kitchen trying to figure out the new cabinet organization system.

"I do," she says.

"I'm not sure how to take that. . . ."

"It's not about you, it's about human behavior. You know how there will be a report on TV of some woman who kills herself and her kids, and everyone acts like that's so shocking?"

I nod. "I guess so."

"What's shocking," Cheryl says, "is that it doesn't happen more often. What's shocking is that everyone says they fell in love with their child the minute it was born, what's shocking is that no one is honest about how hard it all is. So—am I surprised that some lady drowns her children and shoots herself? No. I think it's sad; I wish people had noticed that she was struggling, I wish she could have asked for help. What shocks me is how alone we all are."

She stops and looks at me carefully. "You look different."

I burp the combo of pizza, cake, orange soda, and Londisizwe's tea; I'm surprised blue-green smoke doesn't puff out of my mouth.

"I missed you," Cheryl says. "You know, we don't talk about a lot of things, it's all sex, sex, but I've been watching—you've come a long way."

"How so?"

"You're human now."

"And what was I before?"

"A two-by-four," she says.

I give Cheryl the gift I brought back for her—an old wooden phallus.

"A dildo?" she asks.

"It's an important African symbol."

"Is it supposed to make me think of you?"

"Not necessarily," I say.

"Did the children see you buy it?"

"Nope."

I lie on the sofa with Tessie at my feet, her muzzle on my hip, one cat behind me, another on my neck. As I'm falling asleep, I'm thinking of the village waking up for breakfast. . . .

For several days we are in a zone that is neither here nor there, existing outside of time and geography, decompressing—readjusting. The children sleep, eat, and watch TV.

For me it is a period of reorganization, realizing that things don't have to be as they have always been. I don't want to lose the openness, the sense of possibility that I felt on the trip. For Ashley, Nate, and Ricardo, things can never be as they were; the same is true in many ways for Madeline and Cy as well. For the first time, I understand that, as much as one might desire change, one has to be willing to take a risk, to free-fall, to fail, and that you've got to let go of the past—in other words, I have to finish my book. And then what? Go back to school; study religion, Zulu culture, literature? Become a suburban real-estate agent? This isn't so much about time on my hands as about life in my hands. And it's life as currency. Where am I going to spend it? What's the best value? I'm limited only by what I can dream and allow myself to risk, and by the very real fact of the children—I can't take off trekking the globe in search of myself. It seems pointless to go on for the sake of going on, if there isn't some larger idea, some sense of enhancing the lives of others.

At every opportunity, Ricardo or Nate retells the story of the hijacking; each time, the boys elaborate on what happened, what they were thinking, and what they would have done had the bad guys "tried something." Ricardo would have picked up rocks from the side of the road and thrown them at them—stoning them. Nate would have used his martial-arts training to "take them out." When asked, I offer that I would have attempted to negotiate—to talk them down—limited only by my ability to speak their language. Every time the boys retell the story, there is more to it. This is their unpacking of the event, the dawning of the realization that it was really fucking scary—that we could have been killed, and that, had we been kidnapped, had we been threatened with bodily harm, there would have been very little we could have done. Their retelling of the story makes it clear how powerless we really were. And the fact that when they retell it Ashley says nothing concerns me. Ashley in some ways was the most vulnerable of us—she was the girl, the child, the prize, and the heroine. The boys don't say anything about that part of it, but I think about it—a lot. And I think Ashley does too—which is why she starting screaming on the roadside, and why her survival training kicked in.

Africa seems both so far away and eternally present, like a scrim that I'm operating behind. I keep drinking Londisizwe's tea, which I think is helping.

I am cooking, cleaning, and packing three enormous duffels with a month's supply of sheets, pillows, bug spray, stamps and stationery, shirts, shorts, and bathing suits, while having an identity crisis—one I'm too old to have—against the backdrop of a heat wave and three children who are leaving for camp this weekend. Ashley and I talk about "relationships" away from home and reaffirm that there should be no trading of physical favors between adults and children—she shouldn't fool around with anyone more than three years older or younger, and what she does should be limited to "the soft arts," a phrase I coined for the occasion. Ricardo and I review the plan I've come up with in collaboration with a colleague of Dr. Tuttle's to wean him off his medications and add a variety of supplements. Nate and I go over his summer reading and extra-credit projects.

At dinner, Cy holds up a stalk of broccoli like it is a tree and asks, "What is this? Is it an evergreen tree? Is it a maple? If I can't identify it, I can't eat it."

"Broccoli," Ashley says. "Not a tree, a vegetable."

"Oh, right," Cy says.

"Take a brave taste," Ricardo urges, and he does.

"Oh, right," he says, "I forgot, I used to know broccoli. In fact, Madeline used to make a delicious sauce that went on it."

I ask Madeline if she minds my deviating from her recipe book.

"Not a bit," she says, "I never could eat that crap. I did it for the child."

On the third Saturday in July, Ashley leaves for a month of camp. On Sunday, we all drive the boys to the bus, which is parked in the church parking lot—the same church parking lot where Amanda found Heather Ryan's wallet in the trash. I see the trash cans in the corner but say nothing—there is really no one to say anything to. Ricardo's aunt Christina comes with us to say goodbye; she's made an enormous lunch for him to take on the bus. "Use it to make friends—share," I whisper as we're sending him off.

On the way home, we stop at a nursery and buy a trunkful of plants, a few new roses, petunias, geraniums, some cherry tomatoes, zucchini, and radishes, because Cy says he's always wanted to farm. We spend the afternoon in the yard.

"Do you miss Amanda?" I ask Madeline.

"It's tricky with children," Madeline says. "You have your ideas and they have theirs. There's a lot each of us doesn't know about the other."

We plant a rosebush for Amanda, and later I notice that Madeline frequently talks to it.

In the afternoon, while Cy is napping, Madeline tells me that she used to have a companion, "a very handsome neighbor whose husband also worked long hours in the city. She was thoughtful in ways that never occurred to Cy . . ." she says, her voice trailing off, leaving me wondering if they were lovers or just friends.

We have drinks before dinner: grilled cheese sandwiches and a summer gazpacho that Cy describes as soup waiting to mature and become a Bloody Mary.

There is enormous stillness in the house, an odd hollow. "Awfully quiet around here," Cy says.

And we all agree—it's too quiet.

That night, I come upon Madeline sitting in a rocking chair, her shirt up, a withered old breast extracted, and one of Ashley's babies at her breast. She looks so calm, so pleased with herself, that I do nothing more than drape a blanket from the sofa over her.

"She's still got the knack," Cy says.

"How long will they be gone?" Madeline asks, patting the baby.

"A month," I say.

Monday morning, the pet sitter's sister comes to spend the day with Cy and Madeline, and I return to work in the city.

The dress code at the law firm is relaxed for summer: khakis, seersucker suits, and men in short shirtsleeves looking more like accountants with pen protectors than the finest of legal minds.

The stories are in good shape. Ching Lan has worked hard: each has been transcribed, edited, and copyedited. I go over them once more, make a few small changes, and return them to Ching Lan before lunch for a final polish. Following up on my earlier conversation with Julie Nixon Eisenhower, I phone her and again suggest submitting them for publication. During the course of the afternoon, the decision is made to send them out through the firm to five or six places simultaneously. Given the sluggishness with which most things happen and the hot, then cold, response when I first suggested submission, I'm surprised by how quickly the idea gathers momentum.

One of the partners drafts a letter announcing an exciting new development in the field of Nixon scholarship, the short stories of RMN collected and edited by noted Nixon scholar Harold Silver. The draft is approved by Mrs. Eisenhower, and "SOB" goes out by messenger that afternoon.

In the later part of the evening, my telephone rings. "It's David Remnick from *The New Yorker*."

I pause, waiting for something more, like the rest of the recorded announcement: "We're calling you about an exciting subscription offer. . . ."

"I hope I'm not intruding," he says.

I take the phone into another room, leaving Madeline and Cy in front of the television.

"I knew your brother," Remnick, says, "not terribly well, but a bit."

"I didn't realize," I say.

"So listen," he says, "we're very interested in this story, but before we can go further I need to know if it's authentic."

"To the best of my knowledge it is," I say, and explain how I was contacted by the family and the provenance of the boxes.

"How many stories did Nixon write?" Remnick asks.

"There are approximately thirteen," I say, and then, suddenly, I'm not sure how much I can say without violating my confidentiality agreement.

"Are you still there?"

"I am," I say. "But I should probably go."

"How would you characterize the other stories?" Remnick asks. "Personal, political, similar in tone to the one we've got? Are they really fiction?"

I answer as carefully as I can. When we're finished, I feel filleted but admiring of his technique. I place a call to Mrs. Eisenhower at home. I picture her on the sofa of an old-fashioned formal living room, a faded testament to another era.

"She's not available—may I take a message?"

"Yes, I wanted to let her know I've had some calls from the media."

Twenty minutes later, Mrs. Eisenhower calls back. "I hope you won't take this badly," she says. "We've decided to withdraw the story. The response has been overwhelming; we're going to take a step back and consider what we're doing a bit more carefully."

"Was it anything to do with the quality of my work?" I'm compelled to ask.

"No," she says. "While I was surprised by the extent of some of your edits, when I looked them over in comparison to the longer versions I thought you did a fine job. It's a family issue; we're not sure that presenting my father as a fiction writer is consistent with the Nixon brand." There is a long pause. "As you might imagine, the concept of our brand is not something I thought of before; it used to be all about red and blue, Democrat or Republican. So we're going to give it some thought, and if we circle around, you'll be the first to know. Thank you for your enthusiasm—I know how fond of my father you are."

I press further, thinking this may be my last chance to glean some insight. "As you know, I've been working on this book about your father. I'm curious, has your sense of him changed over time? Did you ever discover things that made you uncomfortable?"

"My father was a complex figure who did what he believed was best for his family and his country. You and I will never know the depth of the challenges he faced. Thank you," she says, "and good night."

I e-mail Ching Lan and ask her to meet me at the office tomorrow at nine.

By 7 a.m., CNN is on the air with an old guy in Oregon holding up a notebook of Nixon's, which he claims his grandfather won when the former President was a poker-playing lieutenant commander in the navy. The notebook is dated 1944, which coincides with Nixon's service. The man reads an excerpt, which I immediately recognize as a fragment from "Good American People."

Leaving the house, I have the feeling someone is watching me. An unfamiliar car is parked nose-out in the driveway across the street; the driver gives me a creepy nod, and I swear I would hear a camera clicking if cameras still clicked.

The elevator in the midtown building that houses the firm stops on every floor, dispensing its Starbucks-cupped, muffin-topped human cargo. I am aware of someone behind me. "Cut too close to the bone," he says over my shoulder. I move to turn; the elevator goes dark and jerks to a stop. The other passengers gasp.

"We're under attack," a woman screams.

"Doubtful," a man mutters.

"There's always a snag," a familiar voice says calmly over my shoulder. "Always something a little bigger than you running the show."

"Tell me more," I say.

"What more can I say? I'm disappointed," he says. "My fifteen minutes are fading fast."

The elevator car lurches upward, the lights blink, the door opens. Passengers surge forward, rushing to get off, fearing there is more to come.

"Must have been a power surge," an old man who has remained in the car says. "That kind of thing used to happen all the time in the early 1970s; we called it John Lindsay's long arm."

Up ahead, scuttling towards the fire stairs, I spot a man in a blue windbreaker, tan khaki pants, and a baseball cap.

———

Ching Lan cries when I tell her the project is over. "I try to be no one when I come here. I am blank for you to write your books on."

"Don't worry," I say, "I will write you an excellent letter of reference."

She sobs.

"And I will hire you to copyedit my book."

"That's not why I am crying," she says. "My career will be fine: I have been offered full-time professional position on a volleyball team, but I told them I had to finish this first. I am crying because I see you love President Nixon very much—despite how he behaves. You work hard, you are so brave. Because of you I have been studying all about China. I learn so much more about my country than I ever knew. I learned about myself through you."

"Thank you," I say.

"What do you think happened?" Ching Lan asks.

"Fear," I say.

"Maybe later," Ching Lan says, "they will try again, and it won't seem so scary."

"Have you ever done that, frightened yourself with something?" I ask.

"No," she says. "I am not so scary. But my father, he doesn't like mice. A mice scares him very badly. He jumps on his pickle barrel like a little girl. My mother has to chase the mouse like a big cat. Can I ask you a question?"

"Of course."

"What do you like so much about China?"

"No one has ever asked me that before. This may sound odd, but I like how big it is—China has everything from Mount Everest to the South China Sea, and how many millions of people live there, how industrious they are, the depth of the history, how ancient, beautiful, mysterious, and other it is."

"Have you ever been there?" she asks.

"No," I say. "Have you?"

She shakes her head no. "My parents tell me they never want to go back, that what is there is from long ago, and that life is very hard. They are sorry for their relatives who stayed, and they carry the sadness with them, but they like it better here."

What I don't tell Ching Lan is that I am also secretly terrified of China: I imagine a dark side that doesn't value human life as deeply as I do. I worry that if I went there something would happen to me, I would get sick, I would rupture my appendix, I would end up doubled over in a Chinese hospital unable to care for myself. I imagine dying of either the gangrenous appendix or perhaps an infection following surgery performed under less-than-sterile conditions. I don't tell Ching Lan that I have nightmares that involve Chinese people wearing bloody lab coats, telling me in broken English that my turn is next. I also don't tell Ching Lan the one big idea that I've not yet articulated. I don't tell Ching Lan that I can't help but sometimes wonder if the current world economic crisis could be directly linked to Nixon's opening relations with China.

When we are done, Ching Lan and I say goodbye to Wanda and Marcel and turn in our badges; goodbye to the office, to the firm, to the men's room, to the elevator.

We go to the deli for lunch; I am not hungry, but her mother insists. "On the house," she says.

I have brought the trinkets from South Africa, which are now like going-away presents. I give Ching and her mother scarves I bought in the airport, and for her father a money clip. Her mother gives me a Hershey bar for the road. "Don't be strange," she calls after me as I'm leaving. "Come back soon."

It's 2 p.m. I've been home all of ten minutes and have changed my clothes and gone out to water the plants when Sofia pulls up.

"Unscheduled stop," she says as she's coming up the driveway. I'm sure she's been circling the block, waiting for me to come home.

"I keep thinking about you and the Big BM." She puts her hands on her hips with a staged sigh.

"It was better than I expected. I'm really indebted—thank you," I say.

"My pleasure," she says. "I learned so much about you and Nate and South Africa! How was the cake? I forgot to ask."

"Perfect."

"I'm glad," she says. "I wasn't sure it would work—different water, altitude, and ovens! I don't know if Sakhile told you, but I sent four extra boxes of cake mix so they could experiment ahead of time."

"You really did think of everything. And all the Jewish traditional elements—I had no idea that was going to happen."

She smiles proudly. "The bars and the bats, that's what I do," she says. "The jerseys looked great, didn't they?"

"Fantastic," I say, "and the whole thing with 'The Lion Sleeps Tonight'—amazing."

Sofia blushes and then reaches out and puts her hand on top of mine, which is at that moment squeezed into a fist holding the spray nozzle. I lose my grip, the nozzle slips out of my hand, and water shoots in a wild circle, abruptly stopping when the hose hits the ground.

"You know," she says, not noticing what happened with the hose, "ours is a much deeper relationship than the usual client-planner."

I say nothing.

"I'm really interested in you," she says.

"I can't."

"Are you not interested?" she says.

"I'm involved," I say, literally taking a step back.

"I thought she ran away."

I say nothing.

"Are you counting an affair with a married woman as involved?" she asks.

"It works."

She contemplates for a moment. "What about a three-way?"

I shake my head no.

"Not even tempted?"

"Can't."

We are in the backyard doing a strange dance: she takes one step towards, I take two steps back; she goes right, I go left.

"I don't believe you," she says. And, impulsively, she is on me, knocking me back into a lounge chair.

I see Madeline glance out the kitchen window into the backyard. "Cy," she screams, ear-piercingly loud. "Man down."

Like the college linebacker he once was, Cy is out the door and down the steps, charging towards Sofia, like a wrecking ball swinging in from the left. He hits hard, knocking her sideways.

A moment passes; Sofia stands up, dusts herself off, and looks at Cy. "Thank you," she says, "I must have tripped over a root." Turning to me she says, "Be in touch," and then she's gone.

I text Cheryl and tell her she was right about Sofia. She writes back asking if Sofia suggested a three-way. "Yes, how did you know?"

"She asked me first," Cheryl types back. "I said it was up to you but that she had to ask." There's a pause. "You know me," she writes. "I'm interested in all kinds of things. . . ."

Cheryl invites Madeline, Cy, and me to come for dinner later in the week—before heading off for a month in Maine. "A yar-becue," she types, "yard barbecue, just Ed and the boys."

Cy and Madeline are excited. "It's been a long time since we were invited to a dinner party," Madeline says, and then whispers loudly that after Cy's fall from grace they were dropped socially by pretty much everyone they knew.

"I didn't fall from anywhere," Cy mutters. "I stole some money. It's more common than you realize."

Madeline and I make a Jell-O mold—with pineapple chunks suspended in green, mandarine oranges in yellow, and green grapes in red. I've never made Jell-O before—it's magical.

We arrive at Cheryl's to find the yard thick with smoke and the dense perfume of hot meat.

The three boys, Tad, Brad, and Lad, are helping their father, who is hovering near something that looks like a cross between a fire pit and an antiquarian outhouse.

"We built our own smoker," Ed says, welcoming us.

"Is that backyard legal?" I ask.

He nods. "Homeowners have rights," he says.

"I hope your neighbors aren't vegetarian."

"I grew up smoking meat," Ed says. "My father and I would hunt and would dress whatever we killed—fowl, venison, and so on." Ed claps me on the back. "I miss having a hunting buddy," he says. "My boys never got into it—maybe that's something you and I could do?"

"Maybe," I say, sure that hunting with my sex-tress's husband is a bad idea.

We sit down to dinner. I've got Madeline and Cy one on each side of me; Tad, Brad, and Lad take the other side of the picnic table, their swelling frames threatening to tip the balance entirely. The boys pass bowls of potato salad, coleslaw, and corn bread while Ed opens the smoker, nearly asphyxiating us all.

"You made all of this?"

Ed and Cheryl both nod. "We like to do it ourselves."

Everything is delicious, beyond pleasant, nearly heavenly. "I don't know how you do it," I say to Ed, when Cheryl is away from the table clearing plates. "I'm a lucky man, Har," he says, having coined a new nickname for me—Har.

"Cheryl and me, we get each other—the good and the bad. Life is long, what's the point of being judgmental? I don't have any hard, fast rules—be happy, enjoy."

And I can't figure out if Ed is a genius or a moron.

Cheryl comes back with our Jell-O mold decanted onto a plate—shaking like a fat lady—and the boys bring out a tub of homemade peppermint ice cream.

We dig in, and all is good until Cy asks for a third helping, and then, when he's done, remembers that he's horribly lactose-intolerant, and we make a mad dash for home.

D espite the summer heat, the ninety-degree days, Madeline and Cy are always cold; they wear cardigans, inside and out. I extract the old window screens from the basement, put them in, and skip turning on the air conditioning. It is like a summer from the past: the heat builds during the day. Tessie lies on the tile floor in the front hall, panting; in the afternoon there are thunderstorms, and at night there's the melancholy tap-tapping sounds of bugs on the screens.

It's near the end of July; everything is elongated, made languid and slow-motion by the heat. Madeline and Cy retreat into a world of long ago. There is something beautiful about their slowly evaporating ghostlike narration, which shows marks of revision, erasure, and locked doors—events long ago put away.

I take them to concerts at the bandshell in the park and watch them dance across the lawn like it is thirty years ago.

"What's your secret to a long marriage?" I ask Madeline one morning.

"We don't burden each other with our feelings," she says. "A woman friend of mine called it staying in the dance."

"The dance?"

"Of courtship. When you are courting, you are your best self, but then, too often, we devolve and reveal our worst selves. Why would you want the person you live with to wake up seeing your worst self every day?"

One day, when Cy is annoyed at one of the babies from South Africa, he fires him, tells him to "box it up and get out. There's no future for you here, sitting around thinking it's going to come right to you. It doesn't work that way, buster. I don't want to see you around here anymore," he says.

"That's not your baby," Madeline says, grabbing the plastic infant from him. "That one is mine."

"Mine," Cy says, surprisingly possessive, grabbing the baby back.

Just as I'm thinking I'll have to intervene, they make up.

"Fine," Cy says, annoyed. He looks the baby square in the eye. "I'll give you another chance, but don't blow it." From then on, Cy walks around carrying the baby under his arm—sideways, like a football. He takes it pretty much everywhere, calling it his brown brother and occasionally his wife.

I give myself until the children come home to finish the book. I set up shop on an old card table in the attic—surrounding myself with box fans that create windy white noise. I weigh down my papers with rocks from the garden. I find the heat inspiring, like being in a boxing gym. Stripped to a pair of gym shorts, I type as rivulets of sweat trickle down my face, the meaty smell of myself ripening pushing me to work harder—ready or not, it needs to be over.

Using a sharp blade to crack the old paint off, I pop open the small window up in the eaves. The glass is wavy; the view doused in rainbow-reflected light makes everything look better than it is. I move about cautiously, careful not to bump my head on the beams. There are things up there from long ago, a World War II uniform, old teddy bears, an ancient crib that I dust off and bring down to Madeline, who immediately takes it and sets up a nursery by her side of the bed for the babies.

The phrase "while you were sleeping" takes on new meaning as I plow through the pages from the past fifteen years, noticing that everything I've written is couched in a protective tone, hemming and hawing, positing and pulling back. Time to rip out the stops—fuck it. Dick Nixon was the American man of that moment, swimming in the bitter supposition that for everyone else things came easily. He was the perfect storm of present, past, and future, of integrity and deceit, of moral superiority and arrogance, of the drug that was and is the American Dream, wanting more, wanting to have what someone else has, wanting to have it all.

I conclude that the 1970s court of public opinion was bourgeois and unforgiving in nature; once a politician's fate had been decided and his number in the global historic pecking order had been assigned, there was precious little room for movement. I wonder if it would be different now: if Nixon owned up (deeply unlikely) and attributed his behavior, his failings, to a traumatic event—growing up in the Nixon household—would he have been exonerated? Is the rise or fall of popularity or historic significance a fixed game?

As I close in on the ending, I find myself thinking about Claire. Imagining if Claire could see me now . . . Would she be impressed? When I stop to think really hard about it, nothing I'm doing would make any sense to her. My fantasy moves on to Ben Schwartz, my former department Chair—Ben, who thought I'd never finish the book—what would Ben think? I belch. The flavor is overwhelming—Londisizwe's tea! This is the last of the pain, the foul smell coming out; these thoughts are the path of the old mind needing to be left behind.

I call Tuttle. It's the middle of the afternoon in early August; he answers his phone.

"Why are you there?" I ask. "I thought shrinks took August off?"

"I'm a contrarian," he says. "I take July. In August I make my nut working overtime, covering for my colleagues who prefer Wellfleet."

We make a time to meet. His office is freezing cold. Across the edge of his desk where last time there was a collection of cups from Smoothie King, there's a row of Dunkin' Donuts coffee cups. "They opened a drive-thru," he says.

"I'm almost finished with the book," I say. "But it's like I'm waiting for something to happen, some kind of relief or sense of relief."

"Are you pleased with your work?"

"I want someone to read it."

"Who is your fantasy, your muse?" he asks.

"Richard Milhous Nixon," I say.

"And what would you want him to say?"

" 'Thank you'?" I suggest, plaintively. " 'The world needs more men like you, Silver. You're a good man.' "

"Do you see Nixon as a father figure?"

"I wouldn't rule it out," I say after a long pause.

"Why can't you just say yes?" Tuttle asks. "What would it mean to you?"

I look to the floor, I break out in a cold sweat, I can't meet Tuttle's eye.

"What would it mean?" Tuttle asks again.

"I love him but I think he did wrong," I sputter.

"Do you say that in your book?"

"Not so much."

"Why not?"

"George is a paranoid bully who doesn't see what's good for him and looks at me as the enemy no matter what I do." I blurt it out, and then there's a very long silence.

"And Nixon?" Tuttle asks.

"I'm not sure Nixon could psychically afford to accept that he did anything wrong. He desperately needed to think of himself as decent."

"Do you think your book is good?"

"Sometimes I think it is a brilliant, reinvigorating discussion not only about Nixon but about an entire era. Other times I wonder if it's just a cultural hairball that took years to cough up."

"Among the living, whose opinion matters to you?"

"Remnick?" I suggest, tentatively. For whatever reason, since the phone call I've been fixated on Remnick.

"Are you really finished?"

"Pretty much. I'm just waiting for something to happen."

"Waiting for something to happen? Like what?"

I have no answer.

"Isn't it up to you," Tuttle suggests, "to make something happen?"

We sit in silence for the rest of the session. As I'm leaving, he hands me a folded mint-green sheet of paper. I'm blank.

"The Psychiatric Evaluation form from the New York Department of Social Services," Tuttle says.

"Thank you."

"I'm open to working with you further," Tuttle says. "Let me know if you'd like to schedule something."

From Tuttle's office, I go visit my mother. In the parking lot of the home, they have set up a large aboveground pool with a wide cedar deck, umbrellas, chairs, and a long wheelchair ramp from the front door of the facility to the edge of the pool, where residents can be deposited onto a slide, and—"wheee"—down they go. "More," a man shouts. "I want to go again. It's like Coney Island."

I spot my mother under an umbrella, holding court in a black-and-white polka-dot swimsuit, wearing Jackie O–style sunglasses, and sipping a plastic tumbler of iced tea.

"Ma," I say. "You look ten years younger."

"I always liked being by the shore," she says.

"Where's your husband?" I ask.

Looking around, I realize that all the men and women are wearing variations on the same suit—basically, a men's version and a women's. All together, they look like a geriatric circus act.

"Big sale," one of the aides says. "Buy one at full price, get as many more as you want for half off—we bought them all."

"Geronimo," a man says, jumping in.

"Don't forget," the lifeguard calls out. "No pushing, no splashing, no pooping in the pool."

"So how are you?" I ask my mother.

"Good," she says. "We went on a field trip to a lobster place and had the early bird, all you can eat. I myself don't eat so much, but Bobby thought it was well worth it. And you, where have you been?"

"South Africa," I say.

She looks at me strangely.

"Nate had been there on a school trip and wanted to go back, so we decided to have his bar mitzvah over there."

"And you didn't invite your mother?"

"I did," I say. "You sent back the RSVP card with some nasty remark about shvartzes written on it."

"I'm entitled to my opinion," she says.

"If you can call it an opinion," I say. "We have another word for it. . . ."

"And what's that?"

"Racist?"

"Shhh," she says. "Not so loud, someone will hear you." We're quiet for a moment. "I don't get it," she says.

"What?"

"Why are you so competitive? Why do you feel like you have to outdo everyone? The wedding at the Pierre"—that was George, not me—"holiday party at the Four Seasons"—George again—"isn't it enough to have a regular bar mitzvah and a nice Sisterhood Luncheon, like we did for you?"

"Actually," I say, not even taking on the George of it all, "my bar mitzvah was a shared event with Solomon Bernstein."

"It was good for your father's business—he got several new clients."

"And several people got food poisoning."

"No one died," she says.

We say nothing for a few minutes. I see Bob in the pool, wearing floaties and talking with another woman.

"So," I say, nodding towards Bob, "is the honeymoon over?"

"It's only just begun," my mother says.

Sofia calls to say she wants me to meet her for coffee. "We need to talk."

"In person?" I ask nervously, thinking our last encounter was a close call.

"I'm not going to pressure you," she says. "I'd like to review the event and expenses, plus update you on what funds have been received. Also, we never discussed my fee."

"Fine," I say. We make a plan to meet in a local diner.

"I hope you're not mad," she says. "I made a Web page about you and the kids and your trip. I set it up so strangers who read about you and Nate can donate. Sakhile once said something to me, there are strangers, people we don't know, who care about us. I found that interesting."

I nod.

"It's amazing—more than a hundred people have sent in contributions, everything from ten dollars to five hundred dollars, people who want nothing in return."

"How much is in the BM account?" I ask.

"As of yesterday, gifts total twenty-seven thousand, three hundred eighty-nine dollars, and eighty-six cents. I think Nate is going to have to pay taxes. I had no idea it would be this much—otherwise we could have set up some kind of nonprofit. Do you want to deduct expenses from the gross?" she asks.

"No," I say, "I am paying for the bar mitzvah separately; whatever gifts were received should be absent of a processing fee."

"It's an enormous amount—I wonder if we should give it all at once—I wonder what should happen?"

"I'll ask Nate when he's home from camp."

"Okay," she says. "So about my fee . . ."

I'm thinking she's coming in for the kill, this is how she's going to get me. . . . I wouldn't capitulate, so now she's going to sting me. I brace myself.

"Usually I charge between thirty-five hundred and five thousand, but in this case, I want to donate a portion of my usual fee. Fifteen hundred would be fine, if that works for you?"

I'm flush with surprise. "That's so nice of you—really generous," I say, embarrassed by what I'd been thinking.

"I wasn't kidding when I said I enjoyed working with you—it meant a lot to me," she says.

"Thank you," I say.

And now she's giving me the look.

"Please," I beg, "you promised."

"Can't blame a girl for trying," she says, smiling.

Every Friday night, I take Madeline and Cy out for Chinese food. Mr. and Mrs. Gao, the owners of the restaurant, ask if I know about any available real estate—the commute from Brooklyn is getting to be too much.

It occurs to me that I could rent them Cy and Madeline's house, which would at least cover the ongoing maintenance expenses. On Saturday morning, I take Mr. and Mrs. Gao to see the house.

"It is an American Dream house," Mrs. Gao says. "It is *Leave It to Believer*," she says. I can tell from the way Mrs. Gao is touching things that she is moved by the very things about the décor that agitated me—to her it is like a museum of the American Dream.

"We can't afford this place," Mr. Gao tells his wife.

"You can," I say. "We'll make it work." I ask what he pays currently and if that includes utilities. I offer him the house, including utilities, for a hundred dollars less a month.

"You drive hard bargain," Mr. Gao says.

His wife slaps him. "Why are you always such a cheapskate?" She wags her finger at him. "Don't ruin this for me." And she turns to me. "Thank you," she says. "We are very grateful."

"I hope you will be happy here."

The August days are bakingly hot, airless; every afternoon is punctuated by thunderstorms that start between five-thirty and six, often knocking the power out. I buy extra flashlights, batteries, and candles and make sure to have dinner cooked by five—just in case.

"What did Amanda die of?" Madeline asks one afternoon as the black clouds are quickly thickening and the first low rumbles of thunder echo through the neighborhood.

"Amanda?" I repeat, startled.

Madeline nods. "What did she die of? I keep thinking of the children with their mother gone—we must take good care of them."

I realize that she has conflated Amanda and Jane into a single missing person.

"It was sudden." I say, "Something in her head."

"She always had headaches," Madeline says.

"It couldn't have been anticipated," I say.

"We had another child," she says, "an infant who passed before she was a year. Amanda and her sister don't remember her—they were quite young when the baby came."

"I think they knew," I say softly, thinking of Amanda's attachment to Heather Ryan.

"It's possible," she says. "They certainly knew something was wrong, Amanda kept making me get-well cards."

The media exposure generated by the withdrawn Nixon short story is enough to get me access to agents. I strike up a correspondence with Franklin Furness, a fellow from an old political family who runs a mid-sized literary agency with a distinct interest in American history and politics. "We like representing those from the extremes—it's the center that frightens me," Franklin Furness writes. "Nothing good comes out of the middle—the action is at the edges." Furness agrees to represent the book and will commence submission as soon as I forward him the final draft.

At 5:37 a.m. on an August Thursday, a time remembered only because that particular clock permanently stopped, a bolt of lightning struck the maple tree next to the house, splitting it with an explosive crash that only the heavens could have wrought. The tree was cleaved in a way that left one half standing as it had for the last half-century and the other half slumped against the house, one fat branch jutting through the wall of what had been George's office, which suddenly looked like an arboretum.

The concussive crash, and simultaneous smell of something burning, hurls me out of my narrow bed in the maid's room, next to the kitchen. I grab the fire extinguisher from under the sink and frantically search the house. After I discover the tree in George's office, I dash upstairs to find Madeline's arms wrapped around Cy, who is sitting bolt upright in bed, screaming, "Papa's fired the derringer."

"Nightmare," Madeline says, patting her husband's back. I hurry back into the hall and pull down the attic stairs.

The smell of ozone, of burnt eggs, of gunpowder, of molecules ripped apart and rearranged, fills the attic.

My laptop sits on the card table, the sleeping screen no longer shows a slide show of the South Africa trip; it is blinking, stuttering, searching for itself— blank.

The wall around the outlet where the cord is plugged in is black; there are fiery singe marks a good foot or more up, marking the boards with a sooty electrical fingerprint.

There is no fire.

Tessie is at the bottom of the attic stairs, whining. Madeline and Cy are standing there in their nightclothes, looking upward. "Shall we call in the cavalry?" Cy asks.

Is this what I've been waiting for?

The book is done. Cooked. There is no more need for perfection, it has simply ended—or, more specifically, electronically imploded.

It's not as though the version on the computer was my only copy: there are others, various versions, iterations, three on flash drives, including one buried in the backyard in a time capsule—a fireproof box that I bought at the hardware store—and another e-mailed to the desk of Franklin Furness.

At another point in time, I would have been hysterical at having lost the changes since my last backup, or perhaps paralyzed, stunned dumb by the blinking eye of the black screen. Curiously, I feel relieved. It is as though something I carried with me for so long has vaporized, a great cloud lifting. I don't have to do anything—beyond accepting that it is over. Finis. I am free. And I am oddly exhilarated.

And then it occurs to me—was the book the foul thing that Londisizwe said I was holding on to, the thing I'd been keeping close like a companion? Is this what lived inside and needed to come out? Is this it?

Just before the children are due to return from camp, a letter is forwarded from the hospital where Jane died, with a Post-it attached. "This arrived a couple of weeks ago, sorry to be delayed in sending it, I was on vacation. Do not feel pressured to engage if the enclosed is not of interest to you. But if you want to respond—I am happy to act on your behalf as a confidential courier. Hope you're having a good summer. Best." And it is signed by the doctor who was in charge of Jane's case.

Hello, My name is Avery and I am writing to thank you for the gift of life. I live in Ohio and was on the wait list for a heart and lungs for a long time before I received your donation. At the time, I didn't know if I would stay alive long enough to even have this chance to write to you. Through your tragic loss, I received an incredible gift, a second chance at life, and want to thank you and your family. I hope that you find comfort in knowing what the heart and lungs of your loved one have provided for me— since the transplant I have gained great strength and can now breathe well enough to walk and to climb a flight of stairs. I was able to return to school and finish my undergraduate degree—it is my hope to continue my education and become a social worker or perhaps a poet. And the big news, I am engaged to be married. For years I have been in love with a wonderful man, but I did not feel able to accept his proposal until I knew there was a chance we might be able to build a long life together. And more recently I have been able to travel, we went to California. It was amazing. Anyway, part of my reason for writing is to say that if you are open to the idea I would very much like to meet you and thank you in person. I know that this is a difficult thing—but it is my hope that seeing the opportunity and joy you have given me will give you some comfort in dealing with the loss of your loved one. I look forward to hearing from you.

Avery

I read the letter and I can't help but cry. I cry for Avery, for Jane, for Ashley and Nate and Ricardo. I cry for everyone. And then I stop. I stop because Cy and Madeline are waiting for me to take them somewhere, Tessie wants her lunch, and the children will be home from camp in a few days and there are things to do. I put the letter away.

The children return, stronger and more confident than before. Ricardo arrives wearing medals for swimming, archery, boating. He is golden brown, slimmer, taller, with a golf swing and a tennis serve, and he is on no medications, instead a regimen of activity plus amino acids and some kind of fish-oil swirl that he says tastes like melted ice cream—I try it and almost vomit. Ashley has breasts that I swear weren't there four weeks ago. She's a funny mix, part girl, part woman, and painfully self-conscious. And on Nate's upper lip there's an unmistakable dark fuzz, and depth to his voice. They are filled with stories of friendships, adventures, and secret languages, the high of the South Africa trip extended through their time at camp, and I see not only growth but a new kind of thinking—things are possible.

Ricardo presents me with a wallet he made for me, pieces of leather whip-stitched together, my initials hand-tooled on the front. Ashley has constructed a shadow box that looks like a TV with a small painted portrait of her mother on the screen. Nate brings remains of animals he found in the woods around his camp—the skull of a squirrel, the skin of a snake—and a dozen owl pellets, which he cracks open, showing us how to identify what animal the owl has eaten.

There are only two weekends left before school starts. I gather the children and tell them about Avery.

"Would you like to meet her?"

"Yes," they say unequivocally.

"So," Ashley asks, pushing for further clarification, "is she like a new mom?"

"No," I say.

"A stepmom?" she tries again.

"Not so much."

"A transplant mom?"

"How about she's just a lady from Ohio," Nate says. "She's not related to us."

"But she has Mom's heart and lungs—don't you think that changes who she is? I mean, now she's more like Mom than anyone, except us."

Nate shrugs. "You know what, Ashley? She can be whatever you want her to be."

"Thanks," Ashley says.

I explain it to the children, and then I try and explain it to Cy and Madeline, who don't quite follow—the best they can manage is to understand that this woman, Avery, was bequeathed something precious that used to belong to Jane.

Cy seems nervous. "I just sold the insurances," he says repeatedly. "I didn't deal with technicalities. When they died, they didn't usually come back. Isn't this more of a trusts-and-estates issue?"

"She's just coming to say thank you," I say.

"Why didn't my mother get to give her organs away?" Ricardo asks me privately that evening. "Is that something only rich white people can do?"

"No," I say, "anyone can do it—but you have to plan ahead, and you have to die in a way that preserves your organs, so they are viable."

"What does 'viable' mean?"

"Your mother died on the scene after a car accident; Jane died in a hospital, where they could keep giving her body oxygen, making sure her organs stayed healthy, and then they removed them as quickly as possible."

"Do you have to be dead to give your organs?" Ricardo asks.

"Usually," I say. "There are certain organs that you have two of, like your kidneys, that you can give even if you're alive."

"I want to give an organ," Ricardo says.

I nod. "That's a lovely idea," I say. "But you can't give any organs away until you're a grown-up."

"Fine," he says, "but as soon as I'm grown-up, I'm giving it all away."

On Saturday at noon, we meet Avery and her fiancé, at the hamburger pub in town. It's a place George used to like to go, because they knew him and always seated him so he could see both of the TVs simultaneously. I've always hated it, because it seemed to be the place where miserable husbands went when they ran away from home—even if only for an hour—to soak themselves in the comfort of other bastards and beer.

Avery and Mark, her fiancé, are already there; I see them nervously pawing through the crème mints by the register when we walk in.

She is small, with short close-cropped hair, like a Jean Seberg or Mia Farrow.

"You must be Avery," I say as we approach.

"Wow," she says. "Look how many of you there are."

"I'm Ashley," Ashley says, extending her hand.

"Nate," Nate says, hanging back, just giving a wave.

"Ricardo," he says, shaking hands with both Avery and Mark.

I introduce Cy and Madeline and suggest that we take a table.

"This feels good," she says, "very familiar. It's almost like I've been here before."

"It's a hamburger joint," Mark says. "They're pretty much all the same."

"I like this one," Avery says.

When the waitress takes our order, Avery asks for a burger well done, and Ashley comments that that's the way her mother used to like them too. Avery smiles.

"So how come you needed the transplant—is that an okay question to ask?" Nate wants to know. "I mean, it's fine if you don't want to answer, if it's too personal."

"It's fine," Avery says. "I have a congenital syndrome. It got worse when I became a teenager. I couldn't go out in the summer because I wasn't supposed to sweat; I couldn't do any sports, no salt, lots of diuretics, Lasix, Digoxin, iron, vitamins. Sudden death was always a threat. I would leave the house in the morning and wonder if I'd be coming back. That's when I started writing poems," she says. "I wrote poems to manage the stress. I even wrote one about coming here today."

Our drinks arrive. Ricardo breaks the ice by shooting the paper wrap from his straw across the table at Mark.

"With the transplant," Nate continues, "do they give you a choice of who it's going to come from? Like, you can get it from this woman or that guy, or . . . ?"

She shakes her head. "There's a very long waiting list for organs. You wait and you wait, and then the doctors have to think it's a good match, and, funny enough, women don't do well with men's hearts."

"Where did you two meet?" Ashley asks, looking at Mark.

"In a cardiologist's waiting room," Mark says. "I was there with my grand-mother."

"Remind me again, how are you related to us?" Madeline wants to know.

"They're not," Nate says, firmly.

"So what's it like in Ohio?" I ask, trying to manage the awkwardness, wondering if I'm the only one noticing.

"Nice," she says. "Very nice. I just realized, this is the first time I ever left the state with my new heart."

"Did they tell you anything about her?" Nate asks.

"No," she says. "It's all kept confidential—it's a big deal, some people really don't want to know. Is there something you'd like to tell me?"

The hamburgers arrive.

"My mother would be happy for you. She liked doing things for others. She was a very generous person," Nate says, his voice cracking with emotion.

When Avery has to go to the bathroom, Ashley goes with her. Later, Ashley tells me that Avery showed her the scar—it goes right down the middle of her, like a zipper.

Left alone at the table, Mark tells us how grateful Avery is to be meeting us. "She's had a hard time since the transplant; she's different in some way and can't quite put a finger on it—she has bad dreams, dark thoughts."

"It's a big surgery," I say.

"Dying is worse," he says, and there's nothing left to say.

"I just really want to thank you," Avery says when she comes back from the bathroom. She doesn't sit down again. It's one of those meals that are over before anyone's really eaten.

Cy wraps his burger and slips it into his jacket pocket; Ricardo sees him and does the same, adding his waffle fries as well. As we're leaving, Ashley asks if Avery and Mark would like to come over to the house. Nate looks stricken.

"Sure," Avery says. "Just a little visit."

I lead the way, with Mark driving on my tail up the hill towards home. I glance at Nate in the rearview mirror. "You okay, kiddo?" I ask.

"No," Nate says flatly. "I'm not okay."

When I pull into the driveway, Nate is the first one out of the car and into the house. The front door hangs open like a hole into the house, an open wound.

Mark and Avery park at the curb as Tessie comes bounding out and stands at the edge of the grass, barking.

"She doesn't like people?" Avery asks.

"She's very friendly, but she won't cross the line," Madeline offers.

"The line?" Mark asks, coming around to Avery's side of the car.

"The invisible fence," I say.

Avery gets out of the car. She stands looking up at the house, but, suddenly unsteady, she wobbles and sits back down in the front seat. "Owww. Owwww."

"What?" Mark asks.

"Tessie," I implore, "stop barking."

"My head," Avery says.

"Did you bang your head?" I ask.

"No," she says, "it just suddenly hurts."

"Do you often have headaches?"

"No," Avery says, as if annoyed with all my questions. "It's not like a headache. It's like something's banging on my head, hitting me. Oh, I don't feel good, I don't feel good at all."

"Just a second," Ashley says, running back up to the house to get something.

"Is this the house?" Avery asks.

"This is where they live," Mark says.

"Yes," I say, knowing full well what she's getting at.

"I think my head hurts because this is the place where it happened," Avery says.

"Seems like a stretch," Mark says. I hear him struggling with the idea that his fiancée is not who she once was.

"It's real," I say, hoping to reassure both of them. "Jane's heart knows. . . ." I tell them about cellular memory and repeat the story of the girl who got the heart of a ten-year-old murder victim: "The transplant recipient began having terrible nightmares, and ultimately the police were brought in; the girl's nightmares were accurate and provided the clues that solved the murder."

"I think we should go," Mark says.

Ashley comes running out with a gift she's wrapped for Avery. "It was something I made for my mom; I want you to have it."

"Thank you," Avery says, her headache clearly getting worse.

Mark starts the car and puts it in gear. It lurches forward—we all stand back.

"I've got to go, honey," she says to Ashley. "Stay in touch. . . ."

"I'm not entirely clear what she wanted," Madeline says, watching the car drive away.

"I never want to see her again," Nate says, when we're all back inside. "It was too weird, like one of those movies you see the trailer for—by M. Night Shyamalan."

Nate is up in the night. I hear footsteps and intercept him in the living room. "What's up?" He doesn't answer. "Are you sleepwalking?"

He shakes his head no, and sits on the living-room sofa. "Why did she come? It's like she wants us to tell her it's okay that she has Mom's heart—that we're sorry she has feelings about it, like we're supposed to make her feel better? How about it's not okay, none of it is okay? How about no one thought for one minute about me or Ashley when all this was happening?" He goes on and on. I don't interrupt. I look at him. I listen. I pat his back. He rocks back and forth, downloading all of it—erupting. Every feeling he's ever had is coming out of him—at various points he's crying, or wild-eyed and screaming. Ashley and Ricardo come to the top of the stairs and ask if everything is all right.

"Yes," I say. "Nate is very upset, but he'll be fine." In truth, I'm not sure. He's exploding; everything he tried so hard to keep in for so long is coming out.

Tessie is with us in the living room, helping too. At some point during the night, we start talking about the trip to South Africa—it seems to calm Nate to revisit our adventures. I tell him about the Web page Sofia made for the trip, how she posted pictures and stories about the experience culled from the e-mails and photos I sent, and that strangers had been visiting the site and making donations. I tell him that there's close to thirty thousand dollars in the account.

"You're just saying that to make me feel better."

"Nate, it's one-thirty in the morning. Why would I lie?"

I take him to his father's computer, show him the page and the comments people have made about being so impressed to see such a young person committed to making social change.

"Is the money real? Do we actually have it?"

"Yes," I say, "it's in a bank account in your name."

"Can I call Sofia tomorrow and thank her? I didn't know how involved she's been. I mean, it's really kind of amazing that someone who had nothing to gain was so supportive."

"Yes," I say, "it's unusual."

"And we should make a time to talk with Sakhile about what to do with the money," Nate says. "Can we e-mail him now?"

"Sure," I say, and we do.

"How about trying to get some sleep?" I suggest. He nods. "Listen, I'm really sorry about today—I wouldn't have suggested it if I thought it would be so upsetting."

"I didn't know it would be," Nate says.

I follow him upstairs and down the hall to his room. "Will you read to me?" he asks.

"Sure," I say. He picks a book from when he was younger off his shelf and crawls into bed. I read to him like he's a little boy, and while I am reading, Ricardo wakes up again and also listens, and when I am done, I kiss Nate good night on the forehead, and then I kiss Ricardo too.

"Do I have to worry about her?" Nate asks as I'm walking out of the room.

"No," I say.

By morning, Sakhile has e-mailed back several times, wondering when we can talk—anytime is good for him. Wondering how much money is coming their way and when they might get it.

We schedule a village meeting via Skype, and I leave it to Nate to tell them about the Web site and the donations.

"How much?" Sakhile asks excitedly via Skype.

Nate smoothly defers a direct answer. "Quite a bit," he says. "Enough to make a difference."

And quickly the conversation becomes about want. From South Africa we hear that the village should have a car or a bus that would run back and forth to the bigger cities.

"A bus is a way out," Nate says. "Let's think of ways in—things that make life better in the village."

"Cable television and a really big TV?" one of the South Africans suggests.

"I'm thinking more along the lines of having a well dug," Nate says, his voice becoming increasingly tense, sad.

"That would be very expensive," Sakhile says.

"Exactly," Nate says, "a once-in-a-lifetime opportunity."

The conversation continues, with the South Africans talking about all the things they might buy, from electric guitars to Vespas and refrigerators.

"Enough," Nate says. "You are becoming just like us: you aren't thinking of your village, of your parents, your children, your future; you're thinking that you want a fancy car and a gigantic TV."

We are all silent.

"The child is pointing the way," Londisizwe says.

"We are not going to resolve this tonight," I say. "Let's give it some thought and talk again soon."

"I feel terrible," Nate says when we are off the computer. "I created a monster."

"You didn't create it," I say.

"Well, then, I fed it," Nate says, disgusted with himself.

"No one is immune. It is human nature to want, for each generation to aspire to more. People confuse things with achievement, with other kinds of progress. It's the measure of success."

"Whoever has the most toys wins?" Ricardo says.

"You don't have to give them the money," I suggest.

"It's their money," Nate says. "It was given to me for them. Whatever we do with it has to be for the village, for the future—food, housing, ensuring the quality of the water supply."

"I'm impressed that you don't just walk away," I say.

"I can't walk away," Nate says. "I started this."

"And you can't blame them. They're from another country, but they live in the same world as we do."

Labor Day weekend is spent packing and shopping for school supplies.

Come Tuesday, we all make the pilgrimage with Nate back to the academy. Nate seems to enjoy giving Cy and Ricardo a tour, and Ricardo asks if one day he might get to go to a school like this. "Yes," I say. "If you want to."

We get Nate set in his dorm room, Cy gives him twenty bucks "mad money," and we head home. The next day, Ashley and Ricardo start at the public school down the road, and by the end of the week Madeline and Cy are signed up for three days a week at a program for seniors.

Even my mother places herself in the autumn mix, informing me that she and her husband are going back to school. They've signed up with OLLI, an organization devoted to Lifelong Learning, and are taking classes in political science and radio theater.

Nobody seems to notice that I am the only one who has not gone back to school. I am now officially unemployed; the feeling is disconcerting—I manage the stress by organizing everyone else.

The house is filled with life. There are people coming and going constantly.

Ricardo gets a pet frog and a turtle and begins taking drum lessons. Ashley resumes her piano lessons. On weekends there are activities such as leaf raking; Cy and Ricardo enjoy creating enormous piles and then either jumping in them or simply walking straight through, and having to do it all over again. We borrow the Gaos' minivan and go on group excursions to see the foliage, or go pick apples and pumpkins. It is all good and mostly uncomplicated—except for the twenty minutes during which Cy goes missing in a corn maze.

I meet with Hiram P. Moody, to discuss the cash flow—he seems to think it's not a problem. "Families are like little countries," he says. "It's an ecosystem, an ebb and flow. Between the money coming in for rent for Cy and Madeline's house, their Social Security checks, and income from investments—they're fine. With regard to Ashley and Ricardo, you function like a human cash machine, but between Jane's life-insurance coverage, George's severance from the network, their previous investments, and the settlement from Ashley's school—you're more than fortunate."

I try to live within my means; they're limited, but I have the benefit of George's full wardrobe, and when my insurance runs out, I pick up a freelancers' health policy, and beyond that my wants and needs are few.

I keep track of all the money in dedicated notebooks—one for each child, one for Cy and Madeline, and another for the household and one for myself—carefully noting each expense and from what source it was paid. Not only does it give me something to do, it protects me from a nagging fear of being accused of mismanagement.

Cy is increasingly frail, more forgetful, and having trouble "containing" himself. All this prompts a visit to the doctor, who basically says, "You get what you get and you can't expect more. None of us last forever."

I ask the doctor to step out of the examining room for a word in private. We leave Cy on the table, his pale, hairless long legs nearly blue, and veined like a plucked chicken.

"What does that mean—'none of us last forever'?" I say just outside the door. The doctor shrugs. "How old are you?" I ask.

"Thirty-seven," he says.

"You got a fuck of a lot of nerve," I say to him.

"What do you want?" he asks. "You want painkillers, you want Valium? You tell me," he blithers on.

"What I want is compassion, some understanding of what it's like to be sitting there in that gown that is one step away from a funeral shroud and worrying what it's all about."

"Right," he says. We go back into the room, and the young doctor hops up onto the exam table next to Cy and says, "Can you hear me okay?"

"No need to yell," Cy says. "I'm old but I'm not blind. I can see your lips moving."

"You're doing very well," the doctor says. "The more you can get out and exercise, go for walks, the better; just keep moving, and enjoy yourself." And he hops down off the table, hands me a couple of prescriptions: a statin for Cy's cholesterol, Flomax for the prostate, Valium as needed for anxiety. He winks at me and is gone.

Ashley, continuing her embrace of Judaica, asks me to please get tickets for the High Holy Days. Having declined to renew the membership at the temple George and Jane belonged to, I find myself online buying tickets from a "liquidator." The idea that one "buys" tickets to an annual religious event bothers me; I'm aware that for many Jews the High Holies mark their annual visit to temple, and it's also when synagogues raise their funds for the year—but it doesn't feel right.

I meet some guy on a corner and pay six hundred dollars cash for two "member" tickets to Yom Kippur services at a conservative temple in Scarsdale.

Excited, Ashley insists we get there early to get good seats. We sit for hours and hours, and when we finally get to the Viddui, the communal confession of sin, I find myself right there with the rest of them, beating my chest, repenting "for the sins that I have done before you." There are at least twenty-four sins: the sin of betrayal, having an evil heart, causing others to sin, eating what is forbidden, speaking falsely, scoffing at others, being scornful, perverse, rebelliously transgressing, the sin of having turned away from God . . . I am pounding my chest along with the rabbi as he recites the litany of our wrongs. I am guilty. I am guilty of even more than I realized I could be guilty of.

"We're bad," Ashley whispers to me. "Just listen to all that we have done, all the harm and trouble we cause."

I sober up for a moment. "We're human, Ashley. We atone because, despite our best efforts, we will always do harm to others and ourselves. That's why each year we ask those we have hurt for forgiveness, and each year we present ourselves to God and ask to be forgiven."

She starts to cry. "It's just so terrible," she says.

"Which part?" I ask.

"Being human."

Out of the blue I get a call from the Department of Social Services with regard to scheduling a home visit for a pending foster-care application. "We had a cancellation; the social worker can come tomorrow, or I can book you for December 23 . . . ?"

"Tomorrow is fine," I say. "What time?"

"Anytime between nine and five," she says.

"Could we narrow it down?" I ask.

"No," the woman says.

"All right, then."

The social worker pulls up at 2 p.m. in a small nondescript car. Tessie barks.

"I don't like dogs," the woman says when I open the door.

"Would you like me to have her wait in the other room?"

"Please," the woman says.

I put Tessie on a leash and ask Madeline to hold on to it. I escort the social worker, and her fat folder, into the house.

"So the boy is already living here?" she asks.

"Since the spring," I say, "at the request of his aunt."

"Where does he sleep?" the social worker wants to know.

I take her to Nate's room and show her the bunk bed—Ricardo's is the bottom bunk, with all the stuffed animals. "He likes animals," I say, showing her his frog and the turtle.

"How does he get to school?"

"He and Ashley, my niece, walk to and from school together."

"Have you completed your advocacy training?"

"Not yet. I'm signed up to start in a few weeks—the classes were all full."

"And have you thought about the impact of a foster child on the family?"

"Yes," I say. "The family is thrilled; in fact, it was the children's idea."

"Your approach to discipline?"

"Firm but flexible."

"I see you have your parents living with you," she says.

I nod and say no more.

"And the small outbuilding in the yard?"

"It's a temporary structure," I say. "A celebration of the autumn."

"The boy cannot sleep there," she says, firmly.

I nod. "Of course not."

"Your application mentions one cat?" The social worker says, as the two cats run by.

"She had kittens," I say, leading the social worker the rest of the way around the house.

"How many children live in the home?" the social worker asks.

"Three," I say.

"Don't forget our brown babies," Madeline calls out, "that's five in all."

The social worker visibly bristles at the phrase "brown babies."

"They're twins," Cy yells, over the narration of the golf tournament.

"The babies are dolls from South Africa," I explain. "Dolls are very good for older people, they think of them as real."

The social worker nods without interest. "If you are approved, you will be paid for board and care; you will receive a clothing allowance; money can be requested for special things, such as after-school programs, tutoring, a winter coat, and clothing for religious occasions. But, given budget constraints— don't ask. To avoid the appearance of servitude, please don't have the child do any cooking, cleaning, anything that might be construed as work for hire." She hands me some papers to sign and is gone.

"I hope you're not going to hire that woman to work here," Madeline says. "Tessie and I thought she had an attitude."

I am in the A&P when Amanda calls. I look around, thinking perhaps she is here, watching me through the loaves of bread, peering over the mountain of navel oranges. I am here often, because we use more groceries than ever before: numerous appetites to cater to, young and old.

"Where are you?" I ask.

She doesn't want to say.

"Are you okay?"

"I'm fine. You?"

The randomness of her call has caught me off guard. I feel intruded upon. "Good," I say. "Funny enough, I'm in the A&P right now; they changed the layout, they put in a new pathway, like a winding country road, it's supposed to make shopping more relaxing, more natural."

There's a long pause. "What else?" she asks.

"I finished my book." I offer myself up, leaving out the part about the lightning strike. "Your parents are doing well; the kids are at school. What have you been doing?"

"It's hard to say," she says.

I find my frustration growing: her opacity, the thing that used to make her seem compelling, the impossibility of knowing what she was really thinking, is now an irritant.

"Can I ask you a question?" I pause. "When 'something' happens, do you want to know?"

"No," she says, definitively, "I really don't. I like not knowing, just imagining. Knowing might change something; I might end up doing something differently. I don't want to be burdened."

"Okay," I say. "Do me a favor. . . ."

"What?" she asks.

"Don't call this number again." I pause. "It's not all about you, Amanda, it's not like you get to leave your parents with a total stranger, like it's a coat check, and then just check back whenever you want, to make sure everything is right where you left it."

I hear the sound of rustling paper in the background. "A couple of things," she says, ignoring everything I said. "Every year, my parents go to West Point for the Army-Navy game—they have season tickets. Have they mentioned it?"

"No," I say. "Not a peep."

"And it's their anniversary on the twenty-fifth of September. Forty-five years."

As she talks, I'm in the dairy section, filling the cart: low-fat milk for Ricardo, lactose-free for Cy, soy for Ashley, and Maxwell House International Instant Peppermint Mocha Latte for Madeline, who described it as her "addiction." As I go up and down the aisles, grabbing bread, crackers, paper towels, Amanda continues to give me details about things like getting the chimney at the house swept, making sure the storm windows go up. She's downloading information, letting each bit go like an autumn leaf, riding the breeze as it makes its way down to the ground. After a few more minutes, I say, "Amanda, let it go, you don't have to worry about this stuff anymore. It doesn't matter—none of this matters, this is all just stuff."

"The stuff of life," she says. "I've been writing it all down so I can pass it on."

"These are operating instructions—not what you need to pass on. I've got to go," I say, preparing to hang up. "Take care."

In the car on the way home, I'm filled with an overwhelming sense of dread—was I out of line? Will she retaliate? I imagine Amanda sneaking into the house in the middle of the night and leading her parents down the stairs, reclaiming them. I imagine myself being proactive—packing everyone up and going underground, like in some kind of witness-protection program. Cy and Madeline are mine now. I'm using them—the children are using them. I can't afford to lose them.

Cy tells me he needs my help. "We have to go on a little trip—back to the old house. I left something there."

"Not a problem," I say. "Whatever it is, Mrs. Gao can bring it over."

"No, we need to go, just you and me, tonight, with a shovel," he says.

"Really?" I ask.

"Yes."

I phone Mr. and Mrs. Gao and let them know we'll be making a surprise visit and ask them to pretend not to see us. As soon as it's dark, we head over there with two shovels and a couple of head-mounted flashlights I have picked up at the hardware store.

Cy marches ten paces out from the basement door and three to the left and starts to dig. "It's about eighteen inches down," he says.

"Here, let me, my back is stronger." He watches me dig for a couple of minutes and then starts digging another hole, about a foot away.

"There's more than one?" I ask.

"Seven or eight," he says.

I keep digging until I hear the sound of the shovel hitting metal.

"Bingo," Cy calls out.

We get down on our hands and knees, and I dust off the top of what turns out to be a .50-caliber military-issue ammunition can, and suddenly I'm terrified.

"You have ammunition buried in the yard—explosives? This could be dangerous. We could blow ourselves up."

"It's not explosives—it's cash. I put it in the ammo cans because they're waterproof. Why do you think I never went along with the idea for an in-ground sprinkler system? It would have wrecked my retirement plan." He chortles.

"Cy, are you telling me that you have seven or eight cans of cash buried back here?"

He nods gleefully. "Yes, I never trusted the markets, so I socked away whatever I could, a little here and there over the years."

"And this isn't the money you stole?"

"No," he says, shaking his head. "I gave that back; this is mine."

"Are you sure about this, Cy?"

"Positive," he says. "Keep digging."

And so I do. I dig for hours; we find six cans.

"That's odd," Cy says. "I could have sworn there were more."

I shrug. I'm nearly crippled, my head is throbbing, I'm thinking I could have another stroke any minute now. "It's enough, Cy. Whatever it is, it's enough."

He nods. "There's ten thousand in each can," he says.

"Sixty thousand dollars?"

"I sold insurance, son, and I was damned good at it. Insurance was big back then, late 1950s, early 1960s. Everyone thought we'd be blown to kingdom come. . . . I was very careful: every bonus, every little extra bit, I squirreled away. Look," Cy says as we're finishing up. "I know it costs a pretty penny to take care of Madeline and me. And Christmas is coming, and I want to do something for the kids—maybe buy them some United States Savings Bonds. And, well, here's the truth, I've always wanted a Lionel train set. Every Christmas, despite my age, I still come downstairs hoping it's going to be there. And you know what, this year it will be, because I'm going to get it for myself. You'll come with me," he says. "We'll go into New York and pick it out." He pauses. "So—you think I've got enough for the train?"

"Yeah, Cy, I think you've got it covered."

Together we fill in the holes and make a plan to come back and repair the damage to the lawn. "Before they notice," Cy says—which is of course impossible, because for several hours the Gaos have been staring out their back windows, wondering what the hell we're doing as we dig up the heavy green metal cans.

"I should have asked you before we started," Cy says, "but I'm assuming that you can keep what happened here tonight just between us."

"Not a peep," I say.

A letter arrives with no stamp, no return address. It's neatly typed on fine blue stationery.

Franklin Furness shared your manuscript with me—he wanted my opinion as an off-the-record fact-checker. I put two and two together and wanted to drop you a line, a note of congratulations. I was pleasantly surprised to see that your belief in the dream survives along with your hope that the hearts of men are not as dark as their behavior might lead one to believe. The smog of history never really clears, there's an enormous amount we'll never know, suffice to say it hasn't been a government by the people for a very long time. It's a company, a multinational—the land of the free and home of the brave as brought to you by the People's Republic of China. Historical forces are underestimated—just like physicists describe gravity as a weak force— the shape of history is surprisingly easily recast. And here we, you and me, once again front and center of the Zeitgeist, the fragrant and foul, mix fact and what you hope is fiction that is bubbling up like an ancient tar pit. And while we might revel in the accuracy of our conspiratorial musings—and, yes, we were right all along; our youthful doppelgängers are at it again. Do you realize that there are now more than eight hundred and fifty thousand people employed with Top Secret security clearances? No one knows who is doing what, and even those authorized to know it all can't possibly keep up. A plan or ten could be hatched, threaded through in such a way that it would take years to unfold with no one person in the lead. This is the new terrorism, buttons pushed made by people just doing their jobs with no idea of the cause and effect, the relation of any one action to another. The drone, just look at the definition—a stingless male bee—aka a powerless man—the most dangerous kind. A strange buzzing by your ear—no longer a humble bee but a fake bug that can be flown into your house, land on your dining room table, or fly right up into your ear and on command, with a computer keystroke, blow you and your house the fuck up and you'd never know why. They are among us and we will never know who they are or what is happening. It is all bigger than any of us could ever imagine. Forty-nine years since the big event—the implosion of American politics, the inauguration of our dark age—and this is where we got to. As you can imagine I am working on a book of my own—seems there are still a few of us thinking along the same lines—carrying baggage, something we need to get off our chests before it's too late. Anyway, all this to say: Congratulations. Good work. The world needs more men like you, Silver.

I read the letter several times. I can't help but be pleased. It's what I've wanted to hear—it confirms my feelings, my suspicions, my hope that it's not all for naught. I assume it's from my "friend" at the law firm, the guy in the elevator—but who is he? Is he someone I should know—a familiar name? I pocket the letter, thinking that I'll do more digging later—maybe there's something in it, a phrase, a way of speaking, that will ring a bell.

Walter Penny calls to say that George has been moved again. "He was having tummy trouble, so we sent him to a place with better medical care. I can give you the address and visiting info—it's been a while since you saw him."

"The incident is still fresh in my memory," I say.

"Did you get the check?" Penny asks, like that should have fixed it.

"I did, thank you."

Walter gives me the prison information. "It's about an hour from where you are, overlooking the Hudson."

I drive up the following day. On the outside it's bucolic, set in the landscape like an old castle or fortress. The parking lot has an employee-of-the-month parking spot with the person's name written in red marker in a white rectangle. As I'm pulling in, I happen to glance at an old house off to the right, and, like witnessing an apparition, I see a dapper fellow wearing an old tan corduroy jacket come out the front door and head towards an ancient station wagon, and I'm thinking it's the ghost of John Cheever going out for a ride.

Bucolic on the outside, but like a furnace inside, sweaty, sticky, with a gamy smell. I pass through the metal detector and into the waiting area. The guards bring George to the visiting area in shackles; we speak through holes drilled in thick Plexiglas—holes filled with the spittle of every criminal's family that has come before us.

"How are you?" I ask.

"How could I be?"

"It was an accident," I say.

"I am not asking for your opinion," George says.

"You look horrible. Walter mentioned that you'd been in the hospital."

"I had proctitis and gonorrhea."

"What is going on in there?"

"I've had to make my own way," he says, shaking his head bitterly. "There's nothing good about this place. My teeth are rotting. I used to get them cleaned four times a year, now my breath smells like shit all day. You sold me out. You gave me up, and for what—Lillian's chocolate-chip cookie recipe?"

"What are you talking about?"

"You took advantage of my sweet tooth; you used the cookies to fuck me over."

"They already had you, George," I say. "I'm the one they used, like a human shield. I gave of myself to protect you. I had no option to turn them down," I say. "They had me by the balls."

"You have no balls," George says.

"Nice, George."

The inmate in the visiting booth next to ours falls to the floor and has a seizure.

"How are my roses?" George asks as the guards move to clear the room so they can attend to the sick prisoner.

"They have black spot. I'll spray again tonight if it doesn't rain," I say as I'm exiting.

On the Tuesday before Thanksgiving, Nate comes home from school with a friend named Josh. The next day, we borrow the Gaos' minivan and drive into New York City. Cy, Ricardo, Nate, Josh, and I head for the Lionel Store while

Ashley and Madeline have a plan to get their hair done and go for lunch. The city is crazy with people, I feel like a tourist—jostled by everything.

At the Lionel Store, it takes a while before the sales guy realizes exactly who the train is for, but once he does, he gets into it, and seven hundred dollars and lots of accessories later, we leave the store—each of the boys carrying a heavy bag. I take the boys out for ice cream. It turns out Nate has never had a banana split. I order two for the table, and Cy scowls at me. "It's my big day," he says. "Let us each have our own."

And we do.

When we are done, we rendezvous with Ashley and Madeline, who have had not only their hair done but their toes and nails as well.

"One more stop," Cy says, as we cram back into the minivan. He directs me to the Eighty-first Street side of the Museum of Natural History.

"I'm not sure how close I can get—they close a lot of the streets ahead of the parade."

"Your best is all I ask," Cy says.

I park in a lot a couple of blocks from the museum and, like a line of ducks, we follow Cy, bumping into people as we go, echoing a chorus of "Sorry, sorry, sorry." At the barricade on the corner of Eighty-first and Central Park West, Cy whispers something to the cop and pulls his old driver's license from his wallet. I glance at Madeline, who seems to know exactly what Cy is doing. She smiles.

"Of course," the cop says, opening the barricade and ushering us all through.

Cy smiles, pleased with himself. We are now among the select few pedestrians on the block where the Macy's parade floats have been laid out in the middle of the street and are being inflated. "There's a hose going right up Betty Boop's ass," Cy points out.

"Betty Poop," Ricardo exclaims.

"How did we get here?" Nate asks.

"I've still got a card or two up my sleeve," Cy says.

"We used to live right here on this block," Madeline says. "For many, many years. Our girls grew up playing in Central Park if it was sunny, or among the dioramas in the Natural History Museum if it was cold or raining."

"Cool," Nate says.

"This parade is the stuff of my childhood," Cy says. "I was here when Mickey Mouse first flew, and when Ethel Merman sang."

"I had no idea," I say as we walk up and down. The children are in awe of the giant floats, Betty Boop, Kermit the Frog, Shrek, Superman all swelling to life. Under bright, nearly forensic white lights tended to by workers in Tyvek suits, the giant balloons are held down by netting, sandbags, and ropes. I can't help but notice that on the other side of the museum there are also floats—and an enormously long line that snakes for blocks—public viewing.

"This is the coolest thing ever," Ricardo says. "Thank you."

It is magical, almost fantastical, and what I'd call the good kind of melancholy—as sweet as it is, it's also sad. We linger until it is dark and cold and our bones have begun to ache.

As we are driving home, they all fall asleep in the car. I am alone and awake. Driving up the Henry Hudson Parkway to the Saw Mill, I see the glowing eyes of a raccoon staring me down at the edge of the road. It begins to snow—first small white flakes, and then fat ones, the size of the doilies under the lamps in Aunt Lillian's house. I open the window; the snow blows into the car, dusting everyone as if with a kind of magical powder.

Thanksgiving. It has been a year—and a lifetime. The table has been set. Ashley and Madeline have handcrafted a cornucopia centerpiece that spills autumnal bounty across the freshly pressed tablecloth: gourds, squash, pumpkins, and, if you look carefully, the silver-buckled Pilgrim shoes Ashley and I bought in Williamsburg overflowing with plump red and green grapes.

Thanksgiving morning, I am up early, laying piecrust in tins. Glancing out the kitchen window—past the stump from the maple tree, which has been chopped, chipped, spit out as mulch, and sprinkled around everything in the garden, like funeral ashes scattered in remembrance—I spot four deer soundlessly tiptoeing through the yard, a father followed by two fawns and the mother. Their tails twitch as they bend to taste the garden. I have to smile. The only deer I've seen near here have been bloody carcasses on the side of the road. Madeline shuffles in, sees that I'm staring at something, and comes to look. She leans over the sink and raps heavily on the glass. "This isn't a grocery store," she yells. The father deer's ears twitch, his tail goes up, and they take off, having gotten word that they are no longer welcome.

———

Madeline asks if I've noticed Cy sitting on the floor of the living room, in his pajamas, hooking up his train set.

"He looks happy," I say.

"He is," Madeline says, confessing that she's glad he got the train now—she doesn't think he's going to make it until Christmas.

"The doctor said he was doing well," I say.

"He's going," she says, "bits and pieces are flaking off. But he's not suffering. We should all be so lucky."

The children are in their pajamas, watching the parade on TV and helping Cy set up the train. Nate's friend Josh is dyslexic. He calls Nate "Ante." Nate explains that whenever Josh texts, he types "Ante" instead of "Nate" and the nickname stuck. My suspicion that they are more than friends is quashed when Nate comes in for breakfast and tells me that Josh is not the average academy student: next year, after Josh becomes Jenny, he'll transfer to a coed school so that the academy doesn't have to address the gender-bender issue.

"How did you become friends?" I ask.

"We're both knitters," Nate says. And then Nate helps me slide the twenty-eight-pound trussed, stuffed bird into the oven. "I wrote to my father," Nate says. "Well, I started to write a letter, but it got really long—eighty pages. I gave it to my adviser, who said it's not a letter, it's a memoir, and he wants me to keep going. Am I too young to write a memoir?" he asks.

There is no right answer.

Between making "holiday punch" and looking for a platter big enough for the bird, I'm texting back and forth with Cheryl—I invited her and her family, but Thanksgiving is big in Ed's world. His sister cooks, and Cheryl and Ed double up on their Plavix and Lipitor the week before. "Be sure to shove a lemon into the bird's hole before you put it into the oven," Cheryl texts.

"Too late."

"Never too late," she writes. "And before it starts to get brown make an aluminum foil tent—save the browning for the last 30 min—helps the skin stay crisp."

"Does anyone use an actual pumpkin to make pumpkin pie?" I ask.

"No," she writes.

Mr. and Mrs. Gao arrive, carrying a hot turducken, which they deep-fried at the restaurant and brought directly to us.

"I have no idea what a turducken is, but I like the way it smells," Madeline says, welcoming them.

"We don't know either," Mrs. Gao says. "We saw it on TV and they said it was very American. We ordered it online."

Ricardo's aunt and uncle come in with a gigantic sweet-potato-and-marshmallow casserole and an enormous glass bowl of ambrosia. As a way of saying hello, Ricardo gives us a long demonstration of what he's learned on the drums.

Ching Lan and her parents have taken the train from New York, carrying big bouquets of flowers and Lucky Break Wishbones for the children. "You know how turkey have only one," her mother says. "Well, now you can have as many as you want, spread lots of good luck. We sell them all week in the deli—very popular."

With each new guest, introductions are made all around. In the middle of it all, Ashley descends the stairs wearing her dress from Colonial Williamsburg along with the shawl and head covering that Sofia got her for the bar mitzvah. She has become increasingly religious, defining herself lately as "Orthodox." I accept the notion as a phase, a heartfelt adolescent identification offering her comfort, and, I hope, part of the progression towards a healthy sense of self.

"I want to light the Thursday-night candles and pray," she says.

"There are no Thursday-night candles," I say.

"But Aunt Lillian and Jason have never seen me do the prayers."

"I hear you, but today is Thanksgiving; the day belongs to our Christian brethren. Would you like to say grace?"

"Let Cy or Ricardo say grace, but I want to speak at the table."

"About what?"

"I'll prepare something," she says, going back upstairs.

"Okay," I say.

Jason and Lillian arrive with the famous cookie tin, laden with product.

"I taught Jason how to make them," Lillian says proudly.

"We did it together last night," Jason says. "Now we can have cookies anytime, as many as we want."

"Are you saying you don't need me anymore, that you only wanted me for my cookies?"

"Mother, I am saying that I am glad you trusted me with your secret recipe," Jason says.

Lillian looks around. "Where is your mother? I thought for sure she would be here—I was looking forward to our rapprochement."

"She and Bob are going out with friends," I say.

"That seems strange, doesn't it? You making a holiday dinner without your mother?"

I make no mention of my anxiety about what would happen, or how I would introduce Madeline and Cy to my mother and Bob. Who would they be to each other? Would there be a fight for turf?

"Well, Bob's children only invited him but not Mother to their Thanksgiving, and their feelings were hurt," I explain. "Of course, I invited them both to join us, but as my mother put it, 'I don't want to burden Bob with the complexity of family, he's suffered enough. We'll go with friends, there's an early bird at a local place. The minivan will take us from here; we'll have a good time.'"

Before we sit down to dinner, we take lots of pictures—group shots in the living room. Almost everyone has a camera or a phone, so we take turns, some friends and some family.

"Should this be our Christmas card?" Madeline asks Cy.

"What's with all the Chinese?" I hear Lillian ask Jason, as we make our way to the table. "I thought he got divorced?" She takes her seat at the table. "Is he running a boarding house?" she mutters. "It's like a freak show, a random collection of people."

I am at the head of the table, bearing witness. I am thinking of Sakhile and the e-mail he sent this morning: "When the road narrows, the guy to the rear of you has the right of way."

I am thinking of George and his proctitis in prison and wondering what they're serving for Thanksgiving dinner an hour north of here. I am thinking of Cheryl and her family. I am thinking of Amanda, wondering if she is in this country or out of this world, and of Heather Ryan's parents having this first holiday without her, and of Walter Penny likely out for a long run before supper.

Stay, I tell myself, as I take a breath. Stay here, in the moment. And I breathe again—deeply. I think of Londisizwe and his tea, and even though it has been months, I burp and the flavor repeats.

I look down the length of the table and see young and old talking, passing platters of turkey and stuffing, sweet and savory, embracing the season. Ricardo hands me the cranberry sauce. "Ashley and I made it," he says, proudly. "We squeeeezzzed the lemons."

"No such thing as too much gravy," Cy says as the gravy boat circulates.

I look at Nate and Ashley and remember Thanksgiving last year, when they were curled in their chairs like spineless lumps, their electronics in hand, eyes focused on the small screens; the only things engaged were their thumbs. I remember looking at them with disdain as they sat inert, unaware of their mother enslaved in the kitchen, their father bloviating at the guests. And now Nate turns to the guests and inquires, "Does everyone have everything they need?" And Ashley asks Lillian, "Can I get you anything else?"

In the living room, the television is on—the movie *Mighty Joe Young* is playing, and I ask Nate to turn it off, and he does. I am surveying the situation, comforted that I can actually feel pleased. In fact, I notice that I feel nothing except benevolence—free-floating good will.

It is Thanksgiving and I do not fear the other shoe falling; actually, I am not even wearing shoes. There is a distinct absence of tension, of worry that something might explode, erupt, or otherwise go wrong. I note the absence of worry and the sense that in the past that absence of anxiety would have caused me to panic, but now it is something I simply notice and then let go—carrying on.

I am looking down the table thinking of everyone I've ever known; every hello and goodbye sweeps through me like an autumn breeze. I am porous, nonstick.

"A prayer?" Cy suggests.

Our heads are bowed.

"Itadakimasu," Nate says in Japanese. "I humbly receive."

"Our Father, for this day, for this food we thank Thee," Ricardo's aunt offers.

"My turn," Ashley says, standing up before the aunt is done. "So, like, it's been a really wild ride," she says. "But there's a book I read this summer and

I wanted to share it with you." Ashley then begins to read from a page she's printed out:

> I do not think of all the misery, but of the glory that remains. Go outside into the fields, nature and the sun, go out and seek happiness in yourself and in God. Think of the beauty that again and again discharges itself within and without you and be happy.

"Very nice," Cy says. "Was that Whitman? Longfellow?"

"Anne Frank," Ashley says.

Cy waits a moment before raising his glass. "Well, I want to thank you, all of you. It has been a very good year for Madeline and me, moving back into our home. I don't know why we ever left. La-hoolum!"

Madeline leans over and whispers loudly to Cy, "Thanksgiving is an American holiday, not a Jewish holiday."

Lillian leans over and, while pointing towards Madeline and Cy, asks Jason, "Whose people are those?"

Jason shrugs. "Dunno."

"I didn't know Claire's parents were Caucasian," Lillian says.

"Maybe Claire was adopted," Jason suggests.

"And where is Claire anyway?" Lillian asks. "I thought they killed Jane, did they kill Claire too?"

We eat, we gorge, we stuff ourselves, greedily devouring everything. Plates are passed for seconds and thirds. Aunt Christina's ambrosia is oddly addictive; after my third helping, she tells me that the secret ingredient is heavy mayonnaise. I skip a fourth serving and load up on turkey. We eat until we are sated and still we keep going, eating until we are in pain, until we are suffering, because that is the new American tradition.

"I don't even like sweet potatoes and I had two helpings," Ashley says, pushing herself away from the table.

"The bird was perfect," Madeline says.

We take a break before dessert; the children work as a team and clear the table.

Mrs. Gao and Ching Lan and her mother insist on helping to clean up.

Mrs. Gao brought Tupperware containers—"my gift to you," she says. "I love these things; they burp when you close them."

I am so overstuffed that I can literally go no farther than the living-room sofa. I lie there thinking of George eating pressed turkey breast, jellied cranberry slices still bearing the ringlike indentations from the can, lumpy gravy, and glutinous white-bread stuffing, and I wonder: Is there pumpkin pie in prison? If there is, does it have any flavor at all?

The children are outside, playing football on the front lawn with Ricardo's uncle and Cy; there are joyous shouts as the pigskin passes from hand to hand.

There is talk of an early snow, freezing rain.

It is three hundred sixty-five days since the warning, three hundred and sixty-five days since Jane pressed against me in the kitchen: me with my fingers deep in the bird; our wet, greasy kiss.

It has been a year in full, and still the thought of Jane fills me with heat. I feel myself rise to the occasion.

May we be forgiven; it is a prayer, an incantation.

May We Be Forgiven.

ACKNOWLEDGMENTS

With great thanks for their support, friendship, and editing skills: Marie Sanford, Amy Hempel, Katherine Greenberg, Amy Gross, Elliott Holt, Lisa Randall, Laurie Simmons, and Syd Sidner, who sat next to me for days and weeks, bringing me way too much coffee, and Claudia Slacik, who quite literally gave me a place to write.

Zadie Smith, who asked the question that got the whole thing going; William Boyd, who picked the first chapter for *Granta*'s 100th issue; Salman Rushdie, who later selected the piece for *The Best American Short Stories 2008;* and Heidi Pilator at Best American Short Stories.

Agents Andrew Wylie, Sarah Chalfant, Charles Buchan, Jin Auh, and Peter Benedek on the West Coast. And lawyers Marc H. Glick and Stephen F. Breimer.

Paul Slovak, my editor at Viking, who met me for lunch many times along the way, and Sara Holloway at Granta, UK, who has been a wonderful friend and editor for the last ten years.

Françoise Nyssen and Marie-Catherine Vacher in France; Carlo Feltrinelli, Fabio Muzi Falconi, and Maria Baiocchi in Italy; Robert Ammerlaan in the Netherlands; and Helge Malchow and Kerstin Gleba in Germany.

Elaina Richardson, Candace Wait, and the staff of Yaddo, without whom I would never write anything. Special thanks to Catherine Clarke, who retired in 2011 after spending twenty-five years at the front desk saying, "Good afternoon, this is Yaddo," in her wonderfully calm voice to anyone who called.

Andre Balaz, Philip Pavel, and the staff of the Chateau Marmont—my West Coast Yaddo.

My colleagues at the Pen American Center, Poets and Writers, and The Writer's Room in New York City.

And my brother and parents—what a long strange trip it's been.